Mark Behr was born in Tanzania in [...] South Africa with his parents. His f[...] lauded by critics throughout the w[...] the United Kingdom and the USA, [...] African classic. *Embrace* is his second novel. Mark Behr died in 2015.

'Behr wants to turn all our received notions on their heads, to discomfit liberal and reactionary alike . . . [his] portrait of the Afrikaner family, with its myriad prejudices and conflicts, is by turns affectionate and exasperated, and rings utterly true . . . the most persistent of the themes [. . . is] the crippling psychic damage caused by self-deception, and the pain and the necessity of facing the truth about oneself and one's heritage' *Spectator*

'Behr's story of Karl de Man, aged 13 and standing at that awkward, yet magical, intersection between childhood and manhood is a powerful commentary on love, sexuality, politics and power . . . [There] are moments of exquisite understanding of the love that is possible between people – flawed people . . . There are layers to this book and layers to almost every chapter' *Cape Times*

'*Embrace* explores not only Karl's transition from child to young adult, but also the fickle nature of both love and memory . . . The ungrammatical, urgent syntax of the child contrasts with the lush descriptions of the South African bush and the musings of the young man as he begins to apprehend the world about him intellectually as opposed to sensually' *TLS*

'*Embrace* is a huge book . . . It is a genuine achievement . . . that Mark Behr manages to sustain his narrative for so long without flagging. This is because the themes are universal' *Gay Times*

'The writing is steeped in zoology and natural history and good allegorical use is made of both: dangerous brute forces stalk the grass in this Eden before the Fall' *The Times*

Praise for *The Smell of Apples*

'Masterly . . . a disturbing story which subtly lays bare the twisted logic of apartheid' *The Times*

'Compelling . . . the disturbing and powerful story of a child's introduction to hypocrisy and disillusion' *Sunday Telegraph*

'Mesmerising . . . *The Smell of Apples* is an astounding first novel' *Sunday Times* (South Africa)

Also by Mark Behr

The Smell of Apples
Kings of the Water

EMBRACE

Mark Behr

ABACUS

First published in Great Britain in 2000 by Little, Brown and Company
This edition published in 2001 by Abacus

5 7 9 10 8 6 4

The author gratefully acknowledges permission to quote from the following:
'Do-Re-Mi' by Richard Rodgers and Oscar Hammerstein II © 1959 Williamson Music International USA. Reproduced by permission of EMI Music Ltd, London, WC2H 'Both Sides Now'
by Joni Mitchell © (UK and British Commonwealth) 1967 Siquomb Publishing Corp., USA.
Reproduced by permission of Westminster Music Ltd., London, SW10 0SW. © (Canada) 1967
(renewed) Crazy Crow Music. All rights administered by Sony/ATV Music Publishing, 8 Music
Square West, Nashville, TN 37203. All rights reserved. Used by permission.
Age of Iron by J.M. Coetzee © 1990 J.M. Coetzee. Reprinted by permission
of Secker & Warburg

A CIP catalogue record for this book is available from the British Library.

ISBN 978-0-349-11300-5

Typeset in Centaur by M Rules
Printed and bound in Great Britain by Clays Ltd, Elcograf S.p.A.

Papers used by Abacus are from well-managed forests
and other responsible sources.

Abacus
An imprint of
Little, Brown Book Group
Carmelite House
50 Victoria Embankment
London EC4Y 0DZ

An Hachette UK Company
www.hachette.co.uk

www.littlebrown.co.uk

to my friends and family
for laughter, moral imagination and trust

I begin to understand the true meaning of the embrace. We embrace to be embraced. We embrace our children to be folded in the arms of the future, to pass ourselves on beyond death, to be transported. That is how it was when I embraced you, always.

J.M. Coetzee, *Age of Iron*

A grand Mass which could also be performed as an oratorio (for the benefit of the poor — an excellent practice that has now been introduced) . . . with slight alterations it could even be performed by voices alone.

Ludwig van Beethoven, *Letters*

I

I

Let's start at the very beginning, a very good place to start. When you read you begin with a, b, c. When you sing you begin with do, re, mi.

Do, re, mi.

Do, re, mi, the first three notes just happen to be, do, re, mi.

Do, re, mi.

Do, re, mi, fa, so, la, te . . .

Oh, let's see if I can make it easier . . .

2

I – no, we, I suppose – lived in the mountain country of the dragon. Here the school gave each of us two hundred Hills a week, the institution's own currency to ensure none of us had real money lying around lockers to tempt us boys or, as Mathison said in our first year, the long black fingers of the Munts. Money unguarded in a locker was a magnet to a black hand.

The Juniors broke up an hour before we Seniors. By the time we got out of Latin and then Art to line up and be paid, the younger ones from Standards Two up to Five were already sated on the sweets and cool drinks they ran down the hill to purchase from the shop in the Dragon's Ridge holiday resort. We qualified for extra pocket money if our parents thought it a good idea or if they could afford it. Mervy's and Dominic's could and did and they shared their extra Friday afternoon purchases with those of us whose parents sometimes did give, sometimes couldn't, or wouldn't or simply didn't. Lukas's parents — wealthy sheep- and horse-farmers from Indwe — did not give extra money as they couldn't see the necessity for more than two hundred Hills a week. Times when I didn't have the weekly extra, Dominic bought me two Eveready torch batteries and a tin of Nestlé's Condensed Milk, even though I never said directly that I didn't have the money. Always Nestlé's, not Gold Cross at twenty cents cheaper, because that had a thicker texture and an odd after-taste as if the sugar had not been properly dissolved. Since our second year, all I had to say on a Friday afternoon was that I wished I had a fix of sweetness and Dominic obliged, always with mock indignation:

'Dreadful for the voice,' he said, jutting out his chin and rolling his eyes. 'But what can I do? You're an addict. I'm your accomplice and willing buyer.'

At the store, like everywhere else, we stood in line. Only two in at a time. This way Mr Buthelezi kept an eye on what was leaving the shop. Our buying done, we stood eating and drinking while we watched the game in the small reserve. A couple of eland, ostriches, zebra and the lone wildebeest bull. Poor excuse for a game pen, I thought, throwing back my head to suck on the tin of Nestlé's. Thankfully the pen wasn't overstocked and it was large, so at least the poor animals had space to move. From the fence we strolled in groups to join the smaller ones already cavorting in the holiday park's Olympic-size pool.

On the high diving board I waited for Lukas down below to pull himself onto the side. From the pen came a zebra's call like bubbles through water. I waved at Dominic on the lawn with the others. He jumped up and called that he'd take a photograph of me in mid-air. I grinned, nodding.

Lukas took hold of the poolside's lip and hoisted himself to his haunches, straightened, pulling the Speedo's fabric from the cleavage between his buttocks. I glanced at Dominic, then back at Lukas, to whom I was about to whistle to watch my combined pike and forward somersault. I caught sight of Mr Cilliers passing with Ma'am. Head unobtrusively turned, he was staring at Lukas, who was turning to face up at me. Lukas didn't see Mr Cilliers.

Behind me younger boys concertinaed up the ladder, waiting, growing impatient. I was by then no longer looking at Lukas. My eyes were taking in Mr Cilliers and blurred in the corner of my vision the object of his gaze. Poised, prepared in anticipation of the bounce, I registered the way he regarded Lukas. It might have been simply the sidelong glance of a man at an arbitrary boy beside a pool of clear blue water – Dominic calling he's ready to take the photograph – but not to me. The gaze had already transposed itself over images and other frames from recent memory and Saturday night movies. Of three men, rigid behind a desk. Of pain; shame; something like resentment. Intrigue. A thought or a memory had flashed through the folds of my brain, or a series of hitherto inconspicuous recollections had stirred into alien symmetry like ripples on a seemingly controlled surface.

It was in the moments after I again became conscious of Lukas's eyes and Dominic's camera on me, when from behind a line of boys was telling me to move and I – barely aware – sneered that I'd drown them if they didn't shut up; when I looked ahead into the sky; noticed the zebra in a straight row at the fence, their eyes concentrated near the shop; bounced twice and shot into the air; tucked my legs into a perfect pike then folded myself into a ball and snapped straight and Dominic's camera must have clicked as I dropped vertically to the surface, cleaved the water and felt a brief sting in my back, swished downward, opened my eyes and headed for the bottom and lingered a second, listening to the humming of the motor and watching air pop from my mouth, watched it rise, felt my lungs burn and shot myself up.

It can be in any of these instants I – through the distortions and ravages of memory two decades later — recall that the initial impulses about Mr Cilliers might have come together for me.

It was not difficult. Within weeks, I had found little excuses to stay for a few minutes after rehearsal. By the time the others rushed for the doors I had already selected a particularly difficult transition, just a few bars, in the first soprano score. This would be my point of access. Over the previous days I had simply lingered for a while, ignoring Dom's call for us to get to the supper line together. At first I did little beyond collecting the sheet music from the piano and squaring off the pile into a rectangle of white geometric precision.

Now, alone in the hall with him and ignoring the pounding fear of possibly being asked to sing alone, I willed myself to speech: 'We can't seem to go from the C to the D sharp and then all the way down to the B on the final eleisons, Mr Cilliers. The words don't seem to quite correspond with the notes, Sir. If we could just repeat those bars — without the rest of the choir — maybe we could synchronise it with the second sopranos, Sir.'

I had anticipated his surprise at this exhibition of sudden interest: never once in the previous two years had I shown more than a remote — even a strained and resentful — commitment to most of the music. I will not let his frown put me off, I told myself. I looked away, continued talking, arranging the music, ignoring the raised eyebrows. Nothing could tell me that subtle, diffident-seeming persistence would not, eventually — even if it took months — be accepted as genuine alteration of character; as evidence that something had happened to transform my sullen tolerance into a full-fledged interest.

Standing in front of the piano, he watched me. He flicked open his score and I felt the initial stirring of relief. Clearly he was paging to the end of the first section. Still standing, he dropped one hand to the keyboard. Played the four notes. I was unsure whether I should smile or frown. Then there was an unexpected pressure, like tears, in the sockets of my eyes and I blinked, repeatedly, certain that crying must not take place now.

'This here? The fourteenth bar before the rondo?'

'Yes, Mr Cilliers,' I answered. I cleared my throat and continued collecting the pages.

In the hours we had stood facing him since that day at the pool, I forced myself to never allow my eyes to venture from his face for a fraction of a second. His rare moments of lapsed vigilance – used till then to inflict a burning pain to the ears or neck of Niklaas Bruin one removed from me – I now grasped as openings through which I could project alert concentration: a hint of a frown; contemplation; my head inclined, nodding. The soft grunt of an alto's fart, the smell reaching all our nostrils at the same instant, was ignored by me, even as I longed to cover my nose and the others giggled without twitching. I now noticed the grey strands in the black curls of his temples and around his ears; had at some time become conscious of the way the hair across the forehead jumped a split second before the jerk of his hands. For the first time I was seeing the extraordinarily white skin against the dark stubble shading his chin by afternoon or at evening rehearsals. I had already acquired the habit, at the moment of dismissal when his eyes swept over us – making us register his feelings at the outcome of the session – to let mine linger on his face. When he showed satisfaction – rare as that was during those initial introductions to the Mass – or if the mood just felt good, I allowed the faintest of faint smiles, something I imagined to resemble awe, to appear at the corners of my lips.

Knowing that the teachers speak amongst themselves, Ma'am Sanders's classroom, even Art where we were allowed a measure of informality and fun, had for me become terrain in which I could be seen investing additional effort. In Latin too, I tried my best, translating every word, learning what is verb, noun, declension, conjunction, nominative, dative, accusative. Checking and double-checking, sometimes even asking Niklaas Bruin for help. And the recorder, once

every two weeks with Marabou! God, that remained the biggest struggle. After two years my Music Theory and note-reading were stuck way
below standard. Barring a miracle there was no way I was going to
catch up any time soon. At most I could practise the prescribed pieces
and forget the deadly breath of the carnivore when she stood behind
me and over my shoulder moved her little baton, bar for bar across the
music, grunting through her nose. Marabou, I knew, could not ignore
how little I had ever known of my instrument. No one could. Yet,
surely, that also meant she would have to see how hard I was now
trying. Effort, in the absence of talent, would have to be rewarded.

Alone upstairs in the library I looked up from whatever I was reading to smile at whomever passed by. Sometimes it was Cilliers himself.

In the dormitory I no longer spoke, joked or quarrelled during
quiet time. Before lights-out I remained sprawled across my bed with
my head to the passageway where Uncle Charlie was certain to see me
pore over the Bible. In the showers I had become first in and first out.
Soon, I suspected, *knew*, they would all have to see that I had emerged
into a reformed patriot, something for them to be proud of; a citizen
they could praise and adore. Exactly what Mr Mathison said whenever
we prepared for tour: 'Behave yourselves like citizens. Patriots who have
earned the right to be in one of the best boys' music schools in the
world.'

The afternoon sun cast elongated shadows of aloes across the
grand piano's shiny black surface. Without looking from the pages –
aware of a deeper flush spreading into my neck and cheeks and no
longer seeing the music in my own hands – I felt his eyes on me; looking into me. The four notes were being repeated, over and over. I
sensed him take in my movements as surely as I could feel the sun's
glare and that other heat emanating from my face. I placed the collected scores in a neat heap atop the organ to one side of the hall. I
turned, allowing my eyes to meet briefly those behind the piano.
What I read from the face was neither smile nor frown; rather something akin to beneweling, a word that might translate to English as

bemusement. I smiled, shrugged my shoulders, then turned and strode from the hall's open outside door.

From that instant, dreading that even suspicion of misdemeanour might throw me back to square one, I began inventing excuses to go as seldom as possible to Dominic after lights-out on Saturday nights. And if, from this sudden change of behaviour and altered routine, Dom suspected anything amiss, he said nothing, himself perhaps relieved that I was for once, for the first time after two years, out of trouble.

3

The aim had been to kill on average one hundred and twenty each night. Frozen in blindness brought instantly by six hundred glaring watts, they stood dazed and trembling. The rifles were aimed, fired, hesitating only to make sure the shot was a kill. Then lifted deftly towards the next.

In the moonless dark the antelope were so easily stunned that the rangers were often able to cull almost double the nightly quota. When the open Land Rovers were filled with carcasses – loaded by Jonas and Boy – the vehicles headed for the park gates where kraals, butchers, hospitals and the nearby school would collect their share. Twice Dademan and Mumdeman came from Charters to collect impala for biltong. Mkuzi's carrying capacity for impala had for years been assessed at twelve thousand head. In the last year we lived there an estimated twenty-two thousand were depleting the yellow grass and shrubbery in a season when the water-holes had long disappeared and become first muddy death traps, then hollows tiled with large chocolaty rectangles that curled up and left empty dustbowls where only zebra and wildebeest still occasionally came to roll. All that remained green around our house was the magic guarri, the aloes and sisal Bokkie had planted, and the tambotie trees from where I collected jumping beans.

Bok's marksmanship was undisputed in the Natal Parks Board. With his .222 BRNO, he could score a perfect hit between the eyes from about 100 yards: a precision that would collapse an animal's legs on the spot where a moment before it was grazing. At home Bok had an intense dislike for men who could not be trusted for a clean kill. Only at home, or when he was alone with me on Vonk or in the Land Rover, did he articulate his disdain for the likes of Wilcox who, time and time again, had to fire a second or even third shot before the animal would either be brought down or cease its twitching and lie still.

'Bad enough, having to kill all these animals. No need to let them suffer.'

For the two months the slaughter took, Wilcox from Ndumu Reserve and Jerome Newman from Mkuzi town came to stay in a tent erected by Jonas and Boy on a flat sandy patch under the water tank and the tamboties. *Spirostachys africana*, Bok read the Latin to me from his manual, and I started learning plant names to show off to my sisters when they returned from boarding school.

Six afternoons a week during the culling, Bokkie prepared a canvas backpack with coffee in a Thermos, three plastic mugs, roast guinea fowl and freshly baked bread in tin foil. At sundown the three men accompanied by Jonas and Boy said goodbye to us before they got into the Land Rover and drove off into the dusk, Bokkie holding Suz by the collar, me Chaka. Lossie, the yard ostrich, seeing the men get into the vehicle, approached, his erect neck and tiny head moving from side to side like a periscope, round eyes vigilant as he took in the entire scene. Then, when the machine started up, he would emulate a mating dance, strutting and genuflecting, his wings lifted from his body, feathers ruffled into a grandiose white and black fan. As the vehicle moved off into the dust road, the bird pattered ahead until, unable to keep up, he swerved behind and trailed upwind for about half a mile as Jonas and Boy laughed and shouted from the back of the open vehicle at the giant bird to 'go home'.

Five nights a week the men would not return until dawn. When grey streaked the horizon and the flashlights were no longer effective, they came home. On Saturday nights they were back around midnight as there was no culling on Sundays.

Monday to Saturday, having woken from the relentless *Piet-my-Vrou, Piet-my-Vrou* in the thorn trees and with nothing on but a short floral mini, Bokkie would have lifted the kitchen's reed wall out onto its stilts and have coffee and breakfast ready: scrambled guinea fowl eggs, impala steaks crumbed and fried in spicy batter and slices of thick white-meal toast spread with whole-apricot jam.

Outside, at the tap beneath the water tank, the men washed the blood off their hands and forearms. They said goodbye to Jonas and Boy and then descended like lions onto the kitchen where Bokkie waited.

I arose when I heard laughter from the table. Too exhausted to sleep, the men told their stories and I, still blinking, came to listen in rapture to the tales of the night. It grew light and their ebullient voices altered into slower, softer and gentler murmuring. As the sun was about to break over the thorn trees and they prepared to go to bed – always and without fail – one of them would say, 'It's not nice doing this to animals; not nice at all seeing them slaughtered.'

The two guests left the kitchen, and I crossed the cool cement floor to fetch a glass of powdered milk Bokkie kept mixed in the fridge. Turning from the fridge I would see Bok's back as he bent to kiss Bokkie's neck where she stooped over the enamel washbasin. For a few moments I might be stung by embarrassment and I might lean, smiling, blood rising in my cheeks, against the cool of the fridge door. My mother would turn to face my father, her arms going around his neck, a wooden spoon dripping suds still held in one hand over his shoulder. His arm around her waist, hand clasping her side, they swayed as if to commence a dance, turned, and I, face pressed against the gentle humming of the gas fridge, would see Bok's hand manoeuvring Bokkie's crimplene mini down over her bum, his bronzed fingers venturing briefly between her barely covered thighs.

Another memory made of Mkuzi. The year before Lena joined Bernice at boarding school in Hluhluwe. Bokkie: a bare foot on the spade in the patch of sweet potatoes below the water tank, cotton hat, damp, covering her short dark hair. The huge silver water tank above her a mirror in the afternoon sun, the mounting three metres above the ground a deterrent for large animals. On the farm in Tanganyika, she told us and our occasional visitors, she had had a huge vegetable garden of radishes, leeks, onions, lettuce, cabbage, rows upon neatly tended rows of fine-leafed carrots. Gardeners. Labour as cheap as water was abundant. Mkuzi, in contrast, was dry. All she grew outside the carefully tended rockery of succulents and cacti was the patch of sweet potatoes and a few bushes of mint that thrived on the tank's run-off.

Behind her our house: Mbanyana. Shower and toilet, kitchen, sitting room and two bedrooms; each space partitioned by a layer of reeds without doors; only concrete the floor, at times our cool refuge from what the adults called the unrelenting heat and us kids only the sun.

By the time we got to Mkuzi, Bernice was seven, Lena almost five, me just over two. When we first came to South Africa and Bok was temporarily with Shell & BP, Bernice had gone to school at Werda Pre-Primary on the Bluff in Durban. Then, when Bok got the Parks Board job, Bernice had to go to boarding school in Hluhluwe. When she came home for a weekend she shared mine and Lena's room, all three of us sleeping on the fold-up camp-beds brought out from Tanganyika.

Bokkie raises herself slightly, weight on the right foot, pushes the spade in beneath the clump of sweet potatoes. She bends down and removes the indigo-coloured lumps, knocking off the soil. She throws the sweet potatoes to one side, onto a small heap. Her chin lifts. Gaze moves to the paddock about half a mile across the stretch of open veld. Even over this distance our eyes must meet. She can see me and Lena; both of us shirtless. I brush Ganaganda while Boy and Lena fill the feed trough with cubes. It has not taken me long to recover my bravado. Two days before, as the first scream reached her ears, she was already out of the house, dashing for the stables from where Boy was running with me in his arms. She had run, *knowing*, for the thousandth time, that it must have been a snake. From afar she had shouted, 'Wat is dit, Boy? What is it?'

And the man had called back, 'Is fine, Miesies, is fine, is not mfezi.'

Thank God, thank God, thank God, a rhythmical incantation as she ran. She took me from Boy's arms, talking softly to pacify me, but I only screamed louder at the same time motioning at my back.

'What happened, Boy? What's wrong, Karl, my boy?'

'Is Ganaganda, Miesies,' Boy answered, perhaps trying to smile re-assurance. 'She kick Karl, here . . .' And he pointed. She turned me to inspect my back.

'Thank you, Boy,' she said, motioning with her head that he was free to return to his tasks.

She blew cool air and the screaming intensified once more before I grew calmer, sobbing faintly into her neck; tears finding the path down her chest.

'Mamma is hier; toemaar, my kind; Mamma is hier, hoor.'

Lena was making her way from the stables. With me still sobbing on her hip, Bokkie balanced on one leg and bent to remove the duwweltjies, first from one, then from the other foot. The hellish burning from her foot soles had not registered until the moment I started to calm down.

'Ganaganda is just a naughty girl, don't worry, my boy.' She could discern the welted outline of the mare's print between my shoulder blades.

'Gana kicked Karl,' Lena announced. Bokkie nodded.

'Oh my baby, it's nothing,' she whispered into my ear, then turned me so that she could rest her lips against the hoofprint. Her breath against me, blowing out, then breathing in, must have taken in the smell of my body, probably mingled with the saltpetre of the horse. She smiled at Lena and started, watching, careful to step on the hot sandy patches where she was able to spy the little devil thorns. Over her shoulder I looked at Lena, following.

Leaving the sweet potato patch, she bends to collect the roots in her arms. She moves past the aloes and succulents of the rockery. One more time I see her looking at me by the stables. Then, with the bare toes of her right foot, she opens the gauze door and swings it wide open, and with a quick step, enters the house of yellow reeds as the door behind her slams shut.

4

Constructed in the design of an unusual L – its foot slightly higher up, rather than at the base of its leg – the school sat in a valley on a hill surrounded by orchards, green mealie fields and uncultivated veld that stretched around to where the mountains became the horizon. Along the ground floor of the foot, east to west, were the administration offices, the dining hall, the headmaster's office and the auditorium with a roof that rose three floors to achieve its spectacular acoustics. The auditorium, where the choirs occasionally rehearsed, had long windows from where one could see across the orchard terraces, down to the swift-flowing water of Sterkspruit and up the hills to V Forest. From the choir benches, one could look up and see the balcony library and walkway, its eight bookshelves spanning the length of the room. When the auditorium downstairs became too crowded during Wednesday-night performances, additional chairs were placed up on the library walkway.

The walkway led to the Junior dormitories. Here the second and third floors of the foot accommodated the Standard Two, Three and

Four boys in dormitories C and D, as well as E, where the five of us stayed for the first year and a half before we were separated.

On either side of the library landing was a door, one leading to the Secondaries in C Dorm, the other opening into a passage to the leg and the conductors' bedrooms. Cilliers's room was the last of these. Continuing along this passage one reached the extension with the music rooms and conservatory. These rooms faced out over more orchards towards Cathkin Peak and Champagne Castle, which rose to almost 3400 metres, the highest point in the Drakensberg Range. V Forest, dense and green, was clasped in the fold of two foothills and below it, closer to the citrus orchard, sprawled the rugby fields on which cows sometimes grazed in the shade of the poplar bush. There we had our forts. In summer the green of the poplars and in autumn their yellow and orange fluttering smudged Sterkspruit's winding waterway from sight.

The bottom floor of the leg that ran north to south was comprised of our classrooms. Built over these were the Senior dormitories: F and G for the Standard Sixes and Sevens. Between F and G was the sick-bay and Uncle Charlie the house-master's room. On winter mornings, when he walked through the dormitories, shouting, 'Wakey, wakey, rise and shine, jeans, T-shirts and black polo-neck jerseys,' the peaks were often covered in snow. Word had it snow had fallen down at the school only five or six times in written memory.

During breaks we had to play on the dusty soccer field that doubled as a parking lot for visitors' cars and the school's two tour buses. On a terrace below this soccer field-cum-parking lot was the dairy and the cowshed alongside the stables and the servants' quarters.

Steven Almeida had not returned after the Secondary Choir's Malawi tour. Into February, poring over the photographs of the tour, exchanging negatives, we speculated on why Almeida had left. He couldn't have failed Standard Five, surely? His family couldn't have gone back to Angola with the war and everything going on there. Maybe they couldn't afford keeping him here? No, they owned a new Audi and they too already had colour TV. And remember his sister Marguerite, how gorgeous she was at Parents' Weekends and at the airport when we came in from Malawi, dressed like a pop-star? No, the Almeidas had money. The remaining five of us, including poor struggling Bennie, had passed Standard Five and were now all teenagers. Being a teenager was a wonderful and dreadful thing to be. It meant we had reached 'that stage', whatever 'that stage' was meant to mean. From the way Almeida had been the previous year we'd accepted he'd be with us to start high school and Senior Choir with Cilliers. He was very, very quiet, but still, he could have said something. How he would have loved to join us on the coming European tour! It would have been just like in Malawi, the six of us at the lake. Look at this shot here of Steven and Dom at the Olvers' piano. And this one here on the cata-maran by the jetty – look there's Ma'am in the background. Skiing in Europe, Steven would have loved it in his quiet way. Only nine months to go. Back down to five as we'd been before Steven, we were again an odd number, which meant having always to try to find host families for three. Had Almeida indeed failed Standard Five, he would have been forced to leave, of course. But there was no way anyone with his brain could have plucked a standard. The loss of his voice, we knew, was an enormous blow to the school – especially with the proposed *Missa* that required the superstar quartet. Not that Erskin Louw was bad in Seconds, he's brilliant, of course, and he's the nicest of the Standard Seven prefects – any of the others would have had Bennie and I caned for gipping hair cuts last week. But at twelve – no, he turned thirteen last April on the Eastern Cape trip, didn't he? – Almeida was the greatest soprano, maybe the greatest voice, the school had ever had. For the year he'd been with us, he moved comfortably between firsts and seconds, wherever his volume and range was needed to fill in: somewhere between a contralto and mezzo, able to surprise an audience by flying up briefly to a coloratura descant. In the Secondary Choir he at times took Dominic's first soprano solos – even though he never had Dominic's stamina above high C. Awestruck at the agility of the handsome Portuguese boy's voice, Dominic would stand in the wings smiling. Then he'd whisper to me, 'He is a god, you know. He could sing the Queen of the Night and put half the fucking world's sopranos to shame.' Blasphemy aside, myself and the others agreed that Steven Almeida had to have in his throat and chest the vocal chords, diaphragm and thyro-arytenoid muscles of an adult. He sang with the voice of an extremely talented and well-developed female soprano, in contrast to Dominic who himself had the voice of an exceptionally gifted boy. All through Malawi the two of them had been looking forward to Rossini's *Cat's Duet* for the '76 programme with Cilliers.

And Almeida was good-looking. 'As handsome as any boy can be before he starts looking like a girl,' I had said to Dominic in Malawi one night. 'Yes, I suppose. But you've got my kinda looks, Karl,' Dominic whispered in a silly American accent, 'and Mom and Dad also think you're a far bigger charmer than Steven.'

And then Almeida, who had said he was coming back while I silently hedged my bets, didn't. And I, who thought I wouldn't ever return to the school I loathed so intensely, returned, lock stock and barrel.

Perhaps, Mervy said, one of us can ask Mr Mathison for the Almeidas' address and write to them. Find out why he left. We never did. Maybe not wanting to know. Occasionally through the year we looked at the photographs, commented, eventually less and less, till Steven was almost forgotten.

All five of us remaining had finally achieved the highest rung of the school's musical ladder: the Senior Choir. Although there were still the Standard Sevens above us, being in choir with them did soften the hierarchy of seniority and the prefect system that remained in place on the passages, the playground, in the dorms, during prep and in the dining hall.

Through the course of the previous two years I had continually imagined the disgrace of being held back, first in the Junior then in the Secondary Choir. In this place and in Bok and Bokkie's minds, I told myself, being held back in choir will be tantamount to failing a Standard. Each annual choral promotion seemed to me a miracle, a relief begged and divinely granted, for it surely meant that the terrifying secret of my inability to sing the high register of the first soprano score had not been found out; that no one other than Niklaas Bruin and whomever else had stood beside me in choir suspected that in each concert I left out at least a quarter of the entire repertoire; that with time the proportion of what was mimed to what could be voiced had been growing. Who knows how long it will be before the tainted F sharp sinks to a thin F; from wavering F to nervous E? There was a nightmare in which I stood through an entire performance unable to utter a note, mouth opening and shutting like a fish on dry land. But the dream's terror lurked not in the guilt or the silence – which I could and did bear rather comfortably – it crouched in the shame of exposure. At Lake Malawi, where with Ma'am's permission we six had sung informally for our hosts, Dominic and Mervy suggested I consider moving to seconds as my voice was rather good in the lower registers. So, now that we were back and starting on the *Missa*, I was thinking of asking Cilliers to be moved. Still, I kept postponing: the mere thought of being asked to sing alone was bad enough. Then of having to see Mr Cilliers's face contort in displeasure as if at a bad smell when he heard in my voice the breathy sounds coming from trembling, inadequate vocal chords – it kept me from asking, left me in the front row. But, I knew I should. There was the overseas tour! And as Cilliers said: SAA Jumbo Jets have no seats for joyriders. The Mass was the most difficult thing we'd done. Already I was more bored with every rehearsal than I'd ever been in the past. For the third year running and to Dominic's frustration, I had deceived my way around beginning-of-year voice-testing by faking acute hay fever.

'Why lie about such a small thing? You're cutting off your nose to spite your face because you don't like choir, that's all,' he said. 'You'd enjoy it if you were in the correct voice.'

'Are you sure you're comfortable in first soprano, De Man?' Cilliers had asked suspiciously in January when, snivelling and with red peppered eyes, I walked into the conservatory and offered my excuse for not testing. 'Else you must come back next week and do the test, okay?'

'I'm fine, Sir. I'm not up there with Webster, of course not, Sir. But I'm very comfortable in firsts.'

Along with the fear of having to sing alone and then being thrown into seconds was the certain humiliation of having to admit that my voice was no longer – had never been – good enough for that front row. That I was being moved from where I'd been standing five down from Dominic for two years. In Juniors and Secondaries I had loved being the tallest in the front row. Especially for performances. Therein and of itself was reason enough to make me perfect the art of opening my mouth with the rest, when necessary visibly straining the ligaments of my neck in a way I knew concealed, if not erased, the fact of my silence. Adding to my sense of Divine Protection in firsts had been the fact that whenever – in a fit of anger at discerning a discord from the front row to his left – a conductor prowled by with his ear almost touching our lips, he had never once passed mine at that terrifying moment where the score showed anything above a high G and I was again treacherously mute. Still, I was wondering whether I shouldn't at once pluck up the courage and go and ask Cilliers to move me to seconds. He was not half the ogre Mr Roelofse had been in Secondaries and there was no telling what might transpire if my ineptitude was exposed before Europe. Out on my arse! Probably thrown back into the misery of the Secondaries with Roelofse and Marabou who were going nowhere but on a tour of the ugly Orange Free State. Seconds isn't bad, of course, I told myself, and Almeida had been essentially a second.

While I pondered my voice and my other approach to Cilliers,

Dominic, Bennie and, again, I remained first sopranos. Voice merely hinting at signs of deepening though not yet leaving him unable to attain the highest second soprano registers, Mervyn had been moved to first alto. Lukas, till now the deepest voice in our other choirs, had again, and to the chagrin of the Standard Sevens, become the vocal foundation of the second altos. Towering head and shoulders over even the older boys, his tall physique, like mine in firsts, had once more also made him the ordering point from which the altos descended. During voice testing Mr Cilliers had noted the altered timbre in Lukas's voice, possibly the herald of a pending break, an occurrence that would end his life at the school. This was something we refused to believe could happen in the year before the overseas tour. If Lukas could hold out – save your voice, don't sing so loud, mime, pretend, I advised – who cared if any of us came back in '77. We had started together in '74 and we wanted to finish at least the '76 year and Europe together. Lukas, as dispassionate as ever, said we were all too precious about Europe. He couldn't understand why we wanted to travel abroad before we'd even seen half of our own country. If my voice goes, it goes, he said, and I'm not complaining about the swelling in my balls. No use crying over spilling the milk, he joked, and anyway, their farm Swaargenoeg with its sheep and horses was all he really cared about.

Each day of the week we sang for almost two hours: an hour in the morning and another before dinner and prep. As a key tour or performance drew near, the Senior rehearsals were to be extended to six days a week and, if required, up to three hours per day. Till now we had not yet been required to spend the additional hours. But Lukas, Bennie and I already dreaded the two months before Europe. We had heard and seen so much of Seniors' pre-overseas rehearsals, first as Juniors and then as Secondaries: hours upon hours; conductors' tempers boiling over; voices and violence booming through the school; canes flying; tears; threats; exhaustion. From the outset we had known there would be no escape. Mr Cilliers, in telling us of the new repertoire, had made no secret of the enormity of what lay in store: a programme almost entirely new; June and July a four-week Transvaal and Cape tour. Then, to celebrate the school's twentieth anniversary, an end-of-year performance of the *Solemn Mass* with full orchestra and the SABC Philharmonic Choir in honour of Prime Minister B.J. Vorster. And finally, after that, a three-week tour of Europe! My first ever trip overseas and the school's first since Israeli and European reviews had begun calling it the best boys' choir in the world.

Dominic and Mervyn, eternally enamoured with music, never sounded anything but sheer excitement at the prospect of the whole arduous year. Quite certain that Beethoven's Mass had never been performed by a boys' choir, Dominic felt that therein already lay for us an historic challenge. Lukas, sardonic and distant, said we'd survive the musical regime as we always had. Bennie said he couldn't care two hoots as long as the European pay-off was good: he wanted only to go to Amsterdam where we'd heard blue-movie theatres bloomed on every street corner just like in the kaffir kingdom of Lesotho close to where his mother lived. Dominic had been to London and Amsterdam more times than he could remember and said he hadn't seen more than a couple of porn shops and they were in districts we certainly wouldn't be allowed near. Dominic himself had always been refused access to the porn places but while he waited outside his mother and father held up pictures and all kinds of sex toys for him to see through the shop windows.

It was the very idea of going to Europe – how epic and impressive the notion in and of itself – that so appealed to me.

'We'll be going to Europe, did you know?' I asked Lena on the phone after the announcement, knowing well she had already overheard Bokkie's excited response.

'Just don't get an even bigger head, Karl,' Lena said. Besides Bok, when he took the rhinos to Texas, I was going to be the first in our family to experience overseas. Of course Aunt Siobhain had been back to Ireland a few times and Uncle Michael accompanied her once from Tanzania when he first went to meet her family in Dingle. But neither Bok's nor Uncle Michael's trips were what I'd call overseas tours. Mine was going to be a Grand Tour of Europe, like something from a novel or a movie. And to think that I'd almost not returned to this place! I smirked. Saying goodbye to Dom and the others at Jan Smuts last year I was dead sure I wasn't coming back. And then, on the very day of the return as I unpacked in F Dorm, fuming at again being divorced from Dominic, Lukas and Mervy in G, the rumour about the tour reached me. A few hours later, as we stepped into Senior Choir's first rehearsal, Mathison and Cilliers had made the announcement. Overjoyed, already seeing myself in the major cities of the world, I at once quit sulking about having only Bennie with me in F Dorm. Even to this enormous and boring repertoire I can submit, I told myself. Not a negative word. Think positive. It's in your own hands. Silently I hoped, of course, that we would have loads of free time to spend at the stables and at the river. But in my diary, as if it would come true if it were written in ink, I asserted my resolve to make my contribution to the choir's success. Instead of homework during prep, I wrote scenes of myself walking through snow in London; eating in dimly lit cafés in Paris and Stockholm where Dominic and I were sure to bowl over our host families and the other patrons with our unusual accents and our charm. In my diary I wrote about visiting the ancient galleries and museums of Holland and England, places that Ma'am and Dominic so often spoke of during Art class and to which I could bring only secondary knowledge gleaned from books. When not engaged in my alphabetical reading of encyclopaedias upstairs in the library, I studied the few texts I could find about the exotic and famous locations where we'd be performing over Christmas and New Year. New Year 1977 – I made a diary entry – you will remember me and my friends eating warm pastries as we walk laughing down the icy canals of Amsterdam. Not watching silly fireworks on the Toti lawn with the Brats and that nouveau riche Uncle Joe.

5

At night, unable to sleep after lights-out and, of late, masturbating, tired of reading beneath the sheets, I tried to drift into my dream of floating like a bird or a dandelion seed or anything that could glide, across the brown Mkuzi scrub. If that didn't work, I went as often as I wished to the Zululand bush where Bernice and Lena returned fortnightly from boarding school in Hluhluwe to spend the weekend at home. On alternate Friday afternoons after we moved to Umfolozi, Bokkie and I took the Peugeot station wagon and for an hour meandered along the dust road through the Corridor to pick up the girls from the bus at the Hluhluwe Reserve gate. The Corridor was where Bok and the other rangers sometimes came on horseback to dart rhino for the Save the White Rhino Campaign.

At the approach of another vehicle, our hands automatically went to the window-handles. Winding up, waiting till the white dust was gone, then down again, letting the air spill back into the hot cabin. If we arrived at the gate before the bus, I'd walk around looking at the maids' crafts. I asked if we could throw coins to the pickanins who stood a distance from the gate, waiting to dance and call 'Sweeeeets, sceeeeents' to the tourist cars and buses entering the reserve.

'We don't have money to wipe our arses and you want to throw coins. You're just like your father. Forget it,' Bokkie said and I dreamt of one day showering coins on the poor dancers with their tatty clothes and snotty noses.

The girls were home for the weekend. Then on Sunday evenings we all returned to the Hluhluwe gate to drop them off. I preferred it when the bus driver was off duty and we had to drop them at the hostel in Hluhluwe, as I could then see the comings and goings of the other kids. But invariably the bus was already at the gate, waiting. The forty-seater diesel, empty but for the driver and the two girls waving from the back window into the Peugeot's headlights and the choking dust, would vanish into the night, not to return for another two weeks.

Bernice, already accustomed to boarding in Grade One with Stephanie since the days in Tanganyika from before I could remember, seemed to take to the routine of being away from home without showing a tinge of trepidation or sadness. At eight she was the smiling big sister whom I adored, who with Bokkie taught me to read when I was only three. Bernice could handle anything. Hidings with Bok's belt, helping with meals, being away from home, picking ticks from my scrotum, reading and telling me stories. But, whenever my siblings boarded the bus, I felt pangs of sorrow on Lena's behalf. I could never quite forget her suppressed tears and unspoken pleas the first time we dropped her in Hluhluwe. That once, she had almost wept and again – but of this I'm no longer certain – after the first weekend as she and Bernice walked towards the bus. Barely six, two front teeth missing. And off she went. Cardboard suitcase in hand. Thank God for Bernice. How could you bear to be so alone without an older sister to take care of you?

'Jirre, she's brave,' Bok said of my youngest sister. 'Resilient. A will of iron for such a little girl.' We drove back through Hluhluwe Game Reserve while Bokkie tried hard to hide her tears. I wondered how it would be for me, when the time came: to leave the game reserve, Bok and Bokkie, Chaka and Suz. Even as I begged to go to school already at three so that I could be as clever as Bernice and our oldest cousin Stephanie, leaving home was a fate too terrible to contemplate.

During the years home alone with Bok and Bokkie, first at Mkuzi then Umfolozi, and in response to my recurring appeals, Bokkie and Bernice taught me to read and write. Visiting Dademan and Mumdeman in Charters Creek, Mumdeman allowed me to show off my talent to their tourists. Once I could string together a coherent sentence, my other games alternated with writing in the grey school jotters brought home by my sisters. Bernice, Lena and I invented Gogga, a secret language only the three of us could understand. All the vowels of a word were kept the same, and ten of the alphabet's consonants were changed: b to bok, d to did, g to gog, k to kyk, l to loel, m to mim, n to nee, p to pop, s to soos, t to tit.

'Loeletitsoos gogo aneedid poploelay witith tithe didogogsoos,' I'd say, and Lena might respond, 'We firsoostit have tito dido tithe didisooshesoos or weloelloel gogetit a hididineegog.'

Our speaking in Gogga could drive Bokkie and Mumdeman to distraction and eventually the language was more or less banned from our home and our grandparents' home. 'You're Afrikaners now,' Mumdeman said. 'You sound like Makoppolanders from the wrong side of Mount Meru when you speak that gibberish. Talk Afrikaans or English and be proud of your heritage.' Lena and I continued speaking Gogga later in St Lucia and in Toti when we didn't want anyone to understand what we were saying. In the Berg I began teaching the language to Dominic. Soon he and I could rattle it off faster than English. And so Dom and I had Gogga and English – even when it was an Afrikaans week in the Berg. Though eventually we seldom spoke Gogga, we continued using it to joke, or, when the need arose for secrecy or simply to tease the others by pretending publicly at sharing something exclusive. Dominic and my Gogga had six further altered consonants: c to coc, f to fick, j to jol, v to vis, w to wow and y to yok. The only other place I used Gogga was in my diary. There I put down the stuff I didn't want in English or Afrikaans. On the off chance of the book being discovered where I hid it in the slit of my mattress, at least my worst thoughts and actions – those I even dared write in Gogga – would be rendered as partly incomprehensible. Once my Latin is good enough, I told myself, I'll graduate to using that as my secret language, even though Ma'am said Latin was a very difficult – almost impossible – language to use for modern discourse and idiom. Its real use lies in enhancing your understanding of the music you sing, she said, and of the English we write and speak, and, of course, it is essential to understanding Roman Dutch law – which was relevant for those like myself and Radys Dietz who wished to go on to university to become lawyers.

*

Umfolozi. When Bok was away taking tourists on trails I played out-side the yard amongst the marula trees and hook-thorns. The latter, which I read about and memorised from Bok's Parks Board Manual, were *Acacia caffra*, names that came back to me once we started Latin during that Senior year in the Berg. I lay in bed and imagined – thought I'd ask Ma'am – that *caffra* was the Latin root of the word kaffir.

In Mkuzi there had been no yard and no fence. Barring a dis-proven sighting on a close-by sisal farm, there had been no lions in the park. In Umfolozi I was allowed out as long as one of the bull terriers accompanied me. While large game like eland, nyala rams and giraffe came occasionally right up to the house, we knew that in seasons of good rain, with antelope abundant and no migration to escape drought, the likelihood of leopard or lion venturing close to human activity was remote. Moreover, there was no way that either Chaka or Suz would let a predator – or even Jonas – near me.

After we left Mkuzi for Umfolozi, and once I had definitely stopped believing that the horse Ganaganda would show up for me to brush, came the horsy game. Sometimes I was the stallion Vonk – before Bok had to shoot him when he fractured his leg. Sometimes I was the mare Ganaganda. A twig between my teeth, I galloped through the bush with a thin stick as riding-crop in one hand while my other handled the invisible reins. Wood from tambotie trees was never used as a bit. I had witnessed in terror and recalled with horror what hap-pened to Bernice in Mkuzi when we thought she had chewed a tambotie leaf or swallowed a jumping bean. And I heard too many times what it had done to the Umfolozi storekeeper, Mr Watts, when the old man had eaten impala grilled over an open tambotie fire. The elasticity of a thin marula branch made for a splendid riding-crop. For hours I would be gone from the yard, Chaka or Suz by my side, or, when Bok was not in the bush, with both of them as my reliable companions. We walked and stalked the veld, played on the boulders above the donkey compound and secretly explored the overgrown cliffs beneath the trail office. After Lena and I saw a leopard there, I abandoned my idea of walking with the dogs all the way down to the White Umfolozi to look for the cave where Dr Ian Player said he had found a young boy's skeleton. Maybe killed in the times of Chaka, when Umfolozi was the hunting ground of the Zulus. From the house you could see the White Umfolozi snaking its dull water and white sand east towards Chaka Zulu's hunting pits. Hidden by hills, the river there joined the Black Umfolozi to flow its course to the Indian Ocean below the St Lucia Estuary, close to Dad and Mumdeman at Charters. Bok promised to one day take me to Chaka's hunting pits, but we never got round to it before we too were transferred to Lake St Lucia.

I played with my Dinky cars in the sand-pit Bok had built for me and filled with the White Umfolozi River sand. The dogs would be banished to the enclosed side garden from where they could do no damage to the elaborate infrastructure of roads, camps and valleys I spent weeks constructing. Bok gave us instructions so that Lena and I could, with roads, towns, hills, rest camps and rivers, map the whole of Zululand between Umfolozi, Mkuzi, Hluhluwe and Ndumu down to Charters Creek on the ocean, where Dademan was the Park Warden and Mumdeman the Camp Superintendent. Sometimes Lena and I removed the Dinky cars, the towns and the rest camps. Then we planted hundreds of yellow broken *Themeda triandra* stalks to represent Chaka's regiments. From up on our hills, smaller impis swarmed down the valleys into the Umfolozi valleys to surround and vanquish the lesser tribes, the evil enemies of the upright and honest Zulu nation.

Sometimes, in our network of roads, a tour bus would get stuck and one of us, happening by on horseback, would be compelled to radio to base-camp for help.

'Umfolozi HQ, Umfolozi HQ, this is Ranger De Man, do you read me? Over.'

'Roger, Ranger De Man, this is HQ, go ahead. Over.'

'HQ, I found a bus stuck in the sand, RF Ndlovu's Ridge. We need some help pulling her out. The tourists are getting hungry. Over.'

'Roger, Ranger De Man, we have your RF. Will send a tow truck. You're far out, could take us two hours to get to you. Over.'

'Roger, HQ,' Lena said one day. 'Don't wait too long. There could be terrorists in the bush waiting to kill us.'

'Tourists won't kill us, silly, the lions will, and the black rhino,' I said.

'Terrorists, imbecile. Not tourists.'

'Roger, HQ, I'll get the boys to start digging so long. Over.'

'Roger, Ranger De Man. See you in a bit. Over and out.'

And at night after we went to bed Lena and Bernice told me about the terrorists. Had heard them spoken of at school. Kaffirs. Black and swarming everywhere through Mozambique and Rhodesia. It was the terrorists who stole our land in Tanganyika. With guns from Red Russia. Terrified, I listened for anything that sounded like a tread outside the window. Was ready to scream and flee the room if I heard a twig trod on in the night. I waited till my sisters were asleep. Rose and ran down the passage and crawled into bed between Bok and Bokkie.

Days Bok and Suz were due back from the bush, Chaka and I awaited them down the hill at the Parks Board office. I watched Chaka closely. When his ears started to twitch and stand upright, I knew: he could hear or sense their approach. He'd snort and from inside his throat make puppy-dog sounds. He'd look up at me, eyes pleading for permission to run ahead.

'Behave yourself, Chaka,' I would say in my gruffest Bok voice. And, if he went on to yelp: 'You better stop. I'm warning you. Enough is as good as a feast.'

A mile away, so Bok would later say, on some footpath edging along a ravine, he would be pointing out to his trailists the performance being put on by Suz. She ran ahead of the short line of people, then, knowing the length of the imaginary leash, would turn, running back past the group to where the donkeys followed ahead of Jonas and

Boy. Down the line again she'd fly, stopping to spin around, then dash back to Bok who strode along with the rifle across his shoulder. Yelps, almost inaudible; small, muted barks; talking to Bok; asking, as she half turned ahead, then flew back again to look up at him. He did no more than shake his head. She fell into step, now silent, beside him. The tourists, smiling, would say:

'Oh, Ralph!'

'Oh, come on, let her go.'

'Poor Suz.'

'Ralph, you're being cruel! You brute.'

'Look, she's dying to run off.'

Then, if he had been satisfied with her over the three-day trail, and if the distance I would have to run alone seemed safe, he'd say, 'Go, my girl.' And the bitch, without a sound, darted from the group, tail a streak behind her. When she'd made distance enough to know she would not be called back, she'd break her sprint for a second and bark, three short sounds ricocheting up the Mpila hill. Beside me, without a second's pause, Chaka would answer and run, sand flying from behind his paws. I'd follow, calling for him to slow down, knowing he couldn't be stopped by anything. Soon, jumping on each other, playful in their nipping and licking, the dogs would return as a pair to my side. Then I run with them, calling them to heel when they try to dart ahead. Rounding a corner or a clump of trees I see nothing but the figure in the path ahead of me. He lifts an arm and I reach out mine and as I near him he lifts me still running and hugs me to his sweaty chest.

Sitting on his hip, I could then look back at the line of people behind us, totally amused by what they had seen. Self-conscious, I'd look away from the hearty smiles, to the end of the line, and wave at Jonas and Boy. Bok sat me down on the side of the path. 'Meet my Philistine,' Bok grinned as the line of people drew together. I nodded modestly as he said:

'This is Sylvia Porter from Louisville, Kentucky.

'This is Professor Jans Groningen from Bloemfontein.

'This is Mike and Rhoda Jones from London.

'This is Senator and Mrs Pat O'Hare from Washington.

'This is Leanne and Joan Hepburn from Cape Town.'

I waited in the grass as Bok and the group moved off and the donkeys and the boys approached.

'Sawubona, Jonas. Sawubona, Boy.'

'Yabona, Umfaan.'

Jonas would lift me and deposit me somewhere amongst the leftover victuals, water bottles and folded tents, astride the front donkey. At the office the tourists were packed off in the VW Combies that had come to transport them first to the camp for ablutions and packing, then on to the airport in Empangeni. Before they departed, and after the final group photo in which I was invariably included, I heard them tell Bok that their lives had been changed for ever; that they would never forget him or the wilderness; that they would write; that Bok must come and visit in *The States*; that they'd be back. Sometimes the women would cry.

6

Amo, amas, amat, amamus, amatus, amant. First Latin word and conjugations we were taught.

By Ma'am. Learnt. From Ma'am.

7

The batteries had begun to dim as I finished *The Day of The Jackal*. Book and torch back in my locker, I lay listening to the breathing and the light snores around me. And the frogs, their croaking bobbing from the orchard into the dorm. *Dormire*, to sleep. Still unable, despite my Mkuzi dream. I wondered if Dominic was. Should have organised to go there tonight instead of lying here wasting my time with insomnia – nice word – waiting for Saturday. I still prefer him coming here, I thought. Somehow feels less dangerous. And once a week wasn't enough. Somnia, somniae, f. Sleep. No, that was dead wrong. *Somnus*, is sleep. Do verbs have a gender? Only nouns. Is sleep female? Insomnia. Must be where the word is derived. Insomnia. Somnambulate if you combine *somnus* and *ambulare*. To sleepwalk. That's what we had decided we'd say happened if we're caught. No one would believe us, I knew already then. Jesus, sweet merciful Father, please don't let us ever be caught. Three faces over a desk. Bok. Bok's Chevrolet parked in the street beneath the Natal Mahogany at the gate. Our new car that couldn't go into the garage as that had become Bok's office. He and Uncle Michael fixed six rows of metre-wide pine shelves to the walls. Easter I'd return. Would Bok see through me? Guess about Dom and the thoughts of Mr Cilliers? Forget it. On the shelves and on the floor, the stock was stored. Almost every inch of wall – other than a section beneath the square of burglar-barred window – covered in neatly ordered rows of curios. From the moment the roll-up garage door opened I would be overwhelmed by the scent of grass, wood and wood polish, and, I thought, the smoke of fires, which was distinct from the smoke of Bok's Paul Reveres. Dusk smells, shadow smells. Curios. Turn on the double-tubed fluorescent ceiling light and the mood was radically altered, changed into that of a rude store room and office: on the shelves and stacked on the concrete floor the entire trade of Bok's Sub-Saharan Curios.

On the broad surfaces to right, human figurines from all over Zululand: men in dugouts, women stooped with children fastened to their backs, warriors carrying spears, women grinding corn in bowls, figures cross-legged on a wooden slab in front of beehive Zulu huts, small black boys extending hands in supplication, begging, women praying on slates of wood inscribed with Biblical scriptures and popular slogans: *The meek shall inherit the kingdom of heaven*; or *Zululand – Wilderness Kingdom*; and, commissioned from the

Zulus through a contact who traded with curio stores north of the Limpopo: *Rhodesia is Super!* Sometimes two or three exclamation marks.

Beside the human figures, the animals. Amongst those, also stock from before the fall of Lourenco Marques: wooden crocodiles, rhinoceros, hippo, elephant, marabou storks on one spindly leg – yes, they did look exactly like Holloway. Warthogs, giraffe, buffalo, lion and cheetah. Some the whole animal, some only the head.

Next, the masks from all over the country. The most profitable Bok bought from the girls in the Eastern Transvaal: masks made us our biggest money. Cheap and easy. Bok, buying directly from the girls, tripled the price when he sold to the curio shops, who in turn doubled or quadrupled theirs. Every tourist seemed to want a mask to take back home: Aberdeen, Bonn, Copenhagen, Dijon, Edinburgh, Florence, Geneva, Hamilton, Ipswich, Jerusalem, Kristiansund, London, Munich, New York, Ottowa, Paris, Queenstown, Rome, Stockholm, Tokyo, Utrecht, Vienna, Washington DC, X, x, x – must be some place in China with an X but Chinese don't come here – Yazoo City, Zurich.

Then, a disorderly mix of ashtrays cut from coloured sandstone; wooden heads and busts of bald indunas and bare-breasted girls; salad spoons; small and large spears.

Against the back wall were the cotton crocheted doilies sown in with beads; then necklaces, bracelets in copper and silver. Postal cable woven and plaited into bracelets. The postal cable bracelets, made from sources unknown and not enquired after, Bok said had been particularly popular of late. On a stretch of open white wall, above these, were the four trophies Dademan had left me in his will: the two Grant's gazelle heads, the small dick-dick and the huge sable antelope with its eyes that followed you everywhere you went in the garage. These, Bok said, we could hang in my room once I returned from the school and went to Port Natal with Lena. For that was where I'd go, to the best Afrikaans school in Durban, not to Kuswag High where

Bernice would matriculate. Bernice had remained there, Bok told family and friends, only because a change midway through high school would have disrupted her studies.

Stacked in piles after the bracelets were watercolour and oil paintings from near the Mozambique border. Less abundant since Frelimo took over. Some of these were on paper and some on canvas, mostly of sunsets and dugout canoes with palm trees and villages. Unlike the paintings in the books Ma'am shows us or those I've seen in galleries while on choir tour, these in Bok's garage have no names signed in the bottom corners.

The semi-precious stones: boxes full of tiger's-eye, amethyst, malachite, jade and onyx. Running my fingers through the smooth stones, letting them slip across my palms, endlessly, daydreaming, thinking of nothing in particular, my eyes taking in the shadows of woodcuts, scents, the play of light on glinting varnish and matt wood, grey silhouettes against white walls.

Beneath the back shelves were the woven grass baskets and to the right of those the rolled-up grass mats and then rows of brown, ochre and black kaffir beer pots in various sizes and shapes.

On the shelves to the left, the cow-hide shields and assegais, many of which Bok commissioned from kraals in Zululand. Then, on the last section of wall to the left of the window, smaller narrower shelves were taken up by ostrich eggs from Oudtshoorn. While most of those were white, Bokkie had written in one of her letters that Bok had asked James to decorate a few eggs with black figures and sunsets, as demand for adorned eggs had suddenly increased.

In the middle of the floor was Bok's huge work-desk with the phone, neat piles of paper and ledgers and a small two-door filing cabinet.

Bok had still been a game ranger when he got the curio idea from Uncle Michael and Aunt Siobhain, though the notion of doing curios as an own business was from after Uncle Michael started his fish and chips shop near the Amanzimtoti Drive-In. The curio idea had been a long time in the make, starting on a smaller scale while we were in Mkuzi. When Uncle Michael was still with the municipality, he and Aunt Siobhain, who was in medical supplies with Lever Brothers, were trying to save money to buy their own house in Toti. Uncle Michael and Aunt Siobhain had different schemes going, one of which was the curios, while the other was the ironing of surgical masks. Aunt Siobhain got the surgical mask contact through her work at Lever Brothers, and she passed on the idea and the know-how to Bokkie in the bush. Bokkie used two irons and an enamel jug of water from which she sprinkled. While she pressed the white tissues into their right shapes with one iron, the other stood with its face up to the stove's gas flame. When a pile of the tissues had been pressed, I was allowed to help her cut-knot-and-fold-in the elastic bands into the masks. The elastic was there to go around the surgeons' and nurses' ears. While we cut-knot-and-folded-in, I usually wore one or more masks, often not only over my nose and mouth, but occasionally over my head, arms and forehead, so that I watched our labour only through slits. Once every two months or so, when our cousins came from the city, Aunt Siobhain collected the masks and Bokkie received five or six rand. That was the one scheme, and it kept Bokkie busy in Umfolozi while Bok took out trails and assisted with Save the White Rhino.

The other was the curios. Uncle Michael would give Bok cash with which Bok bought things mostly from the Zulu girls in the villages outside the reserves or from Dademan's staff at Charters Creek. Jonas's wife Nkosasaan and some rangers in Hluhluwe also spread the word. When Boy and Jonas returned from near Ulundi, where Nkosasaan lived, they sometimes brought along masks and other woodcuts. From Umfolozi the boys could go home more often then they could from Mkuzi, so the curio trading increased. Jonas himself carved crocodiles and hippos on weekends when he and Bok were back from trail. Uncle Michael and Aunt Siobhain then bought these and sold at a profit to the tourist shops along the Durban Beach front. On Friday afternoons we went to pick up my sisters from the bus, the black girls with clay pots, baskets and trinkets had at first tried to sell to Bokkie. But as the girls at the Hluhluwe gate often sold directly to tourists for higher prices, Bokkie never bought. Occasionally a small load of baskets or kaffirpots was dropped off at Mr Watts's store. While Bokkie was ironing masks, she sent me up to Mpila to carry the goods back to the store room beside the carport. A camp guard came to tell her that something had arrived and I would be dispatched. Once, around the time of the hornbill invasion, a guard came to say eight pots were delivered at Mpila. I was sent up while she stayed bent over the ironing-board. She told me to make eight trips – not carry two at a time and to take Suz along.

The eight brown beer pots stood polished and shining in a row in the sun outside the store. On either side of the elegant necks were oval handles. The adorned openings were ridged with different patterns of leaves, beads, criss-crosses and antelope spoor. On the first trip back I balanced a pot on my head as was customary for the black girls. I imagined a blanket wound around my waist, swinging my hips, humming as I sashayed down the footpath. As far as I walked, hornbills followed me, flitting from branch to branch. 'Go away,' I shouted, from beneath the pot, 'I'm not feeding you anymore. Go away.' But they followed, squawking like the plastic toys of Molly Hancox's baby. I managed fine with the pot on my head until Suz got in my way. I caught the pot by a handle as it was about to crash into the ground. The pot had not broken, but the handle came off in my hand. I swore and kicked Suz in the ribs. Fearing another hiding as I'd recently had for feeding the hornbills, I threw the handle into the long yellow grass beside the footpath. The next seven trips passed without incident and I packed the merchandise in the store room with the missing-handle pot at the very back, angled away from the door. Instead of going in to report the completed task I went to the sand-pit. With another kick Suz was banished to the side yard. I knew Bokkie would go out to inspect the goods, but hoped that the longer I stayed away, the less likely she was to discover the damage. I played with my Dinky cars and started building a new guest camp beside the Black Umfolozi.

'Kaaarl,' I heard. She had found it. I ran to the store room, trying to look cheerful. She asked about the missing pot-handle and I said it had been like that when I fetched it.

'Then why is it standing at the back, turned so that I cannot see?'

'It was the first one I brought down, so that's why it's in the back.'

'Well, I don't have money to pay for broken things.'

She told me to get Suz, because we were going to Watts's store. 'Why is the dog locked in the side yard, anyway?'

'I'm playing in the sand-pit.'

'Get her out. We're going up to the store.' Letting Suz out I muttered that she had me in deep trouble and that if I got another hiding she would live only to regret it. I went into the kitchen, where Bokkie had already turned off the stove and was placing both irons on the sink. Up we went, Bokkie striding ahead, Suz trotting in the middle and me behind.

At the store Mr Watts said he'd personally seen to the off-loading of eight clay pots, each with handles attached. Bokkie apologised for bothering and we headed back towards the footpath. She asked how I had broken the handle.

'I didn't break it off, Bokkie! I promise. Maybe it just fell off somewhere along the way.'

Our eyes skimmed the footpath all the way home and to the store room.

'Did you leave the path, Karl?'

'No, Bokkie, I walked straight home. I promise, Bokkie.'

Back up to the store. Nothing. Then, as we went down the path and the hornbills were going crazy in the trees around us, she reminded me of how I had lied about feeding the birds and how my lie had returned like Lena's plastic boomerang to catch me out. For weeks she had been aghast at hornbill droppings and an occasional feather everywhere, in the window frames, all over the veranda, in my bedroom. Discovering for the umpteenth time a ragged cut from the loaf of bread, she had at last asked, 'Are you feeding the hornbills?' I said no, I knew better than to feed any wild animal. Still I continued the feeding: lumps of porridge from Chaka and Suz's bowls – a place the birds were too cowardly to venture near; pieces of bread, either stolen from the loaf in the kitchen or morsels snuck off my own plate while my mother wasn't looking. I lured them into the house while she was in the kitchen, eventually feeding them in my bedroom. If they fought or screeched so that their sounds were sure to reach her, I'd hurriedly shoo them from the window.

'Was that a hornbill I heard?' Bokkie shouted from the kitchen. 'Yes, Bokkie, it was just sitting here in the shade in my room when I came in to fetch my Mustang. It's gone now.' Soon the birds had become so confident they were flying into the open kitchen door, sitting on the bottom door, squeaking at Bokkie who chased them away. Soon I was waking in the mornings with the tick-tick-tick of their enormous bills against the glass pane of my bedroom windows. I feared a glass pane may shatter, a shard pierce me as I lay on my stretcher. This was a full-scale hornbill invasion. Soon it seemed my parents were content that the strange pattern of bird behaviour had developed spontaneously – probably because of the hornbills growing accustomed to me from the hours I spent in the bush with the dogs and in the front garden. Then, while I was sitting in my room one day – the huge birds by then eating from my hand – Bok, whom I didn't know was in the house, snuck down the passage and, before I knew what had struck me amidst the fluttering of hornbills, laid into me with his palm until I was screaming and begging for him to stop.

'I've told you a hundred times not to feed wild animals.'

'I'm sorry, Bok,' I hollered.

'We fine tourists for feeding them and here you sit! The game ranger's son, feeding them in your own bedroom!' I looked at Bok with pleading eyes. 'How long,' he growled, 'before you have the eland eating from your hand! Until they gore a tourist, or one of your pet baboons rips out an old lady's throat!'

'I'm sorry, Bok.'

'And the lying? How many times did your mother ask you whether you were feeding the hornbills? How many times did you lie to her?'

'Twice, Bok.'

'Twice too much! You never lie to your mother or to me, do you understand me? Do you ever, ever hear Lena or Bernice lying to Bokkie or to me?' Licking the salty snot and tears from my lip, rubbing my bum, I shook my head.

'This pot cannot be sold without a handle,' Bokkie said in front of me in the footpath. 'That's one rand gone, flushed down the toilet. One rand that I don't have.' By now I felt sorry for her but could not imagine recanting and again being exposed as a liar. Later, I thought, if she was safely back in the house, I'd go and fetch the handle, say I had found it somewhere on the side of the path where we hadn't looked.

'Your father earns a hundred and twenty rand a month,' she spoke from ahead of me as we made our way down the path. 'A rand is worth ten loaves of bread. That's one-third of our bread money for the month.' Trailing a few steps behind, I cast a glance into the grass patch by the wayside where I had thrown the handle. Every now and again she stopped, turned over a fragment of wood or a stone with her sandal. Eventually, close to the gate and seeming near tears, she gave up, 'I'll just have to make two hundred extra surgical masks.'

Instead of listening to the afternoon wireless serial with Bokkie, I returned with Suz to the grass along the footpath. I went through, inch by inch, trying to get Suz to help. There was no sign of the handle. I had cost my mother the equivalent of ten loaves of bread; had caused the labour equivalent of making two hundred surgical masks. In the long grass – now become sprawling fields where before I had seen only patches – every pebble, twig or piece of dung seemed for a second to be the handle, but was useless other than to fling in anger at the hornbills that now seemed set on tormenting me from the branches. The loathsome object was nowhere. I searched, eventually convincing myself that it must have been in a vast stretch of grass higher up, near the camp. I combed that. The handle had, I felt in despondent certainty, simply vanished. Maybe the plot of land where it had been flung was cursed by the Zulu witch doctors in the olden days. Maybe it was an old kraal or a burial ground and my tossing the handle onto the sacred ground had disturbed the ancestors.

The wireless was on and Bokkie was listening to *Die Geheim van Nantes*. The one iron rested against the gas flame and with the other — a wad of cloth around its handle — she was pressing the tissue of another surgical mask. I waited for a commercial break.

'Bokkie,' I said, on the verge of tears, 'I've looked everywhere. It's gone.' She kept her face averted, pushing down hard on the tissue in a deliberate movement that made the ironing-board tremble on its thin wooden legs. She nodded her head, rigorously.

'I'm sorry I lost it, Bokkie,' I said.

'What?' She asked, turning to hear with her good ear.

'I'm sorry I lost it, Bokkie,' I repeated, almost whispering from the lump in my throat.

'It's nothing, Karl. It's nothing. What is an extra ten hours breaking a back over an ironing-board when the back has been broken so many times it doesn't feel any more? Just shows: better to do everything myself than entrust it to others. If I ask anyone to do anything in this house I'm just making extra work for myself. There you have it, Katariena Maria De Man born Liebenberg. This is your life. This is your cross to bear.'

I stood in silence. Ready to weep. 'I can help you cut-knot-and-fold-in,' I whispered.

'Didn't you hear what I just said? I'll do everything myself from now on. Thank you for offering.'

For two days she barely spoke to me, calling only when my food was ready, saying my name through stiff lips at night as she tucked me in after prayers. I waited for her to stop being angry; to talk to me and to love me again. Then, miraculously, with no explanation, the pot-handle was, somehow, forgotten and or forgiven. On a bright, starlit night, Bok awoke me from my sleep as I had asked as soon as their alarm clock went off. With the Afrikaans service of Radio South Africa from the wireless by our side, we went out onto the lawn where we sat wrapped in blankets with Suz by our feet. The night was not unlike any of hundreds we spent in the enormous silence of Umfolozi with Bok back from trail and just the sounds of the wild around us. But it was also different from any other: that night we were not look-ing at the flickering ecstacy of stars and the seemingly close-by haze of the distant Milky Way. Instead, our eyes were straining at the moon, checking whether we could perhaps see a black spot on its glowing sur-face. We couldn't, of course, and I suspected Bok and Bokkie had known that much all along. But we heard Neil Armstrong, close to that exact instant he announced to the world: 'Houston, Tranquillity Base here. The eagle has landed.' And then, bored from waiting for the man to walk on the moon, I fell asleep. I awoke from Bok saying my name and shaking my arm. Just in time to hear it: 'That's one small step for man, one giant leap for mankind.'

Bok hugged me and Bokkie to him and said: 'We beat those Russians. I knew we would.'

Zululand was wiped from the sand-pit. From Bokkie's green lawn I stepped onto the smooth white sand of the moon — careful to evade the craters — as I practised my message to the world.

8

Eyes, as if entranced, moved nowhere but from the face to the hands poised, fingers relaxed in front of his chest. The piano's introduction neared its close and the fingers retracted, wrists drew closer to the chest, shoulders lifting and now the tension was inscribed in lines on the face, grooved pincers extending around the compressed lips. The eyes closed only to snap into a deliberate glare taking us all in as simultaneously the dark fringe bobbed on the forehead, the arms shot forward and up and in that same instant it seemed one hundred and twenty boys' voices, in perfect unison, sang:

'*Ky-r-i-e*,' over four bars, drawn to a slight diminuendo into which swelled Mike van der Bijlt's second alto *Ky-r-i-e*, echoing ours; then, a tone higher and with increased volume, we repeated *Ky-r-I-e*; his finger flew towards Dominic bringing him in over the end of ours; eyes wide, a harsh whispered crescendo over the end of Dominic; we breathed and then, another full tone up, now in complete crescendo to his fists shaking we repeated K-Y-R-I-E, retracting the D sharp into diminuendo as he brought in Louw from second soprano behind us; closing his eyes, fingers into claws showed he wants crescendo on Louw's first *e-l-e-i-s-o-n*, his hand flew at us quivering and we repeated, now pianissimo, after him. Then, the whole choir with the quartet:

> *Kyrie eleison*
> *Christie eleison*
> *Kyrie eleison*

Louw repeating our penultimate *Kyrie*. Conradie from first alto was about to take it up, when: 'Stop! In God's fucking name stop!' His eyes, still closed, the last words barked after the acoustics had melted and a familiar silence descended in the hall. No one moved. I was not breathing. We waited for the miscreant to be named. It could be any one. Or all of us.

'Louw,' he hissed, opening his eyes; black, flashing and terrible, 'now that you are in Standard Seven and nice and big, let me tell you: you are not singing a fucking death march.'

Silence. Brief relief. My mouth relaxed and I breathed in, then out, allowing my fingers to unbend from the sheet music.

'This is *not* a death march. Nor is it a requiem. Stop dragging,

dragging behind the piano. And stop scooping from note to note and sounding like Shirley fucking Bassey.' He paused.

'Do you hear me?'

'Sorry, Sir.'

'Don't *sorry* me!' Glowering at Louw, he took a pace towards the quartet. 'If you can't do it, fuck off! As jy soos 'n donnerse meid wil sing, get out of here and come back when you can do it properly. Where's the Portuguese diva when I need him? Verstaan jy my, Louw?'

'Ja, Meneer.'

His nostrils flared, his chest heaved. Then, abruptly, immaculately transformed, there was a different voice altogether: 'Later, later, when we get to the Agnus Dei – if we ever get there because this is the most useless choir in the history of the universe – in section eleven, *then*, Louw, you can do your tragic stuff. There you colour your voice black and grey. Just before the *Dona nobis* right at the end . . . in six months' time . . . that's heavy, war-like, guilty, sad. But that's far away. Understand?'

'Yes, Mr Cilliers.'

'All of you, not just him. Do you understand what's going on here?'

'Yes, Mr Cilliers,' in unison.

'I want you to think . . .' And he stopped, turned around and stalked to the far end of the hall. From there, when he spoke at last, his voice carried, echoed from the ceiling along the library corridor and back down to us: 'The crucifixion. Die kruisdood, Christus aan daardie kruis, verstaan julle?'

'Ja, Meneer.'

'The Mass is a re-enactment of the sacrifice on the cross and through it we gain merit from God. We sinners . . .' He was quiet for a while and sat on the back of a chair. 'The Mass continues the work of redemption – throughout time. We are asking to be made worthy through God's mercy. Worthy through mercy to sup from the body and blood of Christ. Just think of that, boys, just let your minds imagine for a moment that you are asking for forgiveness and mercy so that one day you will be allowed to take Communion. The Catholics amongst you do it young, the rest of us only when we're older. But that's beside the point. For now, we all imagine ourselves begging to be allowed at the table. The Last Supper. This is a plaintive mood, it is not one of death. Red. Think the red of dawn, okay? Red voices. Brilliant pink on the high notes, sopranos. And altos, purple on the lows. Purple. There is hope of eternal life, even as each of us knows we are not worthy to enter these sacred mysteries.'

His voice trailed off. He walked back to take his place to the side of the pianist. 'Do you get what I'm telling you to visualise?'

'Yes, Sir.'

'Okay. Right. Goed. From the *Kyrie* before Erskin.'

Later, I faced him where he was seated behind his desk in the conservatory. Light from open windows rested in squares on the lawn. Warm humidity filling the room seemed to palpitate with the ringing of crickets and frogs from the orchard. The sounds peeled off the walls and resounded back down to the river.

'I asked you to come,' he said, and paused for a while looking me in the face, 'because I thought you may have something on your mind.'

I nodded. Stared down at the linoleum floor.

'What is it, Karl? What's bothering you?'

A quick glance at him. Suddenly at a loss for words. Down again at my own bare legs and sandalled feet. Above my knees the hair was standing on end. Jesus. Now that I was here I was terrified.

'Karl?' Reassurance in the voice using my first name. Baritone.

I averted my gaze, still unable to look at him. I turned my face, unseeing at the heap of concert posters and programmes before him on the desk. No, I cannot do this. I'm treading dangerous ground and heading for disaster where I've been before and no, no, I'm not going there! 'Sir,' I blurted, my voice louder and my tone more urgent than I'd meant it to be, 'I'm not doing well in firsts and would like to be transferred to seconds, Sir.' I kept my gaze on my legs, waiting for him to speak.

'Look at me, Karl.' Again the voice was gentle, offering measured reassurance. I lifted my head, found him smiling across the desk. 'You're saying you'd like to be a second soprano? That you're finding firsts too much?'

'Only the really high score, Mr Cilliers. I'll be perfect in seconds, I know, it's not as though I need to go down to alto or anything like that. I'm excellent between B flat below middle C, up to . . . maybe just above the high G. So to test my voice would be superfluous, Sir.'

He chuckled, lifted his hand to his mouth, amused. 'To test your voice would be superfluous.' A smile played around his lips. He nodded. Possibly teasing me.

'That's just my opinion, Sir.' Spoken in earnest. 'I'd hate to waste your time this late in the term when I should have told you already during voice-testing in January. But if you prefer to test me, Mr Cilliers, that's fine.' But please, please Merciful Father, don't let him, don't let him ask me to sing.

'You've never really enjoyed choir, have you, Karl?'

'I beg your pardon, Mr Cilliers?'

'You may go to seconds, of course,' he paused. I am ready to shout for joy. 'But,' he says, 'I'd like to know more about how you feel in choir, generally.'

What must I say? More than a word of truth from me would be suicide.

'I really enjoy the concerts, Sir. I'm not sure why you think I don't like choir, Sir.'

He said he'd been watching me over the last month or so, had noticed a marked change in my attitude. He wanted to know what the change was all about, whether it had been merely because I had wanted to soften him up to allow me to change voices. I felt a flush across my face. Warmth radiating around my legs as if from a floor bathed all afternoon in the hot sun.

Now I would talk for my life: 'Sir, when I came back in January,' I paused, picking through the words, 'I decided I wanted to give my best to the school. If I have a different attitude, then it's because I'm a Senior now and I want to get the most out of my last two years here.' Surely that was good enough. An ample explanation. Whatever the motive for my altered state, surely the point was that I had changed for the better. How wonderful that I had succeeded—

'You can trust me, Karl.'

'Sir?' Still looking at him, I now frowned. His bottom lip was caught between his teeth. Again smiling.

'Is there something else on your mind, Karl? I believe there is, you know.' I yearned to melt into the air. He knew, had known all along the real reason for my coming. My alibi of being moved to seconds – no, not alibi, I had wanted that too – had been seen through. 'As I said, you can go to seconds tomorrow, that's cleared up and agreed upon. No test . . . As you say, it would be, eh, superfluous.'

'Thank you, Sir.'

'But,' he said and stopped. When at last he spoke, asking for the real issue on my mind, I knew that my being there was because of his precise grasp of what I had been hoping for; had been dreading. Now, the realisation of what I had gotten myself into terrified me. Every signal, every pondering look I had cast him over the weeks had indeed been seen. And as I saw it on his face, heard interest from his tone and his searching open-ended sentences, I longed to either retract everything or at once make him understand – believe – that he had misread it all. No, this wasn't what I had wanted. Not really. That was just a little game. A silly teenage fantasy. I wanted to deny even to myself what I had been up to. And it was not too late to back off. No. He was still only guessing. I could say that there was nothing, absolutely nothing else bothering me. But then, I could also find out what he was thinking and *then* back off. I can't do it. I can't do it. I can, I can, can, can, can: 'Sir, do you remember, last year, Sir?'

He frowned. 'What about last year?'

Silence. A drop of perspiration trickling down my back. I must speak. I must. But the possibility, the likelihood, of this thing turning

horrible now threatened to dumb me. I cannot do it. I knew, had all
along; cannot go through with it. Speak, Mr Cilliers, you say something. I must get out. It's all wrong and he's going to cause endless shit.
What am I doing! I must think up something now to make him think
he's misunderstood . . .

'Have you been doing it again?' he asked.

Eyes, terrified on his.

The face was open, even affectionate. Nothing there to say he
would break this confidence. He won't, he won't: 'No. No, Mr Cilliers.
I've just . . . It's just that I've started having dreams.' I felt dizzy at the
tension, the sight of the man in front of me, the fear, the lies. Lies:
saves that came in the very instant of challenge. Not premeditated. Just
there, ready to jump like frogs from my mouth. Talk, cunt. Please talk
now before I turn and run.

'What dreams, Karl?'

'Dreams of those things, Sir.'

'What sort of dreams?'

'It's not just the dreams, Sir. Sometimes when I wake up, it's . . .' A
threshold; another I cannot cross.

'Karl?'

Yes, yes, yes: 'Sticky, Sir.' A faint smile again around his mouth and
eyes. Now I dreaded him asking more about the dreams. Of those wet-
affairs I knew nothing but for Dominic's references and the vast little
Lukas told, most of which I imagined was boast, anyway; I should
have asked Dominic if it's the same as just plain coming. Please let him
not ask; please let him believe me.

'Karl,' he paused and stared from the window, 'do you and the
other boys still do what you did last year?'

'No, never, Sir, I swear, please don't tell Mr Mathison, Sir. *You*
know how we were caned . . .'

'Don't worry. This is between us. I give you my word, Karl.'

'Sir, something else . . .' Terrified, flushed and sweating, I rushed on.
He rose from his chair, came round the desk towards me. Sat down

on the edge of his desk, his feet a metre away from my sandals. He said nothing, waiting.

'I'm afraid you may become angry at me, Sir. But I can't help it.'

'I won't, Karl. I've promised you: this is confidential.'

Again at my feet. Smelt horse from afternoon riding. Passed a hand swiftly beneath my nose. Then quickly, without looking up: 'It's you, Sir. In my dreams.'

I sensed him rising from the desk. Saw his legs straighten and his shoes move off; heard him cross to the big glass doors and peer into the night. I gritted my teeth, too afraid to look at his back. A ridiculous mistake; going to backfire; if only he won't tell, it's still okay; if he talks; oh God, Bok; Jesus; the caning, no, never, the humiliation; so much burst through my mind; my hands contorted to fists and arms clasped to sides; what am I doing, what am I doing; going to piss myself; shaking; I want to vomit. Yes, I'll—

'You dream of me?' With his back turned. Still I could not lift my eyes from my feet. Lead weights balanced on my downturned eyelids. Could not blink, let alone move.

'Please, Sir, I only told you because . . . because I thought maybe you could help me.'

Only the crickets and the frogs. Fingers dug into my palms. If I had nails I could have made them bleed. Oh God, let my palms bleed; cannot stay here, must get out. Without thinking I was saying: 'I must go, Sir. I should not have told you, Sir. I'm sorry. Deeply, deeply sorry if I have offended you, Mr Cilliers.' I waited for the dismissal. I hate you; I'll say you made it all up. That you tried it and when I refused you became angry.

'What do you want me to do, Karl?' His voice as tranquil as before.

At last I looked up at his back; made out that he was looking at me in the black glass. I felt spent. As after a day of diving or swimming or hard riding. Stars, flickering through my field of vision. Dizzy again. Could doze on my feet. Hear my own voice, tired and distant as though sourced from a place not my lips: 'Anything you think, Sir.'

The picture begins to blur as he turns to me. I try to hide the tears by again averting my eyes. Wipe them with the back of fists no longer feeling anything.

9

It was almost dawn. Bok thought it could be rain coming through the thatch, brushing his cheek. Only when the burn of a million white-hot needles shot from his eyes into his head and he screamed in agony did he realise what it was. Hands rubbing at his eyes he stumbled to the kitchen and felt for the red Tupperware jug. He poured the milk between his batting eyelids, over his face; the entire jug. There was no relieving the fire ablaze from eyes to brain. Bleary, bumping against the reed walls he found his way to the bed and felt for the holster and the loaded revolver. He fired two shots through the roof and lay with his face in the pillow, writhing. He heard the footsteps of their running; shouted for them to come in. They found him there in the darkness. With his arm over his eyes he told them he was blind. He told Jonas to take the revolver to the bathroom. The rinkhals lay coiled on the toilet seat. Jonas fired three shots and the snake bounced, twitching, to the cement floor.

Boy had never driven a motorised vehicle until that morning. The Land Rover, in first and second gear, all the way to HQ. From there Willy Hancox took Bok to hospital in Matubatuba. A week later we got home from visiting Bokkie's family in Klerksdorp. Bok, eyes puffy and red, was still wearing dark glasses.

10

Before meals we stood in line on the arched stoep. At the very front were the Standard Twos, then the Threes, leading all the way up to the

Sevens at the back; nine years old to fifteen; the line roughly from short to tall, broken only occasionally by a boy taller than his peers. Like Lukas, behind Dominic and me amongst the Standard Fours in our Junior year. Standard Seven prefects patrolled the stoep to ensure absolute silence in line.

We filed quietly in. Plates were collected from the counter behind which Matron Booysen supervised the black staff dishing food in spoonfuls. Beauty had taken a liking to Dominic ever since we first arrived. Once a term he returned from home with a gift for her. I didn't bring gifts, but my association with him had bought me her generosity. She knew our likes and dislikes. Matron Booysen's eyes, drawn into slits against the smoke drifting up from the cigarette between her lips, scanned the plates to make sure none was favoured. Dominic despised the fish in mushy white sauce: Beauty dug around for the smallest piece possible. I could not countenance Brussels sprouts: Beauty scooped five tiny, shrivelled ones onto my plate.

On lunch duty was Marabou, then our class teacher, whom we still called Miss Holloway. Once we all had our food and were standing behind our chairs, she chose a name to say grace:

'Karl De Man. It's an English week.'

I prayed. 'For what we are about to receive may the Lord make us truly thankful, and may he also grant the teachers strength to say their own prayers. Amen.'

Muffled giggles from the boys at my table. I read Dominic's amused lips: Stupid. The prefect at the head of the table grimaced. Apprehension knotted my stomach. Miss Holloway gave us permission to be seated. Over the clutter of chairs came her command for me to excuse myself and wait outside.

Passing the Seniors, I heard the whispered sneers: 'He's going to fuck you up.' 'Pansy.' 'Loudmouth.' 'Brass-arse.' 'Naff.' Johan Reyneke, leaning back, chair reclining against the wall, blocking my path. To skirt him I turned between two tables, blood rushing into my neck. Behind me I heard Reyneke: 'Fokken rooirok, Moffie. Buys is going to rip the skin off your arse.' I looked straight ahead, chin raised, over the seated heads, too afraid, no, too ashamed to meet anyone's eyes.

The sun fell onto the stoep through the arches that ran the distance of the bottom floor. She let me wait. The glare into the heat of my shame warmed my cheeks and neck. I took a pace back into the shade.

They're all looking. I hate you, Reyneke. I hate you O'Connor, and you Sullivan. I hate you. I hate you. I hate you all.

She stuck her head through the sliding door and told me to stand in the sun where she and the rest of the school could see my disgrace displayed. She disappeared, back to her food. My thoughts crowded into a channel of loathing that threatened to make my body shake; fear brought me back into the sun. I waited. I hate this place. Why did I ever come here? I'm not coming back. Next year I'm not coming back. Next year, next year.

Chairs screeched as tables rose for dessert.

She wants to starve me. See if I care.

'De Man.'

I looked over my shoulder. Sullivan was leaning against the door frame, only his head outside.

'Holloway says you must face this way.'

I turned to the glass doors, glimpsed heads bowed over plates. Looked down at my feet. This afternoon's horse-riding. And what's a caning or missing a stupid lunch with Brussels sprouts, anyway. Look at those ants going into the cracks. Sandal's in their way. Mindful of eyes, I lifted my foot ever so slightly to make way for the line already curved off course to bypass the obstacle. Shifting my weight to one leg, I waited. Guessing at the column's whereabouts beneath the shoe, I lowered my weight back onto both legs.

I felt her in front of me even before her flat black shoes and thin stockinged ankles entered the focus of my downcast vision. I looked up into her face, took in the long beak amongst the wrinkles of rouged cheeks, the strands of sparse grey hair, like an old man half balded. Without saying a word she led me into the corridor towards the auditorium where the teachers ate. She waved me on to wait outside the headmaster's office.

A burst of laughter like bells chiming – Miss Roos, her laugh unmistakable – from the auditorium. She would think the prayer fun. Please let Miss Roos intercede, let her say something. Please let it be Mr Mathison and not Mr Buys. Back against the wall I pinched my bum with all the sting my fingers could muster.

> *Ich will hier bei dir stehen*
> *Verachte mich doch nicht!*
> *Von dir will ich nicht gehen,*
> *Wenn Dir dein Herze bricht*

They let me wait.

Thank you, Jesus, it's Mathison.

'You know what you've done wrong, De Man?' He frowned as he gestured me into the office. He took the bamboo rod from the rack above the desk.

'Yes, Mr Mathison.'

'What have you done wrong, Karl?' He adjusted his gold-framed glasses and sniffed.

'I was precocious, Mr Mathison.'

'Bend.'

I bent forward, arms and hands dangling below the knees. I closed my eyes. Please let it be only one.

> *Wenn dein Herz wird erblassen*
> *Im letzten Todesstoss*
> *Alsdenn will ich dich fassen*
> *In meinem Arm und Schoss*

Ears warned of the approach and I tensed, taking both the impact and instantaneous burn without showing a flinch.

'Precocious. Disrespectful. A show-off. You know the words but refuse to learn their meanings.'

Still doubled down at the waist, eyes now open – Yes, Sir – I stared at the ruffled patterns on the carpet beneath me. I waited for Mathison to tell me to stand up and go. Instead, again I heard it, felt the rip into my bum and the pain up my spine burning into my neck.

Please let him stop now, dear Jesus.

'Okay, Karl.'

I stood upright and turned to face him, resisting the urge to rub myself.

'You must stop being cheeky to the teachers, Karl.'

'Yes, Sir.'

'You know how I hate caning you boys, don't you?'

'Yes, Sir.'

'Why then always force me to do it?' He wore a sad and wounded expression, as though he were the one just beaten by me. I averted my eyes. Ashamed of myself. He gave me permission to leave. 'Thank you, Sir.' For some reason I thought of Bokkie, who always spoke about Mathison being such a smart and well-dressed man. And a sincere Christian. Born-Again, some said. Ideal for a school that, although private, professed to Christian National principles. No, Dom said Dr Webster said, mercifully he's not a Born-Again, just a typical average white South African Christian bigot, no more so, no less. I had never heard the word bigot till then.

Miss Holloway was waiting. Through the auditorium I glided as if on air, looking straight ahead. I followed behind her, noting her long skinny legs kick out like stilts and the little round body stuck oddly on the top, like an avocado stone with matches inserted to keep it suspended in a bottle of water. Tufts of sparse grey hair streaked out from her minuscule head. No I thought, not an avocado stone on matches, a bald vulture, no, no, like a marabou stork. The ugliest bird in the world. Sister to the vulture.

Back to the dining hall. The clamour of dishes from the kitchen

slammed into the silence of the huge empty space. Voices from outside; down at the soccer field.

The plate of food was on the table as it had been left. Only now
the plastic cup had been filled with water. The servants had started
doing the dishes in the adjoining room. I hoped Beauty would not
look in and see me. On the plate I noticed nothing save the hateful
heap of Brussels sprouts. Only four! Dominic, thank you, thank you!
Miss Holloway sat down across from me. I ate the fish, the salad and
the mashed potatoes. After a while, she exhaled loudly and shook her
head.

'If you ate the Brussels with your other food, rather than avoid
them till last, you'd be able to manage.'

I finished chewing. 'Yes, Miss.' By now the rest of the food had all
but disappeared from the plate and what remained were the four
Brussels sprouts. I took a deep breath followed by a mouthful of
water. Still holding my breath I cut one of the little heads in half and
stuck it into my mouth. I chewed and swallowed. I repeated the pro-
cedure: cut it in half, then, one mouth of water for every half Brussels
sprout.

'What do you think you're doing, Karl? That's very unhealthy. If
I've told you once, I've told you a hundred times: stop using water to
swallow your food.' She extended her arm and pulled the cup away.

Two and a half Brussels sprouts still on the plate, pasting their
smell up my nose and down my throat to collide with the food in my
stomach. 'I can't eat them without water, Miss,' I said, looking up at
her.

'Well, then we'll just have to sit here until we *can* eat them without
water, won't we?'

They are in the quad, in the shade of the cyprus, and down on the
field. Bitch. Bitch. Bitch. She knows, she knows, I'm going to throw up.

Matron peered from the kitchen. The serving counter's sliding
hatches shut with a wooden bang. We were now sealed in. Miss
Holloway nodded at the cutlery protruding from each of my hands,

suspended over the side of the white plate. I stuck the fork into a whole sprout. This is your ugly green marabou eyeball. I'm cutting it in half. Bringing it to my mouth, I held my breath. The smell remained, lodged like window putty in the back of my nose while I chewed. I felt my stomach contract. I knew I could not finish the remaining sprout and a half. Little green and yellow planet in a white cloud; the half showing an endless array of folds leading to the exposed heart. I tried to trace the paths to the tightest fold somewhere in the light centre; my head stooped closer to the plate. My eyes started to swim.

I'm going to throw up.

I lifted my head, blinked away the tears, wanting her to see. 'Please may I have some water, Miss.'

'Want me to call Mr Buys? Seems Mr Mathison didn't do his job properly.'

Looking down, ignoring the half, I forked the whole sprout and sliced it in two. Again holding my breath I swallowed, my stomach protesting. Two halves remained.

'See. A little will-power can take you a long way.'

My stomach was convulsing. A burning wave in my throat, swallowed back. I stared down at one half on the white plate, looking for a tiny patch that might be the centre. There was more than one. How many centres could exist in one half of a bloody Brussels sprout? And, the patterns on either half looked decidedly different.

'Please may I stop now, Miss. It's only these two halves . . .'

'Eat your food, Karl.'

The bell rang; end of break. I placed the knife and fork neatly back on the plate and looked at her.

'Get that idea right out of your system. Eat.'

I lifted the fork. Pushed it into the half. Raised it to my lips. Opened my mouth and held my breath. Closed my mouth over the cold mushy blob and tried to think of playing down by the river, feeling Rufus's canter beneath me. I chewed. I could not swallow. My stomach was refusing. I heard the boys fall into line, prepare to go into class. Again tried to swallow. Felt my throat begin to bulge.

'Swallow that food, De Man.'

I swallowed. Half to go.

'Please may I have water, just for this piece, Miss Holloway?' Eyes wide as they could go; pleading. She did not answer, just sat, quietly, head to one side, now smiling at me. I looked at the plate and brought the piece of vegetable to my mouth; felt her look down on my head. Could she see the movement of my scalp beneath my thick hair as I chewed? Dominic's hair, I thought, is so fine you can see his scalp in even the slightest breeze. I lifted my head and met her gaze. I glared at her.

Later, so I would hear from Dom who'd heard from a giggling Beauty, Holloway swore to the headmistress that she had seen in my eyes a glint of hatred. She told Erskin Louw a day or so later – who in turn told Mervyn – that she had never seen a child's glare so devoid of respect, so viciously intent on showing contempt for adult authority. As if plucked by an upward force I half lifted myself from my chair; she mouthed something; the knife and fork dropped to the empty plate and in the same motion she said I seemed to bring both hands to my mouth while my body doubled forward. Most of it caught her sidelong across the chest, but because she flew up from her chair the barely masticated food slid down her front and dripped onto her shoes. Beneath the droplets on her chin I could see nothing save astonishment. I kept waiting for her to wipe her face; to say something. Instead, without taking her eyes off me she called for Matron Booysen and told me to go and wash my mouth before returning to class. When Matron entered from the kitchen I was already approaching the glass sliding doors. Behind me I heard her asthmatic voice:

'Precious! Beauty! Bring a bucket and rags. Hurry up.'

'Oh,' Dominic said as the class sat listening to my story while we awaited the return of a refreshed Miss Marabou, née Holloway. 'That lovely brown and yellow frock of mine from Milady's in Escourt. Ruined, I tell you, ruined by that monstrous De Man boy's fish and veggies.' And we laughed at his gestures and facial expression, more simian than fowl.

'Bring on a pot of Brussels. This is Marabou's vomit marathon!' I said and half the class practised gagging sounds, the short and long bullfrog noises of vomiting.

Right into Standard Six, Marabou might suddenly be stopped in her spindly tracks when from somewhere behind a pillar in the dining hall, the back of a classroom or a tree trunk, she heard a sound exactly like the first wrench of a vomit cut short. Certain that she'd heard it, could not again be mistaken, she looked around. Her long nose was turned up like a red beak, the eyes with green eyeshadow rolling around in search of the culprit. We giggled, stayed down behind cover.

11

wasrond the wold in aty 80 days an bernice was a red shinees and lena eskimow to dademan and mumdeman cum aso to look The red chinese are bad and the yellow chinese are good like we die eskimos kiss their wifves with there noses, so lena hat to rub hers with a boy and everyone at the konsert lafed and lena looked like lena was going to cry on the verhoog. Daar was 'n feetjie was a feary The best in a white dress who lost the silfe sta silver star on the end of her wand. The feari can do not anything without the sta beakose her silver wand does do no toor magik anemo. she walk round and round and said I lost my silver star. Then she sits down again on throne and says I lost my silver star. The poor fairie cried all the time and the dwergies elfs look for her star but they did not find it. so, filias frog told the elves to come on his ship so they can go look for it all over the world. They wend every where in the whole world and everywhere the people were singing and dancing. In america are red indians with feathers in the hair and dance around fires and call each other who, who, who, who, with your hand over your mouth like. In red russia the kossakke fold their arms and go down like this with one leg under them and one kicking out. In one place they wikkel their tummies and make their hands as if they are a cobra going to spit like in sheresaad. The eskimos live in snow houses that's why lena had white fur on her hat. They dance in sirkels and eat raw meat because the fire will melt the snow and then the poor eskimo will all drown, one shot, dead. who's scared of eating a bit of raw meat. The eskimos are the best. No one speaks latin because the romans are dead but I can speak some of it because I know the names of plants in Afrikaans and English and some Zulu that Jonas teaches me but I speak kitchen-kaffir and fanagalo like Bokkie but Bok speaks Zulu better. My best word is Kukumakranka. Kukumakranka. Kukumakranka. Like a guinea fowl got a fright. But it's a flower Gethyllis afra, see, that's Latin. Just like Ebenaceae. Ebenaceae is my lucky word because it is the family, like grampa De Man, and the children like Bok are things like Euclea and the grandchildren like me are Euclea divinorum is magic guarri in zulu ncafuzana this one is easy to remember it sounds like you put kaffir and kosasana together. magic guarri grows all around our house. I can write, see, Bokkie and Bernice showed me even though I'm only four. The arabins ride on camels and they live in the desert where they make oil so filias frog got some for the stove on his ship. in charterscreek Phinias works for Dademan and Mumdeman but that's not filias frog. phinias in charters Creek has funny feet that look like a truck went over them because his toes are all out like krokodyl toes sticking over his pategas. Then they went to a place where they wear long dresses and black suits and do waltzes. One two three, one two three, one two three, like this. Bok and Bokkie have showd me how to Waltz, like this, one, two three, one two three and the two-step where you two-step on the turn. In Israel is where Jesus was born and Filias Frog and the elves sang Silent Night and the shepherds and the wise men and everyone is there. Bernice was the queen of Red China and the king has a big sword and he chops off people's heads who don't listen to him. In Lapland they have reindeer got horns nearly like Njala but Njala are bigger and they live in tents. And Filias Frog and the elves looked everywhere and asked everyone they met on the trip if they know where the fairy lost her silver star. No one knew anything. It was like it vanished. Vanished is when things just go away, like just gone to nowhere. You can vanish things with magic. Like with Euclea divinorum the muntus vanish sickness and with Euclea undulata headaches. Someone put curlers in Undulata's leaves. So Filias Frog came back on the ship and upon their return found the fairy on her throne still weeping and repeating: I've lost my silver star. Then she cries even more when Filias Frog and the elves report that the star, the source of her magic and happiness, is nowhere to be found in the whole wide world. Then the fairy raises herself up from her throne. And *suddenly* a light shines from the centre of the spot where she'd been sitting! She bends down. *Picks up her star* and puts her hand to her mouth. Then Filias Frog and the elves laugh and holler and they say: she's been sitting on it, she's been sitting on it, she's been sitting on her silver star. Everyone from all over the whole world came running onto the stage and I could see Bernice and Lena as they all danced and sang 'Joy to the World' and were happy because the fairy had found her silver star. And because the fairy was happy everyone was very happy and they all lived in consummate joy happily ever after.

From the moment we returned from my sisters' first school play, I insisted we rub noses. I no longer wanted to say goodnight in any other way. Bokkie told Mrs Watts at the camp office she imagined the novelty would wear off, but when Bok returned from releasing white rhino cows at Ndumu, he too could not get his mouth near my lips. An entirely new set of games were added to my solitary repertoire. Lena's Eskimo outfit was in tatters from my running through grass and thorn. Aware of my sister's attachment to the costume, Bokkie stitched the torn gown together with her Singer, and convinced me I could not be horse and Eskimo all at once. Eskimos did not even have horses.

'Can you imagine a horse on the snow? Snow is very slippery and you know what happened to Vonk when he slipped in the mud, don't you?'

At times I would play with her make-up and her old wig, turning myself into a girl, or, with her mascara, by drawing lines along my eyelids and donning Bernice's costume, becoming the Empress of Japan. The colours of her lipsticks and eyeshadows turned my face as beautiful as I thought I deserved to be. I got her to use almost a full roll of precious tin foil to cover a piece of bamboo for which Bok cut a star from an old shoebox which was then also enclosed in foil. When he was home I insisted on their audience as I played the fairy missing her silver star. At first they fell about on the couch laughing; later they got bored and told me to play something else. I perfected the Cossack dance, the cobra dance and I begged Bokkie to teach me the real waltz – no! not the one Bok did with me on his hip while he held my outstretched foot in his one hand; and later the cha-cha, the two-step and the polka.

I begged and my mother would sit, letting me 'do her up'. Tired of these games for a while, I would again return to my Dinky cars and build roads and bridges in my sand-pit outside in the yard. Then, again becoming Ganaganda galloping through the veld. From the kitchen, so she told Bok, she would see nothing except the patch of shiny hair, level with the tips of red grass. Somewhere in the vicinity of my head, she would see the other movement of grass and she'd know Chaka was there. Exhausted and thirsty from running and the sun, I would come inside and drink from the plastic water bottle. I'd take the jotter to practise words and the making of sentences. Bored with that, I'd put *The Sound of Music* onto the turntable. Having learnt that the shiny paths in amongst the minute grooves signalled the end of each song, I would skip to track 4, 'Maria', or to 5, 'I Have Confidence', or 7, 'My Favourite Things', or 9, 'The Lonely Goatherd' to which I could dance pretending to be a goat, or 11, 'Do-Re-Mi' to which I could sing along, the first song I learnt independently of Bokkie and Bok and soon knew by heart. Sometimes Bokkie would let me listen to her Sinatra from where I learnt 'My Kind of Town' and 'Fly Me To The Moon'.

Much was as it had always been in Umfolozi; only now, there was more.

12

In the first year — before Almeida came and we built the river fort and started the kleilat wars — we often played kaffirs and police, mares and stallions, cowboys and Indians (Apaches), racehorses and trainers, hide-and-seek, kings, queens and slaves, and Nazis and Jews. That game could have been Mervyn's invention as he was not only my first Jewish friend but one of the first Jews to attend the school. He knew everything we needed to about the Genocide and was also the one who gave me *The Diary of Anne Frank* to read. Our roles, like our games, changed constantly. Lukas, Dominic and Bennie were the millions of Jews as often and with as much abandon as Mervyn and I were the gas-chamber commissars.

In the grove of young wattles behind the conservatory, any two of us, wielding sticks as rifles, would herd the others into the imaginary gas-chamber. That place, which doubled as our fort, was constructed by tying tips of the still pliable wattle saplings together with clumps of grass. Before the moment of pre-climactic herding, the commissars had first to execute an elaborate search plan of finding and exposing the Jews from their hide-outs. If, say, Lukas and Mervyn had been appointed the hour's SS commissars, we would be given a chance to go and conceal ourselves in the open veld, or in the tall trees that grew on the side of the koppie due east of the school on which stood Mathison's house. Within the Jewish category we rotated roles as the whim took us, with either Dominic, me or Bennie being alternately mother, father, son or daughter.

On any particular day, Dominic could be father, Bennie mother, and me son. I hated being son as the role demanded I obey both Father Dominic and Mother Bennie.

The three of us were sitting in the branches of an old wattle that hung over the hill's gradual downward slant.

'The SS is approaching our hide-out,' Father Dominic whispered and Mother Bennie put her free arm around my shoulders.

From our vantage we could see down the hill, to where the commissars were combing the shoulder-high grass.

'How did they discover our hiding place, my husband?' Mother Bennie whimpered. 'And what will they do to us? Oh, and what about our first-born son?' She now pretended to sob, stroking my hair.

Lukas's deep second alto voice carried up the incline: 'Come out, you stinking Jews, we know you're up there in the ghetto. Give yourselves up and be spared your fate.'

'Never,' Father whispered to the family gathered in the branches around him. 'Remember Masada.' Most of us knew Israel's arid fortress from a framed poster that had been hung in the concert hall after an earlier tour of Israel. Once, before a recital of Hebrew folk songs, Mr Selbourne told us the story of the Jews' suicide, hoping its invocation could inspire us to reach what he always referred to as 'music borne from emotional depth and artistic discipline'.

'Yes, Daddy,' I whispered. 'Let us rather kill ourselves than be taken hostage.'

'Karl,' Bennie hissed, 'you're meant to be a child.'

'Now, now, dear wife,' said Father. 'Let us love each other in our family's hour of despair.'

'Yes, husband,' Mother answered.

'How do they know where to find us, Mommy?' I asked.

'There are traitors amongst our people, my baby. That is how they know we're here. Millions of our people have already been gassed.'

Now, right below us, the commissars looked up. They aimed their rifles into the hide-out. Mother, Father and I were left little choice beyond immediate and unconditional surrender. Forcing us at gun-point down the hill to Auschwitz, Commissar Mervyn prodded Father in his back: 'Come on, you filthy Jews, you're going to have a shower.'

'Mervy, you must call us Hymies.'

'Shut up, you Jewish bitch,' he retorted; and my mother was pushed so that she stumbled from the path into the long grass.

Into the gas-chamber at gunpoint; the metal door latched behind us; my mother grasped my father by the chest and wept: 'This is our end, my husband! Oh, our poor son!'

Outside, the taps moan as the commissars turn on the gas: 'Shhhh, shhhhhh, shhhhhhhhh.'

Soon, no longer able to hold our breaths, we are coughing and sputtering. Increasingly cruel laughter permeates the chamber where we still attempt to huddle together. We paw at our own throats, clawing against the fire rushing into our lungs. The laughs turn to vicious howling as our family's embrace unravels into flailing spasms of slow and dramatic death.

Then we change roles.

13

During the dry season, on an afternoon when there was spite from the sun veiling the world in a thousand gyrating aquarelles, Bok took me to a sandbank in the White Umfolozi to fire my first shot with a revolver. Dressed in only khaki shorts, he steered his Land Rover along the track with me and Bokkie on the front seat beside him while Chaka and Suz panted in the back. I may have chattered about the week past when he had been away in the bush darting white rhino to be transported to other reserves.

Bok pulled the vehicle deep beneath the branches of a fig, close to one of the few pools that retained its water even when the bush and veld had become a patchwork of browns and yellows as far as the human eye could see. The previous time we were close to there, the river had been a churning torrent of muddy water dragging trees and animal carcasses along the angry route we had come to witness. Then Bok had just returned from trail with tourists after being holed up for three days in the Ncoki caves, cut off from Mpila by the rains. From miles away we heard the roar. Bok, Bokkie, me, with Bernice and Lena back from boarding school, sat in the vehicle, agog at the volume, the movement, the speed that turned the spectacle before us to terror. Now it was an entirely different land-scape we entered. At my request, Bok again told of an earlier flood – in the years we were still in Mkuzi – when two game rangers on an inflated tyre tube had seen a Zambezi shark this high up the river.

Bokkie wanted to be in the shade. Above us in the sycamore fig's branches, hadidas had built a nest on a shaggy clump of flood debris. Cautioned by the dogs' erect ears, we looked upstream. Figures as if caught in dancing mirrors, a herd of zebra and wildebeest stooped to drink from another pool in the distance. Bok said we'd have to wait. He didn't want to scare off the game with shots. Bokkie spread a blanket for us to sit where she would soon lie down to read. She took from the canvas shoulder-bag a beer for her and Bok to share and a Tupperware bottle filled with red Kool-Aid for me.

I climbed the fig's trunk. Sliding on my bum, I approached the nest. From below Bok told me to keep a reasonable distance, particularly if there were eggs or hatchlings.

The game slowly retreated from the pool. Bok said we could go. He instructed Chaka and Suz to stay and they found their resting places in the grass beside the blanket. With the revolver in his holster and an empty five-gallon jerry, we moved into the riverbed. In both hands I carried a small red and black box of ammunition. Behind us, Bokkie settled down on her stomach, chin resting on a pillow, her Mills and Boon out before her.

Bok's eyes scanned the riverbanks. Bokkie and the dogs under the fig disappeared behind us. We halted across from a rocky outcrop rising above the bank on the other side.

'Can I take these out, Bok?'

'In a minute, Philistine. I'm going to put up the target. Stay here.'

In the pattern of shade cast by dull-green reeds I waited, watching my father cross the white sand and place the can atop an almost round boulder on the opposite bank. I wished Bernice and Lena were there to see.

14

25 March 1976
Amanzimtoti

Home in Toti for Easter. Due to the June and July tour of the Transvaal and Cape I won't be back here until the October holidays. How I'm looking forward to the Cape! Last year with the inauguration of the Afrikaans Language Monument we barely saw anything other than Paarl and Wellington. This time we'll be there for two weeks. There is so much I want to see there: Table Mountain, Cape Point, the vineyards of Stellenbosch and, of course, Groot Constantia. In Art Ma'am has shown us the most wonderful copies of Pierneef lino-cuts, many of the white Cape Dutch architecture and thatched roofing, the oak trees, outside staircases and gorgeous gables. Dom says the Boland is a lot like the South of France.

Time has flown since my last diary entry. Cociloelloeliersoos has called me only once after that. My excitement and dread was short-lived as he only wanted to ask whether I was catching up in second soprano. Although, he did ruffle my hair (!) and gaze at me rather strangely before I left and he asked whether I was okay not standing right in front of him anymore. I told him I was doing very well, because I am. I'm actually enjoying choir. I told him he could ask

Erskin Louw who is just two down from me. I'm not the tallest in seconds as I was in firsts and now I'm no longer right in front of him and I'm two rows back. I'm now almost as tall as Lena! Bernice found two pimples – my sisters now call them zits – on my right temple last night while we were all watching *Haas Das se Nuuskas*. TV is lots of fun but Bokkie moans like a stuck record-player about Bernice and Lena spending their nights in the lounge instead of doing homework. The SABC is planning to screen the Montreal Olympic Games in July, so I do hope we'll be staying with host families who at least have TV. The moment *Haas Das se Nuuskas* was over Bernice pinned me down on the carpet for my first ever zit patrol! Behind my ears she found at least three blackheads. When she squeezed those it hurt like hell. 'Use a pin!' Bokkie shouted from the kitchen. 'You'll be scarred for the rest of your life! Why don't you kids listen to me? Look at these scars on my face, do you want to end up looking like me?' And Bernice shouted, 'Yes, of course we want to look like you because you're beautiful,' and then she whispered, 'even though you're such a bloody moaner.'

Dominic phoned yesterday afternoon. I told him he has to call during the day because at night we spend family time together. There's no use in angering Bok. Dom is allowed to phone as much as he likes and I'm a little worried he'll call while Bok's here.

I spoke to Aunt Lena, who says Klerksdorp has frost every night. She's sure Great-Uncle Klaas and the other tramps are already heading for the coast. She says Uncle Joe's affair with the bokititcoch Matilda isn't bothering her anymore because she's been Born-Again. I told her that Mathison might also be Born-Again and she said, 'Praise the Lord. Thank you, Jesus, that Karl is in the company of your disciples. Thank you, thank you, Jesus.' Since she's Born-Again she says she knows God is on her side and will stand by her into any further tribulations she and Uncle Joe must pray through to honour the promise they made on their wedding day: through sickness and in health, for better or for worse, for richer or poorer. She says she's praying that Uncle Joe may lose all his millions, so that he may become like Job. God, she says, will never break our backs with the burdens he places as blessings on our shoulders: he merely wants us to bend our knees. She is filled with the ~~holy spirit~~ Holy Spirit and says she's so blessed that she may soon be speaking in tongues. I wonder whether Mathison speaks in tongues. That is something I'd love to hear. Maybe do it myself, though I cannot imagine the Holy Spirit coming near me at the moment. Not with everything Didomim and I are doing and my thoughts about C.

Afternoons I wait at Pahla station for Alette and Lena and we walk home together. On days when Lena stays at Port Natal for sport Alette is alone. Then we can talk about music and books. As usual Lena's doing only sport and no school work and Bokkie has her hands in her hair. Bernice is working hard for matric and she says she wants a university exemption even though she's planning on becoming an air hostess so that she can travel.

For the first time in ages I've had a reasonable report: A's for English, Latin and Art. B's for Natural Science, History, Geography and Afrikaans. Pass for Music Theory. E for Maths. Bok is popisoossoose-did off about the E and says I won't ever find a job if I can't do Maths.

Alette is doing Grade Five piano this year. On Sunday she played the organ in church because Juffrou Sang has the flu. I'm deeply in love with Alette. ~~Her and I~~ She and I speak about Europe often. We've traced our tour in Prof's Atlas. When I'm with Alette I don't even spare a thought for Didomim or Cociloelloeliersoos.

Bokkie's back from slaving in the church garden. I'm off to say hello. Will write again in the Berg next week. Mumdeman has met an old widower whom she's thinking of becoming engaged to. He has lots of money.

15

Quiet time felt an eternity. The words from the page found no place to take hold in the fever that had become my mind. I paged to Psalm 23.

That I could recite by heart, moving my lips, while pretending to gloss the text. I repeated it in my head to the rhythm against my rib-cage. After lights-out, I waited to hear Uncle Charlie's door shut in the passage between the dorms. I quietly rose as if for a quick visit to the bathroom. I snuck past the house-master's chamber and glided into G where Dominic waited, listening to the radio through his headphones. I lowered myself onto his bed, my arm across his belly.

'Aren't you getting in?' he whispered, removing the headphones.

'No, I'm tired from riding. I'll come tomorrow night, okay?'

'Want to listen for a while?'

'Just a bit.'

I stretched out, resting my cheek on the pillow beside him. He handed me one end of the earphones and took hold of my free hand. It was the ten o'clock news. I heard only the reader's voice; of what he said I took in nothing. At the peep peep signalling the bulletin's close, I lifted myself onto an elbow.

'Okay. Sleep tight,' I whispered against his ear.

'Are you okay?' he whispered back.

'Ja, fine . . .why?'

'I wanted you to stay.'

'Tomorrow, okay? I'm already falling asleep.'

'Tomorrow's Sunday?'

'We can make an exception, okay? Change the routine.'

I dropped my head and kissed him. 'Loelovise yokou.'

'Loelovise yokou titoo.'

I got up quietly and slipped back to my bed in F Dorm.

Listening to the fugue of breathing as around me boys began to sleep. Another variable came to mind and I prayed: dear Jesus, just *this once*, be on my side and let big Fat Du Toit not choose tonight for one of his muffled tossing-off sessions. And, if Dademan is somewhere in the ether, please let him not be here tonight to see where I'm going. I waited, anticipated the ritual of squeaking springs. Using hands and feet, I stuffed my blanket and pillow down between the sheets next to me. The squeaking didn't happen.

Soon, hearing Du Toit's light snores, I would rise and pull the covers taut over the dummy in my bed. Barefoot, I would cross the dormitory as if again towards the bathroom. Instead of entering where any wakeful eyes might suspect my figure from going, I will sneak through C Dorm where the Secondaries are already long asleep. I will slowly edge across the stairwell's landing. I will peer around the balcony door to make sure no teachers or staff are downstairs in the auditorium. When assured – absolutely certain no one is moving about in that vacuous space – I will tiptoe through the library and past the Junior dorms.

The passage door will be unlocked as he had said it would.

I'm a big boy now, I'd think and smile a nervous smile to myself. Within weeks, I'd have my own key: an instrument granting liberty of night movement that would initially seem to cost little more than a weekly stop in his bedroom. But it was not freedom I was seeking. In my own turbulent mind, I imagined that mine was the premeditation of a playful revenge and a little adventure – though those alone would not be my dividends. What came before thoughts of freedom or even the attainment of goals, and what for me became my most special discovery, was that squirt tasted like salted almonds on my tongue and against my pallet, that it burnt, long afterwards, quite pleasantly at the top of the throat. Knowing it neither there where I waited, nor understanding it even as it unfolded around me through that winter when I'd have to wear slippers on the cold linoleum passage, I was about to take myself further into that intimate space that in our mountain school, could not but exist at the obscure intersections of love and betrayal.

16

Jonas and Boy live in huts. Jonas and Boy make things with wood and Jonas beats the drums. Jonas makes faces and masks that you can put over your face and little men and Tambotie tables Uncle Michael buys for 10 cents and he sells them for R1.00 in Durban and gives some to us but Jonas doesn't know. Jonas says we can get rich from curios. Nkosasaan makes grass carpets and straw mats. She is Jonas's girl and Jonas says she's fat she's going to have a piccanin. Nkosasaan lives in Ulundi. Boy is not married but he has babies. That's a sin. Jonas and Boy carry guns like Bok. Because Bok must look after them when they're scared of elephant in Ndumu. Because Jonas and Boy are kaffirs and kaffirs don't know anything Bok must take care of them. Kaffirs are dangerous. Kaffirs are stupid. Thick like pap and their lips. They also stink because they never bath. Kaffirs are also niggers and wogs and houtkoppe and boys and coons and baboons and Afs and natives and Zulus and Muntus and Sothos and Xhosas and the piccaninnies hang rocks on their filafoois to make them long like black mambas. Bokkie doesn't allow Jonas and Boy into the house they must wait outside. Me and Lena go to the hut and sit and drink magou with the boys and they teach me the drums and we sing with the drums and how to cut wood for masks and statues. I love Jonas best. Jonas is best on the drums. Jonas teaches me to sing 'Ihashi igabane'. I love Boy too. Boy carries me on his shoulders and his hair is like Lossie's feathers and he smells like fire and grass and if I fall asleep he carries me home. Boy is strong and looks after Bokkie when Bok's away with Jonas on elephant patrols or chasing the poachers. When Bok's away on Save the White Rhino then Boy sleeps with the gun outside the kitchen wall so we can call him if something happens. In the bush the kaffirs know their place. In town Uncle Michael says the Munts are getting restless like in Tanganyika.

17

Mr Walshe slipped his fingers into the spaces between stomachs and girths; adjusted bits and told some to sit up straight and not look like a sack of mielies. He passed over Lukas and me. The two of us were at the stables as often as the system's rotating roster allowed and Mr Walshe knew us well. Moreover, Lukas was his sometime assistant at the dairy. Occasionally, when Mr Walshe was away, Lukas had permission to supervise Junior rides.

The pages of our Bibles, the inside lids of our desks and our pencil cases were brought to life by photos of us on our favourite mounts. Alongside these were photos of girlfriends and pin-up girls cut from *Scope* magazine, which came once a week in the mail for Lukas. In his Bible, Lukas also kept an enlarged picture of Harlequin, his own retired racehorse. My favourite horse was Rufus. I rode him whenever I could, though till '75 the horse would frequently be taken by Reyneke or one of the other Seniors before I could get to the stables. Rufus was probably a boerperd of sorts, yet almost as fast as King, who was part Arab, part thoroughbred. Rufus's copper coat glimmered even in winter's molt and his mane and tail were the colour of bleached thatch. At my request, Lukas instructed the stable boys to refrain from cutting Rufus's mane. The boys respected Lukas both as Mr Walshe's right-hand man and because of his fluent Xhosa. While most of the stable boys spoke Zulu, Lukas said they were none the less able to understand the language of the Eastern Cape and they seemed to take delight from their animated conversations with Lukas, transactions from which I was excluded. Knowing that at one point I had spoken at least broken Zulu to Jonas and Boy, I regretted not having learnt their language properly. Zulu could have been put to effective use with the stable boys.

Lukas alone was allowed to ride King, the farm's strongest most wilful creature. As happy as I was on Rufus, I did envy Lukas the honour brought by his physical strength and prowess as an experienced equestrian. *I do equestrian sport.* Something I delighted, unashamedly, in saying. Home for the holidays it could drive Lena up the walls.

The regular riders constituted a fairly small group. Much of the school up on the terrace belonged to a world whose dwellers seldom ventured down to the parts whence Mr Walshe oversaw the farm's activities. Dominic, for one, had not come riding more than four or five times. The same with Mervyn. Of course Dominic had to take care of his fingers for piano, and Mervy had violin, but still I suspected that even without those commitments neither of them would take much pleasure down there. To me, on the other hand, riding was the reason for being in the Berg. That and the tours. Our fort. And the landscape. And Dominic. When I thought of it, I imagined guiltily that I would sacrifice Dominic, the tours and the forts, but not the horses. Everything about riding, the movement from the horse into my body, the speed and rhythm as the ground coursed by, seeing the world from the elevation of the saddle, the smell. The smell of horse on my hands mingled with leather and dubbin. Prep was a battle as I tried to concentrate on homework while inhaling the odour from between my fingers. After riding I had to be cautious, for the smell of horse, just like that of rain on the dry earth, let something loose in me. I wanted to go wild. Become *boisterous*, a word I'd learnt from Miss Roos.

We walked the horses down, past the Dragon's Ridge holiday resort and over Sterkspruit's concrete bridge. Lukas was saying that the mare Cassandra would foal within eight weeks. I could not wait. Steven Almeida and I had been there the previous year, watching together, when Cassandra conceived by King. For a moment again Steven was back with us, quiet and unspeaking. Again I wondered what had become of him. I leant forward and patted Rufus's neck. Somewhere in the mountains heavy rains had fallen, for the river was swollen and the bridge covered with a foot of swift-flowing water. Thick silver jets spurting from the pipes beneath the concrete crashed into the downstream pool. Wading across, the horses were allowed a brief drink. Once over the bridge, the gradual ascent began. Mr Walshe allowed us to canter as we passed beneath V Forest and took the road's steep curve up the hill onto the grassy plateau. From here the ground rose gradually for another three kilometres before it climbed again into the next layer of foothills and the base of the wide escarpment. At a nod that we're allowed a short gallop, King, with Rufus on his tail, streaked ahead. A good while before the cliffs Mr Walshe whistled for us to rein in.

Where the road became a dead-end we dismounted and secured the horses to a dilapidated split-pole fence. Tied our riding caps to the stirrups.

Not everyone wished to go up the hill to the paintings. Most preferred to stay with the horses and talk to Mr Walshe. He sat with his back against a tree trunk, removed his bush hat and lit a Gunston Plain. Only Ron and Gerhard, two Standard Fives, followed Lukas and me along the short path up through the shrubbery.

'Not past the front ones, Lukas,' we heard from behind.

'Of course, Mr Walshe.' The first overhangs, where the rock paintings could be seen, led to a narrow ledge, completely overgrown, behind which we knew were more overhangs. Somewhere back there, so one of the stable boys had told Lukas, was a real cave, or a series of caves. None of us had seen the cave and we never had enough time to bash through the bramble tangles, old yellow-woods and thick foliage that obscured the ledge where we thought the cave may be. Our party of four, with Lukas ahead, moved on to where the rock face was broken and rugged, overgrown with bramble and monkey ropes, before opening into shallow rock overhangs. Streaks of bright sunlight dappled through the shrubbery, illuminating the smooth walls. A smattering of ferns and moss clung to the rock; from somewhere a trickle of water made damp stains like maps down near the floor; we guessed at the source. Underfoot, sand, refined as white powder, was covered in spoor and droppings.

'They look like raisins.'

'Taste one, see if they taste the same.' Our laughter running along the cliff.

'This is klipspringer. Look at the spoor,' I said, going down on haunches and pointing to the tiny imprint of cleft tracks.

'And dassie over here,' Lukas said. Ron and Gerhard moved to the sand beneath the opposite wall to look at Lukas's find. Ron said something about having read on the back of a Chappies paper that elephant are dassies' closest relatives.

'Durrrrr . . . Steve,' I hissed inadvertently and the du, and the sss, and the tt returned.

'Here's the giraffe.'

They crossed over to me standing with my neck thrown back, face turned up to where the rock folded back to make the ceiling. They chatted while we stared at the fading yellow drawing of the long-neck with the dark markings. The legs were faded, like natural shades in the sandstone. How quiet I wanted it to be. Like in a museum or at a grave site. This, I thought, is sacred ground. I wanted the others to shut up; to hear nothing but silence and feel the spirit of the place. In another lifetime, before any of us were born or even before we'd arrived in Africa, people lived here, ate here, fought and mated – made love – here. The further back into the dusk, the brighter to my eyes seemed the red, yellow, brown and orange drawings. Most were of small stick figures on the hunt: bows and arrows at the ready to release at a young eland grazing to one side of the herd. Deeper we moved, towards the ledge's tangled obstruction. There the drawings made up a dense montage of paintings over paintings of human activity around fires and scenes of the hunt, less visible as the sun was absorbed by the dark. Not a montage, I thought, no, I'm sure this is what Ma'am would call a palimpsest. A palimpsest of imagery. Now beside myself with excitement, I wanted only to go deeper along the ledge.

'Wait,' I said, 'I'll ask Walshe for his lighter so we can see better.' I moved back to the entrance and out into the sun.

'You're not smoking up there?' Mr Walshe asked even as he was taking the plastic Bic lighter from his pocket. I grinned. On impulse I turned to the cliff and belted what I imagined a high G. The dart of sound carried up the gullies, seemed to swirl against the stone and then disappeared somewhere in a faint echo, leaving only us, the grass-hoppers and the birds.

'Sound like a smoker, Mr Walshe? *You* have a go, Sir, let's hear.' Around him boys egged him on. Mr Walshe blew smoke though his nose and handed me the lighter.

'Flat as a sheep being slaughtered,' Sarel Raubenheimer quipped from where he lay on his elbow beside Mr Walshe. 'I wouldn't brag if I was you.'

'Flat like your big black nose and putu-smackers,' I smirked down at him before turning back up the incline.

'Anyway, you're not meant to be shrieking into the mountains,' Raubenheimer called after me.

I turned, a sarcastic smile now hooked to the corner of my mouth, 'Well, run and report me to Mr Cilliers, klik-bek. Let's see what he says.'

'Arse-creeper . . . go any deeper and all we'll see is your feet.'

'I can't help it if I was born with more talent than you, Raubenheimer. Feeling a little lonely since Harding and Reyneke left? No more big bully prefects to take care of you.'

'Be careful up there, Karl,' Mr Walshe interrupted our bickering. 'I want you boys down here in ten minutes.'

'Yes, Mr Walshe,' I answered with my eyes still on Raubenheimer: 'Jealousy makes you nasty.' And with that I turned and trotted up the path. The suggestion that I was sucking up to Cilliers galled me, even as I knew indeed that was what I had been up to. Still, I had not meant for things to be obvious enough for anyone other than Cilliers himself to note. Then again, what the hell! For a moment I almost wished Raubenheimer could know that I had been in our conductor's bed. What a joy being able to challenge Raubenheimer to tell Cilliers — about me shouting a single note into the mountain; accusing him so publicly of petty envy.

And then, in the heat of the afternoon sun, I went cold and fright-ened at my own recklessness. Felt ashamed of myself with Cilliers. Of me and Dom. Swore to God I'd put an end to it all.

'Lukas still up there?' I asked the two who had emerged and were sitting in the sun a couple of paces from the front overhang.

'He's waiting in the back.'

Lukas and I moved farther along the ledge than we had been before, breaking and pushing branches as we went. More water dripped in a steady stream ahead of us, from somewhere behind the screen of branches and creepers. I was about to flick on the lighter to check the rock face when Ron's voice reached us, calling that Mr Walshe was ready to leave. We cursed and carefully backtracked along the ledge.

'We must come when we have more time,' I said. 'I want to find that cave.'

'It's around here somewhere. All the farm kaffirs know about it. We must bring a panga to chop open a path,' Lukas said, and we made our way back to the group.

18

I felt the crown of my head still damp from washing my hair in the shower. And the brittle winter-grass shave around my ears and in my neck from the afternoon's hair cut. How I hated, hated it when you did that to us. To me. Destroyed my hair once a month. So that there wasn't enough even for my fingers to pass through. Robbing me of my looks. When I grow up, I swore again, I will have hair, long blond, into the small of my back. Call me a hippie, a communist, a sissy I don't mind. I hate you all. I could weep from rage at the school. The barber. It would be a week before I could face myself in the — no, I'm not going to cry, don't think of it, think of something, something—

Like a giant undulating shongololo, Jonas's forefinger along the blade's ridge seemed to steer the tip of the knife, grrrts, grrrts, grrrts, into the wood. His grip around the handle applied the pressure to make the tiny incisions, scratches, hollows. Sometimes, for the faint lines of wrinkles on the mask's forehead, he used the fingernails of his right hand, the splintered tips as hard and sharp as broken tortoise shell. He was the smallest man Lena and I had ever seen and when he sat beside Boy outside the hut with us watching his work, I thought his mammoth fingers would be better suited on Boy's body, for the latter's hands, as if through a trick of irony or fate, while every bit as ashen and strong as Jonas's, had in turn nine of the shortest, stubbiest fingers in the world. The tenth, the pinky on Boy's right hand, had been severed by a panga in a fight with rhino poachers. That is why — Bokkie warned the boys — Lena and I were not allowed to carve wood; the blade would slip and cut off our fingers.

We were allowed at the huts of Jonas and Boy's compound until late afternoon. Then, before sunset, one of the men would tell us it was time to go home. Suz at our side, we set off through the bush along the half-mile walk to Mbanyana. Bokkie did not mind our spending time at the strooise, though she made it clear that once Lena went to school and like Bernice brought back homework for the weekends, there would be no sitting around kaffirhutte. The same held for when I one day went to school.

'It's fine while you're kids but when you get bigger it's not a good influence. Anyway, I don't want you turning out like Groot-Oom Klaas, niksnut, good for nothing tramp.' Groot-Oom Klaas was the brother of my Oupa Liebenberg on Bokkie's side. Groot-Oom Klaas, the cleverest man in the family, so we were told, was once a law professor at Potchefstroom University for Christian Higher Education before he suddenly went crazy and became a tramp. Ever since, he just turned up at the Liebenberg family in Klerksdorp whenever he needed money. When the frost bit the Transvaal veld, Uncle Klaas took off for Durban where it never really got cold. Then, with summer's return, Uncle Klaas headed inland, back to Johannesburg and Klerksdorp where the family whispered that sometimes he slept on park benches and in train stations. No one seemed to know exactly what had made Groot-Oom Klaas go mad, but we'd all heard Oupa and Ouma Liebenberg say it was a woman. A dark-haired girl he loved, had been engaged to, who left him for another man. Groot-Oom Klaas couldn't take it and went off his trolley. Others said the madness runs in the family; that it strikes the cleverest Liebenbergs in every generation: just look at Aunt Lena. She had to drop out of school after getting seven distinctions in Standard Nine and could never finish matric. If she hadn't eventually married rich Uncle Joe Mackenzie, what would have become of her? But Bokkie maintained that her sister wasn't mad; she only had mood swings and suffered from anxiety because of epilepsy when she was younger. No, others said: there's madness in the Liebenberg family and it strikes once every generation. They said that Great-Great-Grandfather Liebenberg, whom we kids never knew, used to sit on an anthill in Kroonstad barking like a baboon at the full moon. Then there was Great-Grandfather Liebenberg's brother Serphaas: used to get so angry he beat his wife and eight children half dead till eventually a vein burst in his head and they locked him up in the madhouse. And then there was Great-Uncle Klaas. Bokkie told a story of how when she and her brother Gert went to boarding school in Brei in the Molopo, Uncle Klaas arrived there and stood calling them from outside: 'Katie and Gert Liebenberg! Katie and Gert Liebenberg! Are you in there? Come out and speak to your Uncle Klaas.' Then Bokkie laughed and told us how ashamed she and Uncle Gert were when the teacher told them to go outside and get rid of the old poor white. And then there was Aunt Lena: in and out of Tara in Johannesburg where she had shock treatments that made her better for a while. Once we could all understand the meaning of generational madness, the idea that I carried our generation's mad gene was immediately brought into play, if I recall correctly, by Lena.

Walking back from Jim and Boy's compound, I thought of Lena and I as Hansel and Gretel moving through the bush, escaping from the wicked witch. I ran my closed fist up the thick yellow stalk of grass and then, from my palm filled with golden kernels, dropped markers along the route from the kraal to our house. Noticing what I was up to, Lena said:

'It's the wrong direction, stupid. The birds are anyway going to pick them up and you'll be lost, so wê! And we know the path home and we've got Suz. So stop being stupid.'

I despised her when she was like that. I knew full well she was right; could say nothing other than possibly: 'I'm just playing a game, stupid yourself.' And then add: 'I can't wait for Bernice to come home. She's clever. I like her more than you.'

'And you've got the mad gene,' she said. 'Watch out or you'll burst open your brain.'

I pictured my head bursting like a ripe monkey-apple on a rock, bits of my bloody skull and fragments of brain clinging to the red-grass. 'Then you'll be sorry,' I said to Lena, 'when I'm dead. For teasing me and calling me stupid.'

19

They had dressed up to drop me off for my first term at boarding school in the Berg. Bok wore his long beige safari suit and Bokkie the smock-and-hot-pants of floral cotton; only that day she decided to not wear the hot-pants beneath the smock. 'Don't want to create the wrong impression . . . that we're common or something. Those are smart people.'

'Ag, Bokkie, they won't see anything except your legs, anyway. Don't worry,' Bok said.

The night before they left me we spent with the Therons, who farmed near Winterton. The Therons were friends of ours in East Africa who also came out in the middle sixties. Their sons and daughters attended boarding school in Estcourt and we usually saw them over Parents' Weekends when Bok and Bokkie and the girls stayed over on the farm.

The excitement of the months leading to my arrival at the school now barely overshadowed the dread I felt at the prospect of leaving home. There had been first Bok's decision to allow me to audition; then the weeks of preparatory voice training and a brief furthering of my pauper's knowledge of music theory by Juffrou Sang: 'This white note is middle C next to the white D with the black donkey's ears.' She too was the one who told me that musicality and a good voice alone would not secure my acceptance to the school – and even on that score I wasn't in the top league; I needed to perform academically with straight A's on my school report. I would have to answer in full sentences when questioned by the panel; to smile and look them in the eye, to exude confidence: 'Use that charm, those blue eyes'; to say that I had always wanted to play the piano and to sing in a choir of international renown: 'It won't hurt if you say that you're a little frustrated at singing in a school choir that doesn't sing Bach or Beethoven or Brahms.' Having never heard the names or the music, I copied down the Three B's along with the titles of a piece by each; committed them to memory, practised in front of the bathroom mirror to say the names as though I had grown up with them in my ears and spilling from my lips.

There had been the drive up from Toti with me dressed in the new green Terylene trousers and the brown corduroy jacket Bok brought me from America when he went to see how things were going with the three rhino he had taken to Texas. Then, the horrible waiting where we sat amongst other boys and their parents for my name to be called. Into the auditorium drifted the occasional song from the room where the auditions where taking place. Voices like nothing I had ever heard: heavenly. I knew already I could never make it. And when at last I stood at the black grand piano in the room adjacent to the principal's office, I felt raw terror. All I knew was that my six-month training in the Three B's, to answer questions, to control my breathing and open my mouth aa, ee, oo, uuu, iii, oeee – everything Juffrou Sang had taught me – was wiped from memory as I faced the two men in the room.

One behind the piano, the other behind the desk. Later, in the Peugeot back en route to the Theron farm, I would be unable to describe either of my auditioners to my parents. One, I thought, had been the conductor at the concert Juffrou Sang had taken me to in the Durban City Hall. But during the audition, concentrating, trying only to remember what I was meant to do and say, I took in little but the two men's words that seemed a ready ambush for each of my insecurities.

The man at the piano asked me what I was going to sing and I said, '"Bless This House in D".'

'You mean, "Bless This House".'

'Yes, Sir. I must start it in D. That's the song that was sung in church when my parents got married.'

'How interesting. D . . . and what if you started it in F? Could you manage?'

A, B, C, D, E, F ran through my mind. I was certain he could see me calculating. F was higher than D and I knew there was no way I could reach there without sounding like a squealing warthog: 'I learnt it in D, Sir. D with the donkey's ears.'

The pianist smiled and began improvising an introduction, nodding for me to start when I was ready. Horror, for I had no idea of how to begin without Juffrou Sang's head nodding *one, two, three*. I just began, not listening to the piano, singing and looking into the corner of the room above their heads. I heard my voice, hoarse and breathy, threatening to crack on the high notes. I dropped my jaw as Juffrou Sang had taught me, pushing out my chest and taking deep breaths at the exact moments I had been coached. But the voice — even to my own untrained ears — was not as good as it had been in Juffrou Sang's living room or when I played the Pied Piper in Kuswag Primary's operetta. I knew, even as I sang, that I sounded ghastly. The song was coming to an end without a semblance of synchronisation between voice and piano. I wanted to weep with despondency and for a moment considered breaking off and asking them for a glass of water and another chance. Then the scales, still in the strained voice, and while doing these I decided I didn't want to be at the school, anyway. Between knowing I wasn't good enough and telling myself I didn't belong there, I wanted to get out of the audition and back to Kuswag Primary as soon as possible. Briefly wished I might be accepted only to decline and say I'd rather stay at home.

Then the two men asked more questions. And here, at last, the rehearsed answers scrambled back to the front of my mind.

'You say you've always wanted to play the piano. You're eleven. Does that mean you don't read music?'

Could I take a chance, disregard Juffrou Sang's advice; lie? What if they asked me to show them? No. Just tell them the truth, 'I play the recorder and I've just started learning to read music. We don't have a piano at home, Sir. But we're getting one because my Dad's business is growing. I'll learn to read music before the end of the year.'

'What does your father do?'

'He's a white hunter but he's starting a curio dealership.'

'And you lived in a game reserve?'

'We did, Sir, until I was nine and a half. My dad was a game ranger in Mkuzi, and Umfolozi and at Lake St Lucia. But now we're living in Amanzimtoti, just south of Durban.'

'Did you enjoy living in the game reserves?'

'Yes, Sir. Very much. It would be almost like being there if I could come here – on the farm with the horses and everything and to sing good music, like Bach and Beethoven and Brahms.'

'You have a good school report. All A's.'

'I am very fond of school, Sir. And music also.'

'You go to an Afrikaans school, but you sound English. Where did you learn to speak English so well?'

'We were born in Tanzania, Sir. There we spoke mostly English, but when we came to South Africa we went to Afrikaans schools. My mother is Afrikaans. And my cousins – on my father's side – their mother is Irish so we speak English to them. And Amanzimtoti, where we live, is very English. We're all perfectly bilingual.'

'Do you really want to be in this school?'

'More than anything in the world, Sir.'

That had been it. They said I could go. I walked back to Bok and Bokkie hiding the shameful knowledge that I had not succeeded. I myself was unaware that the ambivalence about leaving home had now again been swept away in the current of desire to succeed at what had been begun. At Kuswag Primary, teachers and children kept asking when we'd hear. It felt as though the entire school and neighbourhood wanted only for me to succeed. The thought of not getting in haunted me into my sleep.

A month later and against every dreadful anticipation the telegram arrived. Lena, Bernice and I took the sealed envelope up Dan Pienaar to open at Juffrou Sang's house. We knocked at the door. Alette opened. She jumped up and down when she saw what I was holding. We went into the lounge, lined with shelves of Prof's books and Juffrou Sang's records. Juffrou Sang came out and smiled as I handed her the envelope. I said I wanted her to open it. The telegram cryptically congratulated Mr and Mrs Ralph De Man on their son Karl being one of thirty new boys chosen over hundreds of auditioned applicants. I would be expected to start in January, the first quarter of 1974. Further documentation would be forthcoming. We jumped around, hugged and kissed before the girls and I ran down the street to tell Bokkie.

'Frank Sinatra!' Bokkie beamed jokingly. 'You're going to be the next Sinatra.' My sporadic fantasies of being a star had not included Sinatra, even though I knew 'Love and Marriage', 'Under My Skin' and 'My Way' off by heart. By then I had wanted to be Rudolf Nureyev. Robert Redford or Rudolf Nureyev. No one I had seen could hold a candle to Redford's smile, good looks and horsemanship in *Butch Cassidy and the Sundance Kid*, which we saw at the Toti Drive-In. Redford as Sundance was charm, looks, adventure, seductiveness and recklessness wrapped into one face. For hours I was in front of the mirror, practising his dry smile, trying to get his lines around my eyes, wishing we didn't have to have such short hair for school, sure that if my hair were just an inch longer I would look like Sundance, blond hair blowing as I galloped through the desert.

At school I was a hero. Kuswag was on the map.

Everything purchased for me – neatly ticked off the school's long list by Bokkie –was in the two cardboard suitcases Bok lifted from the Peugeot's boot.

'Just look at the cars,' Bokkie said softly. 'I mean, where do they get all the money for the school fees?' And later, once we were alone in the dormitory: 'I'm disappointed in these rooms; look at these little lockers and the narrow beds. Where's all the money going?'

'The classes are small; tours cost a lot of money, Bokkie.'

I moved from bed to bed, reading to myself the names pinned to the pillows. Lukas Van Rensburg. Dominic Webster. Bennie Oberholzer. Mervyn Clemence-Gordon.

'But they must make money, Bok, from the concerts and the records and everything. Surely they can do a bit more with the boys' rooms?'

'Bokkie, they're boys. That's part of it. Treat them like boys; prepare them for the army.'

'Ja, but why charge such exorbitant school fees, Bok?'

'Look,' I said, pointing, 'we have a view of the mountains.'

Bokkie continued unpacking things into the small wooden locker with the calico curtain, complaining that everything couldn't possibly fit into the restricted space. Bok came to stand beside me at the window. The flat-topped mountain set against a deep blue sky loomed spectacularly large before us. Clouds hung motionless like mounds of cotton over the foothills and forests. Green. Brown. Blue. White.

'That's Champagne Castle. The view alone's worth the price.'

'Mommy's putting your socks on the bottom shelf for now, and your toothpaste and plasters and so on up here, on the top, okay, my boy? You must keep it neat, Karl. Neatness will score you points.

Look after your things. Everything is marked with your name; nothing has to get lost in the wash.'

'Yes, thanks, Bokkie.'

We heard voices approach up the stairs. The new arrivals introduced themselves as Harold and Janet Webster, their son was Dominic. I shook hands with Dominic, the first of my four roommates. He was shorter and skinnier than me, with huge scared eyes.

'Oh, you shouldn't unpack the boys' things,' Mrs Webster said to Bokkie at the locker. 'Just leave them in the suitcases; most of the clothing has to go to the cupboards downstairs. I've just spoken to Uncle Charlie, the house-master. Lovely bloke. They'll tell the boys what to do after the parents have left.'

'Oh,' Bokkie smiled and started repacking things into my suitcases. The Websters placed Dominic's leather bags in the passage beside his bed.

'You can leave the toiletries and so on.'

'Yes, thank you,' Bokkie answered, glancing at Mrs Webster, who was unzipping a small leather pouch from which she lifted Dominic's things. He and I smiled at each other.

'We're over at the El Mirador, how about you?' Dominic's father asked.

'No, we need to get back to Durban — we're just down the road — so we're not staying over.'

'We'll stay the night and check in in the morning to see everything's okay. But you'll be fine, Dominic. And you too, Karl. You have the best dorm. Look, it's right up here, and it's the smallest. Much better than one of those long halls. You're going to make such good friends. And look at this view of Cathkin Peak.' Mr Webster said that he needed to have a word with the principal and asked Bok whether he'd like to come along. They agreed to meet us later at the parking lot.

'What's your instrument, Karl?' Mrs Webster asked, smiling at me where I sat at the foot-end of my bed. I looked at her, not understanding the question. Bokkie looked up from the suitcase.

Mrs Webster smiled and said, 'What instrument does he play? Dominic plays the piano.'

'Karl plays the recorder, but he's going to learn to play the piano, too.' Bokkie smiled affirmation at me.

'Dominic is quite the pianist. Last year he played with the SABC orchestra, Chopin's First Piano Concerto. Youngest person ever in this country. Maybe you can give Karl some guidance, Dominic, what do you say?'

'Of course, Mum. And stop showing off.'

From my bed, Bokkie stared at Dominic. I could not believe I'd heard right. Mrs Webster pulled her face at us and smiled, 'He's right, I am.'

'That would be nice of you, Dominic,' Bokkie smiled at the skinny boy. I quickly nodded, happy and excited at the prospect of sharing a room with an accomplished pianist, moreover, someone who would help me master *my instrument*. How grown up it sounded; how matter-of-factly grown up: *my instrument is the piano*. This room, I thought, Dominic, everything, is going to be wonderful. Just wonderful.

I waved until the car disappeared in a swirl of dust around the last bend of the road that led up from the valley to the narrow plateau and main road away from the school. I did not weep. Not then. But as I turned and faced the three-storey building that was about to become my home, loneliness pulsed in the rush of blood, shuff-shuff, shuff-shuff, in my ears over Bokkie's voice: 'We'll visit you in six weeks, my boy. Parents' Weekend is around the corner. It will be over before we know it. We'll also write once a week. And we'll phone once a week. Okay?'

And Bok: 'Remember Lena and Bernice, Philistine: they did it at six. You're eleven already. Dr Webster and I have left five rand each as extra pocket money for you and Dominic. It's with the accountant, okay, Philistine?'

'Buy yourself some Condensed Milk, Philistine, okay?'

'Yes, Bokkie.'

Utterly alone, I now wanted them back. To be with them, with Bok and Bokkie; not here in the shadow of this big, angular building with the long, cold corridors and these mountains that suddenly looked exactly like the cruel brutes they were named after. More than anything, I wanted my mother. I tried not to imagine her in the front seat beside Bok, driving away. I knew she was crying. Don't cry, don't cry, don't cry, you can cry later tonight, into your pillow when no one's watching; when no one can hear.

At the edge of the parking lot I waited for Dominic, whom I could see saying goodbye at the open window of a silver Mercedes-Benz. As the vehicle moved off, he came towards me: skinny, sparse brown hair and eyelashes like a giraffe. I again felt myself half a head taller and clearly stronger than the cheeky elf weaving towards me through the parking lot.

'I waited for you.'

'Thanks.'

'Are you going to see your parents tomorrow?'

'No. They'll phone from the hotel. The school wants all parents away by tonight. It's not fair on those whose parents have already left. I don't mind.'

'We'll see them again in six weeks, anyway.'

'I can't wait for Parents' Weekend.'

'Me as well.'

'Me neither, you mean. Are you Afrikaans?'

'Yes, but I'm bilingual.'

'What does your father do?'

'He was a white hunter but he's gone into business now. He trades in curios.' We stood watching each other in the odd silence of the parking lot.

'Mine's a medical doctor.'

'That's nice,' I said. 'Should we go to the dormitory?'

'Dorm,' Dominic said. 'Let's. Maybe the others are there. You can call me Dom, okay?'

'I share a dorm with Dom,' I said and we giggled, more from nervousness than the rhyme.

'Can you believe we have to make our own beds and polish our own shoes?'

'Yes?' And then, realising he had probably never made a bed in his life, probably didn't know a tin of Nugget from a tube of Colgate toothpaste, I quickly said, 'It's easy. I'll show you.'

Had he really played the piano with an entire orchestra, I asked. True, he said, but not Chopin's entire First as his mom had made it sound. Only the second movement. Mrs Webster, he said, liked showing off when he did well but she knew little about music and lots about science. I myself had never heard of Chopin or of a kid criticising his parents like Dom did with such ease. From those first moments I knew we would be friends.

20

That tongue in my mouth. It is that I thought of as I pulled the dummy blanket from the bed and slid down between the sheets rubbing my feet on the sides of the mattress to get rid of the dust and grains of sand from the floor. The size of his tongue; so much bigger than Alette's. Four visits in which he had allowed barely anything but my hand to bring him to climax; then, tonight, the kiss. Most he's done to me. And a little stroking while the breeze came through the glass louvres of his room making the curtains bulge like the dress of a pregnant woman. His fingers lightly up the vertebrae of my spine playing the keyboard into my neck.

No longer afraid of him I was wishing he had done more. Sometimes, when our benches faced him – no, no, not then – rather, in those moments when we walked into the conservatory and I saw him at the piano *before* we started rehearsing; while Raubenheimer took the warm-ups; I felt my face aglow, my legs icy cold, like I was too scared to look at him. Couldn't keep my eyes off him behind Raubenheimer. But that too was not it, I realised already then. It was not fear of him or even awkwardness at what we were doing. It was that I wondered if anyone could guess it. It's like I'm so terrified someone may find out, I thought, but at the same time I'm hoping someone might. But not now. Not now, I asked in another prayer.

Then the kiss, like in the movies, like me and Alette beneath the streetlamp. But the one with Cilliers carried on, on, on. At first I thought I would suffocate, but then I heard him breathing, and I breathed too, and discovered a kiss could last for ever because you could breathe at the same time. I must try it on Dom, I thought.

And I had felt him, again stiff, when he rested on his side against my leg. Quite nice.

I can't believe I'm doing this, I repeated to myself, in class, riding, swimming, with Dominic, down at the forts, during prep. All the time during choir. Sometimes I couldn't think of anything else. Please dear God don't let anyone find out. His tongue felt huge, his dick massive; were adults' tongues really so enormous? The stubble against my cheeks rough, ticklish, but sometimes also pleasant. Next time, I smiled to myself, I'm going to stick my tongue right back into his mouth. Stupid, I should have done it tonight; probably thinks it's the first time I've done it. I'm going to do it to Dominic. Dominic will love it. I'll practise on him and I can use it on Alette. I had to turn onto my stomach and hide my face in the pillow, almost choking in my own stifled laughter. I lay in bed, adrift on air; waiting for something to happen. All of me anticipation. My penis was stiffening. I pushed my hips down into the mattress. I tugged the sheet away from where it folded in beneath the mattress and felt for the diary. No, I didn't feel like writing. Had to try and sleep.

Never, never before in the years at that terrible place had I felt so good. This was going to be the best year. Happiness is in your own hands, Bok and Dr Taylor had said ten months before, and they were right. Happiness was in my own hands. The best.

21

'She was the loveliest girl I ever saw. There were attractive girls in Tanga and Dar, but your mother had a body, jirre, like nothing in Tanganyika. And she looked like Ingrid Bergman. There's a bioscope you'll see one day — I'll ask Uncle Michael to bring it when they come from Toti — with Humphrey Bogart. *Casablanca* it's called. Everyone in Arusha went to see it and all the women started wearing their hair like Ingrid Bergman. A bit longer than it is now. So when I met your mother, I was immediately in love with her. Asked her to marry me that first week. I'm a leg man, you know. Like Uncle Michael is a boob man. I'm a leg man, I mean, look, look.'

From the kitchen table, Bok nodded towards Bokkie, whom we could see through the opening of the elevated kitchen wall. I took in my mother, bent over the cactus garden and rockery, the backs of her brown legs, beautiful to me already then, facing us; her short dress tucked into the side of her underpants. Clearing a few scraggly weeds from around the impala lilies that she had herself planted when we arrived, which were now flowering white with their star-shaped petals lined a deep pink. Flowering in the middle of the drought. Stars of Mkuzi, we called them. Instead of Star of Sabi as Bok's book said. *Apocynaceae*, family oleander. *Amatungulu*, Jim said. We were not allowed to touch them as the sap was poisonous, could cause dreadful stomach cramps and vomiting.

'Now, which man wouldn't want to carry that catch back to his family in East Africa?'

At my insistence Bok was again telling how he had met Bokkie when he'd come to South Africa for army training. How he had married her and taken her to the farm in East Africa. Bernice and Lena, back from Hluhluwe for the weekend, had also come to listen.

'The bicycle shop, Bok. Start with the dance.'

'We had a weekend pass,' he began. 'So, myself, Braam van Aarde, Len Maritz and a couple of the other colonial boys took the Jeep to go to the Friday dance at the Vastrap in Klerksdorp. Braam had gone to the Vastrap on his first pass and came back to camp in Potchefstroom and told us about the dollies. Old Braam had tall stories to tell about the girls — all lookers — he said were interested in him, but we knew he was colouring the truth because Braampie was no oil painting, to say the least. Fate was on my side that night because I was dating Sonja Myburg and she and I were meant to go to the bioscope — the 20th Century — in Potch that night. I think it's still there, in Kerkstraat. Anyway, so Braam and Len convinced me to cancel Sonja Myburg because they wanted me to do the driving back from Klerksdorp. They knew I could handle my grog. None of you kids will ever see your father drunk. I promise you that. Uncle Michael may show himself to Stephanie and James drunk, but you three will not see me in that state. But Braam and Len, I mean, just like Uncle Michael, three four beers and they'd be swinging across the road. Couldn't handle it. So, anyway, we went and we're doing the sakkie-sakkie, and the jive, and then I see this girl coming past me, doing the twist with another guy. And I see her from behind — just like this — white dress with big blue flowers, perfect rhythm, and her face, sort of shy and when she smiles it's a timid smile, like maybe it's her first dance but you can see from her rhythm it's not. So, next number I go to her standing with a group of girls and I ask her to dance. We danced for the rest of the night. Oh, she loved Elvis.'

I could see them in my mind's eye. Bok and Bokkie, just like when Bok put on the Patsy Cline or the Jim Reeves or the waltzes and they danced in each other's arms on the lounge's cement floor. Only in my story my mother wore a long white dress that was wide and glittered like Cinderella's in the illustrations of *The Tales of Grimm*. In the story my father called her Katie like others did, not Bokkie, and she called him Ralph, like everyone else. And Ralph wore a black suit with a yellow rose on his lapel and they were gliding in a big ballroom, sweeping around while a huge orchestra played from a balcony beside a marble staircase that grew wider the closer it got to the dance floor. And Katie—

'I found out she was working in Klerksdorp as the receptionist at Otto's Bicycles. So I got off drill one Friday afternoon and drove from Potch to Klerksdorp. She was there, alone, hiding from me behind an upturned bicycle on the counter. I asked her to marry me. She said yes. A year later we tied the knot. Everyone from Tanga, Oljorro, Dar and Arusha came down for the wedding – all in convoy from East Africa. For our honeymoon we drove back up, a two-week trip in Uncle Michael's new Valiant. Then Bokkie had to learn to speak English and Swahili; I tell you, upesi, upesi.'

'What's upesi, upesi?'

'Gijima, gijima.'

'And what happened to the other woman? Sonja Myburg?' Lena asked.

'Well, I passed her on to one of the other local boys who had fancied her anyway. Worked out nicely, fair and square for everyone.'

22

During the first two years I had neither cared for nor resented the Saturday sessions of compulsory letter-writing. They had become just another – perhaps less vexing – part of the way we lived. No more difficult to internalise as part of our culture than standing silently in lines, not being late for class or choir, not talking during quiet time before or after lights-out, short showers, not washing or wetting hair without Uncle Charlie's permission, no smoking, no screaming, no wet swimming trunks in lockers, hair cuts once a month, always sleeping for two hours in the afternoon before concerts, nothing except the day's prescribed clothing on the body or in the wash, no roaming at the river without supervision, no food other than fruit to be removed from the dining hall, no back-chatting teachers or prefects, not fraternising with the black cleaners and kitchen staff, writing thank-you cards to host families, no playing in the orchards, always being friendly and polite on tour and to school visitors, speaking only Afrikaans one week and only English the next, attending interdenominational Sunday school on Friday evenings and interdenominational church service on Sunday morning, no running along the corridors, no food in the dorms, no hiding in the dorms during PT, no talking during prep.

Supervised by two roving on-duty teachers, the Saturday rooms were silent cells until noon, by which time all letters had to be handed in and checked. Once read and okayed, the letter could be folded, placed in an envelope and sealed in the presence of the teacher, then thrown on a pile. Postage became the school's responsibility. Included in each quarter's account for school fees was the bill for mailing.

I wrote two letters every week: one to my family, one to Alette. Occasionally one to Mumdeman at Midmar. Of late, I'd taken a liking to the epistolary period. During the week I jotted down notes of things I wished to include in my correspondence. My interest in letter-writing had germinated at least in part because of the fondness I was developing for Ma'am Sanders ever since Malawi. As our class teacher I found her fair and generous, lavishing as much attention on the weaker performers such as Bennie as she did on brainboxes like Niklaas Bruin and Mervyn; always inspirational in Latin and Art, where there were only six of us in each class. She was the kind of teacher who went the extra mile: always bringing in supplementary books, occasionally a film. As strict as she was and though our opinions were only rarely asked, I developed a sense that Ma'am took us seriously. That she was divorced from her husband – quite a scandal – and had a daughter at university and a son in the army doing national service all made her that bit more interesting. She was the first person I knew who was divorced. Somehow the fact that Bennie's real father had died discounted his mother's divorce from his stepfather.

Ma'am's twin sister, Miss Hope, was a teacher at Port Natal. Lena, as if warning me about Ma'am, told me that Miss Hope strutted around with her nose in the air, full of airs and graces in addition to which she had favourites amongst the artsy *gatkruipers*. Even without meeting her, Miss Hope sounded as though she may be a lot like Ma'am. Everyone feared Ma'am, as had I before I got to know her. She was tall, quiet, strict, articulate, gaunt, and she herself was the first to say she didn't suffer fools gladly. Since the Malawi tour we had not been allowed to call her Miss as we did all the other female teachers. Instead, she insisted she be addressed as Ma'am! How splendid I found the word, how round and rich and mature compared to the flat, snake-like and spiteful sound of Miss. Miss this, Miss that. Miss mistakenly missed missing miss's miss. *Ma'am*, on the other hand, like *divorcee* and despite her aloofness, sounded like an invitation to conversation and repartee.

Initially it was only my essays Ma'am seemed to find intriguing. But recently, whenever she supervised letter-writing, she had started making light pencil markings in the text, suggesting I rewrite or reformulate certain paragraphs. These interventions never felt like the acts of censure our letters were sometimes subject to by the others — Marabou and Mr Buys in particular. Ma'am allowed us to write what we wanted, in most cases doing little more than a rudimentary skimming of the main points. Once though, she did ask Niklaas Bruin to rewrite a letter that bespoke the awful quality of our food. She told us she hated asking Niklaas to rewrite but that if she did not enforce the rule and if a consequent complaint came from parents she would get into trouble for not catching the taboo. Canings, poor food, homesickness — 'anything that may cause your parents undue worry — when in fact the school takes perfect care of you' — were not to be represented in letters.

Ma'am asked me to remian and clean the blackboard.

'You write wonderful letters, Karl.'

I turned from the board: 'Thank you, Ma'am.'

'You have a gift, you know. You should work at it. And on your drawing.'

I tried to suppress any outward show of the thrill: 'How do you mean work on it, Ma'am?'

'You have all these wonderful ideas in your letters. Particularly in those to your friend, what's her name — Alette? Those to your parents are more reserved, but to Alette, wonderful, just like in your essays. But often you seem simply to blurt things out, instead of being conscious, deeply conscious of what you're writing or drawing.' She showed me a pencil sketch I'd done the previous week, of Cathkin Peak and Champagne Castle behind. Only shadows and light, no strong lines. 'This drawing, the care you took with this. This is brilliant.' She smiled, her green eyes sparkling at me. In that moment I wanted to reach out and touch her cheek. To tell her she was beautiful. Knew that doing so was unimaginable. 'You should write with infinite care. Think on the precise word you want to use . . . Consider each and every image . . . not be so careless. It's not as if you're in some race, Karl. Good writing — more than children — lasts a lifetime and beyond.' My stomach had moved into my throat. If I was breathing it was not through my mouth or nose. It was, for that moment at least, as though God had appeared to me. Like her and I were back at Lake Malawi. The two of us, discussing Art.

She asked me to help carry books to her car. She was to visit friends in Bergville for the weekend. In one hand I grasped the grass basket she was taking along and allowed her to place the books in the fold of my free arm. On the stoep, as we passed the empty Standard Four classroom, she stopped, turned to me and said, 'Carefully. Always write carefully. Carefully, carefully.' She smiled and we walked on.

'Like porcupines mate,' I chirped, and smiled up at her.

'Who's Porcupine?' she half frowned, half smiled at me, her head turned.

'No, I mean . . .' She hadn't caught the stupid joke and for some reason I felt uncomfortable, that I was being overfamiliar, and thought an explanation inappropriate.

'No, it's silly. Nothing, Ma'am. But my thoughts come quickly, Ma'am. I just write what I think.' The stoep was shaded from the noon sun that glared down directly onto the corrugated iron roof. The quad was deserted and I wondered where everyone was.

'Then you will have to learn to go back,' she said. 'Check that you're writing everything as precisely and as creatively as possible. You can always go back and change things, you know, there's always more paper. Just ask.' For a second I wondered whether she was flirting with me. Enjoyed the thought.

Her red VW Passat was parked beneath a wattle next to the two rondavels where Mr Selbourne lived. 'Karl,' she said, opening the back door, 'when you read poetry in class, it is very moving. And you write these letters, packed with information . . .' She smiled again and I felt sure this could be a come-on. 'Why don't you stay out of trouble – as you have over the past few months – and rather concentrate on your writing . . . Observe, take things in rather than waste your time being mischievous.' But then she gave me a strange, almost pleading look, before bending to place the books on the floor behind the passenger seat. This was not flirtation, no, this was mothering. I suddenly wondered whether she knew about Mr Cilliers. They are close friends, I thought. Would he tell her? Never, he—

'Do you know what a sonnet is?' She interrupted my thoughts.

'I'm not sure, Ma'am. It's a poem, I think.'

Leaning back into the car she brought out two books, one fat and one thinner. She handed me the fat one: The Concise Oxford English Dictionary. 'I'll lend you this. Look after it.'

'Thank you, Ma'am. I will, Ma'am.'

'And take this for good measure.' I glanced down at the tatty paperback she placed atop the dictionary. Strips of yellowing Sellotape pasted along the spine and along the edges of some of the pages held the book intact.

'Thank you, Ma'am.'

'Has anyone ever told you that you had a talent for writing?'

I said no, no one had.

'I've seen you up in that little library often, Karl.' Both her hands were resting on the Passat's open door frame. She wore no nail polish and I could smell her familiar slightly spicy perfume. 'You enjoy reading, obviously, have you ever tried writing your own short story? Or a poem?'

'No, Ma'am. I did write a . . .' I stopped myself. 'No Ma'am, I've only written essays for class.'

'You may want to practise some sonnets for Alette.' She winked, her face lighting up into a huge smile. 'Use the dictionary, Karl.'

'Yes, Ma'am.'

'Oh, take a look at these,' she said. From an envelope she turned to lift from the basket, she drew three photographs. 'Just received the first snaps of Graham in uniform. Look how smart he is.' She hands me the photograph, leaning slightly over me to look at the colour print in my hand. 'He had only just completed basics there, look how skinny he is!' A young man of about eighteen, good-looking, smiling from the print, his eyes the same green as the tent behind him. The same as hers.

'He has your eyes, Ma'am.'

'Why thank you, Karl.'

'You must be very proud of him, Ma'am?'

'Oh yes. Very. He's been selected for the parabats. Only the élite go there.'

'Congratulations, Ma'am.'

'Thanks, Karl. And this here is my daughter Jenny. The three of us during Graham's first weekend pass.' She clicked her tongue, pursed her lips and slid the photographs back into the envelope. 'What are you doing after lunch?' she asked, and proceeded into the driver's seat.

'We'll probably be down at the river, Ma'am. Probably fix our fort. And Cassandra's going to foal any day; maybe this weekend. Lukas and I want to be there when it happens.'

'Have a good weekend. Thanks for helping me carry.'

'It's a pleasure, Ma'am. Thank you for the books. And for . . .' I wondered how to show my gratitude for her taking an interest in my work. In me as a person – '. . . the advice about writing, Ma'am.' She nodded, smiled at me, looked ahead and started the car. About to turn away, through the window and over the burrr of the engine, I heard her call my name.

'Who *is* Porcupine's mate?' she asked, smiling.

I shuddered. Stepped closer to the window. How can she possibly know? No, she doesn't. I laughed the possibility off. Wondered whether to actually impart the insipid joke. No, it was too rude to tell Ma'am. Instead, I said, 'Porcupine worked for us. His friend made wood carvings and we called him Careful, because he always carved the wood with a fat blade and said, Careful, careful.'

'Oh!' She laughed out loud, threw back her blond hair against the headrest. 'So, when I said you must write more carefully . . . I see. How original! You see, you *are* a natural. I'll bring you some of my own books to read. This library isn't up to much. Sound appealing?'

'Wonderful, Ma'am.'

With a wink she pushed the Passat into gear. The car crawled from the parking lot up the dust road.

Was she interested in me, beyond my work? I wondered whether perhaps I could seduce her too? Imagined having her and Dom and Cilliers. Jesus! And would her thing be the same as Alette's and Stephanie's? Surely it would go back to normal size after she'd had her children? It couldn't stay enormous, surely, so that I could stick in my entire hand? No, I had seen Bokkie's and it looked quite normal, even after three kids. Vagina. I'd have to use that word if she ever let me touch her thing. *Vagina, vaginae*, feminine, sheath. Radys and I had shared a conniving look during Latin vocab.

As I walked back along the stoep, I felt a flush of guilt or shame. I was obsessed with the filth of sex. How will I ever wash myself clean? I was on a one-way street to hell. And I had lied to her. I had no idea of why I lied. Or told fibs. A better word. In church the next day I would force myself to concentrate on each syllable of Dominee's life-giving, liberating words.

23

The boy is ten. In the passage he stands dressed in his school uniform. His father walks up. He tells the boy that if he ever catches the boy doing it again he will be killed.

24

We cantered towards where we'd descend the plateau. From a distance we could discern two figures moving towards us on foot. I thought they were two men, but then identified the broad rim of a woman's straw hat. A couple, probably on a hike from Dragon's Ridge. Mr Walshe raised his hand and called over his shoulder for us to slow down, move to the side of the road so the couple could pass. We came to a standstill. He nudged his mare and trotted her ahead, lifting his hat in greeting. We waited while he engaged in conversation with the grey-haired man. The school below us was etched in brilliant white against the green veld. This will make a great painting, I thought. Bright blue sky, dark green veld, simmering white building. Only those three colours, each in strong contrast. In severe lines. Impatient for feed at the stables, the horses strained at their bits.

'Keep that stupid animal away from me,' Lukas commanded Craig.

'If he kicks King or Rufus I guarantee there's going to be shit,' I cautioned.

'De Man always knows just a little better,' Craig said, shaking his head and pulling his mouth.

'Doesn't take much round here,' I smirked. I tugged Rufus's reins to get away from Whiskey, Craig's mount. The little gelding was forever kicking at anything that came close to his rear. Safely out of reach I leant forward and swung my crop onto Whiskey's flank; Craig almost came a cropper as the horse bucked, kicked back in my direction.

'Stop it, you two,' Lukas said.

'Ooh, now Van Rensburg has to get his money's worth, again,' Etienne chimed in.

'Shut up, Etienne,' a voice from somewhere. I was no longer interested in the group. Something about the grey man by the roadside seemed familiar.

'Don't want to play cowboy anymore, De Man?'

I paid no heed, drawn instead to the man with the wisps of long grey hair blowing in the breeze.

'Hey, Karl, what's up?' Lukas brought King abreast.

'Who's that old guy?' I asked. 'I've seen him, somewhere.'

Mr Walshe turned his mare back to us. He came closer, with the couple walking at his horse's side.

'Gentleman, let me introduce you,' Mr Walshe said. 'This is Dr Alan Paton. Do you know the man who made Pietermaritzburg world-famous?'

'*Cry the Beloved Country!*' I snapped before anyone else could begin to answer. I knew, I knew! I wished I had my camera.

'Good afternoon, boys. Handsome mounts you have there. Having a good ride?'

'Yes, Sir.' From all around. Then, before another word could pass, Mr Walshe said it was time to get back to school if we weren't to be late for choir. The others called greetings. Dr Paton and his companion waved as we gave slightly on the reins. My eyes remained on him. When the group moved off, I lagged, barely seeing the woman at his side, noting only the smile from him to me. Rufus was now straining and throwing his head. I tugged the reins, brought him around.

'Afternoon, Sir.'

'Afternoon, son.'

'Sir, I want to ask you something, if I may, Sir?'

'Go ahead, son, just watch that horse doesn't walk all over us.' I drew in the reins, holding Rufus a pace behind the couple, who were already continuing their stroll.

'How long did it take to write your book, Sir?'

Alan Paton smiled, as though to himself. 'There *is* more than one, you know.'

I felt embarrassed, but he chuckled and continued, 'Three years, son. Why do you ask, have you read it?'

'Yes, Sir. I found it in the school library. It has your photograph and signature.'

'Thank you, son, I'm glad to hear that.'

From behind came the shrill of someone whistling through his teeth. Mr Walshe was waiting alone where the road disappeared down the bend above the river. I turned Rufus, nodded my head to show I was on my way.

'Can I tell you something, Sir . . .?' I asked. Alan Paton and his companion came to a standstill.

'Yes?'

I cast another glance back at Mr Walshe who was again moving off. 'I'm going to be a . . . an author.'

Alan Paton grinned at me. I grinned back. I remember today that it looked like the wrinkles of his skin drew into circles around his lips pulled back from impressive yellow teeth. Like a beautiful old baboon, I thought, then.

'Good . . . Very good. I wish you well,' he said.

Mr Walshe had disappeared from the bend. The hill's edge, a pencil line against the veld below, was a clean horizon unbroken by human intrusion.

'I must go, Mr Paton.'

'It's been nice speaking to you, son.'

'Thank you, Mr Paton.'

Speaking for the first time, the woman at his side asked, 'What's your name?' And I, preparing to give rein, called back, 'Karl De Man, ma'am.' Then I veered off the road. *These hills are grass-covered and rolling, I recalled to myself, and they are lovely beyond any singing of it.* A mere one week after Ma'am had said I should write! It has to be a good omen, I laughed. Being told I could write and then meeting, by the biggest luck in the world, such a famous novelist. And with Ma'am's words not yet cold. No, it wasn't luck! It was God! It had to be Him! Oh, if only it had been Wilbur Smith instead of Paton! Imagine meeting Wilbur Smith!

Over the beating of hooves the couple cannot have heard my voice as they turned to watch. And who could guess what they thought if they did? A magician, a fool, a show-off careering down an incline too steep for most men on a horse at speed.

25

Lips furled like thick wads of cloth over the leaves, plucked and chewed with jaws swaying gently from side to side – not up and down like people's – and their eyes blinked long black lashes while they looked out across the scented acacias at Bok holding me against him on Vonk's back from where we were watching.

26

Laughter, a word caught here and there, a whistle, shouts, voices carried up from the river and the poplar bush where the rest of the school was at play: swimming, drop kicking the ball through the uprights, talking beneath the trees, mending forts, fishing for trout in the rapids, plotting war against opposition gangs, secretly pelting each other with the kleilat. But the two of us, reclining in the shade of the orange orchard wearing only black PT shorts, as if suspended on a thick carpet of grass under the trees, barely noted the sounds from the other world in the distance. Him on his back staring at fragments of blue visible between the leaves. Me on my stomach. Book held out before me:

> *Let me not to the marriage of true minds*
> *admit impediments: love is not love*
> *that alters when it alteration finds,*
> *or bends with the remover to remove.*
> *Oh no! It is an ever fixed mark*
> *That looks on tempests and is never shaken;*
> *It is the star to every wandering bark,*
> *Whose worth's unknown although his height be taken.*
> *Love's not Time's fool, though rosy lips and cheeks*
> *Within his bending sickle's compass come;*
> *Love alters not with his brief hours and weeks,*
> *But bears it out even to the edge of doom.*
> > *If this be error and upon me prov'd,*
> > *I never writ, nor no man ever lov'd.*

We were quiet for a while.

'Write a poem for me like that, Karl.'

'I could never write poems.'

'And I can never compose like Schoenberg.'

'You will, one day . . . Even though I don't like his music.'

'Abba for you!'

'You brought me the tape.'

'I know your taste: Condensed Milk and Abba – the sweeter the better.'

'Why did you bring me the Abba if you think it's so shit?'

'It was a present for you, not for myself. I wouldn't ever give Beauty a recording of piano sonatas, would I? I give her what she likes and needs.' I thought of the boxes of old clothes and bags of groceries Dr and Mrs Webster brought for Beauty after every holiday. I resented

Dom in that instant and it was on my lips to say that the Websters' charity towards Beauty may not be the source of gratitude they thought. Instead, I said, 'Ma'am says you're a child protégé, like Mozart.'

'Prodigy. Sure, but not like Mozart. When he was thirteen *he'd* already composed sonatas and nocturnes . . . I'm entering my twelve-tone phase. Anyway, she wants you to be a poet, idiot. Why do you think she gave you all those books. How did she know you want to be a writer?'

'She just said she likes my letters home. And my essays, you know how she reads them out in class.'

'You should show her that play you wrote last year.'

I said I had thrown out the play. He opened his mouth mutely and shook his head. He said I was crazy, that his parents had kept even the smallest silliest pieces he composed from age five. 'Why don't you write me a poem, Karl . . . Write me a poem about love. Love and oranges.'

'Love and oranges!'

'Something like the one in the *Groot Verseboek*. What was it? Miss Roos read it to us a few weeks ago.'

'Come on, Dominic.'

'*My girlfriend's in a nartjie, my grandmother in cinnamon, there's someone in anise, there's a girl in every scent.* That one!'

'Don't be silly. And you're not a girl.'

'Poetry is the highest form of literature.'

'I don't care. It's too difficult. I don't understand half of it. You can say much more exciting things in short stories and novels than in poems.'

'Rubbish! Just try it; it won't kill you.' I imagined the stories I would one day write. Like Wilbur Smith, whom Bok and Bokkie read. *When the Lions Feed, The Sound of Thunder.* Or Sir Rider Haggard and maybe even short stories like Herman Charles Bosman I found in the library. Or Alastair Maclean and Robert Ruark. But mostly huge books about Africa; about the bush and wars; and all Mumdeman's stories of what the English did to the Boers. About the last Afrikaner trek to East Africa. The charge of elephant at hunters; safaris; torrid romance between muscular men and ravishing women; millionaire white hunters from America; intrigue; deception; loyalty; wealth, valour. Of a woman as beautiful as my mother or as ravishing as everyone said Mumdeman was as a young woman, who has an affair with a film star who comes to Tanzania to make a movie. Of illegitimate children and murders and safaris. Those are stories I want to write, I told myself. Not boring things like Mr Paton's book, which just goes on and on. Oh, the language is exquisite, but I never properly understood why his book was so famous. No, Wilbur Smith for me. I tugged a leaf from the branch of the orange tree.

Dominic was speaking about a French perfume-maker who created an octave of scents to replicate the octave of notes. Each note had its own smell. If he played a chord, like F-G-C-F, the concomitant scents would be something like musk, lemon, rose, sandalwood. A concert was given that was a complete failure! The patrons came away half dead, choking, and with headaches because of the hundreds of smells they'd had to inhale.

'You could write a book of poems along the same lines. Each poem a different smell. Not each word, because then your readers would suffer the same fate as the audience at the concert.'

'I haven't ever wanted to be a poet. Though maybe a painter,' I said.

'I love when you read poems to me. Call it "The Scent of Love and Oranges — For Dominic".' From beneath his head he pulled a hand and placed it briefly over my nose: 'Squirt and oranges.'

We laughed and he rolled over on his stomach to face me.

'I can't call it that,' I laughed again, placing the orange leaf in the middle pages and shutting the book. 'Do you think,' I smirked, 'the French composer had squirt as one of his smells?' Again we cracked up. 'No wonder the audience almost pegged.'

'What about . . . "The Scent of Ejaculation and Oranges".'

Our laughter swathed by the thick leaves, the branches heavy with the last fruit of late autumn. Somewhere, higher up in the Berg, winter waited.

'You must try and go for it a little longer,' he said, catching my eye. I looked away. 'You'll be able to come, I'm telling you. Begin . . . ad libitum. Keep it amoroso . . . Next time, just relax and don't think of anything except what I'm doing . . . Then affrettando, agitato, oh, oh—'

'It's too much! It should just be oranges and then *the poem* must show it's really about love.'

'Changing the topic, Karl. Anyway. The scent of oranges.'

'Not scent. Smell. The smell of oranges.'

'What's wrong with scent; it's far more poetic to say scent.'

'It's a sissy word. Like something homos would say.'

'Tchaikovsky was a homo. And Britten. And Beethoven kissed Liszt a long sloppy one. Jesus Christ, what do you think we are!'

'Stop saying that, Dominic.'

'Why? What's wrong with you, now?'

'You're blaspheming again and I don't like that other word.'

'I don't care what anyone says.'

'Jissis Dominic!' I heard the pitch of my own voice rising. 'If anyone ever finds out. Last year . . .' I broke off the words, the thought, aware of reaching into a place of which he knew only a skewed lie. Somewhere I would never go again in language.

'Yes! Last year Almeida told you he had heard some Seniors were caned and threatened with expulsion for fucking each other. Probably that ugly Harding and Reyneke. We saw them, it has to be them, so what? You couldn't stand those two anyway.'

'You don't understand, Dom.'

'Sorry that I'm so thick, Karl! I've made a terrible mistake. And don't worry, I've got better things to do than run around and tell everyone you're my boyfriend.'

'I have a girlfriend.'

'Alette? Oh for God's sake. One letter a week never a lover made, if
you ask me.'

'You know very well we're . . . going out.'

'Do you kiss her? No! And does she lie with you under the orange
trees? No! Does she try and make you come? She doesn't, Karl, does
she!'

'Oranges don't grow on the coast. And she'll do the other stuff, one
day, when we're older. And I did it with my cousin. I mean, I stuck it
right in.'

'Fine, but you don't have to stick it in to be homo. Anyway, in the
meantime we're homos.'

'Please stop saying that, Dominic. Please, please . . . Promise me?'

'It's not like I'm going to run and tell the whole school, you fool. I
also don't want to be caned. Did you really do it with your cousin?'

27

At night my parents and occasionally Bernice would take the set of
small silver tweezers from the cupboard and place them on the side of
the bath before lifting themselves down, in front of me. FFuffff!
went the gas geyser as they regulated the temperature by turning on the
hot, then the cold taps. Our bodies copper against the white enamel
tub.

'Okay, let's row!' They'd call and with cupped hands we swirled the
water into a whirlpool around the sides of the bath. When the hot-
water tap was opened, I anticipated the moment the warm water
arrived from the front, reached my legs and churned around my back,
heating my waist.

Then, half raising themselves from the tub, they would turn to face
me and say: 'Time to do those little calabashes!'

Water dripping from my warm body, I stood in front of them as
they took the tweezers and with intricate care began pulling off the

tiny pepper ticks that had gathered in my loins and in the folds of the scrotum during another day of running through the long grass. To prevent one of the pin-sized heads from staying beneath the skin, a dab of Vaseline might be applied to the tick's torso, the oil forcing the red speck to relinquish its grip.

28

With the piano, he sang, emulated instruments while his hands continued before his chest; clarinet taking over from oboe; left hand plunging at us, moving us up by step D E F sharp, the change of harmony, his voice, altering tenor to falsetto again the clarinet, melodic strand, enfolding ours, voices change, Aunt Siobhain's voice, on top of Stephanie, ballet of blue cranes, Patty Pierce, dolls, Camelot on the beach, classroom in St Lucia, Juffrou Sang, Coolie Mary's son brown filafooi with James sucking it in Mary's kaya, candle and lemons under bush, Old Danny Boy, balcony Louis Botha airport, boys are not allowed in girls' bedrooms to get up to mischief, not allowed to sit on Bokkie's bedspreads Lena and Bernice have periods panties stained brown will they have babies, Mervyn laughs and says no must do It to have babies no boys don't have periods wet dreams are not periods, Blue Lagoon they came together and there was a baby, running from Phinias no from Jim's hut, hairy baboon spider in footpath, crying, Suz and Chaka, doing it, getting stuck Bok sprays them with green garden hose they come loose, men on moon at night outside on blanket by marula tree, Americans cleverest beat Russians, terrorists, burn Bibles poor Christians behind Iron Curtain, Christians banished to the snows of Siberia, must pray for forgiveness, what am I doing Dear Jesus forgive me, still love Father will read Bible, must think of it, in excelis deo, will get him back bastard, speaking in tongues, Gloria, Gloria, Cassandra's foal, chestnut coat, all the ooze and the afterbirth Cassandra licking, Lukas laughing so happy about the beautiful foal, huge opening when the legs came out, then the body and head last, thought dead, no, she licks and licks and on its little legs like bending fingers, must concentrate, not let Cilliers see lapses, have not heard, open mouth almost wrong word, keep eyes on him, concentrate Karl, concentrate, will be good, he smiles piece over, how did we get here?

Having heard barely a single note of my own or from the choir around me.

29

Inside hung the thick scents of sisal poles, thatch and creosote in which the timber beams and uprights were regularly dosed against wood-borer and general decay.

Movement in and around the water never ceased: the brown tip of a submerged stick was a turtle's head barely breaking the surface; dragonflies bright red, yellow, green, blue helicopters hovering, dipping their abdomens into the surface and bouncing up, again hanging with vibrating wings, mating in mid-air like they're giving each other piggy-backs; white-winged butterflies in rows at the water's edge. The coming and going of birds: starlings, regal blue shining satin as they bathed and chattered, ruffling feathers and splashing in the small pools formed in the mud by hooves; swallows, white-chested and red-chested, briefly settling to pick up mud for their nests, then darting up, sweeping over the pan and still in flight dipping their beaks and sending ripples over the surface; malachite kingfishers, silent and almost invisible in the reeds, waiting, their telescopic focus below the water's surface, down, the sharp beak scooping up tadpole. Rare though it was to see them, in the peeling green branches of an overhanging fever tree or on the dry white thorn, a fish eagle, its white collar and copper coat aglimmer where it waited for bigger fish to move; diving head first wings streamlined to its side, striking the water in the same instant unfurling its wings that rowed backwards, putting it in reverse, elevating, struggling with the black torso of a barbel, sprays of water as the fish floundered and the burdened bird winged off, settled back on its perch, the fish still struggling in the claws; and then, the razor beak ripping into the black skin, bringing its prey to shuddering passivity.

Bube-hide perched over the water beside a thick bush surrounding the pan. Before the drought the thatched structure with its wooden platform resting on poles cast its reflection to the middle of the glassy surface. During the week and in the off season we spent days there and at Masinga hide just to the south, while Bok with Jonas and Boy did maintenance. Wood had to be treated, sections of the roof rethatched, the winding sisal passage leading into the hide secured with reams of wire, garbage bins emptied and occasionally plastic and bottles collected from where some unthinking tourist had littered the parking lot. The network of game paths leading to the pan were subject to a weekly inspection: poachers, knowing the whereabouts of the waterholes, employed the paths to set their most fecund traps.

At dusk and dawn, game came and went: mongoose dashing for the water in a straight line; vervet monkeys and troops of baboons, barking, cajoling and tumbling in the dust; warthogs, snorting and rolling till their flanks were black and shiny and they trotted off into the undergrowth with tails vertical antennae above them; duiker, ears twitching, eyes alert, dainty. Heard from afar – like fingers flicking the inside of mouths – zebra announced their approach with the wildebeest, legs thin and nervous, retreating at the merest suspicion of danger. Ah, but the arrival of giraffe! Only twice in the years at Mkuzi do I recall seeing them at a hide. An inkling of movement above the tree-tops and I put my hand on Bokkie's arm, pointing with my stare. Then, if I was correct, small heads began popping up above the leaves. The closer they came the more I could see of the magnificent necks, moving from side to side, pausing, turning lazily to gaze sidelong at something beyond my view. Crowned kings and queens, they glided into full view from the bush, flanks quivering where tick-birds clung, legs bending at distended knees and flicking backwards in what was for me the most elegant movement of the bush. Heads turning, huge eyes intently on the hide, and I so hoping they could see me or simply know I was there, loving them, doing nothing to hurt or scare them. If from the distance there were sounds from Bok or the boys – digging, chopping, talking – they tarried before moving down to the water's rim. Spreading the legs as wide apart as I imagined they could possibly go without slipping, splitting; moving weight from side to side, finding a foothold; tipping necks forward; upper lips rippled at the surface and nostrils opened and closed while they sipped for what to me was eternity.

The three of us inside the Land Rover's cabin were silent while we drove back to Mbanyana at night with Boy and Jonas on the back. When it was cold, Bokkie said she wished we had an enclosed vehicle or even just a tarpaulin so that the arme skepsels didn't have to sit out in the wind. The beams roved along the sandy tracks, sweeping the dry bush each time we bounced through a hole or turned a corner. I fell asleep on Bokkie's lap and would not awake till next morning when she told me Bok had carried me in to the stretcher. If awake by the time we got home, I watched as she prepared supper or hovered around Bok sipping his Black Label and listening on the wireless to the Afrikaans service of Radio South Africa.

After supper they sat beside each other on the brown couch, he with his beer, she with a shandy – half Black Label, half lemonade. He smoked Paul Revere and she Rothman's Special Filter in the blue and white pack. When the radio wasn't playing and the hissing of the hurricane lamp not too loud, you could hear them inhale and exhale, or the phu of their lips releasing the filter, and the cry and call of jackal or at times the cackling laughter of hyena. Bok went to the Blaupunkt on the stuffed elephant foot and wound the tip of a coil onto one turntable and inserted the full roll on the other. Bokkie said she missed a little boere-musiek and she would write and ask Oupa Liebenberg or Aunt Lena to maybe send some. I was allowed to press the white perspex button that said PLAY and immediately Jim Reeves, Patsy Cline, Frank Sinatra, Mantovani or a Strauss waltz passed through the reed walls, out into the bush. When the Blaupunkt's batteries started going flat the music began to drag and Bok turned it off. Next day Bokkie placed the batteries in a neat row on top of the roof, where Lossie would be unable to get hold of them. The bird was forever swallowing things from around the house or the kitchen when the wall was up: bits of rope, cups, cutlery, my Dinkies, socks from the washing line. I spent hours scratching through his droppings with a stick to find my little green Lancia or to see if Bok's spanners would turn up. When he imbibed Bokkie's ball of knitting wool, half a day went trying to get him to stand still while we pulled at the wool that came out of his mouth like a long purple worm.

They read to me from the *Kinder Bybel*. Of Abraham and Isaac if I promised not to cry; of Esther, brave and beautiful in a crimson cloak; of Solomon and his wisdom suggesting the cutting up of a baby; of Jesus sprawled bleeding from the cross while the Jews jibed; the tribe of Judah; Joshua at Jericho and the bad woman Rahab who saved the day; of Moses so magnificent in parting the Red Sea; the dreadful plague with frogs in your food and malaria mosquitoes killing Egypt's children; of Joseph and his coat with colours that didn't even appear in the rainbow; of Potiphar's wicked wife; of Jezebel; David and his defeat of the Philistines; the miracle of water into wine.

I knelt at the stretcher for prayers. Earlier I had repeated after them but later did it without their help. I prayed for our family and for Lena and Bernice in boarding school in Hluhluwe. The older I got the longer the list of people to pray for: Dademan and Mumdeman at Charters, Oupa and Ouma Liebenberg in Klerksdorp, Uncle Michael and Auntie Siobhain in Amanzimtoti, all my cousins on both sides, the souls of Great-Grandfather and -Grandmother De Man, Great-Grandfather and -Grandmother Liebenberg, Auntie Lena in

Klerksdorp, Uncle Coen and his girlfriend Mandy. I was terrified of leaving someone off my list lest I unknowingly contribute to death, suffering or bad luck. Unsure whether I was expected to pray for Groot-Oom Klaas, I none the less sometimes did, asking God to forgive Groot-Oom Klaas for turning into a tramp and casting disgrace and shame over the Liebenberg family. Bok eventually taught me the 'Our Father' in Afrikaans and English, because he said it basically covered everything and in that way one was sure not to leave anyone or anything out.

If the Blaupunkt's batteries had not gone flat, I could hear them from my stretcher, over the wail of jackal, and the weeping of the nightjars, doing the polka or the two-step or the waltz, and I imagined them, again, Ralph the prince and Katie Cinderella, floating over a marble floor in a country called Vienna.

I developed, so Bokkie said and I still recall, an insatiable appetite for story-telling by age three. About the time she and Bernice began teaching me to read and write. I can also remember Lena's fifth birthday, when Molly Hancox brought her children to have a party at Mbanyana. I cannot remember that it was Molly Hancox for sure, but the recollection is of a party with two kids who are not cousins from the city. The only other white children living in Mkuzi were the Hancoxes from Southern Gate, so, to my mind, it has to have been them. It *was* Lena's birthday of the year before she went to boarding school, which means fragments of conscious memory from around two and a half: Lena quietly walks up behind a laughing dove that has come to sit on the red ground outside the lounge wall. She bends and picks it up. It sits quietly in her hands while the two children and I draw around her to see. The children want to take turns to hold the bird, but I implore my sister to let it go, to see if it can fly and go back to its nest. When I want to cry, Lena raises her hands, unfolds her fingers, and the dove flaps its wings and flies off into the bush. We all watch its flight. And that's where the memory ends.

Other stories, told and retold at my request, of our lives in Tanganjika, of our great-grandparents leaving the Union in 1910 to trek to East Africa to get away from the British who had won the Second War of Liberation. And Oupa and Ouma Liebenberg who were poor farmers in the Molopo before poverty forced them to Klerksdorp. As much as these family sagas for which I depended on the willingness of adults to tell, I loved to hear the stories from the three thick books Aunt Lena had given us. These were *The Tales of Grimm*, *The Stories of Hans Christian Andersen*, and *The Arabian Nights*. I also remember, from somewhere around the time of Lena going to boarding school, she and I lying on either side of Bokkie while she read us *Hansel and Gretel*. Bokkie broke off reading mid-sentence when the story had been barely begun — because I was already whimpering.

'Mommy's not going to carry on reading if you cry, Karl,' she said, closing the book over her index finger. 'We haven't even got to the sad part, and already you're crying.' I controlled myself, wanting to hear the rest and knowing Lena would be furious if the reading was terminated because of my tears. I managed, for a while at least, not to cry. But by the time Hansel is imprisoned in the cage, being fed to fatten by the witch, I sobbed openly and Bokkie tried to console: 'It's only a story, my child. It's only a story.' There is little memory of this incident other than my tears and Bokkie's words.

Then, from among these I so loved to hear, I adored even more the stories within the story of Scheherazade, the mistress of the Sultan who deferred death by telling tales that would never be concluded by morning so that her execution was eternally postponed. My book didn't say that that's how it worked, but Bernice, who'd heard another version, told me all about Scheherazade. And Bernice, who already knew how many days there were in a year, once calculated for me: two years and 271 days. I thought Scheherazade certainly the cleverest woman in the entire world. Once I could read for myself, I frequently put off the last page or so of the fables, waiting rather for the following day. Then I would read on, making believe that the Sultan would have had my head had I concluded the other story too soon.

Our cousins came to the bush with Uncle Michael and Aunt Siobhain. We got our first Christmas tree: a central stem of aluminium with fold-out wire branches covered in plastic pine-like leaves, about half a metre tall and mounted on a tripod. From two cake tins came the most beautiful decorations imaginable. Silver and golden balls, reams of silver, gold and copper streamers to drape over the green plastic branches. Small Santa Claus, stars of Bethlehem, leaves and red berries of holly, triangles, squares, little boxes in tinsel to hang from the branches. And, a fairy – an angel, stupid, Lena said – in a white satin dress with a wand and a star on its tip, to be placed at the top of the tree.

Uncle Michael brought along a diesel generator, a movie projector and movies we watched against a sheet Bokkie draped against the outside wall. She and Bok, next to Uncle Michael and Aunt Siobhain, sat on camp chairs while we kids with James and Stephanie lay on blankets spread open across the spiky grass. Jonas and Boy, neither of whom had ever seen moving pictures, were allowed to come and sit on one side of the fire behind us kids. For us and the grown-ups at least part of the fun was watching Jonas and Boy's faces, their white teeth shining in the projector's light, just like baboons in the dark, we said.

During the much-anticipated *Casablanca* I fell asleep – for the life of me not having seen any resemblance between my mother and the tragic-looking white-skinned actress called Ingrid Bergman. I thought far more that Bok resembled Humphrey Bogart – less in that than in *The African Queen*, which we all found hilarious. Swimming in the single remaining pool of the Mkuzi River next day, someone was forever screaming that someone else had leeches and the rest of us fled or rushed to aid the one whose blood was being sucked from his body.

But the movie I wanted shown repeatedly, that was set up at least twice while I alone sat and watched and everyone else was around the braai, was one Aunt Siobhain said she had brought as a special treat for me. In it was a young girl with violet eyes whom they said had since become the most beautiful woman in the world; one who was forever getting married and divorced. Her name was Liz Taylor. Able to read for myself the screen titles, I knew her real name was Elizabeth. Virtually from the instant the first images flickered against the sheet, I fell in love with every fibre of my four-year-old body: Clueless about why it was called *National Velvet* and unconcerned with ever finding out, all I cared about, dreamt weeks of having for myself, was a horse named The Pie.

During visits to Mkuzi or when we went to the city, we heard Uncle Michael and Aunt Siobhain say that Stephanie was at *that difficult stage.* I recall Stephanie once receiving a beating for calling Uncle Michael a bastard to his face. I must have been four or five. We were all shocked, but my outward expression was tempered by an unspoken respect for Stephanie's courage; after all, she was only calling my uncle a word everyone else, including Aunt Siobhain, called him behind his back anyway. We all looked upon Stephanie with a tinge of awe: not only was she older than any of us – a full eight years older than me – and already in Kingsway High, but she had breasts and though she no longer walked naked in front of us, it was clear through her bathing suit that she already had hair around her poefoe. The hair, far more than the breasts, we speculated, was why she no longer bathed with us or swam naked in the river. Stephanie moreover, alone among us, could hold court with the grown-ups whenever talk turned to East Africa. And then, tied to these awesome characteristics, Stephanie did ballet.

With the house too small to hold us as well as the clan from Toti, Bok and Uncle Michael put up a two-roomed tent beside the water tank. The grown-ups slept out there and the children inside the house. One night, long after we'd gone to bed, we were awakened by a commotion. James, in bed beside me, screamed that an elephant had charged through the tent and his mother was dead. Stephanie told him to shut up — that there were no elephant in Mkuzi. We jumped up, wide awake from the sound of voices shouting. We bundled through the door to the outside.

At first I saw only the flames leaping up and licking at the base of the water tank. I screamed and started crying. We all cried, including Stephanie. I waited for Bokkie or Bok to come running out of the tent, ablaze. It could not have been more than a few seconds, but the horror of what it would mean if they were dead had dawned on me. Bernice had her arm around me and Lena. Then we saw them: all four adults naked, scurrying from the dark at the tap with jerry cans and buckets of water. Bok shouted at us to get out of the house — in case the thatch caught alight. He ran to the other side of the tank and climbed the scaffolding. While the others went about throwing buckets of water and sand, Bok adjusted the sprout of the run-off and opened it so that it spurted full blast onto the fire. The tent had already almost burnt to the ground; the flames subsided.

What had happened, or so it was said forever after, was that after a particularly heavy bout of drinking Uncle Michael had fallen asleep with a cigarette between his fingers. The stompie had set his foam-rubber mattress alight and by the time they awoke from the smoke the smouldering mattress had turned into a fire that ignited the canvas tent.

James and I now had to share our bed with Lena, three of us, head to toe. Before we fell asleep James leant over Lena's feet between us: 'Did you see their poefoes and their filafoois?'

Lena kicked us to lie still. I bit her foot and pushed James back to his side of the bed. Lena said she'd get me the next day. Bernice whispered for us to go to sleep. I could not understand what James had found unusual in nude adult bodies. There was nothing remarkable for me in seeing my parents naked; after all, there were no doors in our house, not between rooms nor to the bathroom and toilet. Seeing Aunt Siobhain's or Uncle Michael's meant nothing to me, for surely, as

Bokkie always said, if you had seen one you'd seen them all. And surely my parents knew that the squeaking of their bedsprings at night only *sounded* like the rattle of guinea fowl? None of that mattered: it was the fire – that Bokkie and Bok could have been burnt to death, that I could have been left alone with Lena and Bernice – that was foremost in my mind.

30

Late April's first cold night and I, reclining on my side, the sheets bunched onto the floor, lay on the single bed in his room beside him. Back to the wall, my one leg rested over his knee. Above his chest – still heaving – I could see light from the bathroom door slightly ajar. The tip of the white towel protruded into view from the carpet beside the bed. A wind, howling and whistling like hundreds of distant sirens, swirled around the school. Sheets of corrugated iron rattled on the roof and the bare peach tree creaked and rubbed against the window. When I breathed, the warm film forming between my stomach and his side went schluck as if we were being glued together. I thought of Suz and Chaka getting stuck, Bok, the garden hose, spraying the jet at them, getting them to separate. And Cassandra, the blood and ooze when she'd foaled the previous afternoon. The little foal.

'Mr Cilliers?' I whispered.

'Uhhm . . .'

'Are you falling asleep?'

'No . . . Are you?'

'No.'

I had no idea how to proceed. Willed him to act. He must feel it, down there against his leg, why wasn't he touching it?

I slid my hand up over his damp belly; my elbow momentarily brushing his limp penis. My fingers found his hands folded into each other in the tangle of fine hair on his chest. Fingers wrapped around mine, intertwined. Again, I waited, wondering if he could not sense what I wanted. What if he knew but wouldn't? Heedful of the stillness when the wind subsided and all of a sudden again apprehensive, I began to withdraw my hand. A swift application of pressure from there; I read reassurance. I took his hand down his belly, over his thigh. Restiveness from his body against mine; I paused; wanted to let go of his hand.

Once more, I felt him lax, the hand become limber in mine. Down farther. Placed it where for weeks I had wanted. Relief, at least as much as pleasure, when the fingers wrapped into a cocoon around the pulsing chrysalis.

He turned onto his side; propped himself on one arm and rolled me onto my back. I closed my eyes. Felt the warmth of his torso descend even before his mouth reached my lips. Into the movement from the wrapping of fingers I lifted my hips; into the wet of the mouth my head from the pillow. I tried to empty my mind, to feel only the mouth, the tongue, the stimulus of the hand. *Relax. Relax. Relax.* Concentrate. Dom's voice — amoroso, ad libitum, arabesque — no — affrettando, agitato —

Exhausted, I dropped my head back into the pillow, left him panting above me. I know it's there! Why isn't it happening, dammit, dammit. It's just sitting in there but it doesn't want to pop out. I felt his face move, heard him now breathing through his nose. The wind tugged at the roof; branches scratched at the windows.

Lips, stubble, moved across my cheeks, my chin, down my neck, tingles gathered where hair begun at the nape. My neck lifted from the pillow, my nose gasped at the unexpected smell of shampoo in his hair, funnelled it into my head till it was filled to bursting. His tongue, the enamel of teeth broadside against my chest; lips; caresses down my side; my belly. My palms open on the back above, below me; fingertips found heat in the moist down of his armpits. A tremor, a second of incredulity at a mouth in my loins. Memory: something like this. Hands in his hair, hips heaving, and felt it burning I'm going to pee shudders through my body and tug whisper frantic now stop but it's too late and my body shakes and I am dizzy in the silence. A rush of blood coursed a beat through my temples.

An eternity.

I felt cold. Filthy. Disgusting. I wanted to pray. He, down there, sensing something, lifted himself and with his free hand reached towards the floor. Not quite inaudible over the wind, the spurt passing from his mouth into the folds of the towel.

He came up again beside me; placed my head against his chest. I wanted to leave. I never will come here again, never, I swore. *Not even animals; sent to orphanages; San Andreas something; against nature; expelled.* Phrases attacking from nowhere. I was suddenly and irrevocably the child surrendered to Satan. No! Dear Jesus, dear Lord, forgive me. This was a mistake, Saviour, now I know. Never again. I swear to you. Till then he had never touched me. But now, a mouth had been used. I had been given and had taken pleasure. I had allowed a man to spill my seed. Death, that was what I deserved.

Drifted into sleep; let it take me like a fever, a memory of burning cold.

At first I did not hear him speak.

'Sorry, Mr Cilliers?'

'Are you dozy?'

'No, I was just thinking.'

'I said: when we go on tour, next month, you can sometimes stay with me, if you'd like.'

I lifted my head; found the shine of his eyes in the dark. Eased back into his arm.

'With host families?'

'When I'm with one. Or in a hotel. Ever stayed in a hotel? Would you like that?'

'What about choir? I mean . . .'

'It's not unusual for some of you to be put out with a conductor. When there are hosts with a big enough house.' He was quiet for a while. 'Weren't some of you in PE or East London with Mr Roelofse last year?'

'Only because he wanted to keep an eye on me and Lukas. To make sure we slept before the concert.'

'I could do that again.'

'What about Dominic? I usually stay with him or Lukas.'

'You can both stay with me. Dominic may have to run through some solo work with me. Almeida had to do that with the Language Monument last year.'

For some reason I did not want to hear about Almeida. Not now. I spoke quickly: 'But how, I mean, how will we . . .'

'The same way as this, I imagine.'

Silence. I didn't want to stay with him. Never. I would think of something.

'Do you and Dominic do this?'

'Sorry?'

'You and Dominic . . . I'm scratching in his salad, hey?'

'No! Mr Cilliers.' And hastily added: 'Tonight is the first time. I have a girlfriend.' Immediately regretted having said it was the first time.

'Is this the first time you've come?'

'Sort of . . .'

'Except in the dreams?'

'Ja . . .'

He kissed me and I thought I'd choke of the rough, slimy tongue. I pulled away.

'Did you like it?'

'I kiss my girlfriend Alette like this. She likes it.'

'No, when you came. Did you like it?'

If only he would stop talking. Then I could get up and get out of his den.

'I'm sorry it was in your mouth.'

'Don't be silly. I like it.'

Please, dear Father, let him stop being so disgusting.

'You can use my name, if you like.' Then, as an afterthought, 'When we're alone.'

Silence. I started to drift away. Just for a little while. I had no idea for how long I was gone.

'You do know I'm playing with fire, don't you?'

Awake. Nodded my face against his chest.

'This is crazy. Sometimes I think I'm out of my mind.'

'I swear I won't tell, Mr Cilliers. Never. I swear.'

'It's not just the telling, Karl. The whole thing, it's all wrong. All, completely, completely wrong.'

'No one has to ever know, Mr Cilliers. We just never have to do it again.' I closed my eyes, again wishing him to silence.

It's over, anyway. Sweat crackled where we touched. There was a lull in the wind. How awfully quiet outside and in there. I was hot. I dozed; woke.

'I want to open the window, just a little.'

He moved at once, saying he'd do it.

In the faint light I squinted at the body silhouetted against the curtains, lighted from behind by the bathroom glow. The sounds of the wind again rising entered the room and the curtains ballooned, briefly enfolding his body.

He spoke as he turned from the window: 'We fell asleep. It's almost two o'clock.' Kneeling on the sheets he looked down at me and smiled: 'You shouldn't stay too much longer.'

In his gaze I felt it, the unmistakable stiffening, again, still sticky.

II

I

Dearest Daddy, Mommy, Bernice and Lena,

Thank you for the letter I received yesterday when we got back from the Transvaal and Cape Province tour. The Greyhound broke at the summit of Van Reenen's Pass and the AA had to be called to repair the fanbelt. Up there in the freezing wind we waited for about two hours. Everyone went into the bush to do their business. Niklaas Bruin squatted and accidentally did it in his blazer pocket. He's a little freak, so his awkwardness came as no surprise. It stank us out. Eventually, when he owned up, we got the driver to put the blazer in the hold with our suitcases. Niklaas was the most unpopular guy around and Bennie's new name for him is Pong-Pocket. As we only got back here at about six in the morning, we were allowed off school until lunch-time to sleep and there was no choir that day.

After Pretoria, we went to Johannesburg. Did you receive my postcard from the Voortrekker Monument? I stayed with Lukas and Bennie at the Websters, only for one night and we were so busy we barely saw them. We received rave reviews everywhere and Mr Cilliers was altogether happy with our performances. He says we are sure to be a hit in Europe. In Johannesburg Radys Dietz and Eben Stein stayed with a Mr and Mrs Donnelly and while we were there Mrs Donnelly was on TV news with the riots. Did you see her? We didn't, because we had a concert, but we were told she really was on the news. She had gone to take their ~~ousie girl servant~~ maid back to Soweto while the children were burning down their schools. The Soweto children surrounded her car and wanted to set it ablaze and kill her, but she shouted, 'I'm

English, I'm English, leave me alone, I'm not Afrikaans.' Lucky for her the police arrived and the kids ran away. Mrs Donnelly told Radys and Eben they were just like savages, pillaging, murdering and marauding. It was the most terrifying ordeal of her life. One can just imagine. The day they left the Donnellys the maid didn't show up for work and the Donnellys were worried about her. In Jo'burg everyone stays off the streets at night.

To Potchefstroom we had to take a back road so we wouldn't have to pass near the locations. Although we could see smoke rising into the air all around Soweto, they told us everything was calm in the Western Transvaal. Mr Mathison has asked us all to write and say that our route never put us in any danger.

I suppose Aunt Lena phoned to say we stayed with her and Uncle Joe in Klerksdorp. We stayed all over the house and she said it was a pleasure having all five of us there. My friends all liked the mansion very much and wished it was warmer so we could swim. Uncle Joe didn't come to the concert. He was out on the farm . . . But Coen brought Mandy, and Oupa and Ouma also came. Ouma fell asleep and only woke later when we were doing the gumboot dance and Sho Shaloza. Oupa reckoned we were very bright to be singing all the Latin and Hebrew music. I didn't tell him that we hardly know the meaning of the words because I thought it would only disappoint him. Aunt Lena says he cried while we sang the negro spirituals and he cried as usual when we said goodbye. He says he enjoys driving the Mann lorry that he and Coen have gone into business with. Groot-Oom Klaas has gone off by himself again and no one knows whether he's dead or alive. Aunt Lena says if he's alive he could have gone your way for the winter.

As a going-away present Aunt Lena gave me R10, and I still have most of it. From Klerksdorp we went to Kimberley (we saw the big hole), to Beaufort West and Oudtshoorn. The ostrich farm we visited there didn't have rides, so unfortunately that's something I'll have to do at a later stage. In BW we stayed with a man who farms chinchillas. They are the strangest looking things, like a cross between a springhaas and a rabbit. Their pelts are very sought after and I thought they'd make a very warm kaross.

In Cape Town we had snow on the mountains. In the City Hall there we had a standing ovation and we did 'Were You There' as an encore. It is Mr Cilliers's favourite part of the repertoire. After the second ovation we ended with Zoltan Kodaly's 'Mountain Nights'. Because all the host families were taken, we stayed with *friends of Mr Cilliers who have a beautiful house on False Bay. Their surname is Erasmus and the mother used to be an opera singer. When I asked where the tusks and Kudu head were from, they said they came from East Africa. Mrs Erasmus said her husband was born there and I wondered whether you knew them?*

Now we are catching up schoolwork and have started doing extra hours for the performance of the Mass at the beginning of December. Information bulletins are to be sent out to all parents so you can order extra tickets if you would like to invite guests. It's quite a big thing because it will be broadcast live on TV from the Durban City Hall. Do you think Aunt Siobhain and Uncle Michael would like to come, and maybe Mumdeman?

Rufus is well. We are going riding again on Monday.

All my love,
Karl

PS. Lukas sends his regards. We're playing rugby on Saturday against Winterton.

Ma'am called me to her desk. Holding the folded letter she spoke quietly as if wanting the class not to hear: 'When someone has been shamed, Karl, you may think it acceptable to kick him and further humiliate him while he's down and being jeered by the world.' I was stunned; hadn't a clue what she was talking about. 'But for you to stand on his head so that you can gain personal elevation from his shame – that, dear Karl, I find reprehensible. I hope no one *ever* does that to you.'

A frown compressed my forehead; worry; at a loss for what I had done wrong. How had I disappointed her? There was nothing, nothing on those pages I thought that may have offended her. She smiled while she slid the letter into its envelope: 'I will not ask you to rewrite this.'

'Ma'am, I don't understand? Is there something I should have left out?' By now most of the class could figure that I was being chastised.

She shook her head: 'No, Karl, but I want you to know,' and then she spoke louder, 'that I find your and the rest's responses to

Niklaas's disgrace immature and cruel.' She licked the flap and stuck it down with her fingers, closed her eyes to show I could return to my seat.

I walked back to behind Dom without meeting anyone's eyes. Furious at her for letting Niklaas Bruin know his shit had featured in my letter.

2

In our first year, some of us took the floor when Marabou was out of class. Dominic did Liberace behind the closed piano and Bennie did Cassius Clay on top of Marabou's desk. My own favourite performance piece was Langenhoven's poem 'The Moth and the Flame'. Marabou's desk — already cleared for Bennie's Cassius Clay — was huge and out of proportion as the flame, but it none the less did the job. Spreading my wings, flapping them at first leisurely, extending them as I spun and recited, slowly, closer to the flame.

> Oh, oh, oh, the other moths were dumb and dense
> but far from the candle I, I, I will remain
> from afar in the dusks I'll observe
> from this far it is safe and gazing free.
>
> Ah! I need not look from one side only!
> I keep a clear distance and fly around
> then I know from all sides how it looks
> so to care for not getting too close.
>
> My circle is — ever so slightly — skew and inward bent
> but even there where closest I was
> nothing happened! Nothing! So there's no reason
> none! For this wide rim so far from the shaft

The wheel spins ever faster faster faster faster
and the light and the glow begets bigger delight
and the rims grow tauter round the shaft
aaahhhhh, the end of the wheel, aaaahhhhh
is the ash ssshhhh of the mothhhhhhh

As the tempo increased, so too did my spinning and circling, arms flailing, until by the last stanza I was almost running. My body was alive with me inside. Even as I recited the lines, my head seemed to shrink tiny, almost not to exist, as all I felt were my limbs, now loose, now taut. And my heart. Like doing ballet. In the final line I threw myself across the desk to shrieks of laughter from the class. More than once, when Marabou was out, someone would ask: where's Cassius, Liberace or 'The Moth'? And little more prodding was needed to get us going. As the performances had the propensity to turn rather noisy when in fact we were not even allowed to speak, it came as no surprise that one of us was eventually caught. Miraculously, it was Ma'am who came to investigate the din. As I leapt to throw myself into the flame the class roared. Skidding across Marabou's desk I saw a shadow at the door. Unable to stop my momentum I flew off the desk, landed on my hands. My feet were still up on the desk when Ma'am walked in. But instead of calling me out and having me caned, she smiled and called it a superb rendition. She told us to be quiet, and then she left.

It was more than a year till the Malawi tour when I'd speak to the tall, serious teacher again. But I knew she must have remembered the poem, for in September of our Marabou year, during the auditions for new members, when the choirs performed a few songs and a number of boys had to play instruments, Mathison had asked me to recite 'The Moth and the Flame', adding: 'But without the performance I've heard about!'

I stood in the auditorium, delighted, at least in part because I knew

I would never be asked to sing alone or play my recorder. The verses of Langenhoven's poem lent themselves superbly to dramatisation, like many of the twenty-odd poems I had committed to memory by then. So, the recitation in the auditorium – standing still, performing it by voice alone without the running, the spinning and the leap across the desk – was a bit of a personal disappointment. The applause for my solo performance was none the less an inspiration. I learnt more poems, read them aloud in class whenever an opportunity arose.

3

On the shores of Lake St Lucia, Charters Creek perched above the estuary that pushed its salt water inland to where it was fed by the veins of the Mpate, Nyalazi, Hluhluwe, Mzinene and Mkuzi Rivers.

Having passed through the eucalyptus and pine plantations near Matubatuba, the approach to the camp where my grandparents worked for the Natal Parks Board was along a sandy two-track road through lush forests. For stretches of the drive the sky was erased by a ceiling of branches and tangled creepers. Baboon ropes hung like grey swings awaiting young hands and feet. I want to remember that it rained often – afternoon thundershowers – for the land and dense shrubbery was moist and green compared to the tans, browns, beiges, ambers and mustards of Mkuzi and Umfolozi. Here the crests of kaffir-trees – *Erythrina caffra* – broke the green jungle roof in a haze of red and in September the dull crimson crinkle paper flowers of sausage trees augured spring when one barely knew winter had been. The place, Dademan and Mumdeman said, was almost the tropics. Not quite as wet and humid as Oljorro in Tanganyika, which is right up at the middle of the world, but in some ways similar. Charters Creek, for me, was a paradise akin to my imaginings of Eden as taken from the illustrated *Kinder Bybel*: butterflies, flowers and birds; down at the water and on the shore pelicans, flamingoes, seagulls, swifts and sandpipers; in the forest, duiker and bosbok. And, more than anywhere else in a Zululand I remember, the magical grunting call of the purple-crested louries. No sound of the bush was to me more haunting, more mysterious than that of a loury, no bird more beautiful. A sighting of the bird bouncing along a stem or of its aloof wings overhead was always a surprise, always a tiny secret shared, an annunciation of angels.

The camp consisted of eight rondavels and a small administration building from where Dademan and Mumdeman oversaw things in the marine reserve. When I visited, Dademan allowed me in behind the reception's flat latch-door counter and I could speak by radio to Bok at Mpila in Umfolozi. When the office was not expecting the crackle of radio contact from other reserves or HQ, I could speak for short intervals on an unused frequency where no one was likely to receive my messages of poachers being shot, crocodiles dragging piccaninnies to their watery deaths, hippo devastating canoes or a cargo of rhino horns intercepted by me while out patrolling on horseback.

Dad and Mademan's thatched house stood overlooking Lake St Lucia, on a kikuyu lawn up the hill, away from the main camp, almost hidden from sight by the purple extacy of jacaranda, Natal mahogany, pride of India and different creepers. The bush on the landward side was fought back by Phinias, who tended the beds of blue and white agapanthus, tumbling sweeps of cup of gold, golden shower, hibiscus, frangipani, tree wisteria and barberton daisies as big as my hands in red, pink, white, orange and yellow. Mademan's pride was the hedge of *Strelitzia reginae*, with their orange sepals, white bases and blue, almost purple petals which glass-eyes frequented for nectar. Nights were for the call of bushbabies and the nightjars, preceded for the whole day by the emerald-spotted wood doves. Sadly they called: *My mother is dead, my father is dead, all my relatives are dead*. Phinias couldn't make bird sounds, but Jonas emulated the wood dove best: *Don, don, don, I-had-babies-and-they-died, I-had-babies-they were stolen-now-my-heart-is-going-don, don, don, do, do, don-don.*

From dusk the growing clammy, damp smell of the estuary mingled with the fragrance of frangipani, wild jasmine and gardenias from the forest. And there was the hghghg hguum hghghg ghuum of hippo moving somewhere down along the shore. In the morning a scattering of droppings and the trampling of Ouma's flowering clivias or red hibiscus confirmed that they had come to ravage the garden. I feared the hippo at Charters Creek far more than I did white or black rhino in Mkuzi or Umfolozi. I told myself I would always see a rhino from a distance in the veld, or, if it charged, I could let Chaka and Suz's barking serve as protective decoys. With Bok on horseback, the tens of rhino we encountered, white and black, always let us be or stomped off to a safe distance from where they might come to a standstill and turn, snorting, to gaze at us. But hippo: fat, ugly, always slyly drifting and peeping up from the water, came out at night, like dark devils from the sea. Moreover, I didn't have the bull terriers with me at Charters. Mademan's little Pekinese, Skip, would be a joke thrown sky high by a charging hippo. I had heard story upon story of native canoes snapped in half by the cavernous jaws — not only in South Africa, but in Tanganyika and Kenia. Dademan had cines of us at the Mzima springs near Mombasa, where, from within a glass tank, one could view the fish and the hippo underwater. If hippo run that fast under water, Dademan said, imagine what speed they can attain on land — then add fifteen miles an hour to that. Hippos were monsters, as bad or worse than crocodiles. At least the long scaly reptiles were up-front about their evil. You could see they were dangerous. But hippo I distrusted in the same way as I did hyena. It had something to do with their appetite for the night. I myself had no fear of the night, but in the bush I did fear its creatures. During the day, when the hippo lay with their mouths wide open while dentist birds manicured the teeth inside the pink mouths, I was never misled and imagined that far more than being designed for an ecological function the birds were there in cohorts with the night devils to deceive everything and everyone into believing their hosts docile and friendly. The sickle-shaped hippo teeth mounted on our mantelpiece — especially after we moved to Amanzimtoti — had visitors astonished and appalled when they realised they were not looking at small elephant tusks. More people were killed in Africa by hippo than by any other wild animals. It was the first *fact* I ever learnt and I repeated this *fact* over and over to myself and to my city cousins whom, to my chagrin, thought themselves bush children after a day at Charters or Umfolozi. *I was the bush child.* Except for the stray piccanins and little Jeremy Wilcox — and he was so young it didn't count — I was the only child in the whole of the Zululand reserves. I knew the bush and would not let my cousins or even Lena and Bernice forget that. Fact.

Old Phinias, the garden boy, sometimes took me into the forest to look for the louries, just as did Jonas in Mkuzi's forest of figs. Phinias was a bit crippled in one foot and had sleeping sickness because of repeated bouts of malaria. Dademan said he wasn't quite sure about the malaria-story and a more plausible explanation for Phinias's falling asleep on his feet was your typical kaffir disease: *idleness.* Another new word. Still, I worried about Phinias dozing somewhere during one of our bush walks where I may be unable to wake him. I knew there were no large animals to fear. Mostly duiker, the shy bosbok and occasionally nyala and kudu. But there was always a chance of encountering a lone hippo strayed from the river. Or a mamba, the most terrifying and poisonous of the Zululand snakes. But like everywhere, the fear was rarely at the front of my mind; it dozed very far at the back. With Dad or Mumdeman's permission, Phinias walked with me along antelope path where it was possible to hear the louries. If one were deadly silent, there was even occasion to see them, hopping from branch to branch or swooping off into the green. We approached the forest as quietly as possible, my eyes simultaneously trying to look out for birds and Phinias's long toes like a frog's spilling over his mpategas and crunching dry leaves. We would stand quietly and look up, our mouths open so we could hear better, and when they called, our eyes swept the branches in competition to see who could spot one first. Soundless, with only a show of eyes, he or I would signal victory. If the birds were not there, I begged him to sit down and wait with me, for I couldn't imagine returning home without a report of a sighting. If, on an odd chance, we had not seen one, I'd simply bring myself to believe that we indeed had, just briefly, that I had certainly seen one while Phinias was sleeping on his feet. In Mkuzi Jonas couldn't be tricked and would have told me I was a liar. Sometimes we would have to sit for half an hour, and they might stretch out with their arms behind their heads on the leaves and I'd lie down beside them. But while my eyes and Jonas's were searching in the branches, Phinias's soon closed and before long I'd hear the breathing of the man asleep. Jonas also closed his eyes, but I doubted he ever slept. Nothing seemed to pass him by. Suddenly a high-pitched ko-ko-ko-ko-ko-ko, rising in pitch, louder, then transformed to growling and suddenly ending, or a kok-kok or kro-kro-kro broke the forest silence only to be re-called from somewhere in the thickets. Before you could see them fly they tumbled into the centre of a tree, sat quietly, or hopped along the branches. Then you held your breath, waiting for the flight, and, when they swept down, you saw at last the hidden crimson under their wings.

On one of our homeward walks I suggested Phinias go and see the Sangoma to cure his sleeping sickness. Phinias laughed and asked whether I thought the Sangoma could really cure him. I said no, because only people who believed in Jesus were real doctors and the Sangomas were heathen witch doctors who were going to burn in hell. Then Phinias held his stomach and laughed so much he came to a standstill in the sandy track.

'What you laugh at, Phinias?' I asked, but he carried on walking, laughing so much the tears ran glistening down his cheeks.

'Is cause you're not really sick, eh, Phinias? Is cause you have idleness not sleepiness.' But that just sent him spinning in circles, bent over double, his laughter breaking open the sudden quiet of the bush.

4

Sticking loosely together somewhere in the middle as the groups of boys walked along, we had been speaking about the upcoming Parents' Weekend. Letter-writing and lunch were done and under Mr Buys's supervision we were hiking to Copper Falls. Even though I disliked Buys, feared his anger and temper, I was looking forward to the falls. It was a new route to a place we had not been before. Hiking, like riding, allowed me to feel that my being in the Berg was worth while, after all. With Buys at the head and some prefects at the tail, our line stretched for about half a kilometre along the dust road that wound up towards the Champagne Castle Hotel. Buys cut left into the veld and started along a footpath through the green veld.

The six of us talking as we fell into single file to follow the overgrown footpath. Bennie: built like a Rottweiler and as strong as one; short, stocky, arms and legs lined with muscle. Of us all, Bennie had the shortest fuse and he was constantly ready to fight. Mervyn: red curls, freckles on his white face, long arms and legs. Steven Almeida: as tall as me, long slender limbs covered in fine black threads, a head of straight jet-black hair and, I knew, a dense tuft sprouting in the centre of his chest. Lukas: towering in the middle, already looking like a man. Dominic, the shortest, his hair standing upright in the breeze. And me, inspecting them from behind. At an angle from which Champagne Castle and Cathkin Peak together looked like a mammoth flat-topped table, the six of us posed for a photograph, Almeida and Dominic on either side of me.

In two weeks' time our parents would come for the once-a-term visit. It would be the first time I'd seen Bok and Bokkie after the July holiday. They would again stay on the Therons' farm. I found myself hoping they would not come so that I could spend the weekend in the hotel with the Websters.

Mervyn's parents were again flying down from Pretoria in their Cessna and staying, along with Dominic's parents, at the El Mirador. After the weekend Mervy was flying back to record an album and a violin solo for TV with the National Youth Symphony Orchestra. We envied Mervy and Dominic the sporadic liberties afforded by their instruments.

As Bennie's mother often didn't come for Parents' Weekends, he went out with the Clemence-Gordons. Bennie's mother worked as a secretary at the Ficksburg farmers' co-operative where his former stepfather was the manager. Bennie told us it was difficult for his mother to get away on Saturdays when most farmers came to the co-op. I would later think that her absences were perhaps related more to their not having much money and the story about the co-op an excuse. I resisted asking, but as far as I could ascertain his late father left money for his education that enabled his mother to keep him in the Berg.

Lukas. Certainly the strongest among us, he was rarely inclined to show off or prove his strength. He was, I sometimes thought, a friend to all of us and to none. Although he mostly hung around with us, he got along with everyone, was respected by everyone, and despite him being as hopeless as Bennie at school — and that he was caned as much as the rest of us — it did nothing to tarnish his reputation as a solid, reliable companion to all. Once in a while his mother or father came to Parents' Weekends alone as the American saddlers and Arabs could not be left alone on Swaargenoeg.

Steven Almeida. Carrying a makeshift walking stick in front of Lukas. Silent. Soft-spoken. Gentle. Portuguese, and his family had left Angola due to the war. While no one had ever rivalled my friendship with Dominic, I was fascinated by almost everything about Almeida. I was sure the affinity was in part the result of his being from outside South Africa and that it sounded as though his family had been forced to leave their country, just like mine. When we toured Malawi that December, he would be the only one besides me whose passport would show he had not been born in South Africa. Almeida's voice – like good red wine, Mr Roelofse always said – had just garnered for us a standing ovation at the inauguration of the Afrikaans Language Monument in Paarl. In the glaring lights and zoomed onto by cameras practising SABC TV's first live concert broadcast, he did a solo of 'Dit Is Die Maand Oktober' that, despite his odd Portuguese pronunciation, brought the entire open-air pavilion to its feet. Almeida intrigued me. His voice, his broodiness, his Catholicism, and his ability to take cuts, as phlegmatic and seemingly indifferent to pain as Lukas. Almeida would rise after he'd been caned and seem to glide away without twitching a nerve. Lukas, when caned, grinned, though the steely glint in his eyes gave away the fact that he was repressing the pain. Before and after cuts, Bennie seethed, whispering that he'd return to kill the torturers when he was a grown-up. Dominic and Mervyn, whom we teased as goody two-shoes, had probably been caned no more than ten or twelve times. Seeing Dominic caned was dreadful: worse to see than if it were being done to me. Coming up from bending, his face was white and his huge eyes blinked rapidly to prevent tears from brimming over; the eyes of an impala in spotlights. And Mervyn, his freckles hidden for hours afterwards by a red glow: pain, shame, silent, unable to hide or speak a word of the anger and humiliation flushed over his face and into his neck.

From Parents' Weekend, and Mervyn's week off for LP and TV recordings, our discussion moved to those of us who had TVs at home and whether Phillips was better than Sony and whether it was true that sitting too close to a TV screen could make one sterile. Much of our time was being taken up by talk of television: the

SABC was running test programmes in anticipation of January 1976 when South Africa would get regular television for the first time. Not only had we already been on live TV at the Language Monument, we were scheduled for more recordings en route to Malawi when we'd stop in Johannesburg to do *Kraaines*. Karicke Keuzenkamp was the presenter of the show and for the duration of the Malawi tour one heard boys humming 'I Love You Timothy'. Dr Webster called Karicke Keuzenkamp a one-hit wonder, just like 'Four-Jacks-And-A-Jill'.

Within the thicket of trees we could already hear the falls and then the shouts as the front of the column reached the water. Mr Buys's voice, in Afrikaans, found us before we exited the forest: 'Take off your clothes and I don't want to see any wet shorts or shirts when we leave. And no photographs!'

Entering the bright sunlight, the cool air rushing from the falls struck me and turned my skin to gooseflesh. Two thin but powerful silver jets squirted about ten metres over shear rock face to the green rock-pool below. I whistled. My eyes ran along the almost copper granite exposed and shining beside the falls. I shoved to the front of the group.

'This is like a fairy-tale.'

'Don't get all lyrical, De Man,' Bennie mumbled and shoved me playfully from behind. 'Wait till we're in that water. We're going to freeze our balls off.'

We joined a group on a flat boulder and began peeling off shorts, shirts and underpants. Beneath us the first boys approached the water. From the corner of my eye I saw Mervy raise his Kodak Instamatic. Then Buys's voice: 'I said, no photographs, jou bliksemse klein Jood!' And he came towards us, swinging the check shirt he had already removed. Mervyn was silent at the bare-chested man's approach. Buys threatened to remove the film but Lukas protested in English: 'Mr Buys, he only aimed it as a joke. He didn't really take a photograph.'

Buys glowered at Mervyn, then, still showing disdain, turned and stalked off. Over his shoulder he reminded Lukas that it was an Afrikaans week.

As soon as Buys was well away and as Mervyn pulled down his underpants I said under my breath: 'Now, quickly, Mervyn, take it while his jelly arse is turned.'

'Come on, Karl,' Lukas interjected, 'quit your shit.'

'Yes, Baas Lukas,' I whispered and tugged off my shirt.

Unobtrusively, I let my gaze run over them, becoming naked around me. Five sets of loins: Dominic, cut; his so much like mine: standing, rather than hanging, the purple head exposed, the shaft straight and the pubis just showing the first shadows of dark hair. Mervyn, huge, cut, round head like a giant red acorn, shaft white as marble and long red hairs around and on his balls, freckles on his arms tummy and legs, but white where the sun never got him. Lukas, uncut, thicker and darker but probably about the same as Dominic's and mine when the skin was pulled back; his testicles not half the size of mine. Then Bennie: below the belly stencilled like a palm leaf, also uncut, brownish, long and thin, tip dangling from side to side below the tight mauve scrotum. Almeida: dark skin all over his body, the penis small, almost translucently grey and pink like a hatchling in the tangled crotch. My eyes moved up to his face. Surely, surely, I thought, the most handsome in the school. No, not handsome, beautiful. The most beautiful boy in the world. How different it felt seeing him out there than at night during the ritual shower. He looked up, caught my eyes on his chest. I slipped out of my underpants, ashamed at being caught; swearing never to look again, Dr Taylor, will not look, wrong, boy man will be will not ever again, deserve death, everything they want, proud of me, read *To Kill A Mockingbird*, Bernice in Wimpy Bar, we spoke about school, Bernie, don't think. Don't think.

We clambered down the rocks and from the corner of my eyes I caught Buys taking off his shorts. Revulsion at his hairy arse and flabby buttocks. Again, admonished myself; focused on the falls.

'No diving, De Man!' Buys called from behind.

'Ja, Meneer.' As if I'd dive into a pool I haven't explored. Sod.

Everywhere around us were naked boys. Buys warned the little ones to stay away from the mouth of the pool where the current was strongest. We waded, splashing each other, then, bodies half submerged, made surface dives and swam to where the pool was an emerald of shadows and depths. Bennie and I joined some Standard Sixes, taking turns to dive down and see how deep it was. Each of them returned sputtering to the surface, unable to go all the way down. Bennie and I went together. At first I could see him, beside me, down, down, into the green, ever growing darkness and colder water. As my chest tightened I no longer looked out for him and concentrated on the downward flight. My lungs felt like bursting. I was already turning up when my fingers grazed the stony bottom. I grabbed for something to take back, felt pebbles come away into my hand, then brought my feet down as I began to panic and shot myself up, terrified. We broke the surface at the same moment, each waving a fist full of small round pebbles.

We stayed in for a while, looking for warm patches in the water, floating there, then diving beneath the waterfall and coming up to feel the force of water beating on our heads, pushing us down again. All the while I held on to the quarry. We left the pool to laze with the others in the sun.

'Here,' I said to Dominic and Steven Almeida, extending my open hand, 'from the bottom.'

They each took two; left one in my palm. After studying the black and white markings, Steven smiled at me and flicked his back into the water. Dominic dragged his shorts closer, slipping the pebbles into the inside pocket. I passed the one remaining in my hand to him.

Buys told us to stay out of the water so we'd dry off before getting dressed: 'I don't want the conductors whining you got colds.'

He commanded us fall in for roll call. Number off to ensure everyone was there. From one we counted all the way up to 118.

Two short. Numbered again.

Still only 118.

'Who's missing?' He barked over the rush of water. No answer. We followed his eyes skimming the ridge above the waterfall and along the pool.

'Great stuff! All I need now is for two little ones to be drowned!' He hit the inside of one hand with his fist. 'Standard Two and Three . . . Fall in from short to tall and check who was washed downstream.' They scuttled into dining-hall order. All there. Again he demanded: 'Who of your mates are missing? Come on, dammit, we're not leaving here if anyone's lost.' Still no one spoke.

'Okay. Into dining-hall order the rest of you. Four to Seven, move!'

We checked the Standard Fives. All nineteen of us were there.

Standard Sevens; only thirteen.

Reyneke and Harding. A hint of excitement rippled through me.

'Waar's julle maatjies?' he called. No one answered. He continued: 'Come on, were they here? If they're lost we need to organise a search party.'

At last someone broke the silence. 'They didn't come, Sir.'

'And with whose permission did they stay?'

Silence.

'Okay. Okay. Okay. So two of the Seniors are gipping and no one wants to rat. We'll sort this one out when we get back. Start moving there at the front . . .' He sighed: 'But when you get to school, fall in outside. I don't want anyone in the dormitories. We'll see what those two have to say for themselves . . . and to you all when you don't have a movie tonight.'

It was an almost two-hour walk back. Around us boys angrily speculated on how many cuts Reyneke and Harding were in for. Some guessed six of the best. In our group no one except Dominic spoke. In hushed tones he bemoaned the fact that we were getting it for the transgressions of others. None of us responded. Noticing, he too fell silent. Leaving the single file of the footpath, the six of us moved into an extended line on the road.

From *Buys*, I thought to myself: the worst of the worst. Four that will haunt me, make me flinch for the rest of my life, whenever – if – I allow myself a memory. I felt my eyes burn. How I hoped he would give them four. Even three. Two, forget about six! Just two from Buys was the same as twenty from anyone else. I wondered what the others were thinking: were they too sunk in a place none of us had spoken of to each other since that June night, when Dominic was safely away in Europe. For a second I resented Dom; wished he would leave us, for perhaps then we would speak. I wanted to look at them, but feared the looks, suspicions, angers – combinations of these – that might be found there. Buys, Mathison, Cilliers. Monsters, sitting over desk, don't think, they don't know, no one knows, forget it, it's over, don't think, never again. It was almost sunset. On my one side was Dom. On the other Steven Almeida. More than from the others, I desired and dreaded to know what was going on in the silence of the beautiful Portuguese boy's mind.

It was almost dusk when we reached school. Light red sunset hung in the clouds above the hills. Into Standards beneath the stoep's arches. Buys instructed us to be quiet while he went in search of the two culprits.

Soon he came down, followed by Frans Harding and Johan Reyneke.

'Look what I found under the beds in G Dorm,' he announced, grinning and telling a sheepish Harding and Reyneke to face the arches as he led them into the quad. He called for someone to fetch his cane from the Standard Three classroom. Bennie muttered from beside me that Buys was going to give it to them right there, where we could all watch. I felt a pinch of pity for the two. Or for myself. Even as I hoped he'd beat them half to death, I did not want to witness his brutality again. When a grin spread over Reyneke's chops I again felt my heart harden. By the time the cane was brought, Buys seemed to have altered his plan. He instructed Frans and Tommie to drop to the paving stones for push-ups. He looked at us and said: 'You will not be seeing a movie tonight because of these two. Who call themselves *prefects* . . . You will all be punished for the disloyalty of these indolent scinnivers. Say after me: "Suffer, suffer," then I want you to clap twice, then say, "Suffer, suffer," again.'

It was, I told myself, God exacting revenge for Harding and Reyneke's reign of terror. We began: clap, clap, suffer, suffer. One hundred and eighteen boys together with Mr Buys. Clap twice then 'Suffer, suffer' each time Harding and Reyneke went down. Clap-clap up, suffer-suffer down, clap-clap, suffer-suffer, clap-clap, suffer-suffer, and our voices and the clapping resounded up into the empty dormitories and down into the stillness of the black orchards.

After forty, Reyneke was struggling to keep going. At fifty he collapsed. Buys told us to quiet down.

'You better get up, Reyneke. Your Rooinek buddy is still going.'

We laughed. Reyneke got up and started again, as did we, clap-clap as they went up and suffer-suffer as they went down, clap-clap suffer-suffer, clap-clap suffer-suffer. I raised my suffer-suffer above the throng, now wanting Harding to hear me; I didn't give a damn if he killed me later. He had to know how I was thriving on every clap-clap, on every syllable of what was changing to suffffer-suffffer. I hoped Reyneke would outlast Harding; add that shame to this. Clap-clap suffffer-suffffer, clap-clap suffffer-suffffer, clap-clap-clap suffer-suffer-suffer. An entirely new beat. Harding was slowing down; it was now so dark we could barely see, but it was clear the two could no longer remain in synch. Someone turned on the lights. At once Reyneke fell to his stomach, panting into the paving stones beneath his face.

'Kom aan Reyneke!' I shouted, egging him on, oblivious as to whether it was to see him disintegrate or to have him beat Harding.

My two most hated enemies; Standard Seven prefect bastards. My hands flamed. Beside me Dominic was wiping his over his shorts. Behind us Lukas was grinning: clap-clap-clap suffer-suffer-suffer. I wanted to ask Mervyn to take a photograph; decided against it. Mr Buys had his foot on Reyneke's bum, telling him to straighten his back. Harding strained against gravity, now tiring fast, arms barely able to hold his weight. Just a matter of seconds before he too would be spent and down. When Harding collapsed our incantation turned to a long jeer.

'You will carry on until you vomit,' Buys called. We joined in applause. The two boys elevated themselves back on trembling arms. Beneath them wet stains marked the paving. Reyneke was crying, tears glistening in the light, giving him away even as he kept his head down, turned from us.

I felt nothing. Not a moment of pity. Clap-clap suffer-suffer, I got everyone around me going again. Reyneke was on his knees in front of Buys, the sandal again on his bum. It was no longer possible to distinguish sweat from tears. Cry, you bastard. Cry, cry, cry. Then Harding too could no longer come up and the clap-clap disappeared as our chant changed to sufff-er, sufff-er, sufff-er. Mr Buys shouted that they had better start pushing up or the whole school would go for PT. Our chant deepened and the classroom windows vibrated. They tried. Reyneke sobbed. His black T-shirt was drenched and his arms a shining brown with perspiration. I wanted Harding to weep; if only, if only Harding would weep I'd be satisfied. But he didn't; held out. Slowly, barely, but going on. Nothing but voices now chanting suffer-suffer-suffer to yet another different beat. We began a new tempo, improvising, first sopranos almost in sing-song style suffer-suffer, followed by the seconds suffer-suffer-suffer, and then a suffer-suffer-suffer-suffer staccato from the deep alto voices. Harding cracked and fell to his knees. Crescendo forte from the arches. Harding covered his face and his stomach heaved as he sobbed into his hands while we were almost in a three-tone harmony that had caught immediately. I leant forward and looked up and down the lighted arches. Faces slightly obscured by the light from behind us, I could see only the outline of heads moving, bodies swaying, bobbing up and down; all of us.

From nowhere Ma'am – Miss Sanders – had appeared in the lighted quad. She walked over to Buys and our sing-song chant grew louder. She seemed to speak to him quietly. He grimaced. She waved her arms around and put her finger to her head as she spoke. It now looked as if she was shouting at Buys and I wished everyone would pipe down so that we could hear. She pointed at the two boys sobbing on the ground. Buys pointed at the main entrance, telling her to leave. From the arches the volume intensified. Yes, they were arguing. She obviously wanted him to stop, but the more she gestured and shook her head, the louder became our throng. Buys laughed in her face. She brought her finger up, shaking it close to his nose. He brushed her hand away. A roar of approval from the arches. We could see she wanted him to let Frans and Tommie go. Finally she turned around and headed back through the front door. Behind her, Buys half turned to look after her. With his free hand he gave her an up-yours sign that broke up the suffer-suffer as we burst into spontaneous applause.

It was years later, when as an adult the scenes arrived to replay themselves over and over in my mind, I realised that our oratorio of suffer-suffers had happened at least a full year after Ma'am had caught me performing 'The Moth and the Flame' in Marabou's class.

5

'Living under the English was out of the question. Like cookies in a concentration camp,' Mumdeman said, compressing her chin side-wards and down to show her disdain. The lake's quiet schlock was just audible over the crackling fire. Skip's ears twitched at Mumdeman's feet. An owl hooted from somewhere in the mango trees.

'Just before the Peace of Vereeniging – Peace, my foot! – Oupa Mostert called the family together and read the story of Abraham and Sara going to Egypt to escape Canaan's famine. That's what it was, here, after the English burnt our farms to the ground. Scorched-earth policy Milner called it. Murdered twenty *thousand* women and innocent children in the concentration camps – and kaffirs too, mind you – killed almost as many poor kaffirs in the camps. Now they're all lovey-dovey of course, making like none of it ever happened. Slaughtered our livestock: famine, starvation, suffering; poor whites where before the Boers had been a proud and self-sufficient nation. Anyway, to cut a long story short: Oupa told us there were Boers getting together to move north – to our Canaan – out of the evil Union that was nothing but a conspiracy by the English to keep us Boers enslaved. We were being sold down the drain by Botha, Smuts and Hertzog. Big-shot pseudo war heroes; not heroes at all, I tell you, turncoats, gatswaaiers, jackals, de laaste een. But what else could they do, I suppose, the concentration camps were our undoing. Always the English, damn imperialists; like the rinder-pest, impossible to escape once it's taken hold. It was only God's mercy that your Ouma and her four brothers and sisters got out of those camps. Rounded up the Boer children and women while the men were on commando, burnt the farmhouse near Senekal to the ground. But they couldn't break our spirits or our faith. Not the Boer spirit: Not the Mosterts, Van Rensburgs, Labuschagnes, Van Wyks, Lategans and the Brinks. Later the De Mans, De Beers and the Cloetes joined us. It was time for the New Great Trek and we were going to be part of it; just like them a hundred years before us; like the Israelites two thousand years ago; on our way to German East Africa.'

Dademan sprinkled water over the grille. He winked at me as he sipped from his beer while turning over the pork chops. My eyes again fixed on my grandmother.

'And then, Mumdeman?'

'Oupa and Ouma Mostert packed up the little that could be salvaged and we hitched the wagons. Left the farm; just left it there for the kaffirs and the English. Your Ouma was born somewhere just through Mozambique on our ox-wagon, no doctors and nurses like you had in Arusha, Karl'tjie . . .' She paused and smiled at me: 'My birth was the first registered birth of a white child in the whole of East Africa. Ja, your grandma isn't today's child. Ouma-Grootjie Mostert had eight children: four already in the concentration camps and four more of us in the years after the Anglo-Boer — no! the Second War of Liberation, don't let anyone tell you otherwise, Karl'tjie my child. Not a damn must you ever call it the Anglo-Boer War. It was a war of liberation and we lost because of what the English did to us. Two of my brothers and sisters — Susanna and Joachiem — died on the trek north. Your Ouma-Grootjie never got over it; yellow fever in Mozambique. Ag, it was just like it was in the time of the Voortrekkers. New frontiers bring new diseases; new challenges.'

'Tell of the concentration camp, Mumdeman.'

'Ag, no, my boy. That makes your Ouma too sad. Another night, okay, Karl'tjie? Pour another sherry for me, please Angel.'

As I occupied myself pouring the brown fluid — later she would be bound to allow me a sip — I asked Dademan to tell about the World's Fair in America. Chronologically the World's Fair came before the Trek, but Mumdeman had been on a roll and I hadn't wanted to break her stride. On the braai the chops and boerewors sizzled and Dademan cut into the sausage to test whether it was ready. A fountain of juice ignited the flames, and Dademan tipped beer to prevent the meat scorching.

'I was five,' he began, 'just a little older than you are now. It must have been about 1905 and we were still licking our wounds, counting our dead, trying to make do on the farms the English had levelled. One day General Cronje came to ask Oupa De Man if

Oupa would go with them to America for the World's Fair in St
Louis, Missouri. It was to be something astronomical. More than six
hundred veterans off to take part in a restaging of the war. Of
course the English tried to stop it; didn't want the world to see what
they had done to us. You know, the world was on the side of the
Boers — I mean we didn't really call ourselves Afrikaners then, it was
the olden days, so we were just Boers, plain and simple. The world
was on the side of the Boers against the British. The imperialists were
worried that the thing at the fair would be one-sided, you know,
show the concentration camps. All the generals went to America: De
Wet, Viljoen, Kemp. Big show. First the cavalry of both sides came
together separately, then there was the Battle of Colenso in which we
shot the shit out of the pommies. Anyway, we didn't show the concentration camps but we re-enacted Paardeberg — where General
Cronje had to surrender because of what they were doing to the
women and children in the camps. To this day I can remember how
angry Oupa De Man was because that story was never told — about
why Cronje had to surrender. Forget about the truth, just put on a
show so that the English and the Americans can be happy. Tell the
story the way the victors want it. *Might is Right.* Thousands came to see
the show. Over twenty acres on a hill overlooking the whole St Louis
exhibition; horses, cannons, ammunition, the works. In the middle of
America, I ask you. And not a word about the concentration camps.
Bloody disgrace. But the rest was made to look as real as possible,
like dincum battles. It was actually there, even before talk of Union,
that Oupa De Man and Brink and Conradie started speaking time to
trek north again. The English, the English, the English. Like leeches.
One day that story will be told.'

As if wanting to get us away from the war, Mumdeman commenced on the years in East Africa: how they had purchased the
Oljorro land at the foot of Mount Meru from the German government. Mount Meru once higher than Kilimanjaro until the volcano
spat its crest. How they had cleared the land with the help of the

natives; how she married Dademan in the small Dutch Reformed church at Eldoret in Kenya; lived first for months in tents and in wagons, plowing the land with oxen, killing snakes, hunting down leopard come to snatch livestock; burning unwanted bush that in the fertile soil encroached unrelentingly on what had been cleared. Slowly building a home in their Canaan.

Listening to Mumdeman was better than any occasional movie or the fairy-tales and fables that so addicted me. Movies, like fairy-tales, I told myself, *were* only stories. But, what Mumdeman said was all true, absolutely true. And, what was true was real. When Mumdeman spoke of the Serengeti, with Dademan interjecting detail, a canvas unfurled before me, a visual narrative in scope virtually as vast as my imagination: 'We always approached from the East, just as the sun broke the horizon: Oh, Karl'tjie, sunrise over the Serengeti . . . Mm, mmm, mmmmm . . . a hundred thousand wildebeest and zebra, moving in waves across the sprawling savannah. In the dawn you could not see the herds' beginnings or ends, a river of game as wide as nothing anywhere on earth before or since. Here and there, where the herds ran – from playfulness or from being stalked by lion or cheetah – it was like striped currents flowing in the stream, silent, only the sound of birds or the breeze in your hair, because sometimes they were so far away that the sound of their pounding could not even reach us. You might need binoculars to see what was going on. Oh, and the Thompson's Gazelle, hundreds of them, like jack-in-the-boxes up and out of the grass; you've seen on Dademan's cines, but film can't capture the feeling of seeing a hundred golden gazelle leap up and away, bouncing, white tails plumed like ostrich feathers in the morning over the veld.' No one in the world, I was sure, could tell a story as well as Mumdeman.

'And the times we saw the lions' kill on the Serengeti,' Dademan took up, 'too many to remember.' And they would go on, telling and retelling safaris and fishing by the Ruvu; hunting elephant bulls – the size of ox-wagons – with tusks that dragged in the sand; of Ahmed,

King of Marsabit, the biggest tusker that ever walked the East African plains; setting up camp in the Ngorongoro crater; making biltong; of Bok and Uncle Michael getting a hiding for coming from behind the long-drop and throwing in a bag of bees while Grandma's best friend Sanna Koerant was doing a poo; how the Maasai and Somali had the most beautiful girls in Africa; of Aunt Siobhain arriving as a nurse in a white uniform from Ireland in the mid-fifties; of how Stephanie was born and the big party they had to celebrate the first De Man grandchild in East Africa; how Bok was sent to the army in South Africa to learn to fight because the Mau Mau were murdering white farmers like flies in Kenia and how he met Bokkie in Klerksdorp; and how Mumdeman loved my mother — full-blooded Afrikaner girl — 'from the moment she arrived in Oljorro'; how Bernice was born and Bokkie went a little deaf in one ear during the birth; and James was born in the car on the way to the hospital in Arusha because Uncle Michael didn't drive fast enough; and when Lena came and they couldn't believe it wasn't a boy and Bokkie's ear went even deafer.

'And Auntie Siobhain,' I asked, 'when she came from Ireland, did you like her?'

'Oh yes . . .' Mumdeman said, pausing. 'Day I met her I said to her, look, Siobhain, you're not really English, you're Irish, and that's a different beast altogether. Poor Irish, you know, centuries of suffering under the English. Starved by the hundreds of thousands in the potato famine and they had been on the side of the Boers in the war. Ag, besides, by that time the Boer War was a long way off and we all had to stand together against the kaffirs, forgive and forget, I always say. There was the Catholic thing, of course, you know, raising Stephanie and James Catholic and outside of the Dutch Reformed Church, but Uncle Michael himself had gone to the Catholic mission school in Eldoret for a while and it didn't surprise us that he came out half Catholic himself and that he wanted to marry an Irish girl. There also weren't that many whites up there, you know, so the young men couldn't be too choosy. But we liked Siobhain, Catholic of te not, blood is thicker than water.' And from the way they spoke about my cousins' side of the family I deduced that Uncle Michael had somehow become anglicised at boarding school while Bok, who also went to English school in Kenia, sort of kept his Afrikaans. I was never quite able to figure out why Bok, if we were so Afrikaans, spoke better English than Afrikaans or why he, just like Bokkie, Aunt Siobhain and Uncle Michael, called Grandpa Dad, rather than Pa, and Grandma Mum rather than Ma, like real Afrikaners would. I sensed, from all those nights alone with Dad and Mumdeman, that things were never quite the same once Uncle Michael had gone to the Catholic school. It was, so it sounded to me, as though he had come away from there no longer wanting to speak Afrikaans, said he wanted to marry an English girl, somehow thought himself a bit better than the rest of the family.

'And by then Tanzania had gone from German to English anyway. So we were half English, too, I suppose. Almost all we spoke. But were we glad when Bok came back with Bokkie. Full-blood Boere girl. From a poor family – didn't know what money was, I tell you – a woman of courage. Learnt farm Swahili within a year, English, fitted into the Oljorro community like a hand in a glove.'

We had finished eating and Mumdeman gathered the plates. I fed the bones to Skip.

'We went to Tanganyika,' it could have been either of them speaking, 'to get away from the bloody, bloody English. And just when we had a place of our own, the Germans lost the war and East Africa became English. Then, just when we got used to the English running the place; just as everything was coming together for us, farms producing like nowhere else in Africa, just when Bernice was going to school, and you were born, Karl'tjie – jirre, that night Arusha saw a party like never before – the kaffirs came and stole it away from us. Mbuyu, your farm. Your birthright. Gone, overnight.'

And Mumdeman spoke in the way all the Tanzanian expatriates we ever knew spoke: about how she had heard that things had changed with the black government: poverty and disorganisation. How in the streets of Arusha little boys swarmed like flies down on visitors on the pavements and in their cars, begging. And all the visitors could do was quickly turn up their car windows to lock the urchins out. That nothing functioned in Tanzania since the communists had moved in.

Then Dademan said that it had all happened long ago and I should go to bed. Mumdeman got up to come and tuck me in and to supervise my prayers. Before we left the fire, I would go to kiss Dademan goodnight and he would hug me and hold me against him and then he'd frown and feel my shoulder blades and he'd say, 'That all happened in paradise, when you still had wings – you feel, here – where these knobs are; that's where your wings grew when you were still an angel.' I could smell his cigarettes and the brandy and Coke on his breath. I kissed him again, five quick, small, dainty kisses, and said I knew I was never an angel and that he shouldn't tell fibs. And he'd say he was an old man who never even told white lies and I'd see: tonight I would dream I was an angel with wings flying over the Ngorongoro crater and the great savannahs of the Serengeti.

6

Our fort was the furthest upstream, on a slope facing one of the deeper pools where Second Rugby Field ended against the poplar bush. Built when Almeida was still with us. Downstream, hidden amongst poplars and wattles on the school side of the river, was an entire fort village with structures of varying shapes and sizes, fashioned from any material we could lay our hands on. Between forts boys shuffled through the crackling mat of leaves, clearing neat pathways. Up where we were, the bush grew dense where undergrowth and reeds signalled the beginning of indigenous vegetation. We had designed and built our fort around a fallen poplar that had its crest halfway into the river. When the tree fell, its base of tangled roots and a solid block of soil was hoisted onto the surface. I was certain it had been Steven's idea for the clump of roots and soil to form the fort's back wall, but Bennie always claimed it as his. The fallen tree's trunk, a good two metres above ground, formed the structure's central beam, to which we tied layers of reeds, branches and sticks and, over these, thatch as insulation. The front, facing out onto the river, was open. We had initially thought of enclosing that and leaving just a gap for a door. Later, happy with the river view, we left it. Inside we sat or lay on our backs staring at the white poplar beam: talking, sweeping away leaves, rethatching, discussing the pros and cons of lining the walls with mud. We'd thought the poplar would have died, but that afternoon I noticed that the branches were again budding. We chatted about whether the fallen giant had the strength to grow for many more years, or if its crest – and with it our roof – would sag further into the stream; or if, as its roots grew deeper, it might again lift itself. The biggest trees in the world, I told the others, are the giant sequoias in America. They grow to be three thousand years old, I said, and after they fall may take another thousand years to die. Whatever our poplar did in the decades to come, we knew we would not be there to see.

Sitting in the entrance, we spoke about going overseas, how the Mass was sounding, and whether we'd return in '77. The year was far over half gone. Maybe it was true what the old people said: the older you get, the more time flies. Though the nights were still icy, all around us were the first signs of spring. Over the mountains black clouds stacked and the sun fell through gaps in golden sprays that reminded me of the lights that bathed holy men in medieval and renaissance paintings and in the coloured illustrations of the *Children's Bible*. Our task for Ma'am's Art class was to sculpt, in clay, a piece inspired by the work of one of the South African sculptors she had introduced. Mine was the figure of a man, like *Narcissus*, by Fanie Eloff, a picture of which Ma'am had shown us. Dominic chose to emulate the style of Anton van Wouw's *Zulu Head*, only he was making a bust called Beauty Kekana. His figure looked nothing like

Beauty, but I couldn't bring myself to tell him. Mervy lay on his back behind us inside the fort, instructing Bennie who was up on the beam about filling open patches that needed rethatching. We knew this would probably be the last spring we would be there together. Steven's leaving had left five. Who'd be next? For one thing, Lukas's voice was in trouble. In class it jumped and squealed mid-sentence, leaving the rest of us in stitches. And worried. During the July tour his voice had become so tired Mr Cilliers had given his solo part in 'Gonna Lay Down My Sword and Shield' to Mike van der Bijlt. Clearly, there was no way the voice would hold till December. Bennie, carefully perched, tightening ropes and stuffing in handfuls of thatch, said he was definitely coming back. He wanted to postpone school in Ficksburg for as long as possible. Both Dominic and Mervyn's parents were thinking of taking them out as choir took too much time from their instruments and there were better professional tutors in the Transvaal. Mervyn had spun the same I'm-going-to-leave yarn every year — every few months — so we were less inclined to believe that he would really go. Dominic said he may convince his parents to allow him another year, but that he wouldn't dream of staying if I left. I'd been saying I was probably going to stay. What I didn't say was that I might not. That I had been reading things between the lines of Bokkie's letters and from her voice once a week on the phone: even though she never mentioned it directly, I could hear that things were not thriving with Sub-Saharan Curios.

We sat staring at the movement of the water, the reflections of heavy cloud. For the rest of my life, I thought, I don't want to go home, want him for ever, will go away with him, fish small trout near surface, want him, resent being without money and dependent on Bok's big talk, clouds heavy over Champagne Castle, *dance of the rain*, hate you all, won't go home.

'Stop it, Karl,' Dominic muttered, 'look at your mouth,' motioning for me to stop biting my nails. I wiped my fingers on my shorts and tried to clear the mud from my lips with my clean backhand.

'Off?'

'Yip.'

'My dad says,' Lukas said, 'it's probably better to get back into normal school as soon as possible; it's quite a process to adapt from a music school. Settle into high school proper.'

'We'll come and visit you, Lukas.' Dominic said, pressing a hollow into his clay where Beauty's mouth was going to be. 'We'll try and get another tour to the Eastern Cape.' My mind drifted from the conversation. Bok had been saying the same thing as Lukas's father: maybe we should make this my last year, so that the Port Natal academic curriculum wouldn't throw me once I got to the more important Standards. But, as much as I had wanted to get away from the Berg in the past – had begged them after the Malawi tour – I could no longer imagine being anywhere but in the mountains. Cathkin Peak towered like a solid block into the blue, black and white of sky and tumbling clouds. The ridges dropping westward from Cathkin like the scales of a dragon's tail. Maybe. Was that where the name came from? How did the blacks know about dragons, or was it the Voortrekkers who named the range? Bok said . . . But the mere thought of my father oppressed me. I tried in vain to redirect my thinking. Why was what I wanted always and without fail at odds with what he wanted and expected from me. Last December I had wanted out; begged, cried, begged; he sweet-talked me back. Now, I wanted to stay. He wanted me out.

The sun disappeared behind the clouds heaping over Cathkin and Champagne. Someone called from downstream that the whistle had gone. Two Juniors passed close by the fort and Mervy called them to cross the stream and take a photograph of us. For an hour the clouds had heralded an afternoon thundershower. It was close. Dom and I placed our sculptures in the back of the fort on a ledge Bennie had carved in the roots of the poplar. Then we drifted towards where everyone was gathering on First Rugby Field. I watched the moving bank of cloud and recited:

Oh the dance of our Sister!
First, over the mountain-tops she peeps on the sly,
and her eyes are shy, and she laughs softly.
From afar she beckons with one hand;
and her bracelets shine and her beads glitter;
softly she calls

We paused to look at what Sarel Raubenheimer's gang had done to the fort of Harding and Reyneke. It was the biggest of the structures, made of massive logs, square, almost like a log-cabin, though the walls were not insulated and from certain angles you could see right in. The new occupants – again Standard Sevens – were insulating it with grass, and Lukas teased that they were copying our idea. Harding and Reyneke's fort looked good, quite perfect, though I did not like the location, preferring ours, removed, on the outskirts of the village.

By the time everyone was gathered on First Rugby Field the clouds had stacked into black masses and we ran the hill from the river, up past the orchards. Looking back you could see the rain waving in dramatic grey blankets down the mountains. Winds rushed in from nowhere, lifting dust and winter's leaves into flurries. I called for the others to look at the coming rain and as we ran they laughed as I continued:

The big-game chase from the plains,
they dam up on the hilltop
they flare their nostrils
and they swallow the wind
and they stoop, to see her delicate prints on the sand
The small-folk deep beneath the ground hear the swish of her feet
and they crawl closer and sing softly:
Our sister! Our sister! You came! You came!

And I threw my arms into the air as though for a dance. I was about to continue when Buys called from behind:

'De Man. Stop looking for attention and get a move on.'

We ran, my neck ablaze, my hands tightened into fists, up the hill.
I did not look back. We reached the school just as the first heavy
drops puttered down on the corrugated iron roof. From the veranda
in the arches, we watched it come down, smelling the drops in the
dust. Rain, hard, thunderous afternoon showers. Lukas and Dominic
stood beside me. Lukas wished the deluge could be falling in the
Eastern Cape. Lightning zig-zagged over V Forest — we covered our
ears — and thunder rolled down the valley. In an animated voice, gesturing with my hands:

> She informs the winds of the dance
> and she invites them because the yard is wide and the wedding huge . . .

I stopped. From the corner of my eye I'd seen Buys approach to pass
behind us. I dropped my arms.

'De Man . . .' he said, coming to a standstill. I turned around.

'Ja, Meneer Buys?'

'When are you going to live up to your name?' he asks in
Afrikaans.

He stood shaking his head, the huge Adam's apple bobbing, his
gaze was obliterating mine. I grasped at once what he meant and
could kick myself for the moment of lapsed vigilance. His eyes
remained on me. How was I to respond? It was not a question. Nor
did I hear it as a statement. This was his fist in my face, disguised as
eight words. He shook his head again and blew through his lips,
from the movement of the Adam's apple it seemed he wanted to add
more. Instead he walked off, still shaking his head. I turned back to
face the rain.

'Ignore the bastard,' Dominic said.

'Sticks and stones . . .' said Lukas.

We watched as the enormous drops burst against the quads
paving. I mulled over Lukas's balmy words. It was the same refrain

Niklaas Bruin had always cried at us when we were teasing him. I wanted to say to Lukas that he was wrong – him and Bruin – that I preferred, infinitely, sticks and stones. But I shut up, resentment at Buys blurring my vision. I had heard my name said into abstraction, into an idea separate from me, existing now for ever in the distance behind me, moving away, beyond my grasp, down the veranda on Buys's lips. I thought of him going now to his wife. In their bedroom. Kissing her.

After a few minutes, Dominic said he was going to practise in the conservatoire. He left, saying we'd meet at choir. Lukas asked whether I wanted to go with him to the dairy. He and Mr Walshe were expecting an old and very ill cow to calve any day. I did want to see the cow calve, badly, but I had no further inclination to speak – something I would be bound to do if I accompanied him to the dairy. I said no, I had Latin and Afrikaans homework to finish. Lukas left to fetch his raincoat and I lingered for a while on the veranda. Cassandra's foal it was exciting seeing birth, must also see calf, Dr Taylor, will not think of it, will be, he loves me, in my hands, fuck you Buys, fuck you, die, lightning strike you, turn to salt pillar or black charred acacia in Mkuzi after storm water and red mud and black tree so sad so scared, Bok on Vonk, Bokkie's wig Aunt Lena's on the twig, no, stop, kill you – and instead watched the rain dam up on the grass in front of the arch against which I was leaning.

7

Caught by the paw in the wire of a poacher's snare, the sow's struggle was written with deep furrows into the earth, tufts of wiry hair clinging from branches and blood spurted against yellow stalks metres around. Bok and Jonas found her there in the footpath, her body still warm, two piglets trying to suckle from the dusty teats of their mother's carcass. And Jonas pointed to her front paw: blood was congealed only where the wire had cut into her flesh. High above the cut, closer to the sow's thigh, the skin itself hung in loose slithers with strips of meat showing through in red. This was where she had tried to chew off her own leg.

Bokkie mixed powdered milk with sterilised water and I fed the piglets from a baby's bottle. I named them for Jonas's wife and daughter: Nkosasaan and Nkosi.

After three days the little tummies began heaving and once the diarrhoea began Bokkie coaxed me into keeping the little hogs in a box outside the kitchen. On the morning of the fifth day, when I arrived as usual to give them the bottle, I found the little bodies stiff, the grey skins covered in blotches of dried green excrement.

We buried them on one side of the rockery and Bokkie helped erect a cross made of two bamboo cylinders tied together with a strip from her kitchen rags.

8

From up there I could watch it come down past the empty auditorium windows. Aloe leaves became bowls, sent waterfalls into the next, in terraces, farther down and down to below window level at the plants' bases, obscured from view. The rain enclosed the valley in a white haze from halfway down the orchards. If one didn't know, one could not guess the existence of either the river, its poplars, the hills or V Forest. The school was wrapped in veils of water.

There was no one else there. Ever. There I could always be alone. Doesn't anyone else in this stupid school read? We were not allowed around the dormitories during the day, yet for some reason my presence up in the library was never questioned. When someone walked by and saw me, I supposed they assumed the books justification enough. I could not imagine being banished from the library. As public a thoroughfare as it was, the fact that no one else used it made

it my own. From March there had been, in addition to the encyclopaedias, another reason for being up there: if he walked through we
may exchange a few words or just a quick smile or a wink. I no longer
thought of him as Mr Cilliers. He was just him. Or, without ever
saying it aloud: Jacques.

Lightning flashed, struck somewhere down the valley with a whip-
crack. Thunder. As if on cue, the drops beating on the roof became
deafening. I could watch it for hours, but knew that insufficient
reason or excuse to be up there. I turned and stood on a chair. Took
down C from the line of red leather-bound encyclopaedias. The previous year, after the July holiday with Dr Taylor, I decided to read the
entire twenty-five volumes. A–Z. The project was taking longer than
I'd thought. I opened at the pressed orange leaf. Soon I may skip past
C and just begin on D. Couldn't sit on C for the rest of the year.
Sniffed at the dry parchment. My bitten fingernails were encrusted
with the brown and yellow of river clay: *Caledonia, name applied by the
ancient Romans to upper Britain* . . . Wonder how the Romans knew about
Britain? Must remember to look it up. I skipped a long section in italics. Italics, so I had come to understand, more often than not
contained information of such detail it bored me . . . *In poetic and
rhetorical usage the name is a synonym for Scotland.* That's interesting. Why on
earth not keep it Caledonia; that's so much more fun to say than the
short – Scotland – which is nothing more than a muffled dog's bark.
The name rolled around in my mouth. I savoured the different
accents and possibilities: Ca-le-do-ni-a; Ca-le-donia; Caledo-nia. All
endlessly better than what it's called now.

*Calendar: System of measuring time for the needs of civil life, by dividing time
into days, weeks, months, and years. Calendar divisions are based on the movements
of the earth (see EARTH: Motion) and the regular appearances of the sun and moon.*
I skip a section . . . *Calendars, Ancient: The ancient Babylonians had a luni-
solar calendar of twelve lunar months of thirty days each, and they added extra
months when necessary to keep the calendar in line with the seasons of the year.*
Again I skipped what seemed boring . . . *The Roman calendar . . . About*

7th Century BC had ten months with 304 days in a year that began with March. Began with March! Crazy ... skip ... *Calendar, Gregorian. The Gregorian calendar, or New Style calendar, was slowly adopted throughout Europe. It is used today throughout most of the Western world and Asia ... The British adopted 1 January as the day when a new year begins. The Soviet Union adopted the Gregorian calendar in 1918 ... The Gregorian calendar is also called the Christian calendar because it uses the birth of Jesus Christ as a starting date. Although the birth of Christ was originally given as 25 December, 1 BC, modern scholars now place it about 4 BC.* Crazy ... So, Christmas is not Christmas by a long shot. I must remember to tell Ma'am, though I'm sure she already knows. *The Jewish calendar: The starting point of Hebrew chronology is the year 3761 BC, the estimated date of the creation of the world described in the Old Testament.* I wonder if Mervyn knows? I had no idea the Jews have their own calendar. Ridiculous. Who's stupid enough to say the world's only about six thousand years old? As stupid as saying the world was created in six days. Forgive me, sweet Jesus, Father, but it does seem unlikely and I think it may be meant sort of symbolically, even though all the ministers and the teachers and Bok and Bokkie say it is true literally. Skip ... *Islamic calendar ... In the Middle East the Islamic calendar is used extensively. It has a starting date of 16 July, AD 622, the day after the Hegira ...* Skip ... *For information on the Aztec calendar and the Mayan calendar, see AZTEC and MAYA. See also CALENDAR REFORM; CHURCH CALENDAR.* So, who decides what's what if everyone has their own years, dates, times? About to skip on to Calendar Reform, I heard him, over the racket on the roof, clear his throat. I looked up from the book. Found his smile.

'It's rather wet, isn't it?' he asked.

'Yes, it is,' I said, my spirits lifting. 'Lovely the rain, don't you think?'

'In the mood for some starfishing?' He asked, and I laughed. Nodded. He said nothing more, only inclined his head down the passage. He showed me with his fingers to wait ten minutes before following.

I could not take in another word. We had done it only once during the day, and that was on tour. Here I'd never seen the inside of his room in daylight. Choir was half an hour away. We'd have to hurry. God.

Sitting, encyclopaedia open on my knees, I recreated pictures of him as he was the afternoon in the hotel. We were off from concerts for two days. Dominic — who always had to be placed in host families with a piano — remained in Oudtshoorn to use the free time for practice. 'Come with us, Webster,' he invited Dom more than once, 'we're going to a magical place.' And Dominic, as tempted as he was, said he had to stay. It was the year he sat his Grade Eight piano exams, and he wanted to do well.

The night before we had left Dominic told me he was sure Cilliers was interested in boys.

'No, Dom, I don't think so.'

'Well, what are you going to do if he comes on to you?'

'What would you do?'

'I've told you and you called me a pig!' We laughed and we kissed and I swore I'd tell him if Cilliers tried anything, knowing I wouldn't.

We drove to the West Coast in an Audi borrowed from our host family. He said he was taking me to a place he had not been himself, though friends said it was beautiful and very quiet. As we approached the building we were going to stay in I thought he must be mistaken: it bore no resemblance to my idea of a hotel. It was nothing like the Elangeni, the Blue Waters or Malibu that towered over the ocean and where Aunt Lena and Uncle Joe stayed on their annual Durban vacations. The Paternoster, forlorn in the *fynbós* above a flat sea, looked more like a dilapidated and discarded two-storey house that had only been renamed hotel but not revamped to resemble one. There were no other cars. Were we to be the only patrons? I tried to hide my disappointment at the dull building without gardens, no Mercedes-Benzes and BMWs in the tiny gravel parking lot, no fountains, no lifts, no porters running to fetch luggage. I had pictured tall buildings, modern glass windows that slid rather than folded open, Cape Malay waiters in black waistcoats carrying cool drinks on silver trays, a huge room high above the ocean with room service and fresh white towels in the bathroom every day. I said it was beautiful — and wonderful that we were so close to the beach. It could be that he read my face, for he smiled and said it was very European and *quaint*. The word, in and of itself, made me warm to the place. It will still be quaint, I told myself, even if it doesn't look very grand.

He took the suitcase from the back seat and we walked into the small foyer. The receptionist was a young Afrikaans woman who welcomed us with a burr — like the people from the Swartland — in her voice. He said I was his son and that we'd be staying two nights.

'Oudtshoorn number plates, I see. I have family there.' She smiled.

'Pietermaritzburg,' he answered. 'This is a friend's car,' nodding his head.

'Long way you've driven, hey! You must be exhausted!' Heartiness glowed on her face.

He smiled and nodded, pursing his lips in agreement.

'Good that you came today,' she said. 'Lots of space because it's middle of the week. You're probably going to be alone unless some lost tourist shows up. And we're expecting crayfish from the boats.'

'Good, good, good,' he answered and winked at me.

'Your first visit to Paternoster?'

'To the Cape, for him,' he said, gesturing to me. 'His first time in die kolonie.'

I had of course been in the Cape the previous year, though clearly this was not the time or place to remind him.

The receptionist chuckled: 'Have you, Menere, had Cape Crays? Nothing like Cape Crays I tell you.'

'No, no. We haven't have we . . . son?'

I shook my head, not knowing how to respond.

'Single or double, Menere?'

'Double's fine, your nicest room, please,' he said and roughed my hair. 'If he kicks I'll let him sleep on the floor.'

I grinned at her. She asked whether she couldn't send up a klong with an extra mattress just for in case: 'The carpets are threadbare and the nights are cold! Be warned!'

'What do you say, Karl?' he smiled at me. 'Would you like a mattress, or are you going to lie still?'

'I'll lie still . . .' I said, holding his smile.

He looked at her and said no, really, it wasn't necessary to send up a mattress. She handed him our room key and suggested we tell her in advance if we wanted crayfish for dinner. With the place as quiet as it was, there were no plans for dinner and they'd really only be cooking for us. I took the suitcase and we started up the stairs. She called after us: 'You must take a drive or a walk to Tietiesbaai. This way,' and she pointed over her shoulder, 'there's a dust track down the coast. Not flower time, but still stunning.'

He gave me the key. Upon reaching our room he nodded for me to go ahead. I unlocked the door, glanced up at him. The place was dark and a hint of mould hung in the air. From the door he still watched me as my hand glided along the wall feeling for the light switch. A thick blue carpet covered most of the wooden floor. A four-poster double bed stood with its foot-end towards the windows, which were hidden by heavy velvet curtains with a golden sheen. The bed's cover was a patchwork in different patterns and hues of blue. On the one bedside table a radio-alarm clock flashed electronic time and above a huge antique dressing table hung an oval mirror, embossed in gold leaf. I turned back to the door. He inclined his head, indicating he wanted me to go into the bathroom. Had he indeed guessed my initial scepticism? Was he letting me look it over to tell him it was to my liking? The washbasin had small bottles of shampoo and neatly packaged bars of soap. On wooden racks above the white enamel bath and toilet were stacks of neatly folded white towels.

'Does it please you, sir? May I come in, sir?' he asked from the door.

I laughed and said: 'Of course you may, Klong.'

The door closed behind him. He smiled as he passed me. He laid the suitcase on the bed, sat down beside it, and looked up at me. I grinned and looked away, my eyes settling on the drapes.

'As wide as you want them.'

I crossed to the curtains and almost tugged them off their rails. Below me, only a hundred metres away, was a beach whiter and an ocean bluer than I'd ever seen. To one side on the dunes stood a cluster of small white houses where coloured children were playing soccer in a split-pole enclosure. On the shore a boy was fishing with a man a short distance behind him. I unfastened the latches of both windows and smelt the sea as the fresh air streamed into the room, rustling the lace curtains. I felt him behind me; smelt his body, the faint scent of sweat from the hot car. No aftershave. I kept gazing at the ocean and the white beach, deserted except for the boy fishing and the man watching. I felt his lips in my neck and his body push against mine. His arms draped across my shoulders and he kissed my neck, then my cheeks. I felt for his thigh, and ran my hand along his stomach and down, clutching the fabric of his jeans where it was hard against my lower back. He reached around my shoulder and unbuckled my belt, unbuttoned my jeans and unzipped my fly, pushed his hand into my underpants and gently squeezed my stiff penis in his palm. I felt his chin resting on my head. The boy's fishing rod was bending as if he'd caught something. We stood, quiet, and neither of us moved. I wanted it never to change, wished that we could stay like that in the window for ever, would never have to leave that place. The man had moved closer to the boy with the rod, seemed to be talking to him while he tried to reel in the fish.

'I want to tell you to use my name, but I'm concerned someone may overhear,' he broke the silence, keeping his chin on my head, 'here or in choir.' For a while he was quiet, then he said: 'Just now, in the lobby, I was paranoid that you might call me Meneer.' He laughed, his stomach moving against my back.

Facing the receptionist, when he asked me about the mattress, I had thought fleetingly of calling him Pappa or Pa, but couldn't get the word over my lips. My father was Bok and had never been Dad to me except in the letters I wrote home on Saturdays. And that merely formality in a letter so I didn't have to explain to teacher-on-duty that Bok's my father and Bokkie my mother. And writing differed from speaking. In writing I could say almost anything; talking, there were a myriad things I could not even think of uttering. Not Father, Pa, Pappa, Pappie or anything else. Just plain Bok, when I talked to him.

'Do you want to use my name?'

I knew his name. But I could not get my mind around calling him that. Not to his face. Amongst ourselves in choir we sometimes used it playfully or sarcastically. Dominic might whisper: 'Looks like *Jacques* is in one of his moods. Sopranos beware.' Or: 'Something's eating Jacques . . . Having his periods, perhaps?' It was like Jean Jacques of *Freedom, Equality and Brotherhood*, which we were doing with Ma'am in History. The other teacher's name that was a source of playful sarcasm was the Hildegaard of Miss Marabou. Marabou's name lent itself beautifully to histrionic flair: 'Hildegaard approaching!' one of us would whisper and dash for our desk when the hateful woman patrolled the stoep supervising prep or letter-writing. Or, hidden in the branches of the rondavel oak when we first got to the school: 'Hildegaard entering the line of fire!' Then pelting her with acorns from our hide-out, suppressing our giggles as she searched around her, then up into the branches, unable to see us clinging like tree frogs flattened to the enormous branches. Or, when as juniors she chose to sit with us at lunch, Dominic, speaking as if in serious conversation with me, just loud enough for her to hear: 'Quitite tithe ugogloeliesoostit soospopecociesoos, tithisoos Hiloeldidgogaardid, didoneetit you tithineekyk?' And she'd glare, ready to snap, but not sure what handle she had on him. As soon as she took another mouthful of food, I'd say: 'Tithisoos soospopecociesoos hasoos eyesoos loelikyke a bokloelacockyk mimamimboka.'

And when she'd finished chewing she'd set her mouth in disdain and say: 'You two may think yourselves cute now, but wait till you grow up. Just you wait. I promise you. When you grow up, you'll be outcasts.'

'I don't mind calling you Sir,' I said.

'But when we're alone it sounds completely absurd.'

'I can call you . . . by your name when we're alone, if you want. And Sir in front of the other boys. I won't get it wrong.'

The boy was up to his calves in the water. Behind him the man gestured angrily, instructing him on how to bring in the fish.

'Can you manage *Pa* or something while we're here?'

A chuckle escaped from my lips. I said: 'I just won't say anything, I won't call you anything. I can't call you *Pa* – *that* sounds absurd.'

'But if you don't call me Pa you'll sound insubordinate, or disrespectful. You can't just say: yes, no. These people are nosy as all hell. They aren't accustomed to having strangers around.'

'I'll call you *Pa* here . . . *sir* at school, and your name when we're alone.'

'Say it.'

'What?'

'My name.'

I sighed. 'I can't just say your name out of the blue. It will have to be in a sentence or something.'

'Say it in a sentence then.'

'I can't,' I giggled. For a moment it seemed he would let it go.

'Come on, Karl, say my name.' I glanced again at the boy battling the fish, then turned around in his arms and brought my lips to his mouth, letting them rest there, feeling his stubble, again smelling his sweat as we looked each other in the eyes.

'I love you, Jacques,' I whispered against his lips. My voice sounded hoarse and I wanted to cry; not from sadness, but from embarrassment and bliss. I dropped my forehead to his chest.

9

The hidden grain, the layers and rings and twists beneath the bark normally obscured in the deepest recesses of the wood, had been brought to the surface as if burnished till, to us, they looked like tambotie shined with high-gloss furniture polish. Leaning backwards as though they were to sit down on their haunches, the rhino rocked to and fro against the severed trunks, the rough hide of their hindquarters having worn off long ago the splinters and sharp edges of the tree's breakage. With varying degrees of ardour, they swayed, their heads turned up, horns almost slanted backwards; then turning around, rubbing another side or lifting a leg to rub a thigh or a portion of the belly. Each session made the tip of the stump first smoother, eventually shinier, leaving it after years as resplendent as any piece crafted at a carpenter's hand.

I recall at least three rubbing stumps in the Mkuzi veld, all near mud-pans where water only temporarily gathered before it evaporated or was slurped away by the earth's thirst. In Umfolozi I saw a stump once only. It was the time Bok took Tommie Bedford and some other tourists for photographs. Tommie Bedford was the Springbok rugby captain at the time. It was a thrill to meet him and have our photographs taken with him and his girlfriend who had blond hair down to the small of her back. Bok went out of his way to make select trips memorable, guiding visitors to outlying locations most tourists rarely entered; taking them also to places without the reserve like Dingaan's kraal and Isandlwana, to the site of England's most bloody battle against the Zulus. Tommie Bedford's girlfriend wanted to buy beadwork so Bok took them to kraals where Zulu women threaded bracelets, trinkets and necklaces of bright, shiny beads.

People like the Bedfords were called VIPs, an abbreviation whose significance I knew a while before I understood its literal meaning and could fill in the words. When Bok left the Parks Board to become a white hunter with Southern Safaris he frequently took VIPs – rich

Americans and Europeans – to hunt for trophies in Botswana and Rhodesia. One of the most famous was the astronaut Wally Schirra, who went into space before Apollo. Bok told us of how he and Wally Schirra were sitting around the camp fire late one night when Schirra turned to him and said: 'Ralph, you are the first man I've met who has not asked me how it was to walk in space.'

'I know,' Bok says he answered. 'Those things don't matter in the bush.' Only then did they talk about what it had been like and Wally Schirra said that it was there in outer space that he realised the minuteness of human beings within the infinite scheme and time-lessness of the universe.

In our sitting room we had an autographed photograph he later sent Bok. The picture was taken while the spacecraft had been in orbit. On it one could see the whole of Africa and parts of Europe, the continents surrounded by blue oceans and smears of white that must have been clouds. Bernice did a project on planets and took the photograph to Kuswag to show her class. Her teacher said the picture with its signature was extremely valuable and would accrue further in years to come. With the whole earth already mapped, explored and understood, space, Bernice told us afterwards, was man's new frontier and the astronauts its courageous reconnoitrers.

10

It was cold and windy outside, so he went back upstairs to fetch our jerseys. How unusual to wear a jersey on the beach, I thought, wait-ing for him out there in the car. In Zululand and Natal you take off your clothes and in the Cape you put more on.

We drove south along the narrow road pointed out by the recep-tionist. Everything along the way looked different from the Indian Ocean coast. Only fynbos, grass, very few trees. And dryer in a dull green and cinnamon-coloured sort of way, not green and colourful like around St Lucia or Toti. Inland from the coast was veld, unlike Natal where the end of the beach was the beginning of the dizzyingly green bush. The plants at Paternoster were different: small and spindly, succulents, stringy creepers that clutched the surface of the sandy soil. It is all, he said, the function of the winds, the cold Agulhus tide and the less moist climate. Out of the car, the differences became even more stark: here we walked in powder-fine white sand, not the little yellow grains I knew. Beaches with barely any waves were broken by bays between black boulders where huge waves rushed, spurting froth skyward and groaning as they churned and drew back, then came flinging themselves once more against the rocks. The further we walked the rougher the sea became and the waves roared down on the beach, 'like porcupines storming with their quills erect,' I said. He frowned and I showed him how the wind scooped the tips off breaking waves making them look like quills, bending in a forward rush. I could not recall the poem – Opperman perhaps – from which I had filched the image. I left it, allowing him to think it my own.

Dense forests of kelp swayed in the tide. Pieces of green and black stems, broken loose, washed up onto the beaches where we walked bent forward against the wind. The water was freezing. Nothing like Toti or St Lucia where one could swim all year round. We clambered up the rocks and sat hunched over rock-pools pointing out tiny fish, hermit crabs and knobbed seaweed I had never seen before. I picked up crabs and held them up to show him where they carried their eggs. He asked whether I wasn't afraid and I said no, animals and creatures rarely harm you if they know you're not going to hurt them.

'How do they know your intention?'

I said they just know; they can sense it. I said I knew the sea and the beach from when Bok had been a ranger at Lake St Lucia after Umfolozi. But things did look different in the Atlantic Ocean, I said. Here were different kinds of starfish, brightly coloured and patterned, which I lifted from the rock-pools to let sit in my palm.

And anemones, their tentacles long and stringy, ten times the size of the ones on the East Coast. I tried to stick my fingers in before they could withdraw into their tight-lipped cylinders. Running the tip of a finger along the tight folds of the slimy lips feels kinky, I said, and he asked me what I meant. I laughed and looked away.

A sea urchin. Its black spikes a pom-pom in my palm. He cautioned that I should put it down as it was poisonous.

'If you hold it carefully, it won't harm you,' I said and unsuccessfully tried to get him to take it from me.

'If that thing squirts poison into you, your hand will wither and fall off.'

'They don't do it for no reason. It's if they are stepped on or hurt or if they need to eat or protect themselves. It's like porcupines,' I said, 'it's not true that they shoot out their quills. They ruffle them out and run into whoever is threatening them and then leave the quills behind. They don't shoot them out.' I told him about Suz, when she got quills stuck right through her flanks and into her face. Bok pulled them out, but the poison still almost killed her. I knew, and Chaka probably too, that something was wrong one afternoon when she didn't come running from the trail to meet us. There was no Suz when Bok came into sight through the bush that day and my heart sank. Had a leopard at last taken her? Or a lion? A crocodile? Before I could ask, Bok said she was okay. Motionless she lay across the donkey's saddle bags, unable to wag her tail when she saw us. At night she slept beside my bed, all the while making small sounds while Chaka cried and yelped outside my window. I feared she would die. But within a day or two she had regained her strength, was back to her old self, running through the grass; chasing meerkats and warthogs, and barking at eland with Chaka and me when we were out of Bok's sight.

'What if the urchin thinks you're trying to hurt it? It will sting you, you know that.' I could hear he was teasing, patronising me. I didn't believe for a moment that he was really afraid or concerned that the creature might cause me harm.

'A little bit of poison won't kill me! A scorpion once stung me and we just put some Scrubbs Ammonia on and I was fine.'

'Oh, for the invincibility of childhood.'

'I'll be fourteen in October.'

I returned the sea urchin to its pool and we walked back down onto the beach, heading for the car. Waves licked up to where the sand was dry. The tide was coming in. The wind now in our backs. A few paces behind me I heard his voice:

'Karl-who'll-be-fourteen-in October, I love you.'

I turned and pulled a face at him. He laughed and asked whether he was embarrassing me. I shook my head; glad he had said it.

I lay on the bed searching for decent music while he took a bath. Nothing caught clearly, except Radio Good Hope and a few black stations.

After him, I went in and filled the tub almost to the brim. Water splashed over the sides as I submerged my body and head. What a pleasure opening the little containers and washing my hair with shampoo that was not from my cone-shaped Colgate bottle; unwrapping each little soap a different fragrance and new colours. It reminded me of our holidays in Klerksdorp with Aunt Lena and Uncle Joe. Two full-time maids – Ragab and Liesbet – kept the household going there and the bathrooms had bath salts, bubble bath and an endless supply of big fluffy towels. Ragab and Liesbet were superb workers and the mansion was always spotless and fragrant. Once, when Aunt Lena found a grime ring inside the bath-tub she called Ragab from the kitchen. Ragab insisted she had cleaned the bath and that perhaps one of the Brats had taken a bath. Aunt Lena told her to tell the truth or else face the sack. Ragab again insisted she had washed the bath, at which point Aunt Lena grabbed the hosepipe from the washing machine and beat the screaming and begging Ragab all the way down the passage. Lena and I laughed as we followed the two women. By the time they reached the lounge

Ragab had wet herself and Aunt Lena instructed her to clean the mess from the carpets.

The other house I loved was the one I had been in only twice, the second time just a few weeks earlier on tour: it was the home where Dominic grew up and where we'd stayed with the Websters. What classy people Dr and Mrs Webster were, I thought. Both had university degrees and Dr Webster had studied in the United States. Their house in Saxonwold was set on an enormous piece of property that sprawled down to a small lake at the bottom of the garden. The Websters had a speed boat for water-skiing and inside the house was a separate room with nothing except a snooker table. They had thousands of books, whole walls covered from floor to ceiling, as well as the biggest collection of record albums I'd ever seen. Amongst the Websters' albums of modern and contemporary music were a few I knew, as Mrs Webster liked the music I had grown up with. Dominic said his mother was as sentimental in her tastes as I was. But most of the Websters' collection was music Dominic had had to tell me about, much I'd never heard of. He said that many of the albums were from the mid-sixties when his parents had still been socialists – a concept I researched from the dictionary – and Dr Webster had had long hair: Joan Baez, Bob Dylan, The Beatles, Miriam Makeba, Neil Young, Leonard Cohen, Aretha Franklin, Donovan, The Beach Boys, Mercedes Sosa, Pablo Milanes, Janis Ian, Kris Kristofferson, The Monkees, Gladys Knight and the Pips, Ella Fitzgerald, Louis Armstrong.

The houses where I felt at home were where you could fill the tub and then pull the plug, not places teabags had to be used twice, where you were not shouted at for dripping syrup while spooning some from the jar, where you didn't get told you wanted everything you laid your eyes on. Because most of what you wanted was already there.

Jacques had pulled back the cover and top sheet. He lay on his back with his hands behind his head, eyes shut, listening to the radio. From around his waist the towel had fallen open. I thought he had done it deliberately, that he was pretending. I stepped closer to the bed. The motionless eyelashes, the rise and fall of his chest and stomach said that he had indeed fallen asleep. His damp black hair lay in slithers on the pillow and against his upturned wrists. One arm was diagonally below his chest; his legs slightly apart: white, skinny and also covered in a haze of black hair. For the first time in daylight, I saw his penis, limp and pale in the pubic tangle that ran up to his navel. Head to toe I took him in. He was like something from a book I had seen; like Christ or one of the men in the black and white photo romances Bokkie prohibited us from reading. I had gone stiff and stood waiting, wondering what to do. When I looked at his face again he was staring back at me. His eyes ran down my chest and tummy and stopped where I knew there was now a clear bulge in the towel draped around my waist. He smiled and told me – no, asked – whether I would not drop the towel: 'Sal jy nie die handdoek laat sak nie?' Holding my breath, I lowered the white fabric. I walked over to the bed and stood, facing him. Half raised on his elbow, he lifted himself and took me into his mouth. His other hand went around my buttocks and for a while he rocked me. Then I was on the bed; on top of him; my face between his legs; taking him into my mouth; afraid I might choke feeling it grow harder as the head moved through the foreskin; inhaling the smells of soap and moss. His tongue ran from my scrotum backwards. I gulped, almost bit him, closed my eyes. Stubble, sharp and rough like sandpaper, grazed the skin of my scrotum and buttocks. Nothing I had known – ever – felt as good as that. Every nerve of my body, it seemed, came together there and his tongue had found me out. It was too much to bear. I pushed him away, lifted myself off him, keeping my lips around his penis. I moved my head up and down, taking in as much as I could without choking. In an urgent voice he told me to stop, but I continued, refused to remove my mouth. I found his hand and placed it between my thighs. Then I felt it, suddenly, a rush into my mouth. I held it there, not breathing. I wanted to spit it out; feared it could be poisonous. That I would die. Then I felt the burning in my own loins, shudders in my lower body. I had to breathe. I swallowed. Felt it burn down my throat. I lay thinking that mine had probably been over his face or chest. I held onto his skinny white ankles. When I opened my eyes I watched the stiff organ slowly draw back into itself, leaving a silver drop hanging where the foreskin had now drawn into a tiny flower, folded into a closed anemone. 'Long Legged Woman Dressed in Black' was playing on the radio as drowsiness began to overcome me. My tongue ran around the inside of my mouth. It was impossible to know whether at the back of my mouth I was tasting or smelling or, both at once, unmistakably, the scent or after-taste of salted almonds.

He moved, turned his body to face head down next to me. He did not speak; just ran his hand through my hair, stroked my cheeks with his fingertips.

I asked him how old he was and he told me to guess.

'My father started going grey when he was about thirty. We used to pull out the grey hairs and he'd give us one cent for every one. You're going grey, so you must be about thirty or forty, I don't know.'

'Thirty-three.'

Mungo Jerry's voice died away and the *peep-peep-peep* signalled time for the news. A woman's voice said that the schools around Soweto had once again been set ablaze by black children. The police had been forced to shoot. Statistics on deaths were not yet available. The entire township had been cordoned off and Prime Minister Vorster had declared a State of Emergency. Jacques muttered something about ungrateful savages and sat up to turn the radio off.

'Is it okay . . . to —' I whispered, embarrassed, and could not complete the thought.

'To what?' he asked, smiling down on me.

I quickly shut my eyes, then opened them and blurted, 'Is that stuff I swallowed poisonous?'

He laughed, still looking at me where my head rested on the pillow. He shook his head and whispered, no, it wasn't poisonous. Then he was down there, again, his tongue everywhere. I thought I would faint. With hands on his ears I brought him back up to me. He lifted himself and lay with his full weight on me, and kissed me. There was a damp spot where his hair began to curl in his neck; both my hands were there, pressing his face into mine. I whispered for him to put it into me, and he said he couldn't, that he didn't want to hurt me. I said it wouldn't hurt. While we kissed he began to push with a finger against my anus; trying to slip it into my rectum. My body resisted, seemed to contract. Pain stirred in my lower back and abdomen. It opened, slowly, until he could slide in a finger; then two; moved them around; asked how I felt and I just nodded my head. With my legs lifted over his shoulders, I could feel his penis now against my anus. He whispered that I should try and relax. My eyes closed. Gently, he began to push and withdraw. I could feel myself open. At moments I wished him to stop. An excruciating pain; but then, for moments again, pleasant. He asked whether I was all right. I nodded, my head thrown back in the pillow, unable to speak or open my eyes. I was impaled; I could not move; as if every atom of will had been drained from me; that nothing mattered except what was happening in that moment everywhere and nowhere in my body. I was gasping through my mouth; not sure whether I could take it. When he moved too deep, pain bolted up my spine, exploded in my skull; he asked whether he should stop. I shook my head. Now there was a remarkable, overwhelming feeling of lightness, as if I were composed of only air, grounded only where he was inside me. The longer it continued the more I could move; my arms came back to life, brought his face down to mine; I kissed him. Tears ran down my cheeks; dammed into my ears. He stopped. I opened my eyes, saw the fringe tumbled across his forehead; frowning. I nodded for him to continue. I started crying. Again he stopped, but I clasped my legs to his back, urging him to go on. When I sobbed he covered my mouth with his hand.

From behind my closed eyelids and through my tears I saw the world slowly break apart into millions of new colours, and I wondered for weeks afterwards whether I had perhaps lost consciousness, for just a few seconds.

Later, lying curled up against him, he again asked me whether I was all right.

'I loved what you did to my starfish,' I whispered.

'Your what?'

I giggled. He had no idea what I was talking about. I flopped over on my back, embarrassed at having said it. Smiling with my eyes shut.

'What star?'

'My bum, I liked what you did.'

'Your starfish!' He sputtered and laughed in my ear, saying I was too clever for my own good. He went into the bathroom. Now I felt that I was drenched in sweat, as though I'd just got out of a lukewarm shower. I let my fingertips crawl around my anus, certain there would be blood. Nothing. I sniffed. A waft of shit. Lifting myself I checked the sheets. The brown smudge made me squirm. The toilet flushed and I dropped myself onto the mark, hoping he would not discover or suspect what I was hiding.

I moved the orange leaf to the top of the page so that once the book was shut only the tip was visible. Rain was again thundering down on the roof, leaving me wondering whether there may have been a cloud break. I stepped onto the chair and reached to the top shelf. I slid the encyclopaedia in between B and D. I looked up and down the balcony; peered over the balustrade into the auditorium. No one in sight. I stepped down and ran along the passage.

At his door I again checked behind me. I turned the handle and stepped into the room, just as he was emerging from the shower. I locked the door. I asked whether we could open the curtains and the window, just a little, so that we could smell the rain. He cautioned me to whisper. He drew back the curtains a few inches and opened the louvres.

With both hands he ran the towel behind his back. I removed my sandals. In a whisper I asked whether he knew Eugene Marais's poem about the rain. He nodded, smiling. I asked whether he'd like me to recite it for him. He winked and nodded, a finger to his lips.

'Must I whisper the poem?' I asked, smiling, gesturing as if perplexed.

'Yes! Unless you want us to get caught. And we have about ten minutes before choir.' Running his hand down my cheek.

'Okay. I'll whisper it to you. Sit down.' Then, while he sat naked on the bed and the rain again beat down harder on the corrugated iron roof, I began to whisper:

> *The Dance of the Rain*
> *Song of the fiddle player, Jan Konterdans, from the Great Desert*

I recited the dance and I moved my limbs, my body, my clothing, to make visible the words:

> *Oh the dance of our Sister!*
> *First, over the mountain-tops she peeps on the sly*
> *and her eyes are shy, and she laughs softly.*
> *From afar she beckons with one hand;*
> *and her bracelets shine and her beads glitter;*
> *softly she calls*

My hands, trembling, around my mouth:

> *She informs the winds of the dance*
> *and she invites them because the yard is wide and the wedding huge*

My arms open, go up, my body moves from one corner of the room to another, an urgent whisper:

The big-game chase from the plains,
they dam up on the hilltop
they flare their nostrils
and they swallow the wind
and they stoop, to see her delicate prints on the sand
The small-folk deep beneath the ground hear the swish of her feet
and they crawl closer and sing softly:
Our sister! Our sister! You came! You came!

Leaping onto the bed, stooping the way game does to sniff the soil, and the whisper further subdued:

And her beads tremble,
and her copper-rings flash in the disappearance of the sun
On her forehead is the fireplume of the mountain vulture
she steps down from the heights

Step from the bed:

with arms outstretched she spreads the faded kaross

T-shirt removed and cast to the floor, body twirling around the room:

and the breath of the wind is lost
O, the dance of our Sister!

My arms shoot up and my hands reach towards the ceiling: 'See, it's the dance of our sister!' My voice rasps in a laugh-filled whisper and my wild eyes see him come for me in the room's centre. He presses my chest to his and my feet leave the floor and he kisses me as he carries me to the bed. 'You're getting too heavy! You're almost as tall as me.'

*

In choir, smelling him from my hands, I feel how raw my chin is. Know in a day or two it will peel.

I I

'I did learn to speak Swahili, but not as well as Bok who was born there and spoke it all his life. And English, of course. That was a nightmare, because we hardly spoke English in Klerksdorp, you know, it's a very Afrikaans town. We did do English at school – we had to – but writing a few words for exams or reading some books wasn't the same as speaking it. I knew when I married Bok that I'd have to learn because he told me from the beginning that many people in East Africa knew no Afrikaans. So when I got there I just listened, picked it up from Aunt Siobhain – though I never got her Irish accent, of course. Siobhain and I raised you kids together because Bernice and Stephanie were four years apart and of course Lena and James just a few months. Look, let me tell you, Aunt Siobhain and I got along like a house on fire. That's a smart woman, I tell you. Can work her fingers to the bone. No airs and graces. Doesn't touch drink. A heart of gold. That Uncle Michael, though, believe you me, doesn't know what he's got in that woman. Always out at night, drinking with the boys while poor Siobhain has to sit at home with the kids. And a snob, man, thinks he's better than us you know, and then there's this pretence at being English. And Siobhain had a thing for you, of course. Ag, when I fell pregnant we were all hoping it would be a boy – but especially Siobhain – because you know there were the two girls and we really wanted a boy. Also to be friends with James. I told Bok this was the last time we were going to try and you know, my bad ear . . . Anyway we were all sure so everyone gave only blue things for you and there were still all the blue things from when we thought Bernie and Lena may be boys.

That had all been packed into the campher kist and we'd had to buy pink after they were born . . .'

'Couldn't the doctors fix it, Bokkie?' I asked, listening to her knitting needles click click above the half-finished jersey, concentrating on my own: one plain, one pearl.

'What?'

'The ear, Bokkie.'

'No, we tried.'

'Do all women go deaf when they have babies, Bokkie?'

'No, Karl. It's just something that happens to some women. It's usually during labour, when the pressure on your eardrums is so intense. Same thing happened to Ouma Liebenberg: with each one of us that was born she went a little deafer. So when I fell pregnant with you we decided it was the last time, because I'd lost so much hearing with the first two. When news spread that you were a boy all the farmers and their wives came into Arusha and there was a big party at the club into the early hours of the morning. I could hear them all the way to the hospital. Bok was quite a sought-after bachelor. You know how handsome he is and how women always fall for his charms – lots of girlfriends before me I heard after I got to Tanganyika – and a bit of 'n ramkat. Just like we did with Bernie and Lena, Dademan made tape-recordings of you crying and making baby noises and we sent the recordings by mail to South Africa for poor Oupa and Ouma Liebenberg. Ag, later, when we got a letter, Ouma Liebenberg wrote to say how Oupa cried when he listened to you screaming. He has such a small heart, you know.'

'And was it sore, Bokkie, when I was born?'

'Not as sore as with Bernice and Lena. They took hours and hours. That's where the deafness probably came in. But you couldn't wait to get out into the world. Wasn't really even necessary for me to go to hospital, but we didn't know that of course, when my water broke. You just slid out like a little pink bird – nine and a half pounds, mind you – ten minutes and that was it. A smile on your face after only three weeks. Little devil, from the beginning. And you didn't sleep through the night until you were three years old. Not one night did you sleep through until some time in Mkuzi. When we woke the next morning I told Bok to go and check, I was too scared, sure you died in the night or had been dragged off by a leopard.'

'Tell when the Maasai came to dance at the house.'

'Now that was a story! It must have been about six months after we were married because I was already heavily pregnant with Bernie. I fell pregnant five days after we were married. So somewhere on the trip from Klerksdorp to Oljorro; probably at Lake Victoria where we spent two nights resting. Anyway, one afternoon I was alone at home on Mbuyu, when I heard the singing from the distance. I think the houseboy had the afternoon off because I had no one to ask where the singing was coming from. We had a little stoep and I went out and looked down the farm road but there was nothing. The singing was growing louder, no drums or anything, just the singing and then I walked around the house and saw this group of twenty or thirty Maasai running towards the house, singing and spears waving and simis in the air and they were painted and I had heard all the stories about the Mau Mau and I ran inside the house and I couldn't lock the door because we never locked doors there so I had no idea where the key was and it sounded like they were surrounding the house and I ran and hid under the kitchen table. Just praying. Praying that God would spare me and my unborn child. So scared, so very scared. Later it grew quiet outside but I was still too scared to come out from under the kitchen table. I didn't know what they were doing out there. You know what the Mau Mau did in Kenia; killed hundreds of innocent white farmers, slaughtered all the animals they could find on the farms. Witchcraft and things. That was all going through my mind and I wished I had never come to Tanganyika. Then I heard the sound of a truck and I heard Dademan's voice coming into the house. He found me there under the table and almost laughed his head off. He had asked the Maasai to come and dance, so that he could film them on cine. Anyway, the whole Oljorro thought I was a real pumpkin!'

'Did you miss South Africa, Bokkie?'

'I missed my family. Oom Gert and Aunt Lena. But the six years in Tanganyika were the best years of my life. I would go back tomorrow if we could.'

'Did you ever visit?'

'Once. That's when you were conceived. And we wrote letters.'

'Were Oupa and Ouma Liebenberg still in the Molopo?'

'No, they were already living in Klerksdorp where Oom Gert works on the mines.'

'Tell when you were little and the leguan gave the donkeys a fright and they ran off with you.'

'Ag no, Karl, that's enough now. My throat is completely dry. Go outside and play in the sand-pit or take Chaka for a walk. Out you go, you haven't been outside once today. You can't sit in here day and night listening to stories.' I dropped my knitting needles in her woolbag and went off with Chaka to see whether we could find the eland herd.

12

Wednesday-evening concerts were attended by guests from the surrounding hotels. A deadly silence reigned in the dormitories; showers were taken without anything more than muted and hushed whispers; letters were distributed without the usual teasing and fanfare. Sound travels far and God help anyone whose voice reached the auditorium while a performance was in progress. When not our turn to perform, we could hear the music and applause carry through to us in the dormitories. These were some of my favourite moments. Hearing the songs from my bed. Not having to sing.

After Mr Samuels left in our Junior year and we were briefly without a conductor, Mr Mathison appointed me to conduct two of the Junior Choir's Wednesday-night concerts. That was when we did *Oliver* as part of our programme. Richard Benson, the Senior soloist, had played Oliver on our tour earlier but with him away Dominic would be Oliver during the second, lighter part of the concert. Previously Mr Samuels had had me learn a portion of Fagin's role: *'One boy, boy for sale, he's going cheap, only seven guineas.'* Excitedly I told Bok on the phone that I had my first solo part. I tried to growl out Fagin's songs, but eventually Mr Samuels gave the part to a Senior, saying I just couldn't act tough enough to convince anyone I was selling a boy. I lied to Bok on the phone and said the school had decided only Secondaries and Seniors would do solo parts in *Oliver*.

Why Dominic or Mervyn weren't asked to conduct our Wednesday-night concerts I had no idea and didn't really care, even though they would have undoubtedly done a better job than me. We assumed it was because both their voices were needed in the choir. Before one of the performances I was cheeky to Marabou. She slapped me across the face and threatened to appoint a different conductor. Then, midway through the first half of the programme — to what must have been Hildegaard's unmitigated delight — there was a humiliating moment when I couldn't find the right combination of notes for the 'Hodie Christi'. Four or five times I pushed the wrong chord. Eventually Mathison's voice swept through the hall: 'Help him, Mervyn.'

Mervy stepped forward and pressed the correct notes. I could barely continue to conduct: a fool in front of the choir and an entire audience. During break we sold LPs of earlier choirs to the audience. Everyone congratulated me on a job well done. I could hardly hear them. What was going through my mind was the 'Hodie Christie' chord. While we dressed into our orphan outfits for *Oliver*, all my peers said I had made a splendid conductor and that one missed chord was nothing to get stuck on.

Dominic was brilliant as Oliver. In the final scene, when we sang 'Consider Yourself', we bounced him up and down in a blanket. The audience was thrilled and the humiliation of my inability with the chord was forgotten by the time I had to conduct the following week. I never needed to know the notes for 'Hodie Christi' again, though I remember them even today: G, A, D.

13

'The *Jesse Likes* rolled and the rhino were tossed from side to side in their crates. Slipping and sliding. Not a pleasant sight, I tell you. Waves broke over the bows, drenching everything on deck. They lost their footing. Awful, awful. I was concerned they'd break a leg or something. If that happened we'd of course have to get rid of the poor animals.' Bok took another Paul Revere from his Thirties pack and gestured for Uncle Michael to pass the lighter. Aunt Siobhain clicked her tongue and said: 'Shame, shame . . . Poor things.'

Bokkie and I had collected the girls from boarding school in Hluhluwe the previous day and then driven down to stay with our cousins in Amanzimtoti. Bok had been away for an eternity and I'd been beside myself missing him. I took a clipping from the *Daily News* that showed him loading the rhino, up to the camp store to Mr Watts. Mrs Watts asked me to read it aloud to some tourists next door in the small curio shop. The tourists asked how old I was and when I said I was almost six they said I was way ahead for my age. Unsolicited, I said I was going to be a jockey or a film star when I grew up. A woman said one had to be rather petite to become a jockey and that at five I looked as if I might grow up too tall. I said I'd stop eating and remain small. The tourists laughed.

Jonas and Boy, only occasionally on trail with one of the other rangers while Bok was away, had to listen repeatedly as I told them that my father was in America and of how important he was as was the mission to save the white rhino from extinction. I showed them the clipping and read it to them. Showing off my pre-school skills with the word I realised for the first time that neither Jonas nor Boy could read. Using a twig in the sand outside their kaja, I set out at once to teach them how to write their names.

'Look how easy it is,' I said, writing J-O-N-A-S and, a distance away, B-O-Y. They then had to copy their names below where I'd spelt them out. I let them practise, eventually clearing the letters from the dirt and having them do it without my example. They both got it right and days later, wherever we were, would carve their names in the dirt.

The ship barely over the horizon, I started asking Bokkie how long before Bok returned. Soon reaching her fill, Bokkie showed me how to read the almanac. Every morning I was allowed to draw a cross over the day we were in. Then, seven days before he was due back in Durban and after Bokkie had gone up to Mr Watts's to phone Aunt Siobhain and make arrangements for us to stay over, she told me that Bok was going to be a day or two late. Instead of seven days to go, there were now eight or nine. I set my elbows on the kitchen table, sulking.

'You'll just have to be patient, Karl'tjie. Patience is the seed of genius. I'm sure Bok will bring you and the girls presents. Now just bear that in mind.' Sure enough, the prospect of a gift from America contained my frustration. And I had learnt a new word, a new phrase. I stopped moping.

Long before we approached the outskirts of Durban North I had asked Bernice how far to the Blue Lagoon swan. Nearing Virginia Airport, Bokkie slowed down so we could watch the small aeroplanes land. Then, a few minutes later, as we saw the Umgeni Bridge, I looked out for the enormous wooden swan-boat with its long bowed neck and wings coming up its side. We begged to go for a ride and Bokkie said we could ask Aunt Siobhain to go later during our visit.

In Toti, Stephanie put on her record of *The Sound of Music*. At my request she donned her ballet shoes and powder-blue ballet tutu. While Julie Andrews and Christopher Plummer sang 'Edelweiss' she glided and pirouetted and pliéd across the lounge floor. How grace-ful I found the loose-limbed movements – a blue crane spreading her wings, throwing back her long neck in the veld. I longed to join her. She said I could, and we waltzed. When the dance was over I asked whether she would teach me ballet. She said she would, when next they came to visit. She said that if I was a good boy she would lend me *The Nutcracker* – real ballet music – to take back to Umfolozi.

Aunt Siobhain suggested we take a drive to Louis Botha to watch the planes take off and land. It would be a treat for me as I had never seen real landings or take-offs. We went in two cars – our Peugeot and their Cortina station wagon. At Louis Botha Airport we stood upstairs on the open-air balcony. The day was grey and looked as if it might rain. Only one aeroplane was parked on the ground and Uncle Michael said it was a DC 10 that would soon be taken out of com-mission. Across the airfield the huge orange and blue flame from the Shell & BP refinery plumed from its furnace. Bernice recalled that Bok had worked there when we first came to South Africa. A plane that Uncle Michael said was a 707 from Johannesburg dropped into view and we watched its approach to the runway. Its underside was enormous. We watched its wheels fold out. I jumped up and down and shook my hands as its belly descended. Aunt Siobhain touched my head and Bernice told me to calm down. I was certain it would fall and crash into the tar. This was the biggest thing I had ever seen in the sky; a million times bigger than it ever looked in the movies. The wheels screeched, sending up sparks and white smoke as it touched the ground. It careened down the runway and slowed down to turn. A gigantic moth with spread wings – trembling in anticipation of a mate – it came crawling towards the airport terminal. Uniformed men wheeled a set of high stairs out onto the runway and pushed them towards the plane. James said it was for the passengers to disembark. Just like in the movies, only better. Amongst the passengers stepping down onto the tarmac, my eye caught something. For a moment I wavered, then shouted, 'It's Bok! Look there's Bok!' Around me, my sisters, cousins and the grown-ups burst out laughing. They had known all along, had wanted to surprise me.

Bok came across the runway wearing a long white safari suit. I wanted to run downstairs but was told to wait so that we could all make our way together. It was the longest he had ever been away from home since he and Bokkie were married. Uncle Michael teased Bokkie, saying: 'Tonight's going to be like a second honeymoon, or what am I saying, Bokkie?' And she smiled coyly, trying not to look too excited.

When Bok came through the door I saw him see us – I glanced at Aunt Siobhain, who nodded – and I ran past the incoming passengers and jumped up, grabbing him around the neck. He carried me to where the others were waiting and put me down so everyone could say hello. He and Uncle Michael shook hands and he kissed Aunt Siobhain, the three girls and James. Last, he smiled at Bokkie and gave a pace towards her. We all watched. She smiled and he smiled at her. They looked at each other. Then her eyes brimmed with tears and she put her hand over her mouth and started crying. He took her in his arms and held her while she cried and laughed and smiled again, all at once. Holding onto Bernice and Stephanie's hands, watching Bok and Bokkie in the Louis Botha terminal, I thought the excitement would make my flesh burst through my skin.

'From Durban, all the way around the Cape and a week into the Atlantic, the weather was foul as all hell,' Bok said. 'The crew said it was one of the worst voyages they had experienced. The bull and the younger cow were well behaved, but the old one, jirre Jesus, she was a pain in the arse from start to finish. Called her Shetani. Gave me a hard time all the way to Texas. Every day, clockwork, she threw a tantrum when I tried to give her water and eventually she knocked her horn off against the crate. For them to drink I had to push a baby-bath through the bars at the front of the crate. I fed the baby-bath with a hosepipe. As the journey went on she just grew angrier and more temperamental and the wound on her snout grew bigger from banging it on the side of the crate and against the bars. In the middle of the Atlantic the planks of the crate started to loosen and split. I nipped, I tell you, I nipped. I had no M99 tranquilliser, only the antibiotic I had to inject them with to prevent infections. The captain and I shat ourselves about her crate falling apart.'

Bok had brought me a hunting knife in a black leather sheath; two Red Indian dolls for Lena; a record of Perry Como for Bernice; an American flag for Stephanie; a small chemistry set for James; an electric carving knife for Aunt Siobhain; a James Michener book for Uncle Michael, and a gold wrist-watch for Bokkie.

'They knew well when it was feeding or injection time because they heard my whistle coming along the deck. I became very attached to them, you know, three weeks at sea without any real conversation. Can be boring as all hell. Meal-times for me was an ordeal because the crew didn't speak to each other or to me — real sea-dogs, the lot of them. The radio operator and the second engineer were reasonably okay, could make conversation and had the occasional something to say. But the rest, no, I gave up after a few days. When the weather calmed down I spent my time on deck with the rhino or watched a wandering albatross that followed us for two weeks. A wingspan like this . . . Incredible to watch as it glided above the ship. And there were dolphins, often, swimming alongside the ship or playing in the wake.'

'What about the cow and the crate? What did you do about her?' Uncle Michael asked.

'Ah, Shetani! She soon began anticipating the injection. Her rumps started quivering as she waited for the burning antibiotic to be injected. Burns like hell, apparently. She pranced, snorted and buffeted the sides of the crate and it was impossible to be gentle with her. It was interesting, really, each of them had their own personality, just like domestic animals. They were captured at about the same age — a month to three months — kept at the bomas in Umfolozi for the same period of time to be tamed down, treated identically. But still they were different. By the time we were in the middle of the Atlantic Shetani's crate was threatening to come apart and the Captain and me had visions of a broken-out rhino dashing around the decks causing havoc. I had the radio operator call the US coast guard to fly out some M99 but they refused. So we decided that if worse came to worst we would use one of the ship's cranes to pick up the crate and drop her over the side into the sea. The thought horrified me — imagine telling Ian Player I'd thrown a rhino overboard and the hullabaloo from the newspapers! That's when I made the plan with the dung dam. The baby-bath — that's what seemed to make her crazy — so I devised the alternative and scraped together enough dung to make a small dam in the front of the crate. If I inserted the hose gently she seemed okay. But bring the baby-bath near the crate and she'd go berserk. I was glad to deliver three rhinos as promised to the drive-through zoo in Dallas.'

'And America, Uncle Ralph, what was it like?'

'In Texas I was treated like a VIP. Texans are just like South Africans, I felt right at home. Meat-eaters, like us. But of course they call their braais barbecues. And a barbecue is a smart affair over there, not like us who just throw some meat on the grille and have some pap and garlic bread. No, over there it's fish, chicken, steak, all kinds of salads and snacks. 'n Hele gedoente. Lots of millionaires in Texas and they dress up to come to the barbecues. There's one ranch, man, I'm not sure how big it is, but you can't drive around it in a day. Huge farms — ranches they call them — with what, two, three thousand head of cattle on average.' And then Bok told how he flew from Texas to Philadelphia to see Nada and Rashid. The grown-ups and Stephanie and Bernice all knew Nada and Rashid from when they had come on an elephant safari to Tanganyika. Nada was the cousin of the Shah of Iran and they were very well-to-do. Later, Bok said, when he had had the slides developed, we could watch them and get a better idea of everything. About a month later we would see New York from the sky; Bok with Nada and Rashid in Philadelphia; Bok with the rhino on the ship; Bok sitting on a lawn with newspapers about the rhino's arrival in Texas; Bok with a beautiful dark-haired woman who appeared on a number of slides whom he said was Nada and Rashid's niece; Bok with the Texan millionairess for whom the Gladys Porter Zoo was named; Bok fishing with the millionaires in Texas. But already that night at Uncle Michael and Aunt Siobhain's, weeks before we saw the slides, I knew America was an adventure I wanted.

When Bok had finished telling the trip, we went outside to play with our presents and to jump on the trampoline. Lena got to be first on the trampoline and she left her dolls between James and me where we sat on the metal frame. While she gained height, she said that I was really dumb for not knowing immediately that Bok was the reason we had gone to the airport.

I said I'd known all along.

'Ja, I suppose that's why you were so surprised when he got off the plane. Liar.'

'Liar, liar, pants on fire,' chimed James.

'My knife can cut off your stupid dolls' heads! And cut up your stupid chemistry set,' I snapped.

'You're only jealous,' Lena called, jumping higher, 'because I got the dolls.'

'You're jealous because I got the knife!' I said and grabbed a doll and pretended I was going to chop off its head. She bounced towards me and tried to wrench away the doll. I pushed her back onto the moving mat and dragged her down, then punched her against the chest. She bounced a few times then took a sidelong swipe that struck me against the chin, throwing me backwards. I sat up and folded my head into my arms, feigning sobs. The moment she came close I brought my head up into her stomach. She fell forward onto me, pinned me down and pounded her fists against the back of my skull. Screaming, I kicked her on the back with my heels; we grabbed each other by the hair and rolled around on the trampoline.

'Get off the trampoline if you want to fight,' James shouted. We ignored him. In spite of my worming around, Lena got her legs around my waist and clasped me in the dreaded scissors grip. I squealed that she was going to break my ribs; that a broken rib would puncture my heart and I'd bleed to death. I took another swipe at her head, catching her against her forehead. She started pummelling the knuckles of her fist against my chest. James had disappeared.

Suddenly Bokkie was there: 'Fighting like dogs, again! Lena, let go of him!' Lena unwrapped her legs and we sat up.

'Go to the bathroom and wait for me.'

'It was her, Bokkie! I didn't do anything,' I pleaded from the trampoline.

'He's lying. He's the one that started cutting up my doll,' Lena countered.

'You are brother and sister. Have you no shame! The day your father gets back and you're like animals. He brought us all those lovely presents and this is the thanks he gets. Ingrates! Get off that trampoline and get into the bathroom. Give me these,' she grabbed the knife from where I had dropped it. She lifted the dolls. 'You can have these when you've learnt to behave like human beings.'

United in our fear of what was coming we were silent. Off the trampoline, passing James, who tried to hide behind the door. 'Snake!' I whispered, knowing at once he had gone to tell. Bokkie came into the bathroom with Aunt Siobhain's zebra-skin slipper and beat Lena first. When Lena started screaming, I too began to cry and beg, 'Please don't hit her, please, Bokkie, please.' And when the first sting caught my bum I could scarcely hear Bokkie over my own screaming, 'Please, I won't do it again, I promise, I won't do it again, please, please, I promise, we won't fight again.'

Our mother's face was flushed and she glared at us each in turn as she scolded, 'We are in Uncle Michael and Aunt Siobhain's house. Your father has been away for six weeks. He could have died on that ship! Where are you two from? Makoppolanders! Uncivilised little savages from the bush. That's where you're from. Why can't you be like Bernice – or James and Stephanie? How come they have manners like other civilised people? Tell me, Lena, why?'

'I don't know, Mommy.'

'Karl? Why can't you be like Bernice?'

'Bernice is more mature, Bokkie.'

'Don't try and be clever with me, my boy!'

'I wasn't being clever, I was just saying —'

'Keep quiet! One more sound from either of you for the rest of the night and I'll have you back in here. Then your father can come and take care of you.'

She told us to wash our faces and come to dinner.

I heard, for the first time, the word and meaning of *hillbilly* that night. Hillbillies, Bok said at dinner as he prepared to tell a joke in his American accent, are in-bred whites, poor whites, Makoppolanders, who live in the mountains of Kentucky:

'So, this hillbilly naiiimed Wagonwheels had'o go'do school for the first time and it waaas a big deal 'cause hillbillies ain't your regula school-goin' kinda folk. An' liddle Wagonwheels's brother, well thad little fella, he was a real envious of his big bro Wagonwheels an he begged his mama saying a please Mama can I go'do school with big bro Wagonwheels and his mama say no boy you gota wait your place and leta your big bro Wagonwheels paiiive the way. So, thata Wagonwheels wenna off down that Kentucky mountain fo hisa first day o'school and the teacher she ask all them kids to introduce themself and the kids say Andy, Joey, Mary, Betty, Sandy, Randy, Mandy ana when she get to that hillbilly boy and she ass hisa name he say howdy Ma'am my name isa Wagonwheels and that Ma'am teacher she smile and say no boy tel'us yousa reeeaal name and again that boy say

Ma'am my naime it sure is Wagonwheels and the teacher she begin to
frown and she say ina stern voice no boy, you gimme and your classmates here yousa reaaaal name, and Wagonwheels say again Ma'am my
naime is Wagonwheels and that Ma'am wanno teach the boy a lesson
and she take the cane to'is butt and bead ol'Wagonwheels and again
she ass his name and the boy againsay Wagonwheels and thata teacher
she chase him outa class and say you boy you aint settin foot in here
till you come an tell-us yourse a reeaall name, yourse christening in the
Lord's House name. Anna so that Wagonwheels wenna back up that
blue Kentucky mountain and his little brother, well, that liddle fella
heda been waiding at that gate whole day loong and when he see his
big bro cumin up that blue mountain path he jump over that gate and
run shoutin hey Wagonwheels big bro, tell me please Wagonwheels,
whatsa school like, and, Wagonwheels he get this worried look spread
on his face an he look at that liddle brother of his and he say: You
ain't gonna like it, Chicken-Shit.'

On tour from the Berg, it became my favourite joke to tell our host
parents.

14

'This is a song of praise. It's often introduced by the ringing of
bells – listen – then the glorification of the Trinity. Adulation, our
God needs to be adored. Lift up your voices, boys. Listen to each
other. Watch for every entry, this is difficult, once we know it you can
let go, give everything. Smile, look joyful, your voices nearly ringing
with laughter . . . Glory be to God on high. And on earth peace to
men of good will. *Jubilate. Jubilate.* Ready . . .'

He smiled. Nodded.

The pianist bounced on the stool, hammering the keys.

Fingers, darting at us, brought us in. Tempo excruciating; on either

side of me I could hear the Juniors struggle, falling in at the wrong
bars, too soon, with the firsts, sometimes in the middle of nowhere.
The start sounded chaotic; he didn't stop us, let us continue, wanting
us to get through the entire piece. At the diminuendo on *et in terra pax*,
a complete absence of synchronisation; we were dragging way behind
the firsts; nowhere near the altos who seemed to be singing a different movement altogether. Still he let us continue, his hands
everywhere, arms flailing, trying somehow to get us into synch; face
taut; a mask of concentration. First sopranos, entering *Laudamus te*,
scattered and way off key; so too our response. I waited for him to
stop us; he let us go. His eyes were all over us, not focused anywhere;
his gaze paused for a split-second somewhere in the back centre. Me?
No, behind me. And then he closed his eyes, his jaw suddenly jutting
out; still, he continued, bringing us in with his left, thrusting, jerking
the tempo with his right. He was smouldering; I wondered what was
going on in his mind. All through the first section

> *Gloria in excelsis Deo*
> *et in terra pax hominibus*
> *bonae voluntatis*
> *Laudamus te, benedicimus te*
> *adoramus te, glorificamus te*

at the end of the bar, in sudden diminuendo, the pianist stroked the
keys, and he, eyes still closed, sang the oboe over the piano, bringing
the soloists into the quartet:

> *Gratias agimus tibi propter*
> *magnam gloriam tuam*

it was like a miracle: perfect, masterly. Dominic's voice, legato, leading the other three. But when the sopranos took up *Gratias* it was again
without unity, voices strewn about, the sound of s's all over the place.

Irritation in his pursed lips. Again he glanced at the back of the choir; eyes closed, he seemed ready to explode. What was he seeing there? Then, the whole choir, a cacophony throughout:

> *Domine Deus, rex coelestis*
> *Deus, pater omnipotens*
> *Domine fili unigenite, Jesu Christe*
> *Domine Deus, agnus Dei, filius*
> *Patris*

the long piano interlude, allowing us to breathe, relax. He kept his eyes closed, moving into the larghetto, bringing in the soloists, his expression changing, the jaw relaxing, as if he had moved out of himself, into the perfection of their harmonies:

> *qui tollis peccata mundi*
> *miserere nobis*

relief, tangible, when the choir repeated after the soloists and our tempo perfect, pitch right where it should have been from the beginning, yes, yes, we can do it, his face lit up and it seemed he may break into a smile. The soloists began their duets, heavenly, and he did smile, bringing more relief to us, our shoulders dropped, his head nodding:

> *qui tollis peccata mundi*

then the soloists, perfectly:

> *suscipe deprecationem nostram*

his face, now contorted, mirrored the choir's struggle on *qui sedes ad dexteram patris* and now he opened his eyes, they flashed again at something behind me, the back of the choir, fingers bunched into fists; he ignored the soloists:

miserere nobis

we took up the long *miserere*, still he glared up, took a few hesitant steps forward; paused; rushed past the piano, right towards me, the front row of altos scattered; piano and voices instantly quiet; we ducked, into the choir; he reached up with one hand, I saw Lukas fly past me, the hairy hand behind the neck, dragged from the back row. His eyes flashed like a man possessed, clawing around, searching; couldn't see what he was looking for; still dragging the stumbling Lukas by the hair, moved to the wall and ripped off a piece of wooden panelling. The silence broke as the panelling struck the cloth of Lukas's shorts; on the library balcony, maids in blue uniforms halted, cleaning tools suspended. He held Lukas down while his arm rose above his head and the piece of wood panel was brought down, again, again, again.

It splintered into pieces. Eyes darted: us; piano; balcony – the maids began to move, halted; Lukas below him.

'I've been watching you for the past five minutes, Van Rensburg!' He held Lukas down, speaking to his back. 'What are you doing? What's so amusing back there? Tell me!' He pulled Lukas erect and around; held onto the boy's one shoulder. 'Show me! Tell me what's so fucking amusing, before I rip your fucking head off your shoulders. After more than two and a half years, why can't you keep your eyes on me!' Lukas, eyes glistening and face pink, seemed to smile.

'Stop your grinning,' he lifted his hand as if about to slap him across the face. 'Now that you're no longer a soloist you've lost all interest in the choir. Well, you will sing until I tell you to stop. It's not broken yet, when it breaks I'll tell you. Stop grinning, you bliksem.' I wanted to yell at him to stop, that that was the way Lukas looked when he was being beaten; was not grinning, merely resisting tears. He loosened his grip on Lukas's shoulder and dropped his arms. Cast the broken panelling onto a table. To us; glaring: 'I've had it with you all,' he shouted. 'Do you have any idea what you sound like? The audacity you have – the stupidity – of going on singing when you sound like this! I cannot take it any more. I cannot walk onto that stage in four months' time with a choir that sounds like this.' His tirade floundered; he hesitated; went on: 'That's it. You go on, on your own. Raubenheimer, Webster, you and . . . Jesus Christ, I don't care . . . Anyone, and someone else, work out who's taking which voice. Split up the choir and see if you can get it into your thick fucking skulls.' He marched off. As he went, shouting at the roof: 'Come and call me when you're ready. I don't care if it takes two weeks or two months. I'm not coming back till you've got this into your heads.'

The pianist, too, stood to leave. The maids, witnesses to the entire spectacle, now moved off the balcony.

Raubenheimer said he'd keep the first and second sopranos. Dom and Mike van der Bijlt would leave and take the altos to one of the classrooms.

Then he was on the balcony – we looked up – crossing with the bookshelves behind him. Did not look down; stared ahead and disappeared. Why hadn't he just stopped us when he first noticed Lukas looking away? Why work himself up into this frenzy? Why so angry, I've done something wrong. No. Will talk later, poor Lukas, Jesus, look at wall panelling ripped off, pattern of library books, looks like man's head with long hair, sun on piano, smell of pumpkin and custard from kitchen. Fish maybe.

'Who came up with this stupid idea of letting us sing this Mass thing, anyway? It's impossible for a boys' choir,' said one of the Standard Sevens in the row behind me.

'We're not doing it alone,' Raubenheimer grovelled from behind the piano.

'So why does he want it to be perfect, then? The SABC Choir will carry it.'

'We will be doing extracts alone, without the adult voices, during the European concerts and for a record, you know that. It has to be perfect.'

'Maniac. A damn lunatic; that's what he is.'

'Okay. Let's get going,' Raubenheimer said, ejecting air from his open mouth. He scratched his head: 'Our biggest problem is the changes in tempo.' He leant forward and pressed a few notes; marked something on his score. 'I think we've got the *Gloria* entries – they're tough, but just need practice and repetition. The real trouble starts at bar 43 – the *et in terra pax*. Take your pencils and mark the changes, so that you can anticipate. Look at the opening bars – after the *Gloria* at the beginning, at 43 – there is no change of tempo, we keep trying to drag there, it's not a new tempo – on *et in terra* there's only a new theme, quieter but the same tempo – have you got that? Just because we're singing softly doesn't mean we change tempo. It's particularly clear from the seconds, guys you're dragging there. Keep time, count it out in the same time as the *Gloria* repetitions, pianissimo but not slower! And then on *Laudamus te* we go back to the *Gloria* motif but still same tempo, same key, and then, suddenly, the *Glorificamus* at 84 is fugato – a new idea, but still continuing same key and then at 104 – mark this . . . this is where we all keep making a mess, we go into G, there's that B sharp to E sharp. Everything, everything changes here, also tempo. At 84. Draw a huge circle around it. Okay? Juniors, Secondaries? Let's do that section first up to 104. Have you all got it?'

'Jubilaaaate,' in a dramatic, over-articulated whisper from behind me, sending us spluttering and laughing as we started 84.

15

Chaka and Suz chased the baboons up trees where they were darted with anaesthetic and put in cages to be taken to cities for medical research. My fists full of big coloured wala-wala sweets, I stood beside the cages. The baboons stuck their little black hands through for me to feed. Their eyes were like tiny black and white beads; like Nkosasaan's piccanin when she woke from sleep. Some mothers had babies clinging to their bellies. I bit pieces off the yellow and orange balls for them to take and pop into their cheeks. With a whole sweet they couldn't get their hands back through the bars. Bernice warned me not to get too close to the cages; one bite and you're infested with rabies. They looked perplexed; frowns on their brows, as if contemplation of some riddle occupied their minds. Suddenly a black hand shot out and grabbed me by the hair. I tried to pull away but it held; a tight fist around the blond clump. I screamed that I was being dragged into the cage. Bernice tugged me free. I held onto her, still screaming. Around us the rangers and the game guards thought it a joke. I hid my face in Bernice's neck until Bok came and took me from her. He held me as I sobbed; then he whispered: 'Stop crying, Philistine. Look, the kaffirs are laughing at you.'

16

To enhance our learning and make History classes on the French Revolution more interesting, Ma'am Sanders rented the film of *A Tale of Two Cities*. She had given me the book, which I rushed through, reading sections up in the library and others at night by torchlight beneath the covers. The movie was in black and white. Just before the white horses come galloping onto the screen in front of the carriage, the film begins with the same words as the novel: *It was the best of times, it was the worst of times, it was the age of wisdom, it was the age of foolishness, it was the epoch of belief, it was the epoch of incredulity, it was the season of Light, it was the season of Darkness, it was the spring of hope, it was the winter of despair, we had everything before us, we had nothing before us, we were all going direct to Heaven, we were all going direct the other way — in short, the period was so far like*

the present period, that some of its noisiest authorities insisted on its being received, for
good or for evil, in the superlative degree of comparison only.

Having read the novel, I already knew that many of the conspira-
tors called themselves Jacques. There's Jacques One, Jacques Two,
Jacques Three. I couldn't but think of the other one and smile. My
beloved co-conspirator. Only, he and I — and Dominic — were somehow on the other side. On the side of the bourgeoisie. And I knew
that Sydney Carton would sacrifice himself and go to the guillotine
in Paris so that Evremonde could live and return to London for the
woman he loved. The film offered a more vivid picture of most of the
characters than my hasty reading had allowed. In particular of
Madame Defarge. Even more witch-like in the film than I imagined
her from the novel. How terrifying to *see* her knitting while people
were taken to the guillotine. And her sidekick in the movie — a character I didn't recall from the novel — the one who laughed like a
crazed hyena: the ugliest, most evil-sounding creature in the world.
When the film showed the guillotine's blade from the top, suspended
while the drums rolled before it dropped, I felt it was a million times
more terrifying than looking at the dull-coloured illustrations in the
book. The sharp blade up there; the pale white neck of the aristocrat
waiting in the block; the sound of the drums; one held one's breath;
and then the plebeians cheer! Seeing that, I could no longer believe
Sydney Carton would offer himself so that the woman he loved may
be happy. I'd never be able to do it. Not for anyone. How sad, the
entire story.

Lukas took the final spool off the projector. I could see a few boys
wipe their faces, hastily brush tears from their cheeks. No one spoke.

Ma'am stood to turn on the fluorescent light.

From in front of me, the sound of Madame Defarge's sidekick
cackling, suddenly sliced the silence. It was Dominic. In a moment
we were all laughing. Ma'am, after giving Dom a stern look, also
chuckled and moved over to the blackboard. She said it was time we
got back to the curriculum. We were to read Causes, Developments

and Outcomes of the French Revolution for next History period. That section was bound to appear in the test.

Dominic put up his arm. Ma'am nodded for him to go ahead.

'Do you think we'll have a revolution in South Africa, Ma'am?'

Ma'am's eyes settled briefly on the back wall as she pondered the question. In her usual measured, confident tone she answered: 'No, I think not, Dominic. We shouldn't draw parallels between South Africa and France. The French Revolution was about justice amongst equals in the same country. The plebeians had been exploited for hundreds of years by the aristocracy and they wanted a slice of the cake, as it were. Black people in South Africa know that South Africa does not belong to them, they are not citizens of this country. They have full citizenship in the native homelands. No, the situation is not comparable.'

'They must just try, here,' Bennie said, half lifting himself from his desk. 'I'll kill those kaffirs before they've even got out of the locations.'

'Don't use that word in my class, Benjamin! I've told you before: it is a vile and cruel word. Do I make myself clear?'

'Yes, Ma'am. Sorry, Ma'am.'

'Ma'am, they almost killed our host mother in Jo'burg. Kids were all around her car and they'd have done it if the police hadn't arrived.'

'And, Ma'am,' I spoke up, 'look at what they're doing to their schools. Burning their own schools to the ground. It's horrible, Ma'am.'

'Yes, Ma'am,' said Mervyn. 'They say they want to learn but then they go and burn down their schools. And stone white people's cars.'

'They're protesting because they're being forced to learn in Afrikaans,' Dominic interrupted, indignation in his tone. 'How would you feel if you suddenly had to learn Science and Maths in Zulu?'

'I agree with Dominic,' Niklaas Bruin said, a nervous edge to his voice, as he turned, his gaze fastening to mine.

'Aag, Niklaas,' I said. 'You'll be the first to run when they come to take over your house.' I glared at him and he looked down at his desk.

'Why,' Dominic continued, half rising from his desk, 'should they be forced to learn in a language that is spoken by only two million people? English is an international language, and they want to study in English.'

Bennie said there were *two* official languages, not just one: 'English *and* Afrikaans, and why should they not learn both like the rest of us, Ma'am?'

'Because people have a right,' Dominic responded as though the question were directed at him, 'to choose the language they wish to be taught in. That's why!' Annoyance in his expression as he shook his head at Bennie.

From the back of the class someone said: 'We don't even have a choice, what are you talking about, Webster! It's one week English, one week Afrikaans. Now you want to give the . . . the plurals a choice!'

'Okay, that will suffice,' Ma'am interrupted. 'No politics in class. That's it.'

'But, Ma'am,' Dominic said, 'these issues are relevant to the French Revolution.'

'Well, then we can have an organised debate outside of class time. How does that sound?'

Some said it was a waste of time, but most agreed it was a good idea. Ma'am asked us to formulate a topic.

Bennie said we should address the question of how to get rid of all blacks. Ma'am ignored him and suggested we discuss: *The French Revolution and its Relevance to the Republic of South Africa in 1976.*

'Okay, that's our topic. Now we must elect two speakers. One in favour of positive relevance and another arguing negative relevance.' Her eyes slid over the class, stopped on Dom in front of me. 'Dominic, what about you to speak for the positive side, seeing as you introduced the question?'

'Of course, Ma'am, I'd love to.'

'Okay, and who will speak against it?'

'De Man . . . let De Man speak . . . Karl . . . He's the best speaker.'

I had already anticipated that it may come to this and shook my head. As much as I liked debating, I would not speak as Dominic's opponent. I knew I could probably beat anyone in debate – barring perhaps Niklaas Bruin. But talking publicly against Dominic seemed like sacrilege.

'Come on, De Man. Kom aan!'

'Doesn't want to speak against Dame Dominique Defarge . . .' I swung around in my chair and glared at Radys.

'Okay, pipe down.' Ma'am was irritated. 'Honestly, what has gotten into you boys today?' Now her voice altered, was kind and generous: 'Karl, if you don't want to do it, who would you suggest?'

'Mervyn,' I said. 'He's good. Or Niklaas, but he agrees with Dominic so he can't speak against him. Can you, little Niklaas?'

'Karl.' Ma'am glowered at me.

'Mervyn?' She enquired: 'Would you like to do it?'

'Yes! . . . Merv! . . . Clemence-Gordon . . . You're our man.'

'Is it going to be just in front of our class, Ma'am,' Mervyn asked, 'or in front of the whole school?'

'The whole school,' everyone called.

'No, I'm afraid it will be only our class. No politics allowed in school. I could lose my job.'

'If it's just our class, I'll speak,' Mervyn replied. The class clapped.

When we walked from the room for lunch, Bennie slapped me hard between my shoulder blades: 'Why are you letting an Englishman – a Jew – speak for our side. You would have beat Dominic hands down.'

'I didn't feel like speaking, Bennie, that's all. And Mervy's your friend. Why didn't *you* speak if the whole thing's so important?'

'You know I can't debate, De Man. You can . . . That's the difference. Verraaier . . .'

I fell into line for lunch behind Dominic. I felt sorry for him. The whole class seemed to have turned against him – barring Niklaas

Bruin, and who wanted that little sissy on your side, anyway. In the silence of the queue I thought of what Bennie had just called me. What else might lie behind his words? Was he speaking only about today's class? Did he suspect or know something? Could he possibly guess about Mr Cilliers? No, Bennie was too thick; probably didn't even know about Dominic and me. Was it about last year? Was it possible that Almeida had said something, after all, about my treason?

After lights-out, for the first time in weeks, I went to Dominic's bed. We didn't speak, or even really touch other than where our bodies met. For a long while, as I hoped he could sense how I wanted him to feel better, I held him, got him to rest his head on my chest. I wished he would keep out of arguments when he knew his would always be the unpopular view. But I knew it would be to no avail: he was his father and mother's son and Dr and Mrs Webster seemed to care less what anyone thought of them. Didn't they know how difficult they were making his life by teaching him to always be against everything, even things that didn't matter?

I couldn't prevent myself from going stiff, and soon his hand found my erection. He lifted his head and kissed me. I reached down for him. I longed to be on top of him again as I'd been the night in his bedroom in Saxonwold. When he'd asked with his Condensed Milk breath and I'd slowly obliged and pushed it into him. What we did there, and a few times later on tour took turns at, would be too noisy for the dorm. Even as I tried to forget, each moment in G with him remained frightening, the spectre of exposure and terrible shame always entangled in and almost overwhelming my pleasure and desire. Once we'd both climaxed – of late kissing deeply at the right moment to keep each other quiet – we wiped our bellies and hands on the seam of his locker's curtain. A whispered goodnight and I crept back to F, feeling guilty and afraid. At least for a while.

17

I recognised Bokkie's thin blue aerogram even before Uncle Charlie called my name. At the dormitory door, amongst the others, I waited to see whether there was another for me, perhaps from Alette. Uncle Charlie teased Lukas that his pink envelope reeked of perfume. We called for Lukas to do push-ups. Uncle Charlie shook his head and a sssss, tsss, tsss ran through the crowd as he handed over the letter.

I stared at the aerogram. The school's address was slanted diagonally across the envelope. I cannot, cannot believe she keeps doing it like this when I've told her repeatedly it's out of fashion! I ripped open the narrow flaps I knew her tongue had licked, her fingertips folded over and compressed.

> *Dan Pienaar Drive 21*
> *Amanzimtoti*
> *15 August 1976*

This one again, too! It's out of date, I had told her. There's a new rule; it's different now; you start each successive line directly below the previous.

By now so angry it was a near impossibility for me to concentrate on her words:

Dear Karl

Thank you for your lovely letter about the tour. We're so grateful to the Lord for bringing you back safely. And proud of you for everything you are doing and that you're so lucky to see the whole country. I know Lena and Bernie badly want to see the Cape as well. Maybe we'll go one day. You are so privileged and I hope you're working hard.

We knew a Samuel Erasmus in Oljorro, and Mumdeman says he is the brother of the people you stayed with in Cape Town. Samuel Erasmus's wife Betta is on that photograph we have of me and Aunt Siobhain with John Wayne when he came to make the movie in Arusha. Nice woman. She and Sanna Koerant were on the ship with us when we came out and old Samuel Erasmus was the first to escape by plane. That's where Daddy and Uncle Michael got the idea. Mumdeman says the Erasmuses were on the trek north and one brother struck it rich on the Lupa gold fields; the Erasmus brother you met is from that side of the family who were cowards and left Tanganyika early, before things really started looking bad. They were business people, not farmers. Farmers always stay till the last. Mumdeman says she heard from Sanna Koerant that Johan Erasmus went into the army; hot-shot general now. He became a Broederbonder: the right pedigree and money. And too good for those of us who came out poor. Kamstig élite and married the opera star. But Mumdeman says Sanna Koerant says the would-be opera star was no Joan Sutherland! Stinking rich, stripped Tanganyika of its riches and then fled before anything had even changed. At least we stuck it out to the last. Came out with nothing but the clothes on our backs. Mumdeman says you must ask her about them when you see her again. Has lots of stories she got from Sanna Koerant. Sanna had a stroke in the middle of June, they don't know if she'll make it.

Bernie is studying hard for her matric exams. I'm so grateful that she has stopped watching TV. You know, she used to sit and watch the test pattern before six o'clock when it started and then she would stay in front of that thing until the test pattern came on again at eleven. She's applying to SAA but I tell her she'll have to do something about her weight. R30 for her matric farewell dress. Where the money must come from I do not know. Lena is doing well and just plays her sport. She's the only Std 8 in the first netball team and the coach thinks she'll make the Natal team next year. Goal Defence. Bok's business is not going so well at the moment. Because the bantus are rioting and going on there's less interest from overseas in the curios and he's thinking of going into insurance. It has become impossible to get stock from Angola and Mozambique, because Bok's regular sources have disappeared in the wars. It's a pity, because we need specially the musical figurines from Mozambique that have always been so popular. Bok has taken samples to the Zulus near Empangeni to see if they can copy those.

I've asked Mrs Lategan to keep all Leon's Port Natal uniforms for you next year.

Groot-Oom Klaas showed up here on Tuesday and I gave him lunch before he went off again. Filthy and hadn't had a bath in months. I let him sit outside in the garden and tried to find out what was wrong with him but he doesn't talk much, looks at me as if I'm the mad one. He asked about you and I said how proud we were of you being in the Berg and that you had toured to the Cape and are going to Europe in December. He said he was hiking up to the Transvaal because it's now getting warm up there again and then he just left. Aunt Lena may try getting him into rehab again if she sees him somewhere in Klerksdorp.

Bok and I are going shooting at Poinsettia this afternoon. We have a competition against Durban North.

It's only a few weeks before Parents' Weekend, and we can't wait to see you. We'll be staying with Uncle Gerrie and Auntie Babs on the farm. I don't think Bernie will be coming because she has to study for the trial exams.

Work hard, dear child, because remember: they can take everything away from you except your education. I'm ending this letter now, but never my thoughts of you.

> *All our love*
> *Bok, Bernie, Lena and Bokkie*

My eyes were coals seared to the trembling aerogram's incorrect address format. Why can't you listen to me! I know what I'm talking about. Know, I'm clever, ashamed of you, hate you. Eyes squeezed shut I fell back onto my mattress, turned over, pressed my face into the pillow and crumpled the letter in my fist. Damn you, I will not come home at the end of the year, damn you, damn you, Bokkie.

18

He was ten. He was standing in the passage dressed in school uniform with his suitcase in his hand, ready to start walking to school. His sisters were already halfway down the driveway. His father came walking down the passage and the boy looked up. The father placed his hand on the boy's shoulder. It was a firm grip. He spoke to the boy softly. He said many things while he looked the boy in the eyes. He said: 'If you ever, ever, ever so much as think of doing that again, I will kill you.'

19

He ordered a bottle of Boland white wine. One drinks white only with chicken, fish and seafood, he told me; red wine only with red meat. Never err on your order or your etiquette.

With no one else there, it had seemed the small dining room was laid out for us alone. He allowed me a full glass — my first not sipped surreptitiously from half-empties in the kitchen with Lena and cousin James.

He showed me the fish-knife and fork; explained that cutlery is used from the outside, inward towards the plate. I said I knew, that that's the way my parents ate in Tanzania. I said I also knew that the napkin is unfolded from the moment one is seated. Tipping the soup bowl away, rather than towards, we had been taught by the school in Standard Four, before we went on our first tour. And do you know, he asked playfully, that if you drop the serviette, you don't bend down to pick it up or dig around with your heel to find it; you simply ask the waiter for another? No, I smiled, I would have dived down and fetched it, so thank you, Jacques, for sharing your wisdom. A new world of stylish rules was opening itself to be used by me.

While nowhere as big or impressive as the hotel dining rooms I had been in with Aunt Lena and Uncle Joe, the Paternoster Hotel dining room was special in other ways. I sensed the chasmic difference between being in a hotel with Bokkie's sister and her rich husband, and being on the quiet West Coast with Jacques. Paternoster was classy and romantic. Quaint. The Malibu in Durban was a glossy, plastic and superficial holiday resort for the nouveau riche. While Bernice, Lena and I liked Aunt Lena — who had a great sense of humour and showered us with gifts — you didn't need a degree to see that Uncle Joe knew as much about class as a cat of saffron, spending thousands and thousands of rands on dumb racing pigeons. Uncle Joe was a self-made man. He had become big as a building contractor for the Western Transvaal mines — even though he only had Standard Six. Aunt Lena said he had never read a book in his life and that's why he smirked and made snide remarks whenever I read on the beach. Despite my spending half the day body-surfing, kicking ball or playing beach-bats with him and Lena, when I said I wanted to take a break to read he almost flipped and said he couldn't believe I hadn't outgrown my girlish habits. How could a boy as tall and strong as me sit reading like a moffie on the beach? Lots of money, that he has, Aunt Lena said, but he's clueless about anything beyond the building and mining professions. We all knew that Aunt Lena was the one with brains in that family. Not that book knowledge brought wisdom or joy; look where it had landed Uncle Klaas. But neither did wealth. For all their money, Uncle Joe and Aunt Lena's marriage was held together only by the Brats. We distrusted Uncle Joe because Aunt Lena — and the whole Klerksdorp — knew he had strings of affairs, the latest with the little Matilda slut. And that he may be dabbling in illegal diamonds. His perpetual absences from home drove Aunt Lena half crazy. We all knew she would end up in Tara again. That she'd again received electric shock treatments to make her cope with the blues.

The blond receptionist doubled as our waitress. Before taking our order she joined us at table and had a glass of wine and a cigarette. She said she had grown up in Malmesbury. She had dreamt of going to secretarial college in Cape Town, but her parents hadn't wanted her to leave the district so she stayed and found the job with the hotel. Her boyfriend of two years farmed nearby and they were to be married when she turned twenty-one.

She asked Jacques what he did. He answered that he was a high school teacher. When he said he taught Maths she snorted and said Maths had been her worst subject at school. I wanted to say that I too couldn't do Maths — that to my mind it was the worst subject in the entire history of the world — but I caught myself, concerned that she would ask why he didn't help me master the curse.

'And the wife? Doesn't she mind you two gallivanting in the Cape while she's at home?'

'My wife and daughter are in Maritzburg. He and I are on a trip so the girls can spend a little time on their own. You know how it is.'

'Oh yes, and don't I just,' she said. 'Me and my girlfriends just love a night on the town. Alone, no boyfriends, nothing. Just us. It's necessary, sometimes, just to catch your breath, you know. So, you have a daughter, too!'

He nodded. She said she wanted a daughter and wanted her to become a ballerina. A prima ballerina.

'My sister is a ballet dancer,' I said, catching his eye. A fleeting frown cautioned me not to colour the story too much.

'Oh how wonderful! Does she do shows and stuff?'

'She recently danced Gizelle for NAPAC,' I said, nodding my head.

'Oh I'd love my little girl to do ballet one day!' she beamed, dragging on her cigarette. 'Or gymnastics! Oh, there's a farmer up the road with TV, and I went to watch the Olympic Games there the other night. And there was this little girl, Nadia something, you know all those communist names sound the same, who got ten out of ten for her exercises. The first time ever in the history of gymnastics. Did you see?'

'Yes, she was very good,' he spoke before I could continue. 'Shall we get ready to order?'

While he ordered a starter, my eyes skimmed the menu. She asked whether I had decided. Emboldened by half a glass of wine, I glanced at her and asked, 'You don't happen to have any starfish on the menu, do you?'

'Starfish? No klong, we don't eat those in the Cape!'

'You haven't eaten starfish in a mayonnaise sauce?' I asked, my mouth wide in mock surprise, hand over my chest, not looking at him.

She shook her head and smiled. 'Never heard of it. There's no meat on a starfish. You'll break your teeth!'

'Oh, but there are other, extraordinary nutrients in starfish!' I said. 'You lick it and suck it. It's full of rare juices. You should try it!'

'Sounds pretty strange to me,' she said and looked at him.

'Okay. Then I'll have a prawn cocktail,' I said.

She said it was a very good choice.

I kept my eyes on her as she turned on her heel and left the dining room. I grinned and looked him in the face. He was biting his bottom lip, nodding his head, smiling.

'You know how to play the game, don't you?' He spoke through teeth still clasping his lip.

'Maybe they have starfish only on the room-service menu,' I said.

He buried his face in his hands, his shoulders shaking. And I still recall how I glowed, blessed as if the doors had just swung open and life, real life, was beginning at last for me.

III

I

How different their scent and taste. Again, and again, how indistinguishable scent from taste. Could a word exist for that? One I did not know? When things smell like the palate of others or a taste is really the odour of another. Could it be that I, Karl De Man, had discovered another sense: the seventh perhaps? One that exists at the cusp of the tongue and the nose; at that point where sensations can no longer be distinguished. Him: the salted almonds, and if he had recently washed – which he usually had – Palmolive soap and English Leather aftershave. Aftershave, he claimed, prevented shaver's rash. And afterwards, the sweat: at first salty then vaguely bitter in its aftertaste; if I went down there a second time it had changed to moss or humus mixed with saltpetre; and in the black hollows of his armpits – later damp: there, or in his shirt before it was removed, the smell of kakibush and horse. Dominic: rarely sweat, Brut beneath the arms where recently a few long hairs had begun to wisp; always sweet his sweat; soft the pale skin, barely an odour on the belly, and in the fine hair now starting to curl sometimes the faint smell of piss, shit and fresh sawdust.

We had developed a loose pattern in which Jacques was mostly the one to tell me to come and see him. Occasionally I went on my own accord and from the smile when he opened the door to my knock – sometimes just audible over music from the B&O in his room – I was sure I saw the special pleasure he took from my surprise visits. I tried keeping these to a minimum, going there uninvited no more than once a week. For Dominic and I, being together and planning nights was simpler and we generally stuck to Saturdays, though sometimes we slipped in a weekday session. Occasionally I went first to Dominic, then, after leaving him and donning my dressing gown in which I kept the key, headed for Jacques.

Back in my bed, my hand was over my nose; bringing them with me. Sweat, squirt, soap, sawdust, horse: an ensemble of secret smells. I breathed into my right palm where it was always strongest, while with the left, awkwardly, I brought myself to another climax. I did not wipe it as they were want to do. Dragged my fingers up, scooping it into the fold, smearing my cheeks, my forehead, my lips, tasting or smelling myself: different from either of them. In this place we eat the same food, drink from the same taps, but still we smell and taste or that other sense different, I thought. And when about to fall asleep, I willed myself into the dream: I glided over a veld of brown grass that blows in the breeze, at first in all directions, and I know I'm gliding but I don't know what or who or how many I am. Then, if the focus, the concentration was deliberate, the breeze takes all the grass in one direction, the same direction as I am moving, and it goes faster and faster and sleep takes me. When I do not concentrate – underwater breath lungs bursting fire I'm English almonds that woman receptionist garage full of curios breaking Bokkie's pots Bokkie made masks to sell for money Dominic Both Sides Now bilingual Arusha, Oljorro, Kenia ship this mark on my forehead Bokkie says is from when I fell on the Kenia no Kenya ship when we came out, can't remember too small maybe two, fell off Camelot, Lena, giggles, dragged by Camelot, Simba licking blood off Lena's legs, Bernice puts disinfectant, lying to Ouma, Mumdeman and Dademan no Dademan was dead, cemetery, all crying, family, High on the Hill with the Lonely Goat Herd lei odelei, who is the girl in the pale pink coat, blue dress, fairy's silver star of tin foil, fairy's star, fairy-tale, the fairy's tail, the fair tail, dance with Stephanie, ballet, when she was the cat on the stage, Siamese Cat, over Bok's dead body, can Dademan see me, must pray, dear Jesus, let Dademan understand me, not think, don't think about it, bury it in grave, ghosts, no ghosts exist, pagan beliefs, irrational, cannot see from heaven, unspeakable, will still go to heaven, hell, no, no, not think, think of something else, forget, forget it, over, past, finish en klaar – the grass remains tangled, chunky, blowing in all directions, untidy. Then the dream would not take me and I could cast about in the sheets, unable to fall asleep for hours.

In the mornings I stooped to brush my teeth and it had virtually all flaked from my face; here and there around where the hair began on the forehead and temples it was like skin peeling from sunburn. I washed it with only water; no soap. I smelt them on me through Sunday church and the terrors of burning in hell, or, for the entire day in class. Breathing now into my left, the right struggling with trigonometry, fractions; or doing battle in the oblique trenches of language. On the fine blue lines that veined the blank pages with their pink margins. Translating Latin. Memorising the vocab. Thirty new words a week; and *adjectives with the nominative singular the same for all genders*: felix, felicem, felicis, felici. Learning a new language.

2

Boy stole Bok's revolver and is sitting in jail in Matubatuba. Now Jonas goes on patrol and trail alone with Bok. Boy must go to court. They say Boy will go to jail. Boy stole the revolver and was hiding in the location near Empangeni when the police caught him. We go to court to see how they send Boy to jail. Magistrate says Boy was going to help the poachers but Interpreter says Boy says that's not true. Interpreter says Boy says he was going to sell the revolver for money, he was not helping poachers. Interpreter says Boy says he wanted money for his wife and children. No one knows Boy has a wife and kids. He's lying says Bok. I sit in the middle between Bok and Bokkie and it's hot and sweaty where my legs are on the wooden bench and there's nobody else in the court. Everyone doesn't speak and only the Magistrate must ask questions and Interpreter says into Zulu and Boy talks to Interpreter in Zulu and Interpreter tells Magistrate in English what Boy said in Zulu. Then Boy starts crying and Magistrate asks Interpreter what's wrong with Boy. Interpreter asks Boy something in Zulu and Boy cries and says something in Zulu and then Interpreter tells Magistrate that Boy says his wife and children need money and how are his children going to eat if he goes to jail? Magistrate is sweating on his bald pink head like a plucked pigeon. Magistrate says he will show mercy because it's the first time Boy has stolen. Boy will get twelve cuts. Bok blows through his nose and shakes his head. Boy stops crying and he doesn't look at us when they take him away. Bok says there's no justice in this world. Boy won't be a game guard any more and he's only getting twelve cuts for stealing a firearm. What's becoming of this country? Going the same way as Tanganyika. Maybe it was like jumping from the frying pan into the fire.

I'm six and it's time I go to school. I want to go to school but I hate that I must leave Umfolozi and I must go to boarding school in Hluhluwe. The Parks Board boss Dr Ian Player tells Bok he's transferred to St Lucia. Dr Player is the brother of the golfer Gary Player. Gary Player is rich and famous. Save The White Rhino is nearly finished because maybe the white rhino is saved. We will live right across the lake from Dademan and Mademan in Charters Creek. I can go and visit there every weekend with the boat. Now I don't mind leaving here so much because now I will go to day school in Matubatuba. Matubatuba sounds nice. I say it over and over to Jonas. Ma-tu-ba-tu-ba, Matu-batu-ba. Jonas must stay here in Umfolozi. Now no one sleeps on Boy's bed. Boy is gone and I'm scared he'll come and kill us in our sleep. I say to Jonas we will come and visit. Bernice and Lena can come and live at home again and I'll catch a bus with them to go to school every day. I'm getting school uniforms for boys like Lena and Bernice's for girls. To get shoes on my feet Bokkie makes me sit with my feet in her red bucket full of warm water with salts to make

my kaffir heels and toes soft and not any more like leather like
Chaka's impis. I am getting shoes because you need shoes for school
and church and Sunday school. I've never had shoes and always thorns
in my feet. When a long white thorn went in at the bottom and
came out at the top it broke off and Bokkie put green Sunlight soap
with sugar smashed and stuck it on the top hole and bottom hole
with a big plaster to draw out the thorn and the poison. Now I won't
have more thorns because I'm a big boy going to school in
Matubatuba . . . Matubatuba sounds nice. I say it over and over . . .

We pack the truck. Chaka and Suz kill a big waterbuck up at Mpila
Camp. They grab it by the throat and strangle. Jonas brings Chaka and
Suz full of blood by the collars to tell Bok. Tourists saw it all hap-
pening at Mpila Camp. It's a very big thing. Dogs killing wild animals.
Worse in front of tourists. Scandal, says Bok. Bok holds Chaka and
Suz by the front legs and swings and beats them against the wall. It is
not good enough. If a dog kills animals once it will kill animals again.
Chaka and Suz must be put to sleep. Put down it's called. Bok goes
down to the office and I sit outside by the water tank stroking poor
Chaka and Suz. I tell Chaka and Suz to be very brave. They will go to
doggy heaven and I'll see them there one day. Bok comes with the
injection. I start crying but so that Bok doesn't see. I ask if maybe he
will not put them to sleep. Bokkie calls from inside and says I must
come inside I cannot watch it. Bok says no, the boy watches everything
and the boy can watch this too. Bokkie shouts the boy's going to have
nightmares and Bok says the boy's a boy and he must see the world the
way it is. Now I don't cry. Bokkie's eyes water when she looks at
Chaka and Suz. She goes into the kitchen. Bok pats Chaka's head.
Bok's fingers are dirty from packing the truck. I hold Chaka's head in
my lap. Bok looks like he's going to cry. Tears in Bok's eyes. Bok injects
the medicine. Chaka stops looking at me. His eyes go like glass, like
stuffed animal heads. Then Suz. And Jonas comes to watch because
Suz loved Jonas from the trails. She cries. And Jonas shakes his face
and wipes his eyes and walks to his kaya. Bok sticks in the needle. I

stroke Suz's little head. Then she's dead. Bok gets up and goes to the
fence and looks out over the valley to the White Umfolozi. I go and
stand next to him. His mouth is thin. We put Chaka and Suz in
brown mealie bags and Jonas digs two holes and I help him. We put
the bags inside and I help Jonas to fill them up. At night I cry a little
bit. I don't say the Our Father. I pray big. I pray Jesus take care of my
dear Chaka and my dear Suz and please Jesus forgive them the waterbuck and also look after the waterbuck. And don't let Boy come and
kill us because he's angry. In the morning I go to the graves. Bokkie
says when someone dies you put flowers on the grave. I pick flowers
and grasses and yellow monkey-apples and put them on Chaka and
Suz's graves. Bokkie asks why monkey-apples and I say it's an offering
and Bokkie says we're not heathen who make offerings so I throw away
the monkey-apples and put more mauve tree wisteria it's mauve not
purple that Jonas picks when I ask him because its too high for me. I
take the *Kinder Bybel* and sit and read about Jacob's ladder at the grave.
I ask Bokkie why we didn't stuff Chaka and Suz like kudu heads and
buffalo heads and Grant's gazelle. Bokkie says that's for wild animals,
not for pets you love.

At St Lucia we will live at the sea in the ranger's house. And we can
go fishing and see the flamingoes. I will go to Sunday school and to
church for the first time. I'm going to the big world.

The best of everything ever happens: Willy Hancox gives me a
foal, a Palomino. His name is Camelot and he's still brown like all
baby Palominos and he'll turn like honey when he gets older. Camelot
can come to St Lucia because there's a paddock. Bok says he'll teach
me how to ride when Camelot is old enough.

3

Seasons on the Natal coast came and went, quietly and inconspicuously, without the show of the Berg. Summer seemed to me to exist

all year round with the only real change the drop in humidity and summer's afternoon showers. Returning to Amanzimtoti at the end of June 1975 it had been to the new house on Bowen Street, the first we'd owned since leaving Tanzania. Bok borrowed money from Oupa Liebenberg for a deposit, but still, the bank owned the house, of course, even though in Bok's name. It would take me about eighteen months to fully grasp the concept. Bok's curios had been thriving for six months and I was elated to be in Toti – now in a home with a swimming pool, my own bedroom and wall-to-wall carpeting. If only Lukas and Dom could come and visit, so they could see I had my own room. Bokkie refused to have a maid and continued cleaning and servicing the house and its running herself. The house sparkled. In spite of Prime Minister Vorster's belief that it was a communist plot, South Africa was getting television and Bok wanted to be the first to have a set. Evenings Alette would come over and we'd all watch the test broadcasts and the seven o'clock news read on alternate nights I think by Nigel Caine and Michael De Morgan in English and Heinrich Marnitz and Friedel Hansen in Afrikaans. Afterwards I'd walk Alette home to Dan Pienaar and maybe pop in to say hello to Juffrou Sang and Prof.

There was a slight unpleasantness because of my school report: since going to boarding school eighteen months before I no longer came first in class. My marks had dropped from the nineties into the low seventies. The marks, in and of themselves, seemed not to worry Bok and Bokkie unduly. But there was one sentence on my June report that sent my mother first into a rage and then, worse, into a silence. In the report's comments section, Miss Roos had written: 'Karl is a pleasure to have in class, yet, he consistently underachieves, never getting the marks he should. If he can learn to control his uitgelatenheid, I have little doubt that his academic performance would better reflect his academic ability.' Neither Bokkie nor I understood the word uitgelate so she sent me to fetch the Afrikaans/English dictionary. *Uitgelatenheid:*

boisterousness, elation, exuberance, exultation, in high spirits, loud, rampant. Then,
I had to look under each of these in Bernice's *Verklarende Woordeboek.*
The closest to Miss Roos's intention – according to Bokkie – was
obviously: *loud, rampant; uncontrolled.* When Bok came home, that was
what uitgelatenheid had come to mean: Your son is rampant and
uncontrolled. Your son is turning into a wash-out. My father shook
his head and said that unless my grades went up he'd take me out of
the school. I tried to hide my elation, that I had seen the gap, that this
could be my passport away from a place which I increasingly detested.
At the end of my first year in the Berg I had asked them to take me
out, and they'd refused, saying that being away from home was
making me a stronger boy. Where you can't hang onto Bokkie's apron
strings, Lena had said. Now, after Miss Roos's remarks, I suspected
that a weak report was my ticket home. And how badly, *desperately*, at
that moment, more than ever before, did I want to be at home. The
events of the previous six months, while never contemplated, lurked
like invisible spectres in my mind. And then, Bokkie went silent.
With me. That I, her star child, was turning into a wash-out, was driving her to muteness. With me. To Lena, Bernice and Bok she spoke as
if nothing were wrong. But I was invisible. I washed the dishes and
tried to help prepare meals when Bok wasn't home – that didn't help.
I walked over to the church where she was gardening, asked whether
I could trim the edges of the lawn, she only nodded at my presence
and said: 'You must do as you please, Karl.' I mowed the lawns – at
home and at church; I cleaned the pool, I raked the leaves, I weeded,
left the heaps in the driveway where she'd have to see my efforts. Tried
to get her to talk to me. To acknowledge me. She didn't budge.

Great-Uncle Klaas showed up at the front door. I was shocked to see
him. He resembled Oupa Liebenberg in so many ways – once handsome face, the arched nose, the long slender fingers, the thinning
hair – but he was filthy, smelly, with greasy hair and a moth-eaten coat
that smelt of mildew and old sweat. The man sitting there in our

garden looked nothing like on the photographs I had seen of him where he was young, startlingly good-looking, dressed in a black suit and holding three graduation scrolls and wearing a tasselled cap. Great-Uncle Klaas — even after he went mad — had been everywhere in the passage of late Ouma and Oupa Grootjie's cold house in Orkney — beside stark paintings of the Battle of Blood River and a huge pencil drawing of Dingaan's kraal. But the man on those photographs had been tall, strong, with high cheekbones, a well-trimmed moustache and black eyes that smiled pensively at the camera.

We fed him before he would again be on his way. Without the slightest hint of shame, he stuffed a sandwich and a banana into his pocket. He asked how Bernice and Lena were doing and Bokkie said Bernice was consistent and solid, and Lena was also working hard even though her primary interest lay in sport. I knew he was going to ask about me. But, even before he could, Bokkie, looking into the middle distance, said that I was meant to be the clever one in the family but that I had spiralled into mediocrity and for all she knew I would fail Standard Five and have to be sent to a school for the mentally retarded. 'All the talent in the world and he's going to end up a zero on a contract,' she said, shaking her head. 'Maybe you can speak to him, Groot-Oom Klaas, warn him what becomes of the idle.' She went on to tell Uncle Klaas about Miss Roos writing that I couldn't contain my *boisterousness*. A word that seemed now to feature in our family's every interaction. Bokkie whispered how I had disgraced her and Bok with my loud and rampant behaviour. Uncle Klaas laughed out loud. He said boisterous could mean a thousand different things. That it was a positive word as far as he was concerned and that the family should let me be. He said you kill a child's spirit if you try and turn the child into something he is not. With that he got up, burped, patted his stomach and said he would soon be heading back to the Transvaal. Before he idled down the driveway, he asked to see Bok's business. We showed him the garage with the shelves of curios. Because he reeked so badly of sweat, Bokkie and I stood at the garage door while he nosed around, not saying a word. Then he was off, down the street.

We saw him again in Toti the next day, walking down the main road with a bantu by his side. Bokkie slid down her seat and us three kids dived for cover so that he wouldn't see us. We laughed and giggled. And Bokkie was no longer ignoring me. From the Toti library I took Twain's *Tom Sawyer* and F.A. Venter's *Man van Cirene* and *Geknelde Land*. I swam a lot and read constantly at the poolside over Bokkie's warnings that I was destroying my eye-sight through reading in the glare. On a Saturday afternoon, when SABC TV was due to test broadcast a rugby match, I sat at the pool, legs dangling in the water, reading the first letter I had ever received from overseas. Abroad.

20 June 1975
Hotel Auersperg
Auerspergstrasse
Vienna, Austria

Dear Karl

I wish you were here. This place is fantastic. The hotel we're staying in used to be a palace. Gluck used to conduct concerts in the hall that's now the dining room. I have been going to masterclasses at the university and it's wonderful. I'm learning more here in four hours than in a year in the Berg. I wish you were here. We've been to see where Mozart lived when he first came to Vienna for Count Colloredo who treated him like he was a slave. Mozart had to eat with the servants. Can you believe it? Mozart is everywhere. I was invited to give a small performance of the A Minor Rondo, K 511 and it went so well. You would love the Mozartplatz. It has small statues from the Magic Flute. Tamino is playing the flute and Pamina leaning against him. I've been to places where all the famous composers went: Brahms, Haydn, Strauss, Schubert, Bruckner and to Heiligenstadt to Beethoven's one house and to the villa where he composed the Ninth and to Schwartzspanierhaus where he died on 26 March 1827.

It's very hot and I wish there was snow because this doesn't feel like Europe at all.

From here we go to Paris and I'll see where Chopin lived and wrote most of his work. Imagine if you could be here, how much fun we'd have. I miss you. How is Alette and your family? Please send them my regards. I'm not writing letters to anyone else, though I've sent postcards to Lukas and the others and one to Beauty. I think of you when I play. I'll write again from Paris.

Aloelloel mimy loelovise.

Regards
Dominic

I slid the letter into the envelope, reread his fine handwriting spelling out my name. I wondered whether I should be generous and give Bernice the stamp, which was of a statue of Mozart. It was a new stamp, not old like most of the others in her collection, but it would age. I placed the letter between the pages of *Tom Sawyer* and began reading.

Bok came and sat with folded legs beside me in the sun. He asked how it was going at school and how I liked being in the Secondary Choir. It was okay, I said, and Mr Roelofse was a nice conductor, even though he was very strict. Bok asked about my school report. Why I was not doing as well as I had before. Self-conscious at the direction the conversation was taking, I said I didn't know, that I'd work harder and improve. I did not say that it had been years since I had experienced any interest in school work, let alone in doing well. I loved reading – devoured book after book for my personal gratification – but that was all I ever wanted to do with books. Learning from them had come to seem an impossible labour. I couldn't do Maths. I hated Geography and Biology. History was okay. I liked English essay and comprehension, but hated spelling, grammar, concord, tenses. Afrikaans wasn't as nice as English, who knows why. And now I was in Miss Roos's class. I had liked her at first, quite a lot, but something had fed resentment towards her. It was not that I disliked her as I'd disliked Marabou: it was that she seemed to look right through me or as if she was suspicious of me and——

'I think something is making you unhappy in the Berg, Philistine. Am I not right?' Bok cut short my thoughts.

I shook my head, even while wanting to tell him how I hated the place, that I wanted to leave, start high school six months later in Port Natal. But there was no sense in doing it now, in the middle of the year. Not in a hundred years would they take me out halfway into an academic year.

'Then why are you doing so poorly?'

'I'm still in the top ten in class, Bok,' I answered, looking into the pool's turquoise water. I knew I could stay amongst the best without ever opening a book.

'But before you went to the Berg you were always first.'

'There are clever boys there, Bok. Niklaas Bruin and Mervyn. And some of the others. You know how good you have to be to get in there. The curriculum has a much higher standard than Kuswag.'

'But you used to get 90 to 98 per cent? Now you have 72 per cent. That has nothing to do with other boys being smarter, does it?' He spoke inquiringly, trying to soften the judgement in his voice. In his love.

'I can't do Maths.'

'But it's not just Maths. It's everything, even Afrikaans and English.' I was silent. 'And then, this thing about you being rampant and uncontrolled?'

Boisterous, I wanted to say. I glowered at my hands smoothing the book's dustjacket. How in hell has boisterous become rampant and uncontrolled, I wanted to sneer. You're all so thick. I wished he would leave, go and watch the ridiculous rugby game on TV. Anger in me. Like something choking me in my throat.

We sat quietly for a while. Then, his tone still as soft and gentle as it had been: 'My boy, do you remember last year, when Mr Samuels left the school? The telegram?'

I did. I knew at once what he was talking about. Fear sprinted down my legs. 'It is with regret that we have to inform you that the services of Mr Samuels have been terminated due to circumstances.' There had been a few small articles in the newspapers, *Rapport*'s headline: HOMO STORIES IN BERG SCHOOL. The school had adamantly refused comment; but amongst us speculation had been rife about who had been Mr Samuels's boy. Everyone thought it had been Erskin Louw. Someone reminded us how, once when we had been rehearsing 'Kiss Her, Kiss Her in the Dark' Mr Samuels had said we should sing the folk tune with feeling, imagining that we were kissing someone worthwhile. Someone like Erskin. Rumours abounded for weeks that Mr Samuels had been given the sack because Erskin's parents had found out. Dom said he'd heard that Erskin's dad threatened to kill Mr Samuels unless the school got rid of him. Yet all remained rumour and whisper and looks until that too disappeared and we rarely if ever spoke of it again.

'Yes, I remember, Bok.'

'Does any of that still go on?'

I looked into the water. It was as though Bok knew something or wanted to know something that I could either tell him or not. 'Sometimes I hear stories about some of the boys.'

'What do they do?'

How would I say this? Would I say anything? Couldn't he just leave me alone? 'They play with each other.' I wished he would stop, knew he wasn't about to. Not now.

'How do you mean?'

I didn't know which words to use. It had been years since I had had to use any word to describe that thing to Bok. As a child we had used filafooi, but since then an entirely new vocabulary had come into my life, a vocabulary that could not possibly, to my mind, translate favourably into his world: piel, voël, dinges, cock, dick, schlong, John Thomas, willy, penis, dong, ding, tool, horing, boner. I couldn't use any of these with my father.

'How do you mean, play with each other?'

'With each other's filafoois, Bok.'

The quiet was broken only by TV sounds from the lounge. I could sense that Bok was going to push till he had a clearer answer.

'Do *you* – ever do that?'

I shook my head. Petrified. I saw the three men behind the desk, just a month before. Saw Mervy's long johns, red, bloodstained. Couldn't look Bok in the eyes. Lena, an unwitting saviour, called from the lounge that the rugby was about to start. Bok asked whether I was coming to watch. I answered that I'd be up when I'd finished my chapter. He walked off and I opened *Tom Sawyer* again and tried to read, the sun beating down on the white page, eyes squinting. Reaching the end of the chapter I had not taken in a single word. All I had been thinking was that they were in the house, all their eyes on me, searching for something dark and wicked and terrible in me. The thing that made me deserve death. The windows were eyes from which my family pored over me. Accusingly.

I walked around the pool. Terrified. I entered the house. For a few seconds my eyes, blinded from the sun on the white page, could see nothing. I knew they were all in the lounge, watching rugby. Northern Transvaal vs Western Province. Blind as I was, their four figures were to me only outlines, black and white, like the negatives of photographs. I took my place beside Bernice on the couch. My eyes slowly adjusted and took in the room's normal colours and the running figures on our Blaupunkt's screen. It was going to be a long, long, long holiday.

4

Back from my first day in Grade One I announced that I had no intention of returning to school. Matubatuba Primary was certainly the most boring place on earth. No one else in class could read and write! All we did was draw little lines on loose paper – not even in books – while Juffrou Knutsen treated us as if we were babies. My return to Matubatuba Primary, I said, depended on whether I could be pushed up to Standard One with Lena. If Bok had skipped a standard in Tanganyika because he was so clever at school, I could comfortably skip two, and, if Lena didn't want me in her class I could just as comfortably and confidently go into the English stream of our dual medium school.

'Who do you think you are? You're Afrikaans,' Lena snarled. 'And no one skips standards. Windgat, grootbek!' Bokkie cautioned her to watch her language and change her tone or keep quiet. Bokkie said that skipping standards as it may have been done in former times was no longer permitted. Bernice said I would have to be patient until my peers had caught up with me; something she said was bound to happen before I knew it. Be careful that you are not seen as trying to be too big for your boots, she said. Then Bernice and Bokkie spoke about how strange it was for the girls to be coming home after school every day and Lena said she missed boarding school and her friends from Hluhluwe. I suggested that she return to Hluhluwe considering how much she had loved the place. Bokkie warned that she was tired of our quibbling.

Bernice proved right: Within a few months much of the rest of the class had learnt to read and write. One day our assignment was to draw a big red ball and a little green ball, then to write beneath the big red one B-I-G and beneath the small green one S-M-A-L-L. Inexplicably – perhaps because of a brief lapse in concentration – I wrote B-I-G under the small green ball and S-M-A-L-L under the big one. Juffrou Knutsen erased my error, but the shadow of letters remained, showing through the new, corrected version on the page I had to take home. I feared that someone – Lena in particular – would comment on the shadow pencil imprint.

Then, within six months of starting school and to my frustrated surprise, the pleasure of reading aloud in class had somehow turned against me. Altered into an ordeal. Despite the reading skills I had mastered in Umfolozi, I now started stuttering, tripping over words and phrases each time I had to read aloud in class. Again I said nothing at home. On my second report Juffrou Knutsen gave me a C for Reading. She wrote: *Karl has no confidence in front of people.* On the report I had still managed a golden star, but a perplexed Bokkie said my reading would probably drag me down to a silver unless I improved dramatically. To correct the unexpected problem and to prevent me from failing Grade One, I had to read aloud every afternoon for half an hour, even to myself. If I put feeling into the way I read, Bokkie said – emphasise words and sounds – it would possibly put an end to the stutter that came like clockwork each time I had to read before the class. Somewhere around this time I started biting my fingernails; whether from nervousness or because I had seen it from Lena, I don't know. I began reading aloud, sometimes for an hour at a time, putting expression into things as mundane as *The cat sat on the Mat and the pig ate the Fig,* eventually memorising the entire book. I rehearsed constantly, terrified that I was going to fail Grade One. Bokkie shouted at me to get my fingers out of my mouth while I was reading: 'How can you bite your nails and read at the same time!'

What had gotten into me? Why could I not read aloud in front of other children? Faced by that Grade One class of thirty-one kids – more children than I had ever seen together – something had become bigger than my will and ability to read well. I could do adding and subtracting – had been doing that for two years before from the exercise cards Lena had brought to the bush. Moreover, when I had to read to Juffrou Knutsen alone at her desk, I read like the champion I had always imagined myself to be. But reading aloud to the class tripped me up as I began thinking the audience was sitting there ready to laugh at me. Despite my rote learning of the entire book, I continued to stutter and become terrified when faced by large groups of children. The words seemed like traps, gaping at me from the page. I bit my nails, sometimes till the fingertips bled. When I spent a long time in the water taking a bath or swimming, the flesh around the fingernails became soft white and blue ridges. Like undulations in papier mâché.

Singing perie – perie instead of period as we took to calling each half-hour and later each forty-five-minute silence between clangings of the hand-rung bell – became my favourite. It was the second time in my life I had come this close to a real piano. The first was when Bokkie went to Johannesburg for an ear operation and we stayed with her ear specialist Dr Godmillow and his family. The Godmillows were Jewish and Bok had taken Dr and Mrs Godmillow on trail. Dr Godmillow had said he thought he could fix Bokkie's hearing – there was something wrong with the stirrup – a stirrup in the ear, I thought, how extraordinary – but the operation had been a failure and Bokkie's left ear remained deaf. I was not allowed near the Godmillow's piano, because Bokkie said it was a very expensive piece of furniture. Noting my fascination with the instrument, Mrs Godmillow invited me to stand beside her as she played and explained to me the function of the black notes, the function of the whites, how to make a semi-quaver. That the right hand plays the tune, the left the accompaniment. It was so grand, being treated like an adult in the Godmillow mansion by such a smart and important woman. All the while my parents and siblings sat outside in the sun with Dr Godmillow, my mother with a white bandage around her head. We never saw the Godmillows again. We later heard that they had emigrated. To Australia, to start a new life.

I had seen pianos in books, heard them on the radio and on our Jim Reeves, Dean Martin and Gene Autrey records, but it was exhilarating being that close to the big upright instrument in its shiny wooden casing, with its perfectly ordered row of shiny black and white notes. Now, in Singing period, it was magic, to see and hear how, when Juffrou Sang pressed just a black note, it sounded wrong, and then, when she pressed certain black and white notes together, how it became right. I thought of Mrs Godmillow, taking my fingers and pressing them to the notes, her eyes sparkling as I marvelled at the sounds produced from a mysterious process started beneath my fingertips. Single white notes played alone, for example when Juffrou

Sang was teaching us a new song, held no appeal to me, they and their tune sounded thin and boring. But when she pressed a few notes — even two — together, it made what Mrs Godmillow had called a harmony, sounds that seemed to come alive in my body, sounds that made me want to dance and sing. How I wished we could have a piano at home. I loved the new songs we learnt from thin music books and from the big fat guide of the FAK: 'Al die veld is vrolik'; 'Nooit hoef jou kinders wat trou is te vra'; 'Wie is die Dapper Generaal De Wet?' Juffrou Sang, whose real name I no longer recall, also taught us 'Die Stem'/'The Voice', our country's national anthem, and a verse of 'Nkosi Sikeleli Africa', which she said was the Zulu people's. And, to my delight, a song called 'Molly Malone', which, when I sang it to Aunt Siobhain, had her weeping as it was an Irish folk tune she had learnt as a girl in Dingle.

In our new St Lucia house, Lena and I shared a room. Being the eldest, Bernice had her own, where I was not allowed without permission. Afternoons the three of us sat around the dining-room table doing our homework. Reading aloud could not be done there — though I tried it a few times just to get Lena into a rage — and had to be practised in our bedroom or outside on the lawn. Once done, I would go off on my own or wait till Lena had finished. Then we'd take to the outdoors together. Lena, almost without fail, would want to go to the jetty down on the estuary to fish for grunter or salmon. I enjoyed fishing, but only if they bit immediately. My sister, in turn, could sit hour upon monotonous hour, till it was almost dark, even when there were no bites. Lena would rage at me for my lack of patience and tenacity; while she grudgingly fished alone, I could lie for hours on my stomach, doing nothing but looking down at the movement of water and fish beneath the jetty. Lena would tell me how useless I was at baiting hooks — she could do three for my every one. And I'd try to work quicker, but never with success. When Bernice was with us, she'd tell Lena to lay off me, that I could bait a hook at my own pace and that it wasn't hurting anyone. Then Lena would glare at me as though I were a hated enemy.

Many afternoons we were joined by the Pierce kids, who lived in the trailer park. Their father worked for Natal Road Works and they were always moving around. Mr Pierce could hold a fifty-cent piece between thumb and forefinger and bend it into a perfect half. Patty and Sam Pierce were our friends and went to school with us in Matubatuba. They were the only other kids on the bus in the mornings for almost half the way to school, and then in the afternoons the last off before our stop, which was the final one of the route. Sam was in Grade One with me, but in the English class. Patty and Lena were friends too, though they did once have a fist fight on the side of the road. Patty tore the collar off Lena's school uniform and Lena gave Patty a blue eye that stayed swollen for a week. Bokkie gave Lena a hiding for behaving like a Makoppolander in public. For a few weeks we were prohibited from playing with the Pierces.

We did all kinds of things: fished, swam, collected bait, built sandcastles and huge tidal dams, climbed trees, flew kites, played beach cricket with a tennis ball. We loved swimming and although we were always on guard for crocodile and hippo, Bernice, Lena and I disregarded our fears and spent hours in the water. In addition to the sheer pleasure of the cool water, there was another reason for me always trying to get Lena to swim: swimming was the one thing I could do better than her. She was a head taller than me, she could outrun and outsprint me, could pin me down in wrestling, catch bigger fish, intimidate even older boys at school, hit a ball farther in beach cricket, score double what I did in soccer. But in the water I was like a fish. I had taught myself to swim. When I was four she and I had visited the Hancoxes in Hluhluwe and I had, on my own accord, jumped into the camp pool and, to the consternation of Willy and Molly Hancox who were meant to be looking after us, swum to the side. When Bokkie heard about my bravery she was furious and we were not allowed near water without the blow-up water-wings Aunt

Siobhain had to send from Durban. The water-wings went with us in the afternoons when we went fishing. We never wore them. Not once. Simply lied to Bokkie.

And I could swim faster than Lena. Through swimming I had also discovered my sister's Achilles' heel: she was afraid to stay under for very long. I, on the other hand, remained till it felt my head would burst, often leaving me with a headache. Later, when we visited Mumdeman at Midmar, I could swim a length and a half under water while Lena could barely manage a length. Poor James, unsporty as a stick insect, could do only a breadth. At St Lucia I developed the trick of coming up underneath Lena and dragging her down, screaming. This so infuriated her that she left the water at once, waited for me on land, prowling along the shore like an angry lioness. I often daren't leave the water for fear of reprisals – on land I stood no chance against her speed, strength and agility: talents that neither friends, family nor casual acquaintances could witness without heaping praise on the tomboy who was my biggest rival.

Many afternoons I took Bok's new bull terrier Simba and, bearing carrots or sugar, went to Camelot where he was paddocked with two other horses. He soon knew me. I couldn't wait for him to grow, to be broken in so that I could learn to ride. I asked Bok whether I couldn't just try riding Camelot since he had now gotten to know me. Bok warned me to stay away until the horse was old enough to be properly broken in. On occasion Lena or Sam could be convinced to join me at the paddock. I got them to hold onto Camelot's bridle – to which I would tie rope as reins – while I tried to get onto the eight-month-old. If Lena or Sam stood in front of the horse, he would sometimes allow me onto his back. However, the moment my aid tried to pass the rope-reins over his head, he'd start moving and I would jump off. Failure after failure, I never let up. Once, when Camelot unexpectedly bucked, I came a cropper. I struck the ground at an odd angle and thought I'd broken my arm. I screamed all the way home, lied to Bokkie and said I had fallen off the swing at the caravan park, and within days was back at the paddock. I silently undertook that one day I'd lead Camelot onto the beach where falls in the soft sand would not result in fractured limbs. The experiment would have to wait till Bok was away.

As much as I liked being with Lena and the Pierces, some of my time was again spent alone: walking the beach searching for shells, sitting at one end of the jetty reading while Lena fished from the other, feeding and grooming Camelot, or, with Simba, exploring the bush along the estuary. I found a huge wild fig where hadidas and finches nested and soon we and the Pierces formed a gang and built a treehouse. I came to regret having told them about the Hadi-tree, for now the solitude of the place was gone. Suddenly there were all kinds of rules about who was allowed at the treehouse – no strangers; not our cousins when they came to visit; not Lena's friends who sometimes came to stay over. It was our gang's secret hide-out. Lena, thanks to her superior strength, was always the gang leader. There was not much to lead us to – decisions as to whether we'd go fishing, collecting bait, smoking or not smoking stolen cigarettes, playing in the trailer park, drawing up rules for the fort, playing church or doctor and nurse – a game during which I was allowed to touch Patty's poefoe and she my filafooi while Lena and Sam touched each other's. Patty's poefoe was a delight. Once I had started feeling it I could barely stop. When I stuck my finger inside it was wet and slippery, like the inside of an oyster. I wondered what was up there: just loose folds of flesh, blood, or pee? Or, if you stuck it in too deep, would your finger come out of her bum covered in poo? But when my finger came out it was clean: no blood, no pee, no flesh, no poo. I wanted to touch Lena's, but she refused, saying brothers and sisters don't touch.

Lena and I fought almost daily, while Bernice, four years my senior, inhabited a world of homework and older girlfriends from which I was mostly excluded. It felt as though for the first time I was getting to know my siblings. I was rarely alone with Bok and Bokkie. Now everything had to be shared, where before everything – including attention — was mine except for every second weekend and holidays when they had come home from Hluhluwe. But what frustrated me most about Lena was not having to share attention. It was that she was stronger than me. While I could and did inflict pain, she, ultimately, would get the better of me, either during free fights or when Bok supervised wrestling matches on the lounge carpet. Lena had the resilience of a leopard. Even at school boys spoke of her strength. James, who was her age, stood no chance against her. Besides the swimming and my ability to frighten her in the water, my one defence was my mouth: I could sling abuse, in an array of curse words and snide remarks that Lena could neither counter nor countenance — at least at first. Later, when frustration drove me to bouts of verbal anger she began counter-attacking, saying that while I might think myself clever I should remember what happened to all the clever ones in the family. She warned that I was going to burst a vein in my head and go mad like Great-Uncle Klaas. The older we got, the less necessary it was to even use his name, and when we understood that Aunt Lena had dropped out of school because she had epileptic fits and a nervous breakdown, all Lena would say in response to my provocations, was: 'Remember the mad gene.' After Aunt Lena married Uncle Joe and ended up having shock treatments at Tara, Lena would say: 'Remember, those shock treatments.' Having lost my verbal ability to get back at her for what I perceived as her all-round superiority, I told Bokkie that Lena said I was going to go mad like Groot-Oom Klaas and Aunt Lena. Bokkie said it was a cruel thing to wish upon anyone and that Lena would get a hiding if she ever again used it against me. Though Lena continued reminding me of the mad gene and those shock treatments, I no longer reported her to Bokkie. Through an intricate system of trade-offs we had worked out ways in which transgressions could never be reported; I would say nothing about her using the mad gene if she said nothing about me getting it on the hand at school for back-chatting Juffrou Knutsen; I'd remain silent about her catching undersized salmon if she kept mute about me sometimes playing with her or Patty Pierce's dolls. For dolls, along with dressing in girls' clothing, had now been prohibited: sometime before I turned seven, Bok had said I was to stop handling Lena's dolls and that I could no longer play with girls' dresses and tea sets. We were no longer living in the bush, he said, I was now in the eyes. This was civilisation and I could not go about pretending to be something I was not.

Another of our exchange of silences was Lena's for me getting onto Camelot's back, mine for not saying anything about her fishing with sea lice when sea lice were a species Bok was responsible for protecting. Sea lice made the best bait. Both of us knew it. There was no way I would have reported her anyway for I delighted in their use almost as much as she did. The big difference was that fishing was more important to Lena than it was to me. I held the sea lice and the salmon over her head like the sword of Damocles. As she did the dolls and Camelot over mine.

We wandered around the park with Simba looking for Bok, who was responsible for marine conservation and camp supervision. We were often with him when he checked fisherman's fish sizes, tagged turtles that came to breed in the dunes, when he wrote out fines if too many crayfish had been caught or if people took mussels from the rocks without licences. Most transgressions occurred during holiday seasons when the Look Theres came down from the Transvaal and Orange Free State. Because Lake St Lucia's camping resort and caravan park cost only two rand per night, the Makoppolanders – a word Mumdeman now explained had some origin amongst the poor whites of Tanganyika – came down for cheap holidays. They arrived in lorryloads, extended families that seemed to have countless numbers of ugly children and fat aunts and uncles who sometimes didn't have bathing suits and swam in their bras and panties or underpants. Bok spent his days requesting them to extinguish fires they insisted building on the beach and getting them to keep their sheep tied up. Rare it was for a truckload of Look Theres to arrive without their Christmas lamb on the spit still alive in the back of the truck. Bokkie held these people in almost the same suspicious regard as the Pierces. In time she accepted that Lena and I were friends with the Pierces — even though she said she had wanted better for us. The Look Theres, unlike the Pierces, were an unknown entity descended on St Lucia for a few weeks each year, with their wild children and their suspect origins and no addresses of return. There was an iron rule: No Playing With the Look Theres. The rule was never repealed in the years we lived there.

Out of season Lena, Bernice and I went on the boats with Bok through the narrows and into the huge lake. Simba stood at the front of the boat, his mouth drooling in the wind. Up the narrows we beached the boat and went into the dunes to check for traps that poachers set for small antelope. Coming upon fisherman who were not regulars, Bok asked to see licences. Other times he took VIPs out on boats to see crocodile basking on the estuary beaches or hippo drifting near the reed-spiked shores.

I went with Bok to Empangeni or Matubatuba when he had business there or if he needed to see the police about poachers or holiday traffic controls. Once, soon after we moved to St Lucia, he told me to wait in the Land Rover while he went into police HQ for a meeting. It felt as though he was staying away for an eternity and my bladder was telling me I had to pee. I wished Bok would come back. In front of the parking space was an open lot; I wanted to get out but was terrified of leaving the vehicle. Cars zoomed past, huge trucks stacked with sugar cane and timber rolled by making a terrible din, and there were pedestrians everywhere. Frightened of the place, I could not leave the van. Unable to hold any longer I cried, pissing myself where I sat, the warmth spreading up my legs and around my bum. The pee trickled down and I could hear it streaming in behind the seat. I sat in the squelchy pool, weeping. Soon it went cold and itchy. By the time Bok returned the entire cabin, misted up and humid, smelt like

fermenting piss. He scowled and asked why I had not simply opened
the door and taken a pee beside the Land Rover or in the parking lot?
I said I had been afraid of getting out of the Land Rover. Bok said it
made no sense: how could a child who had never been afraid of walking around Umfolozi, where lion and cheetah and rhino and eland
roamed free, be afraid of leaving a vehicle in the middle of a small
town like Empangeni to take a leak? I said I hadn't known I was
allowed to pee in the streets of civilisation. He clicked his tongue and
told me to use my head in future. We drove to the Caltex station on
the John Ross highway. Bok fetched toilet paper to wipe the seat,
which he had to remove. From the metal hollow where lay the jack, his
ropes, his emergency tool kit, he mopped up, shaking his head. I
again started crying and he rubbed my hair and said it was no big
deal, just a little accident and next time I'd know that it was in order
to get out and do it – even in the middle of the street, rather than in
my pants.

Mumdeman crossed the lake from Charters Creek in the little
flat-bottomed boat *Piper* with its fifteen-h.p. Evinrude outboard. I've
been separated from my grandchildren for too long to stay away, she
said. She would wrap a scarf around her head and steer across the
estuary with Skip. Over weekends, Dademan came along and Lena
and I returned with them. Dademan allowed us to steer the small
fifteen-h.p. engine and we'd putter up the lake back to Charters, with
Simba and Skip standing at the bow, Skip's long Pekinese ears streaming out behind him. At Charters Lena fished. I took my book and
went either on my own – for I was now old enough – or still occasionally with Phinias to the forest to see the louries. Dademan made
braaivleis and drank his brandy and Coke and smoked and
Mumdeman drank her sherry and didn't smoke. Dademan told us
about safaris or we watched cines and slides. The cines were our best:
flickering frames of James and Lena just starting to walk; me sitting
in a mud pool playing with the Wachagga houseboy who raised me
in Tanganyika; blue starlings ruffling their feathers in the Mbuyu

bird-bath with Meru in the background; all of us cousins in a dugout drifting down the Ruvu while Stephanie rowed; Dademan, Bok and Uncle Michael fishing; Aunt Siobhain and Bokkie giving each other perms on safari with all the little curlers in their hair and Bokkie waving the camera away; old Sanna Koerant gesturing with her arms to Mumdeman in the Oljorro garden amongst rosebushes, Christmas roses and bright orange and red cannas; Bernice running her first race at school in Arusha; the Land Rovers travelling over the savannah with Kilimanjaro behind; a bull elephant charging at Bok who picks up the rifle and the elephant crashing to the ground with dust flying and a thorn tree collapsing like dry twigs beneath its weight.

Our cousins came to visit from Amanzimtoti. Most nights there was the usual shortage of beds. I frequently ended up sleeping with Stephanie. I knew well what would happen when I shared beds with my cousin. Earlier I had woken and found her playing with my filafooi. It would have turned into a spade and after a while Stephanie would let me lie on top of her. She pushed my spade into her poefoe. A wonderful, wonderful sensation. Her poefoe had little hairs around it − which Patty Pierce's didn't − and because we usually had our heads under the blankets I could smell her: strong; it reminded me of seaweed, salty, slimy, slippery. After the first time we did it Stephanie secured my secrecy by telling me that if I told anyone Lena would die. I found her rationale for my silence ridiculous and told her so: doing it had nothing to do with anyone dying and there was no need to lie to me. I just knew we weren't meant to do it. I had grown up with animals mating everywhere around us in the bush. I have no recollection of ever, ever not knowing that everything and everyone mated − since Mkuzi I had known that Bok and Bokkie did it all the time − what else was going on when their mattress squeaked and they breathed like rhinos through the reed walls of Mbanyana? How stupid Stephanie was to tell me that Lena would die. I knew, without anyone having to tell me, that it would be our secret. Bokkie, who read to me and my sisters from a little red book with drawings of people doing it, said that at home we should call a spade a spade and sex – not the silly birds and the bees – was no big deal and we'd all do it one day when we got married. However, it was not something to discuss with children at school and it was an entirely private affair. The filafooi was a private part and the poefoe was a private part, that's why we didn't show them off or discuss them publicly and only walked naked around the house. Having sex was also not something for children to do because you did it when you wanted a baby, and to show how much you loved the man or woman you were married to. To do it out of wedlock was dirty and a sin. I feared Stephanie and I might be caught or, if I died, that I'd go to hell. After one of our sessions I asked Stephanie whether she might have a baby and she said no, I was not old enough yet to make a baby, although she was. So, we had nothing to worry about; except to keep it as our secret. Afterwards, I had the smell of her poefoe on my fingers. I always went to wash my hands, afraid that someone might smell me. And that, like doing it, I merely added to my deposit box in my collection of secrets: how I had stolen things from Jonas and Boy; how I sometimes didn't pray at night or left out entire sections of the 'Our Father'; that it was James and I who broke Aunt Siobhain's Oljorro vase and not the wind in the curtains; how I saw Bok kiss one tourist lady after the Umfolozi flood, a long, long kiss; how I stole sweets from the camp store to take to Camelot or to eat myself; how I sometimes ate my snot when no one was looking; or rubbed my finger in my bum and smelt it; how James and I had played with Chaka's thing to make him mate with Suz; how I tore the kite that Willy Hancox made and said it was little Jeremy; how I accidentally drowned one of Mumdeman's bantam chicks when I tried to let it swim and then hid its body beneath the red bougainvillea and then loudly agreed that it was probably a boomslang that had eaten it; how I didn't like going to Sunday school because it was boring and the songs we sang monotonous; how I still sometimes dressed up even though I wasn't meant to; how Lena and I used the sea lice for bait; how Bernice wrote letters to her boyfriend Okkie and that I sometimes read them; how I some-times wished Lena was dead; how I broke leaves off trees and grass, snapped them in half to smell or taste the juices even if Bok had told me the plant was poisonous. My little deposit box — hidden deep in my head — never filled; its capacity to take more seeming to increase with each new silence slipped in for safe keeping.

While I have no recollection of taking seriously Stephanie's warn-ing about Lena dying, there is, from elsewhere, a series of vivid memories about my other sister's possible death. One Mkuzi night I awoke to find Bokkie holding Bernice over the toilet bowl while my sister wretched and belched green and red bile. Bok was away with Jonas looking for poachers. For a few minutes Bernice would stop vomiting and lie down on the double bed while my mother wiped her face and forehead with a damp cloth that Lena kept wetting from the kitchen tap. Bernice cried and held her stomach, drifting in and out of sleep. Bokkie asked Lena and me whether we had eaten green mispels or poison apples? Had we drunk too much marog at the kraal? Had we chewed poisonous leaves or twigs? What about tam-botie? Stars of Mkuzi? Or had we eaten from the boys' fire, which might have had some tambotie wood? Had we seen snakes — she checked Bernice's body from skull to toe — had we been close to spiders nests; scorpions? My mind flew through the previous day but there was nothing I or Lena could remember. Bokkie tried to get Bernice to speak, but my sister just folded into a ball like a frightened shongololo and screamed and cried. Bokkie gave her Milk of Magnesia from the blue bottle. Nothing helped and she just vomited more. My mother's helplessness made me wish that Bok were there. Bok would know what to do. When Bernice seemed to calm down and fall asleep Bokkie told Lena to sit with Bernice while she and I went to the kraal to call Boy. Lena said we shouldn't go out because hyenas had been howling close by all night. Bokkie took the revolver and fired a shot into the sky. A while later Boy came running and Bokkie asked whether he had any idea where Jonas and the Baas had gone on patrol. Boy said they were probably north, above Kumahlala. Bokkie said she wondered whether Boy could go and search, or whether she should drive as far as she could and then fire some more shots to alert Bok. Boy said that he would go, but that it was probably better to drive with the Peugeot, because he couldn't run fast and both the horses were away and Mary was too wild to ride. Should she just take Bernice and drive to Matubatuba? What if she ran out of petrol? Did Boy know whether there was extra petrol in the jerry cans? Yes, he said, there was, enough for her to drive to Lebombo Gate and get petrol to fill up for Matubatuba. Bernice was again retching, trying to vomit, but nothing more came from her mouth. Bokkie told Lena and I to stay and tell Bok that she was racing Bernice to hospital in Empangeni. At dawn she and Boy took a funnel and filled the Peugeot tank with what petrol they could find. Lossie stood around in the grey light, ready to run after the car. Just as Bokkie was about to drive off, Bok on Vonk and Jonas on Ganaganda came galloping through the bush. They had heard the shot. Gesturing at Bernice on the back seat Bokkie burst into tears and told Bok his child was dying. It was the first time I heard that someone in my family — outside of great-grandfathers and great-grandmothers — could die. Death of someone I loved was a remote possibility, imaginable only, but reserved for if you were run down by a rhino, or bitten by a mamba — things you could avoid.

We packed a small suitcase and all five of us sped to hospital. On the way Bernice went unconscious. Lena and I cried because we thought she had already died. Bok told everyone to stay calm. We drove in silence, filling the Peugeot at Lebombo Gate and then speeding up the pass on the dust road, on and on through the sisal plantations, till we eventually reached the tarmac road and the first signboard to Empangeni. They rushed Bernice into emergency. The doctors said they had to do tests and we would have to wait. While Bokkie stayed in the hospital with Bernice, Bok took a reluctant Lena back to school in Hluhluwe. Then he and I went back to Empangeni

Hospital. We stayed with friends – I have no recollection of who they were – while Bernice battled for her life. I was no longer allowed to go to the hospital. The doctors couldn't figure out what was wrong with my sister. She was dying. Aunt Siobhain drove up from Toti to fetch me and I heard Bok tell her that it would be better for me to not be there when Bernice died. I drove back with Aunt Siobhain to stay with my cousins. Every night Stephanie came to me and helped me pray that Bernice would live and when I cried she took me to bed with her. For four days they battled to save her life and I prayed for God to forgive me for ever being nasty to either of my sisters and for ever doing anything wrong. Every day Bok phoned Aunt Siobhain at work to report that Bernice was only getting worse. Then, one night after work, Aunt Siobhain came home and said some doctor in Empangeni said Bernice would have to be cut open, so that they could see if something was wrong in her stomach. We all prayed that night that Bernice would not die, even Uncle Michael, who knelt on the floor and didn't have a drink for three days. Aunt Siobhain came home early to say that they still had not found the problem. The operation had been a failure but Bernice's temperature was dropping. Whatever it was had almost poisoned my sister. There was a lot of damage to her insides but they thought she would live. Next day Uncle Michael came home and said Bernice was out of danger. What Uncle Michael and Aunt Siobhain did not tell me – but what Stephanie secretly imparted to me at night – was that Bernice might never be able to have babies.

It was not my big, older sister Bernice I saw on the chair in the Mbanyana kitchen when I got home. It was a tall skeleton covered in shadowy yellow parchment. Like a dry twig that could snap if you touched it too hard: a dying praying mantis, barely able to move without assistance. She missed weeks of school and Bokkie was concerned she was going to fail the school year. She lay in bed for weeks while Bokkie fed her milk and medicine from tens of bottles that caught the light from the reed opening that was our bedroom window. Soon, Bernice was better and we were out in the bush again, at Jonas and Boy's kraal. It was just like old times when she came home for weekends, when she would come walking with me, reading me stories, dressing me up. Only I never chewed tambotie leaves again to see how much I could shit. While I never said it, Bernice, more than ever before, became the sister I loved. Bernice was vulnerable.

On a Saturday afternoon – I must have been about seven – Bok and Bokkie went to Empangeni in the Peugeot to visit friends. That was when Lena and I convinced Bernice to take us for a drive in the Land Rover. With Simba beside us in the cabin, we slipped down the back road near the kayas where we knew no one but the black guards' wives might see us. After a short distance I demanded to sit outside on the bonnet in the spare wheel, where Bok had always allowed me since Umfolozi days. Bernice tried to refuse, saying it was too danger-ous. I responded with the threat of reporting her for driving. She eventually stopped the Land Rover and I got out and went to sit in the spare wheel. With Bernice driving and Lena beside her, we drove up and down the beach road. I sat demanding Bernice go faster. Eventually I was standing up and dancing around on the bonnet. Bernice slowed down and Lena screamed through the window for me to sit down, or else get back into the cabin. I sat down and pulled faces at them through the windscreen. We took a different route home – behind the new holiday cottages – to make sure we were not spotted, and Bernice started speeding. That is all I remember. Next I am in my bed with Dademan and Mumdeman bent over me; I cannot speak or move my face, my tongue feels a fleshy gap where both my front teeth are missing; if I try to speak it's as though my face is tear-ing to pieces. Dademan smiles down at me, holding my hand. He says I am a big boy and I'm going to be fine; that he has given Bernice a hiding for being so irresponsible. Mumdeman says I must be taken to the doctor in Matubatuba to check whether anything is broken, but we must wait for Bok and Bokkie to get home. Bernice comes in with a red face and swollen eyes and says sorry. Mumdeman puts her arms around Bernice, who starts crying. What had happened, so the story slowly comes together, was that unbeknownst to us the Parks Board had made new, higher speed bumps in the road behind the cottages. Bernice, at high speed, spotted the bump just as she was about to strike it and braked, suddenly. I had flown off. A game guard had arrived to find me lights out with the front wheel only a few centimetres from my head. The girls were hysterical because even though they could see me breathing, they thought I was dying. The game guard ran to the office, told the warden who came and saw that I was okay. The warden radioed Dademan at Charters and they had come over the estuary in Piper.

Bok and Bokkie got home to find me lying covered in blood and mercurochrome. They were shocked. Dademan had to restrain Bok from giving Bernice another hiding. Then, in front of me, Dademan asked Bok where he thought we children had learnt our recklessness? How, asked Dademan, could Bok ever, ever, have allowed me to sit in the spare wheel on the bonnet while he was driving? No, Dademan shouted at Bok, it was not Bernice's fault that I had almost been killed! It was Bok's fault! Do you want your son dead – Dademan asked. How, how could a father be so irresponsible? Was Bok so thick that he couldn't guess he'd be setting a precedent for us young baboons?

'If you want the boy dead he can come with Mum and me to Charters Creek,' Dademan said in English. Bok, beside me on the bed, was like a shy boy, not knowing what to say, just mumbling, 'Sorry, Dad, sorry, Mum, yes, I know it was irresponsible.' The doctor in Matuba said nothing was broken and the lost baby teeth would eventually grow back. I was off school for a week. When I got back, still covered in scabs, I was something of a hero, recounting the story everywhere anyone asked or even if they didn't, occasionally throwing in the fact that I, like my older sister Bernice, had survived a near-death experience.

*

And, I continued to practise more reading aloud. Now it was *Emile* and *Pippy Longstocking*. For weeks I tried unsuccessfully to get one of Bokkie's or Mumdeman's dishes to stick to my head so that I would again have to be taken to the doctor, this time to have the pot removed. I snuck a discarded pair of Bokkie's pantyhose from the rubbish bin and put the panty section over my head and wound wire around the legs to resemble long plaits like the pencil sketches of Pippy in the Astrid Lindgren books. Closing the bathroom door, pantyhose over my head, facing the mirror, I was Pippy, reading – with expression – my own story. I felt my reading, and thus myself, getting better inside the bathroom and out: was learning to show the outward confidence I had always felt with my family, but that had fled when I had to read in front of the class. I knew I could get it right and I did: by the end of Grade One I had not only become the most confident reader in class – and better than Lena two years my senior – but I was chosen to be the frog – the main character – in the class play of *The Frog and the Ducks* in front of the entire school hall full of parents. Mumdeman, who, with Dademan came to the concert, said I was becoming more and more like Bok. She told of how Bok used to do Shakespeare in Arusha so well that an American film producer wanted to take him to Hollywood. Who or what Shakespeare was I had no idea, but he or it sounded grand, even as Dademan and Bok pulled their faces behind Mumdeman's back to show Mumdeman was exaggerating. By the end of the year, when I passed Grade One, I had forgotten my erstwhile fear of reading, tried to tutor Lena in putting expression into things: I was now confidence incarnate. I had been chased by eland; I had survived the fall from the Land Rover; I was the frog in the school play; I could read like a grown-up.

Nothing in the world, I believed, frightened me: I, like Bernice, was invincible. Bernice had the pink scar on her belly to prove how she had almost died. I had the missing teeth and the little scar, almost like a frown, between my eyebrows.

5

26 August 1976

Getting warmer. Hate Latin and Ma'am gives too much homework.
Beauty's husband Ezekiel is here. He comes to visit her from the
Carletonville gold mine twice a year. He again has to teach us pronunciation of the ethnic music. In each of our programmes we sing
two or three traditional African songs. Our audiences love the African
songs – they are light, playful, have catchy tunes and magnificent
rhythm. 'Shosholoza' usually makes the audiences mad and it is sometimes performed as an encore. The other big hit is 'Siyahamba'. Then
there's the 'Xhosa Click Song'. And the Zulu lullaby 'Tula Baba'.
Beauty's husband speaks Xhosa, Sotho, Tswana, Zulu and other black
languages of which he knows all the pronunciations. We don't know
the meanings but we sing the words. Last year Mr Roelofse was walking past the servants' quarters when he heard the workers and the
servants singing a tune that took his fancy. He asked Beauty to send
Ezekiel up to teach him the song. That's how we came to sing
'Uyatlhaga':

> *E . . . la, E . . . la!*
> *Umunt' onzima kilomhlaba, Uyatlhaga*
> *E . . . la, E . . . la!*
> *Myekeleni athwalisamende, Uyatlhaga*

All the choirs did it and Ezekiel came to show us how to pro-
nounce the words and to move. Ezekiel said it was a traditional
Ndebele song that the mine workers sang, originally from Rhodesia,
about how people love the land. Mr Roelofse allowed us to jive a little
during rehearsal, just like the Bantus, but when we performed in
public we had to stand stock still without moving. After the first concert we never sang it again: it simply disappeared from our repertoire.
No explanation given. Must get back to my homework.

6

Twice a week after the day Bok spoke to me at the pool, I went to see Dr Taylor in the office on the second floor of Salisbury Arcade. Mornings after antihistamine and breakfast, if Bok had to visit curio shops in the city, I went with him in our new Chevrolet. 'South Africa!' I called out, the first time the whole family went for a drive in the metallic gold vehicle. 'What do you love?' And we all sang: '*We love braaivleis, rugby, sunny skies and Chevrolet.*' When Bok wasn't going into town, I caught the train from Pahla to Durban Central. Twenty-five cents for the return trip: an hour there, five minutes down West Street, an hour in Dr Taylor's office, five minutes back to Durban Central, an hour back to Amanzimtoti. The same train Lena and Alette took to Port Natal High.

Dressed in civvies – my school jeans and hand-me-down shirts from cousin James or Leon Lategan, I walked to Pahla station, taking a book to read on the train. I'd started on *To Kill A Mockingbird.* I liked Scout and Jem, but it was Atticus Finch I wanted to be. I too would defend good black people against evil whites. The train galloped me to and from the city and more than once I wiped off tears for Tom Robinson, so alone against the world. Around the last visits to Dr Taylor I was onto Wilbur Smith's *The Sunbird,* which I got from the small bookshelf in our passage. Over the previous years I had read, or started to read before abandoning from boredom, most of the thirty or so books in our house: *The Washing of the Spears, Game Ranger on Horseback* by Bok's friend Nic Steele, *The Man With the Golden Gun, The Horseman's Bible, Cry the Beloved Country* (abandoned and later read in the Berg), *Reader's Digest Condensed Novels* (Six Volumes), *The Call of the Wild, Jock of the Bushveld, Reader's Digest Medical Dictionary* (paged through and searched through mostly for anatomy), *Trees and Plants of Natal, White Rhino Saga* by Dr Ian Player. All English; not a single Afrikaans one other than the three volumes of *The Arabian Nights,* Grimm and Andersen that I no longer read.

*

Alette and her family had left for their vacation near Uvongo. When Bernice could find an excuse and twenty-five cents she accompanied me to Durban to do window shopping. She waited for me in the City Hall gardens. When she asked what Dr Taylor and I had talked about, I'd say something like: 'Oh about school. Why I'm not as bright as I used to be. What I want to be one day.' On the train home she asked me to tell her stories, any of the many I adapted from others I'd read, or made up in my mind and sometimes wrote down in fragments. Bernice doted on my storytelling while Lena only rarely showed interest. I began telling Bernice the story of the Singing Chameleon, one I had read in a book that was given to me by Molly Hancox when we were just leaving the Parks Board. The collection of stories was still somewhere on our little bookshelf.

After our pool-side conversation Bok had told me he wanted me to meet someone in Durban. A man who specialised in education. I was now turning into a young man and the specialist in Durban would be someone to talk to about things that may currently be on my mind or issues which may face me once I grew up. *Dr Vincent Taylor, MA, Clinical Psychology, University of the Witwatersrand.* There was a reception area but no secretary. The reception area floor was carpeted and led directly into the wide hall and the elevator. The hall had shiny plastic tiles on the floor. Later that year, on the shores of Lake Malawi, I would remind myself of the hall's acoustics. Like the passages of a hospital.

Try as I might, today, it is impossible for me to reconstruct, session for session, what happened there. Like so much memory, there are flashes, moments, images, words. And these I now strain to order into some narrative chronology, for my inventory of consciousness. It can be that I still forget or silence what I choose to disregard or voice what is chosen to tell in a way that fits my logic, my love, my explication, my life, and so, here, specifically, the silences might – as much as I doubt – speak louder than my words. The silence of the waiting room, the rustling of pages of magazines – *Scope, Personality, Fair Lady* –

I paged through while waiting for him, no windows, all these years later placing myself in that room from far away as I now take it to the language of a man.

Dr Taylor asks what I, at twelve and a half, want from life. Boisterously I say I once wanted to be a jockey or a film star but that I know I'm already too tall to be a jockey and not good-looking enough to be a film star. The picture of a dancer is so long disremembered that saying it doesn't even cross my mind. So I will probably become a lawyer even though I also want to be a playwright. I will only become a lawyer so that I have something to fall back on – for the off chance my plays don't make it to Broadway or the West End. I want to be a lawyer like Atticus Finch, or like Prime Minister B.J. Vorster, who was a lawyer before he went into politics. Dr Taylor says I am very wise to go to university, that there isn't much of a future in writing. Only one in a million who want to be writers actually succeed. I say I don't want to be a writer, I want to be a playwright, but that it's fine and I will become a lawyer, as I said. He asks why I want to be a lawyer. I say that I really want to be a game ranger but that lawyers make money. I want to be rich like my Uncle Joe and my friend Dominic Webster's father. I never want to be poor. People say I have a good mouth and a sharp mind, that I argue well, characteristics needed to make a case in court.

He asks what sort of things I write. But something in his voice makes me cautious. I say I've written bits of stories and poems but that I'm only twelve – almost thirteen. I am reading now, to prepare myself for one day when I will write plays and maybe even make movies. There is no better education than to read, I say. He says he has heard about a play I've written. One we performed up in the Berg. I say it was only half an hour long and we only performed it to our class, so it wasn't a big deal. What was the play about? he asks. Something places me on complete guard; something has clicked. How does he know about the play? I have never mentioned it to Bok or Bokkie. I begin to clam up, feel a flush spread up my neck. I am being

led somewhere; being tricked. After thinking for a moment I choose
my words carefully: it was about a peasant who became a regent. Dr
Taylor asks me what sort of regent I wrote about. I say the regent was
a peasant who was a queen who dressed as a king. I want him to stop.
What does this have to do with what I'm going to become or whether
I'm doing poorly at school? He asks why I wrote that specific play. I
say that I was inspired by a piece – a romantic piece of music – my
friend Dominic plays on the piano; it is called *Remembrance*. I'm not
sure, Dr Taylor, I say, but I think it may be by Chopin because
Chopin is one of Dominic's favourite composers although he also
likes Schoenberg. I say: Dominic is overseas now, has been for almost
two months. I received a letter from him in Vienna. Dr Taylor asks
whether I'll bring the letter for him to read. I lie and say I've thrown
it away. Dr Taylor asks me where I got the story for the play from, the
story on which the play was based. I say I made it up, though the idea
was from two other stories, a Chinese myth that I read in *Children of
the World* and one that Steven Almeida told me. Steven, I say, heard it
in school in Angola before they came to South Africa because of the
communists. He is Portuguese. Steven Almeida, I say, is my friend.
Again, Dr Taylor asks what the play is about. I can no longer look
him in the eyes. It was, I say, about a regent who ruled a kingdom in
West Africa. The king ruled for forty years, I say.

'Why did you write a play about that?'

'It sounded like an interesting story, Dr Taylor.'

'What about it interested you, Karl? You read a lot, you could have
written a play about any other story.'

'I have, Sir. I have written other plays. I wrote one about Sinbad,
and Dominic and I want to write a musical about Ali Baba and the
Forty Thieves. Something like *Oliver*, which we performed last year.
Dominic is brilliant with composition and I'll write the lyrics.'

'But you also wrote the story about the regent from North Africa.'

'West Africa,' I say.

'Well, why were you fascinated by that story? It sounds rather original to me, please tell me about it.' His voice has changed. Perhaps there is really no reason to fear or distrust him.

'Maybe,' I say, 'it is because she could only rule if she dressed as a man.'

'So the regent was not a king.'

'She was a king because she was dressed up as a man.'

'And in your play, did she dress as a man?'

'Yes. But only until she was exposed. Someone hated her and they exposed her.'

'At which time it became apparent she was a woman?'

I nod my head.

'In your play at school — who was in the play? All your friends?'

'Not all. Almeida was the queen's peasant husband, who went around searching for her until they were reunited. Dominic played the piano and Mervyn the violin. Bennie was the leader of the servants — slaves — and Lukas and some others were all peasants.'

'And you, who were you?'

'I was the king.'

'The queen.'

'The king-queen.'

And then he leaves off talking play. He asks, and this the writer remembers, these words are not reconstructed, they were the man's:

'You're almost thirteen, Karl. Do you think you are the boy your mother and father wanted?' I do not know how to respond. He is not angry, speaks gently, drawing me in, affirming: 'Do you think your parents are proud of a boy who pretends to be a girl?'

'I don't pretend, Dr Taylor. It's just a play. In a play you can be anything.'

'Do you want to be a girl?'

I shake my head: 'No, Dr Taylor.'

'Do you want to be a boy?'

'Yes, Dr Taylor.' I look down at my hands, fold the bitten fingernails into fists. I do not say: no, I want to be everything. I want to be whatever I want to be. I can play at being whatever I want to play. Leave me alone; you repugnant, bald, old man with glasses as thick as canfruit bottles. Die, die, die, you're old and your life is over you will die soon and the worms will devour your wrinkly old skin and you'll be nothing, nothing, nothing, while I'm alive and living playing whatever I want to play. Nor do I think, Bok, bastard, why do you do this? Nor that I hate you, Buys, just like Buys and Miss Marabou and Miss fucking Roos, doos, boys death orphanages poor Mervy's bloody bum what does this old goat know old ugly ugly man swallowed into the earth, leave me alone, leave me alone, leave me alone. I do not know how to say that. All I know is that I am ashamed of myself. Hate myself. All I can say is both what I wanted and knew how to say from what I knew I was expected to say.

'Well, Karl? Do you want me to help you become the boy your parents always wanted? Don't you think that will make them proud?' What did this man know about me; about the events of the previous term; of my whole life; everything?

'Yes, Dr Taylor.'

'You want to be the boy your parents will be proud of?' A broad, pleasant smile spread across his face.

'Yes, Dr Taylor.'

'Tell me again, Karl, you say it to me.'

'I want to be the boy my parents will be proud of.'

He smiled. Leant forward and patted my knee. He told me I had now passed through the phase of childhood and adolescent games; now was the time to start the real ball game of young manhood. Unless I let go of the pubescent phase my development would be arrested, right into old age, and I would remain a boy for ever. 'Now is the time to let go of the way you've been in the world, Karl. Now you must learn to speak and behave like a real young man. You don't want to crawl around in boyhood for ever, do you, Karl? When you're a thirty-year-old man, you don't want to still be where you are now, do you? Clearly you are a gifted boy intellectually, but emotionally you're underdeveloped, so now's the time to get the emotions and the intellect lined up – so that one is not ahead of the other. That's my job to help you with.' He said he wanted to tell me a little story. Something I should bear in mind – for it would serve as a guiding myth to me for the rest of my life: 'There was once an old, very wise man, who was respected by the whole village. He was blind. Blind, but very, very wise. Everyone came to him for advice. About their crops, about their children and babies, about disease, about the weather. One day, a group of naughty children came to him and stood in front of him with a bird in their hands. They asked the old man: tell us, if you are so wise, is this bird we hold in our hands alive or dead? And what do you think the old man said, Karl?'

'He said they must let it go, Dr Taylor.'

'No! He was blind, and he couldn't see whether it was alive or dead. No, the old man knew they were trying to trick him. He said: I don't know whether it is alive or dead or whether you even have a real bird in your hands. But what I do know is that it is in your hands.'

'It is in your hands,' he repeated. 'Do you understand the moral of the story, Karl?'

I had an inkling, but surely the old man was not saying they could do with the bird as they pleased? What if it was alive and they killed it? I wanted to lie and say yes, I understand completely, but somehow I imagined that if Dr Taylor gave it to me, explained exactly what he meant, I would be saved. I felt my spirit soar. Like the world was being lifted from my shoulders. Maybe I would, indeed, become the boy my parents wanted. Everything was going to turn out perfect. In grasping the story lay my salvation.

'Tell me,' I said. 'Please explain to me, Dr Taylor.'

'It is in your hands, Karl. You want to be a boy your parents can be proud of, don't you?'

'Yes, Dr Taylor.'

'Well. The old wise man is telling you: it's in your hands. You, and only you, can turn yourself into the boy your parents want you to be. It's in your hands. Are you ready for the challenge?'

'Yes, Dr Taylor.'

From the next session Dr Taylor and I started working on my *programme of action*. My *POA*, as he suggested we call it.

1. I was to stop acting like a girl in plays – better yet if I wrote plays without girls in them, or why write silly childish plays at all when I wanted to be a young man? I was going to be a lawyer anyway, wasn't I?

2. I was to go all the way in rugby – learn to be aggressive in the scrum, roar like a lion when I went down in my position as lock; know that the other team was out to hurt me and I should learn to hurt back – don't play dirty, but play hard.

3. I was to stop reciting poetry. Poetry was girlish and unmanly, and, as a substitute, I was to take two weights of lead pipe and build my muscles every night. Become proud of my body.

4. I was to quit acting girlish at school – try and deepen my voice; I was to stop using my hands when I spoke – only girls use their hands when they gossip.

5. I was to stop being friends with girlish boys and as nice as Dominic sounded he sounded a bit queer – did I know what queer meant? And the little Jewish violinist – now he sounded like a real pansy – and you know the things with Jews . . .

6. But my friend Lukas, now he sounded young and manly and I was to be friends with boys like him. Steven Almeida, well, I could work that out for myself.

7. Now, as for my handwriting, write a sentence. 'What is this here?' 'It's an ampersand, Dr Taylor.' 'Why do you use it?' 'I like its shape, Dr Taylor.' 'Look at all those curls and swirls, look at this preposterously curled E, Karl! And contrast that with Bok's handwriting on this cheque.' Now, didn't I think my handwriting was too curly and girlish? It could be manly if I slanted it to the right, like Bok's. Your

handwriting is you, like your name: it is your face to the world. Twirly-wirly handwriting was a dead give-away. At first, when I left Dr Taylor's office and walked down West Street back to the station, it felt as though my head was separating from my body. Or maybe all that was left of me was my head full of new ideas. It felt as though everyone in the city were looking at me, were programmed to keep an eye on me because I was dangerous. Maybe there was a machine in my brain that they could all read to see and hear what I was thinking. Like a futuristic robot or a machine. It was said that in the future machines would be able to think and act like people, and maybe I was such a machine. Which meant they all knew what I was thinking. I tried not to think of anything bad or girlish. I wondered whether to everyone around me my head might resemble a balloon or an outsized egg, drifting on the pavement at head height. I looked into the big glass windows of 320 West just to make sure my torso and my legs were still there, attached to the enormous oval. It was all right; all there; together. Head still the same size. And then I began to see myself as important, as though I had been elected or chosen for some reason to be brought to Dr Taylor; as though I were special and all the pedestrians and people in cars along West Street knew, as they saw me, that I'd been predestined for some or other as yet unspecified greatness.

Bok, smiling ear to ear and rapping me playfully on the back, took me to a friend of his who worked at Isipingo Steel Works near Louis Botha. The man cut four small weights from steel piping. I would take these back to school and build my muscles whenever I had a chance. Just lift them, up and down, for half an hour at a time. If I was shy to do it in front of the other boys, I could do it in my bed after lights-out.

Before my return to the Berg, Bokkie covered the metal piping in orange Terylene fabric: so that they'll be more comfortable for you to hold.

7

A freezing June afternoon; mist from our mouths, even in the class-room. Jeans and polo-neck jerseys. Dominic had already been overseas for about three weeks. Steven Almeida had permission from Uncle Charlie to stay with us in E Dorm while Dom was away.

Almeida and I were held in detention. We had caught and painted about two hundred flies in different tempera colours, kept them in a plastic bag, and then surreptitiously freed them during Miss Roos's Geography lesson. Red, blue, green, yellow, orange flies everywhere. Five hundred times each, on the jotter pages: *I am not allowed to colour flies with tempera and free them in Miss Roos's class*. Detention with Miss Roos didn't feel like serious punishment. She chatted to us while we wrote lines, told us about her family, her husband's job, all the years she had taught at the school. Miss Roos had a big posterior – as she called it – that swayed from side to side as she walked, her face hearty and open and her laugh infectious and loud. With the school since its founding, she and her family farmed on the Bergville road. She was the only teacher who didn't live on the school premises. Her children went to school in Estcourt with the Therons.

We liked Miss Roos as our teacher. She had a great sense of humour, always joking with us – even about sex – and you could hear her laugh travel through the school wherever she went. Unlike the live-in academic staff, she did not seem particularly involved with school affairs or the choir, although she did play the piano and taught Music Theory.

Imagining the lines went faster if the phrase were broken, I'd write fifty *I am not allowed*'s then, once done, beside those, fifty *to colour flies in tempera*'s and finally fifty *and free them in Miss Roos's class*es. The result was that each line looked as though it had been written in three slightly different sets of handwriting.

Leaning into the page, scribbling the lines on the jotter, I heard them through the open window: snorting, neighing, hooves striking fur, clipping into the turf. I looked up. On the embankment above our classroom, King was trying to mount Cassandra. The mare, ears flattened against her head, vapour from her mouth, kicked and pranced; King trotted off then approached her again. He reared – jets of steam from his flaring nostrils and mouth into the cold colourless air – tried to get his forelegs over her rump, only to have her pull out from beneath him while he tried to cling on – still on his hind quarters – the flanks of his magnificent thighs aquiver; chunks of mud flying from beneath hooves. Cassandra's vagina dripped ooze, like she had just been peeing. Beneath King, his penis, thick as my wrist, white with black blotches, curved up, nodding against his stomach, the tip like a swinging shower-head. When he mounted her again, the penis seemed to fling itself from side to side, searching for her opening, squirting juice in streams as the curved pipe tossed around. Cassandra paused, pranced in one spot, stood still and his rod jittered around the opening, still shooting out the juice. I felt myself go stiff. This was what coming was, Lukas said, now I can see it, litres, litres. King was coming, shooting squirt; beautiful; fantastic. I looked at the desk at the front of the class and found Miss Roos's eyes on the horses. She glanced at me, smiled devilishly and said: 'Karl, enough of watching the horses at play; back to the task at hand.' I tried to concentrate on the lines. But knowing they were out there, hearing them, drove me to distraction.

'They're mating, Miss! Cassandra's going to have a foal.'

'I know very well what they're doing,' she laughed. 'But it's none of our business.'

'Please, Miss, can't we watch? It's no big deal. King is servicing Cassandra.'

'You make it sound like a mechanic doing something to a car!' Miss Roos giggled and Steven and I laughed too.

'That's what Wilbur Smith calls it, Miss Roos,' I said, telling her to read *When the Lions Feed*. I kept glancing at the horses, trying to catch a glimpse of Cassandra's spectacular oozing opening, her upturned head and bared teeth, clouds of vapour everywhere, and King's thick sausage ramming in and out, his tail curved, the muscles of his buttocks and flanks shivering as if he'd lost control of his skin.

'Karl. Get back to work.'

'Why can't I watch, Miss? It's not like I've never seen it. You should see rhinos, Miss, it's like a duststorm when they do it . . .'

'They're just mating, as you yourself said. Why do you want to watch it?'

'Because it's beautiful. And anyway, I've done it. In the bush with sheep.'

For an instant, as her smile seemed to disappear, I thought I'd gone too far. Then she smiled again and said: 'You have not!'

'I have. And guys do it in the dorms all the time.'

'What do they do?'

'We . . . they,' now that it had been mentioned, a shadow of doubt settled in my mind. I glanced at Almeida. My erection was suddenly gone. I shouldn't go on. Saying anything had been a mistake. I could see it in her face: even as she smiled. She was too keen, wanted too much to know.

'Karl, tell me.' Her demeanour had changed. She was still trying to be her old jovial self, but the smile was no longer genuine: 'In E Dorm? The five of you?'

'No, Miss! I was only joking, Miss. To see your reaction.'

'Karl, come to the desk.' Her smile had vanished.

'He's only joking, Miss Roos,' Steven said.

'Don't lie to me, you two. I know what you boys get up to. This is very, very serious. What is it you – they – do? Tell me.'

I went to the front of the class, trying to laugh it off: 'Miss, it's just fun. They just . . .' But I couldn't say another word. Whatever we had done had to be kept a secret. Why, why had I not kept my big mouth shut! And after all, it was nothing. It was too small to even mention and all at once too big as well. She persisted. To show her how silly her seriousness was, to hide my own embarrassment, I thought it

would be less grave if I drew it on the blackboard: the surface cold
against my hand, the chalk screeching, little stick men, like Bushmen
paintings, figures just rubbing against each other. Her neck turned to
watch the pictures appear beneath my hand.

'Steven. Do you do this?'

Almeida shook his head.

'Karl?'

'No, Miss. But it's just playing, Miss Roos.'

'Who have you seen doing this?'

'No one, Miss. It's just a story that goes around.'

'Names, Karl. Give me names.'

'It's just boys, Miss Roos. Stories, from before our time.'

'Okay. You can go back to your seat.'

I erased the drawings from the blackboard. Blew the chalk dust
from my fingers as I moved back to my seat. Steven and I stared at
each other. What had I done? What was she going to do with the
information? Neither Steven nor I had mentioned names. Surely, she
would leave it alone. No use in being paranoid; no, not Roos; she had
simply been inquisitive; had such a good sense of humour. Surely,
surely, she would not say a word? I tried to deflect her attention by
asking why we called it a blackboard when in truth it was green. By
force of habit, Karl, as easy as that, now get back to your lines, she
said. What was Steven thinking? Would he tell the others? Not Steven,
surely he knew it had been accidental, not deliberate? We completed
our lines about coloured flies and I went out into the drizzle that had
started, down to the stables to tell Lukas that King had covered
Cassandra. In eleven months' time there would be a foal. So, that's in
May next year, I figured; and what a stunning horse would spring from
King and Cassandra's genes. I thought of Steven's face as he'd looked
when I left Miss Roos's classroom: a black polo-neck jersey folded
high beneath his chin. Cheeks flushed red. Curly black hair cropped
short. His green-brown eyes seemed not to want to look at me.

❋

In the auditorium, where on the choir benches we stood facing Mr Roelofse in the early evening before dinner, I saw her as she waddled through, smiling. One of the maids pointed her down the passage towards Mathison's office. Miss Roos, hips asway, smiling as was her good-natured habit, glided off to seal our fate. Later, that night, after lights-out, while Mervyn wept quietly into his pillow, when we were all too afraid to speak, I would recall her, try not to imagine the conversation she and Mathison must have had behind that closed door.

8

Hoërskool Port Natal
Umbilo, Durban
25 August 1976

Dear Karl

It's Friday afternoon last period and I'm sitting in the music room at Port Natal and writing instead of practising. So, excuse the foolscap paper! How are you? I am fine.

The rest of the school is on the rugby field doing cadets. It's rather ridiculous, they've told us the girls are soon also to start doing cadets. I suppose it can be fun and Lena most certainly loves the idea. It's still not clear whether the girls will have to wear brown uniforms like the boys. Lena can't wait, wants to be a drill sergeant. On the train in the morning she teaches me how to do an about turn and salute. I love your sister. She's the talk of the school at the moment because she's so young and in the first netball team. And the boys love her because of her beautiful legs. You both got your mother's perfect legs. Your legs are going to be like Shaun Thompson's. We saw him surfing the other day.

Only three months to go before you perform the Mass. I'm aghast that they're letting you do it, it is after all the most difficult thing Beethoven ever wrote. It's an hour long; I've been listening to it on record and can see them drilling you all to get it committed to memory — or are you allowed sheet music. Is it tough?

Have you decided whether you're coming to Port Natal next year or are you stay-
ing there? Lena says you'll be coming back and I do hope you do. Lena says Bok is
saying something about you people moving into Durban, to get closer to his office if
he goes into insurance. Have you heard? That will be great, because we're moving into
town to get closer to Dad's work at Durban-Westville. You know he left Durban var-
sity to go there, because he got a full professorship there?

Teaching the little coolies who are always making trouble. Working as hard as ever.

My mother is fine, still teaching music at Kuswag. My mother wants to know if
your voice has dropped or if it's breaking? She still reckons you were her greatest dis-
covery. We haven't seen you in ages. In April. Almost four months. Are you coming
home in October for the holidays or are you going on tour? I miss you, man!

Thank you for the postcards from Oudtshoorn and from Table Mountain. I hope
you thought of me while you were up there. I want to live in the Cape when I grow
up. Maybe I'll go to Stellenbosch to study medicine. I got straight As in July and I've
got to keep it up because some of the medical schools now demand to see grades as far
back as Std 8. More and more people wanting to study, I suppose. We're having bomb
drills now and that means we can stand out on the rugby field missing entire periods
when we should be studying.

Okay, there goes the bell. I must meet Lena at the gate so we can go to Umbilo
to catch the train. Weekend! I'll post the letter tomorrow.

I love you
Alette
xxxxxxx

9

Dishing up our food, Beauty whispered that I was to go and look
under my pillow. After lunch, instead of going to the encyclopaedias,
I rushed to my bed. Below the pillow I found a dirty slip of yellow
matchbox cardboard. With the slip enclosed in my hand I cut quickly
through C Dorm and went into the library. Downstairs the teachers

were still eating. I sat up close to the shelves where I'd be inconspicuous. I took down a book. The scrap of cardboard was adorned with a few sentences in the most exquisite handwriting I'd ever seen:

Karl, Come to the plum-orchard any afternoon around four when the boys are down at the rugby field. I've come to visit.
                                    Klasie.

Grinning, I slipped the note into my shorts. Was someone playing a trick on me? Who was Klasie? Jacques? I didn't know his handwriting. And then, if it were him, how had Beauty known about the note? No, it could not be Jacques, he wouldn't have given it to or even told Beauty; he would have gone and put it there himself. And why the dirty slip of Lion matchbox. Dom? Him and Beauty in cohorts. He is her favourite. Yes, maybe . . . I took it from my pocket to reread. Like calligraphy, each letter upright, curly, each linked to the next, the capital letters exactly the same height, the y's perfect, almost as if the letters were printed by machine. Or by the surest hand in the world. And the name, Klasie, signed flamboyantly. Like Van Gogh. A name that could be signed at the bottom of a painting. Where had Dominic learnt to write like that?

There was no question of my ignoring the note. Who ever's hand had made the beautiful script knew that my curiosity was bound to get the better of me. Or did the sender mistakenly think I might know who he was? It had to be someone playing the fool. A grown-up. It was grown-up handwriting.

I didn't go riding with Lukas. Instead I took *Gone With the Wind* and strolled down to the fort with Bennie and Mervyn while Dominic stayed to practise. I told them about Scarlett O'Hara and the American Civil War. As we entered the fort Bennie said he smelt fire. And kaffir. Look, clearly someone had made a fire near the back. We swept out dead coals and ashes. Mervyn guessed it was probably one of the farm kaffirs who came down to have a romantic camp-fire fuck. Bennie said we should report it to Mr Mathison. The blacks aren't allowed down here in our forts! We decided against reporting; didn't want teachers snooping around our sanctuary.

The ashes didn't interest me. While Bennie and Mervyn spoke, my thoughts were elsewhere. Could it have been Dom, who would sneak down from the conservatory so that we could have a quick toss in the orchards? No; we had done it the night before. And why in the middle of the orchard when there were no leaves to hide us? I looked up, through the greening poplars, across at the orchards bathed in huge brush strokes of white and pink. And why not in the orange grove, where we did it in summer? Attention still on the mysterious note, but trying to hide my preoccupation, I told Bennie and Mervyn that Lukas and I were angry at Mr Walshe for refusing to let us name Cassandra's four-month-old foal. We wanted to call it Sea Cottage for a horse that had been shot at the Durban July Handicap. Mr Walshe felt it was an unoriginal name and the associations with a wounded horse no good. What about Little Prince, I suggested to Mr Walshe, there's a wonderful book . . . But Mr Walshe said the little stallion was only going to be little for a while. What about calling Cassandra and King's foal Dragon's Prince? Mountain for the Berg, Prince to show he was heir to the King.

Gone With the Wind – the thickest book I'd ever read – in hand, I drifted from the fort, saying to Bennie and Mervy I was off to read for a while on Second Rugby Field. Across the deserted field I cut into the bottom of the orchard, then doubled back through the blooming fruit trees as bees and insects zoomed around in the late afternoon sun. How am I to know for sure which are the plum trees? There were a few sections of plum, I knew from summer when the trees were covered in fruit, but now it was just the pink, white and purple of blossoms. Down the overgrown rows I strolled, darting eyes: will it be Dominic, or Jacques? Higher, closer to school.

The little woollen cap stuck up above the kakibos amongst the flowering trees. Back turned to me. It may be a farmhand. But the shoulders were not covered in the uniform of the labourers: no blue overall. The head turned. Then, smiling, he rose. My heart leapt into my throat. No! No, no, no! What is *he* doing here? The scraggly beard, the long filthy hair sticking out in stringy oily strands from beneath the cap. The yellow smile, the missing tooth.

More than a year had passed since I'd seen him in the Bowen Street garden; no, on Toti's main street! My eyes flew over Groot-Oom Klaas. Klasie. Klasie. Klasie. Oupa Liebenberg's name for him. The man before me cast a glance at the footpath in the distance. Then he stepped in amongst the branches, most of him hidden amongst the blossoms. His grin spread. What is he doing *here*? He must go, at once. I'll turn around and run. I felt powerless. It was like a nightmare. Here! Of all places. Bad enough when he showed up at home; but here! I stepped to the furthest reach of the branches.

He moved towards me and I froze.

'Hello, Karl'tjie.'

'Hello, Groot-Oom Klaas?'

'I thought I'd come and surprise you. Halfway house between Durban and Jo'burg. A perfect stopover. Respite from the rigours of the road.'

'How did you know where to find me, Uncle Klaas?'

He chuckled, a ghastly wet smoker's sound: 'I always know where you are. Don't you remember last year, I saw you in Amanzimtoti – where the waters are sweet? Instead of going on from Estcourt direct to Johannesburg, took a side road. Didn't get any lifts, mind you. Walked all the way from the main road to here. Three days and three nights.'

'Uncle Klaas . . . I'm going to get into trouble. Anyone could pass by, down the footpath and see me,' I whispered, motioning with my eyes to the path two hundred yards away. 'We're not allowed in the orchards. This place is very strict.' I lifted the book to my chest.

He stepped back into the wrapping of branches and pink blooms;

into the centre of the row of trees. A phantom in a haze of pink blossoms.

'No one can see me.'

'Uncle Klaas . . .' I began, wanting only to tell him to leave, but could not. A minute part of me felt pity or something humane. And, the proddings of intrigue. Where was he staying? And how did he get to Beauty? This could be an adventure, but no, it was not one I wanted! No, no, he had to leave. This could ruin everything. Suddenly my recent happiness seemed strung in a precarious equilibrium, about to be snapped. Into chaos. Not only was it too dangerous.

It was shameful.

He was mad, sick, disgusting, dirty. He was shameful but felt no shame. Shame by association. That was the problem.

'Where are you . . . staying, Uncle Klaas?'

'Below the ford.'

'In the bush?'

He nodded, perpetuating the smile.

'Aren't you cold?'

'Fire, Karl'tjie, fire keeps one warm. And when it rains there are the forts. Some nice buildings you boys have down there. Yours is nice. Strong and neat. And soon the days will be warm. Summer is coming.'

Oh my God. No. No. I smell kaffir, the ash! He's going into our fort! No, this is too much. He must go. 'How did you know which one, the fort, which one is mine, Uncle Klaas?' I tried to smile, to hide the terror and anger.

'I've been watching you for a while.'

Every time he spoke my heart sank. Sneaking through the bushes, spying on me and my friends, living in my — our — fort. *And soon the days will be warm, summer is coming!* That could mean only one thing: he's planning to stay! For who knows how long!

'Come with, you can see the day place. You can visit there, it's safe.'

'Uncle Klaas, I want to, but, they'll throw you off the farm . . .'

'Only if they find us! And if they chase me, then I can always come back. I always do. Come,' and he advanced from the cover of the tree, walked by me: a whiff of him, acrid, bitter, smoky. Kaffir. 'It's at least an hour before the whistle will blow.'

'Uncle Klaas . . .' I began to protest, but he walked on, the baggy brown slacks swishing through the oliebosse and kakibush. He was not like a man hiding, more like a king who owned the place. I trotted after him, casting glances behind me.

'What's that you're reading?'

'*Gone With the Wind.*'

He snorted: 'Crap. Who told you to read such rubbish?' And without waiting for an answer: 'Proust, Goethe, Wilde, Cesaire, Woolf, Dickinson, Hughes, Whitman . . . If you want to read, why not decent stuff?' Names I had never heard. 'Have you learnt to control your boisterousness? I hope not!' He laughed over his shoulder.

'Uncle Klaas, please, you must speak softly.'

We strode on in silence, cut south, away from the school, then across the river above our fort. Into the broad daylight he strutted, across the open veld on the other side of the stream. I wanted to weep. Out. Out. Out. In the open.

'Don't be scared,' he laughed, as if reading my mind, 'you can always tell them I'm family. Your uncle. Your great-uncle. Surely family has a visitation right?' He strolled on, not waiting for an answer again, clearly not expecting one either. Merely terrorising me.

'You're getting big. You could be a wrestler, you know. Do you and Lena still wrestle?'

'No. We stopped.'

'Pity. She's a strong girl. Why did you stop?'

'She got breasts.'

'She used to beat you.'

'Not after she got tits. I use to hit her on her tits and that stopped the wrestling because Bokkie said she'd get breast cancer.'

'I saw your mum a few weeks ago in Toti.'

'She wrote . . .'

'You have a beautiful mother, you know that?'

'Yes. I know.'

'Just so insecure. Very insecure. Pity. And so long-suffering. Martha the Martyr. Her selflessness will drive you crazy.'

'. . . Uncle Klaas?' The answer was of little interest to me. I would rather have silence, but while we spoke I could try and forget about any number of eyes that may be upon me. De Man and the tramp. Did you guys see De Man crossing the veld with a white tramp? Uncle Klaas rambled on about my mother choking on her silence, always feeling sorry for herself while pretending to be happy, being too dependent on Bok. About Bok being a woman's man with more charm than was good for any one soul. His torn shoes showed red socks, a tear in the calf of his one leg. And I could again smell him. If Bennie knew that this was the pong in our fort! The further we went the greater grew my revulsion and anger at the creature striding ahead of me. Who does he think he is, coming here and speaking like this about my family? He hardly knows us, sees us once a year.

'Your father,' he continued, 'is a basic shit. Not unlike most of the world, I suppose.'

If he didn't stop I was going to turn around and walk away. How dare he – human dregs that he is – come here and talk about Bok in this way? He's mad! Only a beggar. A vulture. Coming scavenging from the family whenever he needed money or food. Well, you won't get a blue dime from me. Anyway, you wouldn't be able to use Hills. As we approached the V Forest road I begged him to wait, to make certain no one was approaching; the riders could be returning at any moment. He chuckled but granted my request. When it was clear there was no one on the road, we crossed into the cluster of pines downstream from the bridge.

'Uncle Klaas, I must go back. The whistle will blow and I'll pick up serious trouble.'

'And then of course cheating those black peasants with this curio business.'

'Bok doesn't cheat them. He creates work for them. Job opportunities and he has to make a profit. Uncle Klaas, I must go back.'

'We're almost there, just come so that you can see where to come and visit.'

Mad! He is crazy. Out of his bracket if he thinks I'll set foot near him, ever again.

Below the ford, between where one could still hear the rush of water from the sluices and above the wattles where the kleilat fights happened, he made his way through the reeds and a thick grove of bulrushes. Uncle Klaas leading me into the bush. We stood in a small clearing amongst the reeds. Nothing except a bundle of clothes and empty tins of curried fish; the evidence of a fire; reeds flattened where obviously he had been sleeping. A blanket; a plastic Pick and Pay bag. Horrible. How could he live like this.

'We need another blanket.'

'You have a blanket,' I said, pointing. 'You don't need another.'

He inclined his head to the reeds, shifted his gaze from me to there. I followed his eyes. The book almost dropped from my grip. There, behind the lush green stalks and leaves, was a black face, glistening yellowish eyes. I stared for only a moment. I turned on the man beside me. Terror, outrage. I shook my head. I was ready to weep. Suddenly I whispered: 'Fuck off, Uncle Klaas. I didn't invite you here. Go away. Don't ever send me little notes again. Fuck off out of my life.'

I turned and I ran, turned left on the road, crossed the drif, ran through the poplar forest to where the first forts began. Here I slowed down and began to walk; clutching the book to my heaving chest. Thinking of the mad gene.

On a rock below the old pump-house I sat down, panting, trying to expel Uncle Klaas from my mind. And the other one. That he brings a black man here! I strolled back towards our fort, past a group of Juniors playing touch rugby, looking around, wondering whether we had been seen. Mervyn and Bennie were gone from our

fort. Across, below the cliffs on the other side, white flowers had
begun to bloom. I stretched my neck, squinted to see what they were.
Had not noticed them there before. Some sort of wild iris, perhaps.
Opened the book — marked by a pressed vine leaf at page 56 — and
tried to read. I had forgotten everything, everything the book was
about. Go back to the first line, the beginning. What a marvellous
sentence: *Scarlett O'Hara was not beautiful, but men seldom realised it when
caught by her charm as the Tarleton twins were.* What an original beginning!
What *is* he doing here! When I write my first book, I will begin with
a sentence of high originality such as this, so that the reader is caught,
spellbound, compelled to read on. That's so clever, so memorable.
Beginnings; so very, very important.

10

Bok, Jonas and Boy went on elephant patrol to Ndumu and Mozi. A
young Bantu had come to HQ to say a lone bull had come marauding from Mozambique and was raiding the maize and madumbi. Two
women had been hurt and a village plundered.

Late afternoon Bok and the boys stumbled unexpectedly into an
encampment of rhino poachers. One of the poachers reached for his
gun and fired a shot that struck Jonas in the arm. Boy fired and
killed the poacher. They rounded up the rest of the gang, put on the
handcuffs and walked them to HQ from where they were taken to the
cells in Empangeni. Jonas's arm wasn't too badly injured and I went
with him and Bok to hospital in Empangeni to have the bullet
extracted. He was given eight stitches in his arm. When Bok removed
the black thread with pliers a few weeks later the scar was blue and
shiny; smooth and wrinkly to the touch of my fingers. Bernice's belly
scar had since gone from red, to pink, to light brown; the same
smooth skin with tiny, tiny wrinkles.

I went to visit Jonas and Boy at the kraal. Jonas made the little masks and statues that Bok gave to Aunt Siobhain to sell to the curio shops in Durban. Boy made grass place mats, some of them decorated with small beads or interwoven with colourful pieces of wool. I grab a mask and a grass place mat and run away with Jonas and Boy calling after me to return their things. Jonas follows me as I run. He grabs me from behind and holds me by the shoulders.

'No steal, Kal. Kal no steal.' Shaking his head, frowning at me.

I burst into tears and say: 'Mina tella Baas Bok wena shaja Kal. Bok shaja wena.'

He has done nothing more than grab me by the arm. Yet, I have threatened to tell Bok that he, Jonas, has hit me. I'm warning him that Bok will beat him. Bok will of course do no such thing, that much I know. But of my power and Jonas's language — or rather our commanding variant of imperatives — I know enough, already at five, to threaten him even as I weep. Yet, the moment when I will grasp the meanings of our daily barbarism, the layers upon layers of brutal significance, as well as when I care enough to inquire with any measure of self-awareness about the boys and myself, that moment is a future telling beyond the pages bound in your hands. For now, Jonas glowers at me, leaves me with the quarry in mine. He goes back to the compound. I to Mbanyana. There I say to Bokkie that Jonas and Boy have sent gifts for us to hang from the walls of our reed lounge.

Within days I'm back with the boys, though I never plunder art from the compound again.

11

Mervyn was the first to be taken from prep. He didn't come back. Then Lukas. He didn't return either. Then Bennie. Then me. I was taken by someone — I have no memory of whom it was, a teacher, a Senior, a prefect — into the night; it was said heavy snow was falling on the mountains. With jeans and long johns — after supper the whole school had been sent upstairs to don the long underpants – we wore T-shirts, our black polo-neck jerseys and grey bush jackets. Whomever it was that fetched me from the classroom led me through the lighted quad, past the dribble of guests arriving for the Juniors' Wednesday evening performance. The Senior Choir was set to leave for Israel's International Festival of Choirs. It was freezing. Instead of taking me through the concert hall, I was taken around the exterior of the building, to Mathison's outside door. The curtains were drawn. I have no recollection of how I got inside, whether I entered after a knock, or whether a voice told me to come in.

Mervyn, Lukas and Bennie's backs stared at me. On the worn red carpet, they stood facing the desk. Mr Mathison told me to shut the door. I fell in beside Bennie. Was our dorm untidy? Had we been talking after lights out? My heart sank at the sight of the three men behind the desk. I could guess, but still hoped against hope that I was wrong. The gravity of whatever we had done was written into the three faces, the rigid postures. On the desk's glass top, lay the bamboo cane, behind it in black leather, the Bible.

Only Mr Mathison, from his seat at the desk, spoke. His voice was sparse, wounded, sad, no anger to be found there: 'What the four of you have been up to is beneath language.' He paused and stared pensively at the closed door. 'Not even animals do this.'

A flash of Miss Roos walking through the music hall.

'How could you defile yourselves like this?' It looked as if tears may at any moment stream down his cheeks.

Through two closed doors, the sounds of applause reached into his office. The Juniors had obviously walked onto stage in the auditorium.

'Where do you get this disgusting behaviour from? Do you have any idea what you have done? Nowhere in the world, in no human society, is this accepted. It is the gravest sin you can ever commit . . . God's Word tells us – in the New and Old Testament, Mervyn – that your kind deserves death . . . This, you know, is why God destroyed

Sodom and Gomorrah. With fire and brimstone from heaven.' He reached for the Bible. Opened it, paged, and read, something from somewhere about our kind deserving death. Suddenly his eyes brimmed behind the glasses, shining in the light. He cleared his throat and stood up. 'In Sodom, every single person died except Lot and his daughters.' Beneath my jersey and bush jacket trickles of sweat ran down my back, my sides. The headmaster was going to weep; he again cleared his throat; eyes still ready to spill tears. 'Do you have any idea what this could do to your parents?'

This could not be happening. This, Bok, Bokkie, dear Jesus what have I done?

'If they ever find out, do you know what it will do to them? It will kill your mothers and shame your fathers to their last breath.' He broke off, stared each of us in the face by turn. 'I cannot, not for a moment, believe that a parent – any parent – would want a child who has dragged himself through such filth. It would be better for you to go to orphanages. That – Lukas, Mervyn, Bennie, Karl – that is where you will be sent to perish before you burn in hell for this unspeakable act.' The Junior Choir was singing, 'Me Who Melech Hakavod', the soloist's voice a thread sliding through wood of doors, the cracks between doors and floors, doors and their frames.

Mathison came round the desk and stood in front of us. He was quiet for a while, seemed again to be searching our faces. When he spoke his tone had hardened; now he was angry; there was no longer a trace of tears. He spoke in English: 'Let me give you an idea of the sort of life you are in for . . . There is a city in America . . .' For the first time in my life I heard of a place called San Francisco; a place of perversion, sin and depravity; a place of satanic orgies and defilements: 'That den of perversion is the Sodom and Gomorrah of the modern world. The kind of people who live there are the kind of people who do the unspeakable things you four have done.' He paused and sat down on the edge of the desk. I blinked away tears. 'But, as providence would have it,' Mathison went on, 'in God's all-seeing plan – that place, that city of sin, has been built on the San Andreas Fault – a fault line that runs through that entire section of America. Do you know what a fault line is? It is a defect, a flaw in the earth's crust, that rubs against itself for hundreds of years, and then, suddenly, it shakes and trembles and the earth quakes and falls in on itself. That fault line is the key that can unlock your understanding of what you have done. And why do you think I'm telling you this? Why do I want you to dredge that fault line? Lukas? Mervyn? Bennie? Karl?' His stare burning into our shame; his silence underscoring our profanity. He removed his glasses, and nodding at us: 'Because the same thing is going to happen to San Francisco, the same thing that happened three thousand years ago to Sodom and Gomorrah. God will drag it into the burning recesses of the earth; it will disappear off the face of the planet, swallowed as if it had never existed.'

He broke off as applause drifted from the auditorium. Slid the glasses back into place. He said we were to be punished for our crime and defilement in a way that we would never forget. He said expulsion was really what we deserved – expulsion not only from the school, but from the human race – but that they had decided to be lenient, mostly for the sake of our parents and to spare the school public disgrace. He said that we would be punished in a way that would stay with us for the rest of our days; a way that would stand as a beacon of light to keep us from ever again venturing off God's blessed path of spiritual and bodily holiness. And then, as Mathison broke off, Buys rose from his chair. I wanted to cry. I had never been caned by Buys. The very reason for our being on earth had been erased by this deed. 'The very reason your parents brought you into the world.' For a year and half I had managed to stay out of his claws; through hundreds of cuts from Uncle Charlie, Mr Mathison, both Junior and Secondary Choir masters: and now it had come to this. Tchaikovsky's 'None But the Lonely Heart' was drifting from the auditorium. How many were we going to get? Six, so it was said, was the maximum. No one had ever heard of a boy getting more than six. And this was going to be six. The severity – depravity – of what we had done warranted six, if God could swallow us into the earth, why, what heavenly reason did these men have to not give us each six of the best? The long johns! Oh mercy, mercy, will help, at least a little, cushion it a bit, please let it help against Buys, no, not much, but it will help, please, please don't let me be first.

Buys took hold of Lukas's shoulder and told him to bend forward and hold onto the desk. There was again the sound of applause. As the choir started on the Brahms lullaby, Buys lifted the cane till its tip almost touched the ceiling. It sang as it sped down, its force almost broke Lukas's grip and he seemed to stumble forward. Dear Jesus, no, no, no. How can they allow this, we'll die, better than telling Bok, Mervyn gulping, why, why, please not six. Then the next one. This time Lukas really held onto the desk; didn't flinch. The third time Buys's feet seemed to lift from the carpet as the cane struck Lukas, whose hands broke loose and he flew forward onto the desk, hands grabbing at nothing. If it's like this for Lukas, we can't make it; he'll kill us. Lukas, coming up, straightened and turned to face Buys. Tears streamed down his cheeks, even as he grinned.

'Bend, over, I'm not finished with you.'

Lukas turned back. Now his shoulders were shaking. The fourth cut ripped into his bum and he let out a cry, came up, swung around and began sobbing.

'Next one.'

Oh my God, only four. Thank you, thank you. Only four. But why four why not three? Dear Jesus, if Lukas cries, how will I take it? None of us moved. Buys pointed.

Mervy. Mervy stepped forward. He bent and looked over his shoulder. Buys told him to face forward. I closed my eyes. I couldn't watch. Not Mervy. I wanted to put my fingers in my ears; tell them that Mervy was going to scream, that the audience would hear. But the choir was singing, I don't know what – any song, Rilke's 'Elegies' by Holst, Poulenc's 'Litanies à la vierge noire', Saint-Saëns's 'A

Salutaris' or 'Tantum Ergo' or Copland's 'The House on the Hill' –
louder than anything till now. And Mervy did – a split second before
the first cut into him – let out a scream and shot upright, clasping his
hands to his bum, already sobbing. Buys grabbed him by the jacket,
turned him back to the desk. Just as Buys was about to bring down
the cane, Mervyn jumped up and almost sank to his knees as he
faced the man with the cane still above his head. Applause from the
auditorium. Buys yanked Mervy up by the hair, and held him down
over the desk. Leipoldt's 'Boggom and Voetsek', through the doors.
He brought down the cane and again Mervyn screamed, turned his
head while Buys held his neck. Mervy begged, howling. After the third
cut, the denim on his bum had changed colour. It couldn't be pee.
After the fourth, Mervy no longer screamed, he just turned around
and sobbed into his arms. I glanced at him stepping back into line,
caught Lukas, who was still crying.

And then it is me. Please God, Jesus, no, no hate, Karl, hate, hate,
be strong, hate, hate, strength comes from hate, don't show them,
show fucking Buys, try and be brave, Karl, don't cry out, whatever you
do, don't cry out. I bend forward. Still Leipoldt, say with them: 'n
hand vol gruis uit die Hantam wyk, wa-boom gnarrabos blare, gister
was ek arm maar nou is ek ryk . . . Instead of holding with my arms
forward, I lean across the desk's surface and clasp my hands backwards
around the overhang, almost resting my forehead on the glass. When
it comes, against everything I will a white-hot iron thrust into my
spine, I stumble forward, shoot upright and am at once crying; breathing through my mouth. I want to beg. Won't beg, will not beg, won't
help . . . But I cannot, cannot get myself to bend again. He takes me
by the neck and turns me back to the desk. Applause, music, if I start
screaming loud they'll have to stop, but I cannot scream, everyone will
know. The second also throws me up and I clasp my bum and sob, my
face now turned to the ceiling. I see nothing. He is killing me. When
I come up after the third, I am howling, looking from man to man, all
three, pleading with my eyes, my sobs, my tears. The fourth, a fist of

fire in the small of my back, dizzying. I almost stumble as I fall back into line. My legs are trembling twigs, I sob and weep, I do not take in what is done to Bennie, I don't care, kill him. The three of us, crying. Then, before I know what has happened to Bennie, he is beside me again. *Te Deum* from Britten's *Requiem*.

Buys must have put the cane down on the glass top and walked back to join the other two. No one spoke. When our crying had subsided, it was Mathison: 'You four stand here tonight, drenched in shame. You are shame itself. That you must never doubt. None of you will ever speak about this again. Do you understand me?'

We sobbed, whimpered.

'Answer me.'

'Yes, Sir.'

'You know what happened to Lot's wife, don't you? She turned into a pillar of salt. Lot se vrou, 'n Soutpilaar, verstaan julle my? Because she looked back.' He paused. 'Don't look back at what you've done, never. Never speak about it, for to speak about it is to look back and to turn into a pillar of salt. You must move on.' He again seemed on the verge of tears. I looked at him but could only catch phrases of what he was saying. Something by Samuel Barber.

'You three, go.' He motioned at the others. 'Back to prep. You have been caned for not changing your sheets. Do you understand me?'

'Yes, Sir.'

'I've had the chance to speak to you three alone. Now, Karl, I want to talk to you.'

The others had left and I alone faced the men. Like for the audition. Mathison said he had reason to suspect that, while I had not been the ringleader, I had egged the others on in our moral decrepitude. He said he had spoken extensively to the others. It was clear that I as much as Lukas had been the one to instigate the immorality.

Then, like another blow, this time final and to my head, he asked: 'Karl. What is this business about goats?'

It is the slaughter. I want nothing; only to die. Please, please, let me die; let me vanish. I want to run. I want Bok, I want Bokkie. They who will not love me. Leave me alone! Let me be! I want to scream in helplessness. I am only a boy, I am only twelve. I am innocent.

'The makwedini, Sir, in the kraals when I was small. They did it to the sheep,' I sob, dragging my sleeves across my eyes, the snot-pit of my nose.

'Then, why did you tell Miss Roos that you yourself had done it?'

Had Lukas said anything? How much did they know? No, they could kill Lukas, and he would not have said anything. Lie, Karl, lie, lie, lie for your life, cling to your tattered dignity.

'I didn't, Sir, I think Miss Roos misunderstood what I said, Sir.'

'That is because they're heathen savages, Karl. It is the most disgusting thing in the world. The poor animals have no choice; it is worse even than what you have been punished for tonight.' Again he takes the black leather-bound book, opens it, reads.

My bum felt like red-hot coals had been thrown in there.

'You grew up in Zululand, didn't you?'

'Yes, Sir.'

'Do the Zulus call their boys makwedini?'

Why was he asking this? I waited. He waited. An answer was expected of me. But what lurked behind his question? I answered: 'No, Sir.' Again I waited. He stared at me, wanting something to sink in to my recognition. That he knew I was lying.

Then it struck me. Oh Jesus, Jesus, why! Why! Why can't you leave me alone, Lukas, umfaan, piccanin, kwedini, amakwetha, what does it matter, I just made a mistake with the word. Just a word. I wanted to cry again; wanted to beg them to leave me alone.

I shook my head.

'No, they don't, Karl, do they? Go.'

My head was going to burst; mad gene, vein in head, Bok oh please not find out, let it be over, cold, my bum, Mervy, snot on my jacket sleeve.

I walked through the freezing dark. Run away, go hide, in the caves, in a shell, in the bush, Mkuzi, why, past the concert hall where the Juniors are singing, maybe, then, for it was somewhere, through the door or through the window, I heard 'Da Drausst Auf die Gruen Au'.

It was not Christmas, but they sang it that night.

Back to the classroom. I registered the schluck-schluck in my veld-skoens; realised that at some point during it all I had pissed myself.

Prep was over; the classroom empty. I walked upstairs to E Dorm. Applause and shouts of bravo, encore. Encore. A million thoughts and images – monkey-brain I might call it today. Somewhere in amongst those I was also struck by something else, something a writer in the retelling may withhold from revealing as a literary device to enhance affect or effect: during the whole eternity the four of us had spent in that office, then me alone, while the men sat there, while Buys had caned us, had sat there shaking his head, nodding and grunting while Mr Mathison read from the Holy Book and told us we represented the lowest forms of earthly life, the other one – sitting quietly with his hands before him on the desk – had not moved. Not stirring, not speaking a word, not twitching a muscle, like a Sphinx, Mr Cilliers had sat there.

12

Jonas held the ram's horns, bending its neck backwards while Boy and Bokkie held on to its twitching feet. Its eyes, bulging big and glassy, blinked rapidly. Then it struggled one more time, threw its horns from side to side. Bok brought the silver blade down onto the jugular – jutting and bulging – and in an instant – as the blade was jerked across – blood spurted in a thick red jet onto the sand. Within seconds the fountain turned first to little spurts from different veins, then to trickles running down the velvety brown hide. The blood

curdled, made knots and blotches in the sand. You could pick it up –
like soft pebbles that disintegrated with a slight rub. Then the cutting
up began. This part for our biltong. That part for the kraal.

13

The back of his head, his shoulders, his back, moving over, hands
above the piano, the piano keys. To his left, beside the organ, the
ensemble, eyes on him, poised, concentrated. To his right, in front of
the long windows, the soloists' heads silhouetted against the late
sun – Dominic, to his left with Erskin Louw, Gerhard Conradie and
Mike van der Bijlt – nodding time. Text from the Apocalypse, the
Book of Revelation. Bassoon and double bass, then the cello and
viola, D-A-E and then the move, gently, to E minor, gentle, gentle resolution to D major, then the brasses setting tone, solemn, careful, D
major, then to B minor; B, orchestra repeats, voices – the magic of
communion is about to happen – almost emulating the instruments:

Erskin: *Sanctus* taken up by Gerhard, joined by Dominic, then
Mike's deep, diminuendo, soft brass, legato, repeated, calling a God of
power and might:

> *Sanctus, Sanctus, Sanctus Dominus,*
> *Deus, Sabaoth*

Then the brass, almost inaudible the repetition of *Sanctus, sanctus* and
he bounces, the staccato and crescendo quartet:

> *Pleni sunt coeli et terra gloria tua*

and the whole orchestra takes it up before Dominic comes in to the
holy of holies with *Osanna in excelsis,* which the others repeat, dramatically, and Dominic's final *excelsis* when at once it is over, carrying

away into the afternoon quiet of school passages. The silence of a boarding school's deserted afternoon. I take them in together: joined in the music, the man and the boy. One's head bowed, the other's up, eyes closed. Intertwined. Auspicious. Dusts twirl and spiral like stars and planets in the rays of white sun.

Unaware of me up there. Looking down on them. How would I choose? It occurred to me that I may have to do that. If it was not already done. I would not think of it; if I do not think it, the choice does not exist. They spoke; the ensemble began to pack away instruments. The other soloists left. Dominic tarried. Voices and laughter. I leant over the balustrade, trying to hear what was being said or wanting to insinuate myself into the intimacy of their togetherness.

'More tremolo . . . High G . . . Needs recitativo drammatico without losing your tone colour. But don't push so hard. Your voice sounds tired . . .'

'There's something here that reminds me of Mozart . . . Requiem . . . My Grade Eight sonata . . .'

'Haydn . . . Sonata form . . . Actually, Handel's fugue patterns . . .'

Dominic looks up. I raise my hand and he his as he smiles. Jacques turns, lifts his gaze, and stops what he was saying. We stare, as if all three of us have caught each other out.

'I thought you were going riding?' Dom asks with his head thrown back.

'We're back early, so I came to listen.' I answer, standing up with my hands on the balustrade.

'What do you think, Karl? Of the Sanctus?'

'Brilliant, Sir,' I say, hating myself for having nothing more original to offer, no way of entering their conversation as an equal.

'Meet you outside,' Dom says, and moves to the door. I turn to go, then look down again at Jacques. His eyes go to Dominic, then skim the hall before he nods at me, signals that I should come tonight.

14

He must have been nine or ten or thereabout. He was at the front door in the passage dressed in uniform with his box suitcase in hand, ready to walk to school. His sisters were already halfway down the asbestos driveway. He heard his mother's voice, angry, furious, growing louder in her and his father's bedroom. He knew what he had done. His father came down the passage and he froze, terrified he was about to be beaten. But the man merely walked up to him and placed a hand on the boy's shoulder. Very gently. He spoke softly. He said many things – most of which the boy would later not remember – while he looked into the boy's blue eyes with his own even bluer. The man may have smelt of smoke or Old Spice aftershave and toothpaste. Before turning and walking away, he said: 'If you ever so much as think of doing it again, I will kill you.'

15

And we didn't. Haven't. Ever, spoken about it.

I found the three of them on their beds. Only Lukas looked up when I came in. Why was Almeida not there? Already in the shower? His towel was gone from the back of the locker; his riding cap was missing; his dressing gown no longer over Dominic's on the hook. Almeida had evacuated E Dorm – I knew it without asking. For the previous three weeks, ever since Dominic's departure, Steven had slept in Dominic's bed. Now he was gone. I knew, again without needing input from any of them, that none of us would even mention his leaving. Almeida must have known: from the moments we were summoned from prep. I had; he must have. Suddenly I hated Steven. More applause from downstairs; long and drawn out. Who had told Steven to move back to C Dorm? Uncle Charlie, obviously. So, he knows too.

Their eyes – and I suppose mine – were still red and swollen.
Mervy's face and neck were the clour of a beetroot, his red hair a
scrubbing brush set in all directions. Only a blind, mad, idiot could
not see our state. Who, for a second, would believe that they had done
this to us for not changing sheets? Anybody and nobody. As much as
I knew the four of us would not ever speak about it, I knew they had
to suspect – as much as Almeida knew – that it had been me. I had
betrayed them. And how, I wondered briefly, how had Mathison
known to not call Almeida? How, how in the wide world of one hundred and twenty boys, did they know it was only the four of us, and
not Almeida? Almeida had been there – that night – yet he hadn't
been called. What had Mathison said to each of them, as he called
them in, ahead of me? Too many questions. Impossible to ask.

D Dorm was preparing for showers. Around me no one moved. I
frowned at Lukas.

'Uncle Charlie said we're to wait. We'll go after them.'

We always go with D. Uncle Charlie knows.

D bundled down their staircase to the showers. Uncle Charlie's
voice called up saying we were to get undressed, put on our gowns and
wait till we were summoned. Of course he knows.

We began undressing. Bennie was the first out of his jeans.

'Fuck, it was sore. Bastard, bastard, cunt, fucker, poes, hoer, moer,
hond, teef, kont,' he whispered. His bum, turned towards me, was covered in a series of angry ridges.

I peeled off my trousers. As I rolled down my long johns I smelt
the pee before I saw the yellow stains all the way down the white hose.

Mervyn whimpered. He was bent forward, looking into the long
johns now collapsed around his ankles. Pink smudges. He strained his
neck to look over his shoulder at his buttocks, and as he turned I
could see first just the pink of his bum and then the purple and red
where the skin had been torn and open flesh stuck through the purple
welts that sat there – an inch above the skin – like crusts of rugged
red candle wax. I checked my long johns. Nothing. Just the piss

stains. I turned my neck, to see my bum. With my fingertips I felt them, corrugations, huge, but mercifully no blood. How was Mervy ever going to sit? Lukas's bum: purple and swollen over the grey of a week before when he and Bennie had got it from Uncle Charlie for untidy lockers.

E Dorm was no longer called to shower with the other Standard Fives. Maybe ten days. I didn't count. The four of us showered alone under Uncle Charlie's supervision. Then he said that starting the following evening we were to go back to the old routine. Showers with D. It was only then I realised we had not permanently been banished. Uncle Charlie offered no explanation. I suspected it had to do with Mervyn's bum. They had only wanted to prevent us from having to explain the chaos of Mervyn's bum, and, to a lesser extent, the damage to our own.

The longer you sat, the easier it became; but it was winter, and the cold seemed to make it worse. Morning PT, which had always been one of the highlights of my day – the mist, the cold, the clouds of breath as we ran through the dewy grass of forest and veld – was horrible that first week: my buttocks were wounds wanting to tear loose and separate from my body. Riding was out of the question. Lukas said I should come with him for he refused to let a beating keep him from the stables. But I couldn't face the pounding of the saddle. I wondered what Beauty thought if by chance she had seen the piss stains in my long johns on washday; or, more than my piss, Mervy's blood, also on his sheets and pyjamas. My and Lukas's bums – perhaps hardy from regular canings and the saddles – began to turn into psychedelic blue, green and yellow tattoos a while before Bennie's and at least a week before Mervyn's. As Bennie was caned as often as Lukas and I, I was fascinated that he, our hardy little Rottweiler, took so long to heal. The saddle, while it probably didn't lessen the pain of the caning for Lukas and me, did seem to have a neutralising effect on the visible damage left afterwards.

*

Had Lukas or I – I wondered a few times before letting that and the betrayal go for ever – indeed been the instigators, that night? Had Lukas and I been the ones to suggest we do It? And if we were the ringleaders, who had come up with the idea first? That was not, by any measure, the way I remembered it, then or now. It just seemed to happen; without suggestion.

After lights-out, Bennie and I had snuck into D Dorm to terrorise Niklaas Bruin. Once Niklaas was crying and after we got back to E, we had pushed each other around playfully and said it was too early to go to sleep. Lukas suggested we get out onto the roof and watch the moon. All five of us, including Almeida, put on our dressing gowns, got out of the window and walked down the side of the slanted corrugated iron roof. A hundred times before, when the fruit was ripe in the orchards, we had thought of climbing down. But it was a twenty-foot drop from the roof to the ground and the gutter was too rusty to fasten sheets. So we had just let it go.

It was cold and we knew we wouldn't stay out long. High above V Forest a veld fire cut a brilliant red X into the mountainside. Lukas said he wished we had cigarettes. We argued about which was north and which south. We looked for north in the stars and said that was where Dominic was now, somewhere in Europe. Lukas and I showed the others how to read the Southern Cross to find true south. We whispered, aware that the school was just falling asleep, careful not to let our movements be heard on the roof. We spoke of exploring the cosmos. Maybe one day someone from Earth would live on the moon or Mars or Jupiter. There couldn't be life in any form on other planets because the Bible said so. I wondered what Dom would have said to that if he were there. Bennie wanted to become an astronaut. For a while we sat arguing about which Apollo had landed on the moon. Bennie was the only one who was certain it had been Apollo 11, citing the collection of silver coins commemorating America's space programme that he had garnered from Mobil petrol stations. It was quiet; just the river, no dogs barking, the fire too distant to carry its crackles to us. We too had gone silent. We went back up the roof. As we entered the dorm through the window, we started pushing each other around quietly, falling on top of each other. Wordless. We pulled down our pyjama pants and took turns to stick our penises into the cleavage of each others' buttocks. Not penetrating, just rubbing. I became aware that Almeida had withdrawn, had gone back to Dominic's bed. While I rubbed against Lukas who lay face down below me, I watched Almeida in the glow of the moon. He lay silently, his back to us. In a whisper I asked why he wasn't joining in, and he whispered back that it was against the Catholic Church. Lukas snorted into the pillow and we carried on, then changed partners and positions. It could have carried on for no longer than maybe ten minutes, nothing more. Just playing. When we were all back in our beds, Lukas announced that I was the best, because I had an okkerneut-piel. But Mervyn is also circumcised I said. Lukas said Mervy's was too big and too red. Like an ostrich cock. We laughed and Mervy told Lukas to get lost with his willy the size of a pinky and how did he know it was red in the dark unless Lukas had been eyeing it in the showers? Our laughter echoed down the stairs and Almeida said we should quiet down before Uncle Charlie heard the noise. Then we joked with Almeida for being too chicken to do it or have it done to him. He didn't respond. I felt something like disappointment – though that concept denotes something too strong – at his resistance to joining us; partly because it broke the unity of our group, partly, and only very, very far in the recesses of my mind, because I wanted to touch Almeida, his dark skin, his curly black head, the ears like brown shells, the small penis in the dense tuft of hair; the chest like marble. I said nothing of this. Instead, said I thought Mervy's was the best because it was as big as a stallion's. We giggled and guffawed some more and then slowly went quiet. As they drifted to sleep around me, I heard the squeaking of Lukas's bedsprings. Knew what he was doing: wanking, tossing off. Was he able to come yet? As he said that day on their farm? *Masturbation* as the dictionary had beneath *mastodon*: *The stimulation or manipulation of one's own genitals, esp. to orgasm; the stimulation, by manual or other means exclusive of coitus, of another's genitals.* And then, to *coitus: sexual intercourse between a man and a woman, a coming together, uniting,* and below that, *coitus interruptus: coitus that is intentionally interrupted by withdrawal before ejaculation of semen into the vagina.* From Lukas's bed came the increase in speed, the loud breathing, the rattling of the bed. Then the quiet.

16

A grey heavy sky.

Bok's Land Rover in the driveway. He was home early. I had taken Simba along to Camelot in the paddock. Lena and Bernice were down on the beach with the Pierces. Leaving Simba outside I went in through the kitchen. House dark and hulled in quiet. I heard something in their bedroom. I walked down the passage. Their door was open.

Bokkie sat on the edge of their bed with Bok's arms around her. Both crying. Bok noticed me and motioned me closer.

'Dademan died this afternoon.' A simple statement through my father's tears. I had never seen him cry like this.

Then, I see myself, throwing my head back, screaming; Bok and Bokkie, holding onto me as I wail, no, no, and we're all weeping, all three of us, them clasping me to them. I break from their arms and jump up and down. How, what happened? Bokkie says Dad has gone to a better place, that we must use that knowledge to console ourselves. At once, as quickly as I had started crying, I stop.

Dademan had gone to Addington Hospital for blood-pressure tests; nothing major, we had been told. Then, so Bok said, while he was still in hospital a blood clot had passed through his heart. Mumdeman had been with him, staying with Uncle Michael and

Aunt Siobhain while he was in hospital. The funeral in Durban would take place in three days' time. We'd be going.

I went outside to wait for Lena and Bernice. Bok said I shouldn't tell them; he would. Simba came running, waving his tail and I sat on the kitchen step and told the dog that Dademan was dead. Dead, I said, Dademan will go to heaven. Maybe it's adjacent to doggy heaven and Dademan would see Chaka and Suz. As I spoke, I began crying again, now as much about Dademan as about Chaka and Suz; about Jim and Nkosasaan and Boy whom I would never see again. Death was like saying goodbye: terrible, terrible, terrible. Death was something I had grown up with, seeing it every day in the jaws of lion, the arrow of a cheetah's speed felling a warthog or impala, vultures clustered on a rhino killed by poachers, the swoop of a fish eagle to clutch its food from the water, hyena laughing like cannibals over their rotten fest. Death, I knew, was part of the cycle of life. I thought I knew it, understood it, when Chaka and Suz had been put down in Umfolozi, as merely the way it was meant to be; no place for sentiment in the bush, Bok said, and I understood, agreed. But this was not the bush; this was not animals feeding to nourish themselves or dogs put to sleep for killing an antelope. This was Dad – Dademan. The man who told me stories of hunting and of the war. Who shot cines of us kids whenever he could. Who let me play with the radio at Charters Creek. Who was meant to come across the estuary on *Piper* and let me and Lena steer it back to their little jetty at high tide. And what about poor Mumdeman? Poor, poor Mumdeman. Born in an ox-wagon in Mozambique, working so hard, side by side with Dad to clear the land in Tanganyika. I suddenly wept tears for everything that had died around me during the years in Mkuzi and Umfolozi. I wanted to go back to Umfolozi, or better still, back to Mkuzi, where there was less death and less goodbye. Then I remembered the little warthogs, Lossie, bitten by a mamba, the horse Vonk shot after he broke his leg, and I didn't want to go back there either. Back to Tanzania, that's where I wanted to go; back to where I had been a baby and Dademan said I still had wings: there, where I was an angel in a land that was paradise. Before memory.

We got off school for two days and drove to Durban. Bok and Bokkie spoke about Dademan being buried in the Presbyterian church even though we were Dutch Reformed. Bokkie said it was a fine idea as a compromise between Aunt Siobhain's Catholicism and our Protestantism. Bokkie said that Aunt Siobhain had written recently anyway to say she was considering leaving the Catholic Church because of its formality and stiff outdatedness. Uncle Michael never went to church, in any case. Aunt Siobhain said maybe by changing to Presbyterian she could get him out of the clubhouse and into church. Now would be a good time, Bokkie said, now that our hard-headed hard-drinking uncle was so vulnerable after Dademan's death. We said nothing about the fact that neither of our parents ever set foot in the Matubatuba church. One of them would drive us there and sit reading the paper, waiting while we were in Sunday school.

A church is a church, Bok said. But Dademan would none the less be relieved to know he wasn't being buried from a cathedral with golden idols and crosses and the adornments of the rich. I asked whether it was true that Catholics stuck big safety pins through their tongues and chanted mantras to Satan while they burnt incense and walked down the aisle. Bokkie turned from the front seat and asked where I had come across such rubbish. I said I'd heard it from Sam Pierce. Bokkie said there you have it, allow the kids to mix with Makoppolanders and you get this sort of idiocy implanted in their brains. And what's more, she said, this business of boys going into girls' rooms had to stop. We were getting too old for that kind of mixing. Lena should probably also move in with Bernice. When we get back to St Lucia, Bokkie said, that's the end of hanging around the Pierces' trailer.

Bernice said Dademan was being kept in a morgue – a new word – a huge fridge where bodies lay frozen and blue. It sounded morbid, scary, perversely fascinating. I imagined a morgue to be quiet, like when one's head is under water. Like Bokkie's left ear. A place one wanted to be and didn't want to be all at the same time.

In Durban I got my first pair of long trousers with a zipper. To the funeral I wore the new check trousers with my black Bata school shoes and Bernice wore an old dress of Stephanie's and Lena one of Bernice's that had first been Stephanie's. Bokkie had to buy a black dress and a hat and Bok wore the black suit in which he and Bokkie were married. At the funeral everyone wept. It was horrible, seeing Uncle Michael and Bok, holding on to each other. It was ugly, ugly, seeing men cry. And Aunt Siobhain, and Stephanie and James. And Mumdeman, now so much smaller than I had remembered her from a mere two weeks before, clinging onto Sanna Koerant. I never again wanted to see an old woman cry but everyone said it was healthy that Mumdeman had not held back. Mumdeman didn't want Dademan's coffin in the church because it would distract our attention from the service and the minister's sermon, which was, after all, the important thing. So the first time we saw the coffin was when we came out of church and set off behind the hearse. All the cars had their lights on.

Brandy and Coke and cigarettes; no sentiment in that; can smell him even now; as I type. Mumdeman sat on a fold-out chair at the open grave while the minister gave another sermon. Bok, Uncle Michael, Oom Gerrie Theron and others from East Africa carried the coffin to the grave. They let it sink with a hydraulic lift. Before they started throwing in the soil, baskets of red rose petals circulated and we all walked around the grave, scattering petals. I tried to think of Dademan inside the wooden coffin. The nose, the De Man nose, the wrinkles and blond-grey hair — my hair — the busy, naughty blue eyes, my eyes, Bok's eyes. Were they closed or open? And what if he wasn't dead? Sam Pierce had told me a story of a woman who was buried alive. They dug her up and found scratch marks on the inside of the coffin. But Bok said that was rubbish; that we just had to accept that Dad was dead. Bokkie said that cremation was the new thing. This burying of people was a waste of valuable land; before you know it the entire surface of the earth will be nothing but row upon row of graves. Mumdeman had a plot beside Dademan. I didn't want to think about it; not Mumdeman, please let me die before anyone else in my family.

Driving back to St Lucia, Bernice told us that her friend Mona said death comes in threes. We should look out; be careful and warn the family. Bokkie told her we were Christians who didn't subscribe to that sort of superstitious belief. That was the property of the heathen who'd eat their words in hell.

Months later the Parks Board transferred Mumdeman to Midmar Dam. We all went over to Charters to help pack. And then, after Mumdeman's stuff had gone off to Midmar, Bok and Phinias carried the cines and slides and my trophies to the Land Rover. The mounted sable, Grant's gazelle and dick-dick heads; the slides and cines, everything Dademan had left me in his will. All to our garage in St Lucia and later to storage when we moved to Toti and then finally into Bok's garage office in Bowen Street.

17

The lead pipes, covered in their orange cloth, lay hidden behind the shoes at the bottom of the locker in my new dorm.

The five of us had been divided into separate dorms. After eighteen months together in E, they had split us up. Lukas was in G, about six beds away from Mervyn. Bennie and I were in F, nine beds between us. As soon as Dominic got back – Uncle Charlie responded to my query – he would go to the furthest end of G. It all took a few days to sink in. At first I felt only the deep loss, the loneliness, brought on by being removed from my friends. Coming back from that holiday Aunt Siobhain had come along with Bok and Bokkie to see the grand school I attended. When reception told us to take my things up to F, I already suspected what had happened. Uncle Charlie, welcoming parents at the desk, said that from now Juniors would occupy the school's small dormitories and no Seniors or Secondaries would reside outside of the massive C, F and G. I unpacked things into the new locker with Bokkie. Bok showed Aunt Siobhain around the building and gardens. There was no sign of Lukas, Mervyn or Steven Almeida. I saw Bennie's name on the bed, down the aisle from me.

As they were about to drive off, I asked to sit with them for just a few minutes in the Chevrolet. The moment I was on the back seat I burst into tears and said I didn't want to stay there. I begged them to take me home. Aunt Siobhain put her arms around me. Bokkie, turning around from the front seat to face me, looked perplexed. She said nothing. Bok shook his head and exhaled irritably. He said I was merely distraught at saying goodbye after such a wonderful holiday at home. I said I didn't want to stay there if I couldn't be in a dorm with Dominic and the others. Bok said I would get used to it; make new friends. I said I didn't want new friends, I had friends and I didn't want to be split from them. Then Bok asked whether I hadn't learnt anything from Dr Taylor? Had Dr Taylor not taught me that happiness was in my own hands? He said I was twelve and a half, I would soon be a teenager, a young man. He said when I turned thirteen in October I would get my first watch; I could have a new, modern, digital watch, they'd bring up for Parents' Weekend. I knew I'd lost; knew I was doomed for at least another six months. I dried my tears, kissed them, and got out of the car. I waved as they drove off. Hating them. Needing them.

At night, after everyone was asleep, I took the weights from the bottom of my locker. For half an hour – until I lay drenched and panting in damp sheets – I built my muscles. The days passed and the heaviness that hung shadows over me night and day refused to lift. The blues, bigger, deeper than they had ever come to me before. Dominic was not due back for another two weeks. And anyway, what was I going to say when he returned? How to tell him that I could no longer be his friend? Better that their plane crash into the sea on the way back from Europe.

I sought a place to be alone, away from everyone. Till then it had not dawned on me that one could be alone in that hateful place where people were everywhere. I need privacy, I thought, and felt wise at such a sophisticated word intruding into my thoughts. Now I discovered the solitude of the library, and with that came many recollections of the library near the Toti station. Initially I thought I would be chased off the walkway. But I was ignored. It became my place. I discovered the encyclopaedias and began my journey from A towards Z.

Nights in the vast impersonality of F dorm threatened to smother me. Sleep eluded me even more than before. Try as I did, the dream of flying refused to work its magic. Mornings left me exhausted and blue. During breaks I sat alone on the rock below the school's signpost. I wondered whether the sadness was the function of losing my mind. Perhaps the mad gene had somehow been activated. Aunt Lena's had started when she was sixteen and Uncle Klaas's only when he was already a professor. Perhaps it struck earlier with each passing generation. If I fathered a child maybe it would be mad already at birth.

There was nothing intimate about F. We looked down on the quad. Cathkin and Champagne Castle were nowhere in sight. While Bennie was only nine beds away, having him close to me meant nothing. Almeida, still in C, no longer attracted me. His aloofness was not sexy or mysterious. He was just the same as me, I thought, withdrawn and sad and miserable. Not mysterious. Certain friends, I saw, meant something only amongst others. I tried to stay out of Mervy's way. I went riding, for there Lukas and I could bond, but even that was nowhere near the same as the eighteen months before our June Walpurgis.

Sometimes it felt as though I hated them all.

Alone they were almost strangers.

The world had turned its back on me and I wanted to do the same to the world. I yearned to be at home. Not with my parents or my sisters, but not here, and not here left me with only one option: home. I went with Mervyn to get extra pocket money. The accountant told me no provision had been made and what's more, Bok had not paid my school fees for last term. The bookkeeper's words struck me like a blow and I stepped back from the window, aware that Mervy had heard. He asked her for another two rand and tried to give it to me. I refused. Why did she have to tell me that? School fees were not my responsibility; and why in front of the others? How angry I was with Bok. How I loathed my father, resented him for the shame he was causing me by keeping me there when clearly we could not afford it. And then dragging me to Dr Taylor, which, I knew, cost money: had I not seen the fucking enormous check? Was my handwriting not now also slanted to the right? Why didn't Bok pay my school accounts rather than cart me to expensive educational specialists? I could already feel the shame of being asked to leave the school.

I missed Dominic, longed for his return almost as much as I dreaded having him there. At night, unable to fall asleep, I practised with the weights.

One afternoon, as I made my way to the library – my new refuge – Mr Mathison passed me on the passage and asked me to come to his office. I had no idea what he wanted from me and at once was certain that it had to do with the unpaid account. For the first time since June I re-entered his office. He said that he'd been keeping an eye on me and that he wanted to entrust me with a centrally important task. A slight thrill. Mathison adjusted his glasses. Pushing them with the tip of his forefinger up his nose. Then he flattened his blue wool blazer across his chest and smiled at me. Would I, he asked, keep my eyes and ears open and come and report to him if I ever heard anything similar to 'the business' of last term.

I said, of course I would. He nodded affirmation. I left the office, momentarily elated.

At night, after a session with the weights and panting in a pool of sweat, sleep again declined to fetch me. I tried to will myself into the dream of floating. It wouldn't come. I felt cold, freezing. When I eventually awoke, I had dreamt I was holding something I couldn't see. Something whose heart was beating against my enclosed palms. Then it started throbbing, like a pulse in my hands and I became frightened. Then, in the next picture it was Lena's hands growing from my arms and then I was on a rhino's back falling into the sea and going down, down into black water, drowning with the rhino's wild eyes sinking beside me and I awoke, sure I had been screaming. I wondered whether the dream had been in black and white or in colour. In the morning my head was thick as if I hadn't slept a wink. When Uncle Charlie came in, calling, *Wakey, wakey, rise and shine, PT shorts, white vests, running shoes*, I was already long awake. Were it not for the dream recalled so vividly, I would not have believed I had dozed at all. Freezing during PT, my head throbbing, I fell behind the troop of runners. I vomited. Steam rose from the frosted yellow grass. The Senior at the back told me he'd walk me back to school. By morning choir I couldn't stand up straight. I told Mister Roelofse I was ill. He sent me to sick-bay. Uncle Charlie said I had flu. I had a temperature and every lymph node was swollen. He inspected all the glands of my body and rested his palm on my inside thigh, then moved it up to my penis and asked whether that too was aching. I said no. He removed his hand.

Friday at dusk, after two days in bed, I wanted to go to the phone to await Bokkie's weekly call or to phone reverse charges. Uncle Charlie said the school had already phoned home. My parents sent their best wishes for my speedy recovery. Auntie Babs Theron visited from the farm. Bokkie had phoned her to come and look in on me. She brought a tartan-patterned tin of shortbread and sat on my bed. She asked me how I was feeling. I said I was fine. Even Auntie Babs, a woman Bokkie idolised for her dignified composure, the smartness of her home and her four well-mannered children, looked different. What was this woman or her kindness to me? She could not save me. Her generosity and charity meant nothing. I lay there wishing she would leave and stick the tin of shortbread up her cunt. Saying good-bye she promised she'd call Bokkie and say I was getting better. 'Eat the shortbread, Karl. It will make you feel stronger. And phone me if you need me, okay? I'm just down the road. You can keep the tin.'

I had no desire to get better. I wanted to die. If I died they'd all feel ashamed of what they'd done to me. I imagined them at my funeral, weeping, loathing themselves for not loving me enough. And then, me rising from my coffin, to be welcomed like Lazarus into the arms of my father who would at last love me. My headache grew worse. At times it felt I couldn't lift my skull from the pillow. I wished I had my antihistamine, for that, I knew, would make me feel better. I refused to eat. Sometimes flushed the food down the toilet. If I got sick enough they would be forced to come and fetch me. Beauty or one of the other servants brought me food. At least once I wept into Beauty's arms, saying I wished I could run away and never come back. She asked what was wrong with me and I said I no longer wanted to be at the school, that I missed Dominic. She asked what she could do for me and I shook my head against the pillow, tears streaming down the side of my face.

If I didn't eat maybe I could get anorexia nervosa like the Springbok gymnast Debbie Bingham. That would show them. I refused to read from the Bible on the bedside table. I knew what I was doing was a sin; I was not treating my body as the temple it was. I didn't care; fuck God, fuck Jesus, fuck the Holy Spirit. I was going to hell and I didn't care. My going to hell was Bok and Bokkie's fault. And Miss Roos's. Doos. I read *The Blue Lagoon*; *The Swiss Family Robinson*; *Twenty Thousand Leagues Beneath The Sea*; *Groen Koring* and *Die Goue Gerf*.

There was some book – maybe the Jules Verne – with French phrases italicised in the middle of the English. It infuriated me that writers would leave entire sections of French in English books without saying what they meant. On that bed in sick-bay, I decided that if I ever wrote a play in English, I'd leave some words in Afrikaans so that people could feel what it felt like to get to an important sentence only to find it in a language they didn't understand. If I, Karl De Man, had to learn French to understand some stupid English novel properly, others will just have to learn Afrikaans or stay in the dark for all I cared.

No one was allowed to visit. I would spread the flu virus and flu was to us in the Berg what the black plague was to the Middle Ages. When not reading, vomiting or flushing food down the toilet, I seemed to be crying. If Uncle Charlie came in I said the red eyes were from the headache. He gave me two Disprins dissolved in water.

It was as if a light beam fell into the room when Dominic waltzed in there, grinning and scolding me for being in bed when he had just returned from the trip of a lifetime. Back from Europe and Uncle Charlie had given him permission to come and visit. I sat up in bed and could not wipe the smile from my face. He brought me Toblerone chocolate and a lovely white and blue T-shirt that said 'Gay Paris' and a cassette of a new group called Abba. He fetched a tape recorder from one of the music rooms and played me the song 'Waterloo'. He said the music was real schmaltz but it was fun and catchy and his mother loved it and he was sure I would too. He showed me photographs of when he had turned thirteen in Paris. He held up the T-shirt and grinned. He said his parents had bought us each one and did I know – and now he whispered – that the word gay was also a secret word for homosexual? I shook my head and said he was surely joking. He giggled and said no, that's why his parents had bought the T-shirts. I fell back into the pillow and turned my face to the wall. How could this be happening? What had I done to deserve this? That the first present I got from Europe was something

I would have to hide in my cupboard; throw away and never let anyone see.

Dom sat beside me on my bed and asked what was wrong. I said I didn't want to be there; I wanted to go and live with Aunt Lena and Uncle Joe in Klerksdorp. I didn't want to be in the school if we weren't in the same dorm. I did not say that I could not be friends with him, whether we shared a dorm or not and that the evil T-shirt from Paris proved everything Dr Taylor had said. I did not say that something terrible had happened while he was away, enjoying himself and his parents' boundless wealth.

Then, instead of anything I had expected, Dominic said: 'Karl, you are not really sick. You are homesick. And that is never going to go away. You must get up. You must pull yourself together. Stop feeling sorry for yourself. I am here.' He didn't smile, pored at me sternly. 'It's stupid that they've split us up, but there's sweet blue all to be done about that. I'm here for you and I love this place. I can give you some of my love for the place. Get up, Karl, please. You are not sick.' I cried, held onto him. I wanted to tell him what had happened while he was away; that he had no idea as to why they had really separated us. That Dr Taylor had said I could no longer be friends with him. But what would it matter?

'Karl, promise me you will get up — for just one week?' He sat closer to me, speaking urgently. 'If you're not better after a week, I promise, I will tell my father to tell Bok to come and fetch you. And if you stay, just think of it, we're touring Malawi at the end of the year, it's only three months away.' Now he beamed, smiling, as he held my hand, trying to inspire me.

That night I prayed to God to let me live and to make me get better. I swore to live a Christian life, to become a good boy. Next morning the symptoms were gone. I told Uncle Charlie I was ready to go back to class. The six of us were again together, during break, down at the fort we were building at the river. And at night, I prac-tised with my weights: I would not write plays or poems, I would try not to act girlish and deepen my voice when I spoke, try not to use my hands, I would do everything to become the son Bok wanted. I would throw away the Paris T-shirt as soon as I left the school at the end of the year. But I was not going to give up my friendship with Dominic. Not for anyone or anything. Surely, surely, God, Bok and Dr Taylor would forgive me that one transgression? Within no more than six weeks I felt the sleeves of my black school T-shirts clinging a little tighter to my biceps.

18

Not long after Dademan's funeral, a telegram arrived to say that Bokkie's brother, Uncle Gert, had been killed when a rock fell on his neck in the mine in Klerksdorp. Silence and tears moved in to occupy the St Lucia house. In the sunny lounge, the kitchen and the bedrooms she swept, polished and shone, Bokkie was inconsolable. Now it was my mother's tears that drove me to a frenzy as I wondered how we could make her feel better. Uncle Gert's death at such a youthful age — as well as the dramatic circumstances of the accident — should have had a greater effect on me than the loss of Dademan; yet, as much as I knew and understood my mother's love for her brother, and also had my own tiny recollections of him and Tannie Barbara visiting with our cousins Kaspasie and Lynette in Umfolozi, my uncle's death signified mostly Bokkie's grief to me. I tried to feel my mother's pain, for pain of my own was shamefully absent. I was only sad when I thought of Tannie Barbara, Kaspasie and Lynette. Bokkie shed tears over the stove and I came and put my hands around her waist. She was devastated; she seemed frayed in a way not even time would recover. Her bottom lip trembled, the corners of her mouth drooped, her shoulders seemed to stoop as they shuddered, her blue eyes had turned into morbid red maps of grief. What would become of poor Kaspasie and Lynette; the mines didn't pay decent pensions to widows, and how was Kaspasie to grow up without a father? And what about Oupa and Ouma Liebenberg: Uncle Gert had been their eldest child and only son. Now he was gone, taken in the prime of his life. And a parent never, never recovers from the death of a child. Fervently I prayed that I would not die before her or Bok, that Bernice and Lena would grow to be a hundred before they died because Bokkie would surely have to be dead by the time she was one hundred and twenty-one years old? Or was it a sin to think that Bokkie would one day die? Was thinking that the same as not praying that she'd live for ever?

Bernice, Simba and I went with Bokkie to the St Lucia Hotel to call Klerksdorp. We stood outside the tiekiebox while she spoke into the receiver, dragging on her Rothmans. When the stack of ten-cent pieces piled on the directory shrunk too short, Bokkie stuck her hand out with a one-rand note and gestured with her wet red eyes to Bernice to run to the store and get more change. From outside the call-box we tried to follow the conversation but Bokkie was crying so much, it was difficult to know what was going on. Then there were long silences in which she only nodded her head or spoke so softly we couldn't hear from the outside of the glass. Simba whimpered, sensing my mother's tears.

'Shocking,' Bokkie said later that night as she retold the telephone conversation to Bok: 'Gert was struck by the rock and the kaffir right beside him lived. Not a scratch.' And so the story was passed down of how if the rock had fallen only a few inches to the other side Uncle Gert would have lived and the kaffir would have been killed. I tried to visualise what it must have been like underground in a gold mine; deep, dark, cold, wet. And then, while Uncle Gert and the kaffir were drilling for gold, how the rock came loose and broke his neck and he died instantly. I preferred the idea of being prepared for death; what if I were to die now, with the reams of sins I committed every day and the deposit box overflowing with secrets? I would go straight – no questions asked – to hell. I would have to resist my boredom in Sunday school. Learn to mean the words recited in the weekly Sunday school verse – instead of just saying them with expression so that I'd be better than the rest of the class.

We three kids prayed together for Kaspasie and Lynette. They were now all Tannie Barbara had left in the world. I undertook to behave myself and not disappoint my mother again; to protect her from all worldly pain. Not since Bernice's near-death experience with the mysterious poison had I seen my mother like this. Lena asked whether Kaspaas and Lynette couldn't come and live with us because they were now half orphan. Bokkie said that they still had their mother and they'd stay with her in Klerksdorp: 'How would you feel if Bok died and someone took you away from me?' A question that ended the conversation and left Lena looking guilty and me nodding my head. Accusingly.

Bok and Bokkie would drive up to the funeral. We would remain behind, as we couldn't leave school for such an extended trip. We wanted the Pierces to come and stay with us but Bokkie said we'd lost our senses if we thought she'd allow any such thing. Mumdeman, still waiting to be transferred from Charters, would cross by boat every afternoon to come and take care of us. Bok and Bokkie drove off in the Peugeot, the roofrack stacked with impala biltong, pineapples, bananas, papaws and avocado pears for the Liebenberg family. I had filled two empty canfruit bottles with shells and sea water for Bokkie to take as gifts to Kaspasie and Lynette.

'That's two,' said Bernice, after Bokkie and Bok had left.

'Two what?'

'Death comes in threes. First Dademan, now Uncle Gert. Who will be next?'

'If we're lucky . . .' Lena muttered and cast her gaze on me.

'Don't say that! Lena!' Bernice reprimanded. 'Death is no joke. What if something happens to Bok and Bokkie's car?'

I could scarcely sleep at night from worry about my parents on the road. I remembered the time Bokkie's cousin Coen had come to take us for a holiday in the Transvaal. It may have been when Bokkie went for the ear operation, because Bok and the girls were at the Godmillow's house and why else would we have travelled in two cars? Near Pongola a kudu jumped across the road and Coen's white Fiat was a write-off. None of us was injured, but we could all have been killed. I worried about Bok and Bokkie striking another kudu, this time being killed on impact. Till the next day when Mumdeman returned from Charters and said Bok called from Klerksdorp to say they had arrived safely.

Grade Two. Knew I would pass with flying colours. No B or C would ever again adorn my school report. Bs and Cs were the property of my sisters. School in Matubatuba had become less boring as time passed; I could read aloud without a stutter; Juffrou Goosen made me class captain; I was always asked to wipe the blackboard; I was the teacher's pet. And something else: by virtue of the separation into Afrikaans and English streams, I was becoming more friendly with Afrikaans boys. I was making other friends and Sam Pierce, while we still played after school, was moving to the margins of my life. Instead I spent breaks with Gysbert Mentz, Johan Richter and Marie Smith, who pronounced her surname with a silent h.

With both parents away at the funeral and only Mumdeman crossing the estuary for supervision, the long-awaited opportunity to take Camelot onto the beach now presented itself. Through threats to and trade-offs with Lena and through pleading and sulking with Bernice, I got both my sisters to accompany me. From behind the seat of Bok's Land Rover we took a long rope to tie to Camelot's halter. Along back roads behind the camp and caravan park, we led the excited horse through the bush, up through the dune pines and down to the beach. Simba ran ahead, spinning in circles, clearly aware that something was up. The long rope was for the girls to hold onto in case Camelot threw me and tried to run away. My faith vacillated between a confident ability to stay on the horse's back by clinging to his mane and a subconscious certainty of being thrown; the latter largely informing my insistence to take him to the beach where I could not get hurt when – rather than if – landing on the soft sand. We led Camelot to North Beach where out of season there were rarely people on the long white stretches. At the estuary mouth we could hear the hum of the dredger pumping sand. While Lena held onto the halter and the rope, Bernice gave me a hand up. I told Lena to let go of the halter and hold only the rope. The moment she let go, Camelot's hind quarters shot up and I slid down his flank, landing on my side in the sand.

'That's it!' Bernice commanded. 'Your little experiment has failed and we're taking this animal back to the paddock.'

'No!' Lena snapped. 'First give me a chance. Karl is too much of a sissy. Why did you jump off? You're meant to hold on, sod, even if he bucks. Coward!'

I flew into a rage, screaming at Lena who was still holding the rope: 'Camelot is mine! You're not getting onto him before I've ridden him. Willy Hancox gave him to me, not to you!' I wept and flung myself onto the sand, begging Bernice not to allow Lena onto Camelot's back. Lena said I was a cry-baby and she hated me and Bernice threatened to tell Mumdeman unless we stopped our fighting. Eventually Lena gave up and Bernice said I could have one more try but if I was thrown that was *it*, we had to get the horse off the protected beach. She again gave me a hand up but before I was even on Camelot's back, he bucked and I landed – face first in the sand – with the girls screaming. When I looked up Camelot was cantering away from the dunes to the sea. Bernice was running after him and Lena, clinging to the rope, was being dragged on her stomach four metres behind the horse with Simba sprinting and barking by her side. Camelot, on the canter, kicked and bucked a few times, then – with Lena still clasping to the rope – took off on a full gallop when he reached the wet sand. He was moving at an incredible speed. I was up on my feet.

'Let go, Lena, let go!' Bernice howled, running. I followed. Lena clung as the horse galloped, then swerved landward, dragging her towards the road behind the dunes. Simba barked, turned, looked back at us, then again followed Lena.

'Let go, the rope, Lena!' I screamed.

Ahead of me, Bernice was also screaming. 'Let go, Lena, please, please, he's going to kill you!'

Camelot was heading straight for the road. Still Lena held, bouncing as she hit the gravel. Suddenly a truck came around a corner. Bernice screamed Lena's name and both of us came to a halt, waiting for the truck to strike the horse. Camelot swerved and the truck, in a cloud of dust, came to a halt. The horse stood still, ears erect, facing the vehicle. Lena, nine years old and as if nothing had happened, stood up, walked up to Camelot and took him by the bridle and started leading him back to us. The driver got out and shook his fist at us. Bernice and I ran to Lena. She was bleeding down the side of her arms and from her knees. Her shorts were ripped and threadbare. Simba tried to lick the blood from her legs.

We lied to Mumdeman and said Lena – covered in red mercurochrome – had fallen while running along the jetty. But then a guard came to say that someone on the dredger had seen a horse dragging a little boy along the beach and they were wondering whether I was all right? So, Mumdeman caught us out. Bernice cracked and said it was I who had insisted and begged and threatened. Bernice and I each got a hiding – though Mumdeman couldn't hit hard and we barely cried. Mumdeman said that while we might lie to the living, we should remember that Dademan could see us from heaven and that he must be heart-broken to know that I – his favourite grandson, to whom he had left the cines and slides and the priceless trophies – had not only taken a horse onto a beach in a nature reserve and endangered my sisters' lives, but, moreover, that I had been able to lie to Mumdeman, the only woman Dademan had ever loved before he was so brutally snatched from us by the jaws of death. *That* she could scarcely believe. 'The recklessness of my grandchildren! Where do you come from? Girls, how could you, older and responsible, listen to a boy of seven when you are almost adults? And, Karl, how is it you go from sitting quietly reading your books to being like Satan's right-hand man? And you, Lena? Meant to be a girl. Why can't you two behave like Stephanie and James? Examples of virtue, those two grandchildren of mine. But you three, given half the chance, would turn into barbarians.'

We had to do homework. We were not allowed to listen to the radio serials and I was not allowed to listen to records for two days. Ouma forced all three of us to learn Psalm 100 so that we could say it aloud to ourselves whenever temptation for recklessness or lying threatened to overwhelm us.

And Bernice said: 'You see, accidents come in threes: first I almost died of the poison; then I almost went over Karl's head with the Land Rover; and now Lena was almost killed by Camelot.' Lena said she thought Bernice had said it was death that came in threes, not accidents. Eh-eh, Bernice said, accidents and deaths. Three accidents, completed. Two deaths, one to go. All we could do was wait . . .

19

The Malawi tour would let me make memories of myself, for the first time, being physically beyond the borders of the country.

Direct recollection – from Lena and the turtle-dove – comes from after our family's arrival in South Africa. With racking strain I try to reach further, deeper, grasping at recall from before two and a half. May there exist something, coded in the most obscure folds of memory – a single moment of smell, sight, sound, taste, feeling, instinct – *experienced* and *recalled*, that might by force of will be salvaged and translated from those first two years in East Africa to now or to the months before Malawi? Might I be witness to myself lying in a wicker cot on the green banks of the Ruvu? The sight of mobiles drifting from the canopy's slats; Bok or Bokkie's face smiling down on me where I gurgle in pleasant recognition prior to and outside of language? Sucking Bokkie's aureole, kneading her filled white breast with tiny pink fists? The first waddling steps on the Mbuyu lawn at ten months? Taking the fall on the Kenia ship that I am told has left the scar on the forehead? But, try as I may, before two and a half there is nothing of which I am or was even then certain: for all I knew I was an orphan adopted in Nairobi, or, in truth of Lena's jest, picked up in a plastic bag from a park bench when they arrived in Durban harbour after the escape. Still, there were the photographs, slides, stories, cines, sagas that had been shown, told, retold, rephrased, dialogued, contested, restated in varied forms. Those meant it was true: it all happened, somehow in some form determined as it may even by what had been sliced off the borders of Kodachrome and flickering celluloid. Bokkie pregnant; Lena and Bernice holding me on the farm's stoep at two weeks with Mount Meru behind us; godparents, Aunt Siobhain and Uncle Michael, holding me in a white lace dress at my christening, Oljorro's Dutch Reformed church behind them; the girls and me on Bok and Bokkie's laps in front of the blue Mbuyu house, Mount Meru always in the distance. Those memories did not exist from conscious experience; only on paper and from stories. They – and the fact that increasingly I saw my father's eyes, my mother's nose, facing back at me from mirrors – attested that I was indeed their child; not John Wayne's son born from a secret liaison with Bokkie while he was there filming Hatari; not an orphan or a European prince abducted at birth or washed onto the white beaches of Mombasa. Not anyone's but theirs. Even if all the stories of the entire family were an intricate landscape of lies, a network of deception designed to protect me from my true genealogy, could so many cines, slides and photographs be fakes? I had decided – trying for chronology and narrative that moved in one direction – that Lena's fifth birthday in Mkuzi was indeed the first. From there, even as I select and border what to tell, everything follows. Occasionally, perhaps from a temptation to project grandiose genius, I contemplate the fabrication of earlier more dramatic memory: the charge of an enraged elephant cow at me and my sisters; being held on John Wayne's hip; being bathed by Rajabu the male servant who looked after me. But, for now, for here, I resist. The truth is that I feel certain, indeed, of my ability to distinguish what is photograph, relayed and retold family story, cine, from what has been remembered from personal experience rather than other representations.

In the weeks after the death wish in sick-bay, in hours when Dominic was in the conservatoire and I not out riding with Lukas, I returned to the library, though now without the despondency that had driven me there after the holiday with Dr Taylor. Simultaneously maintaining the slow progress through the encyclopaedias, there came a wide reconnaissance of the other shelves. *The Three Musketeers* and *The Count of Monte Cristo*, by Alexandre Dumas. *Gone With the Wind*, by Margaret Mitchell, which at 1100 pages was too thick for the short time before the tour, but a book and a film I'd heard so much about from Aunt Siobhain.

Only days before we left for Malawi I discovered a myriad of books and an atlas in which Tanzania was still called Tanganyika and Malawi, Nyassaland. The map showed that the land of my birth was connected to the country we would tour by a huge expanse of water named Lake Nyassa. I deduced that Nyassaland's change to Malawi had something to do with the blacks taking over – just as Tanganyika became Tanzania after uniting with Zanzibar and the black government came to power and we lost our land. While the name Tanzania appealed to my sense of sound and it furthermore seemed to make logical sense to include a z of Zanzibar that rolled so beautifully from the tongue, Nyassaland sounded far more exotic than Malawi; Lake Nyassa more ancient, expansive, expressive, than the current bland Lake Malawi. I found copies of two books by Livingstone, the first

white man to see the lake. 1860. Exactly a century before Lena was
born. There was no time to read the entire thing, but from skimming
I got an idea of how the Yao tribe near Lake Nyassa caught members
of – was it the Mangosa? – and sold them to Arab slave traders who
in turn sold them to merchants from America. How thousands of
slaves died on the ships and were cast overboard in the Atlantic en
route to Virginia, Mississippi and Georgia.

In the far north of Malawi, across the lake, the map read:
'Livingstone Mountains of Tanganyika'. One book contained pencil
sketches of a Zanzibar slave market, as well as of an Arab slave dhow
with three layers of decks where little black figures huddled in their
hundreds; another an actual drawing of a slave caravan by David
Livingstone. In the sketch, all the people were tied together by chains
as they marched through the veld; some of the bigger men have poles
tied around their necks like oxen spanned between yokes and on the
side of the columns other black people carrying guns. I assumed
them to be the traders, or the traders' sentries. It looked ghastly and
I could not believe that a system such as slavery, so brutal, so in-
human, could have existed. On another sketch, by an unnamed artist,
a slave dhow is sailing across Lake Nyassa with both the large fore and
smaller aft sails taut in the wind, huge waves crashing up the sides of
the boat. Waves that size, on a lake, I thought, impossible. There was
a photograph taken of the missionaries, all dressed in white, sitting
with their feet on leopard skins after they had come out from
Scotland to spread the Word of God to the heathen. There were
some wonderful sketches by a man named Thomas Baines, whose
name popped up everywhere. Beautiful sketches – or were they, I
wondered, perhaps paintings reproduced as sketches – Baines had
done of the rapid channels at Kebrabasa, which, the book said was
where today the Kabora Basa Dam stood. Baines, I saw when my eye
caught his name again while skimming a text, had been Livingstone's
official artist and had accompanied the great discoverer. I envied
Baines, imagined how it must have been for him to be both artist and

adventurer. That was what I wanted to be! Not merely an artist, also
an adventurer. Someone like John Ross who at fourteen years of age
travelled eight hundred miles through the untamed bush from Port
Natal to Delagoa Bay and back to bring medical supplies from the
Portuguese to the English. Only a year older than me and eight hundred miles through the bush! No wonder King Chaka adored him. I
wished to know more about John Ross, how he had come to Port
Natal, where he had come from, what he had thought as he hacked his
way to Delagoa Bay: was there a chance he too had faced black
mambas and leopards, had dreamt of painting, or writing, being a
poet or a playwright? And what did they speak of, him and Chaka,
when they were alone in the king's royal hut?

Like the Senior Choir for Israel in June, we were fitted with khaki
safari suits to wear with our bush hats. The Seniors had returned from
the Tel Aviv International Festival of Choirs with the winning gold
medal. The media had it that we were now the world's premier music
and choir school. We had surpassed the Vienna Boys, an achievement
that brought an enormous responsibility: we Secondaries, and the
Juniors who would be touring Rhodesia, had to keep the school's
name in lights. A single poor performance, a spiteful or vigilant
reviewer, could destroy the reputation so painstakingly worked for.
Before we departed, Mr Roelofse brought us a review from an Israeli
newspaper: 'The choir of the Drakensberg Boys Music School was last night
awarded the gold medal at the Tel Aviv International Festival of Choirs. During an
open-air performance of extracts of Verdi's Requiem, as the choir's crescendos and
diminuendos filled the quiet night air, hundreds of frogs from a fountain behind the
stage must have heard the choir's heavenly range. With each rise and fall of volume, the
frogs too let their croaking rise and fall. What supernatural choir is this, that even
nature emulates its magnificent voice?'

Mr Roelofse wanted us to sing like that in Malawi: like a choir that
nature would emulate. He told us that the Malawi tour would be our
ambassadorial debut for South Africa – our country that had been

turned into an international pariah as a result of propaganda. That the Senior Choir had achieved its feat in spite of international opinion, against incredible odds, was to serve as our inspiration. 'We are going,' Roelofse told us to remember, 'into a black country, Africa's one and only black democracy in an ocean of communism. And it is our responsibility to show those people what we were made of. Music,' he concluded, 'is a universal language.' In Malawi we were at all times to be at our most exemplary behaviour. Our every move would take place as if under a magnifying glass and we had to behave respectfully when there may be an occasional black person in the audience. If we spoke – even casually – about the president, we were to refer to him as *His Excellency the Life President of the Republic of Malawi Dr Z. Khumuzo Banda*. Other than South Africa, Rhodesia, South-West Africa and Botswana, Malawi was the only other country in Africa where we were welcome. We were to afford its black president our sincerest respects. Dr Banda was a man of enormous moral stature, who refused to allow the territory of Malawi to be used by the terrorist forces attempting to infiltrate Rhodesia, South-West Africa and South Africa. His people were loyal to him almost to the man. Amongst ourselves we joked about what it would be like if some of us were placed with a black family in a hut. This would not happen as we'd be staying with only white host families and most of our audiences would be predominantly white expatriates. Together with Mr Roelofse, the tour's supervisory staff would be Uncle Charlie, Mr Mathison and Miss Sanders. Or Ma'am, as we were now told to call her. Ma'am's strictness had long reached mythic proportions from the Standard Sixes, and we didn't much look forward to having her with us. But, to me, ultimately, the thought of Malawi, of flying there by plane, of having almost as many days off as performance days, superseded the slight damper anticipated due to the presence of the upright Ma'am. Bennie argued that her going along was a great opportunity for us to check out the chinks in her armour in anticipation of her being our Standard Six teacher. All talk of

Standard Six I ignored. While never articulating my thoughts even to Dominic, I had no intention of returning to the Berg.

Before departure from school, Uncle Charlie spray-painted a single yellow identification spot onto our suitcases — also as precaution against luggage loss once our baggage would be loaded onto Air Malawi along with that of other passengers. Most of my clothing remained in the big lockers beside the F Dorm bathrooms. I imagined Beauty's hands — sometime in January — going through the rack marked De Man, neatly packing jeans, bush jackets, gum boots, T-shirts, black jerseys, underpants, long johns, raincoat and socks into a cardboard box to be sealed, addressed and mailed to me in Amanzimtoti. I was not coming back. There lodged in the back of my mind the thought that I would never see the school again. After Christmas, when we got back from Malawi, I would find an excuse, I would find a way, come hell or high water, to convince Bok and Bokkie not to send me back.

Driving off to Johannesburg in the school's Mercedes-Benz bus, I did not look back at the buildings. Nor at the stables or mountains I had in some way come to love. I had cleared my locker; my suitcase was jam-packed with each thing I owned including the Paris T-shirt, every-thing except for the stuff in the communal cupboards. On the inside of my suitcase, hidden in my two black Bata performance shoes and inside my two veldskoens, lay the orange-covered metal weights.

Before and after the *Kraaines* TV recordings in Aucklandpark, we stayed near Jan Smuts Airport in accommodation provided by Jurgens Caravans. The owners of Jurgens were friends of Dominic's parents.

Uncle Charlie handled all passports. Through immigration we bobbed, wearing our safari suits, sandals, bush hats and cameras. Inside the Air Malawi plane we compared notes on who had flown most often. Mervyn, whose parents owned the Cessna, was automati-cally disqualified from the discussion. I had flown eight times. The first time at seven — when I was the page boy and Lynette flower girl at Aunt Lena and Uncle Joe's wedding. Then six more flights over the three vacations the girls and I had gone from Durban to visit Aunt Lena and Uncle Joe. To Malawi was Bennie's first. Going through turbulence we told him we were going to fall. Mock nervously gasped that the trip was going to turn into the movie *Airport*. The Malawi flight was one of the rare times I recall seeing Bennie terrified. While we joked about crash-landing in some vast unnamed African lake — Kariba, perhaps, which I knew full well we would not be crossing — I drifted into thought about the drama of the crash, how I would swim into the wreckage, pulling my friends to safety. I wished we would crash; I'd be a hero, my face — maybe with long hair that had grown in the months we'd spent on a lost island — on the front pages of newspapers all over the world.

The black air hostesses — the first I'd ever seen — wore little red caps with leopard-skin inlays and Dominic told me to pose for a photograph in the aisle beside the one who served us. She placed her hand on my shoulder. Mervyn pulled a disgusted face and I just laughed and dusted off my shoulder. Dominic and Mervyn seemed to have limitless supplies of film. They were perpetually looking through camera lenses, snapping even the most informal events and gatherings. I saved my twenty-four exposures for the fourteen-day tour: I was going to photograph Malawi and Tanzania on the other side of the lake.

Mid-flight, Uncle Charlie came to where Dominic, Steven and I were seated a row in front of Mervy, Bennie and Lukas. He leant across the seats and showed me my passport. He pointed at my place of birth, *Arusha, Tanganyika*. Dominic and Steven inspected the inscription. I laughed and said it was so long ago I had forgotten. Then he showed us Almeida's passport, which had *Luanda, Angola* written in it. From behind us, Bennie, Mervy and Lukas rose in their seats. Uncle Charlie teased that Steven and I came from darkest Africa. Soon word spread and for the rest of the flight we heard from everyone except Dominic that Almeida and I came from kaffir-countries.

When Dominic asked about Tanganyika, I said I had been no more
than a baby when we came out and that we never even spoke about it
at home. South Africa was our country and, besides, both my mother
and father, as far as I knew, I lied, were born in the Transvaal. In truth
three generations of De Mans were born in East Africa with me
being the last. But there was no way I was going to go into that. Two
boys in the Senior Choir, Sullivan from Rhodesia and Viviers from
South-West Africa, were also from outside, but those countries were
different. They were run by whites. There seemed something shameful in the loss of our land and our citizenship to blacks. Added to
that, perhaps more than that, I felt an unconscious awareness that to
say my father and grandparents had been born in East Africa would,
again, set me apart from an airplane-load of people who were born in
places like Alberton, Benoni, Cape Town, Durban, Evander, Florida,
Genadendal, Heidelberg, Indwe, Johannesburg, Kroonstad,
Loeriesfontein, Malmesbury, Newcastle, Oudtshoorn, Pinetown,
Queensburgh, Rouxville, Somerset West, Tulbagh, Uitenhage,
Verwoerdburg, Worcester – was anyone born in a place beginning
with X? – Yellowwood Park, Zastron. Once, in our first year, when
questions of place of birth had arisen, I had simply lied and said:
Durban. Now, mercifully, no one seemed to remember.

At Lilongwe we were prohibited from taking photographs of the airport. Our bags were opened and searched by the black hands of
uniformed guards. The rest of Communist Africa, so Uncle Charlie
said, was trying to overthrow *His Excellency the Life President of Malawi*
and the soldiers couldn't take chances that we had been used as innocent couriers of explosive devices or anti-Banda propagandist
materials.

   On the bus, along narrow tarmac roads, through villages, I kept my
eyes on the countryside. It was, I could see from every bend in the
road through the windows, just like the Tanzania of the slides and
cines. Baobab trees, tall green grass, sugar-cane fields around mud

huts dotting the hillsides, red dust roads, goats standing on hind legs chomping from the lowest branches of thorn trees, women vendors by the roadside, dressed in colourful wraps frequently adorned with the face of President Banda. Lilongwe proper reminded me of a bigger version of Matubatuba. I wondered whether this was perhaps what Arusha looked like; Arusha at the foot of Meru, just on the other side of a lake we were to see within a matter of days.

Mostly only a pair of us went with host families. Dom and I were lucky enough to regularly be together except when the overeager local tour organisers had already divided us to stay alphabetically. As Dominic was almost at the other end of the alphabet from me, I sometimes ended up with the wimpish Niklaas Bruin. Narrowly I missed being with Steven Almeida, separated as he was from me by only Belfore and Bruin. In one Blantyre suburb, Bruin and I lived with a family who had a black child. I couldn't make out which of our hosts may be black as neither looked particularly dark. One afternoon after we ate at a table with the girl – the first time I had been seated at table with a black – I asked Bruin whether he thought she was adopted. Bruin said it wasn't important and that people were people and what did it matter what colour they were? I said I wasn't saying that the coloured child wasn't a person, I merely wanted to know how our hosts could have produced a black child if both of them were so clearly white. Next day, Lukas reminded us of how Miss Roos had said that even if there was a hint of black blood four generations back in one partner, a couple could still *throw a black*. Or, even worse, a pink. An albino. Best, Miss Roos said, to check your family history and your wife's family history with a fine comb before you have a child. One drop of black blood and a distant acquaintance of Miss Roos had thrown a black. The class was horrified. We teased Almeida with his smoky complexion that he'd better make doubly sure. In our Malawian hosts home, the thought of *throwing a black* now terrified me and I undertook to check our family tree again with Ouma De Man the moment I saw her after our return.

Lilongwe, Blantyre and Zomba. Lilongwe — no longer Zomba as I had read in one of the library books — was now the capital. We were taken around buildings and sights financed by money from the South African government. 'My father's taxes,' Dom said. For the first time, ever, we had numbers of black people, smartly dressed, in the audience. Near Kasungu we visited a cigarette factory processing local tobacco. After warnings about any ideas we might have of smoking, we were allowed to accept cartons full of Malawian cigarettes as gifts for our parents. Mr Roelofse and Ma'am, who both smoked, tried the cigarettes and said they were terrible, but who were we to look a gift horse in the mouth? I took four: one each for Bok, Uncle Michael, Aunt Siobhain and Stephanie, who had also started smoking. Bokkie had recently quit after smoking for fifteen years: I just tell myself I never smoked, she wrote, whenever there's the urge to light up. You never smoked, Katie, I say to myself, why would you want to start the silly habit now?

We sang in cathedrals, school halls and visited monuments to wars in places I could not even then name, let alone now try and recall. As a goodwill gesture we were scheduled to sing for an audience of Malawian schoolchildren. Before the afternoon concert, Mr Roelofse said we'd better be good because these piccaninnies, like all blacks, knew music. They had been born with the rhythm of drums in their bones. When the audience, seated on the floor of the little school hall, seemed unmoved by anything we sang or occasionally clapped in the wrong places, Mr Roelofse rolled his eyes at us and whispered: 'Bushwhacked.' We giggled and he formed a shhh with his lips, motioning us to control ourselves. Even the Zulu and Sotho songs, with their rhythmical charm, left the audience unexcited. The concert was a dismal failure. Mr Roelofse said it was the first and last time he'd allow us to sing to an audience of musical unalfabetes. Someone suggested we should have let Almeida do 'Oktobermaand'. Maybe that would have moved the audience as it had the pavilion in Paarl. 'Jissis,' Mr Roelofse said, 'As hierdie kaffirs nie eers vir 'n Zulu liedjie kan klap nie, waar sal hulle kan klap vir 'n Portegans wat in Afrikaans Oktobermaand probeer sing!'

Off afternoons, when not expected to be sleeping before concerts, we roamed the streets of Blantyre and Lilongwe shopping with our Kwacha for gifts from the markets and street vendors. Made from wood I didn't know the names of, there was a vast assortment of masks, statues of human figures and animals, small tables, beaded jewellery and cotton crochet work. With extra tour pocket money Dominic and I went to an Indian tailor who made two shirts for me of batik. I would give one to Bernice. I bought salad spoons for Aunt Siobhain and beadwork for Bokkie and bracelets for Lena even though I knew she would never wear them. For Bok I got a wooden letter-opener. Much of the art was different from the crafts Bok sold, and I wished I had money to take home samples of things that might sell well in South Africa. I photographed a long-necked giraffe carved from a single piece of wood that stood as tall as me. Perhaps Bok could commission the Zulus to make those, give them the photograph to copy. We could, I was sure, become rich from tall wooden giraffes.

Dominic and I were placed with an old couple who, for their entire adult lives, had been missionaries in Malawi. One evening, when we were in bed after a concert, Dominic asked whether I ever tossed off. Unease pounced onto me like a cat. No, I said. He asked why. I answered that it was sinful. Dominic chuckled and said he had recently started doing it. I kept quiet, hoping we could simply fall asleep. He was venturing into territory I knew to be deadly; he obviously not.

From the bed beside mine came his voice: 'Why have you gone quiet?'

'I don't want to talk about it. That's all.' Then added: 'It's a sin.'

Dominic laughed, again: 'That's pure unadulterated rubbish! Where did you hear that?'

For only an instant I could imagine telling him about the caning. Instead I said I'd read it in the Bible and what the Bible said was the Word of God. I had of course read no such thing, had inferred it merely from one of Dominee Steytler's sermons on the sin of Onan and then there was June with Mathison. And Dr Taylor. And Mathison asking me to report on what I heard. All the same. It all went together, was all intertwined with where Dominic was heading. Where angels feared to tread. Perspiration began to run from my armpits; my palms sweated.

'For shit's sake, Karl,' came his voice, 'there are all kinds of things in the Bible that have zero relevance in modern times. And as Dad says, the Bible says we should love our neighbours as ourselves and no one in stupid South Africa does that! So, why would we worry about jerking off! Is it in those commandment things?' It was more a statement than a question and I offered no response. Inwardly I cringed at the blasphemy. He continued: 'We aren't living in ancient times. Moses has been pushing up daisies for thousands of years. My Dad says masturbation is the most natural thing in the world and I can do it as much as I want. It's magic when you use an orange. Just dig a hole in it with your finger, heat it up under the hot water tap, and voila! Off to paradise.'

Horrified, I turned my back on him; felt my face hot against the pillow.

'And Bok, what does he say?'

'I haven't asked him about it. But I know what he'd say.'

'You know why Friday the thirteenth is meant to be bad luck?'

'It's a heathen superstition, that's why,' I said.

'No! Exactly the opposite, Dad says. It's a Christian superstition, because in the olden days, before Christianity, the pagans were allowed to have sex with anyone they wanted to when it was Friday the thirteenth. Like a special treat, sort of thing. Just imagine how marvellous! Until the Christians came along and because they hated seeing people having a good time, the Christians started saying Friday the thirteenth is bad luck.'

I clicked my tongue, then thought of something: 'If the Christians are so bad, why does your dad let you sing all this religious music? Why doesn't he send you to a school where you can dance around the fires with the pagans at their feasts?'

'The fuckin' Christians have some of the best music because the churches had the money to commission composers, that's why.'

I didn't respond.

'Karl . . .' came his voice, now quieter.

'Yes?'

'Can I get in to bed with you?'

Eyes, squeezed shut, could make none of the panic disappear. I wanted to tell him about the caning; I wanted to say that he had no idea he was walking into a fire; that Mathison had appointed me — chosen me, because he trusted me and because he knew I understood the bestiality of such acts — to report on this sort of thing. But to speak seemed impossible: I saw everything like a long unbroken line of dominoes; if I said one thing, explained one thing, a chain reaction would be set off, everything, my fine artful act of doing and saying some things and not doing and not saying others would tumble. I must just say no; and let him be satisfied with that. What if he grew angry if I said no without explaining? It would have to be a risk I'd take. I was not going to tell him about Buys or anything that happened while he was in Europe. Mathison, Harding, Jesus, a day before we left for Malawi! When for the first time since August Mathison asked me about 'that business'. 'Have you heard anything more about that business?' 'No, Mr Mathison.' 'You didn't hear anything about Harding and Reyneke?' Fear. What if he knew I knew and hadn't told him? I could say I hadn't been sure. 'I've heard things about them,' Mathison said. 'What do you think? You heard anything, Karl?' Then, grasping at straws, knowing the Standard Sevens were leaving the school for good, that I'd never see them again, and Mathison probably neither: 'I heard someone say that Reyneke did it with his girlfriend.' And Mathison laughing, said: 'Oh that's okay, Karl, that's normal. I only want to hear about that other kind of business.'

'No, Dom. You must stop that. You must never do that. If anyone finds out that you do it – toss off – or this business of getting into bed . . . Dominic, they'll kill you.'

I could hear him sit up in bed. He was quiet for a moment: 'Karl, what has gotten into you? We're thirteen! Boys toss off when they're thirteen. It's nature's way of saying you're ready to screw.'

'That's a sin unless you're married.'

He fell back on his back. A faint light from some form of moon fell across his bed. 'You're clueless. Damn clueless, Karl.'

Suddenly, unable to control myself, I turned my head on the pillow. Wanting to hurt him, seeking to invoke an authority outside of Buys and Mathison and the events of that June, I blurted: 'In July, while you were overseas, Bok took me to a man who specialises in education. He's a doctor, and he told me to be cautious of boys like you.'

He was silent. I again heard him sit up; could see the shadow of his shoulders and head above the white sheets.

'What are you talking about, cautious of me?' he now whispered.

'You're girlish, Dominic. I'm a real boy.' I saw no reason to whisper. Call me clueless; I'll show you who's clueless.

'I'm not interested in that shit, Karl. Biiiig boy, Karl. You and Superman. What I want to know is why did Bok take you to see this . . . this doctor?'

'To speak about my career, my subjects for high school, what I'm going to become when I grow up.'

'And in the process of growing up you're not meant to be friends with me?' He snorted and again fell onto his back. We were quiet.

'That was a shrink, do you realise that?' He paused. 'Bok took you to see a psychiatrist or something.'

'Rubbish, Dominic. He's an education specialist.'

'Well, tell me what you spoke about?'

'About how I was going to become a lawyer, how I'm going to lead my life, attain my goals.'

'Yes? And?'

'Why I was doing so badly at school.'

'You do better than me! And I don't do so badly. Or get dragged off to psychiatrists.'

'I'm not doing my best, that's why. I used to get nineties, now I'm in the mid-seventies.'

'And how did you get to the girlish part?'

'I don't want to talk about it any more. Let's sleep.'

'Fine, Karl,' he hissed, sarcasm in his voice. 'Let's sleep. Sleep away your worries, dear friend. Sleep away our friendship too, for all I care. But let me tell you one thing: it's not you that needed a psychiatrist. No, it's your father.'

'Fuck you. You don't know Bok. Keep your mouth off him.'

'I've heard enough to know he's a bloody lunatic.'

'Dominic, say one more word about my father and I'll knock your teeth out, I swear.'

'And Bokkie, what did she have to say about this little exercise?'

'Leave my mother out of it.'

'So, if I'm so girlish, why did you stay friends with me, even after the big education specialist, hey? Education specialist, my arse! Why are we still friends if he told you not to be friends with me? Can you tell me that much? Surely you owe me that?'

I wished only that he'd now leave me alone. Beneath the anger I could hear the hurt in his voice. I wanted to tell him about the caning, to tell him that he didn't understand, about the Terylene-covered weights in the suitcase on the table beside the door to our room, about why I now wrote in a slanted hand.

'It was the presents, hey Karl!' he snapped. 'It was the sentimental Abba tape, the shit, crap, cheap music you love so much, and the chocolates and the T-shirt I brought you from overseas. Thirty pieces of silver, Karl, enough to make you forget your education specialist.'

I wanted to weep. What he was saying was devoid of truth. No, it was not, nowhere, near true. If anything the T-shirt . . . I squashed my face into the pillow. It was because you came back and saw that I was unhappy; it was because you knew I wasn't really ill; it was because you're my best friend; because you accept me the way I am; because I trust you because you're everything no one else in my life is; even if you had not brought me presents, because I know you love me; and I'm leaving, next year, I don't want to be in Cilliers's choir, I'm not coming back. But I didn't say any of that. Only felt my face contort, knew I was going to cry.

'The presents. Jesus Christ, you're cheap, aren't you?' Again sitting up in bed, his words pounding me. I could hear him turn from me, heard the bed sigh as he fell back and turned to the window. Away.

'It wasn't the presents, Dominic. That Paris T-shirt is in my case, you can take it back. I swear,' I tried to say, voice crumbling, tasting the tears, hearing myself answer: 'I'm here because you're my friend. Because I love—' I choked on the words and turned around and sobbed into my pillow.

I felt him beside me, his arm tightly across my back and his hand tucked beneath my chest, his breathing into my ear.

Halfway through a concert, during break, we'd change from the grey flannels, white shirts, blue waistcoats and white bibs into long red cassocks with white overgarments. Much of the second half of the tour programme consisted of Christmas carols. One night in the middle of the first half of the programme, before carols, first Bruin, then Meintjies fainted of the oppressive heat. The Central Africa Presbyterian church, with its enormous dome, built a hundred years before, seemed to smoulder like a massive hothouse. Even with the stained-glass windows opened, still not a breeze stirred. Perspiration stuck the white shirts to our backs. Fringes were plastered across foreheads. Mervy looked as though he'd run a marathon. Plans for cossacks, garments and candles were cancelled. Before the choir went on for the second half, Mr Roelofse and Dominic went on for Gounod's 'Ave Maria'. It had become customary for Dominic, like Steven Almeida with 'Oktobermaand', to get an encore. The audience, as usual went wild. After three or four bows Dominic and Mr Roelofse walked off. They hovered around us outside to see whether the applause would abate or whether they'd have to go on for the encore. Bennie used an LP cover to fan down Mr Roelofse. The audience kept clapping. There would have to be an encore. Dominic asked Mr Roelofse whether he could do something a cappella. Roelofse, obviously exhausted and delighted at the reception in spite of the heat, agreed. Hastily finding me amongst the first sopranos, Dominic whispered that I should stand at the door and listen: 'This is for you.'

He walked back to the front of the pulpit as the audience roared.

A hundred times from backstage I had heard him and Steven sing. There was nothing new to it. But this time it was for me. And it was without accompaniment. With his voice alone, he began a song I knew, though I'd never heard him sing it before. Aunt Siobhain had taught me the words and the melody some time at St Lucia. The song had never been anything but a part of her small Irish repertoire together with the others we all joined in: 'Old Danny Boy', 'Molly Malone' and 'Auld Lang Syne'. Dominic's voice, spiralled in the acoustics, up to the dome and melted through the warm air:

> *Tis the last rose of summer*
> *Left blooming alone*
> *All her lovely companions*
> *Are faded and gone*
> *No flow'r of her kindred*
> *No rosebud is nigh*
> *To reflect back her blushes*
> *Or give sigh for sigh*

I'll not leave thee
Thou lone one!
To pine on the stem
Since the lovely are sleeping
Go sleep thou with them
Thus kindly I scatter
Thy leaves o'er the bed
Where thy mates of the garden
Lie scentless and dead

With Steven and Mervyn in the shadows beyond where the open doors' light fell, surrounded by first and second sopranos, I felt tears in my eyes. For happiness. For something moving. For something so beautiful. A terribly intimate relief.

So soon may I follow
When friendships decay
And from love's shining circle
The gems drop away
When true hearts lie wither'd
And fond ones are flown
Oh! Who would inhabit
This bleak world alone

Again the audience roared. People were on their feet, again calling for an encore. This time, when Dominic came off, he said he couldn't do more. He was exhausted. The rest of the concert – 'Silent Night', 'Deck the Halls', 'Greensleeves', 'Away in a Manger', 'Auf die Gruen Au', 'Joy to the World', the latter in which the audience was allowed to join – was a raving success. Mr Roelofse glowed red from the heat and gratification. Outside, Ma'am Sanders and Mathison too seemed overjoyed and Mathison shook forty boys' hands.

At home that night, I knew something had changed between

Dominic and me. Neither of us said anything. We undressed and got into bed, still sweating. We spoke for a while about the concert. I said that his and Steven's 'Happy Wanderer' had been better than Gilbert and Sullivan could ever have intended it to be. He said breathing in the heat and humidity had made the challenge of joining notes for 'Bel Canto' a hundred times more difficult than it already was. We need black voices in this choir, he said, did you hear when they sang along with 'Joy to the World'? It was as if the heat didn't affect black people in the same way as it did whites. 'Dad will be furious for me saying something like that, but maybe their diaphragms or their lungs have evolved differently from ours. Maybe because they've lived in Africa for millions of years.' He spoke almost as if in thought to himself. I turned off the bedside light.

'I'm telling you. If this choir had black voices, Jesus, no other choir in the universe could come near us. Black boys' voices. And the music would be so much more interesting. Real. What did you think?'

'Blacks don't sing "Bel Canto", Dom, they do the rhythmical tribal music stunningly, but not the sort of stuff we sing. You saw that crowd last week at the afternoon concert. Didn't have a clue about the music. And there's no ways the school would allow blacks in.'

'Of course the school won't, but that's so thick! And blacks don't sing "Bel Canto"! Karl, where have you been? You're as bad as Bennie and Merv. What about the Negro spirituals, how are they meant to sound? Not like rhythmical tribal, for God's sake. And what about Marianne Anderson? Have you never heard that voice?'

'I suppose you're right, it is thick not having them. But they could never afford it.'

We lay silently and I wondered what it would be like having a black boy in choir or in class with us. It seemed fine to me, as long as they didn't take everything over. But where would they find the money? And could they speak Afrikaans or English well enough to cope in school? It was unimaginable. Maybe in fifty years, once we had educated them, elevated them like some of the blacks in America and the other private schools around Durban.

'What did you think of . . .' He broke off mid-sentence, knowing I knew what he wanted to know.

'It was like nothing you've ever done before.'

I could hear only my own breathing and the sound of my heart racing in my chest.

'Can I come to—'

'Yes.'

And he did. We lay there and held each other's hands. He ran his hand down my belly. When his fingers came close to the elastic of my pyjama shorts, I took hold of his wrist, held it back. And even as we did nothing more, fell asleep beside each other on the bed in the missionaries' house, I must have known we had reached a private crossroads. Must have already suspected which turn I'd allow us to take. With our private parts.

After the final Blantyre concert, before returning to South Africa for Christmas, we were to have what I had most been looking forward to: four free days on Lake Malawi.

The first sighting of the calm surface left me mum. Instinct was to look for the other side. From the dusty bus window, I strained my eyes east, then north and south. Nothing. You can't see the other side! It's like the ocean! If this is the eighth largest lake on earth, what could be the largest? Like a slab of veined blue-grey marble, bordered by a darker line of blue where the water met the other blue of the horizon, the surface of Lake Malawi captivated my gaze. Somewhere, up there, beyond the beyond of the fine blue north-eastern horizon, I trusted, lay the country where I had been born thirteen years and two months before. The water beyond the white beaches, bouldered cliffs and trees was more than enough to temper my disappointment at not being able to see that place, nor even Mozambique, which I assumed from the map had to be directly east from us.

Off the bus, we stood amongst our luggage beneath a sycamore fig and waited to be divided into host families. Lukas had asked Miss — Ma'am — to see whether there was a chance of the six of us being placed together — if any host families had a big enough house; we didn't mind sharing rooms or sleeping on the floor. A call for eight — yes, there was a piano — and the six of us, delighted, volunteered. Instead of two more boys for the one additional room, Mathison suddenly stepped into the process and insisted that Ma'am stay with us. I knew why, wondered if the others barring Dominic had guessed at his sudden intervention. This placed a slight damper on our excitement, for, though we by now knew she was not quite the ogre we'd been led to believe, the simple presence of Ma'am's authority meant we would have to be more cautious in the way we behaved and the way we spoke.

A white house on a part of the lake called something like Monkey Bay. Close to Cape Maclear, our hosts told us, where the first Scottish missionaries lived when they came to Nyassaland. Mr and Mrs Olver were Zambian expatriates, now living in England. They came to their house in Malawi only for northern hemisphere winters. While in England, the house here, furnished and lined with bookshelves, was rented to tourists. Year round a staff of two Malawians — Tobie and Chiluma — took care of the buildings. Dominic and I shared; Lukas and Almeida, Bennie and Mervyn, and Ma'am was on her own. Over each bed — covered in white linen changed daily by Tobie and Chiluma — hung scalloped white mosquito nets. From white walls small windows opened for a view of the lake. At a jetty below the house lay a catamaran and a forty-foot yacht, sails neatly rolled, wooden decks polished and bronze fixtures burnished. Mrs Olver said there were snorkels and goggles in the boathouse by the jetty, extra towels in the bathrooms: we should help ourselves to whatever we wanted in the fridges from the kitchen. Fridges; fridges, the plural ran, almost stumbled, through my mind. Lunch, around a table that could seat sixteen, was an assortment of cold meats, fruit, salads, juice and freshly baked bread rolls, served by Tobie and Chiluma, who wore long white Arab-like uniforms. On their heads they wore red fezzes and I wondered whether they might be Mohammedans.

Four days off; four days in which we would see the rest of the choir formally only on two occasions for a braai at some resort.

Floating on my back in the lake beneath the house, I thought to myself that the water I was in had touched Tanzanian soil, or had come from clouds that had been formed of evaporation from northern lakes and rivers. I was so close to there and, while I would not allow anything to detract from the pleasure of the time with my friends in the big house, there was a vague regret at not being able to see the Livingstone Mountains. Who cares, I thought, this is close enough and if we're lucky Mr Olver may take us north up the lake from where I might see Tanzania.

The Olvers had not attended any of our concerts. After supper they asked whether the six of us would sing for them. While as a rule we were not allowed informal singing, Ma'am said the tour was in fact over and there was no reason we couldn't; no reason to save our voices at this point. With Dominic behind the piano and Mervy stroking his violin, we sang Christmas carols while Ma'am and the Olvers sat in armchairs with drinks. Shy as I was to have my voice heard with only five others, I enjoyed the carols and soon relaxed. For the first time in two years, I was feeling music. Allowing volume on the middle range, I didn't even try to reach any of the high notes and left the 'Silent Night' descant entirely to Dominic and Steven. Dom cast a few quick glances at me, frowning when I also left out parts of other songs.

From an open window behind the piano, I saw a full moon above the lake. I left the others and went to find a place outside. There was a flat boulder above the jetty where earlier in the afternoon I had seen wild gladioli and purple foxgloves. Behind me, against the moonlit night sky, candelabra trees clung to crevasses between the rocks and further inland I could make out the silhouette of a baobab. Piano, violin and voices continued, and I wondered how far sound carried over the water before me. 363 miles long, 20 to 50 miles wide, 2200 feet deep. Somewhere I'd read that sound, like matter, never quite disappears. So, our voices, our singing, like all the other voices and singing of thousands of years around this lake, were still somewhere there, nestling on rocks, in the water, on leaves. All eternity's sounds, a dog's bark, a child laughing, the beating of a bird's pulse, and the echoes of these, were suspended or drifting somewhere around where I sat. I sighed. The echo of a sigh. And what incredible sound might be made if it all came back at once! If history's every voice and echo was heard in a single instant? Like a bomb going off, that's what it would resemble. Its volume, surely, would shatter our universe?

From lights across the bay came the rhythm of drums, possibly a band, for it was not the sound of African drums. Pop or rock.

Mr and Mrs Olver had taken us to see the clock tower at Fort Johnston that afternoon. The red-brick tower stood on the banks of the Shire River along which Livingstone had first entered the lake. In the late afternoon sun Mrs Olver took a photograph of the six of us standing in front of the tower, the clock pointing at half past five.

Ma'am and Mr Olver walked out into the night, passing close to where I was sitting. Ma'am asked whether they could join me. She asked why I was so pensive, and I said I was wondering how much farther north I'd need to go to see the Livingstone Mountains. Mr Olver asked why I was interested and I replied it was less the mountains than the country I wanted to see. I had been born there and no one in our family had been back since we left in 1964. Never before, other than in the aeroplane, had I spoken to anyone outside of our family about Tanzania.

'So, your family left after independence?'

'Yes,' I answered. 'After all white property was nationalised by the new government. We lost everything.'

'Except your lives.' Mr Olver said it was just as well we had left. He said Julius Nyerere's Ujamaa policies had failed miserably and the handful of whites who remained in Tanganyika were having a tough time keeping afloat what little business was left. He said Malawi was an African anomaly, though a very bloody struggle had preceded independence from Britain. 'Long and bloody and always against one and in cohorts with the other hand of Europe,' he said, 'like everywhere else on this wounded continent. When Europe decided what would be this country, way back, there were the Germans to the north, the Portuguese over there.' And he inclined his head towards the lake's invisible other shore. 'But that's all gone, only the borders and mixed excuses for nations they left remain. And the history of struggles. One interesting story from close by here is about Tobie — you know, the tall houseboy who served the lamb tonight — well, his great-grandfather was Chilembwe.' Mr Olver lit a cigarette for Ma'am. She said ta, inhaling and exhaling the smoke into the night. 'Chilembwe, backed by the Tanganyika Germans, led what is today called the Chilembwe Rising. He was disgruntled at the treatment of Bantu labourers by white farmers and, one imagines, from seeing that black life mattered to Europe during times of war only — as cannon fodder. So he staged an uprising. He gave strict orders that no white women or children were to be harmed. Lists were drawn up of white men who had to be killed as they slept beneath their mosquito nets. William Livingstone, one of the cruellest white farmers, had his head cut off in the presence of his family. The head was put on a pole and the women and children in nightclothes were herded through the night behind it. Chilembwe, a minister, held his Sunday service with the head hoisted up on the church altar. The European community, in a panic that they were on the verge of being slaughtered, made plans to pack up. The militia mobilised against the rebels. There are conflicting stories about what became of Chilembwe. He was a village boy who had gone through a missionary education: one story holds that he fled and was killed by the militia. Buried in the bush with nothing except his gold spectacles. If you were to ask Tobie about it he'd say he turned into a pigeon and flew off to Madagascar or the

Seychelles. The other story I've heard Chiluma tell is that Chilembwe, at seeing the soldiers approach, simply walked out of the back door of his church. The soldiers who followed his trail found that the tracks of his shoes had turned into hyena spoor.'

Quiet after the story, we watched the slow ascent of the moon over the water from the Mozambique side. Mr Olver lit another cigarette and offered one to Ma'am. She declined. The story had reminded me of the Mau Mau in Kenya; only the Mau Mau had raped and murdered women and children too. I had read about the Mau Mau in Robert Ruark's *Uhuru*, and filled in bits of additional information from family narratives and memories.

'It sounds like the Mau Mau,' I said, wanting to show I knew the history of East Africa, 'who murdered hundreds of whites in their sleep.'

Mr Olver's chuckle rang across the water. 'Seven whites, my boy, that's about all they killed. And we killed *thousands* of blacks in return. Had murdered a million and more on the Middle Passage.' I had no idea what the Middle Passage was and regretted having said anything about Tanzania. After a silence Mr Olver altered his tone and became pensive: 'What a continent,' he said. 'This country too . . . Things here are not nearly all the papers or Dr Banda make them out to be. There is no press freedom here. Women have to cover their legs down to the ankles.' Dr Banda ruled with an iron fist. Then there was also a man called Chipembere, who posed a serious challenge to Banda's leadership. Mr Olver said that Dr Banda countered support for Chipembere by invoking Chipembere's Yao ancestry. I immediately said that I had read about the Yao: were they not the ones who had sold other tribes into slavery? Mr Olver said yes, and that Banda kept harping on the fact that less than a hundred years ago the Yao were in cohorts with the Arab slave traders from North and East Africa. Mr Olver said that by playing on the history of the slave trade in Malawi, the president could justify his links with South Africa and oppose OAU attempts to impose sanctions on us. I assumed sanctions were

something like boycotts, which I understood because of the international sports boycott of South Africa.

Things were also disintegrating in Mozambique, Mr Olver said,
looking out to where the moon sat above the black waterline of the
horizon. Early in 1975 the Portuguese had, after three hundred years,
withdrawn from there, as they had from Angola. Abandoned
Mozambique overnight and left a population of eight million people
with twelve doctors. Angola, Mozambique, Tanzania, now one-party
Marxist states. And he gave Ian Smith and Rhodesia two or three
years, at most. Mr Olver asked Ma'am what she thought would
happen in South Africa. Did she not think it would eventually have a
black majority government? Ma'am said she doubted it: the state was
powerful and the homeland policies on track, with Transkei due for
independence in a year's time. Her son would be going into the army
in January, and that was of course a concern now that South Africa
was involved in the war in Angola.

'Darling, the boys are going to sing again, do come in and listen.'
Mrs Olver's voice reached us from the open lounge doors.

Mr Olver stood up, saying he'd like to hear more about Ma'am's
children.

She and I were left alone outside.

'And you, Karl, what do you think will happen in South Africa?'

This – the enormous question – was not something I'd ever really
thought about. I said I hated politics. I said I didn't really mind
Bantu, that I thought it was unfair that they could not vote in South
Africa or live where they'd like. Bantu were human beings, but they
were not ready to run a country. And then there was the thing that
they tended to take away white land. We now owned a house in
Amanzimtoti, I said – the first since we got out of Tanzania. I would
hate to lose that if the blacks took over.

I asked her about her son, who had just completed matric. She was
going to phone home within a day or so to hear about his results – if
she could get through on these lines. She was proud that he was

going into the army. Of course it was dangerous, but it was service to our country and simply the way things were. I wanted to ask about her ex-husband, why she was divorced, but imagined the question overly familiar or rude. Instead I told her that my cousin James had a British passport, and that meant he would not be required to go into the army like the rest of us when he turned eighteen. 'Don't you think it unfair, Ma'am,' I asked, 'that people can live in a country and get everything from that country and not have to go to the army because they have foreign passports?'

'Yes,' she said, 'it's outrageous.'

'My cousin James says he refuses to die for a country that isn't even his.'

'Well then, why doesn't he leave and go back to England?'

'Ireland,' I said. 'My Aunt is Irish.'

'Back to Ireland, then?'

'That's exactly what my father says. My cousin's a real sissy, anyway,' I said. 'Always doing flower arrangements and he wants to be a florist when he grows up.' Ma'am said she supposed there was nothing really wrong with that, and we laughed when she said James would probably have a tough time being a florist in the army.

'And, what about you, Karl? Do you like flowers?'

'I don't like flowers in arrangements,' I said. 'I love flowers; but in a house I prefer just one flower, like a single rose or even a single bottle-brush or just one twig of bougainvillea in a vase. My cousin makes these arrangements, with green oasis, that are all stiff and formal. Especially protea arrangements; they're so hard and ugly. I hate those.'

She said she didn't believe any flower ugly. Did I know proteas were named for the Greek sea god Proteus, who could change his shape to become whatever he wanted to be? I said no, I didn't know that; and, that I didn't mean I hated proteas, I hated them in arrangements. I pointed out the wild irises and foxgloves growing behind us. She asked what sort of flower arrangements I liked.

'At one of our host families, I saw some paintings and photographs of one red disa in a vase. That's what I'll have in my house one
day. Or in my office on my desk where I work. A single disa in a vase,
so that I can look up at it from my work. Or just a handful of irises,
like Van Gogh.'

Dominic and Almeida were doing 'Dos Allerschonste Kindl'.

'Like angels, those two voices,' Ma'am murmured. Something
about the phrase had an odd or familiar ring. *Like angels, those two voices.*
Where was the memory's origin?

She asked whether I was fond of art. I said yes, I loved painting.
Knowing she was the one who taught Standard Six Art and Latin,
I left out that the few times I'd been in an art gallery I had found
most of the paintings and sculptures devoid of meaning; that
amongst every two or three hundred paintings there might be but a
single one I liked. I told her that Bok had agreed that I could take
Art as a subject in high school as long as I played rugby and did
athletics as well. It was rugby and Art or no Art at all. Or, Bok said,
I could drop rugby if I won the 1500 metres in track. I told her my
favourite painter was Van Gogh, his poplars, and Monet's waterlilies.
She asked whether I knew an artist by the name of George
O'Keeffe. I said no, though it does sound familiar. She said she
would show me pictures, the following year. I thought of telling her
I wasn't coming back. Kept quiet, not wanting to complicate the
moment or ruin the adult conversation. If I were fond of landscape
and flowers, Ma'am said, I'd have to see O'Keeffe. Where's he from?
I asked. She, Ma'am said. Georgia O'Keeffe is an American. *The
greatest woman painter in the world.* And what about Jan Hendrik
Pierneef, and Maggie Laubscher, South Africa's greatest painters,
the ones who drove our national art? Again I wanted to tell her that
I was not coming back; that I was going to Port Natal to start high
school there; that I would look up the painters in Durban and
write to her about my impressions.

She asked what I would like to do when I was a grown-up. I

repeated what I had for years said: I was going to be a lawyer. I now left out the part about writing plays or making films.

She turned to me, slowly, and in the night, I now again hear her voice: 'You know . . . Do you remember last year, when I heard you do "The Moth and the Flame"?'

'Yes, Ma'am,' I laughed.

'There was in your rendition something of the sensitivity and sensibility of an actor. It was as though you understood each word of that poem, as though you yourself could have written it. Do you ever think of becoming an actor?'

I said no, I don't, though I'd been in plays and musicals.

'You should, Karl,' she said, in her voice a note of inspiration, but also a shadow of sadness as my name left her tongue. For an instant, I no longer wanted to leave the school. Ma'am, alone, strict, upright, humourless, attractive in a severe way, she — even without Dominic — might be worth returning for.

The following night we sang again for the Olvers. Noticing me once more leaving the 'Silent Night' descant to him, Dominic asked that I try second soprano. Keeping my ear close to Almeida's mouth, I quickly picked up the seconds' score. I heard my own voice beside and with Steven's. I sounded bigger and richer than ever before.

In bed Dominic suggested I should get out of firsts. That I should ask next year to be moved to seconds: 'How come you've stayed in firsts so long?'

'When we do those voice-tests at the beginning of the year, I've said both times that I have hay fever. So I've never been tested. Besides, I know how to fake the high notes. Look, I just strain these ligaments in my neck, like—'

'It's a complete waste, Karl. You can't even go near a D. You must move. No wonder you hate choir. You're in the wrong voice.' Outside was as quiet as inside the house. Being in the wrong voice was certainly part of it, but there was also the fact that much of the music didn't appeal to me.

'Tonight,' I said, 'when we sang . . . I could hear my voice has changed. Not just that it's deeper. It's not bad, is it, Dominic?'

'Karl, it's useless on first soprano. It's terrific in second. It's developed, idiot. You don't sing for two years every day without developing your whole vocal chamber. You should hear recordings of me two years ago; I sound like any average little choir moffie from Pofadder. Okay, not quite that average. Promise me you'll ask to be transferred, in January? Anyway, if you do the test Cilliers will pick it up. Promise me.'

'I promise,' I said, knowing the promise could not be broken for I was not coming back.

Giggling into my ear, and suddenly changing to Gogga, he said, 'I wowouloeldid popay a mimiloelloelionee tito boke fickucockykedid boky Cociloelloeliersoos.'

I laughed into the pillow and whispered: 'Popigog.' To which he said he couldn't wait for next year when Cilliers would be our conductor and we'd be Seniors.

Sunlight, filtering through the mosquito net, fell across our sheets. The wind sent waves up the jetty and white horses cavorted miles over the lake. Another night in which we had shared the same bed. Holding hands. At breakfast, Mr Olver said the weather was ideal for the catamaran. Tantalising associations flashed through my mind. Catamarans at full sail were things I had seen only in Seven Seas Cane Spirits advertisements screened in drive-ins and on cinema screens: tropical beaches and turquoise water; men and women in wet bathing suits in colours contrasting with their streamlined bronzed bodies.

Mrs Olver suggested we wear T-shirts over our bathing trunks as some form of protection both against the wind, which was sure to be freezing at high speed, and against sun. Ma'am, afraid of the water, declined to join us. She followed us out onto the jetty, the wind scooping up her thin cotton dress, exposing white muscular legs. She insisted on our wearing life jackets for the duration of the trip. Life jackets, I thought, were no more than devices of physical constraint, designed to inhibit physical mobility. How ridiculous it would look, how it would spoil everything, if the men and women in the Seven Seas commercials had to plod around with life jackets covering their bouncing breasts, their rippling torsos. I resented Ma'am for her interference with my idea of what a catamaran trip should be – for forcing us into inflatable straitjackets; a brief wish that she was not staying with us.

Mr Olver instructed us to sit three on the port fin and three on starboard. At his command, we were to move from side to side as his navigation and the wind dictated. Mrs Olver, readying ropes and slowly unfurling the sails, seemed an able sailor, despite her grey hair and a face creased and lined like a tortoise from too much sun. We drifted from the jetty. The others waved at Ma'am. I, deliberately, looked out into the choppy lake.

Mr Olver steered while his wife hoisted the sails. Wind billowed the enormous white sail and we shrieked as we took off into a southerly wind. Shouts of excitement passed between the two fins, the three of us on port trying to make ourselves audible over the wind, the roar of the sail and the crashing of waves. Mr Olver called for starboard to prepare to move to port; the moment all six of us were seated and clinging to the fin, Mrs Olver swung the sail and suddenly we lifted into the air, howling as the port fin flew over the water two metres above the surface. I was sure we would capsize at any moment. Mrs Olver shouted for us to lean back. I closed my eyes and felt the gush of air as my back hung over the side in mid-air. As she tightened the sail the port fin slowly descended closer to the surface and we exchanged glances, signalled relief with smiles just a little too broad. Mr Olver called three back to starboard and I wondered whether we were in for another lift, but nothing happened and we merely sped along at what seemed a miraculous pace. By then we were hanging back on our own accord, our heads skimming the surface as we chattered and laughed. I looked to the fore and aft: we had completely lost sight of land. There was a moment of unease in which I felt grateful for the secure suction of the life jacket to my ribs and the belt tightened around my waist. Looking into the wind made my eyes water so I closed them, leant back over the side, imagined us on a voyage through space. A few more times we were hoisted into the air, screamed, certain each was an occasion for capsizing, but the grey-haired Olvers, smiling and sticking out playful tongues, brought both fins down and we swished along, getting drenched each time the craft sliced the swells. Soon we could again see land. Mrs Olver, agile as a monkey, began lowering the sail and our speed decreased.

Approaching the jetty, we could see Ma'am, rising from the walkway where she had been sitting with a book. We glided in to the choppy waters and Mrs Olver dropped the fenders over starboard and threw a rope for Ma'am to catch. The old woman leapt from the fin and took the rope from Ma'am. She tied the craft to the jetty posts. Ma'am, wearing dark glasses, said she was relieved that her 'charges' had all returned safely. She asked whether we knew we had been away for two hours. Indeed, it had not felt that, more like thirty minutes. Bennie and Dominic told her she had missed out on quite an adventure and she said some voyages were better left to fiction. She said she had called South Africa reverse charges while we were away and, wait for it, she said, smiling, her son Graham had passed matric with five distinctions. We clapped and Lukas and Bennie whistled through their teeth. As I disembarked I looked at Ma'am. I was struck by the way she wipes from her face strands of hair that have come loose from the ponytail in her neck. Beneath her one arm she clutches the book and with the other she tries to hold down the flapping cotton dress. The wind seems to glue her dress to her breasts and between her thighs lies the definition of a perfect V. I found her beautiful — severely beautiful — and into my mind settled a picture of her that remains as vivid as almost any of her the following year, in front of the blackboard or scowling with displeasure at some inanity that I or one of the others had committed in class. Then, while she's looking down on the catamaran, Steven Almeida, with his dark hair wet and the black T-shirt sticking to his torso, walks quietly by her. The two of them smile at each other. And that, too, I remember, as if it all happened in slow motion.

Passing her on the jetty I asked after what she was reading. She held the book up, cautioning me not to touch it with my wet hands, as it was from the Olvers' shelves. It was called *A Streetcar Named Desire*.

'Is it good, Ma'am?'

'It's a fine piece of writing. You should read it.'

'I will, Ma'am,' I said. I'd never heard of Tennessee Williams. The afternoon before we left Malawi I picked up the book from where Ma'am had left it, face down beside her G & T. It was only then that I saw it was a play. Other than *Pygmalion*, which I'd found and read after seeing *My Fair Lady*, I'd never read plays. Yet, even without having read one, without thinking plays – other than Shakespeare's whose I had not read – were much published in books, I had wanted to be a playwright. Till Dr Taylor. Fuck him. I thought then. I'll find *A Streetcar Named Desiree* in Toti's library and read it right under Bok's nose.

Another night under a shared mosquito net. We woke with a start from a knock on our locked bedroom door. Lukas called that we should come down to the jetty for snorkelling before breakfast. We slid into our black Speedos, took beach towels from a rack and went into the passage. Mrs Olver offered us a glass of orange juice after which we ran to the jetty. I wondered what Lukas had thought of the locked door. Banished the thought. The sun was already hot, even though it was not yet eight in the morning. By the time we got to the boathouse, the other four were already there, rummaging through the wide assortment of goggles, snorkels and flippers. We tried going over backwards into the water from the jetty – as we'd seen divers do in James Bond's *Thunderball* – but came out sputtering and forced to readjust goggles and remove water from snorkels.

Underwater plants, submerged boulders, and the movement of fish — orange, yellow, blue. The six of us drifted together, faces down, looking from side to side. I could hear the sound of my own breathing. From above the sun beat down on our backs, below me lay a new universe. Occasionally one of us would dive down and point at something, a plant, a crab scurrying across a sandy patch, a school of hundreds of tiny silver fish. My mind drifted. I thought of Ma'am; having Dom beside me in bed; Almeida snorkelling next to me; underwater plants green and brown, fish darting, no waterlilies, the colour purple, pink, Ma'am, landscapes, fishes, tails, fins like angels. I brought my head up and saw Dominic's head submerged, his flippers moving lightly, his arms behind his back, snorkel turning from side to side, and I saw the skinny back, the shoulder blades rising above the surface, my eyes darted to Almeida, his arms drifting beside him, his bony shoulder blades visible too, like islands around which water swished; Lukas, his hands held behind his back like Dominic's . . . Dademan where I had wings like an angel, voices like angels those two, no Bok's voice saying voices like angels turning into a screaming incantation in my head, *voices like angels, voices like angels*.

I swallowed water and choked. I swam, sputtering, to the jetty and hoisted myself up onto the wooden walkway. I was shivering. If I had a gun, Jesus gun, Bok, Mathison, Buys, Cilliers, Taylor; if I had a gun and you came near me I'd shoot you. Not in the heart. In the face. One at a time. Execution style in the mouth. Blow your brains to splatter against the white wall. The rage of shivers could not have lasted for more then fifteen seconds, but my head was throbbing and I couldn't go back in the water. I stood up and felt dizzy, saw stars like fireflies between me and the lake. I tugged goggles from eyes, held them. Sank down on haunches. I wanted to weep, but there were no tears. More than crying, I wanted to kill: voices like angels; voices like angels, voices like angels it ran through my head even as I kept my eyes on the five backs, the ten shoulder blades, floating farther away from me.

It must have been in the second week of visits to Dr Taylor. One evening at dinner, Bok, in a brief aside: 'Dr Taylor says he was late for his appointment with two Berg boys, two brothers, and when he got out of the lift he immediately heard singing from down the corridor. As he came around the passage corner, he saw a small crowd of people gathered outside his reception area to listen.' Bok chuckled and said the brothers had broken into song while they waited for Dr Taylor. All the secretaries from down the hallway had come out to hear who was singing. 'Dr Taylor says they had voices like angels. He had to ask the secretaries to leave so that he could get on with his session.'

I had not thought of it since July. When Bok told the story all I had taken from it was a vague sense of thrill at belonging in the company of boys with voices like angels. Now, suddenly, a new set of meanings had clawed and scratched their way through my brain: Who were the brothers? It could not be the Stuarts, because they lived in East London. It had to have been before my time. And I didn't care who they were. What was important was that I had not been the first nor the only one who had gone through Taylor's office or his POA. Moreover, I was not the first or only one to go through there from that school. Within seconds a huge puzzle was slipping its pieces into place where I had hitherto not imagined spaces to exist. Nor had cared to think of it as such: Taylor knew about that stupid play, even though I had never told Bok or Bokkie about it. The school had. Of course. And what had Bok known? How had he known to take me to Taylor and not to some other shrink? And how was it possible that I had been taken to Taylor for treatment a mere four weeks after the caning from Buys? Mathison had told Bok. Bok had known all along. That day at the pool, that day he asked me whether I ever did 'It'. By then Bok had already known. This was the rule! Not the exception Mathison had made it out to be. There was the incident with Harding and Reyneke's gang just two months before Malawi. And Harding on the train! Idiot, idiot I am. If ours was an isolated case, why would

Mathison have asked me in July to report if I heard about such things? And, of course, how did Mathison know about Reyneke and Harding if he didn't have other spies running around? But these were splinters of the bigger hatred that held me spellbound. Foremost in my mind was the knowledge that my father had known, that day at the pool, he had known that I was lying to him. How could you, Bok, bastard, sit there and watch me lying to you, not stop me, not tell me that you already knew — even before you came to sit at that swimming pool? As though pretending that your not knowing made it to not be true. And Bokkie, she also knew, for why was there no question or explanation offered about why I was seeing Taylor? You useless, use-less mother. Deaf mute bitch. Oh your deafness is nothing; but your refusal to speak! And the others? Were they — Mervy, Lukas, Bennie — were they also taken to Dr Taylors in their home towns? And none of us is speaking. All of us, co-conspirators in the school's maze of intricate deceit, betrayal and silence.

My stomach heaved. A measly yellow string of bitterness burnt up my throat and slopped into the lake. Wiped away tears. My mouth. Felt the headache gone.

Bastards. Bastards. Bastards. If I can kill you, Buys, Bok, Mathison, Cilliers, I will. I will destroy you. Bit by bit. Word for word take you apart. Through torture. I will find a way. And that school, that grand place of private learning: brick by brick by brick. I will blow the horn, long, intensely at the most sensational pitch. In a concert of my delights, your walls will crumble while only your whores survive as heroes. Your foundations will be exhumed so that your savage song is permanently played for the nation. No, not to that dumb country alone: to the world. Some day, I will chop you all up and feed you to the vultures and the marabous and invite seven continents to witness. To participate in the fest. No, I will not kill you! Live to the hyenas! Like Chaka! Yes, like he did to that old bitch who had done him harm when he was Nandi's child, only a young boy. Whomever that old hag was, I'll get you like Chaka got her. Like nothing more than an old black kaffir girl imprisoned in a hut, you will feel your own arms tear off, beg me for clemency denied, cry out in pain when hearing your own bones crunch in the foullest of the night's jaws.

Tiny fish had risen to hover beneath the jetty. In the shade of my reflection they opened and closed their little lips around the contents of my guts that wobbled away like curdled yellow milk on the lake's mirroring surface.

20

Mumdeman was transferred from Charters Creek to Midmar Dam where she would run Thurlough House for Parks Board VIPs. For Christmas at Midmar, but, mostly, because it was Mumdeman's first in thirty-five years without Dademan, the whole De Man and Liebenberg families converged on the old colonial farmhouse. It was less a house than a mansion that stood on green lawns that to me were as vast as rugby fields surrounded by century-old oak and pear trees. Paddocks where once horses and cows must have grazed separated the gardens from the dam. Here we kids went fishing for blue-gill, bass and, if we were lucky, eels. Across the dam you could see the small game reserve and, on clear days, rhino and eland browsing.

Bok, Bokkie, me, Lena and Bernice; Uncle Michael and Aunt Siobhain, Stephanie and James and Mumdeman from that side of the family; then, from the Klerksdorp side, Ouma and Oupa Liebenberg; Aunt Lena with her wealthy fiancé Uncle Joe Mackenzie; Tannie Barbara with Kaspaas and Lynette; my mother's cousin Coen and his girlfriend Mandy who got angry when we called them Uncle and Auntie. Then Aunt Siobhain's brother and his wife had come out from England where they now lived after leaving Dingle in Ireland. Their surname was Heany and they joined us after taking a trip to the Kruger National Park and the Drakensberg resorts. Then there was Ouma's oldest and dearest friend, Sanna Koerant, the greatest gossip of East Africa, down from the old aged home in Benoni. Sanna Koerant had become a legend in her own lifetime, her name popping up in every discussion where East Africans gathered. Bokkie and Mumdeman warned us not to say anything in front of Sanna, for, before you knew it, the entire country would know every intimate detail of a family's private scandals.

The house, recently restored and refurbished, was imposing: thick walls built from granite chiselled into blocks, a veranda along its front and back; a dull red corrugated iron roof, stacks of bedrooms, two vast lounges and a dining room with a table around which we could all fit. The year's loss of Dademan and Uncle Gert, evident in whispers and hidden tears, did little to dampen the festivities: braais, boat rides on the dam, Bok and Uncle Michael water-skiing, bonfires at night, walks through the forests, drives to the game reserve, story-telling, music and dancing. The Thurlough House maids were off for Christmas, so we children and the women took turns washing up after meals and packing away the new Parks Board crockery.

It was the first time all of us had been together. Mumdeman said we were like the Royal Family in such a smart house. Sanna Koerant said more like right royal Makoppolanders let loose in Buckingham Palace.

Bernice and Stephanie listened to all kinds of new music and Stephanie taught us a dance that was just coming in: the go-go. Bokkie muttered that the music and the go-go had her worried about Satanism and drugs. Pop music leading to drugs leading to Satanism leading to communism, she'd heard it over Springbok Radio. Aunt Lena laughed and said Bokkie was one big walking double standard: 'Remember how you used to piss your pants when you heard Elvis on the radio?' We giggled and Bokkie said she'd appreciate it if Aunt Lena would use proper language in front of us children. Stephanie taught me to sing 'Jamaica Farewell' and she let me listen to a new Seven Single. It was Joni Mitchell. We sang 'Clouds', over and over till I knew all the words and sang it my every waking moment. Bok threatened to beat me if he heard *bows and flows and moons and junes and tears and fears* once more from my lips. We saw one of Oupa Liebenberg's balls hanging out of his blue swimsuit and Lynette whispered that it looked like a huge swollen raisin and I said it was more like a shrivelled guava. James got a fishhook stuck in his toe and had to be taken to Howick to have it excised under anaesthetic.

On Christmas eve afternoon, Uncle Joe, Aunt Lena and Coen and Mandy took us kids to a funfair at the tourist camp on the other side of the lake. Uncle Joe paid for everything and we were allowed to eat as many toffee apples and ice-cream cones and candy floss as we wanted. The girls and I were delighted that our aunt was marrying such a rich man. To us it spelt privilege through matrimony. After we'd gone on all the rides and it was time to return, we headed back to Uncle Joe's metallic silver Mercedes-Benz. Even though Coen and Mandy were great, none of us wanted to go in Coen's goggo-mobiel and I planned to make a dash for the Benz the moment we got close. We passed through a grove of wattles with Uncle Joe and Aunt Lena walking hand in hand in front of us. Campers and other visitors were streaming past us in the other direction. Aunt Lena suddenly swung around. For a second we didn't know what had happened. Then we saw that a wattle twig had ripped off her wig. We kids cracked up, as did some of the tourists, but Uncle Joe walked on as if he didn't know her. Aunt Lena reached up and quickly slipped the wig back onto her head. Colour had drained from her face and she didn't speak all the way home.

That night the table was set with candles and food for Africa. James and Stephanie had arranged flowers in the middle. As we were about to sit down for dinner, Aunt Lena fell down onto the dining-room floor, arms like windmills and unearthly noises gargled from her throat. We were told to stand back because she was having an epileptic fit. Bokkie and Ouma Liebenberg went with her to her room and stayed away for the duration of the meal. Again Uncle Joe made as though nothing had happened. I was asked to say grace and I prayed that Aunt Lena would not be the third death of the year. Everyone looked uncomfortable when I'd finished. Sitting at the children's end of the table Lena said I should be less worried about the third death than about the third mad gene. Away from St Lucia there were, as far as I was concerned, no trade-offs in silence and I went to Bok and reported Lena for saying I was carrying the mad gene. After dinner Bok gave Lena a hiding and, as her screams ran through the big house, I instantly regretted having told on her. Bok brought her to apologise. He left us to make up.

Kneeling at my bed that night with all the cousins and Bokkie beside us, I prayed again that Aunt Lena would not be the third death in the cycle. Bokkie interrupted my prayer: 'What do you mean, the third death?'

'Death and accidents come in threes,' I said, still kneeling. Bokkie smacked me on the back and asked how I could include a heathen superstition in the middle of a prayer to Jesus who had died for our sins precisely so we would be freed of all idolatry and place all our faith in Him. She told me to get into bed and, instead of praying to my loving Heavenly Father on the eve of His birthday, to lie there and think about whether Satan's embrace and the furnaces of hell was actually where I was heading.

On Christmas Day, to Lena's delighted hissing of 'What goes around comes around,' Bok gave me a hiding with his belt for refusing to let Kaspasie play with the perspex pistol I had received as a gift from the Heanys. Bokkie asked me whether I had no shame, being so selfish to my half-orphaned cousin. We played the catching game that we had invented in Umfolozi because hide and seek was too boring. In the catching game one not only had to find the hiders but also pat them on the back after physically wrestling them to the ground. We loved the game, although one of us invariably ended up in tears because the one who was on had either patted or wrestled too vigorously. Stephanie and I hid together so we could do It in the bushes behind the old cow shed. James, who was on couldn't find us and when we eventually came out Lena whispered that she knew exactly what Stephanie and I had been up to. I said she had a dirty mind.

Oupa Liebenberg told Lena, me, Kaspasie and Lynette stories of the Molopo where Bokkie, Aunt Lena and the late Uncle Gert had grown up before they moved to Klerksdorp. As Stephanie and James could hardly speak Afrikaans and Oupa no English, our De Man cousins were cut off from the story sessions and found other ways to amuse themselves. Oupa Liebenberg spoke of the desert and how he farmed with red Afrikaner oxen, with horns as wide as an adult man's reach; how they were so poor they didn't have a car and went everywhere on a donkey cart; of how, one day when he and Bokkie were alone on the donkey cart and he got off to open a gate, a leguan had frightened the donkeys and they had run off into the veld with Bokkie still on the cart screaming blue murder. Oupa also told of how he had joined the Ossewa Brandwag so that they could help poor Afrikaners against the English who owned everything during the Second World War, but how he had withdrawn from the secret organisation when they got too close to Hitler and wanted to plant bombs to bring the Afrikaners to power. He spoke about when he was a young man. About all his brothers, and of how lazy Groot-Oom Klasie always was while the other boys had to work. While the other brothers had to work, Klasie was always walking around with books. I caught Lena's eye: she was looking at me with a wisened smile. Without her saying a word, I knew what she was thinking.

'And there you have it,' Oupa Liebenberg said. 'All that book learning and what became of Klaas? Tramp, a burden on society.'

And Sanna Koerant, sitting on a camp chair nearby laughed and said it sounded to her that Uncle Klaas was just preparing for what lay in store for all of us. She said: 'What you sow you will reap. We saw that in Tanganyika where we had sown the wind and we reaped the whirlwind. Here, Piet, in this country, we're sowing the whirlwind . . .'

'But, Sanna, what are you talking about?' Oupa Liebenberg asked, 'This is the country of our birth. The Christians of this nation have to keep it from the grubby paws of the black heathen.'

Sanna, serious for once, said: 'And what about the black Christians, Piet? Why must we keep the land out of the grubby paws of the black Christians?'

Oupa shook his head and said: 'Nothing in the Word about black Christians; let alone black human beings. The Word says: He created Adam with hair like lambs' wool – like yours and mine Sanna. Nothing, nothing, not a word about *peppercorns*.' And Sanna cackled through her open mouth, threw back her head and almost fell over backwards from her chair. When she had finished laughing, she faced Oupa and said: 'Jirre, Jesus, Christus, God, Fok Piet! Jy gaan jou gat sien!' Oupa looked as though he was hinging on the verge of a stroke. His face puffed up red and his eyes bulged. He said he'd never hit a woman in his life but if Sanna ever, ever again, in front of his grandchildren took the name of the Lord in vain or used such disgraceful language, he would smack her teeth from her mouth.

For a few hours the atmosphere was ruined. Later that night, all seemed to calm down again when we put on boere-musiek and Oupa and Ouma and everyone danced and even Stephanie was allowed to show off the go-go.

New Year's Day: news arrived that Great-Grandmother Liebenberg, Oupa and Groot-Oom Klaas's mother – the woman with the long white plaits and moustache whom I had met on only two or three occasions – had died at ninety-six years of age. Oupa Liebenberg wept and wept and wept.

21

A warm bergwind brought the scent of blossoms from the peach tree outside his room and from the orchard terraces down the hill. My head was on his back, my legs balanced on his, my toes like clothes pegs around the tendons of his heels. Beneath my ear, into my head, came the enunciations of his body. Taking the beat from his back, I hummed, my cheek vibrating lightly against his skin.

Afternoons in Malawi, while Dominic was at the piano and Mervy practised violin, the rest of us took fishing rods from the boathouse. Lena, I thought, would have thrived on the lake. I told the others of the time my sister had landed a twelve-pound eel in the Midmar Dam after battling it for more than twenty minutes. There had to be eels in Lake Malawi, I thought. Mr Olver said there were more than three hundred species of fish. How I would have rejoiced at catching one eel to photograph for Lena. We didn't catch eels, only half a dozen small silver fish which we gave to Tobie and Chiluma, who prepared them as a side dish for one of our meals.

For supper we were joined by an old man from down the lake. We were again asked to sing. We did mostly Christmas carols, occasionally with the Olvers, the old man and Ma'am joining in. Dominic had retrieved sheet music from the piano stool. Amongst the scores was *The Sound of Music*. For 'Do-Re-Mi' Dominic did Maria's part. Mr Olver called Tobie and Chiluma to leave the dishes and join in the singing. We did 'Climb Every Mountain', and 'My Favourite Things', and finally 'The Hills Are Alive', with Dominic and Steven together doing a duel-harmony descant. Tobie and Chiluma, who had sometimes joined in, sometimes just stood listening, returned to the kitchen. Before taking his leave, the old man invited the Olvers and Ma'am to dinner for the following, our last, evening. Ma'am asked whether she could risk leaving the six of us alone. 'Of course, Ma'am,' in unison. And so the invitation was accepted.

Dominic, having enjoyed the singing, now said he wanted me to sing, alone. I declined, claiming I had a sore throat – maybe from the wind on the catamaran.

'Lies, Karl! Your voice was fine a moment ago.' He rolled his eyes, 'Come on! Sing one of those sentimental things.' The others joined in the encouragement. I did want to extend the enjoyment of the evening, to take the pleasure further into the night, to not be a stick in the mud. Still, the fear of my own voice sent heatwaves into my cheeks. I had not sung alone in front of an audience for two years, and even then never to an audience that itself sang with a voice resembling streams of liquid gold. 'Come on, Karl!' I wanted to, but laughed and said I didn't. Dominic said he'd play 'Boulder to Birmingham' – one of my favourites – and that he and the others could join in on the chorus. Dread of me making a spectacle of myself had me biting my lips even as he played the introduction. In mock playfulness I asked Dominic and Steven to help if my voice packed up because of the sore throat. They nodded and Dominic whispered, 'Just sing it the way you want to, forget about Emmylou Harris!' From the moment I began, I was again aware that something had drastically altered in the sounds I was producing from my vocal chords. Not only were they deeper and stronger than I could recall them ever being, they were quite wonderful, and I had perfect control over what I was doing. Indeed, over the last two years something had happened to both the voice's timbre and my ability to modulate, send it exactly where I wanted it to go. To my own ear – now fine-tuned to what was good sound and what was bad – the voice that came from my chest was beautiful, rich and powerful, touching each note perfectly, rising over the others when their voices joined in harmonies for the chorus. The song drew to a close and they applauded.

'You see, I told you!' Dominic beamed. I was elated. The fear, clutched silently for two years, was instantaneously erased and in its place came a slight regret at never having asked for a transfer to seconds. How different all those hours in choir might have been. My voice would never be classical, like Dom's or Steven's. Nor could I see myself a pop star like Elton John or a rock idol like Mick Jagger. But my voice was good. Good enough. More than good enough to enjoy without feeling in the least bit shy. On the contrary. In a flash of courage, I asked Dom whether he knew 'Clouds'.

'"Both Sides Now"!' he exclaimed. 'Joni Mitchell! Mum's favourite from her hippy days.' He began playing. Again, I sang alone:

> Rows and flows of angel hair
> And ice-cream castles in the air
> And feather canyons everywhere
> I've looked at clouds that way

I was again elated by the sound. No, it would never be the voice of a world-class boy soloist, but it was mine, I had control of it, it could do things I had imagined the property of only born talent.

> Moons and Junes and Ferris wheels
> The dizzy dancing way you feel
> As every fairy tale comes real
> I've looked at love that way

Filled with wonderment, less by the applause than by a recognition of what had so inconspicuously become of a voice I had for two years loathed, I wanted us to keep singing till daybreak. Before drifting to bed we entertained the adults with Afrikaans folk songs: 'Ver In Die Ou Kalaharie'; 'My Sarie Marais'. When we did 'Die Padda Wou Gaan Opsit', Ma'am and the Olvers hummed along as it was the same tune as 'Froggie Went a'Courting'. With 'Al Lê Die Berge Nog So Blou', I made my second discovery of the night: I had learnt, without ever knowing it as it had happened, to harmonise – improvise – and not only in predictable and easy thirds.

I am, I lay thinking to myself as I hummed the song against his back, in love with them. This is what it feels like to be in love. When I'm with Dom, I think I am in love with him. When with Jacques, I think I am in love with him. Yes, I want to be with both for ever. Oh and Alette. One letter from Alette, and I miss her and am certain that

I will love her into old age. And I am cheating on her. But I'm not hurting her or anyone else. So, can it really matter? What would she say if she ever found out? She won't. No one ever will. Does that mean I am fickle? What had become of the ever fixed mark? How I would have liked to tell someone, to ask advice, celebrate the good fortune of having three lovers. I did not use the words boyfriend or girlfriend: lover, lovers. Words that rang truer, more pleasing to my internal dialogues. Ma'am, she would be able to give me advice. Could one love three people – equally – at once? Jacques? Dominic? Alette? I am in love with three people, I was sure. All in different ways, but I loved them and I wanted to be with them all. If one of them left me, I'd still have two. Maybe we could all live in a big house one day when I'd finished school. I smiled to myself, knowing, but refusing to accept the thought as nothing more than a flight of my fancy. I could write plays, poems and novels, and Dominic could be a pianist, and Alette a doctor, and Jacques could have a choir. To serenade us at supper. We'd have lots of money so that we could travel to Europe and America and I could take them to the bush. Alette would truly love that. Wild animals. We'd build a big house at the coast or on Lake Malawi; we'd have a private game ranch like Mala Mala and I could be a game ranger and they could go to work every day. I will be fourteen in six weeks' time, I told myself. After this year, only five more years of school, then five years at university. Ten years. Will we all be able to hold out that long?

I kissed him goodnight and rose from the bed. I slipped into my pyjamas and dressing gown. In the passage, I heard him lock the door behind me. I crept back to the library. From behind the encyclopaedias I retrieved my blanket. It was not a very cold night, but I'd thought I may as well get it over while there was a moon. Blanket under my arm, I retraced my steps. Music was coming from his room. Then, into the first music room, careful not to bump into stands and tjello boxes. I lifted myself through the window. Left it slightly ajar. Made my way through the bush behind the school. It was colder than

I'd thought and I tugged the dressing gown to my chest, tightened the belt. Down behind the rondavels, past the stables and the servants quarters. Cut through the citrus orchard towards the ford. Beneath my feet dry oak and plain leaves crunched in the quiet night. Afraid of being heard, I moved into the road. I put the blanket over my head, sure that no one would suspect I was a white boy from the school.

They were no longer amongst the reeds by the ford. I cursed. They've left. No! Of course, our fort! Maybe I should just leave it. God, if my empty bed was discovered. No. The dummy would do its job. Up Sterkspruit I made my way and crossed along the pump-house stepping stones back to the fort side of the river.

22

Joseph Atwood, a man with a little grey goatee stained yellow around his mouth, came to Umfolozi to make a documentary film about fish eagles. I accompanied Bok and Mr Atwood everywhere they went in search of a mating pair in an accessible spot. During the numerous recces, we also took him to the python holes at Mphafa where, like an excited child, he sat for hours with us waiting for the pythons to make an appearance. Bok dropped a handkerchief at the mouth of a hole, its tip just over the entrance; if the pythons were in there and suffi-ciently inquisitive, they'd come up to slowly take the hanky into their mouths, taste it, spit it out and either slip back in or for a while sun their smooth heads on the sand.

We found a nest near Dengezi. High up in the hill was a pair on the verge of roosting. At the foot of perpendicular cliffs, within sight of the white guano stains running from the nest, we set up a camp of three tents that Jim and Boy enclosed with thorn branches to make a temporary lapa.

Bok and Mr Atwood found a site at the top of the cliff from where the filming could be done. While I stayed in camp with Jonas and Boy, Bok and Mr Atwood climbed the back incline with all the equipment. After an hour their tiny figures again popped into view on the ridge above the guano markings. Ropes swung down the cliffs and one by one the two men slid down to a ledge above the white stains where Jonas said he could make out the nest. There on the ledge they made a platform and erected a small cubicle of brown tenting fabric into which went all Mr Atwood's photographic equipment. Bok then climbed back up onto the ridge from where the tripod and huge flat camera were hoisted down to the old man in front of his cubicle. We stayed for a day to watch that all was okay. At first light Mr Atwood climbed the hidden incline and waved when he came back into view. Then he slid down to his perch from where he said he could see that two eggs had appeared in the mound of dry sticks, twigs, down and leaves.

We departed, leaving Boy there to cook Mr Atwood's meals. We returned only once or twice a week to say a brief hello, pass on messages and new rolls of film, or to have a quick braai in the temporary lapa.

Months after Mr Atwood left, when I had long since stopped enquiring when we would see his movie, he returned, bringing along his wife. Against the wall of our lounge he showed the thirty-minute film that had taken six weeks to *shoot* and another four months in *editing* — the first time I heard the word. The movie was called *For Loving Eagles* and while I'd had nothing to do with either its filming or the process of *production*, the entire event felt as though my eyes, my life, were somehow in every *frame*: starting from the eggs, then the hatching, then the little chicks ugly like newborn porcupines, the frenzied feeding, the parents attacking the cubicle, their talons ripping the tenting to shreds; to where the chicks waddled to the edge of the nest, inspected the ledge of the cliff, took the plunge and rose into their first flight. Magnificent. Utterly breathtaking. There were scenes of the camp with Boy; the hoisting up and down of equipment, and Mr

Atwood said this was what good documentary film-making was about: where the person making the film showed parts of the process of production; how challenging it really was to find apt *locations* and relevant species; that animals and birds were shy and not man's friend – contrary to what Walt Disney movies set out to show the world. It was ridiculous to lead people and children to believe in a non-existent world of innocence where animals were abundant, not aloof, not dangerous, not territorial and not aggressive. I wondered why Mr Atwood – having wanted to show the process of making a wilderness film and of how one got *close-ups* of animals – had cut out Bok's handkerchief that had been used to lure the pythons from their holes? But I none the less agreed with what Mr Atwood had said about showing how he had made the film. For weeks afterwards wished I could rewatch it. Thought of it in bed at night. Wished I had been in it.

Once more, Mr Atwood returned to Umfolozi. This time it was to make a movie about Bok as a game ranger. They spent weeks in the bush and again I often accompanied them and saw the fascinating way movies were made. They set snares, then stuck a live impala's neck in and filmed as it struggled. This was to show what illegal poaching did to animals. They filmed Jonas and Boy setting up camp, and later, when I saw the movie, there were sections of Bok on trail with tourists that I had not seen them shoot, and another of Bok walking along a footpath and stepping on a metal trap that slammed shut like hippo's jaws around his boot. They went to the Lion Park near Maritzburg and there filmed a donkey being eaten. That footage was then stuck into the film as if it had happened in Umfolozi to one of Bok's trail donkeys just outside the trailist's lapa. It looked completely real, and Bok was like a real film star. I wished we could move to America and all be in movies. Then I wanted only to be a game ranger acting in movies: out came a shoebox that doubled as a poacher's snare in the footpath. 'Action,' I'd call, then strut down the path apparently looking at game through binoculars. Stepping in the shoebox I'd scream and fall into the grass, cursing the poachers and calling to an imagined Jonas and Boy for help. Suz would be all over me, licking and whimpering: her disbelief suspended time and time again. For a while I'd lie in the sun, telling Suz that unless she went for help, I'd perish once lion, leopard or cheetah found me in the path.

'*Cuuuuut*,' I'd call, then get up and say: 'Well, Mr Atwood, were you satisfied with the *take*?'

'No, Ralph, sorry. Actually, I'd like to do one more take. Perhaps a little more pain on your face when you step in the trap? Do you mind?'

'Certainly, Joseph. We can go on till we get it right,' and I'd begin again, strutting from the bottom of the footpath, Suz at my heels.

How many other texts sabotage memory here? How what was read, seen, feared, loved and believed later, filters now the Joseph Atwood, the Karl De Man of then? The more I thought about the donkey being chewed up – that it hadn't even happened in Umfolozi but that Mr Atwood had the power to make it happen wherever he liked – the more I thought I would perhaps make movies. Better yet, write them, produce them, star in them, shoot them, edit them, and show them. If you did that, you had the power to make a story into fact, fact into story. Just as you pleased, to fool or entertain the whole silly world.

23

Tobie and Chiluma cleared our dishes while the six of us listened to Seven Singles and albums from the Olvers' collection. They and Ma'am were away at the neighbour's for supper. Soon the six of us were dancing to The Beatles and The Beach Boys, with Tobie and Chiluma pausing to watch from the dining room, grinning at us through the doorway. I ran to our room and slipped out of my school T-shirt into the blue and white one Dom had brought me from Paris. When I walked back into the lounge everyone whistled as I clicked my fingers and jigged my hips. Mervyn and Bennie complained that there was no disco music and that The Beatles belonged in the sixties. Dominic invited Tobie to join us and the man roared with laughter. Dominic persisted, imploring him to come onto the floor, but Tobie shook his head and said no, the master would soon be home. Then Dominic bounced over and grabbed him by the arm, both of them laughing, and he tugged Tobie into the lounge. Soon the two of them were jiving around. The rest of us called approval from the chairs, and Chiluma stood grinning against the door frame. After the song Tobie ran from the lounge, in stitches, he and Chiluma clasping hands and giggling while we clapped and called for him to come back for another dance. I found both Patsy Cline's and Frank Sinatra's *Greatest Hits*. After a brief argument about my old-fashioned taste the others allowed me to play just a few tracks. Chiluma and Tobie again stood in the doorway, waiting to see and hear what we'd get up to next. Almeida and Lukas, Mervy and Bennie, and Dominic and I waltzed; big, dramatic turns, with me steering Dominic and shouting direction to the others. When 'I Fall to Pieces' — the duet with Jim Reeves — came on, we all stopped, for alas, the song was not a waltz. From the doorway, Tobie said: 'Two-step, Master Karl, two-step,' and before Bennie in his overeagerness could remove the LP from the turntable Tobie and I were spinning around the room, me leading, him following, like a champion. I wished Bok and Bokkie could see me, now better even than when they had taught me. Tobie was as light on his feet as I must have been in the days my parents had guided my first steps — and now I was leading. It was a terrific moment. Tobie's smiling face and tasselled red fez above me, his torso covered in the long white cotton suit like an Arabian prince, I thought, coming to pay homage at Scheherazade's court. If only I were dressed formally, and not in the PT shorts and T-shirt, what a picture we'd make. Dominic dragged the coffee table from the centre of the floor to the side, opening up a large space across which we could move.

The music and our elegant twirling came to an end. Tobie was immediately bashful, peering at us through his fingers and shaking with laughter. Everyone applauded. When 'A Poor Man's Roses' came on, he and I again swept around the room, this time in ever widening circles, bigger steps, bolder swirls, arching our backs outward, turning away and stepping out from each other, coming together again, interlocking hands and again twirling around the room. As the song advanced, we grew breathless, yet continued as if we had only just begun, smiling at each other. The bystanders grew quieter, even as we grinned at them and each other.

Then, it was a twist, the last song on the album – 'Too Many Secrets' – and everyone including Chiluma came onto the lounge floor. I showed off Oupa Liebenberg's Charleston. Soon we were all doing it, pulling faces, laughing, sticking out our palms to one another, or swinging imaginary strings of pearls. Things fizzled from there and no objections followed my placing Sinatra on the turntable. Bennie and Lukas drifted to their rooms and Mervy, Dominic, Almeida and I remained. This is Gershwin, Dom said, did you know he was a homosexual? Ignoring the question, I stared from the window across the lake. Behind me the music was changed. I would have loved to remain there. Live in the house and take care of it while the Olvers went back to England. I turned to face the lounge. Dom stood, ready to say goodnight. Almeida was going through the rows of LPs. Mervyn was looking at Tobie in the doorway. Tobie's red fez was now gone, his head of hair exposed. Small plaits ran back to his crown. My eyes rushed down his white cotton-clad body even as he kept his on my face.

'Goodnight, Masters.'

'Goodnight, Tobie . . . Thanks for supper. And everything.'

He smiled, turned around and left through the dining room and kitchen.

'I hate it when they call me Master,' Dominic said and left the lounge.

'I'm going to bed, will you two turn off the lights?' Steven asked as he and I pulled the coffee table back to the centre of the room. Ma'am and the Olvers came through the front door. They told us about their supper and asked whether we boys had had enough to eat. As Mervyn and I prepared to leave, Ma'am pointed and asked about the T-shirt I was wearing. I laughed and said Dominic had brought it as a gift for me from Europe. Mr Olver said our shoes were still out on the jetty and he thought it best if we brought them inside lest we forgot to pack them in the morning. Mervyn and I walked out to the jumble of sandals, then made our way back to the front door. In the passage outside the lounge we came to a standstill. It was Mr Olver's voice: '. . . All of them, you know. Borderline cases.' And then Ma'am: 'I suppose that's the million-dollar mystery, isn't it? How to keep a boy sensitive and still make sure he's not . . . You know . . . Happy!' Their laughter rumbled into the passage. I shoved Mervyn and we walked by the lounge door without looking in. We didn't say good-night to them or to each other.

Under our mosquito net, I turned onto my back. I slid my hand into Dominic's pyjama shorts and he moved his into mine.

'At last,' he said out loud and I said shhh, please. We tugged off our shorts. He clasped my erection in his fist and began moving the skin. With his in mine, I did the same. After a while he whispered that he was close. Not thinking, I whispered back – close to what – but he just grunted and suddenly I felt it, wet, warm, and for a moment I thought he had pissed. Then its slippery texture struck me and I knew he had squirted semen, juice, come. This was what Lukas had meant that day with the sheep; what happened before his bed's springs went quiet; this was like King's litres of squirt into Cassandra. How remarkable, how fascinating.

The hard object in my hand was going limp, and to my regret

Dominic had stopped manoeuvring mine, which remained erect. He took the tip of the white sheet and wiped his belly, then dropped the wet section down the side of the bed. He faced me and asked whether I wanted to come. I said it had never happened to me. Snorting, he said it was time I had the experience. Once I felt it, he said, I would be addicted: 'Only difference,' he whispered, 'unlike Condensed Milk and drugs, this has no bad side effects.'

He tried with his hand to bring me to a climax, but eventually, when I heard he was exhausted, told him to give up. Warm and sweaty, we pushed the sheet off us till we lay uncovered beneath only the mosquito net.

He asked what I liked most about him. I grunted, embarrassed by the question, and thinking now of what Mervy and I'd overheard from Ma'am and Mr Olver.

'Come on, tell me,' Dom insisted and I pushed Ma'am and Mr Olver from my mind. The idea of verbalising what I liked about him was somehow indecent. It fell, I thought, like what we had already been doing, into a realm of things boys were not meant to ask of each other. This was the *borderline*. Alette could tell me she loved me and I could tell her in letters that she was beautiful. But voicing intimacies to Dominic in the dark not only seemed impossible, it constituted a further blurring of the space I had allowed us to enter. He nudged me, waiting for an answer. This is my last night in Malawi, as part of this school or as Dominic's friend, I told myself. Just go for it. Just once.

Eventually I said: 'Your sense of humour.'

'Yes. I agree, I do have a marvellous sense of humour. And?'

'And . . . your kindness. And your voice. It was like dew, shining on blades of grass, when you did "Last Rose of Summer".' Above us, the outline of the mosquito net was neatly tucked into a ring from where it spread into a giant magnolia in folds out and over us.

Without my asking he said: 'I love everything about you, your hands — if only you'd stop biting your fingernails, your legs, your feet, your dick,' he giggled, 'your generosity and your energy.' A list of praises washing over me like a breeze from the lake, yet still leaving me slightly embarrassed. No one had spoken to me like this before. Trepidation, the awareness that something was wrong, kept flicking the corners of my mind. His list had brought to my tongue ideas I wanted to speak, about him, though I couldn't: your fingers, Dominic, with round fingertips like little pink gecko's toes, those I love; your cheeky smile, your giraffe eyes, those I love and have dreamt of kissing; the sights you throw when you're having fun behind the piano like when you did your Liberace impersonation in Marabou's class or your concentration when you're just alone with the music; the way your thin hair gets sweaty during hikes and sticks to your temples and the way your temples throb when you're having an argument with Bennie; the way the tip of your nose moves when you speak. Not a word of it could leave my lips.

Then he asked what I liked least about him and I immediately said there was nothing.

'And me?' I asked.

'Your moods. When you're unpredictable. The way you change from laughing and pestering one minute, to going off the next and sitting on your own. Sulking and feeling sorry for yourself.'

I wasn't sulking when I went off alone, I said. I just had to think about things. I needed to be by myself to work through issues.

'Well, still,' he whispered, 'we never know what's going on with you when you become like that. Too much working through issues will drive you crazy.'

He asked what I liked most about his body. He was again venturing where I had not thought of going outside my own silent contemplation. How vast the distance, I could have self-consciously identified that night, between what we can think and feel, and what we can and eventually will and do say. And is what we don't say closer to what may be true?

He prodded me with his elbow. Unable to say that I liked the angle of his neck before me in class, the peculiar shape of, his fingertips as they spread over full octaves, I turned the question around and asked him rather to say what he liked most about his own body.

'My eyes, most, I suppose. And least that I'm so short and so fucken thin.'

'I always wanted to be short and thin,' I whispered, 'I wanted to be a jockey.'

'And you?' he whispered. 'What do you like least about your body?' It was becoming easier. Barriers were falling away.

'I wish I had a chest and pecs like Bennie. And I want to look like Robert Redford or Steven. He's as beautiful as a boy's allowed to be before he looks like a girl.'

'But, my boy, my dea fella!' Dominic put on an American drawl. 'You've got my kinda looks, Karl. And Mom and Dad also think you're far more gorgeous than Steven.' He laughed: 'Bennie's a short-arse, like me. Your legs are great. No, you're much better looking than Steven and you do look a bit like Robert Redford. I wish I was as tall as you or Lukas.'

'I would prefer to be your length,' I said.

'Height,' he said, and laughing, added, 'length is what Mervy's got between his legs.'

'I wouldn't mind having Mervy's length! Fuck, it's huge. Though I don't want it to be red and clammy like his.' When it became a little chilly I dragged the sheet back over us, feeling for the wet corner, bringing it briefly to my nose, trying to place the smell.

'And I love the way you move. So does Mum,' he said. 'Mum says it's so androgynous.'

'What's that mean?'

'It's a mixture between the way a man moves and the way a woman moves, like a dancer.' Blood rushed to my face. I couldn't respond. Did he not realise that this was the last thing on earth I wanted to hear? I felt like kicking him off the bed, telling him to go back to his own side of the room. I would keep my eyes on Bennie and Lukas,

I thought. See how they moved. Get away from the *borderline*. Androgynous was not how I was going to move, could not afford to move.

'Mom says you're going to be as handsome as your father, when you grow up.'

'I don't think so,' I said.

'Why not? He's very good-looking you know.'

'I read somewhere that we're born with the face God has given us, and by the time we're thirty-five we carry the faces we deserve.'

'So? What's that got to do with you being good-looking?'

'Nothing,' I said, unable to express the certitude that I would deserve an ugly face, that I knew the face God had given me had already by that night malformed.

I thought he had fallen asleep, but then he lifted himself, leant over and kissed me on the lips. Again I was embarrassed, but allowed it. Just a peck, not with an open mouth. Only lips against mine for what was less than a second.

The bus took us to Blantyre International from where we boarded the Air Malawi 727 to take us back to Jan Smuts. Having overcome his fear of flying, Bennie told the whole plane that Dominic and I had danced with a kaffir the previous evening. I felt no shame, threw my hands into the air and said I'd do it again given half the chance. And Dominic, speaking loud so that half the choir could hear, said he could understand Bennie's discomfort, for Tobie was after all a much better-looking man than Bennie could ever dream of being. Feeling as on top of the world, finding it unthinkable that I would ever again be unhappy, let alone have the blues, I sat gazing down on the Africa beneath us. No one – ever – had been as happy as I had for most of the four days at the lake. There was the fact that I was not coming back to the school. That I was not sharing with any of the others. I would write to Dominic, explain that I had to start high school in Durban. We would be pen pals, perhaps visit each other in the years ahead. And I could phone him when no one was home.

At Jan Smuts the Clemence-Gordons and the Websters and Bennie's mother were waiting. We all stood for group photos and Dr Webster asked Mr Clemence-Gordon to take a photograph of me and Dom between him and Mrs Webster. The luggage with the yellow dots came stuttering along on the newly installed conveyor belts. Lukas was catching another flight to Port Elizabeth and I was flying on to Durban. We took our cases from the conveyer. That was the last time I ever saw Steven Almeida. His parents were there with his beautiful sister, Marguerite. Lukas and I almost knocked Mervy down with a choir bench as we looked on Marguerite Almeida; her flawless, exquisite face, her long, curly black hair, her huge black eyes and olive skin. Like her brother, she was one of the most gorgeous creatures I had ever set eyes on.

And so the choir and the six of us split up, saying we'd see each other again at the end of January. And Dom, with his parents at his side, came up and hugged me. 'Loelovise yokou,' he said and for a moment I wasn't sure how to respond. He pulled a face and hugged me again, now whispering in my ear: 'Soosayok yokou loelovise mime titoo.' He pulled away. He was standing right in front of me with his parents smiling at us from behind him. I at last managed: 'Loelovise yokou titoo.' The Websters hugged me and said they'd see me at drop-off, end of January.

I tried not to think of not seeing them ever again. I'm going on with my life, I whispered to myself. Uncle Charlie gave me my ticket and said I and the other Durban boys should move to check-in and board on time. We made our way to domestic departures. A thought struck me and I told the others I'd join them in a second, I just needed to go to the toilet. They told me to hurry.

I dragged my suitcase into a stall where I unclipped it and pulled out the Paris T-shirt. I dropped it into the toilet bowl. Flushed. It didn't disappear. I began to panic, worried now that I'd miss my plane. I flushed again, but the tank had not yet refilled itself. I lifted the tank's lid off and set it on top of my suitcase. I dragged the dripping T-shirt from the toilet bowl and dropped it in the tank. Secured the lid.

Ran to check-in. The other two were gone, already on the plane. I boarded the flight. I was seated alone, away from the others. Bok and Bokkie would be waiting. What would they be able to read from my face? Had last night with Dom changed the way I looked? Would Bok smell it on me? Halfway to Durban I went into the airplane's loo and washed my hands, over and over. I stared at my tanned face in the mirror, wondered whether there were lines around my eyes that would give me away. Lifted my penis and scrotum through the flannels, bent my back and neck down as far as I could and sniffed. Undid the belt, dropped the flannels to the floor and washed my loins.

24

There was, to my mind, something gratifying in my return being from outside the borders of South Africa. With the family, awaiting me at Louis Botha, was Alette. She had cut her hair, short, like Lena. The two of them, beside each other, looked more as if they were sisters rather than Lena and Bernice. It was two days before Christmas; hot and humid inside and out, everyone tanned and brown, looking healthy and happy with the world and with me being home.

I said I'd brought gifts; that Malawi had been the most unforgettable experience of my life and that I wanted to live there when I grew up. As we drove off, leaving the Isipingo Flats below us, I listed the cities where we'd sung, told them about the Olvers, the markets, the lake, the catamaran, the snorkelling and that Ma'am Sanders had turned out to be quite nice. Lena said Ma'am's sister Miss Hope was a real pain but Alette said she liked her. Sitting half on my lap in the back seat, Alette asked about the concerts. I said that the one in the

Central Africa Presbyterian church had probably been the highlight. I spoke about the heat, about boys fainting on stage. Lied about us getting three encores. Bokkie said fainting wasn't unusual in the heat of the tropics. She'd fainted regularly while pregnant with Bernice and Lena in Oljorro.

At the Bowen Street house the fold-out plastic tree from Mkuzi days stood on its tripod in the lounge, its plastic fur covered in cotton, glitter and streamers, the fairy with her staff and silver star at the crest. It was decided that we'd not keep the Malawi gifts for Christmas Day and I handed them out, still unwrapped, together with the cigarettes Ma'am and Mr Mathison had not found very pleasing. Bokkie said I was fuelling Bok's filthy habit and if only he'd stop smoking he'd be able to feel how good she felt after almost two years of being free from enslavement to nicotene.

I told them how Lukas and I had stayed with white people who had a black child. The girls laughed at the thought of my hosts having a piccanin, but Bok said he would be the first to let a decent black man move in next door. Someone like Gatsha Buthelezi. The problem was that all blacks were not ready to be civilised like Gatsha – you would go far to find other kaffirs like him – so before you knew it there would be ten families sardined into a house meant for one. Just like the charras of Chatsworth. You couldn't believe how many coolies could fit into one tiny house.

I changed into shorts as it was too hot for flannels. Bokkie said that Uncle Joe and Aunt Lena were coming to the Malibu for a week around New Year. Alette and her family were going to Margate on the south coast, but they'd be back before I returned to the Berg. About my intention of not returning I said nothing. The right moment would, some time over the break, present itself.

I said I'd walk Alette home. Lena rose to join us.

Bok intervened: 'Let them go alone, Leen'tjie, they haven't seen each other for six months and you see Alette every day.'

Lena said no more than a quiet okay, and sank back into the

couch. I sensed the change in her mood. With that one suggestion, my father had, unwittingly, drawn the holiday's battle line between my sister and me. Lena could come along, I suggested, but she now declined, saying she'd see Alette tomorrow. Bernice suggested we all go to the beach if it were sunny. We agreed and Lena asked whether she could phone James to hear whether he wanted to join us.

Alette and I walked down the middle of the quiet street. There were houses only on the west side. On the east was virgin bush all the way to the railway lines. This was home to vervet monkeys, the only wild animals abundant in Natal outside the game reserves. No wildlife stands a chance outside reserves – Bokkie said – in a country where people are so poor they eat anything that moves. Beyond the railway line was Kingsway High where James went and Stephanie had finished matric. East of the school lay the South Coast Highway, then another suburb, then the holiday stretch along the beach front. We turned from Bowen into Dan Pienaar. I took Alette's hand, folding her fingers into mine. The night was us touching, crickets and cicadas, yellow streetlamps with moths and midges, no traffic to push us onto the long grass where one day there would be pavements. I felt a thrill of pride, holding her hand, a rush of excitement at walking alone at night, so publicly as though we were unapologetic lovers. I asked about her parents, her piano lessons, and she enquired more about Malawi, Dominic and Lukas.

We reached the bottom of their driveway. My heart was bouncing in my chest. That this was night, changed everything between us. The intimacies and playful lusts we had over the years shared in the broad daylight of the bird sanctuary, in that instant somehow meant something quite different from even the tiny gesture of holding hands as we moved down a night street. A vision of Dom and I the previous night passed through my mind. Alette and I would kiss, I suspected, something we had never done at night before. When she smiled her teeth glistened. I knew she wanted me to kiss her. We faced each other, a small step between us. I closed the space, leant forward and brought my mouth to her slightly parted lips. After a few seconds I drew back. Now she stepped forward and again rested her mouth against mine. Without letting our bodies touch, she ran her tongue across my top lip. I closed my eyes and began to partake of my first ever open-mouthed kiss. I was overwhelmed by the strangeness of her tongue moving against mine – it was rough, not smooth as I would have imagined – and the movement of her wet lips over and beneath mine. When she pressed her tongue against my front teeth, then again traced the outline of my lips, I felt myself gone stiff and I let my arms take her shoulders, pulling her closer to me. Her arms went around my neck and we pushed our mouths together, now more aggressive. I held her tightly, pushing my erection against her skirt. She pulled away, wordlessly, still smiling. Again I kissed her, pulled her to me; now she giggled and wriggled from my embrace. I thought it silly, that she, who had allowed me to touch her vagina and breasts before, was acting coy. Surely a kiss could not be more taboo than doing those other things? It was, I thought, this thing of the night. The night that changes everything. As if following something of the speculation of my mind, she said: 'We're getting too old for that.'

Her attitude was perplexing. I said nothing and she started up the driveway.

'I'm not going back, in January.'

'You aren't?' She stopped and turned back.

'No. I want to start high school in Durban.'

'Everyone is under the impression you're going back.'

'I haven't told them. So maybe you shouldn't say anything. Not yet.'

'It's only three or so weeks away. You better say something.'

'I will. You won't say anything, will you . . . to Lena?'

'No, of course, if you'd prefer me not to . . . It will be nice having you home. Want to come in and say hi to Mum? She'd like to see you.'

'Maybe tomorrow?'

'I'll come to Bowen for the beach, if it's sunny.'

'Can we kiss one more time?'

'A small one.' We pecked, and she swung around and disappeared through their front door.

Turning to leave I knew there was no way we'd be going to the beach alone. That much had already been clear at home. A stream of lights was coming down Dan Pienaar Hill. Traffic from the Drive-In's ten o'clock show. Drive-ins and cinemas, so everyone said, were not going to survive the coming of real TV in January.

It was obvious – also from Alette's letters – that over the preceding two years while she and Lena had been going to Port Natal together by train, a substantial bond had developed. It was confounding to me, for they took different subjects at school and seemed to have little in common: Lena spent her days on the sports fields, disliked academic life and couldn't even clap the most basic rhythm, let alone carry a tune. Alette didn't dream of touching a netball ball, a hockey stick or of venturing onto an athletics track. She thrived on academics and music was her life. It's the travelling together by train, that's all, I told myself as I made my way back.

It was a sweltering day and Bokkie said we were not leaving the house without hats. Bok sat in the lounge reading the newspaper. He asked whether we wanted a lift to the beach and we said no, we'd walk. The girls shaved their bikini lines in the bathroom and I collected the cricket bat and tennis ball from the servants' quarters that served as our store room. When the girls came into the kitchen dressed in shorts and bikini tops Bokkie told them to go and cover themselves because they were not walking to the beach looking like tramps. What has become of the spirit of Christmas, my mother moaned as she rinsed the empty cool-drink bottles. Christmas no longer exists, she answered herself, it's nothing more than a holiday for fun-seekers and sun-worshippers, that's all, for crass commercialisation and expensive presents. A far cry from the days when they were too poor in the Molopo to even think of gifts – let alone imagine themselves strutting through neighbourhood streets half nude. What is becoming of this world, she asked, the writing's on the wall, just as the Bible says: no more morals, instead a civilisation worshipping Mammon and the sun! I resented Bokkie for what I knew was her hypocrisy. The minute we disappeared and her housework was done, my mother would be in her shorts and out working in the garden, soaking up the sun on her bare arms and legs. If it were not for her bad ear and the fact that she couldn't swim, she'd spend her every free moment in the pool. She, more than even the girls and I, loved the sun, loved walking half naked. In the bush she would wear the teeniest tops and shorts or minis. On occasion she would hang washing clothed in only her panties. It was clear that our code of dress had nothing to do with our own morals. Instead morals had everything to do with the eyes that might witness us in a state of undress. My mind shot back to Umfolozi and Mkuzi, where I could clearly remember my mother as a less complex woman. Where she smoked; where she and Bok danced at night – before the Dutch Reformed Church taught us it was a sin to dance, a sin to enjoy food, to smoke, to dream. To live.

Already from St Lucia I had loathed Sunday school; in Toti I had started hating church, finding brief pleasure only in the drama of the occasional prayer meeting where I would be the one child who prayed aloud amongst the adults, reading off prayers – for rain, for peace, for love, for forgiveness, for the poor – which had taken hours in the writing. But since leaving the bush, Bokkie had seemed to buy into the Church lock, stock and Bible. What had become of the mother I had liked as much as I had loved? Now I loved her, but felt unsure about whether I actually liked her. And Bok, did I love him or like him or neither? It was chilling to wonder whether perhaps I neither liked nor loved my father. The recognition that my mind could even entertain such a separation shocked me. This, like those terrible thoughts I'd had of Bok at Lake Malawi, was something never to be said out loud.

*

The bottom of the big polystyrene cooler box was stacked with ice cubes. Inside, in Tupperware lunchboxes, went the sandwiches and two plastic bottles of mixed Oros. Lena, Alette, James, Bernice, her boyfriend Robert and I. We walked – while I thought of the difference between loving and liking, whether one could love without liking; you could like without loving, yes, but what about the other way around – down past the bird sanctuary, beneath the railway bridge, across Kingsway High's sports fields, dashed across the South Coast Highway. Smelt the water the instant we ascended Kingsway even before we could look down and see the deep Indian Ocean. Not a breeze, just the big unbroken blue taken up by the light blue of the sky, the sound of cars and screams and shouts and laughter from thousands of people in the water and on the beach.

Away from the clutter of holiday-makers we found a spot of open sand where we spread our towels. Most people were crowded around the small platform from where pop music was being played by a four-man band. After a quick dip we heard over the speakers that the go-go dancing competition was about to start. The prize: dinner for two at the Poseidon restaurant. We went over to watch. The line-up included two Kuswag girls with whom Lena and Alette had been in class before they left for Port Natal.

Alette cracked up: 'Oh my Loooord! Riet Malherbe and Chantelesée Visagie!'

'Common as crap.' Lena laughed as the contestants, many on platform shoes, trooped onto the small stage.

Chantelesée Visagie looked familiar, but having been away from Kuswag for two years and with them always my senior I wasn't quite certain. Her yellow tanga barely covered her breasts, the strings as if asking to be pulled swung wildly against her shiny brown thighs. The band – Hammond organ, drums, guitar and voice – played 'Clap Your Hands and Stamp Your Feet', and the line-up of girls and middle-aged women began gyrating their hips, jiggling their breasts, shaking their arms and shoulders. The audience roared, some laughed and the Look

Theres shouted encouragement. My eyes ran along the legs, the breasts. Chantelesée, so I thought, at only fourteen or fifteen – though Alette and Lena later guessed her around twenty-five because she had failed school about ten times – was certainly the best dancer and the most attractive. She had full breasts, which swayed rather than bobbed while she go-goed, and long thin brown legs, smeared in suntan oil. She kept her back upright as if she'd swallowed a rod, at the same time allowing only her breasts to sway, her belly and her leg muscles to quiver. Behind us a Look There called in Afrikaans: 'You practise that in bed, little sister.' And the men around him cracked up.

'Jirre dis common, Lena! Like bleddie Indian mynahs!' Alette said, suppressing her laugh. 'We got out of that school at just the right time or it might have been you or me up there!'

'Bugger you,' Bernice laughed, poking Alette in the back. 'All of us in Kuswag aren't like that!'

'Bokkie would rip the skin off your backside if you did go-go on the beach!' Robert said.

'I'd be grounded for a year!'

Measured by the applause at song's end, the judges announced Chantelesée indeed the winner. Beaming from ear to ear her figure glided over to the MC to collect her tickets. She kissed him and again the crowd roared. Behind me the Look There hollered: 'Bring me a piece of that cake.' And the three girls around me glared at him, shared glances, and Lena's upper lip curled as though she was ready to snarl some angry phrase.

After the go-go, it was Miss South Coast Legs 1975. We implored Lena to go up as she would certainly win. She refused, scowling that she wasn't going on parade as though she were some cow on auction to Free State farmers. Besides, she didn't have her platforms here. We followed the competition – almost all its participants on cork platforms or high heels – and afterwards agreed that the woman who eventually won her dinner for two at the Poseidon wouldn't have stood a chance had Lena been on stage.

'For a weekend in Mauritius or the Seychelles, all expenses paid,' Lena chirped, 'but not for an el cheapo dinner at the Poseidon.'

Swimming, playing beach cricket and lazing in the sun, we fried. Instead of suntan oil, my sisters and I rubbed our skins with Break Fluid. Alette was unable to hit a single ball during cricket and we were in stitches at the histrionics that accompanied her every attempt. James bowled underhand, thinking that might help, but still she swung, scooped and dangled the bat as if the instrument were designed specifically to highlight her awkwardness. She screamed each time the ball left our hands and fell down in giggles after another swing that had again gone nowhere. Lena's batting, in contrast, had us in sweats as we ran, dove, sprinted and dashed across open stretches of sand or tiptoed in amongst Look Theres' umbrellas and towels.

Bernice and Robert spent most of their time on their towels to one side, with Robert occasionally rising to return our ball. They held hands, rubbed Break Fluid on each other's skins and occasionally kissed. It thrilled me to see Bernice, plump and proud as a spring chicken in her floral bikini, kissing him, lying on her towel gazing into his eyes, her knees touching his. She was so obviously in love. I thought of Dom and told myself to forget. Recalling *Groen Koring*, from sick-bay in July, I suddenly wondered whether Bernice and Robert were having sex. The thought of her getting pregnant and everyone saying she had to get married set my mind spinning. Perhaps, as Stephanie had said, she could not have babies after the poisoning in Mkuzi. Maybe just as well. Please let Bernice be infertile. Ashamed of my thoughts, I tried to think of something else. I wondered whether I could pluck up the courage to tell her she should desist from having sex with Robert, that they could just use their hands . . . I saw and felt James's eyes going to the front of my Speedo; wondered whether he was homosexual as I'd overheard it speculated by parents, uncles and aunts.

We sprinted into the sea, body-surfing, and Lena, James and I held

a nervous Alette between us. It seemed Lena was no longer afraid of
water, though I had no inclination to dive down and drag her under
to assess her new bravery. Closer to shore, the two girls did what they
called the dolphin – riding up a wave on their backs, then jiggling
their arms and breasts. When a breaker rolled them they'd scream,
'Oops. There goes my charlie!' and hastily drag fabric back over the
exposed skin. Their altered bodies were a source of fascination: at fifteen, Lena's breasts were smaller, rounder, upright like miniature
rondavels, while Alette's were already larger, heavier, more like
Bernice's and Bokkie's, though neither my sisters nor mother had
large breasts. Bokkie and Aunt Siobhain had heard about the latest
American thing: having breasts enlarged and they both said if they
ever had the money they'd be right out there, having a bit of a lift.

Alette had to use suntan lotion – she wouldn't dream of bringing Break Fluid near her skin – and after an hour or so, on went her
T-shirt. James, his nose already pink and peeling, had taken to wearing a cap. He, like Stephanie, had Aunt Siobhain's translucent Irish
skin. Each time Alette removed her T-shirt for a swim, she asked
Lena to smear her back with lotion. By noon she and James had to
keep their shirts on, even for swimming, as they were being scorched
right through the Coppertone.

Lena and Alette, I could again see, had become even better friends
than I'd thought. A code of intimacy now existed between them from
which I had been excluded. I felt no jealousy, only a hint of rather
pleasing envy. Lena looked more content than I had ever known or
perhaps cared to register: she was radiant, with red cheeks even over
her tan, her short brown hair streaked white from the sun. Her eyes
on Alette were soft and blue. I was happy for her. Proud of her.

Shadows of tall holiday apartments began stretching across the beach
and we packed up and started the route back. At home we washed the
sea water off in the pool. When James and I changed in the bathroom, he said my dick had grown since he last saw it and that I had

almost as much hair as him. I turned my back. He asked whether I jerked off and I said no. I couldn't wait to get out of the enclosed bathroom and away from my pink-skinned cousin. Lena and I together walked Alette home. We went inside and I saw Prof and Juffrou Sang. Juffrou Sang wanted to know everything about the inauguration of the Taal Monument and the Malawi tour, what our audiences had been like, what music we had performed.

'And next year it's the Senior Choir — the crowning glory!'

'I'm not sure that I'm going back,' I said.

Her jaw dropped: 'Why? You'd be silly to leave now! Just when your voice must be at its peak.'

I said I'd think about it. She again insisted that it was, without a shadow of a doubt, worth my while staying in the Berg and that leaving before my voice broke would be a waste of years in training. 'Besides,' she said, 'you don't know what will be left of your voice once it's broken. I've heard boys' voices — some close to as good as your little Dominic friend — changed to nothing but croaking after they became men. Use it while you've got it.'

'I'll give it serious thought, Juffrou,' I said.

'What about a solo in church on Christmas Day?' she gleamed.

'No, please not. My voice is tired after this year. There was the Eastern Cape Tour in April, then October to Paarl and now the Malawi one.'

'We saw you on TV at the Taal Monument. Uh, who was that black-haired boy who did "Oktobermaand"?'

'Steven Almeida. He's Portuguese.'

'Exquisite. I've never heard a voice like that.' And she shuddered, showing her delight.

'He's a friend of mine.' I told them to watch *Kraaines* on Christmas Day, when our pre-Malawi recordings would be broadcast.

I asked Lena how she liked Port Natal and she said she was very happy to be there. The kids of Port Natal had pride in the school and themselves, unlike the white trash of Kuswag. To illustrate the point she told me about Leon Lategan, brother of Anka, from whom she got her school uniforms: 'Leon saw a kaffir wearing a Port Natal blazer that had obviously been discarded. So Leon bought the blazer for five rand from the kaffir and went home and burnt it. Now can you imagine a Kuswag kid taking such pride in their school uniform?'

I said I doubted any of the Kuswag kids would have five rand to buy the blazer in the first place. It wasn't a matter of money, she countered, it was one of character and loyalty to one's school. Pride would not let five rand stand in its way.

We spoke about the pending visit of our aunt and uncle from Klerksdorp, and wondered whether the annual Christmas drama was again set to play: Uncle Joe disappearing, going where we suspected, looking for prostitutes at the Smuggler's Inn at the docks on Point Road. The previous four Christmases had unfolded in the same way: Uncle Joe out every night and Aunt Lena in tears and the depths of despair, alone with the Brats in the Malibu or Elangeni hotel room.

'Does Bok still go to Smuggler's?' I asked.

'For business, he says, to see curio dealers! But Bokkie doesn't believe him. Neither do we.'

I was suddenly grateful that I was seldom home to feel ashamed of my father's going where we knew and he told us there were whores, strippers and rock musicians. Nor to witness the accusations, the silences, or to hear my mother wordlessly slamming down pots and pans on kitchen surfaces.

'Why he has to see dealers in Smuggler's I don't know,' Lena said, a tone of bitterness in her voice.

'Does Alette know he goes there?'

'Are you mad! He's a deacon in the church. Everyone will think we're common, or something.'

I said I needed to go to the Toti library to take out some books and Lena said she hoped I wasn't planning on spending the whole holiday reading.

Christmas morning – the sun again without mercy – was church. Before we entered, Bokkie took me to see the mustard tree she had planted when we'd first got to Toti. The tree had barely grown half an inch.

Juffrou Sang, behind the organ, nodded to us as our family with Alette amongst us marched down the aisle, my sisters in hats, me in my black school blazer and flannels. Bok and Prof came in with the deacons, dressed in their black suits. Kids who had been in Kuswag with me till the end of Standard Three dotted the pews. The sight of them filled me with a sense of superiority: they looked the way they had two years before – the same long pants or Terylene suits on the boys, the same floral dresses and floppy hats and shapeless loose hair on the girls. What a relief to know I wouldn't be returning to Kuswag. That I'd be going to Port Natal Hoër. Juffrou Sang's recorder ensemble – to which I'd once proudly belonged – played a poorly arranged medley of carols that now sounded utterly amateurish. Alette and I nudged each other, shared snide glances and I suppressed a snort by forcing a sputtering cough. Soon Bokkie and my sisters understood the source of our amusement and within seconds all five of us had the silent but uncontrollable giggles. Beside me, Bokkie was the worst, both hands clasped around her Bible were shaking, the fabric of her dress vibrating around her knees. Eventually our entire bench rocked. Bokkie dug her nails into my and Bernice's forearms and whispered for us to stop. Throughout the service we remained calm, but at the end, when Dominee Lourens walked down from the pulpit and the ensemble struck up a frightfully cacophonous version of Psalm 23, the giggles again overcame us. Outside the church we could barely speak to the bystanders and we rushed to the car where we wailed and cackled while waiting for Bok to come from the vestry. The sounds of the organ from inside died away and Alette said she had to be off. Taking her leave she rolled her eyes at having to go and face her mother with platitudes and embellishments about the ensemble's splendid renditions.

For years I had wanted an air rifle and for Christmas I got it at last. In the bush between our house and Kingsway High, Lena and I, followed everywhere by the dog Judy, went shooting: mousebirds, Indian mynahs, sparrows, all the birds that may eat paw-paw, guava and avocado pears from our yard. We were both good shots. When Bok and Bokkie went shooting at the Poinsettia Pistol Club, my sisters were sometimes allowed to fire a few rounds after official competitions were over. In our back yard we now put up a target and held air-rifle contests. I took my time, aimed carefully. Lena said anyone could shoot well if they took for ever like me. But what good would that do if there was a burglar in the house, or if I had to fire rapidly at an enemy? The trick was to aim and fire. No, she said, I'd be useless if a kaffir came into the house. The boys at Port Natal, Lena said, did target practice with .22s during cadette period. She said it was ridiculous that girls didn't do cadets and were not conscripted for the army. She wished we were more like Israel where girls had to do national service along with the boys. She said she'd heard of a military academy for girls at George near Port Elizabeth. Maybe she'd go there after she'd finished school.

At Uncle Michael and Aunt Siobhain's for Christmas lunch I saw Stephanie for the first time in ages. She tore open her carton of Malawi cigarettes at once. She lit a cigarette and took a long draw, exclaiming she could taste East African soil in the tobacco. She and Bernice spent their time in Stephanie's old upstairs room. With only Lena, James and me, the catching game had lost its lustre. We got Bok and Uncle Michael to join us for lawn cricket, and Bok again spent time perfecting our overhand bowling.

Stephanie had, since the Bush days, become a complete stranger to me. She had finished school, lived in her own apartment in Durban's Overport City, and worked as a buyer for Woolworths. Now over twenty, the years between us had become insurmountable. She was a woman, independent, smoking, driving her own yellow Mini that she called Herbie, after the *Herbie Rides Again* movie.

Later in the day Bokkie called upstairs, telling Bernice to come down. Bernice should remember only one Christmas remained before she left our family for good. These last holidays together were moments she would treasure for the rest of her life. As six p.m. drew close we gathered in the lounge to watch the *Kraaines Christmas Special*. Standing up close to the screen I pointed out my friends, Lukas and Bennie. There I was on TV, caught in close up once briefly during 'Away in a Manger', the carol drowned as we clapped and whistled. I looked ghastly to myself — washed out, pale and nondescript. Dominic — skinny as a rake, his mouth as wide as a soup bowl on the 'Silent Night' descant. Almeida — frequently zoomed onto by the camera, drew admiring comments from Aunt Siobhain and Stephanie, while Bokkie and Bernice confirmed that he was an exceptionally good-looking boy.

'What a dish!' Stephanie gasped.

'Like a young Montgomery Clift,' Aunt Siobhain said, providing me the first recollection I have of hearing the actor's name.

'He's my best friend,' I said and believed myself.

Aunt Siobhain suggested we get tickets to see the musical *Ipi Tombi* in the Alhambra. Newspaper reviews hailed it 'a marvellous spectacle of tribal song and dance'. Bokkie said she doubted that we could afford to go, and besides, Uncle Joe and Aunt Lena would be down and they wouldn't be able to take little Joelene and Lenard. At six and four they were the most spoilt brats in the world, those two, got everything they laid their eyes on because Uncle Joe was a millionaire and Aunt Lena wasn't allowed to beat them. Whenever the subject was Aunt Lena's children, each of us had a mouthful to say. Bokkie, in particular, was a bottle of rage. Uncle Joe had, from the outset forbidden Aunt Lena to lift a hand against the children, an instruction and rule that left us agog — not merely because we had accepted our countless beatings, but because the Brats were, indeed, the manipulative centre of the world wherever they went and we followed. Joelene and Lenard would simply demand — question marks never punctuated their speech — and Aunt Lena would have to jump. In the presence of their father the Brats threw tantrums and plates, and Aunt Lena was not allowed any response other than requesting, imploring, begging or bribing them to stop. Away from Uncle Joe, the kids could sometimes be darlings, and little Joelene particularly, bright and charming, could succeed in letting one forget temporarily what she was capable of when her father was around.

'That,' Bokkie said, 'that the Brats run the Klerksdorp mansion, is what gets my poor sister into the madhouse for shock treatments. And of course Joe Mackenzie's whoring. Now, the latest, is that he has the fourteen-year-old daughter of one of his farm foremen . . .' A brief silence followed, not from shock — nothing Uncle Joe did could shock us any more — merely to allow the company to process the man's latest indulgence.

'Well. Why doesn't Lena leave him?' Uncle Michael asked. The same question we'd all asked a hundred times.

'How can she? He'll just have her declared crazy and she'll lose the children,' Bokkie answered, putting down her knitting. 'He's told her so: try and leave me and you'll sit in the madhouse with your finger up your arse. He owns Klerksdorp, that bastard. Owns the police, all the lawyers. Lena can't turn her arse and he knows what she's doing. Night after night she sits in the mansion while he's with the fourteen-year-old slut on the farm.'

'What do the fourteen-year-old's parents have to say?' asked Aunt Siobhain.

'What can they say? The father works for Joe? He's Joe's foreman. The one who pays the piper plays the tune.'

'But she's a minor, for God's sake. What about the police?'

'Joe Mackenzie owns the Klerksdorp police and every magistrate, hear you me.'

'A building contractor for the mines, my arse! I'm telling you today: that's not where he gets his money.'

'Do you still think he's into illegal diamonds?'

'I don't think it, I know it, so does Lena who does all his books. Why do you think he never appoints a qualified accountant for his businesses, lets poor Lena sit there day in and day out? He tells her how to cook those books, I'm telling you.'

'Well, why doesn't Lena go to the police? Tell them about the diamonds, that will stand in any court of law.'

'My cousin Salomo Burger, big shot in the Transvaal Security Police, told me: Joe Mckenzie owns the police and every Klerksdorp magistrate. Now that's coming from the inside, right from the corridors of power . . .'

We were all silent: adults and children alike. In the face of Uncle Joe's money, his power – and our unspoken envy.

Late that evening the phone rang and Bernice answered. When I heard her say Dominic's name I ran to take the receiver. Speaking softly into the mouthpiece, I told him about the air rifle and our day on the beach. He said they'd been skiing on Hartebeespoortdam and were flying to Plettenberg Bay for New Year at the Beacon Isle Hotel. He said Dr Webster wasn't all that keen on the Beacon Isle since that was the place Mimi Coertze had blown a gasket and filed an official complaint when a black waiter who spoke English couldn't serve her in Afrikaans. Anyway, Mrs Webster wanted to go there and Dom's father had at long last capitulated, saying he wouldn't let the memory of a second-rate prima donna's first-rate discrimination ruin the place for them. He said he wished I could come along and I said I did too. Excitedly Dominic told me that while we were in Malawi Mrs Webster had had a chat to Mr Cilliers. We'd be doing some Beethoven

Mass for the Senior Choir's New Year's programme. I'd never heard of the Mass. 'I love you,' he said and I asked where his parents were. 'They're sitting right here. Dad says hi and Merry Christmas even though he believes Christmas is nothing more than a glittering ball of capitalist crap.' Behind Dom I could hear the Websters laugh.

'Well, thanks for phoning, Dom.'

'If I don't call again I'll see you end of January, okay?'

'Yes, and say hello to your folks and enjoy Beacon Isle.'

I could not believe he had told me he loved me with his parents sitting right there. I was outraged. Petrified that the Websters would guess what we'd done in Malawi.

On Boxing Day Alette left with Prof and Juffrou Sang for their vacation. Saddened at her going, it was good to know we'd be seeing each other again after New Year.

Bernice, Lena and I strolled along the deserted Kingsway road towards the Poinsettia pistol range where Bok and Bokkie were competing in the end-of-year competition. Bernice paged through one of Stephanie's old *Fair Lady* magazines.

'I am not going back to the Berg, next year,' I casually announced, having decided it would serve me best to get my sisters on side before broaching the subject with my parents.

'Why? And what do Bok and Bokkie say?' Bernice asked without looking up from the magazine.

'I haven't told them . . . But I want to start high school here. And it's too expensive to stay in the Berg, anyway.' I said I was not blind, that I could see they and Bokkie were in the same clothes they'd been wearing a year before. And one had to be a retard not to notice that Bok's business was failing.

'A bit late, Karl! For you to realise that after two years and thousands of rands down the toilet,' Lena snapped.

'I didn't realise it only just now, Lena. In July — when they took me back — I asked them not to leave me there.'

'I don't remember that,' said Bernice.

'Well, I did, you can ask them. And Aunt Siobhain was there too.'

'You shouldn't have gone there in the first place,' Lena responded, anger more pronounced in her voice.

'Oh come on, Lena, it's an honour and he's developing his talents,' Bernice said and gave me a smile as she turned a page. While she had always taken pride in my being in the Berg, Lena had seemed, within months of my passing the audition, to resent my going there.

'An honour for him and poverty for us,' Lena said.

'Lena, we have everything we need. There's food on the table and you're at Port Natal as well. I'm at Kuswag and not complaining.' Lena said Bernice had chosen to stay at Kuswag. Bernice responded that she had stayed only because she wanted to finish high school in one place rather than start afresh elsewhere.

'And that's exactly why I want to come back,' I said, 'so I won't change high schools midway.'

'Do you think you're coming to Port Natal?'

'Yes, I might as well start—'

'Think twice, Little Nightingale,' Lena spat. I had no idea what had gotten into her. Suddenly she was hissing: 'The boys are waiting for you . . . The whole school knows about you. Where they needed more information I've filled in the gaps. If I were you I'd stay away for as long—'

'Lena!' Bernice cut her short and came to a stop in the middle of the road. The magazine hung open from her hand which rested on one hip: 'Why are you always so hateful to him? What has he done to you? A minute ago you were saying he should come home and now you're threatening him.'

'I never said he should come home. Groot meneer on TV. He could rot in those mountains for all I care.'

'Stop it, Lena,' Bernice said. 'You sound like a witch.' And then she again took to reading *Fair Lady* and we walked on.

'And,' Lena began, 'if you think Alette is going to be your girlfriend I've got more news for you.'

'She is my girlfriend.'

'Maybe now while you're away, imbecile. But a Standard Six boy coming from a pansy school with a Standard Eight girlfriend. Ha! She'll be the laughing stock of the school and they'll kill you.'

'I don't care, they can do anything they want to me. I can look after myself. I've been away from home amongst prefects and Seniors for two years. Do you think I'm scared of you and your friends?'

'You'll eat those words, believe me.'

'Listen, Lena,' Bernice said as the first shots could be heard, the double thump of the echoes bouncing off the hill above the range, 'I have had it with you. If you don't stop terrorising him I'll tell Bok.'

'Bok will say it can only do him the world of good.'

'Well, then I'll tell Bokkie.'

'Ja, that's just typical of you! Run to his protector. Why do you think he's such a little sissy in the first place? It's because you and Bokkie have treated him like he's some special case since he was in nappies in Oljorro. You and her, and the whole family, think the sun shines out of his arse, while we have to sit without new clothes, while we can never go to movies or eat out, while we can never go on holiday because he's flying around Malawi with a flock of fucken fairies. Tell Bokkie, I've got Bok on my side.'

'You are a bitch,' Bernice said.

'You are the bitch and the coward. You speak behind his back as well, about how he's the family pet. You and James and that slut Stephanie — all of you. Why don't you say to his face what you say when he's not around? I'm just saying what the whole family says anyway. No one can stand him! Don't you remember how it was when we were growing up, and we had to work in the yard, while little Mr Ladida sat in the shade reading?'

'That's shit, Lena,' I said, 'I mowed the lawn and raked and picked up leaves as much as you did, and I still do holidays when I'm home. Even now.'

'Karl, ignore her. Bok let you go to the Berg because it's an élite school. For the upper class. For smart people. Just ignore her, she's so obviously jealous of your talents.'

'I wouldn't speak of lack of talent if I were you,' Lena now turned on Bernice. 'It's not as if you're Einstein, Miss Kuswag Standard Nine C.'

'I'm in matric now and I'm a prefect. And better in C at Kuswag than E at Port Natal.'

'Z at Port Natal is better than A at Kuswag. And there's no honour in being a prefect amongst the poor whites anyway. If you were in Port Natal you'd never smell the badge.'

'Ignore the little bitch,' Bernice repeated as we turned a corner and the shooting range came into view.

Now Lena refocused on me: 'You never lifted a finger, in the bush or before you went away. I would go to Bokkie and say, he's not help-ing and she'd say leave him alone he's reading. Have you fed the dog once, cleaned that pool once, raked once in the week you've been home?'

'I scooped leaves off the pool this morning.'

'There's a filter to clean, there's acid and chlorine to be thrown in, there's a bottom that needs brushing, pipes need to be rolled up and put away. It's me and Bernice that work like kaffirs while you're run-ning around with Alette.'

'I have not been running around with her! And she's your friend, too.'

'Wouldn't say so when you're around.'

'Ignore her, Karl!'

'And yesterday, I again had to mow the lawn while Bokkie took you to town.'

'She took me to the library because I wanted to take out *A Streetcar Named Desire*.'

'I don't care whether she took you to take out *A Queer Named Karl*!
Why must I work while you're out on the town, gallivanting?'

'The library isn't out on the town.'

'Just shut up, both of you.'

'Go back to the mountains, Karl,' Lena hissed, 'where you can do
your *equestrian sports* with the fokken hoi polloi.'

'You mean hoity-toity, and they're not all like that. Some guys like
Ben—'

'Oh, cut it out. Go and feel sorry for Bennie and Mervy and
Lukassie and darling Dominickie with someone who cares. I hate you
and I'm sick of hearing your shit stories.'

My face was flushed. We had entered the shooting-range gates and
the discussion was clearly over. Around us people were greeting.
Everyone in English. This and the business world formed the English
sphere my parents occupied, the Dutch Reformed Church and the
girls' schools the Afrikaans.

Bokkie won a silver tray for best rapid-fire shot of the year and
Bok for best all-round male. Afterwards there were speeches and tea
and cake. A paper plate stacked with cake in hand, I went and sat in
the now-abandoned shooting stalls. I despised Lena more in that
instant than in the all the years of our conflict combined. It seemed
clear that she hated me – perhaps even more than I had ever suspected. And, she was only saying what the whole family said, anyway.
None of them, not one of them could stand me. After six months of
virtual unbroken certainty about not going back to the Berg – the
moments with Ma'am and Dominic at the lake had been fleeting, now
nothing even worth remembering, no, something I had to forget, a
flock of fucking fairies! – I now vacillated between wanting to return
to the Berg at once and wanting nothing more than to stay in
Amanzimtoti. Yes, I decided: I had to get back to Toti and go to Port
Natal. *A Queer Named Karl*, what did she know – what – fucking ignoramus! All she could do was throw around a ball along with a team of
equally idiotic baboons. Just like the rest of this family, no one with

one iota of originality. As for that useless James. Oh, how horribly boring this whole family was; how depressing to have to be amongst them all again, like a mouse running in a wheel. Ughhh. But I might as well come back. Get it over with now. I'll survive it, somehow. For all Lena's anger, there was – I knew and couldn't deny it – something true to what she'd said. My education *was* costing more than we could afford even to dream of. I *was* the one who got to travel while they *never* went on a single holiday except maybe up to Midmar Dam from where Mumdeman was about to retire anyway. I did not, *absolutely not,* agree that I was the family pet when it came to working in the garden or around the house. When I was home I was part of the dish-washing cycle, I carried out the trash, I raked and cut the lawn. The only thing with which I didn't help was making food, but that was because it was women's work and Bok didn't like me hanging around the kitchen, like James. Always pottering and thinking himself a chef.

Time was running out. I had to make up my mind and take up the issue with Bok and Bokkie. I had to find a way to stay in Toti. And a way to get Lena to love me. And the family, everyone. To be proud of me. It struck me again: my sister had grown to hate me. For years – even as we fought like cat and dog – she had been the one to defend and protect me. Could she really *hate* me? It was possible, I consoled myself, that she wanted less to hurt me by saying that, than she needed to remind me of how strong she really was.

From the Malibu, Aunt Lena took Lena and the Brats to do shopping and I – as in previous years – drove around with Uncle Joe to visit pigeon farmers in Westville, Cowies Hill and Durban North. Bernice was off somewhere with Robert, visiting Stephanie and her latest boyfriend. I had told Bokkie I didn't want to spend my holiday driving around with Uncle Joe because I could not stand him. My mother said I should cease my selfishness and do it for Aunt Lena: 'Be nice to Uncle Joe or else he'll be nasty to Aunt Lena. Let's see if we can get through one Christmas without him driving her insane. Please, Karl.' At the Mackenzie mansion in Klerksdorp, the double-storey pigeon run was reportedly home to fifty thousand rand's worth of pigeons, some imported from Belgium, France and Holland. Pigeons — and now Matilda — were his life. So, again I was Uncle Joe's navigator. In the early years I had taken a book along to read in the car or in the hours I waited outside Durban's smartest homes while he was in the cages. My reading had irritated him and so the books stayed at home. While he drove the silver Mercedes-Benz I tried to make small talk and to seem interested in what he was doing. Year after year I'd memorise characteristics of specific pigeons that had won major events for him. I would ask after the welfare of his champions and of his most prized breeding pair, which I knew had been brought in for three thousand rand from Brugge. With time, the most important pigeon farmers from the greater Durban area got to know me almost as well as my wealthy uncle from Klerksdorp.

While we drove along, he steered his talk towards sex. On one of our trips he said: 'The size of a woman's mouth is the same size as her cunt, did you know that, Karl?' I forced a laugh and said no, I hadn't known. 'It's a fact,' he said. 'Look at her mouth and you're seeing her cunt.' I was astonished, not about female genitalia's replication on the female face, but that he could speak to me like that. I said I doubted it was true, that it was probably similarly fallacious to men with big hands, ears or feet having big cocks. Cock. Trying to say the word nonchalantly. I did not say Mervy has tiny ears, a left hand that struggled to change chords on the violin because his fingers were so short, that he wore a size three shoe! Uncle Joe asked whether I had ever fucked. I said no, though I had 'touched Alette and some other girls'. I couldn't say the word cunt — not to him. In the company of my friends it seemed I could use any word, not only because they were my peers, but because dirty words never really sounded dirty when used amongst ourselves. In Uncle Joe's mouth, sex and body parts sounded not only dirty, but vile and evil. There was, I thought but couldn't figure what, a difference between why I found it odd to say cock in front of Bok and why I found it difficult to say in front of Uncle Joe. Uncle Joe said he remembered Alette from the previous year and that she was a pretty little thing, just like Lena and Bernice. I thought of him and the fourteen-year-old Matilda. I would have loved to ask him about her: I was fascinated, and repulsed all at once. Then he said I should not marry as divorce was expensive. Even listening to him, I felt, constituted a betrayal of Aunt Lena. I wished he'd stop. My aunt was sure to ask me what we had spoken about and I would be certain to lie about things that could upset her and tell the truth about others that seemed important to her peace of mind.

In front of the Malibu on South Beach, surrounded by thousands of Look Theres we spent hours on beach chairs and under umbrellas. We bought drinks and ice creams almost every time an Indian vendor walked by calling, 'Eyescream-cole-drinks-eyescream-cole-drinks-eyescrreeeeem.' Day in and out Uncle Joe's eyes were on Lena. I observed him closely. The gaze of an old, sly ravenous lion. Inside me a terrible rage was building. When Lena wore her red bikini – a gift from him the previous Christmas – his eyes came alive, swarmed a hive of bees over my sister's breasts, fixed on her pubis, then again ran up and down her legs. My anger was not only against him, but against Aunt Lena who brought this man into our house and into our lives. I adored my aunt and on account of Uncle Joe felt tremendous pity for her. Yet there were moments I loathed her for not leaving him and I blamed her for our having to deal with him and his bestial power. When he asked me to swim with the Brats, knowing I'd prefer to sit and read, Aunt Lena would look at me with pleading eyes, eyes that said do as he asks, for me. Then I'd take the children to play in the shallows, thinking of how I would like to kill their father and drown the two of them. Other times Uncle Joe would give me a wad of ten-rand notes – hundreds of rands at a time – and I, or Lena and I, or the two of us with Aunt Lena, were charged with taking the Brats to the funfair. When alone, I occasionally pocketed ten rand.

Away from their father, Joelene and Lenard could be utterly delightful. Joelene could transform herself from a sulking nuisance into a witty clown. With the beach crowded by hundreds of thousands of Transvaalers sunning themselves and swimming, there were frequent emergency announcements over the beach speakers of children lost. At six Joelene – with Uncle Joe off somewhere on his own – suggested I take her and drop her off as a lost child. To make the announcements a little more exciting we dropped her easy Joelene Mackenzie in favour of more creative names that the monolingual English-speaking life-savers found virtually impossible to say: Oxwagonia Papenfoes-Suikerrietsaad; Kruisementa Dewaal Van Oskraalsuid. Joelene, bright as a button and overcome with energy, would sometimes embellish the story without even our instruction, and, following the crackle of the loudspeakers, we'd hear: 'Your attention please, attention please, we have a little lost girl, six years old with a pink two-piece, her name is Voëlver —' and then we'd hear the poor life-saver asking her to repeat her name and he'd say: 'Voëlverskrikker Vandewenterspoel.' You could hear her behind him correcting his pronunciation and then, a bit we had not even coached her: '. . . she says she has been walking around for two days and she's begging her mother Maria Magdalena Vande – what – Vandewenterspoel or her brother Langeraad-Asparagus Vandewenterspoel to come and fetch her because she's very hungry.' And then I would go up by which time the life-savers had given little Voëlverskrikker Vandewenterspoel hamburgers, cool drinks and ice cream. She'd run from the life-saver and leap into my arms. And turning on my thickest Transvaal accent I'd thank them and ask whether there was anything us Vandewenterspoels from Brakwatersverdriet could do to express our gratitude. We could send springbok biltong, fresh milk, wonderful rich farm butter, maybe half a sheep? And nervously the men in the bulging red Speedos would say no, they were not allowed to receive gifts from the public at large.

At first I had laughed off Aunt Lena and Uncle Joe's suggestion that I sing at the Little Top talent contest on South Beach. There was no way I was going up there to make a sight of myself amongst the amateurs for the fifty-rand prize. I was, after all, a boy professional. Then Uncle Joe said he would double the prize money. My interest was pricked. It crossed my mind that amongst the hundreds of thousands of people on the beach could be someone from the Berg. My worst nightmare, being heard by someone from the school. God, imagine Dom hearing about this. But the thought of one hundred rand, a year's extra pocket money, loomed larger than the embarrassment. Aunt Lena said I should go up in only my Speedo, to show off my body. I refused.

'Come on, Karl,' Lena said.

'You wouldn't go for Miss South Coast Legs! Why must I go up there in only my Speedo?'

But I did. Thirteen years and two months old, with a black Speedo and a tan begun in East Africa. Another world. I had no idea what to sing. Gounod was as out as biscuits in an orphanage. Right, a bit of Britten's *War Requiem*, that would get this audience on my side. Then it came to me: Abba. Dom's tape to my rescue. With the little orchestra jamming it out behind me, I sang — I did — 'Waterloo'. Looking out at the ships waiting to enter Durban harbour, I forgot about the screaming horde below me on the white sand. Dispelled any thought of how pathetic I must be looking. I thrust my hips out as I sang, danced and put expression into every word, every beat. Halfway through the song I knew that barring the entry of Jimmy Osmond or Lena Zavaroni, I would win. The crowd loved it. Screamed and cheered and joined with every chorus.

The winner would be chosen by the measure of applause. When the prize was awarded I could have punched the MC in the face. It was not cash, it was a fifty-rand gift voucher for further voice training.

Backstage I asked the organisers whether I couldn't exchange the voucher for cash. They said no. I was beside myself. Uncle Joe now refused to give me the fifty rand he had said he'd double. I boiled and for the rest of the holiday thought up excuses to go as seldom as possible back to the Malibu and to South Beach.

Angry at Uncle Joe for having done me in and wanting Lena on side, I asked whether she had noticed the way he looked at her. 'Oh the looks are nothing,' she said, 'the other night when I stayed over he took out his old filafooi to show to me.'

'In the middle of the street?' I asked.

'No, fool, in the Malibu, when I stayed over and Aunt Lena was taking a shower.'

'What did you do?'

'At first I just looked at it and thought I'd ignore him. Then, when he asked me whether I wanted to touch it, I had a thought.' Lena smiled and looked away.

'What thought?'

'I took it in my hand and then bent down, like I was going to suck it.'

'You're lying, Lena!'

'I swear. And just when it started going stiff and I knew he was all excited I brought my lips down to it and said: "I just want to send a message to my mommy and daddy at home in Toti," and I started laughing and let it go and he pushed me away and I laughed in his face.'

'Why didn't you tell Aunt Lena?'

'Ag, it would only upset her if she knew he was molesting me.'

The Mackenzies came for New Year's Eve. Uncle Joe brought cartons full of firecrackers: spirals, Catherine wheels, sky rockets, sparklers. So many we wouldn't be able to light half. And as we unpacked the Mercedes, I was still thinking of how to broach leaving the school, getting out of the Berg and back to Toti.

I was sneezing, unable to control myself. Refused to take antihistamine.

After dinner we sat in the lounge playing Monopoly and watching South Africa's first ever TV New Year's message from the Prime Minister. The Brats were getting restless and wanted to light the fireworks. I burst into tears. I stood in the middle of the lounge floor and announced that I didn't want to return to school. Through snot and tears I implored Bok and Bokkie not to send me back. I said I couldn't spend all this money, when Lena, Bernie and Bokkie didn't even have decent clothes. The outburst must have taken no more than three or four minutes. For all that time their eyes were on me: Bok, sitting in the one big chair. Uncle Joe in the other. Lena on the floor playing Monopoly with Aunt Lena and Bernice. Bokkie sitting on the couch entertaining the Brats.

None of them spoke. When my tears dried and I calmed down, I was overwhelmed with shame. I wanted to leave. I turned, left the lounge and went to my bedroom. Bok came in and said he was taking me for a drive. We drove in his Chevrolet through the deserted streets of Amanzimtoti. Bok asked whether I hadn't learnt anything at all from Dr Taylor in June. I was now a young man, no longer a little boy. I was not to throw tantrums and scenes in front of our rich family. Like crapping in your own nest, he said, and I heard Mumdeman.

'And,' said Bok, 'you have to stop turning every cake recipe into a melodrama.' He told me things were going very, very well with his business. That I had to trust him. Happiness was in my hands! I should go back to school, leave adults to worry about adult business, not saddle myself with worries; that being away from home was turning me into a man. I felt better. What subjects are you taking, he asked. I want to take Latin and Art, I said. Why not Accountancy, he insisted. Because I'm not interested, I said. Don't you want to make money, one day, he asked. I can make money with Art, I said. Okay, just for one year and you must balance it with rugby and sport, Philistine, okay? Okay, Bok.

At midnight, the Brats still awake, we lit the firecrackers. I missed Dominic. Imagined the Websters on the beach at Plettenberg Bay as we left 1975 behind.

On New Year's Day as we prepared for church, Aunt Lena phoned to say she wasn't coming because Uncle Joe wanted her to stay with the Brats. Bokkie reminded us that Uncle Joe refused for himself or Aunt Lena to set foot in any church, the Dutch Reformed Church in particular. Uncle Joe, who refused to read the Bible, said that the portals of hell were lined with the dominees, deacons and elders of the Dutch Reformed Church.

With Juffrou Sang away we made do without an organist. Lena shared her hymnal with me and we giggled at the solemn dragging of the congregation's a cappella. I scooped from note to note, putting a sob at the end of every line. Bokkie jabbed me in the ribs. When the last hymn was over and Lena pulled away her hymnal, I whispered: 'Thank you, I've always depended on the kindness of strangers.' She glared at me and shook her head.

Aunt Lena had secretly given us money to pay for *Ipi Tombi* with Aunt Siobhain and James. Aunt Lena had really wanted to come along too, but Uncle Joe said she couldn't leave the kids and he didn't want to pay for her to go and watch kaffir girls dancing around with bare tits. That, he said, he could see for free on one of his farms.

At lunch on 2 January, Aunt Lena and the Brats pulled into the driveway with the Mercedes. It was obvious from her face she had been crying. She burst into tears and said that Uncle Joe had left early in the morning without saying where he was going. Then, at eleven, when they were on the Malibu pool deck, he was back: with the little fourteen-year-old slut Matilda.

'He didn't say anything, just that she was now on holiday with us,' Aunt Lena wept.

We sat in horrified silence. Once Aunt Lena had stopped crying,

Bokkie said, 'Lena, my sister, now you have grounds for a divorce. Leave the fucken bastard.' It was the first time I had heard my mother use the word.

'He'll take my poor children from me. We have no proof that he's sleeping with her.'

'Jirre, the whole Klerksdorp knows he is.'

Everyone around me is doing It, I thought to myself. Everyone is doing It with everyone.

'How do I prove it?' Aunt Lena sobbed.

'Put a private investigator onto him.'

'No one will do it for me, they're all scared of him.' I couldn't understand why she didn't get one from outside of Klerksdorp, from Johannesburg. I was stewing: our entire holiday was again, as had been the case year after year, messed up by the travails of my mother's sister, the Brats and Uncle Joe. And yet, I knew, we kept visiting them, kept inviting them. It felt as though we were their willing prisoners – enjoying their money, the laughs, and that we therefore had to eat their shit as well. Support Aunt Lena at any cost. For the entire day and night it was just Joe and Matilda this, Joe and Matilda that. Matilda, Matilda, Matilda. A fourteen-year-old girl – the daughter of Joe Mackenzie's farm foreman – someone I had never set eyes on, who had nothing to do with me or my life, was determining our every discussion and move. A fourteen-year-old slut named Matilda was ruining my holiday. Not only Uncle Joe, but the mysterious Matilda. What's her story? How could someone we knew nothing about, determine the course of our lives? I longed to see her. To put a face to the name. A voice to her mouth; fill in the silence that was making us all forget it was New Year. When things were meant to be nice.

I had to sleep on the couch in the lounge while Aunt Lena and the Brats moved into my room. Early the next morning, the day Alette was due back from Uvongo, Uncle Joe arrived in an Avis car and asked to see Aunt Lena. They sat out at the pool. The Brats sat on his lap while we stood behind the lace curtains in the lounge trying to eavesdrop. Within ten minutes Aunt Lena came in to say she was going back to the Malibu. Uncle Joe had sent Matilda back on the airplane and had promised that things were going to be different from now on.

'But, Lena,' Bokkie said, 'he's said that a hundred times.'

'Please, please, Bokkie,' Aunt Lena began to whimper, 'support me in this. Remember Saul on the road to Damascus. If God could change Saul's heart, he will, I believe, change Joe Mackenzie too.'

I had to carry the suitcases back to the car and she cautioned: 'Karl, don't say anything, please. Just be nice, or else he'll take it out on me and the children.' None of us said a thing in front of her. The moment they left Bokkie went into a silence, deeper and more horrifying than I could remember from previous times.

Lena and my animosities were forgotten in the glow of a shared outrage. We sat at the pool with Alette. 'I swear to you two today, I will never get married,' Lena was saying, lines to her mouth.

'Me neither,' said Alette.

'And I swear to you too: may God strike me dead if I ever do.' It was as though Lena and I saw — at least on this one issue — the world through the same set of eyes. How surprised I was to contemplate missing her along with Alette when I went back to the Berg. 'Living together,' I continued. 'I'll do that. Dominic's parents say marriage is outdated.'

'Yes, and fuck the Church,' Alette said.

'Dr Webster's right. Living together's becoming the in thing,' Lena continued. 'I'm going to do it too. Look at Coen and Mandy, living together in sin and happy as any couple I've ever seen.'

'My parents,' Alette, began, 'I know you'd never say so, but their marriage is in trouble. All my father does is work, work, work at the university, his students are much more important to him than my mother. They don't speak to me about it, but I wouldn't be surprised if they separate. I think my mum would have done it long ago, but she's scared of the censure of the Church.'

'What's censure?' I asked.

'If you get divorced you're not allowed to go to church for a year.'

'Do you really think they might . . . divorce?'

'Sometimes I hope they will.'

Going back to the Berg — out of the house with my mother's terrible silence, Bok's grandiosity, the whispers of my aunt's tears and faith in a Damascus Road awaiting the most evil man I had ever known — now seemed a wonderful prospect. We would be in Standard Six, in the Senior Choir. And the dreadful Harding and Reyneke would be gone! There would be Dominic. Yes, Dom. This year was going to be incomparable. Dom and I could pick up where we left off. We'd take ourselves back to Lake Nyassa! Why had I ever wanted to leave? To hover with dragonflies high above the pool: to see the whole story from a position of elevation. Idiotic, to think I'd rather be down here, back with the family. And Ma'am. Art and Latin. There would again be Rufus, the river and our new fort. And none of this shit flying around the idea we call home.

25

About that first night I went to the fort, I remember clearly how, from a distance, their acrid smell reached my nose. A good five paces before the snores like branches groaning in the wind sounded from inside our grass and stick sanctuary, I knew already they were in there: smoke, old sweat and sleep, the aromas of the Great Unwashed. Erasing almost every other from the spring night's air. The school's coarse grey blanket would be ruined, that much was certain. No ways it could be salvaged after passing through their foul lives. I'd have to make a plan and get another from Beauty. In the meantime probably freeze my bones off. Sleep even less because of them. One needs eight hours of sleep to function properly at school and in choir, everyone knew that. I was down to about six, sometimes five. If being cold at night kept me awake even more, I'd be a wreck. Exhausted and pneumonic, I may end up in sick-bay. I could see Jacques and Dominic bent over me, worried brows, their thumbs caressing the black half-moons beneath my eyes. My pale and dying skin. 'It was for my starving uncle,' I'd groan, barely able to speak through chapped and peeling lips. 'I couldn't see him suffer any longer. To see others suffer is to me worse than if it were me. There was snow on Champagne Castle. I gave my life so that he may live.' And I'd be a hero. Like Racheltjie de Beer and Wolraad Woltemade. Our country's undisputed national heroes. But before I died, Buys and Marabou and Lena – everyone who'd ever been nasty to me – filed past my bed crying, murmuring how sorry they were for everything they'd ever done to me. I'd turn my head tragically on the pillow and I'd look up at Dom and Jacques and bravely try to smile at them as I struggled with rasping breath to whisper: 'Loving someone means never having to say you're sorry.' No, ridiculous. All that would happen would be me freezing and probably not even getting near death or sick-bay's doors. Thoughts of turning back were now foremost in my mind. This was crazy. Risking my place in the school for someone I barely knew and cared for even less. Now I was down here, I might as well go through with it. Silly to turn around at this point and not give the old fool what he'd asked for. I'd just have to get another blanket from Beauty. But I didn't want to see them. Let them just find the blanket and know it must have been me. Karl, the Good Samaritan. And may God grant that they'd then get out of here, leave, take the blanket with them, back to the Transvaal. The worst would be if anyone found out. Jesus, no. The De Man boy's poor white uncle.

At the fort's mouth I paused for a moment. I flung the blanket awkwardly into the dark cavern and at once turned on my heel and headed off. Inside the snoring had abruptly ceased. I stopped, listened. I could hear mutters and joints creaking. Again I started off.

Had they found it? Did they know it was from me? I slunk back, cat foot over the blotches of dry leaves in the path. By now they had again settled down, the snoring again starting up.

'Uncle Klaas,' I whispered, urgently. 'There's a blanket for you and the other one.'

I heard them sit up. 'Take it with you when you leave. Bye.' Then I ran off, down river and up across the rugby field. Not a light on anywhere in the school or the conductors' chambers. Into the first music room. Closed the window behind me. I passed Jacques's door. The music had been turned off. Already asleep. I wondered who he was. I'd have to ask him. All we do is It. We barely speak.

IV

I

As we went down, my left arm interlocked with Lukas's right. We gripped each other's jerseys, went onto haunches and moved forward for our heads to shove through the two gaps on either side of Bennie's buttocks. My free hand went through Radys's legs, clutched the seam of his jersey and the elastic of his rugby shorts. In the second before we heaved and roared my wrist pressed against the soft mound of his penis and balls. Each time we went down – even before – I anticipated the brutalisation of my ears rubbed against Radys's outer thigh at vasskop prop to my left, and, to my right, Bennie's on hooker. There was the grinding of cartilage, knuckles, the thudding of togs digging in, tearing at grass. Soil, chalk. Huffing, puffing and groaning; the curses, the thrusting: 'Nou boys, nou manne!' Which would drive me to giggles were it not for my silent hatred of the entire enterprise. Of this tangle of limbs and aggression, of this smell of sweat and farts and shit and repulsive male odours, the racket of elbows and knees, of soiled white shorts and bruised grass, I wanted no part. The longer a game progressed, the more automatic my participation, the less aware I became of my own whereabouts. Something in my brain shut down, gave me over, enabling me to while and will away both halves until the final whistle signified only *my* relief. I cared little whether we won or lost, or about what had appeared on the scoreboard. I wanted off the field, through the shower and out and away from that game. My game, my motive – my heart – I told myself, is different from theirs even as I engage in theirs, even as I function within the rules of this savage sport. To my mind there was no escape: I was tall, well built and perceived as strong. I am a strong boy therefore I have no choice; I do not think therefore I am one of you. Dominic, skinny, spindly, was pardoned from play almost without question for he was a musical genius. Mervy – despite being almost as tall as me – was also excused with only rare questions, teases, remarks like sissy, naff, mof. But, I told myself, when these were flung at Mervy or Dominic they were playful, they did not hurt and were not intended to. When they came at me, they were like poison darts. I would not have that; I played to escape the words. Clearly, size alone did not demand participation. There were other codes and expectations, real and imagined, imposed and self-imposed. In my case there seemed to be no substitute which may have approximated even Dominic and Mervy's half-baked and frowned-upon pardons. I might manage to escape a few weeks of play by dragging the swimming season out for as long as some gala could be found. But that I had to play to live was a fate I accepted. I knew I was there only to be seen to be there. The returns on my sacrifice were, I believed, infinite. Therefore I was a lock, with Lukas, who lived for the four months of the year we played this game to which he gave his all, and where he was the captain. If Lukas or any of the other thirteen noticed my disinterest – the fact that entire matches went by without me touching the ball – none said a thing. That I was there seemed good enough. Lukas did say, 'Well played, Karl, good aggressive tackle,' after the rare match in which I had for a five-minute spurt made any contribution. During practices and games, I was mostly quiet, thinking of something else, forcing my thoughts elsewhere. When things got rough and I found myself at the bottom of the heap of bodies struggling for the ball I tried to cover my head, hoping that I would not be injured or scarred by a perspex boot stud, develop cabbage ears or get a fist in my eye. When I did get the ball, I passed it to one of my team-mates at the first possible instant. Having the ball was having the eyes of the team, opposition and spectators upon me. That was something I could not countenance on a rugby field and less and less anywhere else.

On the Cape tour we played a few friendly matches against our host schools. When Jacques attended, which more often than not he did, I became self-conscious in the way I did when Bok or Bokkie attended when I first played at Kuswag. Back then I still enjoyed the game, had excitedly elected to play. But something had since changed. Whatever excited me at ten had long since turned to resentment. Whenever Jacques came to watch, I played like hell, knowing his eyes were on me. When we left the field I felt his gaze, cast him a glance, saw the pride there. But instead of being pleased by the way he looked at me, I felt disappointed, wanted instead that he should know – even as I declined to show – how I loathed the spectacle. I wanted him to say that it was a game for barbarians and hooligans. Instead he glowed, reminding me again of Bok, back from hunting along the Zambezi, putting an arm around me and patting me on the back after a game. At first my father's delight had been an inspiration for playing, but with time that reason seemed to have become inverted.

We played against Upington High and even though we lost, we – and I – had played well. After the pep talk and post-match prayer thanking God for letting us play a brave game, Lukas grinned at me and said he'd never seen me play with such determination.

Dominic and I stayed with the headmaster and his wife. The headmaster had come to watch the game and afterwards he and Jacques spoke while I, seated in the car with my legs outside, removed my togs. Over the car radio I heard that there were now full-scale riots in Soweto. Black children were burning down their schools. While the news entered the cabin, I took off my togs and socks – which I sniffed at as always – and rubbed wool from between my toes and studied the way the nylon fabric had discoloured my toenails and the area around them, swollen from the sweat of an hour inside the togs.

I have no recollection of what did or might have passed through my mind when I heard the radio bulletin. I might have thought of Radys and Bennie's host mother a week or so earlier when the kids had surrounded her car. Of what the Websters may have said the evening we stayed with them in Saxonwold I have no memory at all. I do remember Jacques coming over with the headmaster and winking, saying I had played well, and that he'd see me the following morning at the bus when we departed for Oudtshoorn. And I remember going with him to Paternoster, staying in the opera singer's home in False Bay, going up Table Mountain with Dom, Cape Town City Hall. And then, driving back from Cape Town to the Berg, through the Orange Free State: from the front of the bus where she sat beside Jacques, Ma'am called me.

'Sit for a moment,' she smiled, making room beside her and Jacques. He winked at me.

'What do you see, out there?'

'How do you mean, Ma'am?'

'This landscape, this sky. What do you see?'

The odd question and my being called to the front of the bus to sit beside them did nothing to help me understand what I was expected to say. 'You mean, the yellow grass and the flatness, Ma'am?' She laughed and shook her head, asked where I thought I saw anything flat? She told me to take a minute and look carefully at what was unfolding outside the bus windows. Nervous at my proximity to the two of them and wondering rather about how they had come to call me, I tried to grasp what she wanted from my answer. My cheeks were aglow. The yellow veld, undulating in the afternoon sun, was not flat. Gullies, hills, dams, clumps of dull green trees, here and there a white eucalyptus, empty red fields, an occasional farmhouse or huts dotted the landscape. The sky was an exceptional blue and here and there fragments of suspended white clouds, all at exactly the same height, cast shadows on the yellow, brown and red earth. Ahead of us the tarred road cut a deadly straight track into the distance, disappearing into hills that rolled on into a growing blue range.

'Ma'am?'

'Oh, come on, Karl. I've just been telling Mr Cilliers that you're a born artist! He said this was the ugliest part of the country and I said you – of anyone in this bus – would see the beauty! Whose work is this landscape?' I looked out again, desperate to give the correct answer. Did she mean God? No, Ma'am had never indicated any interest or belief in God. Suddenly my hand flew to my mouth. The cliffs, the clouds! Yes, the dryness, the way the reds and browns and yellows flowed into each other!

'O'Keeffe, Ma'am? Georgia O'Keeffe?'

A victorious smile spread over Ma'am's face when she looked at Jacques and then back at me. 'And . . . is it yellow and flat. Ugly?' she asked triumphantly. From beside her he smiled, staring from the window.

'No, Ma'am. It is exquisite. It took me a moment because I hadn't understood your question.'

'Can you ever again see the Free State as flat and yellow?'

'No, Ma'am. Imagine if O'Keeffe could ever see this. What she'd do with it?'

'She's probably a bit too old now, and I hear she doesn't travel much outside of New Mexico. Anyway, what about you, Mr Cilliers?' she asked. 'Would you be able to call it exquisite?'

'It might take me a while, too,' he laughed. Ma'am thanked me and said I could return to my seat. I told the others about our discussion and Bennie said he hated the south-eastern Free State. That Ficksburg where he was born was good for nothing other than cherries. And also that it wasn't too far from Maseru in Lesotho where one was allowed to gamble and watch blue movies. He said it was a region of perpetual drought. That they'd stand on their veranda looking out towards Lesotho and see all the rain was falling over kaffir country while the white country stayed dry. Dominic told Bennie there was a lesson in that and Bennie snarled that yes, the lesson was that Satan looked after his own in the mountain kingdom. Lukas told them to shut up.

At dusk, close to Bennie's home town, we began to look out for his mother's car parked on the roadside. She had arranged to say hello to him when the bus passed by. At last we saw the green Beetle and Bennie dismounted with Ma'am and Mr Cilliers. 'Come,' Lukas said. 'Let's go say hello so we can get some of whatever's in that parcel.' We piled out to say hello to Mrs Oberholzer. The moment the bus revved itself back onto the road, we had Bennie's box open. Inside were large packets of dried fruit, a litre of Coke, a bottle of peanut butter and a tin of Illovo Syrup. While we chomped on the fruit – saying we'd be farting like pigs in a few minutes – I watched the sun from behind us turn the plains and hollows and the distant Maluties and the Drakensberg to a deep purple, then orange, then black. It was remarkable. How had I ever thought this part of the country boring or plain? Bennie didn't know where the Maluties ended and the Drakensberg began, said he thought they were sort of one. I under-took to look at a map the moment I got back to school.

The rugby season over and I, physically unscathed by the game and free till the following May, had from an unexpected source indeed been graced with the blessing of a scar. With the tiny one on my fore-head almost faded, the new one had come, I told myself, at the perfect moment. Beneath my right kneecap. A sickle-moon lying on its back, this was the mark that could substitute for the lack of the like from the rugby field. New, pink – the stitches removed only two weeks before – it was a bright crease emphasising the kneecap while I stood, then stretching flat, snug and shiny when the leg was bent. Now aware that my injury had not been particularly serious, I retained gratification from the wound being thought grave enough to warrant the stares of Seniors and Juniors as they passed by me on the veranda. For one week only the knee was bandaged; the attention and my overstated limp a source of tremendous pleasure. Only the other four knew that I was overdoing it when I told Jacques that I couldn't possibly stand during choir, that I had to sit on a chair; when I told Uncle Charlie I couldn't do PT even though I was back in the saddle; when I told Ma'am that I'd have to have my leg resting on a chair in class for at least three weeks. There was a sense of disappointment when the bandages were removed and the scar turned out to be less impressive than I had been hoping. Only eight stitches. Will you ride again, everyone asked. I glowed in shrugging that of course I would, nothing would stop me from riding, even if there was water on the knee as the doctors feared. The question of whether I would ride again reminded me of one asked to surfers after they'd had close shaves or been bitten by sharks off the Natal coast: will you ever surf again? Of course they'd surf again, even if it meant sitting on the stumps where their hips used to be.

Why I liked this little scar I did not quite know, though on the most obvious level it was that it had been inflicted by a horse. On our way back from Bushman Paintings, Whiskey – with Alex Snyman on his back and briefly in front of Rufus on a canter – had kicked up. I felt the hoof like a rock through the denim against my knee. Still on the canter, I leant forward, feeling my fingers and the fabric sink into a clammy dent below the kneecap. I brought Rufus to a standstill by the roadside, hollering for the rest to wait. I slid off the horse's back and as I landed my right knee gave way beneath me. I couldn't get the denim's leg up and had to remove my belt and drop my pants. By the time the group was around me, the damage was exposed and my eyes brimmed with tears. The kneecap – a strange pink and white bone like a raw hamburger patty – was half sticking out. I did not wish to cry, but did, shocked at the sight more than from feeling any pain. Mr Walshe dismounted and told me to stay seated in the grass. Tears streamed down my cheeks and I asked whether my walking would too be impaired. Would I lose the kneecap? He told me to look away and, with a now-you-see-it-now-you-don't movement that felt like hell, slipped the kneecap back into place, leaving a gaping and bloody mouth below the knee. Under Lukas's supervision, the others returned to school from where Lukas was to have a vehicle sent to fetch me. Mr Walshe stayed and alleviated my concern about a permanent limp. He said I would be fine and showed me scars on his own body – among them where an ostrich had kicked him and trampled on his neck, almost killing him. I told him about Lossie in Mkuzi, how tame the bird had been, that he died after being bitten, probably by a green mamba.

When the bakkie returned, Lukas was sitting in the front beside the driver. I was loaded in and Lukas and Mr Walshe cantered behind us, out of the dust range, as the vehicle meandered its way back to school.

Lukas and the driver carried me upstairs to where sick-bay had already been prepared. One look at the leg and Uncle Charlie said I needed to be taken to hospital in Estcourt for X-rays and stitches. Perhaps an operation. As I might have to spend time in hospital he sent Lukas to fetch my pyjamas, dressing gown and toilet bag: 'And bring some PT shorts so he doesn't have to go into hospital wearing only his underpants. Hang these over his locker,' he said, handing my jeans to Lukas.

Uncle Charlie placed a temporary dressing over the wound. Above and below the white gauze, the leg had swollen into a narrow oblong ball. He left to organise a mattress in a canopied bakkie in which I'd be taken to Estcourt. I lay wondering over the horror of limping for the rest of my life. Physical deformity was about the last thing in the world I could imagine living with. A limp for a while – with admiration and pity as its pay-off – was one thing. A permanent deformity was quite another. I thought of my mother's ear, how her embarrassment at not hearing well seemed to rub off on all of us so that we too felt embarrassed on her behalf.

Lukas returned, carrying his sportsbag. He sat down on the other bed. Held his hand out to me: 'Here,' he said, a key appearing between his fingertips. 'It dropped from your dressing-gown pocket.'

'Thanks,' I said, casting my eyes to the bag by his side: 'Pass the bag, please.' He handed me the green canvas bag as I felt a flush spread up my neck. Act normal, act normal, act normal. I knew that he was awaiting an explanation. I had none to offer. I unzipped the toilet bag and nonchalantly dropped the key inside. Our eyes met briefly. He knew or suspected something. He wanted to ask, and I floundered to find words before he could. My mind having been so engrossed in my leg, I was nowhere near finding a believable story about the key. Say something, Karl, anything, clear your throat, scratch your head, rushed through my head. Every possible action seemed contrived, certain to enhance my look of duplicity. I was gagged, cornered in every side of the deafening silence.

'Just a key I picked up. This fucken leg hurts, Lukas . . .' Since the kick about an hour before, there had actually been little feeling besides discomfort when moving and the brief moment the disk had been slipped back. Now, for the first time, the deadness was changing to a light throbbing.

'It looks pretty swollen, can you bend it?'

'No. Uncle Charlie said not to. They're getting a mattress put in the back of the bakkie, so I can lie down. Did you bring shorts?' He took the black shorts from the bag and helped me slip them on.

'Do you think you'll stay in hospital?' The key, for the moment, seemed forgotten.

'I hope not. Last time I was in hospital was when I had my tonsils out.'

'Who's taking you, Uncle Charlie?'

'Yes . . . Why don't you get permission to come along to Estcourt? I'm sure he'll come back tonight – even if I have to stay in hospital.'

'What about choir? Cilliers wouldn't let me go.' At the mention of the name, I heard or suspected an inference, a challenge, a demand, a plea for explication.

'It's worth a try,' I said. 'Why don't you go ask him?'

'Okay. Can I say you asked?' Clearly he was hinting; wanting me to respond. He was tormenting me. Or was I imagining it from beginning to end?

'Just say Uncle Charlie may need some help and you don't think I want to lie all the way there alone in the back of the van.'

He rose and said he'd run to the conservatory.

'Won't you see if Dominic is in one of the music rooms?'

'Want me to tell him?'

'Ja, say he must come and say goodbye.'

With me already loaded into the back of the bakkie, Lukas arrived in the parking lot. Jacques — his face flushed — was with him. Dominic not.

'So you went to war with a horse?' he asked through the open back of the canopy. His one hand, dropped casually over the bakkie's side, took hold of my left toes.

'The horse went to war with me, Sir.' My eyes darting to Lukas, who had turned away to speak to Uncle Charlie. Jacques asked whether it hurt and I said it did, though not much. His hand ran up my calf.

'I told you you were not invincible, you little shit,' he said, cocking his head, smiling. I grinned nervously, feeling his hand lingering, now back on my foot; a flagrantly public display of affection and tenderness.

'I've told Lukas he can go with you . . .'

'Oh, great. Thank you, Sir.'

'Come back soon.'

'I will.' He withdrew his hand as Lukas turned back to the canopy's open hatch.

'Bye, Karl,' he said and stepped away from the vehicle. Lukas slid into the back and propped himself up on his arm beside me.

'Bye, Mr Cilliers,' I said.

Uncle Charlie told me to bang on the carriage window if my leg became too painful or if I wanted him to slow down on the gravel road. He dropped the hatch, sealing us in. Then we were driving off, leaving the school behind us in the descending dusk.

'I couldn't find Dominic, but I told Precious to tell him we looked for him.'

I said it was fine and changed the subject to speak about horses and the afternoon's ride.

Requiring nothing more than local anaesthetic, the wound was cleaned and stitched, the leg X-rayed. I was given a bottle of painkillers and we started on the return journey. It was late, maybe around nine, by the time we left Estcourt. In the back both of us were quiet, not speaking much for most of the way. After we left the tarmac road, somewhere around the time we passed the turn-off to Loskop and the Theron farm, Lukas spoke.

'Cilliers was rather upset.'

'When you asked to come?'

'No. When he heard it was you.'

My heart sank. I waited a while. 'What did he say?'

'*Oh my God, take me to him, quickly* . . . Like it was the end of the world, and we almost ran to the bakkie.'

It was the first time I had been spoken to about Jacques as though he had any form of relationship to me other than that of choir master – with me one of his least interesting voices. I was now suddenly intrigued by what more he might have said. About the way he may have looked when he worried about me. Still present was a nagging in my head that Lukas was on to something. To trust myself to ask another word about Jacques would be stupid. There had been again, in Lukas's voice, the tone of expectation. That, deliberately, is what he wanted me to hear from his telling the incident. To refer again to the key would be crazy. No, leave the key at what I'd said.

'He's probably worried about me missing choir,' I said after a silence which had again lasted just a moment too long. 'I'm quite hot in seconds, these days, you know,' I continued. 'Not quite as useless as I was in firsts. Before you know it I'm a soloist.'

Then we laughed; cracked up at the notion. The tension between us was gone.

'And in seconds, just like Almeida,' Lukas said. I laughed, but couldn't quite shake the feeling that he was trying to tell me something.

2

We packed our things on a Bedford lorry to leave St Lucia, Zululand and the Natal Parks Board.

Bok had grown tired of what he called the authoritarianism of the Parks Board system – and he wanted to earn more money. Who could ever get ahead on the hundred and seventy rand a month he had been earning as a game ranger. No free accommodation plus weekly ration of impala or warthog meat would put him in a position to give his children a decent education. He was joining White Hunters Incorporated in Durban to take wealthy tourists along the Zambezi and Okavango to hunt for trophies. There were bags of money in organised hunting, just waiting to be collected.

Few clear pictures remain in my mind of the circumstances under which we left the bush. All I knew was that Camelot was being sold to Dr Ian Player and Simba had to go to another ranger whose name I no longer recall. Everything surrounding the departure seems to have happened fast and memory is now little more than a diffuse haze. No time for long, sad goodbyes to the just-broken Camelot. Nor to Simba, who had to go because we were moving into a flat where dogs were not allowed. I tried to not think about the dog or my horse and whether their new owners were going to treat them well. What had to be focused on was us De Mans moving on, making progress, poised on the brink of material comfort for the first time since Tanganyika.

In Matubatuba I said goodbye to Guisbert, who had become my best friend. We promised to write to each other but never did, the same as the Pierces, whom, I recall, came to wave as the Bedford, loaded with all our stuff, pulled off. Lena and I sat on the front seat beside Bok while Bernice and Bokkie followed behind in the Peugeot to make sure nothing came off the truck. And so we drove towards a new life in Amanzimtoti, the same South Coast town as Uncle Michael and Aunt Siobhain, where Uncle Michael had just opened up his fish and chips shop at the Toti Drive-In.

In Toti Lena and I shared a room in Afsaal flats, where we lived while we waited for Bok to make enough money so that we could rent a house. The small holiday flat above the beach cost ninety rand a month. Lena and Bernice's turquoise Kuswag uniforms were made by Aunt Siobhain on her new Singer with the electric pedal, and my safari suits were selected from the school's second-hand storage. Unlike many of the Kuswag children, we always had money for new school shoes and never had to take second-hands from the bin. My new brown Batas were a source of pride and I shined them with Nugget every afternoon. As in St Lucia, we had to change out of uniform the moment we got home. While our home was now a different place, the order of much remained basically the same: making our beds in the morning, never sitting on bedspreads, setting and unsetting the table, rotating dish-washing responsibilities, saying grace before meals, and 'Thank you, Bokkie, the food was very nice' before we left table. Then it was homework, after which Bokkie allowed me to go off and play and swim on the Toti beach.

Lena and Bernice had friends living in Brigadoon Flats across the road. My sisters were rarely with me in the afternoons. Down Beach Road lived Robbie Merwe, whose father owned the Seahorse restaurant, and he and I began spending time together at school and on the beach. Sometimes Bokkie dropped me off at the Toti library where I spent hours and took out books on loan for the first time. With

Kuswag being a new school — we were still accommodated in pre-fab classrooms — the library there had few books and hardly any in English, which were my favourite.

We attended the new Dutch Reformed church that had recently been built at the bottom end of Dan Pienaar Drive. There was now no escaping either Sunday school or church. Stripped of our excuse about living far out of town, our Sunday mornings were now gobbled up into two solid hours of monotonous worship: Sunday school followed by the murderously boring sermons of Dominee Lourens. Now we're right on the inside of civilisation, Bokkie said, and we have to take serious stock of any bush behaviour we might unwittingly exhibit: 'Keep your eyes on the other kids and the teachers, so that you can see how things are done in the city. You, Karl, especially. At least the girls had the time in boarding school already before Matubatuba. But I'm worried about you.'

On the very first day during sang perie, my new Juffrou Sang said that the new boy had to stand up and introduce himself. I stood and said I came from Matubatuba, where my father had been a game ranger, but that he was now a white hunter. Juffrou Sang teased that a pretty boy like me had to have a pretty voice and she let me stand on a chair and sing. I said I'd sing my favourite song, 'Under My Skin', by Frank Sinatra, but Juffrou Sang said I'd do no such thing. Since when did an Afrikaans boy sing English songs at school? I said Matubatuba had been dual medium. She said this was not Zululand and I had to sing in Afrikaans. After a moment's thought I started with 'Bobbejaan Klim Die Berg', swinging my hips and clicking the beat with my fingers. Her face lit up and she broke into a smile. Afterwards she said I had quite a voice and that she wanted to enter me for the Durban eisteddfod.

I was almost nine and my voice had been discovered. At the flat I told Bokkie, who said I had probably gotten it from Bok who in Oljorro days had been quite a crooner himself. I had no idea that my father had a good singing voice and undertook to ask him to sing with me when he came back from the Zambezi.

While Lena and Bernice were on the netball court, I began to play rugby. Initially I was at eighth man but in the same season was moved to lock. On Saturdays our under-ten A's took the bus to schools in Durban and the Bluff, sometimes playing against English schools on the fields behind Kings Park Stadium. That first season, though I and the rest played ourselves half to death, we didn't win a single match. It was, so our trainer said, because Kuswag was a new school. By the time we reached under-fourteen and started wearing rugby togs, us Afrikaners and our game would have developed and we'd walk over the English opposition. While enjoying rugby, I continually felt some form of envy towards James, who was in Amanzimtoti Senior Secondary where they played soccer. All the English schools had soccer, which seemed so much more civilised. Soccer had no scrum and no tackle. In soccer you didn't seem to get injured. But I knew soccer was an English sport and there was no way I was going to get to play. I secretly wished to go to an English school, but it was clear that we had now become full-blooded Afrikaners. It made no sense to me that Bok's family had been English in Tanzania, that he had gone to an English school in Kenya, and that I was now in a monolingual Afrikaans school. I read almost only English: it sounded so much more sophisticated than Afrikaans. Yet instead of playing soccer in our free time on the beach, Bernice, Lena and I insisted on playing touch rugby and told James that soccer was a sissy sport.

As both Afrikaans and English were compulsory school subjects and James struggled with Afrikaans, I often helped him with home-work, on occasion writing his essays for him. I knew that if one wrote about death and suffering in an Afrikaans essay you did well. Despite all the afternoons and weekends we spent together, there was a clear division between my cousins and me: James went to Cubs and later to Boy Scouts, I went to Voortrekkers. Lena and Bernice went to Voortrekkers, and Stephanie went to Girl Guides. They were Presby, we were Dutch Reformed.

Bok was away from Toti, hunting along the Zambezi, for weeks at a time. Then, even while he was in town, he would often come home late at night, long after we were already in bed. Within a few months after we moved to the flat, Lena and I awoke and heard Bokkie, through our bedroom wall, in tears. We sat up and looked at each other in the pink flicker of the street's neon lights, listening to our mother's words through her sobbing as she spoke to Bok. She said that she was not prepared to tolerate Bok's nights on the town. It was one thing for him to be off in the bush, hunting to keep food on the table and the children in school. It was quite another when he was in town and out drinking and not spending time with us. I wondered whether Bernice in the next room could hear. Bok, pacifying in his most soothing voice, said that going out with clients was part of his work. He had to mingle with tourists and white hunters in order to attract more business.

'Night after night, Ralph De Man,' Bokkie again wailed, 'I sit here with these poor children while their father is out with the rich and famous. You don't care for them or me.'

'Well, you should come with me, occasionally.'

'And leave these little children? You know bloody well I'll never, as long as I live, leave my children at home.'

'We could get a babysitter.'

'With what! We don't have money to wipe our arses and you want to pay a babysitter. And a babysitter at their age, where do you think, Ralph De Man, I'll find one with hair on her teeth?'

A long silence and I asked Lena whether I could come to her bed. She said no. I went next door and climbed into bed with Bernice.

Bokkie wept that she was tired of Bok coming home smelling of drink, cigarettes and other women. She said if it were not that she had to take care of us, she would go out and find herself a job. But what job would she get, she who had no training, had only ever worked in a bicycle shop? The only job she could get was working behind the till at Checkers with the poor white Makoppolanders. Maybe she could get a job cleaning other people's houses like the kaffir girls? Would that make him happy? To see her scrub the shit stains out of white people's underwear? Then she wailed again, sobbed that she was going to leave the following day to find a man that really loved her and her poor children. Now Bernice and I were also crying. After a while it seemed our mother had quietened down. Only then did Bernice whisper for me to go back to my bed, not to worry, that everything would be fine.

And so it came that whenever Bok and Bokkie argued and my mother cried, I went to Bernice's bed. We rarely spoke about it, but when we did it was clear enough through their bravery that Lena and Bernice were as afraid as I that Bok might leave us, leave us alone in the dreadful flat, and Bokkie would become a servant to rich white people and we would have nowhere in the world to go.

Aunt Siobhain found a three-bedroomed house for us to rent at 21 Dan Pienaar, down the road from Kuswag. Just across the street from the church. For Christmas Uncle Michael gave us a sausage dog we named Judy, from a Punch and Judy show that had come to school. Bokkie was to become the church's chief gardener and landscape artist. It was disappointing to hear that she would not be paid a salary. Even though Bok would often be away, Dominee Lourens said he wanted our father to be a deacon whenever he was in town.

Bokkie began landscaping the church garden. After weeks of battling the discomfort of gardening in dresses, she was given special permission from the diocese to wear shorts on church property – as long as they reached her knees. A bunch of narrow-mindeds, Bokkie secretly called the town council. Side by side with Old Gilbert she wheeled barrows, dug massive holes and planted hundreds of shrubs. Amongst the trees she planted was the little mustard bush, which she said was the world's slowest growing tree. It would still be small, she told us, even one day when we kids got married in the Dan Pienaar church. If Robbie Merwe and I were anywhere near the school's fence over break, we could see Bokkie in her long shorts and Old Gilbert in his overalls, bent over the flowerbeds or pushing the lawn mower around the church with its tall steeple.

Soon after we settled into Dan Pienaar, I developed bouts of sneezing that were eventually diagnosed as acute hay fever. The record, counted by Bernice, was twenty-three sneezes consecutively. My eyes would swell up and I began to scratch and rub uncontrollably. When the sneezing and itches became unbearable, Bokkie sometimes drove me down to the beach to swim, the sting of the salt water burning away the itch and bringing at least temporary relief. What allergy I had developed remained a mystery. At Dr Lombardt's rooms behind Checkers, I went numerous times for all kinds of tests. Eventually, even though we had no medical aid, I was sent to a specialist in Durban who said that the hay fever could somehow be caused by my broad septum – probably from breaking my nose at six. When I grew up I'd have to have a nose operation. For the first time in years we referred back to the fall from the Land Rover.

Next, Dr Lombardt made tens of little pricks on my arms – I wondered whether the stepladder of pricks was going to go up from the pulse all the way to my face – and applied various drops over the punctured skin. A number of these turned into angry welts and it was decided that I was allergic to house dust, dogs, cats' hair, pollen and grass. The results sounded dreadful to me, for they basically meant I was allergic to my whole world, including Judy the sausage dog. I was given a prescription for antihistamine tablets, which brought on not only the end of the itches and sneezes, but a remarkable calm from within which all the world seemed relaxed and controlled to me. When I went to boarding school, I would take along a huge supply of antihistamine. To my surprise, I never needed the tablets in the Berg, nor on tour anywhere else in the country. Also in Klerksdorp, during holidays when we visited Aunt Lena and Uncle Joe – where I was surrounded by cats and dogs and an enormous garden full of flowering plants – I never once took a pill. With time I didn't bother taking the tablets to the Berg. But the moment I set foot in Toti I couldn't survive without swallowing antihistamine at least once or twice a week. Soon the doctors claimed it had to be something very specific to the Natal coastal climate: maybe the fumes from Shell & BP's funnels, or the plant at Illovo Sugar Mills, or maybe the ocean itself. Be it as it may, antihistamine alleviated all symptoms and everyone said the hay fever was something I would in time outgrow.

Our neighbours on Dan Pienaar were two Catholic girls who went to Amanzimtoti Senior Secondary with James. They were Mary-Alice and Betty Preston. Mr Preston worked for the municipality and they had a pool in their back yard where we sometimes swam.

My best friends at school remained Robbie Merwe and Felix Van Zyl whom we called Vlakvark for a reason I cannot today fathom. Both were in Voortrekkers with me. After team meetings on Friday afternoons they were allowed to come and play at our house until their fathers collected them around sunset. Robbie told me that the excrement of the Indians – charras, currymunchers – in Chatsworth stank worse than any other human excrement because of the quantities of curry and spices the Indians consumed: 'It eats away their insides, so they shit out parts of their stomachs and intestines each time they crap. That's why they're all so skinny and why their shit stinks so much. Stay upwind from Chatsworth,' he said.

Many of my leisure moments were spent alone at the edenic Kingsway Bird Sanctuary where I took my books and sat reading. The sanctuary held a number of tortoises and rabbits in pens, while ducks, geese and peacocks roamed free on the lawns and beneath the evergreen trees. Lena would join me and from a hide-out in the bushes we soon started secretly to fish in the lake. Fishing was strictly prohibited in the sanctuary, but what no one saw couldn't hurt us.

I got my first non-family kiss in the sanctuary, around ten, from Alette who was then twelve. She lay down beside me in the grass and allowed me to stick my hand into her pants and feel her poefoe, like a snail, sticking pleasantly to my fingers. I was stiff and she stuck her hand into my pants and we looked at each others and when she asked whether it was my first time I said yes, it was. There was no need, I thought, to tell her about the little scrubbings with Stephanie or Patty Pierce.

Lena and I also became friends with Glenn and his sister Thea who lived right up Dan Pienaar. Glenn was in class with Lena and Thea with me. After homework we four went to the bird sanctuary or played touch rugby or the catching game. When Bok was home from safari, he played cricket with us and taught all of us and cousin James how to bowl overhand. Great was my delight to discover that Thea did ballet, an activity that had captivated my imagination from Stephanie's days as a dancer. Stephanie had recently quit, because, as Aunt Siobhain said, she was now interested only in boyfriends. I begged Bok to let me take ballet classes with Thea in Athlone Park. Bok said I could slip into tights and start ballet as soon as I wanted – over his dead body. I hated him for it.

Above Thea's bed was a poster of the greatest ballet dancer in the world. Pretending to go to the toilet I'd leave the touch rugby games we played to gaze at Margot Fonteyn. She had white feathers in a band around her ears, her breasts were tiny, almost flat, and her long legs jutted out of a white ballet tutu, ending below the silk-laced ankles in slippers on what Thea called 'point'. This was her in *Swan Lake*, though to me she always looked more like a flamingo than a swan. It never crossed my mind to ask what made Margot Fonteyn great, the greatest. That seemed self-evident from her grace and beauty on Thea's wall. At home I practised in the passage, almost breaking my toes as I tried to land on point from jumps. Down the passage I danced and spun, knocking my knees against the walls, pretending I was Margot Fonteyn. In the Toti library I came upon a book with large ballet photos, and there I saw old grainy shots of Vaslav Nijinsky and a handsome man with flaring nostrils and a wild fringe that made him look like a horse. Rudolf Nureyev. These were the first male ballet dancers I'd seen: in tights, muscular, white, their scrotums pulled into swallows' nests where their legs joined. And Nureyev looked wild, like an animal. I wanted to be him. In one photograph he had his bushy hair pulled back by a nylon Alice band and on another by what looked like a hairclip to keep his hair from tumbling into his eyes. I wished we had the money to go to the Alhambra to see NAPAC's ballet where Mrs Willemse took Thea during 'the season'. Now I wanted to see male dancers. I took the book from the library and showed Bokkie the photographs of Nureyev flying through the air in *Spartacus*, of Nijinsky prostrate and painted in the *Afternoon of the Faun*. I asked her whether she would ask Bok a last time whether I couldn't just try ballet once or twice. If I weren't the best in the class I'd stop. I promised. She said no, I'd heard what my father had had to say on the subject and she herself didn't think it a good idea for a boy to do ballet anyway. And what's more, best for me to stop gesturing so wildly with my hands when I spoke, because that could also create all sorts of suspicions. And if I didn't stop she would ask my teachers to tie my hands to my chair. And she'd heard that boys who did ballet only ended up being full of sights. And that wouldn't look good in a big boy like me. I wondered if I were smaller, not as tall, whether maybe then I'd be allowed to dance.

Some afternoons Mary-Alice and Betty came over, but they were prohibited from playing touch rugby as Mrs Preston didn't want them breaking bones or being scarred for life. At their house I was introduced to the music of their idols Donny and Jimmy Osmond and David Cassidy, whose denim-clad bodies and faces adorned the Preston girls' walls. At receiving my first pair of bell-bottom jeans — hand-me-downs from James — I begged to have purple and orange braid sown all around the floppy bottoms but Bokkie said only drug addicts and hippies wore braid. May I have a peace sign then, I begged, but Bernice said they'd learnt at Sunday school that a peace sign was a broken cross — symbol of the Antichrist. No, a witch's foot, said Lena. What about Stephanie, I cried, she has a peace sign on her jeans. Well, the whole family knows where she's heading, Bokkie said. Only when James got new jeans with gold and silver braid in a mandala pattern did Bokkie reluctantly give in and allow braid — a very narrow blue strip with white traingles — around the hems of my bell-bottoms.

I developed — from all my reading, Aunt Siobhain said — the gift of the gab. It stood me in good stead on the neighbourhood streets where there was a form of open warfare between the English boys of Amanzimtoti Senior Secondary and us Afrikaners from Kuswag.

'Afrikana, rotten banana,' they hollered at us. And I, in perfectly modulated English, would retort: 'We can change to the Queen's English whenever we want, but barring plastic surgery you will never be able to change your ugly faces.'

'Oh, listen to the little professor!' one of the English boys would smirk.

'Rather a professor than a poofter!' I'd sneer.

'Listen who's talking, you little naff. Big talk in front of your sister!'

'Rather humiliating when a girl is your physical superior, isn't it?' I again spoke in exaggerated vowels, standing closer to Lena, putting my arm around her who would never, under other circumstances, have indulged such displays from me to her.

'Rockspiders, that's what you Dutchmen are. Go back to Holland!' they shouted at us.

'We were here in 1652, before you rednecks. You only came in 1820, why don't you go back to England, imperialists!' I barked.

After once beating up James at school, the English gang sent a message with him that I was going to fall on my face if they ever got hold of me alone. I felt sorry for James. Being our cousin in the

English school could not be easy. Yet, blood, so we knew, was thicker than water. Despite his pleas for me to stop calling his schoolmates names, I persisted, becoming more and more scathing and sarcastic. The gang rode past 21 Dan Pienaar on their racing bikes, and we would stop our cricket or touch-rugby game and stand in our yard, yelling abuse at them. When they turned their bikes and tried to come onto our property we threatened to call the police.

'How can you call the police, you don't have a phone, Rockspider!' one shouted, pointing out the absence of telephone cable to our home.

'We can go to Betty and Mary-Alice's phone,' one of us countered. 'They are decent Englishman, not like you scum.' We, the Afrikaans kids, were trapped in our yard by the English. Only the division was never quite so clear, for James was with us, and he was English as were Mary-Alice and Betty.

The boys got me alone, one day, when I was reading at the tortoise pens in the bird sanctuary. With Lena fishing in the bush, far on the other side of the lake, I knew my luck had run. Three of them surrounded me, shoving me between them. A foot struck me in the back, a fist against my chest, and a shoe in the stomach as I fell to the ground, panting for air, hoping only that I wouldn't cry. Then, an angel of mercy, Lena sprinted down the grass embankment, her eyes ablaze, hissing for them to get away from me. I lay gasping for breath, too afraid to move.

'You're only a girl,' they jeered. Lena, with the speed of a leopard, jumped at them, her fists flying, her foot catching the biggest of the three in the stomach. One tried to grab her from behind but she swung around, got hold of his neck and threw him to the ground.

'You better run,' I shouted, still cowering on the lawn. 'She's going to kill all three of you.'

'We can't hit girls,' one said, slipping his nose between his fingers, running them up and down at the same time thrusting his hips. Lena rushed, headbutting him in the face. He stumbled back clutching his hands over his nose and ran. At once all three were running and Lena was after them. I shouted for her to let them go. She grabbed the back one by his shirt and spun him around. He shouted as Lena flung him into the slimy water run-off. Almost slipping over the fall into the pool he managed to grab onto a branch and drag himself up onto the side. He screamed and ran off, crying that if he got bilharzia our poor white parents would pay the doctor's bills. Lena shouted that if they ever touched me again she would break their arms.

'We're not poor,' I called after him. 'And we've got more brains than all you Soutpiele put together!'

The discarded book back in hand, we crossed the lawn and snuck into the bush so Lena could resume her fishing. She said she'd known there would be trouble when from across the lake she saw them pass through the gate. We baited our hooks and cast in from our secret place. Our rods were bamboo poles; our hooks pins stolen from Bokkie's sewing kit or from Pahla Hardware. Soon forgetting the closeness of the shave, we were again laughing and Lena was certain the English boys wouldn't come near me again. Together we sat preparing new verbal assaults for me to sling at them the moment opportunity arose. A phone had now been installed at home – though we were never allowed to make calls – and I suggested that next time we should actually call the police.

'Poor James,' I laughed, 'he's really gonna get it at school this time.'

'Do him good,' Lena smirked, 'to get those little white fingers out of the flower arrangements. Little dandy.'

The thin makeshift bamboos to which our lines were tied, the wine-corks as floats, were a far cry from the rods, reels and coloured floats we had used from the jetty at St Lucia. All sold off with the move to the city. What a sad excuse the lake of Kingsway Bird Sanctuary now seemed for all the places we had called home before leaving the Parks Board.

'Are we really so poor, Lena?' I asked, putting a clump of bread on the hook and suddenly wishing we were back in a place where I had barely needed to know what money was. How I envied Robbie who at break bought a packet of Fritos or an ice cream every Friday when he received his pocket money. Imagine being allowed to get pocket money!

'Bok says we're going to be rich. And we already have more than some of the Kuswag kids. Just ignore the Souties, Karl. We'll have our day.'

'In heaven,' I said.

'Before that, I jolly well hope. I'm going to marry a rich man, someone like Uncle Joe.'

'He'll make you mad.'

'Aunt Lena was funny before she met Joe Mackenzie. Anyway, I'll divorce him and take his money. And remember I'm not the one with the mad gene,' she said, glancing at me with a twinkle in her eye. I asked her to stop and for a while we sat in silence, watching the corks, waiting for a bite.

'Do you ever think of heaven?' I asked.

'No. Do you?'

'Yes,' I said. 'Shall I tell you what it's like up there?'

'Okay. But not one of your long-winded, boring stories.'

'Heaven is where no one speaks,' I said. 'People just look at each other and they know what the other is thinking without saying a single word.'

'Karl, jissis man, you're crazy. What about the angel Gabriel, he spoke to Mary?'

'Real angels communicate without words.'

'Since when can people understand each other without speaking?' she asked, shaking her head and squinting in the glare.

'In heaven they can. It's a little like that Englishman – showing you the sign with his nose. I mean, he didn't say a word and you knew what he meant.'

'So, that's sign language, like for the deaf. It's still a language.'

'But heaven will be without signs even. And no one will be deaf.'

'Oh please, Karl!' she clicked her tongue, irritated. 'Rather tell me what we'll eat and drink in heaven.'

Paraphrasing, adapting, changing and adding to my memories of *Charlie and the Chocolate Factory* and drive-in sweet commercials I started, wondering briefly whether she'd notice and catch me out: 'There'll be lots and lots of chocolate. As you come in, right beside the gates: huge, huge, huge slabs of Nestlé Peppermint Crisp and Cadbury's Whole Nut, and it will hang like fruit from trees. I'm seeing the Mopani branches bent almost to the ground from the heavy chocolate harvest. And we'll walk on marshmallow stepping stones across cream soda rivers, I can see us now, crossing like we're playing hopscotch — and the hippos are jelly babies and the fish all kinds of shaped Smarties. Without saying anything we're picking our fill of Aero and Chocolate Log from the branches, wide like the wild figs in the forest of louries. The next stream is Coca-Cola, and the next one Fanta, spurting from orange fountains and we're sailing on a lake much bigger than this in a boat made of sweet wafer and, Lena, you're taking a bite from the life vests that are made of marzipan. The boat's masts are inlaid with cherry's — maraschino — and the sails are vanilla ice cream sprinkled with Flake that's melting in the sun and we're just opening our mouths and it's dripping between our lips . . . And it tastes like Mevrou Dominee's brandy tart sauce . . .' I paused, my own mouth watering. I looked at her.

'That's more like it,' she said. 'Put in some seafood — prawns and crayfish mayonnaise — savoury stuff, things like that . . .'

It could be said that if Juffrou Sang had not selected me to sing the lead in the *Pied Piper of Hamelin*, I may never have learnt to read — in my desultory way — sheet music and may never have ended up going to the school in the mountains. But that's second guessing the route I may or may not have followed, and I am not taken to doing that — ever. What in life is done is done, what is written is written, what is regrettable is regretted, who was loved can never be unloved, and to rewrite this life other stories will have to be told or this one read differently.

To perform the Pied Piper I not only had to learn four solos, I also had to play the recorder. By learning the recorder, Juffrou Sang was of the opinion I was at least learning the rudimentaries of music, despite our not having a piano at home. The newly built house where Juffrou Sang lived with Prof and her daughter was at 27 Dan Pienaar, just down the road from us. Through the many afternoons there as I practised my solos and mastered the recorder, I got to know and increasingly like Alette, whom I knew was the top student in class with Lena. According to Lena and Glenn, Alette was a bookworm and a bore who looked as clumsy as an anteater when running on the netball court. The two of them would never be friends, and, Lena warned, it would stand me in good stead to remember that Juffrou Sang and Prof were snobs who thought themselves better than the rest of Kuswag and Dan Pienaar. The drip Alette was already well on her way to being a real culture vulture – just like her pretentious mother. And, Bernice said, she's an only child, and only children are always spoilt rotten.

Within a matter of months Alette had become one of my closest friends. Her and Lena's class were on a playground separate from ours, and while we rarely spoke to each other at school and she seldom came to our home, our afternoons at their house were spent playing recorder duets, singing, and me occasionally just sitting listening to her practice the piano. Her long brown hair was always tied in two severe ponytails behind her ears, she had stocky legs and even at that age a matronly walk – yes, Lena was right – rather like her mother. She had a pointy nose that turned upwards and small round eyes like a monkey. She was plain incarnate, and I was old enough to know. Yet, as time went by and the more of it we spent together, her laughter at sticking a bow in my hair, her cleverness, her interest in how we had lived in the bush, her musicality, the way we sang together and played the recorder, became to me intoxicating. I found my eyes drawn to her mouth, the way her full lips — Lena said she had poetoe-smackers like a black girl — were outlined with a tiny ridge like a light pencil line. My heart leapt when she walked into church and sat down somewhere near the organ. I began picturing her walking down the isle in a glittering wedding gown while I stood below the pulpit in a black suit with a red rose in my lapel.

Lena's and Glenn's displeasure did nothing to still my growing passion for Alette or Juffrou Sang. On the contrary, my sister's scowl, her exclusion from my going over to 27 Dan Pienaar, may in some ways have added to my bliss.

As we were the only kids on Dan Pienaar who received no pocket money, we, together with Glenn and Thea, Betty, Mary-Alice and James, decided to put on a musical in the neighbourhood. A fundraiser for me and Lena. Bernice had to stay home for homework, something I regretted as she, unlike Lena, had quite a good voice. At my suggestion that we invite Alette, Lena baulked, saying she wouldn't participate if Alette came along. Mary-Alice, Thea and I wrote down words to songs from *The Sound of Music* on foolscap pages with sheets of carbon between for multiple copies. We all dressed up and took to the neighbourhood streets, me shimmering in a blue chiffon dress borrowed without consent from Mrs Preston's cupboard. Itching on my head was Aunt Lena's old wig and my face was vaguely obscured by Mary-Alice's communion veil, attached to the wig by one of Bokkie's hairclips. I was Maria and the rest of the troop doubled in various roles: they were the nuns' chorus singing 'Maria' while I danced across lawns up and down Dan Pienaar Drive. I did Maria's solo of 'I Have Confidence in Me', and Betty and Glenn did 'Sixteen Going on Seventeen'. Mary-Alice, who had a good voice and with her long hair insisted we call her Isadora Duncan, was breathtaking as the strict Mother Abbess. Even though we hadn't initially planned it, Mary-Alice threw in a performance of 'Long Haired Lover From

Liverpool', which drew howls of approval and applause from all over the neighbourhood. James and Thea, now nervous and withdrawn in public as they had never been in private, switched roles as any one of the Von Trapp children. Lena, self-conscious about her singing despite our protests that it was fine for a musical, acted as the purse-keeper, collecting five cents from each yard for every performance. We did 'Do-Re-Mi' and ended with 'Climb Every Mountain' marching out of the yard, back into the street. We were the Von Trapps fleeing from the Nazis, a group of professional actors, a troop of minstrels from the Middle Ages. Under my leadership we went from lawn to lawn — careful to stay out of sight of Alette's house.

By the end of the afternoon, we had made two rand. Lena and I were ecstatic. We had more money than we'd ever possessed. I already knew what I would buy. Thea had told me of a CNA in Durban that had a poster of Rudolf Nureyev on sale for one rand twenty. It was in black and white, unfortunately. But that made the poster cheaper than if it were in colour and it was now, unexpectedly, within my reach. I was sure Mrs Willemse would buy the poster for me next time they went into town. I could see it, glossy and vivid against the wall, above my bed where at night I could lie looking up at the man leaping skyward. And who cared if it was in black and white; I would simply imagine that it was in colour and it would be so.

At home we excitedly told Bokkie and Bernice of the day's extraordinary windfall. I said I was getting a poster of Rudolf Nureyev for above my bed.

But instead of sharing in our delight or praising our resourcefulness, Bokkie was beside herself: 'We are not poor whites! We don't stick hippy posters against white walls and even less do we run around the streets begging for money!'

'James was also with us,' I said, hoping the complicity of Aunt Siobhain's son would bring her to a different insight.

'I don't care about your English cousin! We're Afrikaners and we have different values. It's all those years at St Lucia under the Pierces.

You two have today single-handedly ruined our reputation in this neighbourhood! How can I show my face on the streets again, face the Dameskring at Bible Study? That *my* children go around the neighbourhood collecting money! Wait till your father gets back from safari! Just you wait.' Rather than beating us – a fate we would have preferred infinitely – she told us to get rid of the costumes. To our horror, she sent us back through the neighbourhood to return the money and offer apologies for our behaviour. From a distance she followed, standing at the bottom of each street or driveway, supervising us as we slunk to front doors in the dusk.

When Bok got home Bokkie forced us to tell him, in our own words, how we had shamed the De Man family. This was not the bush, Bok said, and we had to learn to abide by the codes of the city. Even as he spoke, it looked as though he might start laughing, and we knew we were safe. Then his expression went stern and he said that if he heard that I was in a dress or a wig ever again, or that I'd danced across the neighbourhood lawns, he'd beat me so that I'd remember it for the rest of my life. And somewhere there, in the humid haze of the long Toti afternoons, I slowly danced less. Sang more and again read more. Often still wondering how much smaller I would have had to have been for them to have allowed me to be a dancer.

Lena and I, Glenn and Thea took turns at stealing small things from various shops at the new Pahla Station shopping centre. Sweets from the café, and from Pahla Hardware Dinky cars, penknives, hammers and nails, pins for fishing, candles, pieces of perspex, ropes, pliers – all of which went into the fort we had started under the overhanging fronds of a datepalm at the bottom of 21 Dan Pienaar. Here we stockpiled in case the kaffirs took over the country. The four of us in a secret gang from which everyone else was excluded. When the kaffirs came we would be able to live for weeks on the loot we had amassed beneath the palm.

For months I had my eye on one of Pahla Hardware's miniature

Primus stoves, an accessory we all wanted for the fort. As the size-able Primus was too bulky to fit beneath our shirts, we were all too afraid to attempt the theft. On a day when the shopkeeper was somewhere along the back shelves, I picked up the Primus, held it confidently to my chest, and glided out into the street. When the others came out and found me in the bush behind the shopping centre, they could scarcely believe their eyes. Now we needed fuel! We at once sent back Thea to steal a bottle of methylated spirits and Lena went off to relieve the café of a packet of marshmallows. Beneath the palm, we melted marshmallows over the Primus and I lit all the candles, saying we needed flames to create a more festive atmo.

Again perusing the shelves of Pahla Hardware a while later, I slipped a leather pencil bag down the front of my shorts. Just as I was leaving the shopkeeper stepped in front of me, blocking my way. She asked what I had hidden in my pants. I said nothing, that she had a dirty mind and she'd better let me out. She said she was going to call the police unless I removed whatever was in there. Pushing past her and making a run for it seemed stupid, as the whole neigh-bourhood would know who we were. Red-faced I extracted the pencil bag and handed it to her. She said that she'd had her eyes on us for quite a while and warned that not one of us was to set foot again in her store. If we came near there she'd call in the police and make sure our parents were informed of what common thieves they had for children.

I strutted out in shame, enraged that I'd been caught, but relieved at the escape. Furious that I had spoilt the central source of our raids, Glenn smacked me behind the head and demanded to know why I had stolen a pencil bag in the first place. Lena warned him not to lay another hand on me. Then she slapped me against the head, commanding that henceforth I steal only things that could reasonably be shared by the whole gang.

'One needs a pencil bag,' I began to explain, but was cut short by

Lena who snapped: 'Don't say *one*, like it's all of us. Stop talking like a ladeda! You may need a stupid pencil bag but the gang doesn't.'

Something happened in the Kingsway Bird Sanctuary with its lake and its sprawling acres. A few times during afternoons when I sat there reading, my eyes began to water and I'd move from the sun into the shade. But even in the shade they watered. Without feeling as though I were crying, I knew that I indeed was. Might my eyes be watery because of the spitting bugs in the feather trees; was I developing another form of hay fever? Did I need glasses? Then, one day when James accompanied Lena and me to fish, there was a moment in which I almost began to weep when I heard a peacock call. Sure enough, the next time I was alone and their call ran through the trees, my eyes watered and tears brimmed over and ran down my cheeks. When the tears disappeared, a cloud hovered over me – even when the sun was shining. And then, afterwards, I developed headaches and had to take two Disprin. I knew that Aunt Lena's headaches often landed her in hospital where she had to be injected with Voltarin. When I told Bernice and Stephanie, they said it was nothing to worry about, I was merely into the blues. For the blues – I discovered – it helped if I took antihistamine. The tablets did not make me feel drowsy as the prescription warned. Instead, like small miracles, they made me feel as if I was in complete control of my world, as if nothing around me really much mattered.

3

Agnus, second declension masculine, an endless word over ninety-five bars. Dei, second declension genitive, possessive. I named them while his hands brought us in. Qui – has to correlate with lamb of God, masculine – all the while scratching the mosquito bites that itched and now felt like many more than three, as though they stretched all the way up the side of my thigh. Tollis, second person, Pecata, second declension, neuter, and Mundi, second or third declension genitive of second Deus, Deum, Dei, something nominative plural. Miserere — what the hell does it take, genitive, take pity on me, passive, indicative, imperative, subjunctive, is it active or passive? Must be an odd word, nobis, dative, donna nobis, give to us peace. The last movement. Here we're bringing everything to a head. This is the body of Christ, broken for you. Communion is taken. Again I scratched at the bites, trying not to move my shoulder or arm, to seem concentrated, while wanting badly to drop my pants and look. Could it have been a hairy caterpillar or a poisonous leaf rather than a mosquito?

Ma'am had brought a message to class saying I was to go with Mr Cilliers to have my stitches out in Estcourt. He — she said — had an appointment in Pietermaritzburg to see someone from the SABC orchestra to discuss the December performance. He — I at once wanted to believe — must have invented an excuse so he could be the one to take me to hospital. I would be out-and-out surprised if we went anywhere near Maritzburg! We drove off in his Mazda 323 and yes, he said, the meeting in Maritzburg was real. Disappointed that I was not indeed the ordering point of his life, it was none the less satisfying to know I'd be missing half my classes and that I'd be having the full day with him. Our first since Paternoster.

The mountains stood in a blue haze. The veld an unrestrained verdant, almost neon, where but a month before across the yellow and red of winter, black residues of fire had scabbed the horizons. Off the gravel road near Estcourt was a sign pointing to the Gerrit Maritz Memorial. I said I wondered what it would have been like for us to have been part of the Great Trek, to have come over these awesome mountains to face the Zulus. If only the Boers had come twenty years earlier we would have dealt with the regal Chaka, not the evil Dingaan. Chaka was the greatest Zulu King. The first adult book I read when I was ten, I boasted, called *The Washing of the Spears*, spoke of Chaka as one of the greatest leaders the world had ever seen. This, exactly here where we were now travelling, was where the first Boers had settled after leaving the Cape Colony under British rule. The Napoleonic Wars. How crazy that what Napoleon did in France determined what happened here on the southern tip of Africa. From near here, right here somewhere, Retief had ridden out to meet Dingaan who murdered him. Then, the Boer commando to face the Zulu hordes at the Battle of Bloodriver. We were driving through the blood, sweat and tears of Boer history. 'Don't you think that's incredible?' I asked. 'That all of this, and right where the school is, and all the hotels, and even where our forts are, each of these roads, are all places where blood has been spilt?'

'No, my boy,' Jacques snorted, and placed his hand on my leg, 'I'm a Cilliers. That's why I'm here and not dead like Retief. We Cilliers men already stayed at home with the women and children over a century ago.' We laughed. I said I thought I may have wanted to go on commando, especially with the horses and being out in the wild. He said commando constituted more than horses, cowboys and crooks, and the great outdoors. That I had a far too romantic idea of war.

In Estcourt we stopped to have my knee inspected and the stitches removed. I could see the scar wasn't at all bad but kept up the limp. He asked whether I was hungry and when I said no bought us ice-cream cones with Flakes in the centre before we went on towards Maritzburg. How's the wound, he asked and I put my foot on the dashboard, lifting my knee so he could see. Sore? Resting his hand on my thigh, pushing the shorts higher. Not any more, I said. I'm sure it will get better if you keep your hand there.

The campus was crawling with students dressed in jeans and shorts and leather sandals. I felt like I could be somewhere in America, in a movie. The buildings were lovely, like relics of an era gone by, and I imagined being a student there, scurrying into the entrance beneath the red-brick clock tower on my way to write a Roman Dutch law exam. When I told Jacques how attractive I found the buildings he asked whether I had ever seen Hilton College, the private boys' school just up the hill. I said I hadn't, and he suggested we stop there on the way back to the Berg.

At the College of Music he collected annotated sheet music from a secretary and then took me into an office where I met the SABC orchestra's chief violinist, a man whose name I can no longer recall. He shook my hand and said he had enormous respect for us doing this complex piece of music. Then he and Jacques spoke about the strengths and weaknesses of the orchestra and the alterations Jacques had made in orchestration. They drew up a tentative agenda for the three-day rehearsal and the recordings due to take place in Jo'burg end of November. A timetable and meal plans were discussed. I sat listening, taking in the office and the two men intensely engaged across the desk from each other. As we left, the violinist said he'd see me in Jo'burg and that I was to wish the choir well. He and the other members of the orchestra and adult choir were on tenterhooks to meet us all, to hear us sing.

Back in the car, Jacques again asked after my knee and I said it was fine. We spoke about the concert, barely two months away. It would be the biggest he'd ever conducted. He wasn't sure whether he was excited or afraid. No, he said in response to a question, he wasn't really concerned at the live TV broadcast, more about the arrangement he had done of Beethoven's work. 'The Mass is something of a sacred cow,' he said, 'and I'm not sure how the audience or the press will respond to a boy quartet and to the sections without the adult voices.' We were good, he said, but perhaps it was just as well the SABC choir was with us. It was, he had admitted to himself already when doing the arrangement, too much for boys to do alone. I asked whether he was happy with how things were going. He said yes, we were outdoing ourselves. Sometimes he couldn't believe how we — and specially the Juniors — had managed to get our heads and voices around sections of the Mass any adult choir would find a challenge. 'But don't tell them I said that!' he laughed. 'I don't want any of you resting on your laurels. Better to keep you all guessing. That's my experience with any performer. The director, the conductor, the maestro, should not give affirmation too soon. That keeps the performer on his toes. Here's the Hilton turn-off. What's the time? Want to go have a quick squiz?'

'It doesn't matter, if we're late, we can miss it,' I said, but he took the off ramp. Left, then crossed the bridge over the highway. Following the narrow tarmac road we passed through green rolling hills. The neat white buildings of Hilton College sat like an extended English Tudor complex on perfectly tended lawns amidst rose gardens and enormous trees. It looked centuries old, like how I imagined Oxford or Europe where we would be performing over Christmas. The entrance, from which ran a winding road up into the buildings, was marked by an ornate metal gate.

'It's like a hotel complex,' I said.

'Hilton College is money being educated to make money,' he said and smiled. 'Wouldn't you like to come to school here?'

'Yes, but it must cost a fortune! If our school looks like it does with all the money our parents pay, this must be ten times more. Look . . .' Two or three teams were doing warm-up exercises, running, falling onto their stomachs, doing push-ups, kicking a soccer ball, sprinting to where two trainers waited.

'I'm not sure what the school fees are, though I doubt they're much more than ours. Ours is an arts school, Karl, you know there's no money in music. And the people who come to this place and Michaelhouse and Kearsney have been sending boys here for generations. It's a family business. Enormous endowments by grandfathers who want the place kept up. They leave half the money to their sons and the other half to the school. That's why it looks like this. And we're only twenty years old. Maybe with time things will develop in our part of the woods.'

He had gone to Pretoria Boys High, he said. Not a bad school, but nothing like Hilton. And he spoke briefly about growing up in Sabie in the Eastern Transvaal, where his parents were carpenters. That's near the Kruger Park, isn't it, I asked. Yes. Both his father and mother made furniture. Yellow-wood, stinkwood and teak. All cut from the forests in the region. He told me to take a look at his dressing table when I next came to his room. It was stinkwood. A gift from his parents. I asked whether he had siblings and he said he had a younger brother with whom he was very close. His brother and his wife, he said, had recently joined the family business. 'We're a very close family,' he said. 'I admire my mother and father. And they think my brother and I the best things since sliced bread. Like all parents, I suppose.' His father had bought him a piano when he was six. While his mother remained in the workshop on a Saturday, his father had driven him all the way to Pretoria once a week for lessons with the best tutor in the Transvaal. Late afternoon, driving back to Sabie, he would practise what he'd learnt on the dashboard of the car, humming or singing the score while his father behind the wheel kept time, like a metronome, tick-tick-tick-tick. His being the Berg's senior conductor made his parents very proud. They were coming to the Durban performance, as were his brother and sister-in-law. And they'd be at Jan Smuts to see us off when we left for Europe. 'Take a look on my dressing table,' he said, 'there are photographs of them all stuck to the mirror.' I responded that we never had the light on in his room and that I was never there for long enough to go around inspecting the furniture or the pictures, a plaintive chord stringing my voice.

'Ooh, la, la,' he said, putting his hand on my head. 'Are you feeling a little neglected?'

'No, I'm just saying . . .'

'We can't, you know,' he said, 'get much more than pleasure — simple pleasure — from each other in a place like this. It's too danger-ous. In Europe you and I are going to spend more time together. How's that sound?'

'Wonderful.'

*

The sun was an hour or less above the mountains to our west. Injasuti, Cathkin, Champagne, Ndedema Dome, Gatberg, Organ Pipe Pass, the Pyramid, Inner Horn, Outer Horn, Cathedral Peak, the Saddle, up north into Mponjwana, the Inner and Outer Needles, Ifidi Buttress, Mount Oompie, the Amphitheatre, the Sentinel and Mont-aux-Sources from where all the country's rivers sprang and the Drakensberg inexplicably turned into the Maluties. Six, eight deep, they drifted into paling purple rows, diffuse layers of horizon. God, how in that instant I adored you. How I could have wanted to love all of you: your wealth, your poverty, your black and white and brown and yellow and tan, your talking in millions, your cities, locations, your passive and angered and indifferent, your children with games and songs and bombs, mothers, fathers, your ancestors, your health and disease to envelop from every conceivable side my body and let your grass and sandstone and trees and water and air enter each pore of my skin; take me; how then, I thought, I would one day write verse upon verse to celebrate your splendour even beyond the precision of human words.

On the dust road from Estcourt he glanced at his watch. He asked whether I had ten minutes to spare. I grinned and nodded. Knew at once what he meant and said a quick yes. For half the day I had wanted to touch him, my penis going hard and soft sporadically throughout the trip. Now, as if permission had been given for my desire to take flight, as if I'd been told my lust was not out of place, I slid my hand between his legs. Self-conscious, stared from the front window. We turned from the Loskop road. Heading down a deserted road into a pine plantation I wondered whether the land belonged to the Therons. Amongst the pines were scattered patches of wattle and old eucalyptus, their white stems peeling biltongs of bark. For a moment I was thrilled at the prospect of us being discovered, perhaps by one of the Therons. Trespassers, caught in flagrante delicto – while the crime still blazes! The car hidden from the road, we sat back in our seats. He leant over and kissed me. I worried that my breath might be smelly this late in the day, wished I had brushed harder in the morning.

'Let's get out,' I whispered, turning from his face, but he, trying to keep his mouth to mine, said it was too dangerous and we had to hurry. His hand was inside my shorts. I felt embarrassed feeling how wet I must have been even before he touched me. I wanted to be outside where we could lie down on the mat of copper pine needles. Where we could kiss and cuddle, and I could be on top of him.

'This is too uncomfortable,' I said, trying to hold my breath and putting my hand onto his. 'Please, let's get out.'

'Okay,' he smiled, 'but this must be quick. We're going to be late for choir.' He leant against a wattle and pulled me to him. I had never smelt him like this, unwashed, skin and sweat mingling with pine and eucalyptus. He knelt in front of me. I looked down on his head of black curls, the lashes resting on the white skin beside his nose, which broke the arch of his lips around my penis. His nose seemed broader than my shaft in his mouth and for some reason I felt the need to thrust my hips, to hide the whole thing from sight. I held onto the tree, my fingers clutching the rough bark. Closed my eyes. Feeling myself close, I stopped him. Tried to pull him up, but he had to do it himself. Then I turned him so that he was backed to the tree. I knelt, smiled up at him and felt the excitement of being almost adult, so able to manoeuvre him. For an instant I wished again that we could be seen. He cautioned me to be careful of my knee, not to get dirt in the wound. His trousers were down around his bandy legs, the penis arching out, the head half exposed, a crimson-purple emerging from the gaping grey foreskin. I took it in my mouth, and almost gagged as it touched the back of my throat or the glottis, had to pull away. I worked the foreskin with my left hand while my right was in my own loins, letting go when I was too close. I wished I could take longer to come, more like him. He moaned and I pushed my forehead against his belly, enjoyed hearing his sounds. I removed my lips and with both hands kept at it, watching the crimson head now covered now exposed by the foreskin, beautiful, his hips pushed forward and then the squirt, shooting, dripping over my fingers, his hands in my hair, again putting my mouth over it, licking him, shivers from him, bringing myself to climax, looking down, watching me leak over my fingers onto the pine needles. Feeling instantly dirty and disgusted with myself.

'We're late. We're late!' he said, pulling a face and tugging up his trousers and tying his belt. I rose and pulled up my shorts, spotted the three red welts of mosquito bites on my upper thigh. I brushed grains of dirt from the wound and now felt my knee ache. The back of his shirt was stained by gum from the wattle. I pulled off the long slither and stuck it in my mouth, chewing, wanting to get rid of his taste.

We raced back up to the main road. It was almost sunset and we knew there was no way we would be on time. Dust flew behind us. He told me to fasten my safety belt. Seemed angry. We didn't speak until he had parked the car in his bay and we walked swiftly towards the entrance. The sound of the Mass choir in warm-ups came from the auditorium. 'The Maritzburg meeting took an hour and a half. Okay.'

'*Just over* an hour and a half,' I said.

The choir's eyes did not move from Raubenheimer as Jacques and I walked into the hall. I cut through two rows to mount the middle bench. My voice joined the voices around me. My eyes joined the eyes on Raubenheimer; did not venture to Jacques who stood with his head bowed, listening. When Raubenheimer was satisfied he stopped us. Said, 'Sir,' as he nodded to Jacques and took his place in the front line.

'Good sound. Thanks, Sarel,' he said and nodded to the accompanist who moved to the piano at once.

'Open up at 82. The minor chord. Apologies for being late. The meeting in Maritzburg lasted longer than I'd anticipated.' I wanted to smile. That was it. It was true because it had been said. By him.

I was still scratching ... *miserere nobis* ...

'The priest has already said this is the body of Christ, this is the blood of Christ, okay?' He nodded at us. 'For the Catholics,' he went on, 'it is not a symbol, it is the real thing, you are literally eating the body that has been sacrificed for your sins. It's almost the same for us Protestants. But for us it's a symbol, okay? But you also believe in redemption and being saved because you have Jesus inside your body. You've eaten of the body, at least symbolically. When we join with the orchestra I want you to listen very closely to the instruments . . . Incidentally, they're all looking forward to hearing you . . .' And all I could think of was getting upstairs to see why my thigh would not stop burning. I was now certain it had to have been a hairy caterpillar. The moment we broke up I'd run to dab on some Savlon to stop the irritation.

At supper Dom and Lukas asked about the trip. I told them the doctor had said my knee was fine – maybe a bit of water on it; that Jacques and I had had an ice cream; that the meeting at Maritzburg had lasted a boring eternity. Mervy wanted to know about the violinist and I tried to describe what he looked like; gave as full a report as I could, elaborating on the timetable for the Jo'burg rehearsals and recordings. Saying how excited the violinist had said the Philharmonic was about the joint performance. I said I'd missed most of the meeting as I'd been walking around the campus talking to students.

During prep I raced through the Latin homework Bruin said Ma'am had given. Then fell to work on an essay I was trying to write in the style of Herman Charles Bosman.

Unannounced, Dom came to my bed that night.

'Why didn't you say you were coming? It's not Saturday,' I whispered, our heads beneath the bedspread.

'I missed you today,' he answered. 'Where's your torch?'

'In the locker. No, let's leave it, okay?'

'Okay.' We faced each other in the pitch dark. When he spoke I smelt the toothpaste from his mouth. Moved my head closer to his, till our lips almost touched.

'I missed you too,' I said.

'I'm envious, you know,' he whispered.

'Of what?' I asked. He said he envied me spending the day with Cilliers, and me getting to meet the lead violinist. I said there was nothing to be envious about. It had all been quite laborious and I'd have preferred to return to school after my stitches had been removed. Dom said he didn't believe me, whispered that I must have felt happy meeting the violinist. 'You've begun taking our music seriously, Karl. Haven't you? So you must have felt a little grand at meeting the big shot?'

'I suppose, yes. But I didn't even know he was the big shot.'

'He's the leader of the orchestra.' Dom said and I answered that I hadn't realised.

Dominic changed the topic and said he was about to start serious rehearsing for his Grade Eight exams. That he had to use every free hour behind the piano and every hour in bed to sleep. 'I really need to concentrate. I don't think we should do this again till after my exams. Okay?' I whispered no, it was not okay, but I understood. In an instant I was concerned that he suspected me and Cilliers, was at once afraid that he was withdrawing, that he no longer cared for me and was finding an excuse to keep from seeing me.

'Dom, is everything okay? Is something wrong, or is it really only the exam?' He brought his mouth to my lips and kissed me, moved his arm over my back and pulled himself closer.

'It's only the exam. You know I'd tell you if there was anything else. I love you.' Again we kissed. 'I've got four works, Karl. The Bach prelude and fugue I'll do with my eyes closed, but there's the complete Mozart sonata, you know. Then the big romantic Schumann and a modern piece. I'm not worried about the usual scales and the rest, but the works are going to be tough.'

We fumbled loose the top buttons of each other's pyjama pants.

Shhh, I said. We were being too noisy. I wished we could have our own room, as we had on the Cape tour. Where we could do everything to each other, speak, breathe, without the overbearing fear of discovery. Where we had used spit to lubricate each other all over without fearing the squelches and Dom had brought a tin of Condensed Milk to bed one night. Where we could go all the way with each other like the night in their house at Saxonwold when he read me sonnets. Here, in the Berg, it was only the dry-hand waltz, not even sucking, and I now badly wanted to have him in me again, or me in him, his legs clasped round my middle, the pillow beneath his bum, his face smiling up into mine telling me he'd love me for ever. I thought of telling him about the key. Yearned to let him know. Then we could go outside and do it again somewhere in the bush. Decided I wouldn't. Simply too dangerous and I couldn't believe he'd want to do it in the wet grass where he'd easily pick up a cold.

After he left I tossed and turned, unable to fall asleep, my mind a hive of teeming thoughts. I wondered whether anyone would disbelieve Jacques's story. Would anyone suspect he'd lied? What makes anyone think someone else is telling an untruth? Omission, is that different from an act of direct lying? No, it was feasible that we'd been held up in Maritzburg. What if his car had been seen parked in the Therons' pine plantation? My thigh itched. I took the torch from my locker and beneath the covers tried with my bitten nails to push crosses into the welts. Still unable to sleep, I got up. Might as well go and check if those other two were still here. I let myself out of the music room. A few steps away I turned back and left my slippers outside the window. No use getting them mucky and facing questions from Uncle Charlie.

The Milky Way was a haze of low-floating mist while around and before it in the black a million stars sparkled, winked. Dew-wet stalks licked at the hem of my dressing gown, bare calves and feet as I trotted towards the rugby field. Left, right, scanning the road that divided

the orchard from the flat playing field, half expecting to see the outline of one or more farm workers trudging towards me. Across the
field, cat-foot over landmines — blots of dark cow dung — I reached
the river. I slowed down, catching my breath. Soon the sky above me
was hidden by the ceiling of poplars, the stars now winking only
through the gap above where the river gurgled over rocks, making its
way to near Winterton to join the Little Tugela.

Our fort sat hunched like a mirage against the grey soil. From
inside again their smell. But now not only theirs. Instead, mingled
with the smoke and urine, the air smelt of something sweet, like wild
gardenias or honeysuckle. Through the thatch came the sound of the
two men asleep. I sniffed the air for the source of sweetness, remi-
niscent of the night scents of Mkuzi: surely *Turraea floribunda* cannot
grow this high up in the mountains? I came to a standstill at the
entrance to the fort, snores now clear from the inside. Across the
stream, in crevasses midway up the sheer four-metre rock face, clusters
of white flowers were budding. Glowing in the night against their
sandstone home, their white heads all that was visible beneath silhouettes of pines and poplars dotting the opposite shore. That must
be where the scent comes from, I thought. For a while I stood quietly,
straining my eyes towards the other bank. Could it be? No, I could-
n't quite make them out, but they were clearly not growing on a tree.
Must be bulbs, I thought, something whose name I don't know.

4

Juffrou Sang and Alette came to tell Bokkie about a concert of the
Drakensberg Boys Music School. The performance was to take place
in the Durban City Hall. My mother, in shorts, apologised for her
appearance saying she'd been gardening all day. Against Juffrou Sang's
hearty protests, my mother asked me to turn on the kettle and wait in
the lounge with the guests while she made herself presentable. Juffrou

Sang and Alette told me about the school in the mountains. Bokkie came back in a dress, her hair brushed and colour on her lips. Juffrou Sang told Bokkie she'd like to take me to the City Hall concert; however, if Bokkie and the girls would like to join, we could have an outing – make an evening of it – maybe have coffee at a restaurant afterwards. Prof, as she called Alette's father, had something on at university, so it would just be 'us ladies and the children'. Beaming with pride, Bokkie said she would really like me to go. She said she was eternally grateful to Juffrou Sang for exposing me to a little culture and developing my talents. She'd tell the girls about the concert, and, if they were interested, we could all go. While they drank tea, Juffrou Sang complimented Bokkie on the interesting collection of African curios in the lounge, particularly the two clay Maasai heads against the wall, and Bokkie explained the simi and the beadwork – a necklace she had brought out from Tanzania. 'And that was our view from the farmhouse,' she said. 'Mount Meru.' Pointing to the painting above the never-used fireplace.

Juffrou Sang left and Alette stayed so I could show her our record albums. She skimmed through, Jim Reeves, Mantovani, Perry Como, Nat King Cole, the Strauss waltzes, Heintjie, the Gunter Calmen Choir, Patsy Cline, Min Shaw, Kobus and Hannelie. Then her eyes caught the two flat cartons of opera: *La Bohème* and *La Traviata*. Joan Sutherland. We'd never listened to these two sets of records and I had no idea how they'd come to be in our house. Alette told me the story of Violetta. A woman who never thought she could be loved, but fell in love with Alfred. The story sounded sad, intriguing, and I now knew that opera had a story. She asked me to play one of the records from the *La Traviata* collection. As the orchestral music drifted into our lounge Alette threw back her head and smiled. She loved it. I said I hated it. It sounded forced, pretentious and difficult. Why not just read the story or have music with a nice tune. She said I should listen attentively. This – classical music – I would hear at the concert of the boys' choir. Now was the time to begin developing my ear. She listened with her eyes closed, said, *La Traviata* was by Verdi, a great Italian composer. I grew bored, wished she would leave or that we could go to the bird sanctuary. I wanted songs with a clear tune, that you listened to while you sang along or read a book. It was absurd, sitting down, doing nothing but listening like a meerkat on an anthill.

Bokkie returned to the lounge. She told Alette she'd given the concert some thought and that she would like to go and take the girls along. She said she was wondering whether Alette knew how much the tickets would cost. The tickets were two rand, Alette said. Bokkie nodded and left. Alette invited me to come over to their house whenever I wanted. She would let me listen to their collection of classical records: concerts recorded in places called Carnegie Hall and Covent Garden, arias (one new word in a series of new concepts and ideas) by world-famous singers like Maria Callas, Ivan Rebroff, Renata Tebaldi, Elisabeth Schwarzkopf – no, she laughed at my question, forget the silly Mimi Coertze – musicians and composers like Bach, Stravinsky, Paderewski, Rachmaninov, Beethoven.

At dinner, Bokkie told me and the girls she would take money for the concert from housekeeping. She and Mrs Willemse were planning to bake koek-sisters that we could take and sell around the neighbourhood. Lena said she wasn't sure she felt like sitting through a whole concert and I said fine, if you want to stay common for the rest of your life, why don't you just go and stay at Glenn and Thea's while we're in town. Lena answered that she could see I was already under the spell of the culture vultures and thinking myself a snob. Bokkie told us to be quiet: 'We're all going together, or none of us will go.' Bokkie and Mrs Willemse baked. We kids walked around the neighbourhood selling half a dozen at fifteen cents, sometimes charging twenty at the bigger, newer homes and pocketing the five cents we had overcharged.

Dressed in our Sunday best – though neither Bokkie nor the girls wore hats — we waited in the lounge for Juffrou Sang and Alette to collect us.

All the way to Durban, Juffrou Sang spoke about the unique choral experience we had in store; about the exclusive music school in the Berg where boys sang, played different instruments, farmed and did horse-riding. While still teaching in Port Elizabeth Juffrou Sang had succeeded in getting one boy into the school: any South African music teacher's dream. Of every hundred applicants only one was successful. And so, already long before we took our seats in the spectacular white hall with its delicate cornices and boxes in which sat the mayor and other VIPs, I was acutely aware that I was about to hear in unison the greatest boys' voices in the country. My chest swelled at knowing that my musical talent was of a calibre — I had not as yet dreamt myself ever being part of such company — that Juffrou Sang had found me and my family worthy of bringing to witness a group in possession of uniform tone, voice, compass, and a mastery of range that placed it in the same league as the famous Vienna Boys.

I had seen the inside of the City Hall once before when all Kuswag's Standard Twos had been taken to a special daytime performance of the Durban Symphony Orchestra. The event had been put on as an educational concert for Durban's primary schools. Wearing the uniforms of some private schools like Durban Girls College and Marist Brothers were a handful of black and Indian children, their dark skins and black hair visible a mile off amongst the blonds, browns, reds, auburns. I can today not recall what music the orchestra played, but whatever it was did not succeed in keeping Robbie, Felix and me from being bored to death. From where we were up on the second balcony, Robbie and I sat spitting down onto the rows of children below, then hurriedly pulling away from the balustrade and feigning attention. Getting out of the hall into the sun once the concert was over brought huge relief and at home I confessed to my parents and sisters that symphony music was not for me.

I now sat between Alette and Bernice, glancing down at the

programme that Juffrou Sang had purchased for us. Alette whispered
small details about the various pieces on the programme: 'In
Memorium', by Antonio Vivaldi; 'Psalm 23', arranged by Dirkie De
Villiers ('one of South Africa's best composers'); 'Ave Verum Corpus'
by Cherubini; 'In the Merry Month of May', madrigal, traditional,
English; 'The Virgin Martyrs', Samuel Barber; 'Let My People Go',
spiritual, traditional, negro ('a lighter piece, powerful rhythm, you'll
like this one'); 'Ceremony of Carols', Britten; Copland's 'An
Immorality'; 'Schlafen mein Prinzen', lullaby, Brahms ('wonderful
soprano descant'); 'Laudate Dominum', Wolfgang Amadeus Mozart;
'Three Mottets', Maurice Durufle ('I'll play these for you at home,
Mum has them on a record of the Edinburgh Ensemble'); 'Nature
and Love' by Tchaikovsky ('one of Russia's greatest and most dramatic
composers'); 'Die Berggans', 'Die Duiwel en die Slypsteen', 'Rooi
Disa', by Boerneef ('the best-known Afrikaans choir songs');
'Sanctus', by Saint-Saens from his *Requiem*. The scope of Alette's commentary was as impressive as it was daunting and I sat spellbound at
her knowledge. Together we read the short biography beneath the
black and white photograph of the gaunt-faced conductor with the
dark hair with his hands raised in front of him. I took the booklet
from her hand and looked over the photographs that made up its
centre. Boys with long-haired sheep in Wales; with black riding caps
on horses galloping; with the Eiffel Tower behind them in Paris;
snorkelling in the Seychelles; milking cows on the farm in the Berg.

The applause began as the line of boys in their blue waistcoats and
white frilly bibs walked onto stage. In neat rows they mounted the
benches and although there must have been forty of them they
seemed no more than a tiny gathering of birds on the huge stage
beneath the enormous organ pipes. Then out came the man in his
black suit and the applause thundered again as he crossed the stage
and in front of the boys took a bow. They sang standing with their
hands behind their backs, not like me at eisteddfods with my arms by
my side. Most of the music was in German and Latin. Nothing

sounded familiar to me; in vain I waited for them to sing something
I knew. After songs where we were meant to clap I joined the audience
in thundering approval, yet found little as interesting as Juffrou Sang
had led us to believe it would be. Within half an hour I was disil-
lusioned. The music was heavy and boring. Nothing I liked. I had
never heard a record of such choir music – we had only the Gunter
Calmen Choir on record – and these songs were all in incomprehensible languages, without tunes or movement. The whole thing seemed
stifling. Singing a few solos of light songs at the eisteddfod was fun.
A few songs with the Kuswag choir too, or in the school operetta.
That I thrived on. But this programme was awful. The voices were, I
could tell, brilliant, but they sang nothing I liked. Yes, that was the
problem, I thought, I could hear how good the choir was, and when
a soloist sang I could scarcely believe a boy's voice capable of such
sound or skill; but the songs themselves, like the long motionless performance, bored me. During break I ventured a cautious opinion on
the songs. Alette giggled and said I should not call them songs. They
were *pieces*.

The encore's applause died down and we shuffled out of the City
Hall with the rest of the audience, all beaming, smiling. Many
people were obviously acquainted with each other. Juffrou Sang
looked at me with wide, excited eyes. So much had been invested in
it: Bokkie's housekeeping, Juffrou Sang's expectations, walking
around the neighbourhood selling koek-sisters. Before Juffrou Sang
had even asked I said it was wonderful. What a privilege to be in such
a school. And an honour, added Juffrou Sang. I did not say that it
was not the music that attracted me, but rather the photographs on
the programme. Of boys on horseback; touring the world. That it
was on a farm. She asked whether I would like to attend the school.
I said yes, but that the voices were too good for me. She said if that
were my attitude I would never get in. If I believed I could, I would.
She would help me. It is a private school, she said, and it costs a lot

of money. Bokkie said she doubted we'd be able to afford it, but she'd speak to Bok when he got back from the Zambezi. It would be an enormous honour for Kuswag if I were selected, Juffrou Sang said, and everyone in the car concurred. Within seconds I had forgotten that I didn't want to sing, that I hated what for me was the tunelessness of classical music, which was all, like Verdi's opera, monotonous and incomprehensible.

I told Mary-Alice and Betty that we'd been to the concert. They said that they had a cousin at the school, he was older than them. His name was Frans Harding. They had heard from Frans that the boys sang for hours and that they even went to school on Saturdays. That you had to be bright or else you'd fail with all the touring and what not. I countered with the pictures of the farm and the horses. 'Don't be fooled by the tours and the horses, Karl,' Mary-Alice said. 'Frans says it's singing, singing till after the cows come home.' At this, I decided I did not want to go to the Berg. Kuswag and Toti were good enough for me. Here I had all my friends, Voortrekkers with Robbie and Felix, Judy the sausage dog, the bird sanctuary, my family. Here I needn't fear the boarding-school goodbyes I remembered from Mkuzi and Umfolozi. No, I was not going to audition. I'd stay here. Robbie and Felix said they were glad I wasn't leaving.

5

Swaargenoeg's farmhouse, brilliant white with a corrugated iron roof, perched on an incline above a series of small gullies and lower hills. Upon completion of their agriculture degrees at Stellenbosch University, Lukas's two older brothers had each been given a neighbouring farm. Swaargenoeg, Lukas said, was going to be his. His bedroom was adorned with posters of the pop group Bread, *Scope* centrefolds, horses on show, mounted trophies of impala and kudu, and two racks of shotguns.

The other eight of us slept on bunk beds in a rondavel outside the main house on the winter lawn, yellowed and prickly from nights of frost.

Instead of sleeping before the concert, Lukas and I went to the stables. Twenty-two stalls stood behind a neatly tended garden of blue agapanthus, red-hot pokers and aloes. Inside: Arabians, American saddlers and English thoroughbreds. I now saw in real life Harlequin, the horse of which Lukas kept the photo in his Bible along with one of his girlfriend and another of the whole Van Rensburg family. The stables made up the centre of the farm's stud and my eyes would not leave the magnificent animals. Even the horses used for rounding up sheep were in the same glorious condition I'd seen in Bok's *Horseman's Bible* and Uncle Joe's *Farmer's Weekly*s. Holidays in Klerksdorp, I had cut photographs of horses from the *Farmer's Weekly* and *Landbou Weekblad* and imagined owning my own farm, organising my own stables and sprawling paddocks with cross-pole fencing.

The Van Rensburgs' saddle room represented the sort of ship-shape organisation I would have wanted for my own: whitewashed walls, floor shiny with a fresh coat of green enamel paint, hooks for bridles, thongs and saddles neatly lined and the whole place smelling of dubbin, leather and horse. Saddling the horses, I contemplated living in – owning – a place like this. Being given a farm for graduation. The very idea was mind-boggling. I thought of the Brats, and that their lives – however undeserving – would continue to be something like this and better once they inherited the Mackenzie Millions.

Winter-yellow veld, only here and there dotted by sparse patches of shrubbery and lone thorn trees, spread like an endless moving kaross in the breeze. We cantered across open plains, through gullies and walked down eroded ravines from where soil had been washed, carving an otherworldly architecture into which echoed only the gentle puff of hooves, our horses' snorting and solitary birds. Into the quiet, Lukas spoke of how he had come to know every inch of the farm since childhood: this is where vultures tore a lamb to shreds while the ewe tried to fight them off; those are the jackal burrows; that dolomite ridge in the distance is the favourite camping site for him and his Voortrekker team; there – where the aloes dangle down over the krans – his father shot a leopard two years ago, maybe the last one in the region – when we get home look at the skin on the floor in the foyer – pity to have had to kill it but it was taking a sheep every other day; that's where the makwedini pass through after being circumcised; this is where an early Xhosa kraal stood, you can still see the foundations and all the doors facing east to protect them from evil spirits; from here to that dust road – can you see it about four kilometres away – the veld burnt last year, that's why it's greener than the camps we've just come through; this gully becomes a raging river whenever the spruit floods, every seven years, like clockwork. Lukas could not understand my and Dominic's dream of leaving South Africa and travelling all over the world; he loved this landscape like his own life.

'Everything I want is here,' he said, and told how his parents had once taken a European vacation only to cut short their trip as they had so missed the farm.

It's easy to love something you own, I thought. And yet I saw at once the error of my thinking: I thought to myself that the only place I had loved as he seemed to love the farm was the Mkuzi low veld and Umfolozi. Even though we hadn't owned one inch of the land and the bush, not a single wild animal, and even though we hadn't money to wipe our arses or even dream of going on European vacations, and even though we lived in a reed house without ceilings and doors, I could not imagine that Lukas's passion for their farm, their land, their gullies, their ruins, their horses, their everything, could be any more intense than whatever I had felt for the wild thorn bushes, the ficuses, the Mkuzi River's dry bed, the yellow flakes peeling like skins off the fever trees, the impala, steenbok, nyala, vervets, baboons and the warthogs. January's sweet scent of acacias in bloom. And that was lost.

One need not own something in order to lose it. No, loss was not the preserve of those who owned. And what of Tanzania, I wondered. There we owned. And lost. Could ownership enhance the feeling of loss?

Harlequin had been retired from racing after an injury from which he had since recovered completely. I rode a mottled filly, Tarentaal, who had a mouth harder and a stride more powerful than I'd ever felt in my arms. Giving her free rein on the gallop to keep up with Harlequin brought on a dizzying rush of fear and excitement. Lukas laughed as my admonitions gave away my nervousness. Getting the filly to slow down as we neared a fence was like fighting the devil, both hands struggling to saw the bit, my shoulders pulled forward. My hands were trembling. We walked the horses down a barbed-wire fence, leading towards where Lukas said the road ran between Indwe and Dordrecht. Up inclines and down eroded gullies, chatting, looking at the occasional lizard and at flowering aloes and birds; after a brief reassurance from Lukas, giving Harlequin and Tarentaal free rein to walk where and as they pleased.

Below wherever the horses were taking us lay a little valley over-grown with shrubs and trees. A flock of sheep dotted the opposite hillside, some looking up at our slow approach. With my trembling hands on Tarentaal's saddle, I thought of how I had arrived in the Berg and joined the advanced riders after telling Mr Walshe I'd been riding all my life. That had of course been a lie, for other than my time with Bok on Vonk's back in Mkuzi, I had never been on a horse for longer than between two and thirty seconds at a time. Camelot had been broken in too late for me to ride. The lie about my skill with horses, like my fear and terrified concentration during those first rides, was never exposed. While I did on occasion come a cropper, it happened to me no more than it did to any of the others.

Lukas suddenly raised his hand, bringing a finger to his lips.

'Look,' he whispered, pulling a conspiratorial face, 'the makwedini.'

Through the trees we could see two teenaged boys on a small ridge clasping an ewe. From behind, a third standing with bare buttocks on a rock below, was thrusting at the sheep's behind, clearly engaging in an act of copulation. We quietly dismounted, tied the horses, and snuck up on the three whose laughter was the afternoon's only sound. The two holding the ewe looked up. Huge grins spread over their faces and they pointed at us, making the one who was copulating turn his neck to see.

Lukas greeted them in Xhosa and they spoke back, I able to recognise only his name amongst the foreign and beautiful clicks, clocks and tstsssts. They let go the sheep's head – I could now see that a thin orange rope tied her neck to a tangle of forest bramble – and the copulator rose and hoisted the tatty trousers around his waist. What was going through Lukas's mind? How could he be so informal with boys just caught in this act? They chatted and laughed with Lukas, walking up to us and nodding at me, acknowledging my presence without saying a word I could understand. All three were taller than us, possibly a year or two older, I thought. I found it difficult keeping my eyes off the copulator's unbuttoned fly, knowing that what was behind the fabric had just been extracted from an ewe. The discussion trailed off and after lifting their open hands towards us, they left, laughing and shoving each other as they disappeared amongst the trees.

'They didn't untie the sheep,' I said. I went up to where the ewe stood quietly tugging at sprouts of green amongst the yellow grass.

As I fiddled with the rope, Lukas asked: 'Want to give it a try?'

I looked down at him. Snorted in disbelief. Letting go of the orange rope I said no ways, I wasn't sticking my thing in where a black dick had just been digging around.

Would I tell, if he did? Of course not, but I couldn't believe he really would.

He told me to hold the sheep and then proceeded to drop his jeans and underpants. At the sight of his penis dangling out from beneath his black T-shirt I shook my head, smiling. 'You won't do it, Lukas. I bet you won't do it!'

'Watch me, watch me. Want to take a bet?'

'A hundred Hills when we get back to school,' I said, still dis-believing his intention.

We giggled and I rolled my eyes while he massaged his penis. 'Two hundred Hills,' he countered, 'and if I don't do it, two cans of Condensed Milk for you.'

'Fine!' I said. 'Lukas, your dick's going to fall off from VD!'

'I've done this fifty times and never got VD. Very delicious!' he said, putting on a black accent.

'Bullshit! Have you really done it before?'

'I'm telling you, more times than I can remember.'

Losing two hundred Hills, I thought to myself, is worth every moment for what was happening before my eyes. Who knows, maybe I'll do it too. His penis was now erect, and I again shook my head and smiled as the blue-grey glans nodded from between his fingers. 'Jou piel lyk soos 'n bloukop-koggelmander.'

'Die koggelmander soek 'n bietjie skaap-poes,' he sniggered and we cracked up. My fingers slid into the cool layers of the ewe's fleece. Now on the rock, Lukas manoeuvred his penis into an opening I could only picture from where I sat on my haunches above him. The ewe's body didn't move, only her long bottom lip, side to side as she continued to chew.

'Jissis, this is nice,' he said, moving while his hands rested on his hips. I too was now going stiff, conjuring the feeling of my penis slip-ping into the slimy hollow of the ewe's vagina.

'What's it feel like?' I asked.

'Come on, Karl, have a try. It's just like fucking a girl.'

I rose, letting go of the ewe whom in any event seemed unper-turbed by what was going on. I pulled down my jeans and Lukas made way for me.

'Already ready, you shit!' he said, a knowing smile as his eyes took in my erection. 'Parmantig, nè. Talk of a blue-headed lizard! Purple more like it.' And he suddenly sang out: 'The purple-headed mountain, the river running by . . .'

Moving aside the tail I stepped onto the rock. I had to lift myself onto my toes to reach and slid my penis into the pleasure of tight, warm, moistness. I at once began moving my hips, in and out, staying still for a moment, then again moving. This, as far as it depended on me, could go on eternally. Barely had I started, when Lukas said he wanted another go. 'Wait,' I said. 'Go and catch your own sheep.' His laughter broke the afternoon quiet and he told me to stop being greedy and move over. Reluctantly I withdrew and allowed him back. My penis had now taken on a will of its own, bobbing its head, shiny with the ewe's juices, seemingly begging to be held and stroked by my hand. Holding onto the ewe with one hand, I could not let go of the demanding source of pleasure between my thighs. It was emitting sensations, sensitivities and pleasures I had never suspected it of hiding.

Amidst grunting and shuddering before he finally pulled out, Lukas said: 'I wish I could squirt.' He pulled up his pants and fastened his belt. It was the first time I heard the word, though in the moment said nothing of it. Again I took a turn, going for it till it felt my head was coming free from my shoulders and I thought I was about to pee like in the old days with Stephanie. I pulled out. Inside my jeans the erection still strained against the nylon underpants, now alive with need. We untied the ewe. Lukas stroked her head and kissed her on the forehead, patted her on the rump and she trotted off through the trees, bleating towards the flock.

Back on the horses he asked whether I had come. I asked what he meant.

He explained that *coming* was when you squirted the fluid *that makes the girl pregnant*. Any time within the next few months or year, we would be able to come after *tossing off* for a few minutes. His brothers had started coming around the age of thirteen. They told him that coming was akin to an out-of-body experience, like losing your mind and going to heaven.

'If you lather your hand with soap, in the shower or in the bath, and just keep doing it, you'll feel, at a certain point, something wants to happen and you have to stop. It's at that point that you're supposed to start coming.'

'Can you see the sperms?'

'No, but there are millions in the squirt. My brothers showed me what it looks like under a microscope.'

'I've seen them in books, but I thought one could see them swimming in the squirt like tadpoles,' I said.

'No ways, they can't be seen with the naked eye. Each time you squirt you shoot out billions of sperms. So you could populate an entire country with one squirt.'

Until Lukas imparted this information, I had been certain that pregnancy resulted simply from inserting a penis into a vagina. To my mind, ever since the days in the bush, a man or a male animal reached a certain age at which the penis secreted an emission that resulted in pregnancy. And that the pleasure of sex lay simply in the gripping warmth of penetration. Now I was hearing about an additional level of ecstasy: coming, squirting, shooting, pumping. The climax. That was needed for pregnancy. 'What if the ewe got pregnant?' I joked.

'Well, we didn't squirt. And it's impossible, anyway. Animal seed isn't compatible with human semen. Although, you know, my dad says there have been tests with gorillas in laboratories that show that kaffir semen is compatible with gorillas'.'

'That's complete rubbish,' I said.

'Ask my father. I'm telling you, they've done tests in America.'

'How can theirs be different from ours? What about coloureds? White and black semen is the same because we're all *Homo sapiens*.'

'More *sapiens* than *Homo*,' he laughed. 'Anyway, why do you think coloureds look like gorillas?'

'They do not.'

'No Hotnot woman ever became Miss South Africa, has she?' he asked.

'They and the blacks have their own competition. Miss Africa South.'

'Better that way,' he said. 'Keep all the gorillas in their own zoo . . .'

'Lukas, you're a pig. They're people just like us.'

'Maybe like you, not like me,' he sang.

'Have you ever seen Somali or Maasai women? My father says there are no more beautiful women in the world than those in north-east Africa.'

'Sounds to me as though your dad's a kaffir-boetie.'

'He's not.'

'Is he a Prog?'

'No, he's a Nat. But he and my mom don't agree that blacks should be treated badly. My father once took Gatsha Buthelezi on safari.'

'My dad hates the Nats more than the Progs. He's HNP. The Nats took one of our farms to give to the Transkei,' he said. 'And my mother too. It's easy for you people in the cities, you don't have to work with the numbskulls every day.'

'When I grow up I'm going to vote PFP, like Dom's parents,' I said.

'What? They want to give everything to the kaffirs.'

'Not true. They want a federation, with a qualified vote for blacks. It is not right what we're doing to black people in this country,' I said. 'Letting them live in locations and everything.'

'They don't have to live in locations,' Lukas countered. 'Why do you think the government gave them the Transkei? It's their own choice to come and work in South Africa. Fucking parasites.'

Ahead of us brambles and a row of prickly-pear cacti broke the monotony of yellow grass, the pear's bright purple ovals clinging like Easter eggs to the sides of the thorny leaves. I asked that we stop to pick some of the fruit as they were my favourite. Lukas said we were late and had to get back, that he'd send one of the housemaids to pick and clean some for after the concert. To me saying I had thought forest bramble grew only in the Drakensberg, he responded that it was all over the farm, a pest, really, ripping at the sheep's wool. The Xhosas, he said, call it umQunube. On the Q his tongue clicked loudly against his pallet. *Rubus pinnatus*, I said, from the family Rosaceae. I said the word umQunube aloud. Lukas laughed, showing me where and how to place my tongue, upturned into the hollow of my pallet, rather than at the front, close to my teeth. I practised, corrected by him, saying the word aloud, until he told me I had it right.

We galloped home, reaching the house just as the others were rising from the afternoon sleep. Astonishment, anger, envy on all the faces at our daring. Almeida, quiet and with sleep-filled eyes, shook his head. Dominic smiled: only he knew that I never slept; not once during the hundreds of hours of compulsory afternoon naps when I instead lay reading.

In the shower, regretting the loss of Tarentaal's smell from my hands, I brought the bar of Palmolive soap to rich lather, then, penis in hand, fantasized about moving it in and out of the compliant ewe.

Blue velvet curtains, the orange blue and white flag, proteas in beastly symmetrical arrangements. The new Indwe school hall was filled with farmers, wives and children from the surrounding district, all smartly dressed. It was rare for the small town to receive a visit from a group as renowned as we were, and the choir was given VIP treatment. Halfway into the first half I yawned on stage and Mr Roelofse glared at me. I wondered whether I'd be caned during intermission or after the concert.

During intermission Dominic and I left backstage to sell record albums. Neither Marabou nor Roelofse said anything about the yawn. In the foyer Lukas introduced us to his girlfriend Maryke. I could not believe she was the same girl who looked so attractive on the photograph in his Bible. This Maryke had hair like straw and terrible acne crusting along her jaw and temples.

*

Halfway to Port Elizabeth next morning, the bus pulled off onto the roadside. From beside Marabou, Mr Roelofse rose and peered over the seats towards the back of the bus. He said that there were two amongst us who had not slept the previous afternoon. *The Two* had not brought their side for the choir. One of *The Two* had yawned throughout the Indwe concert and ruined the school's reputation. Were *The Two* going to speak up or was the whole choir going to be caned?

Sitting one forward from the very back across the aisle from each other, Lukas and I stood up.

'De Man, again, leading Van Rensburg astray.' I held Roelofse's gaze. 'Why are you here in the first place, De Man? Your voice is useless, you should rather go home and recite "The Moth and the Flame". And you, Van Rensburg, just because you were on the family farm, doesn't mean you're free from your obligations. Rammetjie-uitnek.'

He told everyone to disembark and line up on the tarmac. Baking-oven! Jesus, I couldn't believe he was going to let us crawl through there.

Thirty-eight boys disembarked and fell into line on the tarmac behind each other, facing the two of us. Ahead of us, legs apart, torsos inclined slightly forward, was a tunnel that didn't worry me. The tarmac did. There was no way we were going to crawl hands and knees. Baboon walk, instead. We went through, hands and feet, occasionally lifting one of the shorter boys, while they beat us on the buttocks and back. It was not the burning bum that angered me, nor the occasional flat fist on my back, it was the damage to my palms from the tar road. I seethed. Angry at myself and desperate to know who had gone and told. The bus was already winding its way along the road again when I realised that all the while I had been saying a word over and over to myself: umQunube, umQunube, umQunube. Like a verbal amulet.

In PE Marabou announced that Dominic and I would not be staying together. Instead, Lukas and I were placed out with Mr

Roelofse. In our hosts' home – the Morrises, I think – Roelofse stayed in the room right beside Lukas and me. We were already lying down for the two-hour sleep, whispering guesses about who had chirped, when Roelofse came in and said he'd come in every few minutes to do spot checks and ensure we slept the full, traditional two hours.

I had not slept once the previous year. Try as I initially had, sleeping during the day eluded me. At night I was able to muster no more than six or seven hours at most. So, during afternoon sleeps, I had taken to reading rather than tossing around. My buddies slept through the countless afternoons of host family bedrooms in towns and cities as we criss-crossed the country. And I remained alert through the adventures of Heinz Konzalik, Louis Lamour and Robert Louis Stevenson. Drifted into thoughts of life alone or with one or two friends on an American ranch or on a South Sea island. I introduced Lukas and Bennie to Louis Lamour, whose name they later kept dropping into conversations. I would eventually try and convince them to read 'more complex' works. 'More complex' was the concept I would eventually use to undetectably turn my ascent of 'higher literature' to a boast. Now I lay contemplating the ease with which Lukas had gone through the bakoond, how he had come out smiling; while I had felt little pain, but could choke on the force of humiliation. Resenting Lukas and whomever had split, exhausted from the baking-oven, loathing Roelofse for referring to my recitation, I did eventually fall asleep – the one and only time in the years at the school I was able to in the afternoon.

After the concert, Lukas bought Mr Roelofse a carton of Benson and Hedges Filter. It seemed the man's attitude towards both of us softened considerably. Later, I would tell Bok and Bokkie that boys bought cigarettes for the conductors – that Mervy's mum had given Mr Roelofse a small krugerrand to be mounted as a signet ring; Bruin's parents were donating tennis trophies to the school – and Bok said that was arse-licking, that he would be livid if he ever heard that

I had done something like that. Despite what my father said, I knew that if I had the money I would buy carton after carton of cigarettes for Mr Roelofse or any of my teachers. I'd shower them with kruger-rands. If that would make them like me.

6

And I asked Mumdeman to let Phinias wait until the dandelions were in seed.

Once the lawn was covered by miniature silver ballerinas on a stage, I would pray for wind. When in the afternoon the blowing swept up from the estuary, lifting the pirouetting and swirling into a mist of movement, I'd dance with the seeds while Phinias began mowing and the smell of Kikuyu came in the sap that turned my toes and footsoles green. The fine parachutes drifted and sped over the garden, and I moved among them while Phinias spun up and down the lawn, the mower revving, revving, sputtering when it hit a moist patch. Then Phinias had his foot on the machine, and pulled and tugged, just like Bokkie at home when she mowed. The smell of mowed lawn hung in the air – and dog shit if he went over where Skip had done his business – and the fairies and snowflakes were caught in spiderwebs or settled in the wet bright cut green grass against the bark of the kaffir tree or the huge tree wisteria, or twirling, up-up-up and away in gusts of wind.

7

A pear-shaped stone with hollows for a grip and a rounded, worn point that looked as though once it may have been sharpened. Lukas, who uncovered it deep along the overgrown ledge, said I could keep it. Delighted at the find and my ownership, I didn't mind that we

again had no time to do a proper search for the hidden cave. In the
library I paged to find a sketch and a description of what it might
once have been used for. Archaeologists placed the Bushmen in the
category of the Later Stone Age, which lasted from 16,000 years ago
till the present. Books maintained that the little wrinkly people once
roamed the entire stretch of land now called the Republic of South
Africa. As I'd learnt in Standard One Geography, the Bushmen were
hunter-gatherers and dancing, acting, making musical instruments,
singing and dressing-up and storytelling occupied much of their
time. As people of the Stone Age they made all manner of implements from rock. Indeed, many such implements had been collected
from the Drakensberg and placed in museums around the world.
Much of what I read recalled my Geography lessons from when I first
got to Kuswag: ostrich eggs used as water bottles; mysteriously
poisoned tips on arrows; arrows carried in quivers; no domestic animals; dances around camp fires. But, now, in these few texts, there
were descriptions of rock art. One book mentioned an artist named
Walter Battis, who said of Bushmen art that no artists had said more
with paint by saying less. I pondered the truth of the words, undertook to ask Ma'am, found myself in agreement with Battis: how
extremely simple the little figures against the rock ledges are, yet we
can see that they are moving their hands, flexing arms and legs. Even
while the paintings have very few details, we can imagine almost
exactly what's going on in every scene. I wished the Bushmen of the
Drakensberg and Umfolozi were not extinct. Umfolozi? I don't
remember seeing Bushmen paintings there; do I? I imagined riding up
to the caves and finding some of them sitting around a camp fire,
others painting against the back of the cave walls.

In vain I searched for a sketch of the implement Lukas had found.
Most pictures in the books were photographs or reproductions of
paintings. The ox-wagons in some rock paintings, so the books held,
indicated that the Bushmen lived just over a hundred years earlier,
when the Voortrekkers arrived in this vicinity from the Cape Colony.

But, I wondered, who knows the age of my stone implement with its patterned indentations? How long since the hidden ledge had been used, before being abandoned and allowed to be overgrown? Or was it always like that, had it always been a secret hiding place, like a fortress against the marauding Zulus and the Boers with their guns? Could this rudimentary chopper, or ax, or digger, or weapon be as much as 16,000 years old? I must take it to Uncle Klaas, I thought, tonight, to show him and ask his opinion. Leaving the library I collected sheets of paper from the art cupboard, a pencil and a sharpener from our classroom and went to the music room where Dominic was practising. He formed his lips into a kiss when I entered, but continued over the keyboard. At a desk behind him, I made myself comfortable and placed the implement in a sheath of sun spilling across the flat surface. First I drew the shadows with the pencil point longways against the paper, then the outlines, the hollows and the rounded end. Once the drawing was completed, I signed it De Man in the bottom right, and on the second sheet started again. The sonata stopped and Dominic turned, came over and placed his hand on my shoulder as he watched what I was doing.

'Where did you find it?'

'Above Bushmen Paintings, along that hidden ledge.'

'Did you find the other cave?'

'No. But we will. That one's for you,' I said, lifting the pencil and handing him the first sketch. He smiled and said he'd thank me later, rolling his eyes suggestively, and returned to his seat. The piano started again and I dropped my head, adding a longer shadow beneath the object's sharp point. The second sketch signed, I left, waving at Dominic, and went to place it on Ma'am's desk.

The stone tool was inside my dressing-gown pocket when I went on one of my surprise visits to his room. I heard the muted chords of Scarlatti. The door opened and he was in front of me. A frown quarried into his forehead beneath the wet slicked-back hair. Tonight there was no playful smile at seeing me. Instead his light grip drew me into the room without the usual roughing of my hair. Unable to ignore the change in our routine, the cool reception, I let the implement remain in the warmth of my pocket, my hand folded around its smooth, furrowed surface.

Jacques forced a half-smile and a nod, at the same time pulling me down to sit beside him on the bed. He stared into my face, as if searching for something there. 'I'm worried,' he said softly, then got up from the bed and briefly paced the room.

'What's wrong?' I asked in a whisper.

He turned to look at me intently. Now he smiled, but again, it was the concern that shone through.

'Have you told anyone?'

'Told anyone what?' I asked.

'About this?' motioning with both palms upwards in a gesture that said: of us, of you and me, of this coming to my room.

'No, I swear. I promise,' shaking my head.

He returned to the bed and sat down beside me, still staring. 'Don't be scared, Karl. You know you don't have to be afraid of me. Have you told anyone – Dominic, or any of your other friends?'

'No, I promise you. I haven't ever even thought of telling a soul.'

'Does anyone suspect, do you think?'

I shook my head.

'Has anyone seen you leaving the dorm?'

'No, Jacques, I swear. No one can possibly know. What's wrong?'

He said he was worried, couldn't quite tell why, but for a time we would have to be watchful. It's merely a feeling I have, he said.

My mind raced, thoughts somersaulted as I searched for a slip, a lapse in vigilance, a word spilt. 'No one knows,' I tried to reassure myself as much as him.

'How can *you* be so sure?' he asks.

"Cause unless we've told anyone, no one can know. And I haven't; you must believe me.'

'I do. Over lunch Uncle Charlie said something to Sandra — Ma'am — about boys moving around at night.'

'But they do, some of them. That's not me he's talking about.'

'Who then?'

'Probably Knowles going to Stein, or anyone else. I'm sure Knowles and Stein have something going on.'

'Knowles and Stein? What a couple!' He suppressed a laugh.

'You won't say anything, Jacques, will you?'

'How could I?' And without further explanation he seemed re-assured. He pulled me closer and kissed my lips, my eyebrows, eyelids. I shivered and clung to him when his tongue ran into my ear and he reached over me, fumbling, to turn off the bedside lamp.

Later, he reiterated that my sneaking to his quarters had become too dangerous: 'Let's just give it a few weeks. Come only when I tell you.'

'Well, should I leave right away?' I asked, sarcasm in my tone. He pulled me closer and said no, he wished I could stay till dawn. Satisfied, I snuggled into his neck. Niggling doubt, questions about whether I had done something wrong, I pushed to the back of my mind. Could Lukas have remembered the key? No, this was other boys sneaking around. Nothing to do with me and my key.

I told him about the afternoon's drawings, that the Stone Age implement was in my dressing-gown pocket to show him. I moved to retrieve the object, but he held me back, saying he'd look at it later. For now he wanted only to feel me beside him.

I lay in his arms as we listened to Scarlatti, played on piano instead of harpsichord.

'It is beautiful,' he said.

'Mmm,' against his chest.

He told me of Domenico, son of Alessandro, how Domenico and Handel were contemporaries and friends. 'The music can mean anything,' he says softly. 'Or if there is meaning, it is hidden by the way the composition communicates whatever it wishes to our senses.'

I try to understand what he says, mulling over his words. Can the music truly mean anything? What a peculiar thing to say and what a strange question to be asking myself. 'What are you thinking?' he asks, turning over onto his stomach, his eyes glistening at me from the pillow in the dark. I am thinking of Dominic's hands, how they cross at the wrists, running over each other like baboon spiders. When he plays Domenico Scarlatti. 'About what you just said,' I whisper, 'whether it's true.'

'Well, what goes through your mind when you hear Scarlatti?'

The truth is that I've never thought about it. About Scarlatti or anyone else. In choir, when he gives us an image to hold on to, like with parts of the Mass, of hundreds of people weeping, or in folk songs or madrigals of girls dancing and laughing around a maypole, that is the picture I take and try to imagine. Fabrications of my own I do not have. And even my accepting of images to go with music, that too is new, for last year and the year before the conductors could ply us with ideas and images that either made no sense to me or mattered not at all: in one ear and out the other as I frequently willed parts of concerts and entire rehearsals over. It has been only now, in the months that I've been out of first soprano and in second, in a voice where I am able to sing every note, hear mine meld with those around me and give body to the sound of the whole, that images are starting to make sense, that I have begun to look forward to almost every practice session and each concert. That it is not only the idea of Europe that appeals to me, but performing to the educated audiences who carry in their ears the musical traditions of a thousand years.

'Is the art of music different from other art? For example, the drawing you made this afternoon?'

For a moment I think. 'Drawings, they stick around. But music, once it has been played, disappears, it's over.' I speak into his face and wonder whether I have smelly breath; can't recall having brushed after showers.

'Yes, music is an instant. It does things that words or paint or photographs can never do. Play it again and it is entirely new. Ma'am agrees with me, I think,' he says. I contemplate his idea that when you hear a piece a second time it's entirely new. I want to say that I disagree, but I'm not sure whether I do, afraid that my thoughts might not be relevant to the issue being discussed. Maybe I'm not understanding anything he's saying.

'Come on,' he prods, 'what do you say?'

'If I hear the Scarlatti again,' I say, terrified of sounding stupid, 'I will be unable to hear it without thinking of this moment I first heard it, here with you.'

'Ha!' he laughs, turning his face from me. 'You'll soon forget me and listen to Scarlatti uncontaminated.'

'I won't ever forget you,' I say, running my hands around his shoulders, lifting myself and lying on top of him. 'So,' I say, 'even if it disappears, when it comes back, it's not new.'

'That's why we protect ourselves from too much experience. Ignorance is bliss. The more we have under our belts, the less likely we are to see the world as black and white.' His words come and I try not to let him know what I'm thinking. I remain silent. This is a difficult series of concepts. 'But what about the first time you hear a piece?' he asks. 'Then you have no associations to drag the music away from the here and now? Then it is pure, and beautiful in and of itself, surely? Isn't that the function of all art: the attainment of beauty for its own sake?' Again I remain silent, wondering about the question.

'No, it's not, Jacques. Because when I hear a piece for the first time, like when we started the *Missa Solemnis* with you, I already associate it with other pieces, just a few bars here and there. Or it puts me in a mood because I can't sing without knowing you, there in front of us are,' I pause, 'my lover.' The word, as well chosen as it was, sounds awful and out of place. He tugs me to him, kisses my head. 'But that has nothing to do with the music,' he says, 'and everything to do with you, Karl.'

'I can't help it,' I say, a sadness, an embarrassment at having said something wrong, fingering my mind.

'So, you're saying nothing is inherently beautiful, everything is subjective. Like beauty is in the eye of the beholder.'

'I suppose . . .'

'So, if you don't see beauty, it means there is no real beauty or no really great art.'

For a moment I struggle to follow the logic of his argument, unsure that is what I meant. His conclusion sounds wrong. For surely, surely, there are things that everyone on earth would agree are beautiful? Like the rock paintings, even if the books this afternoon said they were functional as much as aesthetic – words I was yet to look up. Or the flight of louries, in the instant they open their wings, when from below in surprise you see the hidden red – no, crimson – fold out from where you thought there was only green and purple. Yes, surely, the flight of louries is something that will move every human with its beauty. Forget about the Big Five! Who decided what was the Big Five anyway? Change it! Add new names. The Big Six! The Big Six is what it should be! But still, it's really like Basil Hallward says: *Every portrait painted with feeling is a portrait of the artist, not of the thing he paints!* Overseas the imbeciles wont even know what a lourie is! Yes, I've just copied it into my diary! I want to tell him that when I first saw him, even long after I first came to his bed, I never thought him beautiful. Handsome. Yes, I had found his face so plain, had feared him and perhaps, perhaps even hated him after that night in Mathison's office last year. Is that possible! That I once saw him and the beginnings of us together in a light so different from what he and we have become? Since March, the way it was then has been almost forgotten. On that diving board, when, from the way I understood his eyes on Lukas, I had suspected he was interested in precisely the things he had seen punished last year, I had thought of adventure and maybe a little revenge. And then, within months I fell in love with him, have come to need being with him, have come to find him ravishing, cannot now get enough of him: how rapidly he grew on me, spreading under and over my skin like lichen or moss — *parmelia reticulata* — in a perfect habitat. And then, that he is different from Almeida and Almeida's sister, whom I saw and instantaneously found beautiful, with a look that tells you: I have never looked like that, I don't now, and I never will. A physical beauty that sears itself into memory. Like Dorian Gray. Steven and Marguerite Almeida. For a moment I want to ask him whether he remembers Steven; wonder, if Steven were here, whether he would have still chosen me. And I remember that it is I who have chosen him. And then Alette and Dominic, who also only with time became beautiful to me, only as I got to know them. That Alette's short legs don't matter, that her laughter does, and her white teeth. Or the prints in Ma'am's books of Georgia O'Keeffe's paintings! How at first I hadn't a clue what made them special, had thought Pierneef's paintings of the high veld so much better. But, the longer I looked at *White Birch* and *Cottonwood Trees in Spring* — trees I have never seen, that are not indigenous to this country — how her paintings had since altered the way I see most trees and vegetation. Afternoons, when I look at the poplars down on Sterkspruit's bank, I see cottonwoods in spring. And there are photographs a man took of O'Keeffe, of her hands, that reminded me from the first time I saw them, of Bokkie. Something in the woman's face, the dark hair, in her strong fingers, the thick unplucked eyebrows, the way she looks into the camera like she's studying us and it's not us looking at her, that now makes it impossible to look at my mother and not wonder whether if she were not so shy and hurt she might have been a painter. How I resent her for not. If Beethoven could write this whole mass while not hearing a single note, what could Bokkie have done if only she tried? Instead of cleaning the house and Hoovering the floors till they shone like mirrors and feeding us all the time or slaving in the stupid church garden. And the flowers, how I can never think of a vagina again without thinking of an iris or a red canna, or how I can barely look at some flowers — lilies and cannas — without thinking of vaginas. And, her *Bleeding Heart*, like me now on top of him, my penis pushed back, down over his buttocks. That is what makes her a great artist, I think: that the world I see will never be the same after I have looked at it through her eyes. Yes, isn't that what Ma'am means? That the artist has lent us her eyes, to look and see something as she saw it in a way that none of us has seen it, but all of us now can, even if we still see it differently. Oh, how I want to be a Great Artist! To be mentioned in the same breath as Georgia O'Keeffe or Oscar Wilde. Yes, the reviews will say, there is a hint of O'Keeffe in De Man's early work, but look, by the age of twenty-eight, maybe twenty-nine, he had certainly established his own, unique style, which changed the face of creative work the world over.

The rise and fall of his back beneath me tells me he's fallen asleep. Stroking the shoulders I whisper that I must go. In a sleepy voice he tells me to wait a few weeks before I return. He will let me know when he again thinks it safe. While I search for my pyjamas in the dark, slip my arms into the dressing gown, I wonder whether he has begun to distrust me. Is my assurance through the invocation of Knowles and Stein not reason enough for him to let go of his fear? 'I love you,' he whispers, standing naked in the dark behind me at the door, his fingers brushing my neck as I, without answering, leave.

The moment his door shut, I turned and walked down the passage to the first music room. The smell of fresh paint and new linoleum filled the dark. Avoiding the music stands and instrument cases, I felt my way to the window. Beneath my fingers the panel swung open and I edged my body through the opening. From the outside I shut it, taking care to leave a gap into which a finger could later be inserted for re-entry. I removed my slippers, pushing them beneath the tufts of grass overhanging the water duct. Barefoot, I turned right and slunk down the white walls of classrooms, the conservatory, and headed towards the river. Once amongst the poplars I began collecting branches and dry twigs.

At the fort, I whispered Uncle Klaas's name and dropped the bundle. I heard both of them stir almost at once: grunts, fabric against fabric, limbs creaking, the blanket catching against a piece of wire in the thatched walls. Uncle Klaas mumbled something — either to me or to the man beside him. The black man, whom I had started thinking of as the Silent One, said nothing, barely making a sound. It was too dark on the inside for me to make out the way they slept. In the afternoons, when we got there, no trace remained of them other than the smell of smoke and kaffir Bennie or Mervy commented on. I pretended to ignore the remarks. Or, when the smell was overwhelming, feigned perplexity.

'You again, Karl.' I now made out the words, 'What you whispering for?' muttered over the sound of his fumbling for the matches. He groaned, sat up and I heard him crawl towards the opening where I'd gone down on my haunches, waiting. From the structure's mouth, their smell united with the creaking of limbs as Uncle Klaas sat down, the outline of his shape folding in its legs. The Silent One moved invisibly behind him. Soon I could make out both their shapes against the dark inside of the fort. Before Uncle Klaas struck the match, there was pawing at the thatch, a swish, and I knew a clump of the grass my friends and I had painstakingly tied had been extracted from the walls. Piece by piece this place would be dismantled, I knew, and so in the afternoons I would pick more grass, try to fill in the gaps left by their nightly forage. Box and a match in one hand, Uncle Klaas struck the sulphur, holding the tiny flame to the thatch, which immediately danced into flames. He tugged more grass from the wall and I held out some of the smaller twigs. These he held over the flames and then placed the fire right in front of me. Around us the night had gone quiet, only twigs and thatch crackling beneath the filthy white fingers with the long fingernails bordered in grime. The face, illuminated by fire: beard tangled and the one cheek engraved with sand. The Silent One, wrapped in the school's grey blanket, his brown face dark and still knotted with sleep in the flickering shadows.

Uncle Klaas looked up from the flames, signalled for more wood, and his eyes twinkled like black beads in the yellow light. Devilish eyes. Handing him twigs, I sat outside, my back to the river, facing the two men inside our fort.

'Up again,' he said and I grinned. The first time, when I'd brought my blanket, I angrily swore to myself it would be the last. That if they didn't leave soon, I'd report them. But the night after my stitches were removed I had returned, had woken them and Uncle Klaas had at once sent me to collect twigs — no fuss, no shock or surprise, as if they had been expecting me. Now each time was the same. The Silent One's face a blank slate, and Uncle Klaas always a little amused. Each time I was there, I tried to get him to speak about himself, to tell me about the Liebenberg family, about why he stopped being a professor and became a tramp. Each time I asked about my late great-grand-father and great-grandmother, he said they had existed in his previous life and that he had nothing to say about them or the university. I said I had seen photographs of him in my great-grandparents' passage when I was small. That's a time in his life that was over, he said, he didn't think of it for it amounted to nothing more than unnecessary baggage. Then I let it go, afraid somehow that my questions would push him to madness. One in each generation. And I felt pity for him, for even as he refused to speak about the Liebenberg family, he was so clearly part of them: a younger — filthy — replica of my Oupa.

'I came to show you this,' I said, lifting the implement from my pocket.

Careful to evade his touch, I handed him the stone. A smile, a snig-ger, plays at the corner of his mouth. His eyes still on the tool in his hand, he tells me to collect more wood. When I return with three thick branches, the Silent One has the implement in his palm. He turns it around, seems to become disinterested, says something in a language I neither know nor understand and hands it back to Uncle Klaas. From below the blanket the Silent One pulls a brown paper bag and tears off a slither to make their zol. First he flattens the paper by rubbing it against the tattered jersey that covers his chest. Once satisfied, the long black fingers dig around in the orange packet of Boxer, spread it on the brown paper. From another crumpled packet his forefinger scoops a tangle of dull green twigs, which he mixes in with the tobacco. This, I knew the first time already, had to be dagga, though I didn't ask, offered no comment, telling myself that if I were caught down here with tramps and dagga smokers, I would at least be able to say I held no knowledge of what they were smoking. That I had come only because of the pity I felt for my uncle. That I was hoping to convert him to Christianity. If the two tramps don't tell me it's dagga, I won't be responsible. How was I meant to know what dagga looked like, smelt like, anyway?

Uncle Klaas hands the matches to the Silent One. Soon he is inhaling, leans forward and passes the smoking brown zol to Uncle Klaas. My great-uncle hands me the Bushmen tool and silently drags at the zol, its head going red, bits of ash fluttering down to his lap. That these two have not burnt down our fort is a wonder. Who, I speculate silently, would get the blame if this place went up in flames? Uncle Klaas holds the zol out towards me; as usual I shake my head. He has continued to offer it to me, even though I have told him more than once that the shortest route to expulsion from the school is through smoking.

'Don't you think you'll be expelled as it is — for being out here at night?'

'I'll say I felt sorry for you,' I answered. 'At worst I'll get caned.' And suddenly a thought had struck me and I had wanted to say that I could do as I pleased. Because Jacques would protect me. But of course, I didn't. In the months I'd been going to him, and especially after the Cape tour, I had occasionally wondered what benefits might befall me from being the choir master's boy. But nothing had happened to set me apart from my peers. Yet, I had become aware that even if I were not getting tangibles, there was the privilege of the weekend at Paternoster, the privilege of going to Maritzburg with him, oh, and one silly ice-cream cone and something else to lick on! And the privilege of sharing our secret. The privilege lay in the security, I thought. That I can feel safe and happy because of Jacques.

A thrill of horror had run through me as I watched Uncle Klaas and the Silent One smoke dagga the first time. This was crime committed before my eyes. The Silent One getting a glazed look in his eyes, Uncle Klaas becoming more and more animated. How aware I was of the sinful and illegal nature of what they were doing, but to use the words sin or law in Uncle Klaas's presence seemed not only a waste of breath, but a certain way to activate his scorn. In Geestelike Weerbaarheid classes we had been shown scores of movies on the effects of drug use. One scene from these: hippies in America, walking down streets, shouting like hooligans: Make Marijuana Legal! Make Marijuana Legal. Since Kuswag's Sunday school days I had been told that drugs opened the portals of hell. And here, too, often during Friday night visits by Dominee Steytler or Minister Shaer, we were read to from little religious tracts that cautioned against smoking, drugs, sex and rock music. Until Malawi I had collected these, saved them in the back of my Bible, read and reread them: The Sin of Smoking; The Sin of Sex; The Sin of Premarital Sex; The Sin of Drugs; The Sin of Jealousy; The Meaning of Revelation. And Dominic shook his head and rolled his eyes. Now the leaflets remained there, ignored. I read rather Song of Songs, Psalms, Proverbs, which I found poetic and often inspirational. A hundred times I had thought of bringing the tracts down here for Uncle Klaas to read, and each time something told me he would laugh in my face, that the codes we were taught to adhere to would be derided and ridiculed in his terrible world. Uncle Klaas was beyond salvation. And who am I, I asked myself, to speak of sin? As much as I cared for Dominic and Jacques, I knew what we were doing was wrong, that as sure as my name was Karl De Man I was going to burn in hell for doing it, for loving them. Dominic didn't believe in heaven and hell and I'd never touched on it with Jacques. The longer I was with

Jacques and Dominic, the more frequent became the moments I doubted, the less I cared that God would send me to hell for this; and, it's just for now, I told myself over and over, when I leave here, there's Alette, whom I really love. Surely the fact that I believe in God the father, his son Jesus and the Holy Ghost, that I try to obey the Ten Commandments, surely that will make him forgive me if I were to suddenly die in my sleep? The Ten Commandments says nothing about lying with a man as one does with a woman, even though Mathison had read those passages the previous year from somewhere in the Bible. But, those are just a few little passages, and is what we are doing hurting anyone? It was not a commandment. As Dom says about loving your neighbour as yourself: 'If God was real, very few white people in this country would see the inside of heaven.' So, if I burnt in hell, I'd at least be surrounded there by everyone I knew. Barring Dom and the rest of the Websters, but Dom would be there for this other thing anyway and his parents probably because they're atheists.

'What's your interest in this thing?' Uncle Klaas asks, bringing me back to the present.

'I'm interested in the Bushmen,' I answer. 'Do you know that there are hundreds of Bushmen paintings in these mountains? I even read today there are some in Umfolozi, though I never knew that.'

'Are you certain this is a Bushmen piece?'

'Who else's can it be? I'm looking it up in books at the moment.'

'Are you not afraid of the Bushmen spirits?' he says, smiling, his teeth yellow but in a perfect row.

'Christians don't believe in ghosts, Uncle Klaas, and neither do you.'

'Oh, but I do. Spirits, not ghosts. Especially the spirits of the murdered. They are everywhere because they have not been laid to rest.' I wonder whether it is the mad gene or the dagga talking.

'Aag, Oom Klaas, that's an old wives' tale and you know it.'

'Do I? No, Karl'tjie, these mountains of the dragon are alive with spirits. You should beware walking around at night all on your own.'

'I've never been scared of the dark.'

'Know what genocide is?' I shake my head. He starts telling me of how the Zulus under Chaka and later the Boers under Retief exterminated the Bushmen like vermin.

'But, Uncle Klaas, that's because they were slaughtering the Boer oxen.'

'Which were grazing on their hunting grounds.'

'Well, I'm sorry that happened, Uncle Klaas, but it's got nothing to do with me.'

'But you go around carrying a Bushmen implement? You tell me you're interested in their paintings? Or are you interested in the paintings only because their creators are gone, dead. Because they pose no threat to you?'

'I find them beautiful. The simplicity appeals to me.'

'The people or the work?'

'What?'

'What do you find beautiful and simple – the people or their work?'

'The work, of course, Uncle Klaas.'

'Precisely, how much simpler the art is if you don't have to deal with the people who created them.'

'I've started reading about them, so I am dealing with them.'

He laughs and says I'm not half as bright as he expected.

'Well, why don't you leave, then!' I'm suddenly furious. 'Why did you send me the note then, in the first place!'

'You came to me, I only told you I was here and invited you for a meeting. I merely said we needed another blanket. I did not force you here, did I, Karl'tjie?'

'I didn't ask you to tell me you were here. I could get into deep trouble for being here.'

He ignores me.

'Are you a Christian, Uncle Klaas?'

'You speak like a child whenever it suits you, Karl. Listen to yourself.'

'And you like a madman when it suits you. Do you think I don't know that you're mad! How you went to the boarding school in Brei where Bokkie and Uncle Gert were, and how like a madman you stood outside shouting, "Katie and Gert Liebenberg, I'm looking for you."'

He laughs from his stomach, shows no sign that I have wounded him, instead he says: 'Oh, yes! That little school at Brei, so your mother remembers! The school consisted of only one classroom. It was easy to know where they were!'

'Didn't it ever cross your mind that you were an embarrassment to my mother?'

'A madman and an embarrassment. Mmmm . . . so that's what the family says about me. Tell me in which classroom you are and I'll come calling. Make certain history repeats itself . . .' he says, laughing, the folds of his filthy jersey undulating against his chest.

'You're joking, aren't you, Uncle Klaas?'

'Only if you want me to be.'

Suddenly I am terrified that he will show up at the school. Already I hear his voice: 'Karl De Man, ek soek jou!' And the eyes of everyone darting towards the horrendous source of the voice standing on the quad's lawn. Instantly I alter my tone, change the subject.

'Do you like choir music, Uncle Klaas?'

'We can hear you people, right down by the ford in the mornings and afternoons.'

'We're rehearsing Beethoven's *Missa Solemnis*. It's to perform in Europe and for Prime Minister John Vorster in December,' I say. 'The concert will be broadcast live on TV.'

'They still start you early,' he says, gazing into the fire, nodding his head.

'Do you know the *Missa Solemnis*, Uncle Klaas?'

Again he nods and for a moment I see a shadow pass over his gaze.

It is the first time I am aware of feeling any sadness for him, on his behalf. Sadness is different from pity. I don't know how, but it must be. Could it be that he had been a music lover before he went mad and that he is now recalling a time when he was a professor in Potchefstroom? There is so much I want to know about this man. I am fascinated by him as much as I fear him. He yawns and says it's time for them to get back to sleep, else they'll oversleep and I wouldn't want anyone to find my embarrassment of a madman uncle sleeping in my fort, would I?

'I am not embarrassed,' I answer and look quickly at the Silent One, who has already started making himself comfortable. Like an old mangy dog. In my blanket. Even if he doesn't understand a word of Afrikaans, he too must know that I'm lying. As I stand to go, I say that we're doing a Wednesday-night concert in the auditorium. They could stand in the orchard beneath the building. 'You'll be able to hear well from there.'

Uncle Klaas smiles.

'And,' I say, turning to go, 'we even do some black songs that he'll like.'

Behind me I hear Uncle Klaas scratching together sand with which he'll extinguish the fire.

8

Almost ten. At the front door dressed in school uniform with suitcase in one hand and lunchbox in the other. About to open the bottom door to catch up with his sister already at the end of the asbestos driveway. Heard his mother's voice in her and the father's bedroom. She slammed the door of her closet. Father had just returned from a trip. Boy knew why the mother was angry and thought of quickly slipping from the door so they'd think he had already gone. But he wanted to push them, to test their limits, see how far it was to the brink. Then his father called his name and came walking down the passage; caught the boy as he pretended to try and slip from the house. The father walked to within a few paces from the boy and stood shaking his head from side to side. Inside, the boy felt the excitement of fear and the anticipation of humiliation and possible pain. Caught a whiff of Old Spice. The father looked at the boy with loathing, with hatred, his blue eyes icy, ragingly calm. He spoke softly and when the boy looked provocatively down at his shoes he shouted at him to look him in the eye like a man. He asked the boy why he did this. The boy refused to answer. The boy wished the father would die, but only after he had been beaten and shamed. The man said: 'If you ever even think of doing it again, or if I or your mother ever even suspect you of doing it again, I will kill you.' Then he turned around. Pleasure spread across the boy's face as he heard the man walk away down the passage. The boy could not see because through his smile the tears blurred the driveway from which his sister had long disappeared.

9

Head resting on one elbow, Ma'am marked our essays while we completed a History test on the French Revolution. Political causes. Social causes. Religious causes. Intellectual causes.

Political: 1. The government of the old order was ineffectual. 2. The monarchs were corrupt. 3. The nation was excluded from government. 4. The masses had heard about the examples of England and the American Revolutions. 5. There was too much administrative unwieldiness. *Social*: 1. Inequality. 2. The royalty and the Church élites were unreasonably advantaged. 3. Dissatisfaction was rife amongst the Third Class: the farmers, workers and skilled labourers were oppressed and exploited. 4. The rich burgers of the cities, the bourgeoisie, were dissatisfied. (I want to be part of the bourgeoisie.)

5. What the hell is five? Leave it open for the moment. *Religious*: 1. The Church owned 20 per cent of the land while the majority of people had nothing. 2. The Church was not obliged to pay taxes. 3. All posts in the Church were occupied by the royalty. 4. The philosophers were criticising the Church. 5. What the hell, Jesus, where's five! Leave it for now. *Intellectual*: 1. French philosophers like Descartes and Locke argued that reason was grounded in nature. This gave rise to Natural Law. 2. New images of rationalism and enlightenment took hold of people's imaginations. 3. A high premium was placed on the human mind and reason/rationalism. 4. Human beings were placed centrally and the rights of mankind were grounded in reason once reason was purified of superstition and preconception. 5. Faith was to be grounded in reason. There, good. I tried to remember the two I was forgetting. My mind was as blank as the page on which anything could just as well be written.

Last period on a Thursday afternoon. When I get out of here, I thought, Lukas and I are going riding. I hated myself for not having studied for the test; relying on one reading of the relevant chapters. I drifted from anger at a lack of academic memory into daydream; reverie; from somewhere also taking her in as she sat there, reading our stories. Still see her, recall wondering whether she had yet come to mine? A full two weeks of prep I'd spent on it, checking words, phrases, creating metaphors: *His Name Was Henk Willemse*, my story was titled. Henk Willemse was a show-off who refused to accept that an ostrich male protecting his nest was stronger and more cunning and more deliberate than himself. One day when Henk Willemse was again showing off to his farm workers how he could outwit a breeding pair, a huge male with plumage 'that moved like the black thunder and snow clouds of the Swartberg' rushed down on him and with his front toenail cleft Willemse open. The essay was peppered with words like koppie instead of hill, Afrikaans words here and there, and 'the district', 'people said' and 'it was said that', which to my ear epitomised the way Bosman wrote. The essay took its name from the first sentence: 'People of the district still remembered that the heap of stones surrounded by red aloes on the koppie covered the bones of a man named Henk Willemse.' The rest of the essay told how Willemse terrorised the ostriches by removing eggs and often entire nests and how he then finally met his dreadful fate 'at noon on a summer's day when the Karoo was closer than ever to the desert it tried not to be'. The paper's last sentence – in which at least an hour of writing and rewriting had been invested – was to my mind certainly the best I had ever written: 'Years later, witnesses who had not even been there said that as the ostrich's thick grey toenail slid through Henk Willemse's chest and stomach, the contents of his guts spilt over the hot Karoo sand like the contents of an enormous exploding pomegranate.' I knew she was going to be pleased. I badly needed an A for English and another for Art – the only subjects into which my prep hours had been going. Latin would be a B. Somewhere during the term Ma'am's Latin had started to lose me. Prep had become a struggle: I could do nothing but write and paint and draw. The prefect on prep duty, noticing the movement of my arm and hand gliding across white paper, would ask what I was doing and I was always, always doing Art homework. I rushed my way through Maths homework, Natural Science homework, History homework, Geography homework. Latin translation and vocab. Afrikaans and English grammar. My Afrikaans essays were good, but my understanding of grammar and my spelling hopeless – no hope for an A there. Miss Roos came in to teach us Afrikaans. Try as I might to find an original point of access for the essay topics she gave us, I couldn't produce anything of interest to me or her. If Ma'am had taught us Afrikaans, I felt certain, I may even have liked the language. Might even have wanted to write books or poems in Afrikaans. I loved reading and reciting Afrikaans poetry. Loved the sound of a roughly rolled r and a g almost growled from the throat. Nothing in English sounded as earthy or brought out the same colours in words as these letters in Afrikaans. But Miss Roos didn't carry the inspiration to class or to me that Ma'am's mere presence did. I hated the way Miss Roos was always laughing at Dom and the other English boys for getting an Afrikaans word wrong. Or the way she'd interrupt one to point out an 'anglicism' or a 'direct translation' that 'makes a mockery of pure Afrikaans.' No, Miss Roos could never inspire me to be a writer or to love and respect language. Ma'am had the gift of imparting words with the tenderness of poetry. And not only to me. Even Bennie and Lukas, who had always detested English because they spoke and wrote it so poorly, who had almost failed English every year since Standard Four, were now getting respectable C's thanks to Ma'am's extra afternoon classes. They now could even speak it less formally and without all the Afrikaans words stuck in the middle. Their whining about how they hated having to do an extra language had all but ceased.

Oh, why had I not worked harder. The term's report was again sure to be one of shame. At least there'd be a pass for Music Theory, which I was no longer failing. The October holiday was just around the corner. I'm going home, I thought and cringed, no Cape tours to keep me away like in June. I'll blame my report on choir, all the extra hours we're putting in for Europe.

When Mathison knocked, she and we looked up. She pushed back her chair with us as he walked into the classroom and waved us to take our seats.

'May I see you, for a moment, Sandra,' his usually formal voice, gentle and firm all at once.

'Eyes on your own work,' she said, placing her red pen on someone's open essay. 'Niklaas, you're in charge. I'll be back in a moment.'

But it was not Ma'am a few minutes later who stepped back into my thoughts of ostrich toenails and my struggle for two further causes of the French Revolution. Mathison himself quietly entered and sat down behind her desk. His gaze swept over the bowed heads. When his eyes met mine they paused for a moment – accusing, questioning, as if suspicious that I may be cribbing – then moved off and stared silently from the window into the corridor. One brief glance and my wool-gathering had been disturbed. My heart, within moments, was throbbing above my ribs. I looked down onto the page, tried to write but remained stuck. Tried reading over the points on the page. *Someone knows, like a blue revolving light in my head. They'd found out. 5. The heartlessness of the royalty and their . . .* I couldn't complete the deceptive sentence, mind reeled, panic registered in the sudden sweat of fingers around the pen.

'Can we hand in, Sir?' Bruin timidly from the front.

Let them eat cake. Poes. Gatkruiper.

'Bring your papers to me and then go back to your seats. You have another ten minutes.'

. . . refusal to give the people food. No, I couldn't remember anything else . . . *write two more I've already written and hope she either doesn't see that I've repeated them or thinks I didn't know I was repeating. I could always say I'd inadvertently repeated, look up the correct ones in the meantime and spit them out were she to ask or even just frivolously list them in order to show her I knew.* Tried to ignore the consternation, the heaviness in my legs. The bell rang and the last of us handed in. Mathison told us to remain in our desks: *something serious has happened which he has to discuss with us. Monkey-brain. Not in front of the whole class, God, what is it, Jacques, Dominic, Uncle Klaas? Uncle Klaas may be dead in our fort; some workers found them and the police have come from Winterton. Please, please let me be—*

'I'm afraid I received a phone call a while ago with very bad news for Ma'am. And for the whole school.' *His face is ashen, voice sombre, deep, severe. Cannot have anything to do with me. No, not through a phone call.* 'I've just had the terrible task of telling Ma'am that her son Graham has been killed in Angola.' *The classroom is tongue-tied. The suffusing quiet of death's news brought in the afternoon. My paranoia instantly erased. My mind returned to Ma'am:* 'I'll be back in a moment.' *Jesus, Holy Merciful Father. Stunned; no one moved. The headmaster's eyes a flagging metronome over the class.* 'It is a

tragedy for Ma'am and our country too . . . I want you all to be cir-
cumspect with her for the next few weeks.'

'Where is Ma'am?'

'She has gone to her cottage. There will be funeral arrangements
and she'll probably be away for a while.'

Abruptly the room was a cacophony of questions as if a flock of
hadidas had been disturbed from their roost: how had it happened?
Where? Was he the only one? How is Ma'am taking it? Is there anything we can do? SWAPO? Terrorists? Kaffirs! We must have a
collection for a wreath. How old was he, Sir? And Mathison answered
that Ma'am's eighteen-year-old son was killed during training, during
manoeuvres in Angola; killed by his own instructor, that it wasn't an
enemy killing, though of course he wouldn't have had to be in the
army if the enemy wasn't there. He said there was a dire lesson for us
in the death of Ma'am's son: South Africa was under siege. We would
have to be prepared to bring our side, if needs be, to sacrifice our lives
in defence of our civilisation and our entire way of life. 'For most of
you this is the first death of a soldier you knew. I can assure you it
will not be the last.' He got up from the chair and sat on the desk. 'If
South-West Africa goes, there is little hope for our country.
Mozambique is gone. Angola is gone. You boys are only thirteen –
some fourteen – but you have to realise that you are our future. The
protection of this country is in your hands.'

When he said class dismissed, none of us moved. Only he rose,
with both hands squaring off the sheath of test papers he lifted
from the desk. He walked to the door, our tests held comfortably in
both his hands. 'Ma'am is a strong woman,' he said. 'Her first words
to me when I told her, were: at least Graham didn't die in vain. He
died for his country, for us all, yesterday.' Then Mathison was gone.

I stared at Dominic's head in front of me: it was moving from side
to side. We remained still. Some staring at their hands. Others straight
ahead. Tapping a pen on the desk. Bruin and Smith lay down on their
arms.

'Webster . . . I hope you realise,' through the silence Radys Dietz's voice ripped a bayonet, 'that it's because of people like your family that Ma'am's son is dead.'

Dominic turned. The class's heads, eyes, moved as if on a ball to Radys at the back of the class, then to Dom. We were all quiet.

'What?' Dominic asked, his top lip a snarl.

'Because you're spoiling the kaffirs. I know what it's like in your house. Those maids think they're white. And the way you are with Beauty, bringing her presents all the time. You people are creating all kinds of expectations by spoiling the kaffirs. A poor kaffir is one thing, a kaffir with aspirations is quite another.'

'Shut up, Radys,' Lukas said, and he and some others broke the tension by pushing back their chairs and preparing to leave. Radys too rose. Bennie got up. He seemed deliberately to walk out at the side of Radys. Our eyes moved between them and Dominic. Slowly the room ran almost empty as boys drifted from the door. Soon only Bruin, myself and Dominic remained. Bruin, who forever insinuated himself into Dominic's life, stood up and took a seat at the desk in front of Dom.

'I don't know how Radys could say that.'

'Neither do I,' Dominic said and suddenly his shoulders were shaking. I jumped up and pulled a chair closer to him. He lay on his arms.

'Dom, don't take Radys seriously,' I spoke quietly from beside him, wishing I had spoken before Bruin and that Bruin would get up and leave us alone.

'I don't,' Dominic answered through the tears. 'It's Ma'am I'm worried about. She loved Graham so much and now she's lost him.' Again the silence whispered its gloom over the room.

'God, it must be a shock to Ma'am. I wonder whether he suffered, or died instantly,' Bruin thought aloud. He closed his eyes.

'Mathison's right. He's the first person I know that gets killed in a war. Well, I mean I didn't know him, but I did sort of, through Ma'am,' I said, rising to put away my pencil case inside my desk.

'It's awful,' Dominic said. I now sat down at the desk in front of him to his right.

'When my mother's brother died,' I said, 'she said my grandparents would never get over it. A parent never, ever gets over the death of a child. If I were to die, it would kill my parents.'

'Karl,' Dominic said, a note of irritation creeping into his tone, 'let's think of Ma'am and Graham for a moment, rather than ourselves.'

'I'm just saying, Dom—' Lukas had come back to say he was going down to the stables. Was I coming? I shook my head. Instead of leaving, Lukas walked to Dom and put his hand on his shoulder, clasped it briefly and shrugged at us: 'Look, guys, it's terrible, but it's done. All we can do is support Ma'am. And remember, he gave his life for us.' When Lukas had left I suggested to Dominic that we go outside. I wanted to be with him away from the presence of Bruin.

Past the parking lot where there was no sign of Ma'am's Passat. We sat on the rock below which the school's name was burnt into a wooden sign in rigid black letters: *Drakensberg Boys Music School.* Above it, the dragon, our coat of arms. Dominic stared ahead of him at the stables and the servants' quarters. The riders had already left. I glanced over my shoulder to make sure the sign and the aloes blocked our backs; shifted my arm so that it rested firmly against him.

'I feel so sorry for her,' he said, and again his bottom lip quivered.

'So do I. She was so proud of him. She showed me a photo of him once. At least she still has her daughter, Dom, think of that.'

'Lynn . . . I wonder whether she's been told.'

'Do you think Ma'am's down at her cottage?' I wondered whether she knew the instructor who killed Graham; how she would ever forgive the man who had accidentally shot her boy.

'I suppose . . .'

'It would be the wrong time to go to her now, perhaps tomorrow.'

'She'll probably be going to the funeral. God, it will be awful for her. I hate funerals.'

'I've only been to one. When my Grandfather De Man died.'

For the only afternoon in all the time I knew him, Dom did not go to a piano to practise. In moments like these, he said, doing something like a Grade Eight in music seemed so banal, our lives and everything we did nothing but a big rush into a void of senselessness. We baked in the sun, sometimes talking, sometimes letting long minutes slip by without words. He wondered where Beauty was, whether she had been told. We spoke about fearing death. I said I didn't mind dying but that I wished Bok and Bokkie would die before me – not because I didn't love them – but because it would ruin especially my mother if I, or one of my sisters were to die before her. Dominic said he was terrified of dying, of becoming ill, getting cancer and feeling your own body being eaten away by some force you didn't understand or even know the cause of. I'm not afraid of dying, I said, as long as it comes quickly without me knowing, that it is not a long drawn-out process of suffering. Cancer was the worst. Then Dom said the last way he would like to die was through being shot, even though that would probably be quick. I said yes, it must be terrifying being a soldier, although Mathison had a point: at least Graham died for our cause.

'Our cause my foot! Mathison's dead wrong if he thinks I'll ever be a soldier,' Dominic spat. I tugged two blades of grass from the side of the rock, passed one to him and chewed at the crisp base of the stem between my fingers.

'I don't want to go to the army either,' I spoke through the chewing, 'but that's the way things are.' Then, without checking myself, unable to keep the thought off my lips: 'There's no way out and I cannot face the scorn of not going. Bok will want me to go; he was in the army for three years in Potchefstroom. He says it makes a man of a boy.' Suddenly I thought of Henk Willemse in my essay. Considered going to drag it from the pile, rewriting the story of the bursting pomegranate. Now aware of how what I wrote might disturb Ma'am – conjure in her mind's eye an image of Graham being

shot, killed by a hand grenade or a landmine, his stomach spra
over—

'Yes,' Dominic interrupted my thoughts, steel in his voice, 'Dad
says the army makes a man of a boy in the same way as rape makes a
woman of a girl.' I chewed on the meaning of Dr Webster's words.
Dominic went on: 'Dad will do everything to keep me out. Send me
out of the country. Anything. He says our presence in Angola and
Namibia is utterly unjustified. A breach of international law to protect a racist system. I won't set foot in Angola or Namibia without a
passport.'

'South-West Africa?'

'It's real name is Namibia,' he said, flicking away the grass.
Namibia, I mouthed to myself. A better name, nicer sounding, named
probably for the Namib Desert. 'And,' Dominic said, 'South Africa's
real name is Azania.' For a while I was silent, tasting the new name:
Azania. 'Dominic, where do you get that rubbish?' I asked. 'This
country became the Union of South Africa in 1910, and in 1960 it
became the Republic of South Africa. Where do you get the idea that
it's Azania?'

'Mum says that name is on the lips of the protesting children who
get shot by police in Soweto.'

'I thought they were burning down their schools because they
didn't want to learn Afrikaans?'

'That too. You'll hear all about it when we have the French
Revolution debate.'

Azania. Az-ania. Azaiinia. Azanea. Yes, I thought, that too is a
better name than South Africa, which sounds like a direction rather
than a place. But I am all too aware of what happens in countries that
change their names. Tanganyika to Tanzania. Not worth the risk
merely because it sounds nicer. A place is more than its name. But, if
that's true, then why not just change it, anyway? It's the principle
that matters. The principle of who gets to name it. So, it's not the
name, but from whose mouth it comes. 'You know, Dom, when the

blacks get hold of the name of a place it leads to trouble. The farmers in Tanzania lost everything. And look what's happened since Lourenco Marques became Maputo. All the whites had to leave, and just remember Almeida's family fleeing from Angola with only the clothes on their backs. I'm sure that's why he didn't come back this year, because they didn't have the money to keep him here.'

Dominic didn't respond. After a while, he spoke: 'Angola is still Angola, isn't it?'

'Yes, but who knows for how long.' Then he turned his back on me and said we should be ashamed of ourselves, taking only self-interest from Graham's death. It should be her and her son we're crying for, he said; instead we're thinking only of ourselves. Again silence came and sat with us. Dominic said he wanted to go and call his parents. I asked whether he would like me to come to him tonight. He said no. Sex was the last thing on his mind. Not for that, I said, just to be together. No, let's leave it till after the piano exams, he said.

Choir, so it reached us by word of mouth, had been cancelled. A gesture of respect for Ma'am and Graham. A horrible damper sat over us during prep, in the showers, and through quiet time. Tonight's was not the usual silence of discipline enforced through the cane or the threat of the cane, of censure or the threat of censure. This was the quiet of mourning and respect. Ma'am must be down at her chalet, I thought. Who was with her, Jacques, Mathison, Marabou? And her daughter, where was she? How was Ma'am mourning? I tried to imagine her pain, her tears, her despondency. All that came when I tried to visualise Ma'am was Bokkie's face, contorted at the death of Uncle Gert; my own doubling over and screaming at hearing Dademan had died. More than anything I wanted to talk to my mother or Bernice or any one of the others, to hear what they were thinking and feeling: Bennie, Mervyn, Lukas and Dominic. After lights-out, the deep sadness stayed with me. Tears welled in my eyes as I thought of Graham, of

Ma'am, on the phone, calling relatives. Weeping. How did one announce a death? Had Mathison done it correctly? I buried my head in the pillow when I saw Graham's photo, now ghostly white — no, probably smeared with the camouflage Bennie said was called Black is Beautiful — and dead with a gun wound that had ripped open his chest, his heart and lungs dangling out in a horrendous fruit salad. It is the heart where he is hit, I imagined. Or was it his head? What if his face had been blown away? I wept; realised it was less for Ma'am and her son than it was for myself. I am weeping from fear for myself; for something that lurked at least four years away in my future.

I now wanted to be with Dominic or Jacques. There was no way I was going to be able to sleep. I didn't want to sleep. How could anyone sleep on a night like this? I was angry at Jacques. This idiotic fear he had of allowing me to come to him. Weeks — at least two — since I had last been there. And Dominic, the rawness of his sadness, he seemed to take Graham worse than all of us. After supper he had phoned his parents. When he came into prep he passed me a note saying they sent their regards. Then, as we made our way upstairs in silence — none of the usual horsing — he held me back and said: 'Mom and Dad send their love.'

'What did they say about Graham?'

'Dad said it's a time to separate the personal from the political. Certain things, like the loss of a child, are above politics and I should pay no attention to Radys. Mum suggested we respect Ma'am's need to mourn: mourning is an intensely personal thing.'

'I agree with your folks.' I thought about what Radys had said, that Dominic's family was spoiling the natives or plurals as they were now called. Stupid, I thought, I don't know what dying in Angola has to do with spoiling the blacks.

'Dad still thinks I'm right, though. Radys is a reactionary. Loelovise yokou.' As we said goodbye and he turned right to G, I left to F.

'Loelovise yokou titoo,' I had answered, wondering about the meaning of the word reactionary.

An hour after I guessed everyone asleep I again rose and donned dressing gown and slippers. Wounded and brooding at Jacques's fore-warning that I was not to come to his room unsolicited, I slunk past his door, silently wishing he would come out and see me.

'My teacher's son has been killed in Angola. His name was Graham Sanders.' I announced from where I sat at the mouth of the fort. Uncle Klaas stared into the fire. He offered no response; his sleep-creased face expressionless, the news no concern of his. From the opposite bank the scent of flowers twitched in my nostrils. My neck turned, searched the dark above the sandstone embankment. I had still not made time to cross over, climb the bank and identify the blooms. During the day, when they didn't seem to smell, I almost forgot about their existence.

I awaited a response to the news of Graham's death. Nothing forth-coming. Uncle Klaas took the zol from the Silent One. He held it to his lips half hidden by strands of the scraggly moustache. He didn't drag on the brown paper cylinder; only held it there, staring pensively into the flames at my feet. He may as well be, I thought, some ghostly ver-sion of Oupa Liebenberg after a day in the sun on the tractor: same sad blue eyes, same prominent nose with the perfectly shaped nostrils that flare when they're thinking, same full lips turning down at the sides as though in perpetual readiness to cry. This is like Oupa Liebenberg. Only skinnier. And with the filth, the long greasy brown and grey hair like rats' tails under the woollen balaclava, now rolled up onto his fore-head. Sitting in his great-nephew's fort beside a black man also in tatters and also a rolled-up balaclava or some other woollen cap.

'Did you come and listen to the concert?' I asked. His eyes lifted towards me then sunk back into the flames. What was up, tonight? Why the withdrawal, the uncommunicativeness, when other nights he'd been quite pleasant and receptive to chat?

As long as I didn't sit too close to either of them I didn't have to cope with their smell. It made no sense, I thought, that they, down here on the riverbank of all places, would not occasionally wash. Scrub themselves. It was impossible to decipher from Uncle Klaas's skin what was dirt and what the ravages of age, madness and living wild. The Silent One's black-brown skin looked dusty and tired: clearly that skin had not seen water in days, weeks, months, years perhaps. They wouldn't even have to submerge their bodies, I thought, why not just wash hands, faces and hair? I looked at the Silent One's hair sticking out around the dusty balaclava that sat like a crest on his crown: grey and black, salt and pepper, long strands, like wool or down sticking from a frayed pillow slip. And what of their other ablutions? I was intrigued by what they must do after defecating. Leaves, or stones, like we used as kids in the bush? Or was even that too sophisticated for them? The picture of them squatting, standing up and pulling up their pants without a second thought stuck with me. Shit caking like mud in their trouser pants. That could be part of their smell: unwashed starfishes, shitty trousers. My throat contracted; I swallowed. Over the previous weeks I had seen them only once – the first time – during the day. And then Uncle Klaas had looked at his worst – at least the firelight at night softened the dirt, the age. If he could have a hair cut and get rid of the greasy rats' tails; that's at least part of why he looked so much older than Oupa Liebenberg. But the two men before me were creatures of sleep, day and night, seeming to wake only to smoke, light and stoke the fire when I arrived. Of what they might eat I had no idea and was too guarded to ask. Afraid I may be assigned the task of fetching and carrying. And yet I did feel pity for them – and the tickle of excitement at the idea of sneaking food from the dining hall right from under the noses of Marabou and Matron Booysen. So far Uncle Klaas had asked nothing save the blanket. And then even he had not asked, had merely said: 'We need another blanket.' And he had known, somehow and through my protests, my curses, that it would be brought. The blanket had been barely spoken of.

If they were to stay another few weeks, they'd have food aplenty. Stealing, thieving from the orchard. And the school would think the broken branches and half-eaten apples, plums and pears the result of some of us boys getting up to mischief.

'I said my teacher Ma'am Sanders's son was killed.' Again, nothing but the river, the crickets, the frogs. Then Uncle Klaas muttered something to the Silent One, who responded in barely a whisper. At last Uncle Klaas took a deep drag from the zol, held it in his lungs while I waited for an answer that might come once he'd exhaled. But again he said nothing to me. Grumbled at the Silent One in a language I didn't know. The mad gene, I told myself; at work again. I did not understand any of the words that occasionally passed between them, and Uncle Klaas offered no translation: theirs was a secret language, it could have been from any part of the world or it may not have been a language at all. Gibberish or another type of Gogga, for my gratification and entertainment. Frequently I had felt that I would have liked to speak to the Silent One, through him find out more about my uncle. And to have asked where he came from, where he grew up, how he met Uncle Klaas. But there seemed to be no will on the part of this old black man to converse with me. If Uncle Klaas was to be believed, the Silent One spoke neither Afrikaans nor English. When I asked Uncle Klaas the man's name and what language he spoke, I was told to ask him myself.

'What is your name?' I asked, not even getting him to look me in the eye. 'Me . . . Karl,' I said, and you, Jane, almost, but of course didn't. 'What language do you speak?' Again he didn't keep his eyes on me for more than a moment. 'Hey, what language do you speak?' He again ignored me, or pretended not to hear. 'How,' I hissed at Uncle Klaas, 'can I ask him anything when he doesn't understand a word I say? He doesn't even know I'm speaking to him or about him. Is he deaf?'

'He can hear you,' Uncle Klaas said. Sensing that my great-uncle was taking a turn towards the incorrigible aloofness sometimes brought on by the dagga, trying to make me guess what he meant, I changed the topic. He and I spoke for a while about *The Picture of Dorian Gray*. A smile played around his eyes and the stringy lips. He seemed delighted at what I was reading, seemed to forgive my earlier engagement with the doings of Scarlett and Rhett. Now I asked him please to translate what had happened to Ma'am's son for the Silent One. Surely, this was news important enough to justify some form of dialogue? Trialogue? Still he ignored me, instead taking another drag from the zol that had been passed back to him by the black hand. With a languid movement of his arm, he holds out the zol to me even before he exhales.

I take it from the grubby claw extending towards me.

'Suck softly and not too deep, as though you're breathing.' He spoke, smoke spurting from his mouth and nostrils, from his beard, an old flightless dragon. 'Then hold it in your lungs.' Doubtful of what I was about to do – aware of crossing an enormous frontier from where there may be no return – he saw the hesitation. 'Gently and slowly,' he said, 'then you won't cough.' The wet brown paper was against my lips – cool to the touch, their spit – and I shuddered. My mouth closed around the damp and I dragged feebly, watched the tip turn red, saw the ash grow, felt heat beneath my fingers, breathed in slow and deep like at an extended pause preparing for a long high note, and then, starting to panic at the burn in my chest, let the smoke rush from my lungs, watched in relief through teary eyes as it came from my mouth in a clear white jet. I waited for the hallucinations I had heard and read and seen so much of in the films that warned of the dangers of drug use.

'It's doing nothing,' I said. 'It's just like a cigarette.'

'So,' he said, over the disappointment in my tone, 'Graham Sanders is dead.'

'Yes, Uncle Klaas, killed by his own instructor in Angola. It's terrible.'

'And since when did you start caring for Graham Sanders?'

'Uncle Klaas? He's Ma'am's son. Ma'am is my favourite teacher.'

'You should expend the energy caring for the living that you do on the dying . . . Then the world would be quite a different place. But then, there's such drama in death, isn't there? A spectacle of grief that gets your tears flowing, and can make you believe you really cared. As if your tears show how deeply human you are. When in fact you've never cared for the life, death's drama can make you and your witnesses pretend – believe – you did. It's like a concert, hey? Nothing that happened before matters, just what happens on stage . . . What are you people doing there, in the first place?' he asked, again passing me the brown zol. I took another drag, this time more successfully. Still hoping to make some contact with the man in the back of the fort I leant past Uncle Klaas and handed it there, felt skin like sandpaper graze my fingers. Again I awaited psychedelic colours, swirling and throbbing beats like rock music in my head. Still nothing. I'd anticipated I would be rolling around on Sterkspruit's bank by now murmuring, I am an orange, peel me, peel me, please peel me.

'What?' I asked.

'What are you people doing in Angola?'

'They're protecting us from the terrorists,' I say. 'You know that, Uncle Klaas.'

'Do I, really?'

'And, it's not *you* people, Uncle Klaas. You're one of us.'

'I am what I want to be. I'm neither here nor there. Don't drag me into the quagmire. People make war because they're afraid or because they want to protect things. I'm not afraid of anything and I've nothing to protect. Also not the lie you're all in on.'

His provocation, his indifference to things important, did not infuriate me tonight. Feeling as if I could not get a hold of him, had no way of communicating with him, didn't bother me. I was sitting in the lap of a huge and extraordinary calm. Like I'd swallowed a whole handful of antihistamine. Uncle Klaas was speaking from a place in a nomanclature that didn't make any sense, but couldn't irk me.

'It's easy for you, Uncle Klaas, because it's not your child. How would you feel if it were me?'

'This war will be over by the time you're old enough to be stupid enough to go and fight.'

'Bok says it's like our Vietnam.'

'What's *our Vietnam*? An American metaphor? A mere allegory? Is that what Vietnam has been reduced to? Or is it a place where America's poorer boys killed hundreds of thousands of Vietnamese who were doing nothing but trying to live, where there was life before America came to make war, before France came to conquer and pillage. In Vietnam there will be death, love and life after and without America.'

'What?'

'You know what happened there: the terrorists won.'

'They won't here . . .'

'And why is that, Karl'tjie?'

I lie down, legs to the water, face to the fire, chin resting in my hands. Smiling into the flames, I say because we have God on our side, because we're fighting to safeguard Christian civilization from the fate that befell the countries behind the Iron Curtain. I go quiet at the thought of the Iron Curtain. The Iron Curtain. Like tightly packed metal bars of a prison. Slicing Europe in half and Russia at its heart. There people live to stand in long queues for food in the blistering snow and are hunted down for being Christians. Behind the Iron Curtain. There people are martyrs for Christianity, spreading tracts and Bibles, in spite of the fact that being caught with the Word of God means incarceration, banishment to Siberia, torture with electrodes and hot needles inserted beneath fingernails, and frequently death and assassination. The Iron Curtain spreading down Africa, bringing poverty, chaos, communism, starvation, famine, wars. The loss of land. The state gives you a house and if you don't like the house get out! and live on the pavement. You can't own land under communism. Just like in Tanganyika. Julius Njerere. Ujamaa. Uhuru.

Everything taken by the black state. No freedom to move as you please. Rules, rules, rules. There's a song, Little Boxes, Little Boxes we all get put in boxes, our Sunday school teacher said it's about what communism does to people, making them all the same. Nothing left, taking away. I said to Uncle Klaas, communism means the loss of land.

'Whose loss of land?' he asked, and leant back, taking the zol from the Silent One, dragging on its dregs and stubbing it out in the sand.

'Our land,' I said, rolling onto my side, still staring into the fire. 'In Tanganyika, they stole our land. Bok is struggling. Since they left Tanzania, we've never had money.'

'Is that the story? That they took your father's farms? That's why you left?'

'It's not a story, Uncle Klaas. It's the truth.'

'Your father and mother left before their farm was taken. They ran because they were afraid their farm may be taken.'

'Rubbish, Uncle Klaas. That's rubbish.'

'Your parents were afraid that the people of Africa would take back what had been taken from them. A thief always fears thievery.'

'They stole it,' I say in a whisper, 'after we had worked it free of the bush, turned it to civilisation. Everyone's, the Therons down the road, Uncle Michael and Aunt Siobhain's, all the whites' stuff was national-ised.' I left the word hanging, hoping he'd realise I knew what I was talking about. There was to my mind something extremely mature about the discussion.

'They were planning to recover what you had stolen from them,' Uncle Klaas muttered. 'Britain, the nation of rapists, knew that when they handed it back to Nyerere. They didn't even need a liberation war. You people knew what was coming—'

'Me?' I laughed. 'I wasn't even born when we got that farm! Neither was Bok. Dademan gave it to him. But I had nothing to do with it, if you please, dear Great-Uncle Klaas. My hands are clean and my pockets are as empty as yours. The . . . plurals stole my birth-right.'

He laughs, and asks why a minute ago I had said they stole *our* land, which *we* had cleared for civilisation. Now I am saying I had nothing to do with it. If, he says, you want to stake a claim on the good parts, you have to take ownership of the bad parts too. I raise my head and look up into his face. He casts his eyes at me: 'You have everything you need, Karl. Self-pity doesn't become you as it seldom becomes anyone. Stop pretending that you're poor. Most black people are poor. And some whites of whom you are not one.'

'I don't care,' I said and fell back onto my arm.

'Have you ever been in the locations?' he asked. 'Have you ever gone hungry? Have you ever done your homework by candlelight or with a kerosene lamp? Have you ever walked to school through frost in winter with bare feet? Have you ever been shot at by the police?'

'They're accustomed to it,' I said, giggling, trying to undermine his moralism, his self-righteousness.

'To what?'

'It's their culture, to live in small houses and walk to school. And we walked to school in Toti. Bernice still does.'

'And being denied your language and fired at with machine guns?'

'No, and I won't ever be because I don't go around burning down schools,' I said, sitting up and shaking my head irritably. I was bored. I was still not hallucinating, but had begun to feel slightly queasy. A bit nauseous. I moved back from the fire.

'What if you had to go and live in a black homeland, overnight?'

'Uncle Klaas, this is our country. I'm not letting them take it away from me again. I love each tree, each mountain, each animal and all the rivers here. Why must I give it all up!' I now wished the Silent One was not there. Then I could talk more freely.

'This obsession of yours with loving the land! Ha!' He throws his head back. 'It's enough to make me giggle, Karl'tjie. You all pretend to love the bloody mountains and rivers and the soil because then you can forget your disdain for people. And yourselves. What you call love for the trees is no more than a detraction, an alibi, a pretence at not hating humanity of whom you're a part!'

'I don't hate anyone, Uncle Klaas.'

'You will have to destroy your schools, shoot your teachers, you will have to kill your parents, you will have to die, to live truly in this country.'

At first I wanted to say that I'm willing to do that, then, the sentence sounded ambiguous. It didn't make sense. 'How can you expect me to kill my parents? How will I live in this country if I'm dead? You're mad, Uncle Klaas.'

'You won't be dead, but you will have died. Your mother will not be dead, nor will your father, but you will have killed them. Only then will you be free.' I stared into the coals, trying to remember what he had just said. It was a complicated sentence. 'Those who deceive themselves as deeply as you do will have to go through that. For many others, thank the gods, it will be easier.' He's going into his mad state, again, I could tell. I wondered whether the mad gene hid in the veins of his neck somewhere from where it just snuck out of its cellular lair to occasionally feed on his brain, making him talk mad. Turning my back to them and the fire, I sat watching the drift of the river, the clouds, the half-moon. I felt hot, feverish. I think I should get going, but I'm not sleepy. I glance at my wrist-watch. Almost midnight. Without announcement I remove my dressing gown, my pyjama top and shorts and stand naked, facing the river. A snort from Uncle Klaas and I turn to look across my shoulder. Both men's eyes are on me. I smile. 'It's October,' I say, 'surely a boy's got to have a swim.'

I edge my way down the slight incline, my shadow from the fire casting a long wobbly dance across the water. My toe tells me it's freezing. Smell the flowers. I decide to dive — shallow, for the water's flow is light this early in the year. I dive just below the surface and gasp for air as I come up and stroke across to the cliff. I cannot get a foothold on the slippery rock face and fall back into the stream and race back.

'It's still too cold and shallow,' I stammer, scurrying up the bank. Now shy of my own nudity, of the penis shrunk to a drawn-in mopani worm by the cold. Grabbing the dressing gown I turn away and rub the rough fabric over my torso, legs, back. Then my hair; wish it were long, so that I could throw it forward and dry it . . . Sniff, clearing my nose and upper lip. With the dressing gown held in front of me I collect my pyjamas and quickly dress.

At the back of the fort the Silent One pulls the balaclava over his face, lies back and settles down to sleep. From where I sit, closer to the fire, holding my hands out to the flames, I am able to look at my great-uncle's profile. Oupa Liebenberg. Uncle Klaas. Yet he is nothing like my mother's father. A man I associate with tears. Oupa Liebenberg, the one who weeps when he's happy, weeps when he's sad. The man in front of me is one I cannot imagine crying. Of that I'm glad. He looks as dried up as a piece of driftwood, as though there cannot be any moisture left anywhere in his body, let alone in his tear ducts.

'When last did you see Oupa?' I ask. He mutters that he doesn't remember. He remembers only things that are useful to remember. But from within the indifference I can hear defiance in his voice, sourced in an old wound perhaps, and I wonder why he persistently declines speaking about his brothers and my grandmother. Or anyone else of his generation. Commentary about his nieces and great-nieces and nephews and great-nephews he has: my mother the silent martyr, my mother's late brother Uncle Gert: 'If he hadn't died in the mine the workers would have killed him anyway,' Uncle Klaas said of Oom Gert one night. 'So the rock on his neck saved him that suffering.' But his most vicious loathing is reserved for Aunt Lena, the biggest victim and most manipulative woman on the face of the earth. All her Christian gobbledygook. Her depressions, her suffering! She out-suffers the world, my god she's an evil woman. 'She's played that Liebenberg family like a fiddle since she was ten years old. The epilepsy, the dropping out of school. Good thing she had to marry

Joe Mackenzie. Now she'll know what it is to suffer.' Did Aunt Lena really *have* to marry Uncle Joe, I asked. Uncle Klaas changed from Aunt Lena to my cousins Lynette and Kaspasie, the most talented kids in the family but who were likely to come to nothing because of Aunt Barbara's conservatism, her lack of imagination. The Brats, born with diamond-studded spoons in their mouths, wasted on them, the girl Joelene — what an idiotic name, that's the Afrikaner nouveau naming there — would be a victim like Aunt Lena, the son a wash-out like his immoral father Uncle Joe.

Yet it is not my aunts, uncles and cousins I am interested in hearing of. Those I wish to hear of he never wants to speak about. I look at the tattered and bruised replica of my Oupa sitting in the firelight, feeding the fire the last of the twigs. How my grandfather hates this man. And his other brother, Great-Uncle Janus, both of whom he had to put through university by himself dropping out of school. A hundred times I have heard from Oupa and Ouma and others in the family what a mad old dog Uncle Klaas is. What a selfish arrogant snob Uncle Janus who, the moment he had his degrees, left the Western Transvaal to get away from those who had sacrificed their lives for his education. And the old mad dog here beside me. No degrees could inoculate him against the madness that drove him to trampdom.

I recall a time when Oupa and Ouma left Klerksdorp to again try and make it as farmers near the Soutpansberge. Bokkie and Aunt Siobhain drove Lena, me and James up there in the Alcamino truck. Little Kaspasie and Lynette were there for the holiday as well. The two nights our mothers stayed before they left, Oupa and Aunt Siobhain communicated through Bokkie, because Oupa couldn't speak English and Aunt Siobhain knew no Afrikaans.

'We were not allowed to vote,' Aunt Siobhain said. 'The English only allowed the rich landowners to vote.' Then Bokkie would say: 'Hulle het nie stemreg gehad nie, Pappie, net die rykes met grond mag gestem het.' And Oupa would say: 'Ja, kyk hier is ons mos ook soos kaffers deur die rooinekke behandel.' And Bokkie would say: 'Here, he says, we were treated like blacks by the Pommies,' and Oupa would say, 'in ons duisende ons vrouens en kinders uitgemoor in die konsentrasie-kampe, die Engelse,' and Bokkie would say: 'The English murdered thousands and thousands of us in the concentration camps, you know, his mother was in the concentration camp in Bloemfontein.' And Aunt Siobhain would shake her head and say: 'That's the English for you. A million and a half people died in the potato famine, because the English insisted we should pay taxes. Even today, Dingle, the ugliest town in the world where I grew up, is underpopulated because the English took our pork, beef and grain while hundreds of thousands starved,' and Bokkie said: 'Pappie, sy vertel hoe daar hongersnood was onder die Iere omdat die Engelse al hulle kos gevat het, amper twee miljoen mense dood, dis nou die Katolieke, Pappie weet, want die Engelse is mos Protestante,' and Oupa said: 'Ag kyk, Bokkie, die boere is mos maar ook Nederduitse Protestante, en dit het nie die vuilgoedse Engelse van ons rugge afgehou nie,' and Bokkie would say: 'Siobhain, he says that the Afrikaners were Dutch Reformed Protestants and that didn't even help us against the English, they just take what they can from whomever they can.' And Oupa would speak about how he didn't get his first pair of shoes until he was sixteen years old and Aunt Siobhain said she didn't taste ice cream until she came out to Tanganyika to escape the poverty of Dingle, and Oupa would say they never owned a house, always rented, and Aunt Siobhain would say they had a house but no food, that she was malnourished until she became a nurse and could eat hospital food in the nurses' home, and Oupa would say he went for months eating only porridge to put his useless brother Klaas through university, then the aptly named Janus, and Aunt Siobhain said her family had gone for years on potatoes. And then Oupa would cry, tears streaming down his face, saying he didn't know how one nation could be so cruel to another and Ouma would put her hand on Oupa's arm and Bokkie would signal with her eyes to a bewildered

Aunt Siobhain that it was okay, that Oupa cried often and very easily.

The Silent One was snoring.

We cousins stayed on after Bokkie and Aunt Siobhain left. We spent our days with the air rifle, shooting mousebirds and sparrows, occasional baboons to frighten them from Ouma's vegetables, and, when the baboons became scarce, Kaspasie and I fired a few shots through Ouma's dresses hanging on the washing line. 'Now everyone will think Ouma's wearing lace,' Lynette chirped when a scowling Ouma discovered the damage. Lynette and I listened in on the party line, eavesdropping on the district gossip. Or, in the shade of the mulberry tree, we sat on a doek and played Monopoly or Scrabble or Snakes and Ladders. As if by divine intervention on Ouma's behalf, we were told that during one of our forays into the bush, we had shot across farm lines and had shot out a piccanin's eye. The next-door farmer had rushed the piccanin to hospital where the pellet was now lodged centimetres below his left brain lobe. Ouma, in a state of head-shaking agitation and terrified muttering, got us to pray and do Bible study for two hours a day. While in the afternoons she lay on the bed listening to serials on the wireless, she had four of us in the corners of the bedroom and the fifth directly in front of her against the wall, each with a Bible or hymnal, and then at night, by candlelight for there was no electricity, we again had Bible study and prayer for the dying piccanin. If he died, there would be a court case, and we'd probably all end up in reform school. Lynette, Lena and James ganged up against Kaspasie and me, demanding to know why they would be sent to reform school for something the two of us had done. I countered by saying we could never know who had fired the misguided shot, as all of us had used the air-gun, Lena more than anyone else. And James, useless with a gun, could easily have mistaken a piccanin for a baboon. We prayed incessantly and never again touched the rifle. One day the neighbour's van pulled up and the five of us stormed towards him with Ouma shouting at us from the stoep to get back into the house.

Kaspasie was the first to reach the van. When he asked how the piccanin was doing the neighbour didn't have a clue what Kaspaas was talking about.

Ouma stood on the stoep laughing at us.

Boiling, I tried to convince the others to run away with me. Lena and James were too cowardly, but I managed to get Kaspasie and Lynette to follow suit. We packed our little suitcases and took off down the dust road. I had the Monopoly set under my arm. The idea was to walk to Louis Trichardt, fifteen miles from there, and then to hike back to Klerksdorp. When we were no less than a mile from Ouma's home, we saw Oupa's bakkie heading towards us. We knew Oupa was out ploughing, so it had to be Ouma, whom we knew hadn't a clue in the world on how to drive. Yes, it had to be her, for the bakkie groaned along in first gear as she drew near.

'Run,' I shouted at Kaspasie and Lynette, who fled into the bush while I ran along the road, suitcase in one hand, Monopoly in the other. Glancing over my shoulder I saw Ouma jump out of the bakkie and run after Lynette, grabbing her by the dress and dragging her back to the truck. I decided to make a dash for it. Behind me I heard Kaspasie scream as Ouma reeled him in. Soon the bakkie was near me and Ouma hooted for me to stop. I kept going. I heard the truck skid in the dust and then Ouma was running after me, brandishing a quince branch, shouting: 'Stop you Moerskont! Kom hier, Satang!' I was exhausted. She caught up with me, beating me as I dropped the Monopoly set. Money was blown in all directions, into the veld, up into the thorn trees. Ouma chased me around the Monopoly board that lay open in the road, beating me with the stick. When she got hold of me she took me by the scruff of the neck and forced me to pick up, one by one, the fluttering pieces of colourful money, spanking me with the quince branch for every one I retrieved.

By the time Bokkie and Aunt Siobhain came to collect us three weeks later, the story of the neighbour's piccanin, and of being chased around the Monopoly set in the veld had turned from anger into humour, and Bokkie said I deserved the beating both for shooting holes in Ouma's dress and for venturing to run away into a landscape that had no life for ten miles around.

That was the first and last holiday on the farm in the Soutpansberge. The farming didn't work out, just as it hadn't when Bokkie was a girl in the Molopo. Back Ouma and Oupa went to Klerksdorp. Then Oupa tried selling sunflower seeds and they moved to Kroonstad where he was born. Then that didn't work out because the market was against him and they went back to Klerksdorp. Then he worked for a panel-beater in Potchefstroom but the boss was a cheat and they went back to Klerksdorp. And each time Ouma packed up and moved house. Then he worked as—

I am asleep, wake from something, register where I am. Freezing.

Uncle Klaas too has nodded off. The fire is nothing more than a faint red glow. I poke Uncle Klaas's leg with my toe and say I'm going back to school. I glance at my watch. Suddenly nervousness takes hold, fear crawls up my spine, tickles my neck. I walk past things lurking in the bush beside the footpath. For the first time in hours I think of Ma'am's son. Terror grips my chest, makes me shake and shiver as I begin to run. Sprint up the hill. It is almost two in the morning when I slide into bed. For the first time in my life I've been afraid of the night. Afraid of the fear.

10

'Hello?'

'Hello, my child, how are things?'

'Fine, Bokkie, how are things there?'

'Not much news my child, just this thing with Ma'am's son.'

'Ja, it's terrible, Bokkie. Did you hear it on the radio?'

'No, it was on TV last night. Big news. You know her sister — Miss Hope — teaches Lena at Port Natal. Him and another boy from Florida, terrible.'

'Ja, Ma'am has left to go to the funeral in Pietermaritzburg and we're going to sing.'

'Ag, that's good, Karl'tjie, this must be a bitter pill for that poor woman to swallow.'

'Ja, Bokkie. Apparently he wasn't killed by terrorists, it was in a training accident.'

'Oh they didn't say that on TV. Just said killed in action in the operational area. And how's your knee?'

'Fine, all the swelling's gone. We heard yesterday from Mr Mathison.'

'My boy, I'm so glad you're going to sing at the funeral.'

'We're singing with the Infantry School choir. He's being buried with full military honours.'

'That's good. Bok wants to say hello quickly. I wrote to you, okay, Karl? We'll phone again next Friday. And you say your knee's okay now?'

'Yes, Bokkie, it's fine.'

'And tell the bus driver to drive carefully, okay?'

'Yes, Bokkie. Bye, Bokkie.'

'Philistine?'

'Hello, Bok.'

'How are you?'

'Fine thanks, Bok, how are you?'

'Fine, fine, everyone's fine here, healthy, business slow due to the riots but picking up. We're all shaken by Ma'am's son. Graham, right?'

'Yes, we too. We're singing at the funeral.'

'That's good. So, how is school?'

'Fine thanks, Bok.'

'Are you working diligently, Philistine?'

'Yes, Bok. We have a temp, Mr Loveday, while Ma'am's away.'

'And how are Lukas and the others?'

'Everyone's fine, Bok. Lukas's voice has started breaking so he's out of choir.'

'Really! That's amazing. He's only thirteen.'

'He turned fourteen in May. He spends choir down at the dairy now.'

'How about yours?'

'Sorry, Bok?'

'How's your voice?'

'It's fine, Bok. I love being in second soprano. We went riding to the Bushmen caves and Lukas and I found a Stone Age implement. It's a sharp rock with indentations. It must be a Bushmen tool, I'm looking it up in the library.'

'Oh that's very nice. You should hold onto that. A museum would be interested in buying that. Lena won a few trophies and broke some records at the Inter-School Athletics.'

'Yes, Bok. We decided I'd keep it because I'm more interested in the Bushmen than Lukas.'

'That's good. Okay, quickly say hello to Bernie and Lena, and we'll see you in a few weeks, Karl. I've got you one helluva birthday present.'

'Thank you, Bok. Are you or Bokkie coming to fetch me?'

'We'll see, my boy, we haven't worked it out yet. I may be in the Eastern Transvaal buying stock.'

'Okay, Bok, thanks for phoning.'

'Bye, Karl.'

'Bye, Bok.'

'Hello, Karl!'

'Hi, Bernie, how are you?'

'I'm fine, but, as you've heard, everyone's saddened by what happened to Ma'am. Lena says it was announced in assembly at Port Natal. And it was on TV. Lena says Miss Hope is going up to the funeral. Are you people singing at the funeral?'

'Ja, I told Bok and Bokkie.'

'Look out for Miss Hope, she'll be with Ma'am. Maybe you could go and introduce yourself, because she'll be teaching you English when you come to Port Natal next year.'

'I'm not coming to Port Natal next year.'

'Anyway. Go and introduce yourself if there's an opportune moment.'

'Okay. Are you still going to Tech, next year?'

'No, I've applied to SAA. Bokkie said she wrote to you. I'm trying to lose weight for the interview.'

'That's nice, then you'll go overseas often.'

'Yes, later on, but one starts out on domestic flights. Are you excited yet about Europe?'

'I can't wait. We're doing rehearsals for Africa!'

'I'm going to share a flat with Stephanie at Overport next year. Listen, I must go, it's getting expensive. Here's Lena, but don't speak for too long, okay?'

'Bye, Bernie.'

'Bye, Karl, and go and say hello to Miss Hope, okay?'

'I will, bye.'

'Hello, you!'

'Hi, Lena, how are you?'

'Fine thanks and you?'

'Fine. How's school.'

'Okay. I won all six of my events and broke the hundred metres hurdles and shot-put records, did Bok tell you?'

'Yes, that's great. So you broke two records?'

'Yes, I'm rather proud of it.'

'So am I. It's wonderful. Did you get trophies again?'

'Yes, just one, the Alice Brown trophy for the hurdles. It was donated by the coffee creamer people. Imagine winning the Alice Brown trophy.'

'I'll see it in a few weeks. Were you the victrix laudorum?'

'No, idiot, only Standards Nine and Ten qualify for that. Next year. When are you coming?'

'It's from Kruger Day till the eighteenth. Is it the same as yours?'

'No, we break up now, so we'll already be back at school by the time you come.'

'That's a pity.'

'How's Dominic?'

'Fine. He's practising for his Grade Eight, so I don't see him much.'

'Well, say hello to them.'

'I will, and they said I must say hello as well. How's Alette?'

Fine. Also busy practising for some piano exam.'

'Grade Five.'

Did they tell you about the thing with Aunt Barbara and the cheque?'

'No, what?'

Well, big family drama: while Aunt Lena was doing the books for Uncle Joe's business they found a cheque missing for two hundred rand.'

'Yes?'

Anyway, it turns out Aunt Barbara had stolen a cheque and forged Uncle Joe's signature and then sent Kaspaas to cash it at Volkskas.'

'How did they find out?'

The teller at Volkskas remembered that it was a white boy in a Volkies uniform and then they just put two and two together. But Uncle Joe didn't call in the police or anything. Just basically let Aunt Barbara know that they knew. Anyway, I must go.'

'Will you tell Alette I say hello?'

Ja. They're moving to Durban, at the end of the year.'

'She wrote and said they might. I'll be home for my birthday, maybe she can come over for that.'

No she won't! I know what you're getting!'

'Tell me!'

No! It's a surprise. Listen, I must go. Bokkie is having silent fits about the phone bill. See you in a few weeks.'

'Okay. Bye, Lena.'

Karl!'

'Ja?'

Remember to go and say hello to Miss Hope, she'll be your English teacher next year at Port Natal.'

'I'm staying here next year.'

'. . .'

'Lena?'

Bye, Karl.'

'Bye . . .'

I I

In areas the Umfolozi lawn did not reach, right beside the walls of the house and beneath the Marula tree in the front garden, ant-lions burrowed conical craters in the powdery sand. If one very gently dropped a grain or small stone into the crater, the ant-lion, mistaking the movement for the approach of prey, would emerge from its hiding place and if fast enough you could flick out the little devil with a stick. Or if you blew, very gently, in the middle of the crater, sending the sand flying out in a neat fountain onto the surface, you stood a good chance of blowing its cover and exposing him down there, bewildered and hurriedly digging deeper. Ant-lions – real lions hiding out in caves – constituted favourite game in my private reserve contained between the rectangular slates of two empty apple-boxes. Ant-lions were low-maintenance, like impala (ants), and seemed to take care of themselves. Dung-beetles – the elephants of the reserve – on the other hand, needed to be kept happy with twice weekly supplies of donkey dung, which I collected from down at the stables. If the dung was dry, I invariably found rhino or eland droppings close to the house, somewhere along the road to Emoyeni Hill. To make the dung-beetles' lives more interesting, one side of the game reserve had a steep incline, and it was there where they had to go to find their dung. Up there on the cliffs they rolled their symmetrical balls and then tried, with varying degrees of success, to control the descent into the plains where impala roamed the low veld. Chameleons (dinosaurs), leaf bugs (rhino) and stick insects (crocodile), I knew, changed colour. These were caught and held in an old shoebox where Lena had once kept silk-worms she fed from a huge stock of mulberry leaves in the fridge. Because of their propensity to escape, the dinosaurs, rhino and crocodile were not let loose into the game reserve unless I was driving around.

From the school stationery brought to Umfolozi by my sisters, I took glossy red, blue and yellow paper and placed a selection of creatures on the bright surfaces to monitor their responses. Unlike in their natural habitats where they could go brown, green, mottled autumn and beige, my experiments in the shoebox proved that they could not adapt to the paper colours I set up for them as challenges. The stick insects refused to alter from the brown state in which I had first caught them; the leaf bugs died within hours – still the green they had been on the leaves. And, instead of turning blue, red, yellow, the chameleons went a ghostly off-white, their big eyes looking sad and troubled, even as they hissed and opened their yellow mouths in a display of anger and displeasure. Bok said I was going to kill them. He said these creatures could only do so much to adapt and then they die. Or they bite or sting. Forget it, he said, a chameleon – even if it tried – cannot ever turn blue unless you do something artificial, like paint it, which means you're closing its skin's pores, and its predators would see it a mile off, and it would die. Still, I tried, believing that if I slowly moved a slip of blue under them, so that perhaps they didn't notice, I could trick the chameleons into turning blue, my favourite colour. Eventually two chameleons did indeed die and responding to my disappointment Bokkie shouted: 'If your father told you once, he told you a hundred times: even a chameleon cannot turn blue. It will stand on its head and sing the national anthem through its arsehole before it turns blue.' And I went outside and buried the chameleons in the canna beds that Bokkie had planted to line the yard fence. I prayed for the souls of the chameleons and for forgiveness that I had murdered God's innocent creations. Then, extending the burial into a grand ritual my mother came to witness wearing the one church hat she owned and had not worn since Oljorro, I let my captives go free: caterpillars, stick insects, leaf bugs, frogs, lizards, ladybirds, shongololos, earthworms, butterflies, dung-beetles: into flowers, branches, onto rocks, amongst leaves, singing, as I lifted them from the box: 'All things bright and beautiful, all creatures great and small, all things wise and wonderful the Lord God made them all.' When

Bok came back from trail he told me he was proud of me, not only for liberating the creatures, but also for having learnt a wonderful lesson from my own experience.

12

11 October 1975
Bloemfontein

Dear Alette,

Last night was the inauguration of the Afrikaans Language Monument in Paarl. We left there this morning and are now in Bloemfontein. Tomorrow night we're giving a concert at the University of the Orange Free State. Our hosts are Mr and Mrs Schoonwinkel. Mr Schoonwinkel has an electronics company in town.

The ceremonies at the Language Monument were broadcast live on TV and while we sang I wondered whether you were watching and what you thought. The Monument's monolith rises like a concrete finger pointing to God from near the top of Paarl Mountain. Day before yesterday, we went to the open-air amphitheatre below the Monument for a dress rehearsal. It was the first time that the Mass choir was officially conducted by the Senior Choir's conductor, Mr Cilliers, and there was a lot of to-do about us being on TV for the first time and so on.

After rehearsal all 120 of us visited the graceful monolith that starts from a broad base and gets narrower closer to the top. A hearty Afrikaans lady gave us a conducted tour of the whole thing and explained what each part of the architecture symbolises. The tall monoliths made up of three sections symbolise the brightness of Western Civilisation with its languages and cultures. Then there are three concrete mounds, like flattened beehive huts, which represent the Cape Coloureds from Africa and their language and culture. The monoliths and the mounds are connected by a bridge where the two connect, just like the Afrikaans language is the bridge between Africa and Western Civilisation. There's a little wall as well symbolising the Malayan influence on Afrikaans, as they are neither from here nor there. There's a bubbling fountain celebrating the two languages of Afrikaans and English, our country's two life-giving cultures which make up one nation. On the programme it says our nation stands 'powerfully before its future task as, in the burning bramble-bush of time, it is aware of a Higher Presence'.

Our guide herself said she had spent her life researching and fighting for the rightful place of the Afrikaans language in a world under attack by English. She grew up near Dal Josafat where the First Afrikaans Language Movement got started in the olden days. Because of unity Dr W.J.B. Slater of the 1820 British Settlers spoke on behalf of English-speaking South Africans.

Performing in the amphitheatre was wonderful. The programme opened with prayers and the singing of Psalm 146. Cobus Rossouw recited 'Ek hou van 'n man' and Babs Laker 'The Dance of the Rain'. Adam Small did 'Nkosi Sikelel I Afrika' and Nic de Jager did 'The Fallen Zulu Induna'.

The Windhoek Youth Choir was there, all the way from South-West Africa and there were also Cape Coloureds and Malayans like the Primrose Choir. There was a spectacular air show by the SA Airforce's Harvards and Silver Falcons and a salvo of military cannons to celebrate the power of Afrikaans. After us there were other choirs and someone read the same speech that Eitemal did in 1949 at the inauguration of the Voortrekker Monument in Pretoria. Then, at night, eight torches which had been carried from all over South Africa arrived at the amphitheatre and were received by Prime Minister Vorster.

When we sang the audience was enthusiastic and the fact that we could feel the heat of spray and TV lights on us made it even more special. We sang the Boerneef cycle. Whenever we sing 'Die Berggans Het 'n Veer Laat Val', I think of you. 'Rooi Disa' is also lovely. Have you ever seen a disa? Then, because it was October and because of his astounding voice, Almeida garnered for us a standing ovation with John Pescod's 'Oktobermaand'. As it was live TV and we weren't allowed to do encores with the rest of the programme to follow, we left the stage while the audience was still on its feet.

I'm becoming sleepy, so I'm off to bed now. I'll post this tomorrow when Mrs Schoonwinkel takes us into town to see Jaws. Have you seen it yet? Grrrr . . .

See you soon for our short break. We Durban boys are coming home by train.

All my love
Karl

xxxxxxxxxx

10 October 1975
Wellington

As usual I am not tired tonight, so I'm writing in my diary. Dominic, our hostess and her children are asleep and I'm sitting at the dining-room table. Mrs Heese with whom we're living is a widow with four daughters. She is a schoolteacher and loves reading, so I am surrounded by hundreds of books. I wish I lived in a house like this. Tonight was the inauguration of the Afrikaanse Taal Monument. The Monument's monolith rises like a concrete finger pointing to God in heaven from the top of Paarl Mountain. Yesterday, we went to the open-air theatre which is right below the monument for dress rehearsal. It was the first time that we were conducted publicly by Cilliers. Cilliers is an all-too-strict choir master and I'm glad I'll be out of the school before I have to sing in his choir. I don't think he's quite as bad as Roelofse, whom I am sure still cannot stand me. All around us TV people were busy putting up lights, testing cameras and talking on walkie-talkies, so everybody in choir was looking around and Mr Cilliers was getting angry. I hadid loelaneedidedid upop soostitaneedidineeog rigoghtit inee fickroneetit ofick Hardidineegog. Eviseryok fickewow mimineeutitesoos, he fickloelicockykedid mime bokehineedid mimyok rigoghtit ear aneedid popineecochedid tithe sooskykinee ofick mimyok neeecockyk. I titriedid neeotit tito soosquirmim bokecocausoose tithatit wowouloeldid havise gogotit-titenin mime ineetito titroubokloele wowitith Cociloelloeliersoos. Mr Cilliers suddenly became enraged at our lack of concentration and the noise the TV people were making and shouted at the organisers to get the TV people to shut up or else he'd remove the choir from the stage. Atit loeleasoostit tithatit outitbokursoostit gogotit Hardidineegog tito loeleavise mimyok bokurneeineegog ear aneedid necockyk aloeloneee.

After rehearsal an Afrikaans lady gave us and the teachers a conducted tour of the Monument, explaining what each part of the architecture symbolised. The ~~tall~~ monolith symbolises the birth of a new language, Afrikaans, the shorter one the Dutch ~~from which~~ whence it came. ~~Little~~ Mounds at its base ~~are for~~ indicate the influence of other languages on Afrikaans, a very important gesture of goodwill to the Hottentots, the Malayans, the French, the Portuguese, our guide said. When one of the English Seniors said Afrikaans is a completely bastardised language Ma'am Sanders snapped at him and said that there is no more bastardised language in the world than English. Our guide herself had spent her life researching and fighting for the rightful place of the Afrikaans language in a world under attack ~~from~~ by English.

Performing in the amphitheatre was ~~indeed~~ wonderful indeed. The sun was setting and turned the mountains above Paarl orange and then indigo as we marched in rows onto the stage. A slight breeze played in our hair as we waited for Cilliers to come on; at times it caught in the microphones suspended from the dome beneath which we stood. Eviseryoktithineegog wowasoos soospopoiloeltit bokecocausoose Hardidineegog wowasoos agogainee bokehineedid mime. Titugoggogineegog atit mimyok neeecockyk wowhiloele Cociloelloeliersoos mimotitioneeedid fickor usoos tito soosmimiloele fickor tithe TitVis cocamimerasoos. Asoos wowe bokowowedid Hardidineegog wowhisoospoperedid fickor mime tito soostitopop acoctitineegog loelikyke a queer fickor tithe wowholoele ofick Soosoutith Afockricoca tito soosee. I hatite Cociloelloeliersoos fickor wowhatit he aneedid tithosoose otither titwo did tito usoos inee Joluneee. Ifick tithere wowasoos a wowayok toto kykiloelloel tithemim wowitithoutit gogetittitineegog cocaugoghtit, I wowouloeldid dido itit. The audience was enthusiastic and the fact that we could feel the heat of spray and TV lights upon us made it even more special. I cannot help wondering whether we were better than the other performers, though, of course, at a festival like this, there is meant to be no competition. We sang the Boerneef cycle. 'Die Berggans Het 'n Veer Laat Val', 'Waarom is die Duiwel vir 'n Slypsteen Bang', and my favourite, 'Rooi Disa':

Red Disa come and tell me
what you received from above
that you stay pure eternally?
Faith, hope and love

Until tonight I didn't know what a red disa was. I have always thought it was the name of a girl with red hair! Then in the car after the concert Mrs Heese spoke about the Boerneefs and asked whether a Valie like Dominic and a Durbanite like me had ever seen a disa? When Dominic said no, I also said no and then, when she said they grow on the slopes of Table Mountain I knew they had to be flowers. Personification, of course! At home she brought out a book and showed us what they look like. It is part of the *Orchidaceae* family, red, like a huge open heart, and it is sometimes called the queen of orchids. From now on, whenever we sing 'Rooi Disa', I will picture the flowers, red and brilliant, swaying in the mist in some rocky crevice on Table Mountain. From Paarl we could see the outline of Table Mountain, not nearly as flat as I thought from photos. I am disappointed that we are so close to it and didn't get time to go into Cape Town. Dominic and Mrs Heese say it's one of the most beautiful cities in the world.

Because it's October, I suppose, but mainly because of Almeida's astounding voice, the audience gave us a standing ovation for 'Oktobermaand'. Didomim & Bokeneeneeie soosayok titheyok are soosure Aloelmimeidida aneedid Coc havise a tithineegog gogoineegog. It was live TV so we weren't allowed to do encores so we left the stage while the audience was still on their feet, shouting encore, encore, more, more. In moments like that, when we sing music I love and when the audience goes wild with appreciation, I am excited and grateful about being here, proud of being part of the school and the joy we bring. Mrs Heese has just come in to see why the light is still burning. She said I could stay here and be her son, as she had only daughters. Then she brought me a glass of milk from the fridge and asked if I were allowed to drink milk for it could be bad for my voice, and I said, not at this time of night. Now that ~~shes'~~ she's gone, I wonder what happened to her husband. I must go to bed now. Dead tired.

13

At inspection Uncle Charlie discovered that my blanket was missing. Instantly paralysed by shock and real surprise — for I had grown accustomed to sleeping beneath only the sparse warmth of the bed-spread — I was caught off guard. Then, before I could stutter some incongruous denial, I managed to come up with a lie. I said there had been a tear in the blanket — right in the centre — and that I had given it to Beauty to mend.

What if Uncle Charlie spoke to Beauty before I could get to her? I rolled around cursing myself for not having said I had no idea where the blanket went, that I hadn't even noticed, that it had vanished from my bed; the buck would have stopped in a place I wouldn't have had to deal with. An hour long I debated using the key to go down to the kayas, waking Beauty, telling her the story, getting her to help keep me out of trouble and the cane's reach. Then I decided against it for fear some of the other workers would see me, and try to ingratiate themselves with Mr Walshe by telling him I had been outside in the night. And there was no way or reason to retrieve the smelly thing from our fort. Disease, smoke, fleas: it would be smelt from the other end of F Dorm. Fear, like fingers, reached for me: and then they'll find out about the key, and Uncle Klaas, and the dagga, and Jacques, no, no, no, not that. I willed myself to stay awake, wading around my mind in search of a story to lead me safely from the labyrinths of paranoia.

By the time Uncle Charlie came through at six a.m. calling, 'Vests, T-shirts and running shoes,' I had been awake for an hour. Dressing at the speed of light, one takkie still in hand, I rushed downstairs before the whistle. Behind the food counter Precious was setting out our breakfast dishes.

'Morning, Precious,' I smiled, slipping my foot into the takkie. 'Where's Beauty?'

'Scullery,' she said, still laying out the thick white crockery.

'Could you call her for me, please, Precious?' Glancing about for Mrs Booysen she went to fetch Beauty. I tied the shoelace. I watched for Beauty's blue uniform behind Precious leaving the scullery.

'Is coming,' she says in response to my frown.

'Thanks, Precious, you're an angel.'

Beauty's appearance is met by a huge smile of relief. She too smiles at me.

'Morning, Beaut! I'm so glad to see you!'

'Good morning, Karl.'

'Beaut, I need a favour! I need another blanket in the dorm. I lied to Uncle Charlie about what I did with the other one. I said I gave it to you to mend.'

'Where is your blanket?' she asks, displeasure altering smile to scowl.

'You know where it is,' I say, signalling with my eyes that I cannot talk in front of Precious.

Beauty shakes her head: 'Eh, eh.'

'Remember that note?' I whisper. She nods. 'I gave it to him. And to the one that's with him.'

She's now glaring at me, says nothing. Precious looks up. Our eyes meet.

'Will you put a blanket on my bed, please, Beauty? And don't tell Uncle Charlie I lied.'

She shakes her head.

I cannot believe what my eyes are seeing. 'Please, Beaut, I beg you.'

'No! Why do you drag me into your story?'

I am at a loss for words. This is the last thing I have been expecting; not how I had seen my escape unfolding. Nor is it how I know Beauty, stern but always smiling, always ready to help. Dominic. She's still shaking her head as she prepares to turn and leave. I cannot let her go, this has to be resolved before PT.

'If I were Dominic you'd do it.' I try to sound wounded, rather than have her hear the fear rising in my voice.

She turns back. Again glares at me. 'Dominic wouldn't tell stories about me. I'm not doing it.'

'I gave it to one of your people, Beauty,' I try again, giving her a smile that is still not returned. Still she glares. The whistle. The stampede of takkies down the stairs. The time on my side gone, I grab at a brutal straw, my voice calm and deliberate: 'You better put a blanket on my bed. If you don't, I'll report to Mathison that you gave me a note from a black beggar.' Outside, the stampede had turned to small staccatos as the last of the little ones came down.

The woman facing me remains unmoved. 'Please, Beauty. I won't tell. Just give me a blanket, I'm cold at night and I'm going to get into trouble. I must go to PT now.' She turns away.

Passing by the chalets where Ma'am lives, I catch up with Dominic, Mervy and Lukas. In the toilet, I answer Dom's enquiry about where I've been. They are speaking about Ma'am, about the coming funeral. I pray that Beauty will still, somehow, do what I have begged. If it's not there by tonight, I'll ask Dominic to speak to her. I'll think up some story about how it disappeared.

Going upstairs after PT, a neatly folded blanket has been placed at the footend of my unmade bed. My spirit soars; I can leap for joy. Once the sheets have been shaken and smoothed, I throw the blanket over, neatly folding it in with the sheets beneath the foam-rubber mattress. Then the bedspread, also tucked into neat triangular folds.

At lunch I try to mouth a thank you to Beauty as she scoops in our food. Her smile is for Dominic ahead and Bennie behind me in the queue. Her eyes refuse to acknowledge me.

*

An hour I have free after riding and before choir. The hour when the sun falls far through the auditorium windows almost up to where I sit. Engrossed in the last few pages of *Dorian Gray*, I am none the less aware of an off chance Jacques might pass through alone before choir. Then we may, I hope, exchange a few words. From even a brief one-to-one interaction I may get some indication of how long I am to be banished from his room. Up here for less than fifteen minutes and Beauty passes, bucket in hand, mop in another. I look up from the book. Smile: 'Thank you, Beauty. For the blanket. You look like Carol Burnett with that mop, Beaut,' I try to lighten the moment.

As at lunch, she seems to ignore me. Then, as if she's changed her mind, she pauses mid-stride, turns, paces back towards me and with her jaw set square, seethes: 'Don't tell stories about me, do you hear.'

'I'm sorry, Beauty. I had to think of something. I would have been caned.'

She looks at me, unfazed by my explanation. My excuse. In the moment she prepares to turn I say: 'And what's more, I wouldn't have given the blanket to them if you hadn't given me the note.'

'Don't tell stories about me; you still don't understand.'

'Listen, Beauty. There's no need to be angry, it's all sorted out. No big deal.'

'Don't tell stories about me; you understand!'

'You would never speak like this to Dominic, never. You would lick his arse if he asked you. Just because of all the little presents he brings you every term.'

'Keep your mouth off me.'

I rise from the chair: 'Listen, it was for one of your people – the black man – I took the blanket. Stop being so ungrateful.'

'I am not interested in what you have to say about me, what do you know about me, nothing, white boy, shut up about me.'

'Who do you think you're talking to? Get out of here or I'll report to Mrs Booysen that you've been carrying secret notes. Mathison will give you the sack . . .'

'Uzokuzwa mfanawomlungu kuyoquma nhlamuana esinye ziyofekela, hey – I . . . Hei – i . . .' She turns and walks away. It is as if I've been stricken by lightning, clueless about what she has said.

'Go and fuck yourself, black bitch,' I whisper, just loud enough. She doesn't stop. Glances over her shoulder and walks away. Anger, like a hot blush, through my face and arms. Then realise it is not anger. It is shame. Fear of her mentioning to Dom what I have done, how I've spoken to her.

When Jacques does walk by, he only winks at me. Does not tell me to come, does not say it's time for a bit of starfishing. I am grateful. Resentful. My heart is turned into a knot: disappointment, shame, humiliation.

I run after her. Through abandoned dormitories. Hear women's voices behind the kitchen. Run down the stairs. Find her amongst some of the other girls at the scullery door. Peeling oranges.

'May I speak to you, Beauty?'

The women go silent. She stares at me. She does not answer. Stares me down with a smile.

'I'm sorry,' I say. I turn and walk off. Hating her. Ready to spit in her face if she were to come near me. I have turned the corner of the kitchen when from behind I hear their laughter; a loud and spiteful exuberance they know I cannot miss. From an upstairs window I gaze down and see them still behind the kitchen in their blue overalls, seated with their backs against the white wall. Only Beauty is standing. I watch, cannot hear their conversation or their laughter this high up through the glass. All I see are the palms slapping blue-overalled thighs, the heads thrown back, brown faces smiling, teeth and tongues: Beauty, accentuating the swaying of her hips, grotesquely minces up and down the length of the scullery wall along the path I have just walked. The seated maids double over. Muted by the distance and the glass their howls none the less reach my ears. They smack the concrete with their open hands. Beauty turns on her heel to face her audience. Her mouth is pulled into a flamboyant pout and her wrists are drooped and flapping, eyelids batting. Without hearing a word, I know what she's doing, have witnessed it on playgrounds in classrooms in shower rooms on sports fields and in dormitories, have seen it done to others and denied it could be done to me, have done it myself to others. Again I hate her and the others. Hate everyone enough that I feel verged on weeping with pain and shame. Able to kill from rage.

For one solid hour five bars. Over and over and over. *Dona nobis pacem, dona nobis pacem, dona nobis pacem.* I wanted only to be elsewhere. Out and away from the beastly school. The blues had me, I knew. But it was not blue I saw or felt. I was in a grey tunnel, which swirled in black and white clouds. In prep I was able to remain chirpy, laughing and fooling with the rest of the class who all seemed in high spirits after being released from choir's monotony; Cilliers's ability to hear a single bar fifty times until he was satisfied and only he could really hear any difference or improvement from the first time we'd done it. Bastard.

After lights-out I did not for a moment contemplate leaving the school. I was terrified and exhausted. I wished it were already holiday. Just to get away from the place. For a while at least.

14

From walking in the veld and from Tony Poolie's record *Call of the Wild*, no, another title I don't remember I learnt to emulate the calls of birds and wild animals. Having mastered a new one, I'd go to the kraal to show off to Jonas and Boy. Jonas would correct me, teach me others: the hoopoo, the fruit bat, the elephant, the nightjar, the bush-baby. One I was never able to master. He did it in a way that if you closed your eyes, almost like reeds vibrating in the wind, you could hear a flock of guinea fowl pass overhead.

15

The six of us had left our fort, then still under construction, to take part in one of our kleilat fights. Kleilat was banned. Before our time a Senior had almost lost an eye, and so the fights took place in the utmost secrecy as far as possible from the rugby field where Teacher On Duty hovered, reading, talking to boys, or, if it were Buys, playing touch rugby with the Seniors. After rains, the groves downstream had perfect black clay to be moulded with grass or feathery wattle leaves into projectiles that stuck to the end of one's lat right till the moment it was meant to fly off and sting an enemy skin. Moreover, the wattle grove was far enough from the rugby field so that if at all heard, our muted cries would from upriver easily be mistaken for the play of campers down at the holiday park. So there we could scream, shout, holler, our sounds like dassies and birds ringing through the thickets as we sprung from behind tree trunks and shrubs, pounced, swinging a pliant green wattle sprout, which swished like a whip through the air, sending off the clammy bullet to slap its target between the shoulder blades, on the stomach, head or on an exposed leg or arm. T-shirts were stripped off and left in a heap well before the wars commenced, for while the smudge of wet clay on black cotton was at first visible only as a damp patch, it showed up like a blob of lint in neon the moment it dried in the sun. Cheetah slinking through the bush, our white bodies spotted where the lats had found any part of their target. These markings would be carefully washed off before we again slipped into our black PT shorts and shirts. Through the bracken we moved with stealth, hid behind shrubs and platoons of hundred-year-old tree ferns, lay quietly on broad branches, waiting for our prey to pass beneath us. While in these games most allegiances seemed to break down, and even the best of friends fired klei projectiles at each other, myself and a number of others still reserved our most vicious flicks for the most sensitive skins: Bruin and Mervyn. While many of us spared or pretended to spare Mervy, Bruin was undisputed fair game: not only because he was the class's cleverest and biggest arse-creeper, but because a hit, even a touch almost anywhere on his body, resulted in squealing like that of a baboon hit by a slingshot or air-gun. No matter how distant one's hide-out from the scene of the hit, Bruin made sure everyone — we feared even Teacher On Duty — knew he was not only wounded, but that he was experiencing the impact of the hit as beyond the limits of play and directly in the realm of torture. Lukas got Steven against the neck: a brief shriek pierced the afternoon, followed by the cry 'Almeida hit,' and Almeida was out for five minutes, which was the rule, sometimes changed to two or three minutes, depending on how much time we had. Mervy got Smith, Fritz got me, Oberholzer got Jimmy, and we'd sit out the minutes, then rise, on the prowl again. But not Bruin. He'd scream or fall to the ground, writhing in pain. We'd all be forced to leave our hiding places and descend on him, trying to calm him, ensure him he was not having a heart attack, that his vocal chords had not been destroyed by a huge projectile that struck his chest, or that the ball of clay that struck his head from Bennie's lat had not contained a sharp stone that might have caused him permanent brain damage. 'Watch out or your screaming might indeed burst a blood vessel in your brain,' I sneered at him and he looked at me with red, pleading eyes. Bruin awakened something in all of us, though I in particular felt my buttons pressed by him. That afternoon it was Goossen who flung the klei: in flight the projectile must have split in three as Bruin was caught by shots on his chest, temple and one in the eye. There was no whining, no crying before or after Goossen's cry: 'Hit. Bruin dead.' But within moments Goossen's voice, in Afrikaans: 'You guys! Come! I think Bruin's really hurt.' It had been a good day. At least fourteen of us Standard Fives were there. As soon as he knew we were all gathered around, Bruin presented us with a muddy smudge stretching from his right eye into his ear. 'I'm blind, I'm blind,' he cried, 'my eye is gone.' He wiped his eye furiously, tears streaming down his face. With much pleading, assuring, washing his eye with water brought from the river in willing hands cupped together, we got him to stop. Soon he and we could see that indeed he could see.

Then, well before the whistle and while the sun was still warm enough to dry us, it was into the water, scrubbing mud that lay hidden in the folds of nostrils, in hairlines, behind ears. Bruin called from the bank: 'My T-shirt's gone from the pile.' We ignored him and carried on washing. All the time Bruin searched through the bracken. Soon it was clear from Goossen's smirk that he had hidden the T-shirt. When Bruin's search delivered no results, he again resorted to tears and wailing: 'I can't take any more of this. I can't.' He stomped his foot on the riverbank while he glared at us in the water, his eyes red and his cheeks puffy.

'You're going to burst a vein in your head,' I teased and around me everyone laughed. From the grassy knoll where he stood crying Bruin was threatening, as he so often did, to get his father to come and fetch him, so that he could leave the school, his cheeks now a raw pink, the white of the eye that had been struck lined crimson, like the flesh of an almost-ripe plum. When we got out of the water Goossen must have quietly retrieved Bruin's T-shirt and thrown it into the shrinking pile. Finally, with all dressed barring Bruin, one T-shirt remained.

'Searched like your arse!' Goossen sneered at Bruin, who dashed forward to clutch the garment to his chest.

'Freak!' I sniped as the group started off, the snivelling Bruin following at a distance. I caught Almeida's eye. Although he said nothing, I read an accusation there, something that told me he found the way I tormented Bruin unappealing. Ugly. I looked away.

Moving upstream the participants drifted apart. On route back, some of us stopped to look at the impressive fort of three Juniors. Their place was rather special, one of only a few that lay below ground level. Built into a deep donga with steps leading down into the chamber, the roof was made of stumps, reeds and a leaf covering, so that it resembled its environment, almost like a trap for big game in the Olden Days. The way I imagined Chaka had done in Umfolozi, or like the pit used to capture King Kong on his island. Planted at the fort's four corners were bamboo poles with red flags, warning off anyone who might inadvertently step on the roof and fall the five feet into the donga. The boys took us inside, down into the large cave-like cavern where nine of us comfortably sat. It was more than double the size of ours, in which we six and no one else could possibly fit. Light came in through two windows in the roof. Into the sides of the donga shelves had been chopped. On these were an assortment of river pebbles, empty cool-drink tins, rope, plastic bags and a slingshot. In an empty peanut-butter jar stood the bloom of an enormous blood lily. We praised the Juniors for their resourcefulness and then left, talking about how we could enhance our fort by extending the thatch along the beam closer to the river.

We crossed and headed along the footpath of cleared leaves, upstream. We were approaching the powerful structure of Harding and Reyneke, a blockhouse of huge logs. It was Dominic who snorted and pointed. I saw it, through the openings between the logs. Inside, in the dusk, four or five prefects, standing up, bare buttocks, movement. Hands shaking like pistons in front of loins. We walked on, quietly, as though we had not seen anything.

'Did you see that!' Dominic exclaimed. Still none of us spoke.

'They were tossing each other off!' Still waiting for a response. It was Almeida who gave it, as if on all our behalves: 'Ignore the pigs.'

Dominic giggled and told Almeida to not be such a prude. Mervyn changed the topic by again commenting on the craftsmanship of the Junior fort we'd just visited, and Bennie wondered whether we could better enlarge ours by digging a cavern beneath the clump of hard soil around the roots of the poplar. Lukas and I said nothing. Approaching our fort I could not contain an urge to know what was going on amongst the Seniors. I had to see. I circled away from our group and once out of my friends' view ran back towards the big fort. From a distance, I watched for a few moments, wanting to make sure that they were indeed doing what Dominic had seen. I could see the white of arms moving in the dark, an occasional laugh. Harding's voice, muted, saying: 'Hey, not so hard, Mike. Ouch . . .' I walked quietly to the door of the fort. Placed myself at an angle from which I would have to be seen. I stood watching them, my heart pounding. They were each busy with themselves. Raubenheimer, with his back towards me, muttering that he was going to win. It was Harding who saw me and in the same instant lifted his erection and quickly pulled up his pants. They all looked up. Raubenheimer swung around. Pants were drawn up. Faces ashen.

I stared only at Harding and Reyneke, I as speechless as they. Afraid my voice would not come out, would shake. I cleared my throat, not to speak, merely to break the silence, let them know I was not a ghost. I could not have been there for more than four or five seconds, though it felt an eternity, seemed I was seeing them through a haze.

I turned around and started off. Back upstream, my legs weighted down. Mixed with my terror was a sense of exhilarating satisfaction. As well as a blind anger. Let them stew. Let them wonder how much I saw and heard. I was not quite sure of all I'd seen or of exactly what they'd been doing. What would they do to me? Nothing! I've got the bastards by the balls. From behind me came rapid footsteps swashing through the dry leaves. I waited to be struck by a fist in the back, refused to turn around and face my attackers, ready to spew that if they touched me they'd only be in deeper shit. Reyneke was alone: 'Listen, Karl, tell Mathison about me, but don't say anything about Harding, Raubenheimer and Cooke, please. Tell on me, but not on them.' He now walked backwards in front of me. I was terrified, but acted as in control of the situation as I knew how, trying not to meet his gaze. I smirked, shaking my head. I had no intention whatsoever of telling. Wanted them only to know that I knew.

Reyneke grabbed me by the arm and forced me to stand still, facing him.

'Karl. Please be reasonable.' He looked me deep in the eyes, his cheeks flushed. It was to me as though I were really seeing him for the first time. He was no longer the big man who with Harding had been terrorising me for almost two years. He was in front of me, his eyes direct, but not fearful. I wanted to see fear, humiliation. Where were the others, why had they sent Mr Reyneke? I hated Harding more than Reyneke. Harding, the cousin of Mary-Alice and Betty. It must have been a month or two after I arrived. It was pocket-money day and I was with Lukas and Bennie, standing at the fence of the game camp, watching the zebra and eland. Harding and Reyneke, then in Standard Six, arrived with their purchases. Lukas was speaking about the zebra. We were minding our own business. Reyneke was telling Harding that the boo boooh, like the growling of a lion, was coming from the eland bull in the distance. Turning to them I said: 'No, it's from the ostrich, over there, look, you can see its beak and throat, watch, it's puffing.' It was the first time I had spoken to either of the Seniors, and had not thought it a transgression. The next day I was stopped by them on the stoep. Harding, in front of Reyneke, said: 'You're the fairy in the red dress. You ran around the streets of Toti in a red dress. My cousin told me.'

I denied it flat.

Did not dream of saying it had been Harding's auntie's blue chiffon.

But they kept up the story. Once. Twice a term. In front of teachers, my friends, my enemies: 'Tss, tss, De Man. Where's your red dress?'

'Take your hands off me, you disgusting pig,' I now said to Reyneke, pulling loose and starting off. For an instant I thought of asking him, blackmailing him and Harding, to never again mention the dress. But I couldn't, couldn't ever do it. To ask them to keep quiet about it would mean it was somehow true.

'Karl, come on, we were just having some fun.' He spoke from behind me.

'Then why are you afraid?'

'Tell on me, then, if you must tell. Not on the others. And we can just deny it, we're Seniors.'

'I wasn't the only one who saw you.' And with that I walked off, leaving him behind. I was terrified and elated at the power I wielded over them. I wished I'd seen them doing this when I had first arrived at the school. I thought of the night with Buys and Mathison and Cilliers. Did not know why it would have helped had I known about Harding and Reyneke then, but somehow it would have lightened what Buys did to us and the humiliation of Mathison's soliloquy.

The whistle blew and I waited in the pathway for my friends. Almeida was ahead as they cut across Second Rugby Field and I started towards them.

'Karl,' a voice behind me I recognised at once as Bruin.

'What do you want?' I said, trying to move off before anyone saw me hanging around with the class sissy.

'I want you to stop teasing me. Please stop while I'm talking to you.'

'The whistle went, didn't you hear.'

'Why must you always pick on me?'

'I don't always pick on you, Bruin.' As we made our way through the bush. Dominic and the others had spotted me and curved towards where I was emerging from the trees.

'It hurts me when you speak to me like that.'

'Why don't you go tell the others to stop terrorising you? Why come and speak to me?'

'Because you're the worst. I don't mind the others, but it hurts most when you do it.'

I felt uncomfortable and wanted him to stop.

Hastily I promised never to tease him again. Less because I felt guilty, than as an incentive for him to desist from the intimacy, the moment of familiarity I felt he was trying to create.

Two people in one afternoon asking me to refrain from repeating something: one the school's biggest bully boy, who looked like he was shouldering people out of his way, even while he stood still. Who had been at me, out to shame and humiliate and infuriate me at every corner. The other the weediest, drippiest, creature in my class, who whined, and studied himself half to death. Got nineties for everything, whose grades I knew I could eclipse if I worked a tenth of the time he did.

Both wishes would meet my agreement. Reyneke because I merely needed him to lay off me. He, like myself, was leaving in two months' time. He because he was at the end of Standard Seven, I because of my hatred for the place. Two months of peace, at least, I thought. And then Bruin. I rarely teased Bruin again. Not in Malawi a few months later, nor when I indeed did return to the Berg again the following January. I tried to ignore him, mostly. Tolerate him. For each time there was an opportunity – like later when he shat in his blazer pocket – I would see, before my mind's eye, again this afternoon's pleading, the desperation if not of trying to get me on his side then at least of trying to neutralise me. Today, facing the text, I again see the beginnings of a wasps' nest in his ear where he had not properly washed out the klei – something I would have told anyone else of. What I did not know consciously then – though perhaps by not teasing him again it had registered somewhere – was that I never again wanted to hear in another's voice that desperation to please – ever. What I did not wish to recognise, then, and for years to come, were the frightening echoes of my own.

Days later the Natal boys caught the train home for a short break. It was no more than a six-hour trip from Estcourt. I was in a compartment with Harding, and for some reason had ended up sitting on the top bunk beside him. Somewhere along the journey, while my nose was in whatever book I was reading, he leant over to me and whispered: 'I think I'm dying.'

'Why?'

'I'm going stiff.'

I looked back into my book. I ignored his palm crawling up my jean-clad thigh. He began rubbing my crotch. I slowly lowered the book, found his eyes. I shook my head. He withdrew his hand. He sat up. Smiled, and red-faced stared down and out from the window. Neither Harding nor Reyneke ever cast me another glance in the last months they remained in the Berg.

16

We looked at each other's and in Aunt Siobhain's little mirror to see what it looked like when you do a poef and it opens like a brown snake coming out of its hole and then James put the Coke bottle there and you can smell it and it slipped into the Coke bottle and down the glass like chocolate with nuts and then we didn't know what to do so we took the bottle with poef downstairs but Aunt Siobhain was in the passage so we went back up to the second storey with the poef bottle and we didn't want it because it stinks, so we tied it to a string and I went outside and in the passage Aunt Siobhain asked me why I looked as though we're up to something and I said no, I just wanted to go and sit in the garden for a while and then James let the poef bottle out of the window by the string and I took it and untied it and hid it in the bottle-brush that comes from Australia till he came down then we buried it beneath the rubber tree — the rubber tree comes from Brazil — and it was our secret.

17

For the first time since March I remained after what had now become a two-hour-long evening practice. Behind him the maids had begun laying the teachers' dinner tables, hurriedly putting down plates, knives, forks, water jugs. Three hours a day we now faced him from the benches. These two plus one before lunch. By the time we left for Europe the one hour before lunch would probably be up to two. I myself had become engrossed in the music. I could feel myself comfortably go on for another two hours a day, not at all concerned by the regimen that Bennie bemoaned. Not the Mass alone was bringing delight; even well-known pieces we'd sung in previous years of which I was now learning the second soprano. Exploring the music, the nuances of my voice, seeing how our score supplemented that of the firsts and the alto voices, mastering and understanding each transition that initially seemed impossible or once seemed boring or had been taken for granted. Music was now an adventure into genius for me, its discoveries an enigmatic plain of pleasure. That I was singing what had been composed by Ludwig van Beethoven more than a century earlier suddenly mattered to me. I listened with enthusiasm when Dominic and Mervyn spoke about why or if the Mass in D was superior to Bach's B Minor Mass. I paused outside classrooms and music rooms to soak up the music streaming from clarinets, oboes, violins, cellos, flutes. Nichols playing a rondeau on piano by an unknown fifteenth-century composer. Mervy's bow stroking out a sonata by Biber. Lukas struggling with a Corelli that Mervy had performed publicly by the age of nine. I tried to memorise details from our music theory lessons, to copy as little as possible from Dominic, to forget in class that the knowledge was being imparted by Marabou's beak and that Bennie, Lukas and I were her 'most idle students ever'.

Amidst the excitement of mastering the world's most complex mass and of beginning my own private love affair with music, I missed Jacques. When my attention lapsed in a moment he was occupied with the other voices, trepidation came to me. A fear of sorts that I might never again be alone with him. A fear that could not be stilled even by my new-found passion for identifying notes, harmony, patterns, instrumental accompaniment, voice. Almost without knowing it or why, I was now again collecting sheet music, putting away music stands, straightening benches. Deep in conversation with the accompanist, he had none the less noticed me tarry. The bell rang for supper. Still I hovered. At last the accompanist left, and he came closer to me, smiling, asking from across the room how I was.

'I'm fine, and you?' I answered, dropping the Sir I had planned to use as a jab. Standing right in front of me, he said he was fine too, though thoroughly preoccupied with the Mass and the overseas tour arrangements. Only nine weeks away.

'Are you happy with the Agnus Dei?'

'It's sounding magnificent. Absolutely. Even though I'm hard on you boys. What do you think?'

'It's great and we're enjoying it. Long hours and all.'

He believed Durban City Hall would be a formidable perform-ance. A dress rehearsal for Europe. And Europe! The continent was bound to be impressed with the Mass extracts and the school had just received a telephonic enquiry from the Amsterdam Symphony Choir as to whether or not we may want to repeat there.

Is there something different to the way he speaks or looks at me? So clinically enthusiastic. So professional. As if I were just another choirboy. Weeks I had not been with him – and I now wanted him. As secret as my thing with Dominic had to be, at least we could talk, all day, and when he was not rehearsing we could try and be together as frequently as we dared. But with Jacques, I was feeling I was left out in the dark, waiting, wondering when he would call. When he had completed his monologue on what a phenomenon we'd be in Europe, I, trying to sound playful, obscuring my insecurities inside our joke, said softly: 'Haven't been starfishing for quite a while.'

He threw his head back and laughed. Looked around and in a tone instantly serious, said: 'It's dangerous now. And I'm busy as hell, Karl. You should be studying for tests, shouldn't you?'

'I want to come tonight,' I said, now begging with my eyes.

He frowned. Shook his head as he looked at me: 'It's too danger-ous, Karl.'

I wanted to ask why. What had happened that had positioned him at such a distance from me? On the other side of a chasm? But I did not have the courage to engage further with a mind that seemed made up. I felt weak, fearful, as though I had no voice in this relationship. Not even to talk, let alone insist on being allowed into his bed. He was again the conductor.

'I'll let you know, soon, I promise,' he tried to reassure. For an instant I believed him.

'Oookay,' I smiled, hiding my disappointment by pretending to blow up my mouth, act fat-lipped and merely frustrated. The holidays were looming. Then, I wondered, what would happen afterwards? Practice, practice, practice. His preoccupation with the tour and the Durban concert was not going to disappear. It was bound to get worse. What if I didn't get to see him alone before December? And what if not even in London, or Amsterdam?

'It's a promise. I'll see you soon,' he repeated.

I turned to leave the hall.

I began to wonder about him. He'd told me he was from Sabie, about his parents and his brother. But that, and what it said on our programmes of his career as a conductor, was about all I knew of him. What subjects did he do at school? Had he been to the army after university? Did he have a girlfriend? And had he ever had another boy, like me? Had he ever done it to Almeida, as someone had said last year? Would I ask him that? All the questions I never asked in the nights we'd been together. How I now wished we had spoken more. I wished I had asked his favourite colours, his favourite food, his favourite music. Then again, no! Who cared about talking when we could rather do everything we'd done since March. No, I told myself, I don't want to converse with him; I only want to touch him.

Afternoons I still went to the library. He occasionally walked by and then hope would fill the air, only to dissipate as he winked and still did not stop for more than a minute to chat and never to say that I should follow him. I was becoming angry. Thought of writing him

a letter. Began writing, abandoned the idea when nothing looked
right on paper and the whole idea of a letter seemed childish and sentimental. Like something from an Abba song. No, I thought, making
love to the music he conducted would become my substitute for
touching him or communicating in any form. I could act tragic, like
Callas scorned by Onassis who married Jackie Kennedy. Turn life
into a play. But the substitute act failed to relieve. It became almost
unbearable to watch the movement of his hands in front of us.

And doubt arrived.

I wondered whether he'd found someone else. Was another against
his back at night? Was it the way I kissed or did I stink or something?
During breaks I drifted to the parking lot, checking whether his car
was there. What had happened; what had I done wrong? What had I
done to deserve his distance, why had I been cast aside and who, who
in the school had taken my place? I began to reconstruct our every
shared moment and brief conversation of the past nine months, little
pockets of words that could confirm that his current aloofness was
indeed merely a temporary preoccupation, like Dominic's with his
Grade Eight, and not a rejection. After midnight I glided through the
dormitories to check whether all the boys were in their beds. I snuck
to his room and listened at the door. I could not bring myself to leave
the school and visit Uncle Klaas and the Silent One at the fort. That
place I knew would bring no respite before Jacques had taken me
back. I mulled over and chewed on how his withdrawal had begun,
with some unknown fear he said he had, how it had now shifted to an
excuse about the Prime Minister's concert and the overseas tour.
Excuses, each and every one. In choir, while we practised a sequence
of Negro spirituals, he got angry because we were moving around
while singing. He shouted at us to stand still, to not rock like kaffirs
around a camp fire. And who, I slowly began to ask, am I to think
that I was unique! Who else might have keys to that door? Who else
could be doing anything, *anything*, in this place at night? Suddenly I
wanted him to get angry. I imagined he might call me, would need me

to calm him down. I began to think I must do something, to provoke him, so that he'd be compelled to beat me: in that way he'd have to take notice of me. I could test him. He could touch me again.

18

A range of beautiful hills; not mountains! The short winding pass had been tarred, up there where the Peugeot — roofracked and piled high — skidded in the mud as we left. Not mountains. Hills! With its dust road and scattering of huts and patches of crops. Kilted sentinels, aloe candelabra blazed against the green foliage and dark of crags and rocks, breaking the skyline where hills met blue sky. Piccanins and ntombis, cupped hands, calling sweeeeets, sweeeets, getting waves and smiles in return. Already five when we left there for Umfolozi. Donkeys with lopsided ears loitering at the roadside, cattle in the road's centre facing the Alcamino, unconcerned, till we smacked their flanks through open windows and they grudgingly made way for the van to pass. Lena seven. Bernice nine. Less than a decade before and these had been huge mountains shaping a deep dry valley. The Lebombos. Highest point on my horizon. The beginning and end of a world I remembered as my first. Before Tanzania, which had happened before but had left no memories other than those relayed. Beyond the Lebombos lay Mkuzi village in the shadow of Ghost Mountain, the sisal plantations, giants' sheets the cotton fields hung out in the sun, and then the dust road leading up to the tarmac along which Bokkie and I drove to collect the girls from boarding school in Hluhluwe once every two weeks.

And this is green. Greener and denser than it had ever been in my memory. The only vivid and permanent greens I remembered were the lime of fever trees and the deep shiny bottle green of magic guarri around the house. And! The Forest of Figs. That was always green specked with the red and yellow of fruit, and the shafts of sunlight dappling the sandy floor where the blackseed grass stayed green. Other than that I remembered only browns, yellow, ochre, the mustard of dry *Themeda triandra* and the white sand and stone of the roads we drove, the tracks I walked.

Like the mountains and the valley through which we were driving, the game reserve gate, where Bok stopped for us to have a pee before entering, was smaller and less imposing than I remembered. To my one side Stars of Mkuzi — *adenium* — still in full white and crimson bloom and on my other, Bok, who said, yes, they should have finished flowering when the rains came; rarely see them this late, as we shook ourselves, dropped legs of shorts, and returned to the Alcamino which he had left idling. And then we drove in through Mkuzi Gate, Bok and I, back there for the first time in so many years. How will we see animals in the long grass? Can it be, Bok, can it be that so much time has passed and that in all this time we have never been back? Yet, it also felt as though I had never left. As if parts of me had been there all along; parts that now came alive. Something had happened in the chemistry of my brain, was sending signals into the skin, the hair of forearms and the nape of my neck, into the eyes. No, we'd never been back. Not after Umfolozi. Not after St Lucia. Never since being in Amanzimtoti. But how I'd been there! This could not, I imagine, be merely the function of nostalgia: surely the other senses are activated during childhood in ways similar to the conditioning of the head, the ears, the tongue, the nose?

The Alcamino's pick-up was chock a block with the curios we had been purchasing from kraals around the Matubatuba plantations and north, close to the Josini dam. Packed neatly into boxes. Each article wrapped in *Natal Mercury* or *Daily News*. Most of the stock on the back consisted of the new Zulu ethnic pipes which would make or break my father's business. If these didn't make him rich — or at least provide the capital for him to buy en masse for the export market — he was going into insurance: 'It's time to play big,' he said. 'Play ball with big money and the place to do that is the insurance industry.' Without fail, his good looks, his charm and certitude overrode in my mind Bokkie's eternal worries, her silent irritation when to our visitors he gave away as gifts curios that had cost him — us — dearly. 'He'll give away the shirt on his back, and the clothes off our bodies,' she muttered. 'He still doesn't know he's not the fat cat he was in Tanganyika.' And so I was letting concern go, had decided to enjoy this break, even as I anticipated that within these two days he would tell me that I would not be returning to the Berg the following year. That there was no money. I am not going to think about that now, I told myself, I have no need to immerse myself in that other life of mine when I'm here. In paradise. Anyway, I would find a way to go back. I would not leave Jacques and Dominic. The past ten months had been the happiest of my time at the school. And Jacques would come around. He would, I knew, let go the groundless fear that someone may find out. And here: Bok and I had two days together before he took me back to the Berg.

This, then, was the gift they were giving me for my fourteenth birthday. Nothing I could have imagined could have felt as right as this. Who cared about the silly European tour! About a bad school report!

Two days earlier I had taken *The Brothers Karamazov* to the bird sanctuary. The place no longer held the attraction it once had. It looked smaller and was better tended: less like the bush, and more like the neighbourhood park it indeed was. The area around the top of the lake, where Lena and I once fished in secret, was gone. Cleared and transformed into lawn with benches and walkways. There were still the ducks, the peacocks, the rabbits and the tortoises. Before the birds and the tortoises seemed to provide for me some link to the very bush where I now was with Bok. But in the bird sanctuary I was seeing the creatures only as unhappy prisoners: sad, in poor condition, trapped between fences. I returned home without having read more than ten pages of the novel. I changed into my Speedo and for a while scooped leaves off the surface of the pool, watching the shadows dance on the bottom. I fetched my drawing pad and sat sketching, in between working on Dominic's orange poem. At hearing the postman open our golfball postbox I ran to meet him. Tearing open the envelope I knew contained the dreaded report, I saw at once the letter the school had included. Heart racing – what could it be – fear dissolved into anger and disappointment as my brain took it in:

10 October 1976

Dear Parents and Boys,

Due to pressure from Europe it seems likely that the International Choir's planned December tour will be cancelled. It has been brought to our attention that a series of protests and demonstrations are in the planning at a number of the venues where the boys are scheduled to perform. While we continue in dialogue with our European hosts in an attempt to resolve certain questions, it is of paramount importance that the safety of our boys be placed first. We trust that you will understand and support the school's governing body in whatever decision is ultimately taken.

Sincerely,
Royce Mathison,
Headmaster and Chairman of the Board.

My heart sank. This was not possible. How on earth, how, how, how could this be happening? What had I ever, ever done to deserve this? Bernice: behind the closed door of her room, studying for exams. Bok: in Durban, business. Bokkie: working in the church garden. Lena: at school. I went to the phone. Would have done anything to speak to Jacques, hear from him whether it was true. I called Dominic, in Saxonwold. He was out and I left a message with Prudence, the maid, asking that he call me, urgently. An hour later he called: yes, he hadn't yet received his report or the letter but Mathison had called his father last night and told them the whole story. It doesn't sound good. The tour was in all probability off and Dr Webster said it was almost certainly because of the black children being shot in Soweto and other locations all over the country. What does that have to do with our tour, I asked. How can Europe host a bunch of all-white children while hundreds of all-black children are being shot and held in prisons, Dom answered. Dr Webster said that South Africa may as well wipe international contact off its stomach until we learnt to respect black life. He and Mrs Webster were ready to emigrate. Perhaps go to Canada or Australia, but Dominic said he couldn't see that happening. Just another idle threat his father had been making ever since Dominic could remember. I wanted to scream at Dominic that I wanted to go overseas, that I didn't care about black kids who sabotage their schools being shot or stupid rich Dr Webster wanting to go and live in Timbuktu! I asked how piano was going. And so we let overseas go, spoke about other things.

And this, this — scent of dust road and grass through open windows, the silver-green leaves of marulas in pink-white bud, the kaffir trees' leafless stems, grey bark and red feathers against the blue sky — felt as though I was home. If I emigrate, I will come here, I smiled contentedly to myself. I will emigrate or immigrate home, whichever is the apt term. I was ready to forgive Bok everything. I had not thought of the Berg much since I'd heard we were coming. The blow of the European tour possibly cancelled, had lighted, lifted. When Bok suggested I come on his stock-buying trip I had at first cringed but said nothing of wanting rather to stay home with Bokkie and the girls. My anger at Bok had not subsided, and his invitation to accompany him to Zululand was clearly a sort of pay-off for the selling of my trophies. Then, perhaps sensing my reluctance, they had given me the incentive: your birthday gift a trip to Mkuzi and Mfolozi. Just you and Bok. Two days. Two nights. Yes, who cares if the overseas trip goes down the drain, now!

A yellow-billed hornbill sat almost in the middle of the road, digging with its beak into a heap of dry rhino dung. Bok slowly edged around the bird. I leant across him to get a better view from the driver's window. The beady yellow eyes rolled at us, head lilting from side to side, curious, tame, its legs as if covered in long johns hidden in the dung. Bok, his breath smoky in my nose, asked if I could remember the Latin without *Roberts*. Only the *nasutus* part, I answered, which I remember from nasal. Check it in *Roberts*. No. It's the grey hornbill: *Tockus nasutus*. This one is *flavirostris*.

'Remember the hiding you gave me in Umfolozi, for feeding the hornbills?' I asked, again lifting myself over him.

'And for lying about it.' Our laughter, startling the bird.

'I was scared of you. That's why I lied.'

'Didn't stop you from feeding the birds. And don't think you're too old to stop being scared of me.'

'I'm almost as tall as you, Bok. Soon I'll be able to give you a taai klap.'

'Don't get too big for your boots, my boy,' lightly punching my buttock, and we again laughed as I rubbed the spot in mock agony.

Then we saw who remembered: distribution. I checked it in *Roberts*. Status. Both right. Habitat. Both right. Habits. Food. Breeding. Female lays eggs inside hole in tree stump, male sits on eggs and seals himself in, leaving only slit for feeding from female. Male on eggs for twenty-four days – I said twenty-one – before they hatch, he stays another twenty to twenty-two days after eggs start hatching and then he leaves and I said *he* reseals the entrance but Bok said no the chicks reseal from the inside and then male and female together feed the chicks. We checked it in *Roberts*. Bok was right: chicks seal themselves back in. 'This drawing has more pink beneath the throat than it should.' I said, looking from the page at the bird on the dung. It was still eyeing us. Back in the book my eyes glimpsed the lilac-breasted roller. Troupand, in Afrikaans, a name I had never understood. We sat for ten minutes, taking in the hornbill. We drove on, slowly, ten kilometres an hour, our eyes scanning the insides of the bush, the veld. Again it was as if I'd never been away. A giraffe's head above the thorn trees! And quickly we saw them all around us, both sides of the road. Fifteen over a stretch of two hundred square metres. He turned off the ignition. We sat in silence. Watched their lips move, strained to hear the sounds of their crunching.

'Eleven,' he said softly, almost to himself, but also for me to hear, 'we had only eleven giraffe when we were here.' His eyes were slit against the glare on his glasses. Memory, thought, concentration, awe, tenderness, nostalgia, in the lines around his eyes reaching to the spread of grey in his temples. It was in this moment, there, in this way – even with the gold-rimmed glasses that came after the rinkhals spat in his eyes, with the salt and pepper of his temples where before it was dark brown like chocolate – that I remembered him and us together: in his Land Rover or on Vonk's back, his one hand holding the reins, the other arm pressing my back to his stomach. Nothing that had since happened mattered there. Other than being there, being able to see where we spent those years which were the happiest time I'd had on earth. The beautiful genesis of memory.

At HQ we went in to speak to the camp warden about allowing us to visit Mbanyana. When he and Bok saw each other it was like brothers embracing after a decade-long separation. Hugo Reynolds. He remembers Bok and Dademan from when he was at Fanie's Island and Dademan at Charters. They shake hands again and laugh and reminisce about the old times. When Reynolds hears we're going up to Umfolozi tomorrow he grins: 'Do you know who's chief warden at Mpila?'

'No idea,' Bok answers.

'Willy Hancox,' and Bok says, well, Willy's done well for such a lousy shot and they speak about the culling of '67, or '66, no, no it was '67. Bok tells Mr Reynolds about his business. They talk through the old guard: Ian Player now running the Wilderness Leadership School. Mumdeman at Midmar but retiring and probably remarrying! James White, cancer at only forty-four. Helena, his wife, also leaving the Board now. No, our reed house, Mbanyana, has been demolished.

But he'd love to take us out. Bok says no, we can go alone. Mr Reynolds asks Bok whether he's sure, because there are quite a few leopard now, and lion, that come and go.

'Hell, Hugo. I still know this bush like the back of my hand.'

'There's no road to the house any more. Will you find it?'

Bok says he'd bet his life and Mr Reynolds says it's fine if we go alone but he would feel better if Bok took a rifle, just for in case: 'Not because I'm concerned for you, Ralph,' he teases, 'lions don't like old sinewy meat, but it's your son I'm worried about.' Bok takes the rifle and slips a few rounds into his safari suit pocket, thanks Mr Reynolds, who says Bok should come and *chew some fat* again once we get back from the Mbanyana site. 'There's nothing much left there, Ralph. It was levelled about six years ago. Just parts of the floor, I think.'

'No problem,' Bok answers, 'I just want to show this Philistine where he grew up.' At which Mr Reynolds winks at me.

If I remember correctly we do not go to the rondavel to drop off our things.

On the tourist map we're given at reception I see rivers and the Msumu pan. I have no recollection of the pan, I tell Bok. And he says that's quite conceivable, for while it was always there, it often had no water while we lived here. I say that I had somehow thought the dry stretches close to the Forest of Figs were part of the Sand Forest. Now, the map shows me the Sand Forest is way up here, close to the camp. Then I do recall huge surfaces of silver water, surrounded by reeds, with crocodile and hippo and herons. But these I thought were taken from St Lucia, Charters Creek. Maybe I do remember the pan, after all. He drives by Bube and Masinga, saying we'll stop here on the way back to camp.

He parks the van by the roadside about a kilometre above the Fig Forest. I am relieved that we have the rifle; don't know why. I have no sense that we're walking in the right direction. Through grass and bush, no footpath even. And then we're surrounded by enormous bushes of magic guarri, and Bok says, here we are, and at first I think he's wrong, but then there's the sisal that Bokkie planted – the only exotics, how they've expanded – and the tambotie trees, Bokkie's rockery overgrown. And pieces of the house's floor, big slabs of cement, cracked and overgrown with duwweltjies and creepers. The grass is tall, up to my waist, and I say it was never this green and he says no, it wasn't. He takes me to where the water tank was; over to where the stables were, so much closer to the house than I remember. Here the road came in, you can just make out that the shrubs are a little shorter than those around. Impala and duiker spoor everywhere. The bush takes back its own very quickly. And this is where you shot Vonk, here, close to the road where he slipped and broke his leg, and here is where we put up the tent for when we had visitors, and the little vlei, I ask, where Jonas and Boy lived? Vlei, he asks. Yes, I remember pink lilies and a small marsh. And he says no. I'm wrong. We walk deeper into the bush, no more than a hundred metres, and again I'm agog at how close they were. A loud shouting distance, really. No vlei. But I remember the pink lilies, here, somewhere.

Back to the broken slabs of cement. We stand around, he sits down on an anthill and lights a cigarette. I go into the shade of the tambotie trees and scratch in the grass, looking for jumping beans. Nothing but birds; cicadas – when I was very small I thought it was the magic guarri screaming.

'Do you realise what a privilege it was, growing up here? And Umfolozi. St Lucia?'

'I do, Bok. I think I was the luckiest child in the world.'

'You think of it often, don't you?'

'All the time . . .'

He calls me from my scratching beneath the tambotie. Tells me to come and sit with him. I sit in the long grass, holding the beans in my fist, waiting for them to begin their movement.

A silence, then he clears his throat, and for a moment I fear what he might say. Some ambush. A flash of him coming to stand by me at the pool; puking in Lake Malawi. Instead he asks me when, under what circumstances do I think about the bush. I say whenever things are tough, when I begin to feel unhappy. I do not say, *Roses on raindrops and bows on white kittens, showers that drip in my eyes and my mittens.*

'And you, Bok. Do you think about it?'

He says he does, but we're living a new life, a different life. We have to accept that this is over, just as we have to accept that Tanzania can never be rewon. We have so much now, he says, and I'm getting a good education. He lights another cigarette. We sit quietly, the smoke reaching my nostrils, making them twitch. 'You're also very privileged to be in the Berg. You've lived in some of the most beautiful places in this country,' he says as in my palms the beans begin to throb. I say it's true.

And my mind drifts.

To the muddy lot where Jacques's bay was empty when Bokkie arrived to fetch me a week before. Though relieved to leave before the school ran empty, I'd been hoping to say goodbye to him. From the moments of a farewell I might have learnt something of what was going on in his mind, of why I was still being kept at arm's length. Still there had been no occasion for me to get close to him alone. Forget about visiting the room I have grown so fond of.

'Look after your voices during the break,' at the end of choir the last night and with that he turned to leave the hall, even before we descended the benches. 'Have a nice holiday, Sir. *Hou lekker vakansie, Meneer,*' called after him as he waved and disappeared. And so, over the next morning's happy scene of hellos in which Dominic and Lukas joined me to greet Bokkie was spun an invisible film of sadness. Over the delight and pleasure of my mother's presence and at the prospect of the holidays ahead lay the uncertainty of where he and I were heading. Of course, I realised too that we had never really known where we were going, but the fact that we had had our rhythm, our way of seeing each other once, sometimes twice a week, was enough for me. How I enjoyed those nights. And maybe, after all, that was our only destination: the pleasure of those nights. But while that system lasted, it felt as though we knew — or I at least knew — that it would always stay that way. If it has all ended, I told myself, then he could at least inform me of the change. This is what makes the thing with Dominic different: that he tells me where he's at, and I can speak to him about anything. Almost anything. Some day I'll tell him about Jacques. Not now. Because I promised Jacques I wouldn't. Though I'm almost sure Dominic won't mind. He'd only wish he could come along, join us. Imagine that, the three of us together!

Carrying my suitcase, accompanied by Dominic and Lukas, we took my mother to see our drawings and paintings Ma'am had stuck up with pins in the back of our classroom. Bokkie asked how Ma'am was doing. We said she'd be back after the break. Spoke about how frail she had looked at the funeral. How we'd been giving the substitute teacher Mr Loveday a hard time. Against the back wall's large bulletin board, amongst posters advertising concerts, projects on Geography, History and Science, was our art. Mine: a pencil titled: *Erm-Lilies at Sterkspruit*; another of a conductor's chest, his hands held at the ready, *Untitled*; and another, *V Forest*. Dominic's: two pastels, one titled *Pedal*, showing a detail of three piano pedals, and another, *Pillars*, showing the front of the school from the quad. Bokkie said she could see how we had improved since last Parents' Weekend.

'You don't do Art, Lukas?'

'Nee, Tannie. Accountancy and German. Dominic's with me in Accountancy.'

We walked on to the car and Bokkie noted that the cypress in the quad had not sprouted leaves. Its smooth bark, glistening on bare branches enveloped by the tangles of red and yellow roses drooping from the night's thundershower. We crossed onto the wet lawn and smelt the huge open flowers, our faces coming away covered in drops and yellow pollen as Bokkie said she wished she could get roses to grow like this in Durban.

'What's wrong with your eyes, Karl?' she suddenly noticed as we wiped our noses. 'They're bloodshot. Have you got pink-eye or something?'

My eyes were examined.

'They're not sore or anything,' I said.

She looked at the other two and said only my eyes were red. No one else's. Maybe I just didn't sleep well. Or! Have I been reading secretly by torchlight, again? No. I said, truthfully, because I hadn't, hardly, for almost nine months now.

'Lukas!' she exclaimed in surprise as her eyes swept down him from head to toe: 'Why does it look as if your jeans are frightened of your shoes? And you, Dominic, look at yours!' They smiled, bashful at her observations of their bodies' change. Then her eyes were on me: 'And, Karl, look at the distance between your hands and the sleeves of that jersey. You're starting to look like a scarecrow, my child.' Laughter, before she added, 'I can't believe how you boys have grown.'

'Lukas isn't even in choir, anymore, Bokkie. His voice is breaking. He's a big man now.' At which Lukas threw a playful punch at my belly.

'You told Bok on the phone, Karl. So you're not going overseas, Lukas?'

'No, Tannie. Though maybe they'll take me as a bench boy.'

'Where's Mr De Man, Mrs De Man?' Dominic asked. I watched Bokkie in her green tracksuit with white takkies. She said Bok was in the Eastern Transvaal, buying stock. Her hair had been curled and it was cut short against her head. Her straight long brown hair was gone, and so also the ponytail that swung down her back. And with it any resemblance I had wanted her to have with Georgia O'Keeffe. Little golden earrings bobbed from her ears and her pink lips had obviously just been painted in the Chevrolet's rear-view mirror.

'How are you getting home, Dominic?'

'Mervyn's dad's flying in with the Cessna this afternoon, Mrs De Man. So I'm flying up with them and Mum will collect me from Pretoria.'

'I don't know how you can stand flying in those small planes! I had to go in one once and I said never again.'

'It's fun, Mrs De Man! Flying's the safest form of transport.'

'Oe, no, Dominic! Not in those little things.'

'En jy, Lukas, hoe kom jy by die huis?'

'My mum will probably be here any minute, Tannie. She left Indwe at the crack of dawn and we're driving back the moment she gets here.'

The sun was breaking through the clouds.

'Long drive,' Bokkie smiled. 'Say hello to your parents for me, hey? And you people must drive safely, these roads are like soap. There's the sun now, hopefully dry the world out a bit.'

Dominic followed me to the boot. Lukas stayed at the front with Bokkie, who settled into the driver's seat.

'I'll phone you over the holidays,' he said. His hand resting against mine.

'Please do. As often as you can. But call during the day, so we can speak properly.'

'When I'm not practising.'

I pulled a face at him.

'Thanks for coming last night,' he said, adding that he'd miss me. I smiled. 'Are you going to write?' he asked, and I, misunderstanding the question, answered that a letter to him wouldn't get to Jo'burg before we are already back at school. 'Not a letter, silly. Are you going to write short stories or poems? That fucken orange poem you still haven't given me.'

'Maybe. Depends.' I said, closing the boot and moving to the passenger side.

'Lóelovise yokou.'

'Loelovise yokou titoo.'

'You still owe me the one on oranges.'

'Okay, Dom. Will you phone, though?'

'I promise.'

Bokkie had started the car. She leant across me and smiling told

Dominic to tell Mr Clemence-Gordon to fly the plane safely. Through the windscreen I waved at Lukas. We drove off. I turned back. The two of them were still standing in the parking lot. Bokkie stuck her arm from the window and waved. They waved. Then we were gone. The gravel road to Winterton had been turned a slip-slide along which Bokkie steered the Chevrolet carefully. Mud battered the undercarriage. An occasional car with muddy registration plates signalling towns all over the country crawled towards us, some waving as they passed. Within ten minutes, and in response to my questions, I had been given an overview of the family. Bernice: studying like never before as her matric exams are starting in three weeks' time. She no longer goes to school and is at home every day, studying. She and Robert don't see much of each other at the moment because of the pending exams. He really is a sorted-out young man, solid job as supervisor at Illovo Sugar Mill, earns three hundred rand a month, and Bernice has been accepted to SAA as an air hostess – she could *start* at three hundred rand – conditional on her passing matric and loosing seven kilograms. Lena: struggling at school but trying her best as usual. Bokkie is grateful that the sport seasons are virtually over so Lena doesn't have to come home by train to Toti when it's almost dark. Alette? Hasn't been around but Lena and Juffrou Sang at church say she's well and just deeply involved in preparing for a big music exam. Grade Five, I said. Dominee and Mevrou Dominee: just back from another very successful trip of Israel with wealthy members of the congregation and they put on a slide show last week, with Mevrou Dominee – who is so well travelled and knowledgeable – doing an informative and moving narrative about Jerusalem, the birthplace of Jesus, and the continued suffering of the poor Jews under the godless Arabs. The church garden: looking more beautiful than ever, and Bokkie gets compliments from all around and the *South Coast Sun* ran an article and some photographs but of course one never gets a good idea of a garden from black and white photographs in a newspaper. Oupa and Ouma Liebenberg: well, though Ouma fell and hurt her hip but luckily it wasn't broken. Ouma repeats herself, over and over. They are getting old now and Bokkie doesn't know what the worries about Aunt Lena and Uncle Joe — who are the same as always — must be doing to those two old people who have tasted nothing but suffering their entire lives. Two kaffirs broke into their house in Klerksdorp. Stole the radio and the electrical blankets Aunt Lena specially bought for them. Oupa has become an electrician in Klerksdorp, when will those two old people settle down, they're meant to be retiring, but there's no money for retirement. While the rich Joe Mackenzie goes out night after night to the farm and spends it with that little fifteen-year-old bitch Matilda. While Aunt Lena and the Brats stay at home with the revolver on the bedside table because of all the black school unrest in the Transvaal. And Lever Brothers was burgled last week. One doesn't know what's becoming of this country. Joe Mackenzie is the crazy one, not Aunt Lena. Any man who goes around with a fifteen-year-old must be crazy. Aunt Siobhain and Uncle Michael: fine and Uncle Michael is starting another fish and chips shop down at the Toti station, he's doing very, very well, that man can work himself half to death, but they're picking the rewards and they're about to build an extension to the house. James: doing fine and when he finishes school wants to be an interior decorator, he has recently begun painting eggs, with all kinds of motifs, then varnished. Bok gives James ostrich eggs and he paints these with Zulu motifs and these are sold as traditional African Art. He painted his room with a dark blue wall with a motif across it. 'Very with it! You know,' she said, rolling her eyes. And over her dead body would her children paint their walls. Walls are meant to be white. And Aunt Siobhain has bought one of these fridges that gives you water through the door and James flounces around with a glass to show off the gadget and says: 'I only use one hand.' Hulle sal hulle ook wat verbeel! Stephanie: moved from Woolworths to repping for Kentucky Fried Chicken. Calls herself a PRO for KFC! Earns three hundred and fifty rand a month. Mind you, sold everything to go to London on a

sudden trip, but she'll be back in a week's time. Stephanie thinks
she's getting too good for the family and goes from boyfriend to
boyfriend. How Bokkie wishes Bernice would not share a flat with
Stephanie next year. No morals. Bokkie's cousin Coen and his girlfriend Mandy: have built a yacht to sail around the world. Now those
two have their heads screwed on right, not much money, but no children and no responsibilities and they're going to see the world. That's
what I wish for my children, Bokkie said, that you kids will get an
education and see the world. Not saddle yourselves with marriage —
let's cross our fingers that Bernice doesn't lose her head and just
marry Robert — there's no reason you kids shouldn't just live with
your boyfriends and girlfriends. She's getting sick and tired of the
conservative Afrikaners in Toti. Going to that Dutch Reformed
Church is like going to a weekly fashion parade. Bok: curios are not
doing so well and he might go into insurance with Old Mutual and
we might have to sell the house because Bok must now repay Oupa
Liebenberg the money he borrowed and we may move to a flat in
Durban which means Judy — at which point my mind spun, my ears
rang and I no longer heard what she was saying. I don't want to think
about going to a flat. Not another flat. I tried to clear my mind of my
father. Glance at him, now, sitting here beside me on the anthill,
lighting his third Paul Revere in less than ten minutes. Both of us
quiet, each deep in our own thoughts.

While Bokkie spoke, steering the car with both hands on the
wheel, gearing down around each bend, I briefly entertained the
thought of asking about Uncle Klaas, whether there'd been any news
of him. What if I told her that he was back there, just behind us? Or
if I were to tell her that she should turn the car around because there
was someone down at the drift who wanted to see her.

'Will you and he be here when I come back, Uncle Klaas?' For two
weeks — since the night of the dagga — I hadn't been down to them.
Only their day smell in the fort told me they were still there. Then,
the night before Bokkie came, I went. To my question of whether they

were staying, Uncle Klaas grinned and said he didn't know where they'd be. They move as the whim takes them. At once I had again found his vagueness — so deliberate — appalling. I had not come down there looking for more vagueness. Tell me something certain, give me some advice, I wanted to hiss. Why had I gone, looking for what? All I ever found there was aloofness, distance, the rhetoric of his madness. Nothing of the intimacy I needed and simultaneously dreaded getting from the old tramp.

He again gave me some of their zol. I tried to blow smoke rings. Bok blowing smoke rings at Mkuzi, through which we tried to stick our fingers before they dissolved. After a while I felt calm and wonderful. This can be the zol, I thought, but still no hallucinations. I said a cheerful goodbye. He said goodbye, without sentiment, and for the first time the Silent One smiled at me: an enormous grin without more than three teeth in his top gums. I rinsed my mouth in the river. Broke poplar leaves in my palms and walked back across the rugby field as the lightning started and almost at once thunder rolled down from Cathkin Peak and resounded from hill to hill. I have indeed grown fond of him, I smiled to myself, slowing my gait as I began the climb, hoping then that the rain would catch me. I enjoy his company, he is clever, he has read more books than both sides of my family put together. Dostoyevsky, he says. You must read Dostoyevsky. And in Toti I had gone to the library and found *The Brothers Karamazov*. The old librarian, there since we first came to Toti, big-eyed and full of praise at how 'mature your framework of reference has become, Karl'. Uncle Klaas is a genius: a fact that the madness cannot erase. But is he really mad? Yes. No. He seems to know who he is. I trust him. If they are gone when I come back, I wondered, will I continue to go down there in the midnight hours when sleep refuses to take me? Will Jacques ask for me to return this key? And so, for in case he does, I have had another cut in Toti. I'll-cut-a-key-in-Toti, cut-a-key-in-toti, I hummed to myself and laughed out loud as I walked to the school, lingering along the way, waiting for the rain. I assured myself it would not make a difference if Uncle Klaas and the Silent One were gone when I return. While much of the attraction for going to the fort at night will leave with them, I will still go, just for fun, and when I get back it will be warm enough to swim. Midnight swims. Maybe tell Dom and Lukas. Uncle Klaas seemed to me as I neared the school – despite everything the family had said over the years – normal, civilised and clever. As I got into the music-room window the first huge drops struck my head and the shoulders of my dressing gown. Past Jacques's room, ignoring the urge to knock. I will not go begging to that man. I'll ignore you, give you a taste of your own medicine. Bloody homosexual. Through the library, through C, towards F, then, instead of going to my bed, on a whim I slipped into G.

'You're wet and you smell of smoke, Karl,' Dominic mumbled, still waking.

'Shhh . . . You're dreaming,' I whispered, and kissed him, taking in the musky smell of his breath, the mustiness of his sleepy skin. 'I'm not Karl. You're Butch and I'm Sundance.'

Bok amidst the sounds of doves in late morning. His eyes rove from the magic guarri to the patch of seedless *themeda* and young thorn trees where Mbanyana's reed house once stood. The rifle is propped against his knee. What, I wonder, is going through his mind? A hundred thoughts of everything he did here. I am seeing him in his khaki uniform, the green epaulettes on his shoulders: *Natal Parks Board*. On Vonk's back with Jonas beside him on Ganaganda. Jonas, holding me by the shoulders, his hand over my mouth as the black mamba rises in the footpath in front of me. On a whim I tell Bok the story: Jonas and I were returning from the Forest of Figs, alone, because Chaka and Suz always frightened the birds. I was in front of Jonas, walking across a short cut where there was no path. Suddenly the snake was up, right in front of me, its head above mine, its eyes seething. I tried to scream and turn but found myself stunned, unable to move. Within seconds the snake sank down and rippled away into the shrubbery. I stood stock still for what seemed an hour. Only then when I again tried to move did I realise I had not frozen: Jonas's one hand was like a clamp around the back of my neck, the other over my mouth. And when he let me go I was shaking, weeping, clinging to his legs. He picked me up and carried me screaming half the way home, all the time patting my back with his open hands, soothing me with words I didn't understand, the tone of which meant I was safe. 'And then,' I tell Bok who has turned around to face me, 'when we were near here, and I was again walking next to him, I asked him not to tell you or Bokkie about the mamba.'

'Why?' Bok asks. 'What a stupid thing to do. You could have both been killed.'

'I was afraid I wouldn't be allowed back down to the forest.'

'You know he probably saved your life? That's why he grabbed you. To silence you.'

'I know.' We sit quietly. Bok says what a good kaffir Jonas was. One of the best game guards the Parks Board ever had.

'And there was another time,' I say, now enjoying seeing Bok's surprise, 'in the krans beneath the office at Umfolozi. Lena and I were down there with Suz or Chaka, I can't remember which.'

'You weren't supposed to be there, you know that.'

'We never went back, Bok. But before that Lena and I even took Stephanie and James down there.'

'What happened?'

'We were playing under the overhang and then I saw Lena in front of me, like she'd turned to stone. I looked up and there, on the cliff above us, was a leopard, looking down on us. Lena grabbed the dog by the collar and just whispered, "Kom," and we walked up the foot-path, both of us too afraid to look back, afraid of what was behind us, could be coming at our backs any moment. When we got to the road we ran home, with me already telling her from behind not to tell you and Bokkie, because I might be locked up in the yard for the rest of my life.'

Bok sits shaking his head, a smile around his lips. 'The things you kids got up to. Damn right you would have been kept in the yard. What else?' And I tell him that was all, the only times we were in danger, other than the time the eland chased us, but that he already knows about. And I say at least I never threw bees into a toilet where an old woman was relieving herself and Bok laughs and says that's only because there are no more long drops around. He rises, lifts the rifle wordlessly, and still smiling inclines his head towards the road. I follow, slipping the tambotie seeds into my shorts pocket. I can plant these in Toti some time, see if they grow. Maybe Bokkie wants to try some in the church garden. And I must show them to Dom. I walk behind Bok to the van, following his swishing through the grass, neither of us looking back. Of my life, I realise, my father knows nothing. As little as I of his.

As we drive back to HQ to return the rifle, we register what's around us, the impala – remember how we had to cull thousands – the nyala that Bok says have chased away the abundant bushbuck because they had to share from the same height of shrubs.

I wait in the van while he walks into HQ to return the rifle.

At the Loskop road Bokkie slowed down the car even further, slipped into second gear and carefully took a left turn towards the Therons' farm to stop in and say a quick hello to Auntie Babs and Uncle Gerrie. I thought of Jacques. Told Bokkie about my knee, that it had healed perfectly. Pulled up the jeans leg and exhibited the scar. We wound our way along the slippery road through pine plantations and through fields of young mielies until reaching the sign 'Rust en Vrede – Gerrie en Babsie Theron'. The mud still smacked against the car's belly, down the oak lane leading up to the lawn and the house. The farmhouse was shaded by huge jacarandas now in full purple bloom. Wet blossoms popped as the tyres pressed them into the lawn. The magnolias and seringas too were covered in flowers. Monet, I think, would have found things there to paint. 'Must have heard the car,' Bokkie smiled and waved as Auntie Babs came out onto the veranda even before we'd parked the car.

'Welkom, welkom julle,' she called and announced that she had fresh scones and tea ready in the kitchen.

'Good rain, you've had, Babsie!' Bokkie said. 'Gerrie must be happy for the crops.'

'It's going to be a good season for mielies,' Auntie Babs answered from the stoep. 'Gerrie is just out now, checking on the tractors. They get stuck all the time with rain like this. I've sent a girl to go and say you've arrived. He wants to say hello. How are the roads from Winterton?'

'Very slippery, but not as bad as I've seen it before. Ooh, *Herder*, but your garden is looking lovely, Babsie.' Bokkie glowed as Auntie Babs offered us seats on the veranda.

'It's the rains, Katie. And you, Karl? *Mense* but you've grown tall! You're going to be the size of your Great-Grandfather Mostert. He was the tallest man in East Africa, we always joked that he had Maasai in him.'

I smiled, uncomfortable, proud. Bokkie said that I was sure to be taller than Bok, who was six foot one. And Auntie Babs said she couldn't keep up buying new clothes for her youngest children and thank goodness they stopped growing around eighteen when they went to university.

'And how are things at school, Karl? Looking forward to the holiday, I'm sure?'

'Ja, Auntie Babs, very much.'

'And there's the overseas trip. I saw Miss Roos in Estcourt last week and she says the International Choir is the best ever.'

'One would hope so, with three hours a day in rehearsal. Hey, Karl?' Bokkie said, before I could answer.

'You and Ralph must be proud of him, Katie?'

'Proud and waiting to see this term's report!'

'And next year it's Standard Seven?'

'Yes, Auntie Babs.'

'How time flies! It seems only yesterday you were here for the audition.'

'That's three years ago, Auntie Babs.'

'Frightening how time flies, hey, Babsie?'

'Amazing. Are you staying next year?'

'I think so, Auntie Babs.'

A maid came onto the veranda bearing a tray with four china tea cups, a white teapot covered in a down cosy. On the one side of the tray was a silver plate filled with scones and a small glass container of strawberry jam, another of fluffy cream. I watched Auntie Babs — sophistication, grace and patience, my mother's self-confessed ideal woman — as she poured tea for us and asked us to help ourselves to the scones.

Their talk centred around their children. Auntie Babs's two sons and two daughters. One already at university in Bloemfontein, the pretty daughters, all planning to go there. Bernice's plans for next year with SAA — she loves working with people, Babsie, you know. Lena's sport, she wants to go to the Military Academy at George. And about what's happening to whom of the old guard from East Africa. Bokkie, about Mumdeman, retiring from the Parks Board and might marry a rich Englishman — a Mr Shaw — and about Uncle Michael and Aunt Siobhain. Stephanie who's overseas and James. Sanna Koerant, so Auntie Babs said and Bokkie confirmed she'd heard, has not recovered from the terrible stroke in June and no one knows how long she'll live — looks like she's got Parkinson's disease. Shakes and trembles and sputters that the end is nigh. 'You know what I mean, Katie, still the old Oljorro Sanna?'

'Santa Sana!' And we all laughed.

'Same old skinnerbek until she breathes her last breath.'

And I thought of Mumdeman once when I was nine, when I told her how Bokkie wept when Bok stayed out drinking with tourists; Mumdeman told me to never *shit my own nest*, like Sanna Koerant:

'Always telling everyone what was going on in her bedroom and in her life. Every fight, every disagreement, every little detail of her life.' Ouma said, 'Everyone in East Africa from Mombasa to Nairobi knew what was going on in Sanna Koerant's life. Now that's shitting your own nest, Karl. What goes on in your own bedroom is private. That's why we call those things private parts. Never shit your own nest.'

'Yes, Ouma.' But now I wonder if they are so private why is everyone so concerned about them. Why were we beaten for what we did with our private parts if they're so private? Why did Mathison ask me to report to him about other boys if those are private parts? Why were Harding and Reyneke so afraid of me telling, if those are private parts? Why must I sneak to Dominic and Jacques at night? Why does Dominee Steytler preach Sunday after Sunday about the sins of the flesh? No, they're not private, Ouma, as much as we keep them covered, our private parts are more public then our faces. Our private parts are the most public parts of our bodies.

And I tried not to hear Bokkie as she told Auntie Babs all was going well with Bok's business. Tried to block out the overconfident tone in which the complicated rationale for him now thinking of going into insurance was presented. While they spoke, I savoured my scone, each bite from the fork, my eyes in every bed and tree of the incredible garden. Everything was dripping, leaves dripping, branches dripping, the roof dripping: tick, tick, blob, blup, tock, bip, bip, ts, ts, ts, tick, blop, blop-blop, tick, tsss from rain gutters: watertunes as the sun again wanted to break through and shine. Cups of white magnolia drooped after the rain, as did the roses, heavy and overturned with drops perched like balls of quicksilver on the petals. Seringas' scent clung to every breath. Dahlias too, shy, their heads bent down, away from last night's showers. Azalias and rhodedendrums, all bright but spent. Part of Aunt Babsie's garden's beauty was that it seemed to go on forever, even though I knew from Parents' Weekends that it ended after about an acre, against the cultivated fields of mielies and kaffircorn. The sun broke through the dark clouds. At once bright shafts of light fell against the mountains from which the mist was lifting. Then, for a minute a few drops again fell from the sky – drowning the drip-drip – even as the sun broke more cloud. Jackal marries wolf's wife. The lawn was like wet green lucerne and purple velvet where the jacaranda blossoms had been knocked by the torrent. The sun shone, the clouds dissipated, and within no more than the time it takes to drink a cup of tea, eat both halves of a scone, the garden's tempo of dripping had changed to something slower, quieter, as if pausing; waiting for the bluster of birds and beetles, the breath of bees and butterflies. The mist had lifted from the mountains and I was struck by how the shapes of Champagne Castle and Cathedral Peak had altered from the angle at which I was seated. The two mountains, together, no longer looked like one flat bastion of rock. From the Therons' stoep they were separate from the surroundings and from each other. From there they were all merely parts of the Drakensberg's sandstone range, blended in as if they had no life or form of their own. From there Cathkin Peak was nothing like the rectangular mammoth it was from the school, a mere ten kilometres up the road. It is the angle, I decide. The shape of a mountain is determined by the angle from which it is viewed. It has no shape of its own. Like Table Mountain too. From Paarl, at a distance, it is completely different from when you're standing below it, say at the Cape Town City Hall or on The Parade facing its ragged cliffs. Or from up there, when you're seeing Cape Point, False Bay and the Hottentot Hollands Mountains and the blues of ocean and the blues of sky become the world's most spectacular dome. And how different again it all was from behind, at Muizenberg, and how must it not look from Robben Island? Changing, changing, all the time. A million different views. Quite remarkable.

When after forty-five minutes Uncle Gerrie had not shown up from the fields – I'm sure one of the tractors got stuck, Auntie Babs said – we took our leave and Bokkie promised to pop in again when they brought me back in ten days' time. As I walked ahead to the car my mother whispered something to Auntie Babs. Probably, I realise now, that it would be Bok and not she dropping me off.

Where is he? I alight from the car and stand outside, looking at the cycads. Two nyala ewes tread carefully in the shade. I hoist myself onto the rim of the van's pick-up and sit in the sun, watching the antelope.

I relayed to Bokkie the funeral procession in Pietermaritzburg, Ma'am in the black dress, aided by her twin sister and her daughter Jenny. The husband from whom she's divorced. Soldiers, brass instruments and drums, flags and tears. Bokkie made clicking sounds with her tongue. Sounds of pity for Ma'am. The horror of a parent losing a child. Ja, Bokkie said, sounding like Ouma Liebenberg, she doesn't know where it's all going to end. What It and End she was talking of I had no specific clue, yet I believed the It and the End had to do with everything that was going on in the entire world: the onslaught of the Antichrist. The communist threat. The threat of poverty. The threat of losing our house. The threat of the Arabs. The threat of the Americans. The threat of the Dutch Reformed Church. Of permissiveness. Of narrowness. Of blacks. Of time. Of war. Of sex. Of age. Of parenting. Of childhood. Of middle age. Old age. Comets striking planet earth. Going deaf. Exposure. Revelation. Love. Everything in the whole entire history of the universe. I felt her gaze turning from the steering wheel to me. I glanced at her.

'My child, I beg you to get your fingers out of your mouth,' she said, casting her eyes momentarily back onto the road. 'Let me see.' Again looking away from the road and shaking her head at the sight of my fingertips: white, torn, uneven, flesh curling backwards, cuticles broken and upright, miniature antlers.

'I thought you said you'd stop? Just like Lena, fingers always in her mouth. You both have the most beautiful hands, but you insist on mutilating yourselves. I just don't understand it. It makes no sense. Can you explain it to me? You're almost fourteen years old; have you any idea what it looks like when a young man has his fingers in his mouth the whole time? Like this,' she says, looking back at the road and pulling her lips from her teeth, running her painted red finger-nails to and fro across her clenched bit.

'Nice? Hey? What do you think it looks like?'

'Like a baboon eating watermelon,' I said, and we both laughed.

'Well, there you have it, Baboon,' she said.

Lena and my nail-biting is a leitmotif that has run with our lives since each of us first started school. When I went to the Berg, Bokkie was convinced that learning the piano would force me from the habit as I would be ashamed of my fingers on the keyboard. Great was her horror when instead of quitting nail-biting I quit the piano. Once, in my first year, she had brought Juffrou Sang along to fetch me from the Berg. I had been taking piano for two months. While I was show-ing Juffrou Sang the school she asked me to play, to show how much I had learnt. I played a short piece on the auditorium's grand and made about five mistakes in the space of fifteen bars. Juffrou Sang acted impressed, but Bokkie seemed wounded, embarrassed. When I announced later that holiday that I was giving up piano and going back to recorder, Bokkie looked as though I had informed her of someone's death or of a rape. Or as if I had bitten her in the heel.

'Why?' Bok asked, his tone cautioning that I had better offer a plausible excuse. 'Why do you want to stop?' I said I couldn't master a new instrument while I was trying to train for swimming. Sport was keeping me from music.

'There's no swimming in winter,' my father said, his face ex-pressionless.

'There's rugby,' I said, and he nodded his head, expression altered to a mixture of hope and mistrust.

I myself know all too well that quitting the piano had nothing to do with swimming. Even less with rugby. At best, the summer swimming season could be stretched to eliminate a few weeks of autumn rugby. The problem with piano, rather, was that it had not come as easy as I had imagined: sitting down, my fingers running up and down, no heavenly sounds emanated from beneath my hands through the strings. No, piano was like learning anything else. Moreover, there was Miss Holloway, her wheezing vulture breath — halitosis, Dominic corrected me — threatening to make me throw up. But even Marabou herself probably had little to do with it, for she taught the recorder too, anyway. The long and short of it is that I could not concentrate on anything that needed to be learnt from scratch. Maths had gone well until we started fractions. Music Theory was fine because I had started learning it from Juffrou Sang, and those basics carried me through the Berg. Thank God Music Theory required only a pass/fail and I had managed by the skin of my teeth. I had the attention span of a mousebird when faced with new things I had to commit to memory. Reading, drawing, riding, writing, swimming and dreaming I can manage for hours, I thought. But I read something once, only, and, if I don't get it, grasp it and commit it to memory, I find myself unable or unwilling to repeat. Only since Ma'am has been re-marking my essays, has been inspiring me to develop my talent as a writer, have I been willing to go back and rework, rewrite, reimagine, reconceptualise, redraft. I loathe Maths, I loathe rugby, I loathe the recorder, I loathe anything I cannot do well. I love reading, writing, drawing, swimming, riding. Beyond that the world, academics in toto, might as well not exist.

And I'll bite my nails. Even in my sleep I'll bite my nails.

We passed Midmar and spoke about Mumdeman's retirement. About Mr Shaw, the wealthy Englishman from Durban North who had asked her to marry him. Then Bokkie told me that the Lategans had bought my East African trophies. 'Just to help out a little bit and we were sure you won't worry because it does help to keep you in the Berg.' I didn't respond. I glared from the window. The broken stripes in the middle of the road, flashing by, seemed to torment me. I

looked out of the passenger window. I tried to see how I would paint
the green hills of Howick and Merryvale as they glided by and not
the Grant's gazelle heads, the dick-dick, and the sable antelope that
were what Dademan had left me. All he had to leave me. My inheritance. That's it, my entire inheritance gone to the Lategans, the rich
cunts who give Lena their daughter Anka's old school uniforms. I
wanted to cry, I wanted to scream: 'How could you let him do it?
How could you let him sell what was mine without asking me! Just
like he sold Camelot, mine, all I had, without asking me.' Seething, I
felt my mother's presence around me in the car. To keep me in the
Berg! Fuck you, bitch! I was the one who told you and him, begged,
begged – wept and made a fool of myself – that I didn't want to go
back to that school, that deformatory! When that fucken excuse of a
father of mine had sworn that he was going to make it big; that I, as
a child, should not worry about adult business, that I could go back
to the Berg with a smile on my face. How I detested you, Father,
looked up against having to face you when we got home. Cad, liar,
fuck-up, smart Alec, bastard, cunt, poes, shit, kak, hoer, fokker, doos.
And Bokkie, you useless, useless, mother. What do you do to protect
me from him? Whimpering with that thinness of timbre just like
Grandfather Liebenberg in those moments before he is about to cry.
Again. 'We were sure you won't worry because it helps keep you in the
Berg.' I feel like slapping you. Feel my hands around your beautiful,
useless neck. So, you do not want me to worry. But you must know
that I will. Both because of what I know and because of what I don't
know but am wise enough and you know am wise enough to infer
from between the lines, the noise that comes thundering through the
interstices of your silences. You and he: tell me not to worry, but you
know, ensure, already in the instruction, that I will worry.

All I wanted in that instant was for you to turn that car around
and take me back to school. To Jacques. Or to Dominic. Yes, to
Dominic. I didn't care if I ever saw Jacques again. Liar, traitor. User.
Bok. I wanted to go to the Websters and live with them in comfort.

With Dominic whom I trusted. Or I could live on the loose with Uncle Klaas. Anywhere. Anywhere where worry is elsewhere.

Like here. I walk up to the reception area, looking for Bok.

He is talking to Mr Reynolds. I browse the shelves. Go back out into the sun.

But for a few minutes around my arrival and the braai at Uncle Michael's, Bernice hardly left her room for more than a sandwich at lunch and later for supper. She now has a desk in her room, so she no longer uses the dining-room table. Though already in the past having seemed to me in a world removed from my own, Bernice now was slipping away definitively. Bernice's preparation for matric exams, I told Lena, is her ticket even further out of our lives. Bernice's commitment to her studies, to trying to get a university exemption even though she will never go to university, I had found inspiring. There were days she came out with swollen eyes, as if she were worried sick or had been crying, and I wanted to comfort her, impart my knowledge to her, tell her that I would go and write the exams for her. It struck me as profoundly adult, to be studying for exams like that, to the exclusion of all else. For a day or two I was attracted to the idea of committing myself to my school work, getting A's for each school subject, including Maths. Wiping Niklaas Bruin off the map. I saw myself sitting in Bernice's old room, which will become mine once she has left the house. Unless of course we end up in a flat. Around me I saw bookshelves and pens and pencils, large ledgers and maybe even a typewriter. Then I realised it was not myself immersed in schoolbooks I was dreaming of, it was a vision of myself one day when I am a writer. I will be working like this, day in and day out, without taking a break. With a wife or a maid bringing in cups of tea or real freshly squeezed orange juice. Not the Oros concentrate I mix and top up with ice and quietly take in to my sister's room.

There were occasional phone calls from her schoolmates. Stephanie called when she got back from London. Within minutes of Bernice being on the phone with our cousin, Bokkie was slamming down pots and pans in the kitchen, muttering, loud enough for us all to hear: 'Wouldn't say that lady was on the verge of writing matric exams.' And after replacing the receiver Bernice came into the kitchen and said: 'She only wanted to tell me about her trip.'

'Stephanie's so-called trip will not get you through matric exams.'

'We were also talking about my exams, Bokkie.'

'What does Stephanie De Man know about your school work?' Bokkie snapped. 'She was a zero on a contract at school and now she's trying to turn you into the same.'

And Bernice left quietly. Back into her room.

Sunning myself on the Alcamino's bonnet. Still waiting for Bok, I wonder what Bokkie knows about Stephanie's 'so-called' trip. Am I, after all, not the only one in our family who knows why she went?

Alette I saw only a few times. When I went to meet her and Lena and walk them back from the Pahla station. Her pieces for the Grade Five exam are tough but she's in top shape and hopes for a distinction. I told her about the Schumann Dominic is preparing. She asked about the funeral in Pietermaritzburg and I spoke about the music we sang; that Mathison had cancelled our proposed debate on the French Revolution as a gesture of respect to Ma'am and because it bordered on bringing politics into schools. Lena said the old spinster Miss Hope told her she had seen me at the funeral. Then I told them about the prac teacher, Mr Loveday, who came for two weeks to stand in for Ma'am. How I had introduced myself to Mr Loveday as Oscar, and Dominic introduced himself as Johann Sebastian. And for a few days the whole class and thus also Loveday had called me Oscar and Dominic Johann Sebastian. After one lunch Loveday came back to class and told us he knew my name was Karl and Dominic's was not

Johann Sebastian and he didn't find the joke or the class's complicity the least bit amusing. I told Alette that something had started happening in my reading: I now see that Wilbur Smith is entertaining. It's like being in an adventure. But writers like Oscar Wilde, and John Steinbeck — you must read *Dorian Gray* and *East of Eden*, Alette — are genius. For they tell their stories in ways, in words, that you will never forget because they resonate with our own lives. Wilbur Smith is cheap and easy trash.

We said goodbye to Alette in Dan Pienaar and moved on to Bowen. Lena and I started speaking about Coen and Mandy, about how exhilarating that they've sold everything and are going to sail around the world. 'Much better going for a few years than just for a week like Stephanie,' Lena said. Clearly, she doesn't know, I think, or else she would have let on then. While we don't see Coen and Mandy often, we adore them. They are with it, not old-fashioned. Uncle Coen once told us outright that he has had himself 'fixed' so that Mandy won't ever get pregnant. It's called a vasectomy and Bokkie says that's the way of the future.

Lena spoke about how tough it was playing provincial softball. Softball was not a school sport, but she's sure she'll get full honours for sport next year. Next year is Standard Nine and she's hoping that when she goes to matric she'll be a prefect. When she asked whether I was coming to Port Natal next year I answered that I'd like to stay another year in the Berg. Without saying anything out loud, I could see resentment in her expression. 'I won't take Bok's money.' I said, 'I'm going to ask Aunt Lena if she won't pay.'

'And where do you think she's going to get that kind of money?'

'From Uncle Joe.'

'Do you think he'll pay to keep you there amongst the moffies?'

'He doesn't have to know she's paying.'

'Dream on, Karl De Man,' sounding too much like Bokkie when she's angry with Bok and she drops the Bok and calls him Ralph De Man.

'Aunt Lena,' Lena continued, 'can get hundreds of rands. Not thousands.'

And then, when we walked in the gate and passed beneath the Natal Mahogany, there was Bokkie, calling out that I am now the same height as Lena. At once we stood back to back – she's wearing shoes, I shouted, ever so slightly elevating myself on my toes, making myself an inch taller than my sister. Indeed, two days before my fourteenth birthday, and it was the first time I could face Lena, eye to eye. But, somehow, I am not proud of it.

Still no sign of Bok. I begin to feel irritated. I remember other times I have waited for him while he was doing business. Waiting, waiting, waiting for Bok. Waiting for the money.

Poor cousin Stephanie: Before she got back from London, Bernice took a break from studying to come with us for a braai up at Uncle Michael and Aunt Siobhain's. James took me upstairs to show me how he paints his eggs. Uncle Michael has built him a drawing- and work-table that folds out from the wall. I envied him. Above the work-table, on the walls, were racks with books and bottles of paintbrushes and paints. The books, mostly of watercolours and pastel landscapes, do nothing for me, though I said they are 'really good'. Kitsch is the word I had wanted to use. James's own drawings are all like magazine illustrations, good, but unoriginal. They tell me nothing of what he sees. James probably doesn't even know what an Impressionist or Expressionist is.

Then James closed his bedroom door and said he wanted to tell me something I was not to repeat. To anyone. I at once recoiled, thought he might confess to me that he was homosexual. Something that had been said about him since he was about seven and started doing the flower arrangements. I wanted to get out of the room, did not want to know anything about his urges, which have always felt directed at me. Since we were kids, always trying, trying to get a glimpse of my dick, always trying to touch it in the pool, or when we showered together. I find him repulsive, unlike Stephanie, whose cunt I can still fantasize about slipping into, smelling. James's urges seem as though they could rub off and infect me and make me sick. Like his kitsch art. If I were to look at it for too long, spend too much time in his room, I may start to paint like him.

Once I had promised not to tell, he spilt the beans: Stephanie was not in London on holiday. She had actually gone to her Irish uncle in London for an abortion. He overheard it when she was begging Uncle Michael and Aunt Siobhain for money. She had no idea who the father was. She had to sell Herbie to get enough money to go because abortions cost thousands. And it was illegal in South Africa. If anyone finds out, Stephanie could go to prison.

'Promise you won't tell,' he again begged. I again swore, half hearing myself, thinking only of how ghastly, how horrendous, to fall pregnant. Fall pregnant, like falling into shame. Falling in love. Falling asleep. Falling ill. Falling apart. Falling pregnant. My mind embroidered, flying between Stephanie and my sisters: what will happen if Lena or Bernice falls pregnant? They'd probably just do what black women did if they don't want a child: stick a knitting needle up their vaginas and dig around in the womb till they kill the foetus. The thought horrifies me. Again I swore not to tell a soul and then moved from the room, down the passage, descending the stairs as if levitating. What if Bernice fell pregnant and didn't tell? Had the baby and gave it up for adoption? What if she thought she couldn't have a baby because of what happened to her at Mkuzi? But say the doctors were wrong and her insides were okay after all! Would I tell if it happened to me? The shame of it. Sheets of shame descending like drapes over our house, enveloping the family. And if the story were to get out? The church! The disgrace of the extended family: shame by association. When Lena was my age and I spotted sanitary pads in her cupboard, I imagined that she may be pregnant. I went to Bernice who explained that Lena had started having periods. Menstruation, that's all. Before getting to Dominic and the dictionary, I had for a while imagined that men too had periods. Dominic said that the closest men got to periods were wet dreams.

By the time I was outside in the yard beside Aunt Siobhain's papyrus bush, pregnancy had become my worst nightmare. What if I had made Alette pregnant? Though that was impossible for we had only touched each other, never stuck it in, and a girl cannot get pregnant without penetration and orgasm. But what if it happens to one of my sisters? I am certain that Bernice is doing It with Robert. Everyone does It. But everyone knows that FLs break. Lena, who doesn't have a boyfriend, is on the pill for her skin, but as for Bernice, she has the smoothest complexion in the family and there is, I think, no way Bokkie will allow her on the pill. Yet, Bernice is the one with the boyfriend. I had to speak to her. She had to go on the pill at once. I thought again of Alette saying to me after Malawi: 'We're too old for that now.' One step further and this could have been us. I think of Jacques and Dominic. But that was just playing, jerking off. No, if you stuck it into a starfish, could that not pass for fucking? Jacques and Dominic and I; that's full-on *laying with a man as you do with a woman*. I must become a good Christian, it cannot go on like this. My sins will catch up to me. What if a car runs me over, and I die?

The thought of Stephanie having an illegitimate child, of one of my sisters being *put in the other time, knocked up, having a bun in the oven, being on the pole*, depressed me. I must warn them that boys are after only one thing. That is all we speak about at school. They should take a lesson from Stephanie. And don't stick knitting needles up yourselves, Lena, Bernice. Tell me, I'll find the money, I promise you, I will, to send you to London for an abortion. Bernice, I repeat to myself in the Mkuzi sun, has to go on the pill. How stupid this backward country is! Not allowing women to have abortions. How far ahead of us America and England are.

I never got around to speaking to either of them, I think as Bok comes grinning down the selasto path towards the Alcamino where I sit on the bonnet. Waiting.

We've dropped off our bags and groceries at the rondavel and had a quick sandwich. As we head for the hides and the Msumu pan, Bok regales me with the tales just relived by him and Hugo Reynolds in the warden's office: when a ranger lost all his front teeth as a roll of barbed wire fell from a truck and struck him on the mouth near the Umsunduzi – Hugo says he still takes out his dentures to show everyone when he tells the story. When Boy shot the poacher through the artery and the man bled to death; Jonas is apparently still a guard somewhere in Umfolozi. The Parks Board is planning on settling elephant into Hluhluwe and the two reserves may, after all these years, be joined into one including the corridor. When the white rhino calf got stuck in the mud at Masinga hide and how Jonas and Boy had to distract the cow's attention so that Bok and Willy Hancox and the other rangers could pull the calf free. The impala culling – Willy has probably forgotten what a lousy shot he was, Bok laughs. Taking poachers to the Ubombo police station, at least twice a month – Hugo Reynolds says poaching is worse now than before and they're trying to expand co-operation with the LPs – local population. How sad Bok was when he had to shoot a black rhino cow close to our house where she had almost been strangled by a poacher's lasso, strung between two lala palms; I thought it was white, I say; no, black, saddest, most difficult moment of his life, shooting that cow, more difficult than shooting Vonk or putting down Suz and Chaka. How horses are no longer used to follow up darted rhinos – now it's helicopters – which makes it so much more effective and efficient. Another problem now are the bush fires, seems many are deliberately set to chase the game north across the Mkuzi River where the LPs can kill them off. In his day they made thorough, broad fire breaks; they had to, it was the worst drought in human memory. All the catches they made of nyalas, warthogs, impalas, for export to the few private game reserves in the region – there's increased interest in those; soon they'll be popping up like mushrooms, not necessarily Mala Mala smart, but just small private game reserves where the wilderness can be protected and appreciated. Ian Player has done his part, expanding the way South Africa and the world see the necessity for protecting wilderness. Tourism is the future for South Africa. I listen with rapt attention, even as our eyes scan the innards of the bush. Wish he could be back here. Work here.

I am closer to Bok now than I have been since we left Umfolozi. I want to hold him here, keep him here, never again have to experience him outside of this. This is the way I want him. Never again in that garage of his that is his office where I take in a man who only resembles the father I want. Behind his desk in the centre of the garage, surrounded by his shelves of curios. Where I want to find a way to stop kissing him and Bokkie hello and goodbye. Where I've outgrown kissing them. Here I could do it. But not there on the phone. Where his manner is that of a man who pretends to own the world, where, but for what Bokkie has told me, I could, without blinking, for a few hours believe that he actually does. Here, where his strident knowledge of the bush is always tempered by either love for it or his humility before it. Not near where the empty white space on the back wall above the trinkets and bangles has nothing other than dust ovals, outlines like scars, no, wounds, marking the spots where once my trophies hung. Wounds about which he says nothing, and I do not consider asking. Where I do not want to hear him tell me a story that will only succeed in making me feel worse. Let the dust ovals against the white wall sit between us as an inheritance lost that will eventually grow scabs that for some reason will make us both feel better; whether because I do not wish to see him shamed into lying, again, or whether it is because my not forgiving him makes me powerful with the brooding indignation of self-righteousness. I do not know and don't care to explore further the issue of what was mine and pilfered. Where, when at first he asked me to accompany him on this trip, I had wanted to say no, I have to work on Latin, for I cannot, for a moment, imagine what we will say to each other. But then, his overzealous demeanour, as though offering me the riches of King Solomon's mines, tells me he is going north to collect from the maids the smoking pipes he has commissioned, for ethnic pipes are in high demand and even though the Zulus don't usually make them — they're really Xhosa — they will be a hit if marketed overseas as authentic Zulu crafts. Where he *knows* the pipes will be a major success. Where I am not concerned with the pipes. Where I already know they will fail. Where he and Bokkie have to seduce me by confessing that it is my birthday gift, that we'll be coming to Mkuzi and Umfolozi, before I am thrilled and ready to jump into the van. Where I am not concerned with my father's absence. Where I take unbridled delight in it. Where my school report is ridiculed: A for Art, A for English, C for everything else other than Maths, which has dropped to an all-time low: an E. Where all he can say is: 'This is the first and last year you'll be taking Art. You will spend that time from now on doing Maths.' Where Bokkie says: 'We might not be able to afford Parents' Weekend in November but it's not necessary for you to say anything to Lukas or Dominic about why we're not coming. Perhaps you can just say Mumdeman is ill or that we can't leave Bernice while she's writing matric exams. Auntie Babs can come and fetch you to the farm for the weekend, or do you think maybe you'll go out with Lukas's family?' Where I say I'll go with Lukas's family but know I'll go with the Websters, and I try not to look at my father, who again doesn't say a word. Lets his lackey bear the bad tidings. Bokkie of the bad tidings. Where she calls us to supper while Lena and I are watching *The World at War* and when we don't move she mutters that instead of eating our fingers in front of the TV we should come and eat the food she has slogged over. 'Look at the two of them, like baboons with those fingers in their mouths,' and both Lena and I drop our hands, but only I get up and go to the table, saying sarcastically, 'We plan to eat till we reach our elbows. Then see if you'll still love us.'

And Bokkie glares at me, and I knew then already, that when we left to come here, she would weep as we drove off, and I'd regret, deeply, the night's cheek. And again Bokkie calls Lena, now louder, to come and eat because the food's getting cold. And Lena still doesn't look up from the TV and says: 'Just wait, I want to finish watching this.' And Bok jumps up from the table and slaps my sister across the face. 'I will not have you speaking to your mother like that.' And I hate him. If I had a sharper knife, I could plunge it into his back. Let him ever, ever, smack me through the face! I will find a way, Jesus Christ, I will find a way to destroy this man, somehow. And where, less than an hour later after a silent dinner, he and Lena are again the best of friends, as though nothing happened. And I alone am left hating him. As though on my and Lena's behalf.

But here! Here, here. Beside him in the Alcamino, it doesn't matter and that's where I want to keep him. He speaks a hundred experiences and memories and plants and birds I knew nothing of, and his talking grabs me like a fist enfolding my Adam's apple: my recall forms but a tiny selection of imprints from his: his life here, their life here, my life here, intersecting but divorced. If we were to write them down, his and hers and mine, what would be the same? What would be different? And as mine are fewer, drawn from the time I was five and younger, does it make the place more or less real for him or for me? And if all our memories — no, the world's memories — could be written down or even just manifest as they were thought — then what would become of us? If the thoughts of each one who has lived from when we came out of the sea or from dust or a rib whatever you want to believe was breathed out into the world for all to hear or see? How would we distinguish anything from everything? And if we included the thoughts of Jonas and the black people, the millions of them! Thoughts in words, voices in words, memories in words, histories in words: a mist of words littering the world. Words covering amoeba and algae, the waves, sand, the leaves, the plants, the animals, the people, the books, the air. The globe, the universe, and the universes that lie behind it. And not a single one's words will be ignored! Memories and thoughts will be written on everything in a hundred thousand languages, Cantonese, English, Maori, Arabic, Xhosa, Afrikaans, Sanskrit, Hebrew, Zulu, Spanish, Ndebele, Hindi, Swahili, and even languages no longer spoken. The language of history and musicology and art and science and geography, and memoir, and novels, and love, and families, and film, and conflicts, the language of birds, of insects, of animals, and biology, and the hunt, in pictures, in poems. In grunts! And signals from before we wrote or even thought in language, let alone through alphabets in a time before calendars or time. The words would envelop everything and turn into tides that bump up against each other like waves breaking and the memories would go to war like storms and hurricanes and histories will be clouds colliding in trenches and tearing veins and fault lines causing lightning and fires that burnt to cleanse everything till we'll know a single word means a million things. An Armageddon of the word. Of thought, memory. From where it will all begin again, repeat itself over and over, also because a single word left out is a lie, a single voice silenced betrayal. Until from the cycles of chaos something evolves that will not require language. Something that will communicate without sound, perhaps with only touch. The epoch in which we will be nourished by and live from a nail tracing an eyebrow, a cheek. A knee resting against a thigh. Toes meeting in the grass. A palm on a belly. The lifting of a hair from where it has landed on a shoulder. An orifice opening for the rubbing of a finger. Footsoles on warm sand. One nose brushing another. A shadow catches my eye. 'Rhino at ten o'clock.' At once Bok brings the truck to a gentle stop. It is a cow, being led by her calf. Right in front of us. Bok turns off the ignition and we sit quietly. Do nothing but watch as they graze from the sweet grass on the side of the road where the water run-off makes the grass grow longer, greener.

Bube and Masinga hides. Both he helped build when we first got here.

The detail — reeds, creosote, thatch, spoor of antelope in the white sand and silence broken only by the chrrrk of bulbuls and the mournful call of Namaqua doves — at each hide is the split image of my memory: no smaller, as I was expecting after the Lobombos, the gate and HQ. Bok points out the tree orchids in the ironwood above Masinga. Now even those, the way their feet are spread and clutching, almost hidden in the branches above the footpath, are loosed from somewhere I have not fetched them but in the moment of seeing I remember for the first time from a place they were hidden.

We sit for an hour, alone. Baboons cavorting, a nyala bull pronking all white mane and tail as he sniffs an ewe, kudu, ears flapping off ox-peckers, alert, staring at the hide, orioles, bright yellow swinging from branches. I want to say I wish we had the binoculars but catch myself: they, along with his camera, were sold in another month of bad business. Babblers, like a car trying to start and pipits, which I briefly think are crowned hornbills till the second part of their song comes and from the bush the little flock settles at the water's lip for a drink. A murmur of voices coming down the reed alleyway; heads up, ears erect from the waterside; we glance around; three tourists coming up the stairs; back at the water, everything poised for flight; floorboards creek and someone laughs: in a second everything is gone. Bok keeps his eyes on the water and in the bush. I turn and glare at them, shaking my head, wanting them to see in my anger their stupidity. Slowly the movement begins again: impala, turtles climbing back onto branches from where they have slipped. The whispers behind us. I swing around and put my finger to my lips, imploring them with furrows in my forehead to be quiet or get out.

To the Forest of Figs. Pass where we parked this morning to cut through the bush to Mbanyana. On our right the silver blue of Msumu through the fever trees. The cry of spur-winged geese. Pelicans bobbing in the waves and flamingoes gliding in to land.

'The Mkuzi River is full,' Bok says. 'You don't remember this much water, hè?'

'It's completely different,' I say, now unable to remember ever having been here. We park where the road dead-ends and walk along a rhino path to where he says the forest is. I think of Jonas, holding my hand, walking back from here. I know it happened, I can see us, but the surroundings are foreign as if each bush colludes to make me forget. And when we get to the first stream it is full. This is only a tributary of the pan, my father says. The Mkuzi proper is further east. This never existed, I say. There was no river or tributary here. Watch out for crocodiles. He removes his shoes and socks and I take off my sandals. We wade across. From here it starts to look familiar: the reeds, the bigger fever trees, more ficuses, some with red fruit growing from the stems. This is it, I remember this tree, here, on the right, it had ibis nests in it. Yes, Bok says, you're right. Ahead of us are the yellow, green branches of the fig forest. It was over here, somewhere just here, that we saw the mamba, I say. Well watch out, Bok answers, they grow very old, it could still be here. I laugh. A hippo grunts to our right. Bok points. On we go, now the forest is in front of us. Yes, yes, this is it: this same path, we walked every time he came to show me the louries. Up a slight embankment and we're looking down into the water of the Mkuzi. 'This is the long arm of the pan,' Bok says. 'It reaches up north a good two or three miles.' There is no trace of the little path along which we walked right through the dustbowl that I had never thought was part of a river or the pan. Downstream again the grunts of hippo, water squirting. We cannot possibly cross. Jonas, taking me in there, how we lay on the leaves, looking up, waiting for the louries. And Phinias at Charters. Images of the two black men now almost indistinguishable. How badly I want to go in there. 'Please, can't we cross,' I ask. 'I really want to go into the forest.'

'You can hear the hippos, Karl. And there are crocs everywhere.'

'Can't we find a place where it's shallow and narrow?'

'It will be two hours' walk to go up the arm and then cut back the way we came another two hours. Night within an hour. But let's look down here.'

He leads me up and down the footpaths along the bank, again cautioning me to watch for crocodile. This was never a river, I say, taking in the sounds of birds, the sweet musty scent of ficus, remembering Jonas's fingers clearing the fruit of the insects, passing them to me to bite out the sweet flesh from the peels. Jonas picking the red fruit to later clean and eat with his pap. Was Boy not with us? I cannot recall. No, it was always just the two of us.

'It was always a river. But it was dry when we lived here.' And then they're calling, two, four louries at once, their voices hidden from the branches into the water and up to us. Bok too stands still, turns around and smiles.

As the sun falls behind the trees from where we've come, he says we must turn back. I'm cautious of leopard, he says. There are now quite a few in the reserve. In our time only one was spotted.

The flames of the fire we have built dance in front of Mkuzi's night bush. We sit listening to the sounds of hyena whooping near Mahlala.

'Maybe I should become a game ranger,' I say. For a while he's quiet.

'You are the most intelligent in the family,' he says at last. 'You can be anything you want to be. You can be rich and famous. Use your brain, become a doctor or a lawyer. Don't waste your mind on the meagre income of a game ranger.'

'What if I go mad, like Uncle Klaas?' I ask and think of telling him about the tramp at school.

Bok laughs: 'That's the Liebenberg blood, not the De Mans'. You're a De Man.'

I remind him how Lena teased me about bursting a blood vessel, letting the mad gene into my bloodstream.

'She's a joker,' Bok says. 'That's not why you're not studying any more, is it?'

The report. That's what he's been waiting for. Has this, after all, indeed all been the drawn-out approach to his ambush? I try to ignore the niggling of doubt, my inability to trust him. I speak the truth: 'No. I find school boring. This is what I want to do, just live alone in the bush. Sitting here, like this, it would not bother me if I never read another book in my life.'

'You're an intellectual, for heaven's sake!'

'So is Dr Player. He's a game ranger and a writer. And Nick Steele wrote a book.' From our little bookshelf: *White Rhino Saga. Game Ranger on Horseback.* At ten or eleven, when was it, yes, ten, before I went to the Berg. Now, as much as it has thrilled me in the past to be thought clever, I find myself resenting my father's opinions. They are only ways to point out my failures.

'How will you support a family?' he goes on. 'You know that's why we left the Parks Board. To give you kids a decent education. Tanzania too, we could have stayed on but it was no place to raise kids.' Guilt's load unpacked on me! I am responsible for the loss of Mkuzi, Umfolozi, St Lucia. It is not I who want to be rich, I want to say. It is not I who asked to leave Tanzania or this! It is not I but you who went from shooting wild animals to protecting wild animals to shooting them to wanting to make money! Why is everything my and Lena and Bernice's fault? And why must Tanzania, an absence, something I don't know, always be invoked to explain our lives? Can't we, for once, live now, wipe out the past? 'A game ranger and a writer,' he says. 'Now, with that combination you're making sure you won't have money to wipe your arse.' We don't have money to wipe our arses, I want to cry. Who are you to speak! I would, a million times over, exist rather in this bush without money than live entangled in your lies of fantasizing about non-existent riches.

'I don't mind being poor,' I say. 'I only want to be happy. And this' – I gesture with my eyes into the shadows of the veld – 'is all I've ever wanted.'

'How will you be happy without a career?'

I say that I will have a career: I will be a writer and a game ranger.

'And what sorts of things will you write? All writers are dead poor.'

'Not Wilbur Smith,' I say, agitation growing in me.

'You want to write like him?'

'No. Like John Steinbeck and Oscar Wilde and . . .' while I'm talking a thought strikes me, 'and like Georgia O'Keeffe.'

I wait for him to pick it up. He doesn't, and I taste bitter victory. Ignoramus. Idiot. I want to allow myself to force out a laugh, to tell him that O'Keeffe is a painter, and who, who does he think he is to sit and advise me about things he knows about as much of as a vervet of Shakespeare?

'Ernest Hemingway,' he says, 'Dademan took him on safari in East Africa. Did you know that?'

'No,' I say. 'I didn't.'

'There was another woman in Kenia, what was her name, famous writer. Do you know?'

'No.'

'Karen Blixen. That's it. Swedish royalty.'

I resent his trying to tell me what to read. I am not interested in his silly uneducated opinions. I have Ma'am and Uncle Klaas, neither of whom know anything about Swedish royalty, for God's sake.

'And how will you educate your children if you're a poor writer?'

'I don't want children, Bok. Never.'

'That's just a phase, Karl. We all go through that and then we ultimately get married and have kids. If you don't have kids, what will you leave behind?'

'My stories,' I say. 'That is all I want to leave behind. What I want to say is that I'll leave my art with a capital A. Yet the word, *Art*, is one that doubtlessly will anger him. And what if I don't leave a damn thing? Why must I leave anything? Leave, leave, leaving things behind for what?

'Bokkie and I think it's time that you come back to a normal high school next year. We know you wanted to come back last year, but we thought one more year away from home would be good for you.' The ambush has been sprung. He waits for a response. At the very least to see me squirm.

How I hate this man.

'What do you think, Karl?'

'It doesn't matter what I say.'

'Of course it matters, that's why I'm asking you.'

I cannot be bothered to tell him how deeply I want to go back. How music has opened to me this year. And how I am happy there. 'I'll do whatever you and Bokkie want me to do.'

We fall into a passive argument. He asks why I'm now sulking. Having silent fits. I say I'm not having silent fits but that when I asked them to take me out last year they wouldn't. Sent me back. If I now said I want to go back, what difference would it make? And then he proves my point: 'We think it's time to come back now.'

And I know: next year, I'll be back at home. Fourteen years old, arriving at the Hoërskool Port Natal. Where Lena said she'd make sure I had a reception committee: every high-school bully waiting.

'I'm tired,' I say. 'I want to go to bed.'

'Well. Tomorrow's Umfolozi.'

'Yes, Bok,' I say, leaving him alone at the fire.

'Don't you say goodnight, Karl?'

'Goodnight, Bok.'

'Goodnight, Karl.'

I get undressed, neatly folding my T-shirt and shorts at the bottom of the bed. I read from *The Brothers Karamazov*. When I hear him coming towards the hut I put down the book and turn over. He leaves the door open so that Mkuzi can come into the rondavel. I hear him undress behind me. Every movement I picture: stripping out of his shorts, hanging them on the closet door, he never hangs things on hangers, making my mother crazy. The shirt being unbuttoned, also hung over the door, then the sounds of underpants, elastic, thrown onto the suitcase. And then his footsteps to the light switch. Off. But he doesn't go to his bed. Moves outside. Naked. And I hear the hissing sound of his pee hitting the grass, gurgling into the soil. A middle-aged dog marking his lost territory. For a moment I feel pity for him: my charming handsome father. Turning grey. I could, in this moment, weep for him. Then he comes inside, mattress creaks as he lowers himself onto his bed. Soon he is breathing deeply across the room from me.

Now it is quiet. I let myself forget about him, Dimitri Karamazov, the Berg, my mother, my siblings, and I dream my dream, smiling, of being something that can fly at speed over the brown veld of Mkuzi.

Driving through Hluhluwe to Umfolozi; no more than fifteen kilometres an hour, our eyes in the bush. Our sporadic talk is rarely about anything but the past: Dad and Mumdeman, the Charters Creek years, and how good it was to have had them so close to us at St Lucia. Skip, the Pekinese, what became of that dog? Was with Dad and Mum since Oljorro. Came down with us on the Kenia ship from Mombasa. Yes, the dog went with Mumdeman to Midmar, died there. And Mumdeman now thinking of marrying old Mr Shaw. On a whim I ask Bok where I was conceived. He laughs. Says it was when they drove down to visit Oupa and Ouma Liebenberg in the Molopo. A three-day trip, not much to do on the road. The back of the Peugeot. Could have been anywhere crossing one of the borders between Tanganyika and Zambia, Zambia and Rhodesia, Rhodesia and Bechuanaland, Bechuanaland and the Republic. With the girls asleep on the front seats. And Bernice, where was she conceived? On our honeymoon at Lake Kariba. She was born just nine months and eight days after the wedding. I know, I say, because I've calculated. He calls me a little sigabengu, laughing, and asks what I think of him and Bokkie. I say I'm not thick, I know what people get up to. Not your mother, he says, she'd never do anything like that before she was married. I do not say that I do not believe him. I do not say that everyone does It before they're married. Nor do I ask him about him. I don't want to know about him. For then he may ask about me. And to ask him about him would be to betray Bokkie; to know more about him from his own mouth than I already know from the tears of the trailists; from one night when he didn't come home while we were living in Afsaal flats after leaving St Lucia and he walked in sheepishly the next morning and offered a smiling excuse about his car having broken down; and all I could picture for days afterward was his naked body heaving into some woman not my mother. And Lena, I ask. On elephant safari, next to the Ruvu in a tent, or in the Mbuyu house, he says, smiling, hugging a pleasant memory somewhere deep in himself. I was conceived crossing borders. I was not conceived in a place with a name. I belong nowhere. The thought appeals to me.

Very little game. Almost two hours of slow driving and nothing more than a couple of impala, a steenbok and a bateleur, high against the blue, adrift on thermals.

'When we come this way again, maybe we could do St Lucia,' he says. I answer that it would be nice. I tell him about the time when Mumdeman was in charge of us and we took Camelot down onto the beach, when Lena was dragged along the shore and almost run over by the Bedford. I tell him how she clung, like a dog holding onto a sack, wouldn't let go, even when she was hopping along on the road's gravel surface. Bok is in stitches, saying he's never seen a kid, boy or girl, as tough as Lena. I think no, neither have I. Lena reminds me of Bennie, I say. Yes, she's quite a tomboy, he muses. 'Mumdeman never said a word, to me, anyway,' Bok speaks as we drive up the winding pass to Hilltop, where Dad and Mumdeman were briefly stationed before going to Charters. Then along the white road that snakes south-west, up and down hillsides, through drifts, through the corridor towards Umfolozi's entrance. Passing through the corridor between the reserves, he speaks about the continued struggle to get the two reserves connected. At the sight of dust from an approaching vehicle, our hands go automatically to the window handles. Allow the car to pass, wait for the dust to settle and then wind down again, letting the breeze spill in. Where will these people from the corridor be resettled, I ask. No one ever lived here, he says. I remember huts in the corridor, definitely, I counter, from the days Bokkie and I drove along here to collect the girls from school, huts, kraals, women balancing inkathas on their heads, I'm sure. No, he answers, no record of people ever having habitated this area. So, it's not the same struggle here as it was to proclaim most of the other game reserves. There people had to be moved from their ancestral lands. To be resettled somewhere in what's left of their Zululand, he says. Shakes his head and sighs. Through Nyalazi Gate and up towards Masinda camp. I wait for the sight of the Black Umfolozi, but he says no, don't I remember it lies between Masinda and Mpila? No, I say, I'm sure it's just around this corner, down this dip. I'm sure . . . Until we head up onto Masinda Hill and see the river, thick, brown, a python coiling its way southward to near Chaka's Hunting Pits. Then we're crossing the low-lying bridge with its little concrete towers. No more than blocks. Here Bok once let me stand to pose for coloured slides he took of me. I wish they had told me before I left the Berg that this was to be my birthday surprise. I would have brought my Kodak Instamatic. The riverbanks are lined with heavy green sycamore figs, deep swaying reeds. He stops on the middle of the concrete structure. The water hisses beneath us, white foamy whirlpools where it exits beneath my arm. The cry of a fish eagle, recalled, our eyes on the riverbank, the sky, no sign of them. A breeze sends a ripple through the reeds. Bok speaks about the floods, when he and a group were stranded in a cave for two days. I recall how, months after the flood, he had taken me to shoot with his revolver. He says he can't remember it. I don't believe him.

The river behind us, he turns left ignoring the No Entry sign at the junction to the rhino bomas. The place is deserted. He hoots, but no one emerges from the huts or from the little house where Len

Sawyer once lived. We get out and walk to the pens where the white rhino are kept. Here Shetani and the other two were tamed before he took them to America. He shows me which were their pens. The rhinos look up as we approach. One snorts, tosses her head from side to side. Len Sawyer kept two rhino calves in his house. They slept on his double bed with him before he got married and his wife put a stop to it. On this stretch of hard red soil, Lena, Bernice and I rode around on the back of the baby rhinoceroses, laughing, showing off to tourists and grown-ups, never imagining childhood could ever end.

At Mpila we go into the office. The receptionist tells us Willy Hancox is off for the weekend up at the warden's house but he asked her to phone the moment we arrived because Reynolds from Mkuzi called to say Bok was coming. When Willy arrives, he and Bok shake hands, calling each other by their Zulu names. 'Ubejane!' 'Shaya Kabi!' And then I recall that Jonas had a Zulu name for me, one I could not, even at that return, remember. They stand outside Willy's van, smoking. I ask whether I may go down to the house. Willy says of course – the ranger who lives there is on patrol at Sontuli but his wife should be in. Bok says he'll join me there in a minute. I leave them at the Parks Board truck.

Downhill, past Mr Watts's shop, the path I must have walked a thousand times. Through the trees the beige water of the White Umfolozi becomes visible. Now the Watts's house is no less than forty metres from ours, which I recognise only by the water tank close to my old bedroom. It seems as if everything beneath the endless ceiling of the sky has been compressed. A miniature of memory. Everything seems to shrink when you get older. Nothing is as big as when you were small. Mumdeman is getting smaller, not only because I'm getting taller, but because she's actually shrinking. The marula tree has been chopped down and the fence looks dilapidated. Bokkie's old vegetable garden is there. More trees, bigger than I recall, more bird sounds. Wood-hoopoes and bulbuls. Dull brown warblers and pipits, families so closely resembling each other I never quite got to distinguish.

Hesitantly, wishing Bok were here to do it, I go and knock. A woman in a loose-fitting cotton dress opens the door.

'Hello,' she says, clearly surprised. And then with a smile: 'Are you lost? The camp's up there,' and she points up the path I've come. The path I made with Chaka and Suz. Where once I lost a pot-handle. Where hornbills followed me.

'No,' I answer. 'My name is Karl De Man and my father was a game ranger here. We were the first people who lived in this house.'

'Oh, really? Well, come in, I suppose you'd like to look around.'

'Well, I just wanted to look at my mother's garden, if you don't mind.'

'No, not at all, go ahead.' She follows me out. Now I see that she's pregnant. Her heavy belly moves from side to side. It looks as though she could split open at any moment.

'I'll just leave you to it, okay?'

'That's fine, thank you very much.'

'Tell me, did you say De Man?'

'Yes, my father is Ralph De Man. He was stationed here.'

'Is he *the* Ralph De Man?'

'What do you mean?' I ask, smiling.

'Quite a reputation,' she says and walks back to the house. Suddenly I hate her.

I move around the side of the house. Sand-pit gone. Look down to the arm of the White Umfolozi, now just down the hill from the house: it had been so far, then. The hills hazed in the distance. The river's water is a deep blue, reflecting the sky from here, again becoming the brown, beige and dull white where it bends, south and west. Right below me now, its green banks of figs and reeds were places I would never have been able to reach on my own before. Bokkie and I went there for picnics, sometimes taking our cousins and Aunt Siobhain and Uncle Michael. Bok's hair short, and wet, like a waterbuck emerging from a pool. From my right, a lourie, crimson wings spread out as it swoops out of the branches and I stand still, watching its flight as it glides down the hill, disappearing up the hill, its call almost like a grinding. My eyes follow along the path I walked with Chaka and Suz to get down to the office and the donkey's pen. And the krans where Lena and I saw the leopard. How had I almost forgotten? Now, since we've been back and I told Bok, the memory has come to seem important. A telephone pole, down the hillside, where I don't recall one before. My eyes run from the pole along the wire to the house. There's a phone inside. Hours upon hours in this veld, around this house, on these footpaths, the aloes and the rocks. The rock where I hammered in nails, building an infrastructure of game pens, bomas. I walk there, it is closer to the house. A milkweed's hairy fruit — Bok-se-balle we called them — sway like Christmas decorations in the breeze. I don't pop them now, not wanting the sticky latex on my hands, instead take the balls into my hand, feel the sensation of the hairs on my palms, the inflated skin like a gallbladder give slightly when I squeeze. Jacques. *Gomphocarpus* something or other. Above the rock the two aloes I remember, both with dry flower-pods. Must recently have flowered.

The crunch of Bok's footsteps through the grass behind me.

'Lyk dit soos jy onthou?'

'A lot,' I say. 'Just the telephone pole wasn't there. And these aloes have grown.'

'I'm going down to the office, are you coming along?'

'No, I'll stay.'

'Willy Hancox invited us for a braai tonight.'

I look at the hill where the warden's thatched house stands. 'At the house?'

He answers yes as he makes his way down the footpath.

'Did he say anything about Jonas?' I call after him.

'He's way over at Okhuko. We won't be able to see him. Maybe next time.'

'Jonas called me by a Zulu name, Bok, can you remember what it was?'

'Magangane . . . The naughty one.' And suddenly it comes back, as though I've always been able to hear Jonas laugh as he speaks something to Boy and all I can understand is the name Magangane. 'Magangane, ey!' and the man's head shaking out his laughter.

I want to tell Bok what the woman in the house said. Then decide not to, knowing that he will be somehow thrilled by something that nothing but angers me. He disappears behind shrubbery where I remember some warthog holes. I go down there. They have not been abandoned. Instead of following him down to the office where I used to meet him and the boys coming back from trail with the tourists, I head back up towards the house, cast my eyes at the garden. No more shrubs, not the yellow and purple alamandas Bokkie planted, no more kannas. How would O'Keeffe paint the view from here? One day I will. Title it simply. Something like: *View From Our House at Umfolozi.* Or: *Umfolozi View, October.* Or just: *Umfolozi.* And I sit on the rock beneath the aloes, my shadow tucked firmly beneath me where the heat of the stone burns through the cotton of my shorts. The hills above the river, smoky, growing fainter and fainter in the distance. One could do that by dabbing a half-dry white paintbrush across the detail. Closer to the river, the shrubbery of thorn trees and acacia looks like a thick layer of fresh green peppercorns, here and there becoming sparser, showing up the pink sand and yellow grass over which they grow. In the distance, where Black and White Umfolozi come together, Chaka's Hunting Pits. A place of terror, slaughter, laughter and blood sport. Ivory for the English at Port Natal. Not an elephant left in this wilderness. And there's Momfu, where they found an ancient wall and tools at the back of the cliffs, and behind the wall the skeleton of a young boy who had been walled up. The boy's head was smashed in and then the wall was erected. Why had they killed him? What did he know that they wanted him not to tell? What did he have that they had to kill him to take it from him? Dry riverbanks with patches of grass and reeds. Zebra crossing the sand, even from here I can see their tails flicking. Is that a giraffe, there, behind that ochre and green spot, yes . . . The Umfolozi Valley swims before me as tears well in my eyes. I place my face into my arms, watch as tears drop to the rock beneath me, the blotches shrinking as they evaporate in the heat. I hear the birds, hundreds of them, sounds I have forgotten. I knew. I sit with a stick, drawing in the earth amongst the green patches on the rock.

Bok asks whether I've been crying. I say no. It's the heat. Sweat in my eyes.

From Mpila we drive westward. See more rhino. Still no lion. The numbers have grown since we lived here. North-west. Bok says it's a good time for me to start learning to drive. He stops the Alcamino. I get out as he slides across. I walk around the front and get in behind the wheel.

'Do you need the seat forward?'

'I think I'm fine, Bok.'

The vehicle moves well, I'm doing well, battle occasionally to co-ordinate clutch, steering, gears.

'Where did you learn to drive?'

'Just from watching you and Bokkie.'

'When I was your age I was already driving into Arusha.'

The road dips, declines south-westerly. The sun is in my eyes as I head for the Mphafa water-hole. Ahead in the road are three giraffe. I gear down and the motor idles while we watch. Then the bull at the back makes an odd jump, lifts his front legs and mounts the one with lighter markings in front of him. Also a bull. Younger. The back bull's penis, long and thin and pink moves around as if searching. Now Bok snorts and leans over and honks the horn and says: 'Stupid randy things.' The animals move off the road and I look after them, wondering whether—

'Let's go,' he says.

I slip the Alcamino into first gear and move off. Speed up, gear into second, third.

'Were you with me that time we saw the lions mating near here?' he asks. 'You know, they carry on mating for weeks, with neither the male nor female hunting or eating . . .' Again the road drops and I struggle to find the brake, tug at the gear lever. 'You're going to burn out the clutch. Brake, Karl. You're ripping the gearbox apart, dammit!'

I stall the engine and the truck comes to a halt. I say I've had enough, I want to look out for game.

'Het jy nou jou gat gewip?'

'No, Bok. Of course not.'

Near sunset we leave the vehicle and walk towards the water-hole. Why Reynolds in Mkuzi had insisted we take a rifle to the sight of Mbanyana, I don't know. Here, amidst the favourite terrain of lion, my father and I – without Chaka and Suz – are walking along a path. We step into a grassy knoll and then the water-hole is below us. Suddenly – my heart in my throat – impala jump in all directions – I relax – gracefully, ballerinas splitting, high, over bushes, in mid-air. Ahead of me Bok turns, smiles and nods at me. Zebra, bubbling somewhere downstream. The sandstone krans over which water sometimes runs, not now, boulders perched on top. When will they fall? Now, or a hundred thousand years from now? And what does it matter in the scheme of eternity? Eternity like a bird that comes once in a thousand years to rub its beak against these rocks. And when at last there is a little hollow, the depth of a one-cent coin in the ridge of the boulder, then eternity would only have begun. So the boulders at Mphafa, when they fall in a hundred thousand years time, would have been sitting here for no more than a fraction of a second in the history of the world, but still for a fraction longer than humankind roamed earth. An infinity longer than the time in which the little yellow brushes with pink stems of *Acacia burkei* were named that, or swartapiesdoring, or black monkey thorn or – Bok, what did

Jonas call the swartapiesdoring? *Babampala. Babampala.* A beautiful word in whose hollows the bushbabies live.

The water-hole's glassy surface is a mirror of deep green acacia, black stems of tambotie, lighter green grass, patches of blue from the sky, the cliffs reflected showing their undersides, yellow-orange stalks and bushes near the water's edge and lengthening shadows of branches replicated like a photograph superimposed and upside down. In the descending sun's light, the bush has become greener, denser. The dull, like green glass churned by waves, has been replaced by a luscious tropical density. The sky in the water is bluer, the dry grass almost red and gold. Francolins screech and baboons bark, then suddenly go quiet. 'Could be leopard or lion,' Bok whispers, inclining his head to the noise. I purse my lips and he asks whether I'm afraid. No, I say, of course not, pulling my face and looking back down into the shadowed pool. Nothing more comes to the water-hole. We sit in our own silence in the sounds of this enormous world.

We build a fire outside the hut. He has a drink before we're due to go to Willy Hancox at the warden's house for the braai. The Alcamino is behind us and Bok leaves the door open to listen to the news. The sounds of zebra and nightjars are broken by the voice of Jeanette Hanekom, reading the Radio Port Natal news. There's an insert about the American election. Gerald Ford is running against Jimmy Carter. When the news is finished I turn the radio off and shut the bakkie's door. Bok says it spells trouble for South Africa if the peanut farmer is elected. I ask why and Bok says Carter is a bleeding-heart liberal who plans on cutting trade with South Africa. I say I think the PFP is morally the most justified political party in South Africa. Bok's eyes stare at me from across the fire. As if I've gone out of my mind.

'Don't you know what the communists did to East Africa?'

'The PFP are not communists. They want a federation.'

'That's the first step towards black majority rule. And that spells a socialistic future here as it has all over Africa. I don't need to tell you again what happens under socialism.'

I'm sick and tired of hearing about Tanzania this, Tanzania that. If it was so glorious, why were the blacks so angry that they took our land? 'It's more moral than what we're doing to the blacks,' I say. 'I know what you mean, Bok, but it's not right what's happening to the children in Soweto.'

'Those so-called children are burning down this goddamn country! Are you still hanging around with Dominic Webster? Let me tell you, under a socialistic black government in Tanzania, we lost our farms. Everything. There is not a single black country – barring Malawi and Botswana – where you're allowed to own anything. Everything belongs to the state. You can have a crap and your crap belongs to the government. Do you want that? Do you want everything to be taken from us for a second time? Answer me, Karl!'

I remain quiet, afraid, but for once do not want to bend before his anger. We don't have anything for them to take, anyway, Bok. The bank is taking the house back, anyway. 'Did they take our farms, Bok, or,' now almost in a whisper, 'did you leave before they could take our farms?'

He is rattled. As much as I am terrified. I was – he must hear – hoping to expose a lie or a story that has become lore. And in so doing I'm accusing him of being a coward.

'We left when we saw there was no hope. Our farm was next on the list. One and the same thing.'

Uncle Klaas was right. The land had not been taken. Not yet. Our flight was pre-emptive. The whole family has been in on the lie. Should be ashamed of themselves. And then, as if knowing exactly how to deflate my judgement he says: 'I took my wife and daughters . . . and the son I thought I had,' he pauses, 'and we put a few measly possessions on a boat. My wife and daughters, and the son I thought I had came by ship. I, like a number of others had to flee in secret by plane. And in this country, this country of hope, I again joined my wife and daughters because I loved them and the son I thought I had.'

I hang my head in shame. My father is angry, but more, he looks as if I've pulled his heart out. I do not know where my allegiance lies. Without looking him in the eye, staring into the flames, I speak: 'Maybe it was wrong for them to take your farm. But that doesn't make right what we're doing to black people in this country. That is what you and Bokkie have always taught us.'

'Exactly. Your mother and I have taught you to respect good black people. Not kaffirs, but good blacks. Many blacks are the salt of the earth, not like some whites. And that's what the homeland policy is for, so that they can live separately in their own countries and be governed by their own people. And when they have developed sufficiently, they may even get a vote in South Africa. But look at the way the schoolkids are behaving.'

I say I don't feel like going to Willy Hancox. Does he mind going alone?

He says I'm going. And if I don't, I want to say, will you do to me what you did to Lena? Slap me across my face till I submit. I'm feeling sick, I lie. I have a headache and I'm nauseous.

'Well stay here then. Jissis . . .' He gets up and goes inside. Gets dressed into longs and a shirt. I hear the bunch of keys, a six-pack of beers in his hand. Before going to the truck he comes and stands in front of me, forcing me to look up into his eyes.

'And you will carry on playing rugby, do you hear me?'

I look at him: 'I beg your pardon, Bok?'

'Do you hear me, Karl?'

'Why, Bok?' I ask, less about the rugby than to understand why he is speaking to me like this. About *rugby*, when a second before we'd been on *Jimmy Carter*. How did we get from an election thousands of miles in another country, across the Atlantic Ocean, to me playing rugby?

'Because I say so,' he says and smiles, cocking his head at me.

I avert my eyes. I stare into the fire.

'Because sport builds character. Because art turns people into lazy perverts. Because you're a strapping, big, strong boy. Look at your body; you were born to play team sport. Contact sport.'

I was not a big strong boy when, when, who knows when you started hating me, I want to say but cannot. With a smirk, a sneer of suppressed rage, he paces forward until he is almost on top of me. Again I have to look up when he speaks: 'You will play rugby until you become the man I want you to be. No communist kaffir-loving queer will ever set foot in my house. Tell that to that artsy fairy Dominic Webster and his family too. With my compliments. No, actually, I don't care whether you turn into a PFP or a communist or an HNP or anything. Go to Botswana and marry a black girl and breed coloured brats. Go to your federation — of socialist soviets — for all I care. But you will be a man, I tell you. Even there. If it's the last thing I do to you, with my last living breath . . . I will make you a man.' And he turns on his heel; walks off into the Umfolozi night.

I stare at the fire. Ignore the Alcamino driving off. CKQ. At first I try to laugh it off, tell myself how original his alliteration. CKQ, a trinity of K sounds. Probably accidental alliteration, he doesn't even know he did it. And then the rhyme: artsy, fairy. You could have been a second-rate poet, Bok. A flock of artsy fucking fairies. You and Lena. A great poet would have added Philistine.

But then the memory of his snigger returns. Gets me. His cruelty. Deliberate cruelty. The one thing Blanche Du Bois could never forgive. And me neither. Forget about ever taking me back to St Lucia. This is enough. I will forgive you everything, Bok. The affairs, the lies, the deception, the shrink, the beatings, the grandiose pretensions, the distortions, the duplicity, the stupidity, your collusion with that school, the assault on Dominic, whom I love more than you have ever loved anyone. Selling off Dademan's gift to me and bringing me here with what is probably my money anyway! But not the joyous brutality of that smirk. For that I will never forgive you. That smile, that sneer of unmitigated power: the way you used yours in this instant in this place I have loved more than any place on earth.

That is unforgivable.

The first unforgivable thing I have to hold against my heart. Nothing anyone else has ever done to me or I to them is unforgivable. Only this. For this thing you have no right to ask forgiveness, from me. Or from God. Ever. God who doesn't exist anyway, but whom I now wish did, so that he could cast you into the eternal flames of hell so that from across the rivers of heaven I can watch you scream and plead.

The flames dance. The long shadows of trees and shrubs run into the bush. Elbows resting on my upper thighs. I displace my elbow from where it is being bored by something hard, uncomfortable in my PT shorts pocket. I think of what he told me in the truck: that I was conceived crossing borders. And now I hate him for it. Not even a clear place of conception. It is your fault that I belong nowhere. Still staring into the flames I push my hand into the elastic and bring the round objects from my pocket, stare at them in my palm. Tambotie seeds. Jumping beans. Six or eight of them. Mkuzi tambotie. Like small balls of dung, rolled by baby dung-beetles. Within seconds the heat of my hand and the fire has them jumping. And then it strikes me: in his coffee. If I ground them and mash them. Just a teaspoonful over his cereal or in his coffee tomorrow morning. No one would ever know. No one would think it had not been an accident. That he accidentally chewed some tambotie. I could say, yes, he was chewing a twig of some sort at Mphafa. If he had eaten here tonight, instead of going to Willy Hancox, I could have strewn it over his meat, like peppercorns.

I'll keep them, for in case. One day. Some time.

I go inside to fetch my sketch pad. He has left his pack of Paul Revere 30s on his bed. I open the packet and take two cigarettes to

the fire. Light one with a twig and blow out the thick jet of smoke.
A natural.

Ever since autumn, once, twice a month I've been working on
Dominic's poem, but cannot get it to sound right, let alone finish.
Seven months and all I am left with is a long list of words: behold the
orange, circular, skin, smooth, indentations, smell, lemon, navel.
Tonight I add something at the beginning of the list: Dearest, behold
the sphere in your hand: circular, skin, smooth, orange, indentations,
lemon, navel, green patched. And I stop, again unable to continue.

I get undressed, now wrapping the tambotie in a handkerchief
that I slip into the toe of my veldskoens. Into the cool and crisp
sheets of the Natal Parks Board, small rhinos etched into green
stripes as monograms. I turn over on my stomach. My thoughts are
of the Berg: school, of choir, of Ma'am, of Dominic, Jacques. Of
Bok's smirk. How did I become your son? What wires were crossed,
where, that you and I have been given each other? What is there in me
that you are so afraid of me? I sit up. Bok, afraid of me? Jesus, I'm the
one who's scared of him.

Lie down. Get Bok out of my mind by willing myself into my
Mkuzi dream. Floating, floating over the brown grass that turns
green and greener and greener, and I'm floating I'm gone and beneath
me is the grass and I come down towards something in the veld and
it's Bok's desk just sitting there with hundreds of curios on shelves in
the grass and then there's something lying on top of the desk ledgers
and papers and accounts and amongst these is Jacques, with his legs
open and naked and his penis stiff on the black hair of his belly and
he asks me to put mine into him and I'm standing at the edge of the
desk, my hips thrusting, thrusting and he's telling me he loves me
inside him and then there's laughter and it's from the curios, the
masks, laughing with lips moving and I'm looking at them and my
penis is enormous like a stallion broad like a rhino horn from my
navel down going in and out of Jacques and then the curios of giraffe
and elephant and baboons start to move, still wooden statues but

they're animate and they run away and hide in the bushes above a river and I'm walking towards the river looking for the animals and the louries while I'm still inside Jacques who has his legs clutched to my waist and on the other side of the river to the right is Dominic and to the left is Uncle Klaas and behind him the Silent One and they're all calling, 'Come' 'Come,' and waving their arms for me to come and then behind the Silent One there's Jonas, smiling at me and I go into the river and pump my squirt into Jacques who dissolves in the cold water while my body shudders. And I wake up. The sheets beneath me slimy and uncomfortable.

Bok, back from the braai, is snoring in the bed across the rondavel.

I do dream in colour. Now I know it. In the colours of Gauguin or Dali.

19

Assembly in the quad on the first day back and Mathison makes it official: the European tour is off. A last-minute bid to arrange a trip to Israel has failed because of the short notice and restricted time. Mathison says he knows this is a big disappointment to us all and to the country; to Mr Cilliers, to the school – particularly to the Standard Sevens who are in their final year here – but for those who're staying, he promises, there will be a magnificent overseas tour in 1977. And, a donor – someone who has requested to remain anonymous – has donated two television sets to the school, so from next year we'll be able to – applause from the Juniors and Secondaries, most of whom were not part of the International Choir anyway.

I wonder where Jacques is. What is going through his mind. After all the work of the year, all the excitement and planning, the long hours. I wish to see him. To speak to him alone.

Muttering, cursing beneath our breaths, we walk away from assembly into the classroom, which smells of chalk dust and our absence.

Even though we have for a week been warned that a cancellation was on the cards, the actual announcement, hearing it from Mathison's lips, has nipped the bud of lingering hope.

'Mathison's out of his mind,' Dominic says as we take our seats. 'There will only be more cancellations in future. There won't be an overseas tour in 1977 either.'

'I disagree, Dominic,' Bruin turns his neck and speaks from the front row. 'I'm sure we'll always be welcome in Israel. You heard what he said. It was only because of things coming to a head so late that we couldn't go there.'

'Who wants to go to Israel, anyway?' Dominic throws his hands in the air. 'And why do you think we'll always be welcome there!' stressing the last four words dramatically,

'Israel is South Africa's friend,' Mervyn says from his seat near the window. 'And it's the home of my people. The Jews and the Afrikaners have very similar histories.' Dominic rolls his eyes while Mervyn speaks. 'It's true, Dom,' Mervyn goes on. 'Both suffered the horrors of concentration camps and both overcame adversity because they were chosen by God. Do you think it's pure coincidence that Israel became a state in the same year as the government was elected here? 1948 is a great year for both countries.'

'Israel . . . Our home away from home.' Dominic almost sings the phrase.

'You can stop being sarcastic, Webster.'

'Yes, Bennie!' Dominic turns to face the back of the class and snarls, 'Sarcasm is too indirect! I should say: our racist fascist home away from our racist fascist home!'

'Millions of Jews were murdered in Hitler's concentration camps, Dom.' I speak softly, not wanting to join in the discussion but hoping Dominic will stop before he has everyone up in arms.

'How can you speak to Mervyn like that?'

'Ignore Webster.'

'Easy for you, Dom, you've been overseas how many times?'

'Fokken kommunis.'

'Kafferboetie.'

'Anti-Semite.'

'Big shot soloist. Wise guy.'

A glow has spread up Dominic's neck. Suddenly he interrupts the fiery antagonisms: 'Why must you always revert to name-calling? Why don't you argue with me? Give me fucken arguments instead of silencing me with names.' All heads are turned towards him in the centre of class. 'I am not the one who's disappointed by the cancellation of this tour. As far as I'm concerned we're only getting our due.' His eyes fly from Bennie, to Lucas, to Mervyn, across the rest, up and down the rows, and eventually settle on me: 'If you all are so upset: why don't you think? Think for a change, instead of running like lemmings towards the cliff. If you can't feel with your hearts, then at least think with your heads. The one thing my dad has taught me is the difference between treating symptoms and addressing causes. The cancellation of this tour, like all the shit with the sports boycott, this ugly war in Angola, is but a symptom, idiots! It is a symptom of the rotten state in which we live. And don't think for a second, not one moment, that this will end here. No ways! Dad says it's going to get worse and worse and worse, until this fascist government is brought to its—'

'A good morning to you too, Dominic.' Silence as we turn to face Ma'am, who has stepped into his tirade.

'You use the word fascist too easily,' she says as her skeletal frame glides towards her desk. Her blond hair is tied in a bun at the nape of her neck. She no longer seems to be speaking to us. A soliloquy to the walls, covered in our art, our various projects: 'Such use of the word slights the trauma of every victim of the Second World War. In particular, the suffering of the Jews who died and of their families who survived.' She pauses, and again, now almost as if in contemplation to herself, continues: 'South Africa is not systematically murdering people as Hitler and Mussolini did while the other countries of Europe were expelling their own Jews to be sent to Hitler's ovens. Other things may be wrong here, indeed they are. Severely wrong.' Her gaze shifts from the back walls, to her desk, then runs across us. Again she pauses, stares from the window into the sun up the embankment. In profile it is clear how thin she has grown: the side of the face shown to us is sunken, the chin angular and jutting. 'So much of what's happening in this country is wrong and cruel.' She now places her satchel and basket on her desk, turns to look at the class, then at Dominic: 'You will not use the words fascist or Nazi in my class when you talk about what's going on in South Africa. Not unless you use them with enormous circumspection. What is happening here is hardly different from what happened under European colonialism in the rest of Africa, the East and the Americas. And time will show that as bad as this system is, it does not rank with the major crimes of world history, let alone of this century. You may want to take a look at Uganda. Or Biafra. At the Defiquane. Stalin's pogroms. The conquest of America. And even then, you may want to use words like authoritarian, autocratic, despotic. Yes, racist. Not Nazi, not fascist.' Then, with the timbre of an exhausted voice, she says: 'It's good to see you all again. Good morning, boys.'

'Morning, Ma'am.'

'I'd like to thank you all for singing at Graham's funeral. It meant more to me and my family than words can ever say.' No note of self-pity or pain in her deadpan voice. If behind the composure there lies fragility — as there must — she hides it by walking up and down the aisles, handing out our essays, apologising that she's taken so long to get them back to us, asking whether Mr Loveday did a good job and whether we behaved ourselves. I smell her as she glides past me: talcum powder and a faint trace of perfume.

From my report's A in English I know I must have done well with 'His Name Was Henk Willemse'. Smiling a nod, she hands me my book. 19/20. While she tells us to get out our Natural Science textbooks, I skim through her lengthy commentary, excitement like bubbles in my blood:

Karl, I always look forward to reading your essays and once again your rich writing has filled me with consummate joy. And also a little regret at my own lost dreams of being a novelist. This is your first essay without a single spelling error or a split infinitive! You have come so far this year that I'm want to say you're even more talented (and infinitely more disciplined!) than I thought at first. Having said that: I am not sure what to make of your use of a Bosmanesque voice: remember you must develop your own artistic signature. As an exercise (such as those we've occasionally done in Art), emulating the elements of style of another's work is very effective. Just be cautious that you do not stifle your individual development and creativity in the process. Find your own voice. Now is the time. It's time for you to fly the roost! I quote here for you from an essay by Isaac Bashevis Singer. It is from the foreword to Hunger, *the exquisite novel by Knut Hamsun, something you may want to read:* 'Writers who are truly original do not set out to fabricate new forms of expression, or to invent themes merely for the sake of appearing new. They attain their originality through extraordinary sincerity, by daring to give everything of themselves, their most secret thoughts and idiosyncrasies.' *Dare to be sincere in your writing, Karl.*

S. Sanders

Evaporation and condensation. Only snatches reach my ears. *It's time for you to fly!* The longest commentary she has ever written me. It's time for me to fly! I return to her red-ink handwriting. Over and over, hiding the Essay book behind *Natural Science For Standard Six*. Only that one sentence matters to me. I hardly see the rest. A rush of adrenalin that makes it almost impossible to sit still. Through Maths. Through Latin – Karl are you paying attention? Yes, Ma'am. In front of the class she gives scarcely a hint of her emotions. But for the loss of weight, the tired voice, there is no evidence that she has suffered or continues to mourn. At the funeral pain was all over her face, borne on her hunched shoulders. Now that is gone, and the old, steely resolve is back in her eyes in the upright, graceful carriage. When she turns to write on the blackboard, the gauntness of her profile is again obvious, her nose seeming more pronounced than I have remembered. Under what circumstances did she mark my essay?

And also a little regret at my own lost dreams of being a novelist.

The saddest line, I think. Is it in there, somewhere, she tries to relate to me a hint of her heartbreak? How I want her to know that she is always in my thoughts. How I adore her. I should get us all to make some gesture of condolence, for we all must see that she is not over it. As Bokkie says: 'A parent never gets over the death of a child.' Kaspasie and Lynette can speak about the death of their father, even Aunt Barbara can laugh and tell anecdotes about how Uncle Gert was. But Oupa Liebenberg only weeps. Uncle Klaas. Are they still here! I think of taking the essay for him to read. No, I'm not going to sneak out. I'm going nowhere until Jacques tells me to come. In front of me Dominic has been quiet since Ma'am broke him off. Is he angry about her intrusion into his outburst this morning? I would love to speak to Ma'am alone. Let her cry against my shoulder, to give her strength, to say she may take me as a son. That she is the mother I always wanted. Through Geography.

At short break I hand Dominic Ma'am's commentary. He is wearing new jeans, a new charcoal black T-shirt, new veldskoene. His entire wardrobe has been replaced. Struggling to suppress his anger at her, he none the less congratulates me on Ma'am's evaluation, saying hard work always pays off. He himself has to practise like hell. The Grade Eight is weeks off.

The question about spending Parents' Weekend with the Websters I put off for now. When the time comes, I'll use the Bernice-is-writing-matric excuse.

'Are you angry with Ma'am?' I ask.

'Disappointed in her.'

'It must be a difficult time for her, Dom.'

'That doesn't give her the right to treat my opinions like shit. And she's not the first mother to lose a child.' He speaks about black mothers, hundreds, grieving all over the country for their young children who are being killed because they're fighting for the right to learn. Hoping to still his rage at Ma'am, I suggest he see her intervention merely as her giving her opinion. Just as he was giving his.

The bell rings for choir.

Staring at the floor, he sits listening from a chair behind Raubenheimer, who takes us through the warm-ups. Ho-ho-ho-ho-ho-ho-ho-ho-ho-ho-ho-ho-ho-ho-ho-ho-ho-hooo, breath, semi-tone up, hi-hi-hi-hi-hi-hi-hi-hi-hi-hi-hi-hi-hi-hi-hi-hi-hiii, breath, semi-tone up, mo-mo-mo-mo-mo-mo-mo-mo-mo-mo-mo-mo-mo-mo-mo-mo-mo-mooo, breath, semi-tone down, fi-fi-fi-fi-fi-fi-fi-fi-fi-fiiii, breath, semi-tone down. His hands are folded, fingers plaited into a clasp. Ankle resting on his knee. Beige longs, leather shoes. A green long-sleeved shirt rolled up, exposing his hairy arms and the curls on his chest where the shirt is unbuttoned at the throat. His hair has been cut. The stirring of desire, again at seeing him. Feel myself go stiff, from just looking. My legs feel warm and heavy, waiting for him to look up and tell me something with his eyes.

'Okay,' he says, rising. Raubenheimer immediately falls into the front line.

Someone, now filling the tallest spot in the back formerly held by Lukas, asks Jacques whether there's any chance of us still going overseas. He smiles and says no, it is definitively off and there's nothing to be done about it. Shrugging his shoulders. We must get on with it and put everything we have into the Prime Minister's concert and the album recordings. A mere six weeks away. He tells us to open our scores at the Agnus Dei.

My spirits soar as we begin to sing. Our voices fill the hall, the windowpanes rattle in their frames, it is only a wave of sound, harmony as we take up *Dona nobis pacem*. There are moments I hear my voice carrying the second sopranos. He notices and gestures to me to be careful, lifts his hand towards the second altos, nods his head vigorously. The sombre and painful B minor key is in direct contrast to the way I am feeling: I am on a high, I am ready to fly. I take him in, miss his fingers up my spine, yet it's as though nothing really matters other than the richness of our singing and beating within it like wings Ma'am's opinion of my essay. Into E minor. He stops us.

'Beethoven wanted it to be clear here. Look at the orchestration, can you see the trumpets and the drums – that we're struggling with the tensions between war and peace. The resolution is unclear. *Lamb of God, who takes away the sins of the world, have mercy upon us.* And then here, *Give us peace.* Here,' he points from bar 268 onwards, 'remember that from that B flat we've got trumpets and war, almost like a march from the orchestra, and from there it is again the deep, deep prayer for peace that takes over. We're prostrating ourselves before God, begging for peace in a time of war.' He touches the accompanist's shoulder and lifts his hands. And I'm wondering whether there is a chance I could spend Parents' Weekend with him, rather than with Dominic. Maybe a part with him, a part with Dom.

Along the broad gravel road to Champagne Castle, at a canter, slowing to a walk in single file as we reach the S bend, cautious of possible vehicle traffic coming from above. Somewhere in my mind there's a memory of a rider and horse being struck by a car – a movie, a book – maybe still a Secret Seven or a Famous Five, a short story – making for disease whenever we're riding along a road. My fingers in the reins above Rufus's main are blue. From rubbing graphite dust into paper to create gradated tones of blue for the table-cloth around the empty vase Ma'am had us draw.

She has become more aloof as the week passed. Art class, the last on a Friday afternoon, has always been the source of pleasant concentration, discussion, and occasionally laughter. Today's mood was quiet. No whiff of the passion I usually sense she controls or is holding back, giving it to us in small select doses. Today it was not passion she was holding back, instead it seemed like more sadness and more of the sharpness that has been growing towards Dominic. In contrast to the way she treats him, my every word is taken seriously. She answers me, engages, smiles, encourages. But Dominic she virtually ignores, though not so obviously that one could be certain. Curt. She is curt to him, not sharp. Always leaving room for doubt as to what she means when she acknowledges something he says. We're doing pencil, charcoal and carbon drawings. The history of graphite. How pencils are graded according to their hardness and softness: 8B, the softest, to B and up to 8H, the hardest. Different textures of paper. She showed us how to combine pencil and crayon, shade and texture by rubbing lines, blending different colour pencils. The illustrations of Lewis Carroll's *Alice in Wonderland* and sketches by Degas, Leonardo Da Vinci, Picasso and Rodin. When Dominic said he had visited Rodin's home in Paris, where the Master's sculptures adorn the garden, and that he had seen the original sketches for *The Kiss*, Ma'am looked at him with tired, irritated eyes and said: 'It is an education to travel, isn't it, Dominic?' And then she'd gone on, leaving Dominic and the other four of us perplexed. She told us to draw the huge metal milk jug around which she draped a piece of blue velvet. Our prac was done in silence. She barely moved around to look at what the five of us were doing, offered no suggestions, no comments. Today she may not even have been there.

I stare at the blue against my fingertips. It has stained right into the grooves where I bite the skins around the nails. There it is a dark ultramarine, a lighter cobalt blue the farther it goes from the nails until the skin is again flesh colour against the dirty leather of the reins and the copper of Rufus's coat, the thatch of his mane. These blue fingers against the bridle and the red or copper coat, I think, that's something I should draw.

Choir time Lukas now spends down at the dairy with or in place of Mr Walshe. In the evenings before supper he supervises the milking and the horses. In two weeks' time he wants to shoe the horses and there's a Jersey cow about to calf. He says he'll monitor her closely and let me know so that I can be present for the birth.

I ask what he thinks the matter with Ma'am. He pats King's neck, glances at the Juniors behind us and says it's obviously Graham's death. 'But what about the way she treats Dom?' I ask. 'She's always curt with him, cutting him off. He's always been one of her favourites.'

'He's a bit brass-arsed lately, that's what's gotten to Ma'am.'

'He says she's not the first nor the last mother to lose a child. He says you just have to go to every black location to see the grief; hundreds of mothers mourn for fourteen-year-olds, killed by the police.'

'Those kaffirs are burning down the country. I feel fuck-all for their mothers. Graham was trying to *protect* this country. Ag, anyway, who knows, I haven't noticed anything.'

'You wouldn't notice if the school burnt down now, Lukas. What a life. The only thing you see is what's going on in the dairy, hey!'

'Don't be so sure of yourself, De Man.'

'I envy you not having to sing anymore,' I say automatically, then realise I don't mean what I've just said. Every moment of choir has become a treat, each session something to look forward to.

'That's what a man gets for having such big balls,' he says, turning on a gruff voice.

'Kak, Lukas! Yours are no bigger than mine.' And I go on to ensure him that according to my knowledge the break in a voice has nothing to do with the size of testicles.

'Why do you think the castrati had such high falsettos?' he asks, tipping his riding cap at me.

'They had no balls, they were castrated! Still doesn't prove anything about ball size. Mervy's balls are like goose eggs and he was a high alto. And what about Johan Rademan! Fifteen years old, dick like a hosepipe and balls down to his knees and he goes even higher than Dom.'

*

With Dominic now all but sleeping behind the piano, Mervyn, without my asking, buys my weekly tin of Condensed Milk. Mr Buthelezi punches in two gaps and I walk from the store, sucking from the slits. Mervyn takes a sip and says he cannot understand how I drink the stuff. I say Dominic says it's because I'm a sweet and sentimental fella.

Past the game pen, where I mimic the zebra, getting them to look at us with ears erect, we walk from the holiday park towards the river and the rugby field. I tell him about Mkuzi, about the rhino cow and calf, the herd of buffalo we saw wading in the mud of the White Umfolozi. The purple-crested lourie, gliding downhill and disappearing in the bushes, its purple head resplendent in the sun, its wings spread out like fans. That Chaka wore the crimson feathers in his head-dress, alongside the feather of a blue crane.

On the embankment above the pump-house, arum lilies grow in clumps of thirty, forty flowers, the enormous creamy spathes with yellow stamens a natural garden in the wet soil. Into the marsh we plod, pulling the long stalks from their waxy green bases. Half the stalks we'll cut off. Place the bunch on Ma'am's desk. On a piece of cardboard I have sketched in charcoal and then coloured with pastels the blue fingers, the brown reins in black and burnt umber and then Rufus's mane Venetian red faintly glossed with again raw umber. On it I wrote, inanely: Welcome back, Ma'am. Then I got the whole class to sign. I tried to compose a verse, just a haiku or a couplet, but nothing has wanted to come. For days now I have been unable to write a word. That I'm *ready to fly* seems to have had only the opposite affect: I'm not ready to write a word, let alone fly with the word. I keep at Dominic's orange poem, finding new words in the encyclopaedias. There's an essay due in a week's time, titled: 'A Remarkable Vision'. I toy with the sight of the White Umfolozi from our front lawn, or the movement of animals at Bube. Or the dream. God, the dream I had in Umfolozi, with all the colours, and Jacques! I know it could be interesting, but I couldn't possibly write that for her. That quote she has given me, seems, if I understand it correctly, to suggest that I should write about the dream. Yes, the dream, surely, is my inner-most idiosyncrasy? A few times I try, but give up, knowing it is scandalous. I could never give it to anyone to read, let alone Ma'am. So I have begun working on another dream, one I fabricate, of a man trying to cross a river, trying to achieve a state of perfection. The card, together with the flowers, will go to Ma'am. I was thinking about using a small watercolour I did last term, called *Poplars in Spring*, but have let go of the idea because of her comments about me having to find my own style. Bennie comes walking up from the rugby field with Radys and a group of Standard Sevens. He sees us and runs through the long grass to join us. Soon, our arms are filled with flowers. The three of us make our way back up the hill, occasionally stopping to shake ants and bugs out of the deep open spathes that look like white rhino ears or ice-cream cones with an orange waver straw in the middle.

I sit at a desk in the music room while Dominic's head is bent over the keyboard. There is growing resentment from many in class about his blasé attitude towards the cancelled tour. Increasingly I see friends going silent when he's near. Bennie, who has become more and more friendly with Radys Dietz, refuses to play a game of tact, making sure all note the way he leaves any group at Dominic's approach. Dominic himself either is or pretends to be indifferent.

Parents' Weekend is three weeks away and I'm yet to ask about spending it with the Websters. On the phone I have lied to Bokkie and said Lukas has invited me to join his family at Cathkin Peak Hotel. Nor have I told anyone that I will not be back next year, that I'm going to Port Natal. I plan on writing a letter to Aunt Lena, asking her whether she might be able to pay for me to stay. If that works, any announcement on my part would have been premature. To tell Dominic or Lukas – or anyone – that Bok doesn't have the money to keep me here or even to drive up for the last parent weekend is unthinkable. To tell him that Mumdeman is ill would be a lie of com-mission. Lies of omission are something else. Those I indulge in, also to Dominic, with little more effort than it takes to sneeze. Then, also, in my mind's shadows hovers the treasonous possibility of not spending time with the Websters at all. Of instead getting Jacques to take me on a hike into the mountains. If I were to tell Jacques that my parents couldn't come — because we're so poor — he may take pity on me. Allow me to come to his room as often as I wish. No. I can do without his pathetic charity. And now, for the first time I feel a tinge of guilt. Not towards Jacques, but towards Dominic. Clearly I am keeping my options open, and that, maybe, is the worst reason I'm not asking him about the weekend. That flicker of hope and thudding desire, that maybe the thing with Jacques is not, after all, quite over. I cannot understand the recurring need to be with him. At home and in the bush I barely thought of him. But setting eyes on him, finding him still ignoring me, has fuelled my love; my lust. No. I want him to want to be with me. To want me. How I'd enjoy saying: no, I'm sorry, Mr Queer, I've tired of you and I love someone else. Or, better yet, to take the key and place it on the piano in front of him, letting him see I'm through with waiting for him. I could do that, for I still have the extra one cut in Toti. But even as I think these thoughts I already know there will be no following through into action. I miss being with him too much. Yearn. Even once more, even just one more time starfishing! Yet, I also treasure the moments with Dominic. Wish we could be alone, that his exams are over so that we can again lie in each other's arms and talk and kiss and play and tease. I love them both. I want them both. I cannot possibly choose. At night, disallowed from visiting either and sure that Uncle Klaas and the Silent One have left, I stay in my own bed. I masturbate, sometimes twice, three times in the space of two hours. My fantasy is often one of penetrating Steven Almeida. Then I alternate between doing it and being done by Jacques, and when I receive a letter from Alette, it is her I hear saying yes, yes, oh god, yes, as I suck on her lips and run my tongue to her belly button. Occasionally I am sucking Harding's dick or Reyneke is licking my starfish, groaning that he wants me to stick my dick into him. I imagine Marguerite Almeida, her long hair loose on a white pillow and her brown breasts hard in my mouth, her vagina tight and hot around my penis. I can think myself into kissing or stroking anyone or anything. I picture Cassandra's dripping cunt, my one hand guiding King's sausage into her or me, on a small hill, with King's dick gliding in and out of me, his come flying over my back. Or of Dominic, sitting on top of me, his rectum opening and contracting like an anemone around my middle finger, his hands flat on my chest, his head thrown back, groaning like the night in their house. These are fantasies I can never discuss with anyone. During breaks we talk about tossing off, compare boasts on who takes the longest, who can ejaculate the quickest. Who has fucked a girl. But each image that comes to me so easily makes me feel ashamed and guilty. They confirm that I am a child of Satan. I can fantasize about Harding, of him lying beneath me, and I can wonder where in the world he is this year, and then the moment I have ejaculated can hate myself for wanting to have had sex with him. A fantasy is as good as a sin. And my sins are unutterable. I am as good as standing in hell. But a fantasy is not reality! I could never be fucked by King. He'd rip me apart. It's just something to imagine and enjoy. No. That's already a sin. There is no hope for my salvation. Wiping my belly I am ready to grab the Bible from my locker, read by torch under the covers. When I was with Dominic or Jacques, when fear had spread its ugly thorns in my mind, I told myself that at least hell would not be so bad with either of them there with me. Or I'd simply think of something else, like the bush, of wild animals, or of my life as an artist. But alone I have the fear of Dademan or Uncle Gert having access to my perverted mind, or Great-Grandfather and Grandmother Liebenberg. That they're there, in the dorm with me, watching as guardian angels, horrified at the scenes playing out in the mind of their grandson and great-grandson.

His fingers or his back tired, Dominic takes a break. We talk about everything. Especially the Grade Eight and how afraid he is. There are those who say he's way too young to play the Schumann and they're probably just waiting for him to make one mistake. Of Schumann or Dom's ability to play the German's music I have no clue; but I tell him it sounds breathtaking, faultless, perfect. Words I think not only apt, but words that may boost his confidence. Whether he is truly good enough or even almost good enough to play the Schumann I don't know, though Mervyn tells me he is. Mervyn tells me Dominic is world-class. And amongst all the talk of and rehearsing there is Ma'am's strangeness towards him, which he says he's sure is a passing thing. He tells me of his holiday, boating on the Vaal Dam where Dr Webster taught him to water-ski and they worried all the time about him breaking an arm or a finger. Mine with Bok in Mkuzi and Umfolozi. 'I never knew your father was a ranger,' he said, surprised. While saying I was sure I had mentioned it often over the years – that of course he has known – I suddenly realise that the bush is something I rarely speak about outside of our family. Just as I never speak about Tanzania. As much as they are constantly on my mind, I never speak about them. But because I think about them so often, I assume everyone knows.

Having sworn him to secrecy I have confided in him about Stephanie's abortion. He said an abortion was nothing to be secretive or ashamed about. Mrs Webster has had three and she tells the whole world. He said she refuses to go on the pill because it muddles a woman's hormones and every now and again she and Dr Webster have a little slip or the French letter tears and off she goes to London. He laughed, threw up his hands, and turned back to the keyboard, at once taking up where he had left off. As if he had just told me his mother went down the street to buy Kentucky Fried Chicken. His world, the Webster world, I think, is a world apart. No. A different galaxy from the one where I live.

Trying to catch up on Latin and Maths homework. Stuck in translation, unable to remember the gender of *sagitta, sagittae*, I lapse into daydream. Staring at Dominic's slender back beneath the black cotton fabric, the vertebrae of his spine visible with every movement of the flexing shoulder muscles, the white neck and short hair, head bowed forward nodding time, the fingers seem to run from his sides, again, like spiders crossing hot cement. Pulling a double page from the back of my Latin exercise book, I write: *Achilles Heel – Removing the Dampers.* Then begin to draw his heel and sandalled foot, tipped from the toes on the sustaining pedal. I go down on my haunches and study the hollows on either side of the tendon running down the back of his foot connecting to the heel, see the way the calf muscles tremble, ever so slightly with every suppression. He senses me behind him and still playing asks what I'm doing. Drawing your foot on the pedal, I answer. He tells me to kiss him in his neck. I say I can't, not here, where there are no curtains and anyone can walk in. I scold him jokingly for banning me from his bed. He stops playing, swings around and kisses me, biting my lip when I try to pull away. I taste blood in my mouth.

More and more he speaks about Canada. Dr Webster is beginning to sound serious about emigrating. Please don't go, I say. He says I can come and live in Toronto with them after I've finished school in Durban. You can become an exchange student, he says. You can apply to Rotary or to be an AFS. What is an AFS, I ask. American Field Scholar, he says, my cousin was an AFS. Easy as pie. And then, he says, you can stay on afterwards, Karl, yes, we can put up house together in New York or LA or Montreal. And we can learn to speak French. *Voulez-vous coucher avec moi, ce soir*? I don't want to live somewhere else, I say. This is my home. I only want to see other places, not live there. I do not say I know what happens to people who leave their countries of birth.

'Once you've been overseas,' he says, 'you'll want to stay there for ever. And we'll live together.' Overseas. For ever. Together. I stare at him, not allowing myself to dream of it being a possibility. 'We'll have a flat, an apartment as they call it, overlooking the Hudson. Or

the Tiber, or the Thames,' he says. I am too shy to ask what he is talking about. Ashamed of my ignorance. 'I'll be an acclaimed virtuoso
like Paderewski or Rubinstein. And you'll be a famous poet like who,
who do you want to be?'

'Dominic, stop it. It's never going to happen. And I don't like
living in a flat anyway.'

'Okay, we'll have a house on Long Beach, looking out over the
ocean. And we'll have only four rules in our house. Same as Mum and
Dad.'

'What?'

'No Bibles. No Sexism. No Racism.' He pauses.

'What is sexism?' I ask, tentatively. I know racism is to do with
black and white and Indian and coloured, and I know sex is mating
and male and female. But I've never heard the word sex with this
suffix.

'Sexism is treating women differently from how you'd treat men,
just like racism is discriminating against people because of their skin
colour.'

'But women are different from men. They're mothers and home-
makers.'

'Says who! My mother went back to being a researcher a year after
I was born. Prudence raised us. That's why I'm so fond of Beauty. We
were always taught to respect all people irrespective of race, colour or
creed.' I think of us in East Africa, each with our own houseboy. And
Tobie and Chiluma, in Malawi, doing the housework for the Olvers.
But those are black people. I have never heard of white men doing
housework.

'Women are meant to have children, take care of the family,
Dominic. That's the way it is all over the world. And it says so in the
Bible.'

'Exactly! That's why that irrational, stupid book is banned from
our house.'

'Why aren't you allowed to read the Bible?'

'We're allowed to read it, like I'm allowed to go to church and Sunday school here. But we have to go to the library to read the Bible.'

'Why doesn't your father want you to become Christians?'

'Oh, it's not my father. It's actually mostly my mother. She says that God was created by powerful people to take all the pleasure out of the world and to make people fearful. Where people are enjoying themselves there is no fear. And where there is no fear, there cannot be a God. My parents want me to never be afraid.' I think about Uncle Joe. He too refuses to go to church, to read the Bible. But that is for other reasons. What those are, I have no idea. I must ask him about it some time. I wonder if they'll be coming down for Christmas. And Uncle Klaas, what he—

'Want to hear rule Number Four?'

I nod.

'Wash the cucumber before you put it back in the fridge.' He waits for me to laugh. 'You don't get it, do you?'

'No, what's so funny about that?'

'If you've had the cucumber up your arse, Karl, you've got to wash it before you put it back in the fridge, Silly.' I tell him he is disgusting and he says, don't tell that to me, tell it to my mother, she's forever saying it to my dad when he's in a bad mood.

Labouring over the essay, which is giving me no pleasure. Every word, every image sounds contrived: *The ~~man~~ boy crouches ~~desperately~~ in the grass above an enormous gaping precipice. On the opposite bank stands a figure, a statue of incomparable perfection, shimmering like green marble sculpted beneath ~~Rodins~~ a master's hand. The ~~man~~ boy reaches out, but almost stumbles and suddenly draws back, afraid of falling down the sheer cliffs. Below him, in the dark quagmire of swirling black mists, anything may lurk, waiting to devour him. Still the statue ~~urges~~ beckons ~~for~~ the man to cross. He thinks of leaping, takes a few steps back to make a running start, but then sees and knows the chasm is too ~~huge~~ wide.* Unable to continue, not knowing what to do with the man for two more pages, I go back to Dominic's orange poem. That, too, seems impossible, as my list simply grows longer: *Dearest, behold the ball in your hand: circular, skin, smooth, indentations, lemon, navel, green patched, China, California, scent, nostrils, peel, spray, segments, juice, Vitamin C, ~~Marco Polo~~, fruit, colour, yellow, orange, moist, fluid.* I know I must abandon the poem. Some things just cannot be written, like some paintings cannot be completed, as Ma'am says. But to admit defeat, only days after I have been told I should fly! What if I can never again write? What if instead of being a writer I am really a painter? Suddenly I dread coming near words. I have been chasing an illusion, something for which I really have no talent. That I will after all end up a zero on a contract. Be nothing.

I go to Ma'am for advice on both essay and poem. She laughs and says I'm far too young for writer's block and that I must simply keep at it. There is nothing she can do other than tell me to keep writing and to remember that no one told me it would be easy. 'Take heart,' she smiles, handing both back, 'there are seeds of promise in these pieces. Enormous potential. Now go and do it.' Affirmed, I go to the orange poem and add *seeds* to the list. But as inspiring as Ma'am's words are, I remain unable to progress. For some reason I take to a silent blaming of Bok. And eventually also Jacques and even Dominic for my inability to produce something that will impress the breath out of Ma'am. Justify all the hours she puts into me. If I didn't have to worry about next year and if I didn't love Dominic and Jacques, then I wouldn't have so much on my mind. Then I'd be able to fly. Riding offers only a temporary escape from my malfunction.

Because of her absence at the end of last term Ma'am was unable to round off our classes on the French Revolution. After she's handed out our answer papers from the test we now all again remember, she reads to us a description by someone who witnessed the outcome of the Revolution first hand. 'This is an eyewitness account,' she says, opening the book at a marker, 'by the philosopher who has had the most profound impact on the way I see the world. He was an Irishman, like James Joyce, Bernard Shaw, W.B Yeats. He too, like many great men of their time, was persecuted for his beliefs.' Ma'am reads slowly, allowing each word to sink in: '*Yielding to reason at least as forceable as those who were so delicately urged in the complement of the new year, the king of France will probably endeavour to forget these events and that complement. But history who keeps a durable record of all our acts and exercises her awful censure over the proceedings of all sorts of sovereigns will not forget, either these events or the era of this liberal refinement in the intercourse of mankind . . . This king, to say no more of him and his queen and their infant children (whom once would have been the pride and hope of a great and generous people) were then forced to abandon the sanctuary of the most splendid palace in the world, which they left swimming in blood, polluted with massacre and strewed with scattered limbs and mutilated carcasses. Thence they were conducted into the capital of their Kingdom. Two had been selected from the unprovoked, unresisted, promiscuous laughter, which was made of the gentlemen of birth and family who composed the king's bodyguard. These two gentlemen, with all the parade of an execution of justice, were cruelly and publicly dragged to the block and beheaded in the great court of the palace. Their heads were stuck upon spears and led the procession, whilst the royal captives which followed in train were slowly moved along amidst the horrid yells, and shrilling screams, and frantic dances and infamous contumelies, and all the unutterable abominations of the furies of hell, in the abused shape of the vilest of women . . .*'

The reading completed, silence reigning over the class, Dominic steps up onto his chair. He is about to speak when Ma'am commands him get down at once. Instead of doing as she says he strikes a pose: his wrists limp and palms held upward as if in fateful acceptance or supplication and says: 'Oh, Madame Guillotine, my head, for thee.' Giggles are cut short when Ma'am barks: 'Sit down, dammit, Dominic. I cannot stand effeminate boys.'

He doesn't flinch. Our eyes move between Ma'am and him. Then, slowly, he descends, keeping his eyes riveted on Ma'am. With both feet back on the floor, still looking Ma'am in the eye, his hands at his sides, he says: 'Yes, I'm sure you cannot, *Madame*. You obviously have a preference for boys who play with guns.'

Slowly, he takes his seat.

At first I too am stung only by his cheek. The audacity not only of talking back at her, but of his defiance. Then only does the deliberate meaning of what he has said hit home. Maybe to all of us at once, also to her, for suddenly: 'Get out,' she says. 'Get out of this classroom.'

'I will not.'

Silence. No emotion on her face. 'How dare you resist my authority! And how dare you, *now*, speak to me about guns . . .' Again she tells him to get out. Again he says he will not. 'You will leave this classroom, or else I will go.'

'It's up to you,' he says.

And to our consternation, Ma'am begins to pack her bags. Her lips begin to tremble, and then, abandoning her things on the desk, she flees the room. For a few seconds we sit in stunned silence. All eyes on Dominic. Then, as if on cue, Bennie and Radys fly from their seats and swoop down on Dominic from behind. A thud as his head crashes against wood before the desk itself with him and the other two crashes and fists fly. Then I'm around my desk, on Radys, tearing at his shoulders, trying to get him off Dominic. Shouts ring out as I feel an arm go around my neck, throttling me. Through eyes popping from my head I see more bodies joining the fracas. I throw my head back, smashing it into whomever's face is behind me. Gasping for air I turn around, ready to punch my assailant. It is Lukas, holding his nose. I drop my fist.

I turn back and grab Radys around the neck. From the corner of my eye I see Marabou peering through the door, her jaw dropped in disbelief before she hurries out.

'Stop it!' Mervyn and Bruin's voices. 'Holloway saw you.' A fist catches me on the temple and I see stars, wonder where Dominic is, beneath all the bodies. Then Mathison's voice fills the room: 'Get up, all of you. This instant.' Noise as chairs and desks scrape and half the class seems to rise off Dominic, who is the last to get up. His nose bloodied. We stand behind our desks.

'What do you think you're doing?' Mathison asks. Dominic takes his white hankie from his shorts, rights his desk and chair and sits down. Mathison glares at him. 'What, I ask you, is going on here?' Silence. 'Van Rensburg? Tell me.' His eyes now on Lukas.

'It was a disagreement, Sir.'

'And since when do we resolve our differences like animals instead of civilised human beings?'

'Since so-called civilised human beings dropped an atom bomb on Hiroshima,' Dominic says through the handkerchief over his nose, his elbows on the desk.

'Who do you think you're talking to, Webster? Stand up when you're talking to me.'

'You asked a question and I answered it, Sir. And I am dizzy so I'm afraid I won't stand.'

'All of you, go to my office. The whole class. Come on. This insolence will not be tolerated.'

'I'm not going to be caned, Mr Mathison,' Dominic says, his voice rising from his desk over the rest of us moving to the door. As if on order, we halt.

'I beg your pardon?'

'I am not going to be caned, Sir, that's what I said.'

'You will get up off your butt and into that office this minute!'

'You'll have to use force to get me there, Sir. Either before or after I call my father.' And with that Dominic, now clutching the blood-stained handkerchief in his fist, rises and walks down the aisle, passes those of us who've already lined up at the door, and walks from the classroom. Mathison is clearly at a loss for words.

He clears his throat: 'I'll deal with that insolence later. Get going to my office.'

Ma'am sits weeping in the staff dining room. Marabou is with her. Mathison goes into his office while we line up outside. One by one my classmates enter. There's a thud and Mathison calls: 'Next.'

Bennie comes out, holding up one finger and grinning. And so we go in, next, pause, thud, pause, next, pause, thud, pause, next, pause, thud, and with each next we get closer to the door. Boys enter, exit, walk by smiling and return to class. He hits me and I walk out grinning. I pass the line and whisper to Mervyn that it's a joke.

Ma'am has disappeared from the teachers' dining room. Back in class we're all laughs. Bennie and Radys pull down their pants to show there's barely a red mark. An esprit de corps. Unified by our punishment and talking about the rumble in which most of us were punched, throttled or flung to the floor. Lukas gets us to straighten out rows and chairs.

'Waar's daai Webster?' Radys asks. There's a sudden lull in the buzz.

'Where's your little friend, De Man?'

'Calling his daddy. Daddy, they want to hit me, do something, Daddy, give them some more money, please, Daddy.' Radys in his dreadful Afrikaans accent, deliberately mocking Dominic's rounded English vowels. Most of the class is of the opinion that it would be sacrilege if Dominic is not caned. Moreover, what he said to Ma'am is unforgivable. As is his cheek to Mathison.

'Coward, that's what he is.'

'Afraid to take it like a man.'

Ma'am comes back with red eyes and we commence the last lesson of the day.

Dominic doesn't return and I sit wondering where he is. After class I sneak to the dorm to see whether he's there. I ask if anyone has seen him. No one knows anything. I see Beauty entering C Dorm. I run to her. She is sorting our laundry.

'Beauty,' I begin, immediately aware that I'm speaking to her for the first time since the abortive apology behind the kitchen, 'have you seen Dom anywhere?'

Instead of answering, she turns her back, continues folding socks and sorting them into dorms. Each sock marked at the toe. She reads the name, throws it on the relevant pile.

'Beauty, I don't see why you still have to be angry. I'm not angry at you any more.'

She casts me a glance and shakes hear head.

'Okay, Beauty! So I'm sorry about the incident with the blanket.'

Still she doesn't respond.

'And for the library,' I say.

She remains silent, occupied in her job.

'For what I said in the library.'

At this she straightens her back, drops a bundle of socks and looks at me. She folds her arms across her breasts. 'What did you say in the library?' She seems to taunt me, defiance or a challenge in her tone.

'I won't ever say it again.'

She glares at me. Wordless. Waiting.

'I told you to shut up . . . Beauty, I'm sorry, I should—'

'Go and fuck yourself, black bitch . . . or I'll report to Mrs Booysen!' she says. Stands, looking me in the eye.

'Yes, but I didn't mean it. I was just so afraid, Beauty. I'm sorry, really.'

'He was in here a while ago. He's very sad and he's gone to the river.'

'Did he say anything, Beauty? About phoning his father because of what happened in class?'

'Madam Sanders has to say she's sorry. Or else Dr Webster is coming to fetch Dom.' My heart sinks. I ask how long ago Dominic left and she says about fifteen minutes.

'Thank you, Beaut. And, Beauty . . . I won't ever speak to anyone like that again. I promise.' She nods her head and goes back to folding. 'I promise. Don't you believe me?'

'We'll see,' she says.

There is nothing I can do to make it right. Nothing I can say. I run down the corridor, through the library and past the music rooms and the sound of pianos, violins and flutes. Tears sting my eyes. Dominic, Dominic, no, you mustn't leave, please, please don't leave. I'll speak to Jacques! Yes! Yes! Yes! He won't let you go. Don't go. Please don't leave me here alone.

*

I find him at the fort. Facing the river. Cheeks red and swollen. He says his parents are coming to collect him tomorrow unless Ma'am offers him an unqualified apology. His father has congratulated him on telling her off. He will not be going to choir tonight. His father has said for him to start packing unless he hears from Mathison and Ma'am by prep. Dr Webster has spoken to Mathison and given the school an ultimatum.

We crawl to the rear of the fort. I lean with my back against the clump of roots, looking around for traces of them. Their smell is here; they must be down at the drif. Dom sits in front of me, leaning against my stomach, our hands intertwined on my knees. Ma'am's words come to haunt me. The loathing in her eyes as she spoke: '*I cannot stand effeminate boys.*' Like a white-hot branding iron through my body, into my soul. Yet, she is the one who is my mentor. She is the one who is turning me into a writer. I am rattled, I have no idea what to think or do. I am suddenly afraid of being seen with Dominic. And Dominic: '*You have a preference for boys who play with guns.*' I have no idea where he gets the courage from. How could he even imagine standing up to Ma'am? And to Mathison! Refusing to be caned? I ask whether he thinks Ma'am will apologise. He says he doubts it and in a way hopes she doesn't. He's tired of this place anyway. What about finishing Standard Six, I ask, it's so close to the end of the year. And what about the Mass! What about the soprano solos? The Grade Eight exam?

'There are ways to let me play my exams. And any of the private schools in Jo'burg will take me. As for the Mass: let Johan Rademan squeak it out,' he says, giggling and turning to lay his face against my chest. 'You'll still love me, Karl, won't you? Even when I'm gone?'

'I always will,' I say. 'I can't see that Ma'am will apologise. It would set a precedent, Dom.'

'It's not that, Karl. This fucken system is too strong to collapse from one apology. But you all, all of you, should have refused to be punished. By allowing yourselves to be caned, let alone caned for Sanders's spitefulness, you're all making the system function exactly as it's meant to.'

'That's what I'm saying: if she apologises it opens the floodgates for us all to refuse to do as they say.'

'That's not why she won't apologise, Karl, listen to me! This place can't apologise because it doesn't even know that it's wrong to speak to anyone like she spoke to me. They're all equally blind to their stupidity. They all believe their own lies. God I loathe this place. I'm starting to hope we go and live in Canada.' I hear the river. Finches or weavers somewhere in the poplars above our roof. I am heartbroken. 'She knows nothing,' he continues. 'Nothing, she knows nothing about Gounod, the fucken queer who wrote the music I had to perform at her son's fascist funeral. Like half the shit we sing here! Composed by the effeminate men she can't stand. Like half the fucken books she throws at you to read, Karl! Written by the effeminate men she can't stand. Like half the fucken painters she purports to teach us, painted by the fucken effeminate—'

'Stop, Dom, please stop,' I say, my voice breaking. 'I don't want you to leave,' I whisper. And suddenly I'm the one crying.

We walk back up the hill together.

He goes to the dorm.

I go to choir.

Rademan joins the quartet. I open my mouth but cannot sing. I must go and speak to Jacques. Tell him to intervene on Dom's behalf. But when choir breaks up he's gone before I can get to him. A staff meeting has been called. I'll go tonight. Whether he wants me there or not, I'll go and speak to him, demand that he do something. I'll threaten him.

At supper the dining hall is abuzz, Juniors, Secondaries and Seniors. Dom is nowhere. Everyone is outraged at Webster's conceit. The whole school is against him. Rademan is an instant hero. If only I could go to Jacques. If only I could be with Dominic. He is not in prep. Is he in the dorm? At the staff meeting? With Mathison? Is Ma'am there? When I hear the Juniors troop up for showers, I ask the prefect on duty for permission to go to the toilet. Instead I sneak to G Dorm. Uncle Charlie is at the Junior bathrooms, supervising showers. Already from the door I see Dominic bent over a suitcase. This is not happening. No. I go to him and sit down on his bed. He smiles. Goes on throwing things into the case. He says he hasn't heard anything from Mathison, so he's called his parents again. They've told him to pack. I say Rademan is awful on the high notes. He says he heard, and smiles, let them hear if they cannot feel. Let Ludwig turn in his mausoleum.

I ask whether I can come to him tonight. He asks whether I've lost my mind.

'Please don't leave in the morning without coming to say goodbye.' And as I speak I again begin to cry. He steps away from his suitcase. He's biting his lip, eyes flooding. He hugs me. We both weep. He sobs against my chest. My face is pressed into his neck.

In bed I want only to go to Dom. Ma'am's words. Try to block them; erase them; excise them from memory. They were never spoken, not by you, Ma'am. Madam. That's Adam with an M at the front. Bitch, bitch, bitch. I wish it were you who died and not Graham. If only you had died in a car crash none of this would have happened. You have destroyed my life. With one sentence changed my destiny.

Dom wasn't in the showers. Radys saying they could give Dom shit all night; make his last night here hell. And Uncle Charlie, for once his ears open rather than his eyes on every set of loins: 'If I hear a sound from G tonight, if I hear one whisper against Webster, you boys will not sit for a month.' I weep into my pillow, terrified at being left here without him. I must go and speak to Jacques. He must make sure Dom stays or I'll threaten to tell about us.

My hand trembles as I knock. Bach from his room. He is not there. Relief. Bastard. Bastard. Where are you when I need you? Down there at that bitch's cottage. I go back to bed. Want to go to Dom. Should I? What if we're caught; tonight of all nights? What's going on in G?

Uncle Klaas. He'll make me feel better. No use lying in this bed unable to sleep. I will not sleep tonight. I'll keep coming to Jacques's room until he gets back. I will watch the sun rise. Be there for Dom when he leaves.

Deposit the slippers outside the music-room window. There's a light on in Mathison's office and for an instant I want to turn back. Decide against it. I am thinking how I would like to run away from here. If Dominic leaves, if Jacques doesn't do something, I'm running away. I'll ask Uncle Klaas what he thinks. The night is warm, almost hot, and though there is no moon the stars light the sky.

I wake them. Tonight they come outside. We light a fire on the riverbank. On the other side the white flowers have opened. Stars against the rocks. Their scent a bridge across the river.

'So, you're still here, Uncle Klaas?'

'You'll know when I'm gone.'

I tell him that the European tour has been cancelled. He shows no interest.

He asks how everyone is at home. I say fine, though we're moving into a flat and selling off the house and Bok is going into insurance. 'Insurance against what?' he asks, laughing from his belly.

The Silent One has rolled a zol.

I tell Uncle Klaas that I'd like to run away, from school and from home, just like he did. Even to my own ears the notion sounds childish. Preposterous.

'I'm not running anywhere. Haven't ever.' He says. I don't say I know better. That I know the story of how he ran away because his girlfriend rejected him. Instead I explain that I don't want to stay here anymore, nor do I want to go home. I know I have to, but I don't want to. I don't say anything about Dominic.

He laughs and says I can never run away. I must stay and face my demons.

'What demons?' I ask, irritated at his lack of understanding, empathy.

'At home and here,' he says.

'I have no demons. I want to live like Coen and Mandy, on a yacht or in the bush. Away from everything.'

'Why don't you want to go home?' he asks.

'I am not the son they wanted,' I say, quietly. Again I want to weep.

'Are they the parents you wanted?'

I shake my head, but cannot answer. No, they are not what I would have wanted. I am so grateful for his question. Yes, I am not what they want, but they are not what I want. The knife cuts both ways. But how, how does that help me? What comfort does knowing that bring?

He passes me the zol. I drag, deeply, hold it in my lungs.

'How uncourageous you are, Karl. After all. Not quite a coward, but how uncourageous. How like all the rest – in spite of the boisterousness. I thought for a moment you would be different.'

'But I don't want to be different,' I say, my voice beginning to crack. 'Precisely. I want only to be the same as everyone around me. I want to blend and not be seen.' I don't want to be despised, I want to cry to him, for being effeminate. With the smell of zol, I take in the sweetness from the other side of the river. The beautiful white flowers, reaching me through the walms of smoke.

'You cannot be ordinary until you know how different you are. You cannot be different till you know how ordinary.' Stop it, I want to cry, you are full of contradictions. One moment you're kind to me and the next you're so spiteful. Just like Ma'am. You are making me mad. You want me to go mad like you and Aunt Lena.

I stand up and undress. I swim across. Cannot reach high enough to the flowers. In the night I slip from the rocks and fall back into the water. Stronger since a month ago. It has rained. The boulders are too steep. Swim back. Water is lovely. Back at the fort. Put on pyjama shorts. He has lit another zol. Again I drag, in silence. Now my head is spinning.

'You should be happy.'

I can tell he's being sarcastic. Still I respond as if he may be serious: 'Then why am I so unhappy? I feel as though I have nothing or no one.' I want to say that no one loves me. That Dominic, whom I love, is leaving. And Jacques . . . I must go, I must go and speak to Jacques.

'It is because you wish not to know who you are. And I cannot teach you that. You must make that journey yourself. And yours, I can tell, is going to be a long voyage with an inordinate cargo. The cargo of those who try to swim against the tides of themselves. Against yourself, you, like this country, will have to drown.'

You are meant to be helping me! Stare at the Silent One; you just sit there too. Help me. Stand; remove pyjama shorts. Dive back into the water. I come up the riverbank and stand naked by the fire to get dry.

'We have nothing to pack up,' he says. 'Everything of importance is here,' he points to his stomach and to his head. 'Nothing to carry, nothing to drop. Nothing to win, nothing to lose. But for those like you . . . those who deceive themselves as deeply as you choose to deceive yourself, there will first have to be loss and recognition. For you will allow your every weakness to be exploited, and more, your wilfulness will force you to go in search of those whom will do you greatest harm, from whose feasts you will rise, bloated, to do your own. To try and obliterate what you could have loved most.'

I spread my dressing gown and sit down by the fire. Naked.

He leans over for the bag of Boxer next to me and I smell him, his ghastly breath, the bitter sweat. In the firelight I see the fingernails, black and dreadful. I hate him.

In an attempt to hurt, to assert some power over him, I ask: 'If you are so free, why did you run away from home when you were young?'

'I never ran from home. I will never run.'

'You ran away, don't you remember? After your girlfriend left you for another man?' He throws his head back and laughs. Mad, like a hyena in the night. Passes me the zol.

'So! That's the story, is it?'

'Everyone knows, Uncle Klaas. Have you forgotten?' I drag, hold it in, cough. Pass to Mr Silent King.

'I never ran, they chased me.' He says. Without a whim of either sadness or self-pity. Instead he smiles at me, his teeth and tongue shining in the firelight. I feel afraid, shake, as if catching a cold. Again I shiver.

'What happened, Uncle Klaas?'

He takes the zol from the Silent One, inhales, holds it in his lungs and passes the hot stub to me.

'Great-Grandfather Liebenberg, and Great-Grandmother — let us not forget her — they chased me out. For loving.'

'What do you mean, they chased you for loving?' Flick the butt into the river. Tss.

'For not loving a girl.'

'But you said it was for loving?' Suddenly the story, the one I have grown up with, is unravelling. My heart beats in my mouth. I now want him to stop. I do not want to hear the rest. He leans over to the Silent One and rests his hand briefly on the man's exposed ankle. Then he leans towards me and runs his hand up my arm.

'In some ways you and I, Karl'tjie, are alike. You — I.' The pronouns connected by a dash. 'Do you understand?'

It is ghastly, I do not want this. Or to even know this. He smells like a cesspool, sour, of piss. I shudder and start putting on my shirt. Rise to slip on my pyjama pants, turn from him. Stumble. This is what will happen to me. This is how I will become. Dressing gown. This is what I will be. As Bok says: a white man who cannot make it in this country is not worth being called white. Out of here, away. I walk to the edge of the river, leaving them by the fire. Suddenly I feel a wave of anger, raw hatred for him. I imagine him coming up behind me so I can push him in. Let him drown, drown, drown.

'I have already drowned . . .' his voice like thunder reaches me. I fly around and stare at him, tighten the dressing gown's belt around my waist. He is reading my thoughts. As if he is sitting in my brain. I want to weep, when I see his face, white and righteous in the firelight. He looks like the devil. Satan. And his disciple. My eyes glance at the Silent One. *Bible says nothing about peppercorns.* I am terrified.

'Some can live without first feeling the water in their lungs, but others need to go down. We,' he casts his eyes to the Silent One, 'will not drown, for we already have. You still want to walk on the water. Until you've gone down as deep as you ever will to a place where you will face yourself in all your naked horror, you, who fear so much, yours will be a story about the failure of love.' The voice, like an animal growling, must be the voice of Satan.

'There once was an old blind shaman,' he continues, 'the sage of the clan. Everyone came to it for advice. Up there,' he points, 'just below those overhangs. About their children and babies, about disease, about the weather, about their dreams. One day, a group of children came to it and stood in front of it with a bird in their hands. They asked the old shaman: tell us, if you are so wise, is this bird we hold in our hands alive—'

I do not need to hear more! Dr Taylor! It's the story Dr Taylor told me! I will not listen, he's the Devil, he knows everything about me, I will not, do not want this. 'Stop it, Uncle Klaas. Stop it.' I scream, dizzy, as if I'm about to faint.

I turn and run. From behind me he calls: 'It's in your hands, whether it's alive or dead, it's in your hands!' I run downstream, now sobbing, terrified of the night, terrified of every shadow. I will not be like this, I will not be chased from my house and turn into a tramp. I will look after myself, I will take care of myself, I will get out of it all, I will not be what he is. How dare he, how dare he do this to me?

I run through the fort village. I am lost, look for the school's silhouette against the hill. When did I cross the river? I have crossed, no, only imagined that I have crossed the stream, but find myself still on the school side, then along the road, my feet in the dust, and the clouds heavy, like it will rain, the sounds of the night, Bokkie's voice, Beauty and the blanket, beast, fairy-tale, illusions, stories, Dademan, tears, crying, too much Ouma, Ma'am, Jacques, will go to no, no, no, must stop it all, not become like Satan, San Andreas, Jesus is merciful, sissy, pansy, music no more singing, over, love him, I love too much and Dominic, no, Uncle Klaas, hate, failure, effeminate, leave me alone, please go away, sobbing, the smell of flowers, from a garden, like a park, I'm an impala I will survive. I stumble, my hands grab at grass. Sprawl. Instinct. I get up, toe bleeding, Jesus, help me, save me, cannot go through life like this, hairclip, cut it off, Madame Guillotine, Dom, Bok must love me, be proud like Lena, Stephanie, poor Stephanie, money, no, no, don't think, enough, enough, slow down, into orchards, pull yourself together Karl, Karl, Kal, kal, al, al, l, l. Mathison's light still on. Jesus! Careful. Walk, slow down, not afraid, never been afraid of night, nothing here, no wild animals, no ghosts, walk, calm down, down, down, yes, calm down, walk, breath, deep, in, out, in out, deep breathing, clear my mind, Agnus Dei, qui tollis peccata mundi, misrerere noba — nobis — Dona, nobis, pacem, yes, turn up here, go this way, summer, lovely evening, quiet, crickets, breathe, breathe, go back, yes, Karl, quietly, calmly.

I pick up my shoes from outside the music room's window. From the night I climb into the smell of linoleum on the floor, fresh paint. I exit the room and go down the passage. Walk past Jacques's door, hear the music, try to ignore it. I will not go begging to him. It's over. This whole life. But I cannot resist. I turn around and walk back. I can hear music, Brahms's Adagio from the Violin Concerto in D. I can say it's on behalf of Dominic. I've come to speak to you about saving Dominic. I knock on his door. There is no reply. I knock again, louder. He must be here, for there is the music. Still he doesn't open. I again want to cry, knock again. I cannot knock louder, one of the other teachers may think it is at their door. I know he is in there; can feel him. Then think of the B&O hi-fi, how it can be set to repeat over and over. I will go and check if his car is in the parking lot. I again exit the way I have come, run along the dust road behind the school. Yes, it's there. No. The car is not there, where is he? I go back the way I've come. It is the allegro. Again knock. I need him, just this once. I put my head against the door and weep. I need you to help keep Dominic here. Please, please open, want to scream, no, no, no, calm down. Breathe, breathe, relax. I resolve again, no, it is over, I remind myself of the run from the river, Uncle Klaas. Satan. It is over. Only a few more weeks. No more. Nothing.

My hand fumbles in the dressing-gown pocket. Flies to the other pocket. The key is gone. Tears flood my eyes. I have lost it. Somewhere along the road I've lost the instrument that will allow me back into this school. In the passage, in front of the locked door, I suppress a sob. If Jacques were here he could let me in with his. I must go back the way I've come.

My brain is throbbing against my skull. It is nowhere. I go up and down the route I came, in the night, trying to remember exactly where I ran. Up and down. Back up. In two hours it will be light and I will still be out here. They will find the dummy in my bed. Then — Yes! Praise the Lord, thank you, Jesus, thank you, where I stumbled, I find it. Relief washes over me. Credo in unum Deum patrem, omnipotentem, factorem coeli et terra, visibilium omnium et invisi-bilium, and slowly the fear subsides.

I unlock the library door. Credo in unum Dominum Jesum, Christum, filium Dei unigentum, qui tollis, no, no, et ex, what declen-sion, dative, enter and turn to lock the door behind me, patre natum nobis pacem ante omn —

The lights go on. I swing around.

Mathison is standing at the opposite end of the balcony, one hand on the light switch. For a mad moment I tell myself he is block-ing my way and I need only to walk past. He cannot keep me out of my dorm. This is my school. His other hand is in his trouser pocket.

This, I would think later, was not the posture of a man who was there accidentally. He had the composure of one who has been wait-ing. Confidently. For quite a while.

V

V

Hooded glances and open gazes from below up at the balcony where the Prime Minister has taken his place amongst his entourage. Cameramen behind shiny television cameras, rotating their lenses from aisles and down the sides of the hall. Now tipping the shafts to forty-five degrees to zoom in on the South African leader, then again slowly drop the angles, panning across the elegantly dressed audience, the orange, white and blue flags, the triangular arrangements of protea and strelitzia. The enormous stage glows with super troopers, sprays and spots illuminating the seats on which members of the orchestra are tuning instruments. Behind the grand piano with its lifted wing, above the orchestra, are the choir benches, eight deep. Into the hall's white cavern, up into the galleries, resounds the tuning of cellos, violins and violas; the vibrating of a bass trombone as its tubes slide and its master shares a nod and quick smile with the timpani behind him to his left. Three notes of a clarinet tumble from the ceiling with its floral cornices.

A middle-aged man dressed in black evening suit crosses the stage and holds up his hands. His teeth sparkle into a smile; he requests the audience to not look into the television cameras should they become aware that they are being focused on. The audience laughs. He reminds them that this is a live broadcast that will present no second chances and also that no clapping should occur until the Mass's fifth and final movement has been completed. While he speaks, last-minute arrivals are being hurried down the aisles by ushers in white shirts and blouses, black slacks and long skirts. From the foyer the sound of the final bell.

The house lights are dimmed and the hall hulled in dusk. Silence falls, broken only here and there by a cough, the rustling as pages of a programme are folded. Eyes remain on the orchestra seated in the extravagant white light.

Applause when the mayoress, smiling, in a long black dress and a double string of pearls, walks to the centre of the stage. Standing behind a microphone to the left, she lifts a piece of paper and dons a pair of delicate reading glasses, throwing her head back as if clearing strands of hair from her vision. An elegant movement. 'Honourable Prime Minister, Dr John Vorster, honoured guests, ladies and gentleman, and citizens of South Africa who join us this evening in their homes through radio and the year-old gift of television. Welcome to Durban, proud ocean city and holiday getaway of all South Africa. And also – let us not forget – centre of culture and arts.' Applause from the audience and the mayoress again smiles and nods. 'But, we are not gathered here this evening to listen to orations or public sermonising. We are here to celebrate and enjoy the universal language of music. Indeed, in all the world, the only truly unifying form of communication is the language of music.' Applause breaks her stride and again she smiles, nodding at the audience and into the camera of the centre aisle. 'Dr Vorster, it is an honour for every citizen of this city to welcome you in our midst this evening.' Applause. 'On behalf of the city, may I present to you and the country the South African Broadcasting Corporation's Symphony Orchestra and Philharmonic Choir, joined tonight – in celebration of a wonderful school's twentieth anniversary – by the internationally renowned choir of young gentleman from the Drakensberg, united under the leadership of Mr Jacques Cilliers.' A loud round of applause and she briefly inclines her head and leaves the stage.

Applause again as almost at once the choir begins filing onto stage: boys in azurite waistcoats and white bibs, alternating in rows with the adults of the SABC choir in sky-blue togas. Somewhere in the middle of the hall, an observant audience member might notice a father nudge a boy seated beside him dressed in the school's black blazer with its badge of the dragon; a woman in the row behind leans forward and squeezes the boy's neck. The boy, smiling coyly while his eyes are glued to the stage, in turn leans lightly against the girl beside him who in turn does the same to the girl beside her who in turn elbows the taller boy – also in the black blazer – beside her.

Only when the two-hundred-strong choir is ordered and standing with arms held behind their backs does the applause abate. Then it begins again as the orchestra rises and the conductor enters the lights. His black suit, white shirt and charcoal hair are aglow beneath the spots. A good-looking man. He bows at the Prime Minister's box. He lifts his arm towards the orchestra and choir, signalling them to bow. While the applause continues the conductor shakes the hand of the lead violinist and the orchestra is again seated. The hall goes quiet only when the man turns his back to the audience and faces the orchestra and choir. At a nod from the man, four boys step forward and take their places behind microphones just in front of the violins. The choir's face lights up. Teeth glint in the stage lights. The conductor's profile is in view as he and the solo quartet silently converse. Four heads nod at him. He again faces the choir. Then he turns and seems to say something quietly to the lead violinist. The violinist rises, places his instrument on his seat and moves to the microphone of the skinny soloist on the left. As he adjusts it to a lower height, the audience laughs and the boy's smile can probably be seen to the very back of the top gallery. Once the violinist has again taken his seat and placed his instrument against his chin, he nods.

The conductor lifts his hands.

His head moves from side to side, taking in orchestra and choir. He nods, hands show the time and in the instant the conductor's hair jumps and his arms fly forward the orchestra eliminates the silence with the thudding of drums the lashing of trumpets and Karl's skin is turned to gooseflesh. His eyes dart from the back of Jacques's neck and shoulders to Dominic's face, a fresh pink bloom beneath the lights into the dark. There they remain. On his left sits Bok and Bokkie. Then Mumdeman and her fiancé, Mr Shaw, who Karl met tonight for the first time. Stinking rich, apparently, and after they're married he's taking Mumshaw on honeymoon to Europe. To his right are Alette, Lena, Lukas and Juffrou Sang. In the row immediately behind are Uncle Michael, Aunt Siobhain and James.

Karl counts silently for the second alto entry to precede Dominic's *Kyrie.* The voice rises, leaps, then tumbles into the hall. Tears well in Karl's eyes. He blinks a few times in quick succession. His mind drifts, even as his eyes remain on Dominic, then settle momentarily on Jacques and then return to Dom. He knows each note. Can fall in with the second sopranos, and all the others too, he now realises. Without knowing he is doing it, he anticipates automatically each major instrument entry. How different this mass of sound; how enormous in the joining with the adults. This overwhelming volume was what Dominic spoke of when he came back from Jo'burg bearing news of the rehearsals' success, of the flawlessness of the recording sessions at the EMI Brigadiers Studios.

Finding Karl and Lukas milking in the dairy, Dominic had fallen at once into a story of the days the combined boys' choirs had spent with the adult choir in Johannesburg. The two who had remained behind on the farm had heard the buses arrive but decided to wait to greet their friends at supper. When Dominic walked into the dairy ten minutes later, Lukas joked that it was probably the first time he had set foot there for three years. 'Damn right!' Dominic responded as his eyes took in the rickety beams of the old shed and then came to rest on Karl hunched over the bucket at the flank of a black and white Friesian: 'I don't know how you can stand the smell and the flies. Anyway, you don't know what you missed.' Despite his avowed aversion to the dairy and its activities, he went down on his haunches beside Karl. 'You do that well, hey, Karl,' whispered and chuckling. Then, speaking loud enough so that Lukas on the other side of the walkway could hear, he told about Mr Cilliers's masterful control over the two-hundred-strong combined choir; how he consistently and patiently signalled the adult voices to diminuendo while allowing them, the boys, a slight crescendo. Dominic spoke about how starkly different the Mass was with full orchestration and with the added colour of adult voices for whom Beethoven had originally composed the piece. And then the recordings, that a year of hard work, of hours upon hours of repetition and bowing before Cilliers's out-bursts and violence had paid off thousand-fold. 'This Mass is going to be world-class. Ludwig would have shat himself with satisfaction,' Dominic said and briefly rested his hand on Karl's knee.

It is as glorious as he said. More. Perfect, perfect. How I wish I could be facing here rather than there. Skipping the alternate rows of adults, he runs his eyes along the faces of the boys. One hundred and eight-een. In all likelihood he will never see most of them again. Most of these have rarely meant anything to him. They were but names and presences. Faces in the wall of choir voices. A rare few of them trained for galas with him. A number were regulars at the stables. A dozen or so with Lukas and him in the rugby team. His only real friends Bennie, Dominic, Lukas and Mervyn. For all he had cared the school might actually have existed of only himself and the four of them. Yet now he sees each face as a composite part of his world. Remove one and the world is irrevocably altered. A world he is now set to leave. For the first time since he'd stopped singing, he allows thoughts of loss; allows regret and sadness, thick and clotting like old blood through his veins. With self-reproach he takes in each face as he prepares his leave: The solo quartet: Dominic, Beloved, Dearest. Again he blinks. Erskin Louw. Gerhard Conradie. Mike van der Bijlt. On the stands above and behind the orchestra: Ronald Gardener. J.P. Vermeulen. Patrick Moore. Roelf Sianagi. Johan Rademan. Toings van Breda. Laurie Donohue. Lloyd Heyns. Jonathan Thompson. Casper Wigget. Marcus Smith. Alex Snyman. Gideon Fichardt. Tom Spencer. Niklaas Bruin. Mathew O'Leary. Henkie Geldenhuys. Radys

Dietz. Fritz Naude. Bryan Keating. André Marais. Peter Wilmot. Steve Dugmore. Ryan Burgess. Jannie Prinsloo. Riaan Mastenbroek. Mark Bosman. Faffa van Niekerk. Eben Stein. Gert Malan. Peter Muller. Ron Isaacson. Jelly-face Johnson. Peter-John De Waal. Neil Barry. Sean Aucamp. J.J. Cartwright. Sarel Serfontein. Craig Nichols. Barrie Hansen. Rudie Campher. Deon Cilliers. Ian Stoltenberg. Joseph Sniegowski. Pieter Opperman. Michael Sayers. Bennie Oberholzer. Daniel Smit. Percy Johnstone. John Cooke. Stony Steenkamp. Mervyn Clemence-Gordon. Mervy. Max Brown. Jean-Pierre Kotze. Armand Gouws. Errol what's your surname. Johan De Wet. Christopher Jones. Paul Shaer. Marius Theron. Van van der Merwe. Frik Olivier. Sprinter Snell. Braam Naudé. Graham Schmidt. Neville Kotze. Bernard Fischer. Fanus Du Preez. Connor Bruce. Brendan Baker. Naas Stein. Jaco Terblanche. Abel Pauw. Stephan van der Spuy. Clive Macpherson. Gilbert Erasmus. Anton Olckers. Wimpie Jansen. Herman Knudsen. Petrus Meintjies. Craig Kirchoff. Sarel Raubenheimer. Leon Du Toit. Sam Roberts. Christo Scholtz. Wessel De Jager. Cameron Burton. Theo Dippenaar. Llewelyn Connery. Kevin Field. Percy Johnstone. Tommy Mijnhard. Gerdus Serfontein. Coca Cola McCarthy. Peet van der Westhuizen. Charl Oerder. Hennie Potgieter. Paultjie Kruger. Andreas Voigt. Nathan Hammond. Jakkie De Villiers. Joe Knowles. Douglas Cochrane. Ettienne Mensing. Richard Ehlers. Rodney Tait. Stoffel Smuts. Paul De Waal. Gustav Edison. Royce Glover. Benjamin Davis. Charles Spontini. Louis Coetzee.

Each name. To mind as if passed over his lips a hundred times. Now he wishes for a moment to speak with each. Alone. To say in some way he will miss them. As much as they frequently disliked each other, hated even. Now it's all over. Nothing of that matters. A type of little death. 'You should spend the energy caring for the living you do on the dying . . . That will make the world a better place. You pretend you ever cared.' Fuck off. I did. Always. In my way.

He wishes he were beside Lukas rather than Alette. Even without being able to speak, he is sure he would be in a better position to sense what his friend is thinking. Feel what Lukas is about not being on that stage. And this, after all, is the last. After all that, this is how it ends. How bleak. Grim. Grimm. It is beautiful; it is breathtaking, and despite being here and not there, he is still part of it. It would have been ideal to have Lukas on his right and Alette on his left and maybe Mumdeman beside Lukas on the other side. Mumdeman must be out of her skin with pride. Mumdeman in the multi-coloured robe of soft silk that Lena said made her look like the Messiah. 'There's only one Messiah, Lena,' Mumdeman said with a scowl of displeasure, 'and you'll know when you come face to face with him.'

Since Karl had introduced Lukas to Mumdeman in the foyer, she had taken an immediate liking to her grandson's friend. That Lukas sprung from farming stock was all she needed to hear before she began reeling off tales of her own girlhood as daughter to a pioneer farmer in East Africa. Lukas, ever the listener, was soon eating from her hand: how she and the Mostert family had left South Africa and how she was born just through Portuguese Mozambique on an ox-wagon. And that when she marries Mr Shaw in two months' time he's taking her to London and then for a trip on the Concorde to Paris. 'From an ox-wagon to the Concorde! All in one lifetime,' she said as a group began gathering around the De Mans in the foyer, spellbound by Mumdeman's stories. She told what Karl had never tired of after hearing them a hundred times in a hundred different versions: how they had cleared the bush to create a civilisation in East Africa; that at one point there were as many as two thousand white families between Kenya and Tanganyika. 'None of the mod cons you girls take for granted,' she said, smiling at the younger women in the group: 'These hands,' turning her palms up, pulling back the silk sleeves, 'I cleared a farm with these two hands. Look you can see, they've never really recovered.' And she asked the bystanders to touch the inside of her open palms. 'Ten thousand hectares.' Lukas asked what they had farmed, and she spoke about thousands of acres of vegetables. And

Lukas, clearly delighted, prodded for more. Karl, himself gratified at the audience, intervened and asked her to tell how she had wrestled a crocodile in Lake Tanganyika. Mumdeman proceeded, and Mr Shaw smiled and put his arm around her back as she grew more animated and another group joined the widening circle. From crocodile wrestling she went to picking custer apples and being chased by wild dogs, said again that today's women could learn a thing or two from the way she grew up. During a lull in her stories, someone, upon seeing the two boys in the black school blazers, asked: 'And why aren't the two of you singing?' As one Lukas and Karl answered: 'Our voices are breaking.'

And Bok said yes, these are the big boys, turning into men, a proud smile shared between him and the onlookers. Karl took in his father, dashing in his black deacon suit, beside Bokkie, as gorgeous as ever in silver lamé. Bokkie whispered to the children, 'Don't look, there's a TV camera on us,' and Karl, Lena and Bernice tried to ignore the light that suddenly fell upon them and the movement of the camera from whence it shone. Alette pinched Karl and he flinched, acted even more engrossed in the stories.

The storytelling was finally broken when Ma'am, in a long burgundy dress with a low-cut neckline, joined the group accompanied by her equally tall sister Miss Hope. Ma'am and Miss Hope shook a few hands. Bok and Bokkie introduced Ma'am as the boys' teacher and Miss Hope as Lena's English teacher at Port Natal. From the look of pity that Aunt Siobhain and Juffrou Sang cast at Ma'am, Karl knew that Bokkie had signalled to them that Ma'am was the one who had lost a son on the border. The group grew further with the addition of Uncle Charlie and Mr Walshe, the latter whom the boys had driven down with in the afternoon and now saw for the first time in full evening suit with tie. Lukas threw Karl a playful glance, indicating his surprise at how smart the two usually informally dressed men now appeared. Introduced respectively as the house-master and the farm manager, Mr Walshe in particular looked uncomfortable with the suit, the tie and the public glare. Karl listened bashfully as Bok and Uncle Charlie spoke about his and Lukas's departure from the school. Intending the bystanders to hear, Bok joked that the house-master must be happy getting rid of the two Philistines. Uncle Charlie, smiling, said no, neither Karl nor Lukas were the worst cases he's had and surely would not be worse than he'd have in future. And on his own accord Mr Walshe said how he'd miss Lukas and Karl, not only for Lukas's help on the farm, but for the boys' cheerful presence on the rides.

'Karl's quite a horseman, Mr De Man. He sits a horse like he was born there.' Karl was happy that Mr Walshe's deep baritone carried well, so that each word could be heard.

A couple stepped forward, their young son, collared and tied, standing between them. They asked whether the boys minded if they asked a few questions, as they were thinking of auditioning their son. Karl looked at the tiny dark-headed fellow in front of him. The boy gave a confident smile. He was probably eight or nine at the most, and to Karl's enquiry the father answered that the boy was seven, but if he auditioned next year, he would be nine and qualified to go year after next. Either to the Berg, or to Hilton or Michaelhouse. Aware of the eyes and ears of their teachers around them, Karl and Lukas spoke of the special time the past three years had been for them, what unique opportunities for travel and education they had been given. 'It is an education to travel, in and of itself,' Karl said, refraining from looking at Ma'am. Tough, being away from home, Lukas said. 'One gets homesick sometimes. Are you ready for that?' He smiled, and when the boy nodded his head rigorously the witnesses laughed. Karl and Lukas assured the parents, and thus also everyone within earshot, that being in the Berg was the best, most unforgettable experience anyone could ask for. 'And we have tours, which Hilton and Michaelhouse don't.'

'Good luck.' Karl and Lukas said as the parents stepped back and led off the beaming boy.

Miss Hope asked Lena to introduce her to Karl. He shook the woman's hand. She smiled and offered that she was looking forward to having him in her English class at Port Natal. A friendly and familiar smile, he thought, that made her resemble her twin sister. Also the smile of someone who has heard a lot about the one being introduced. But for when she smiles — and her height — Miss Hope looks nothing like Ma'am, Karl thought. One would never have believed they were twins. Although he clearly remembered Miss Hope from the funeral, there it had been to Ma'am that his attention was drawn. And to the coffin and the tragic drama: military trumpets and drums as Graham's flag-draped coffin was carried into church on the shoulders of six of his platoon. Naval, air force and army officers in uniforms standing to grim-faced attention as the organ pipes vibrated Bach into the floor, causing windows and pews to shudder as if the earth were quaking. Enormous protea and strelitzia arrangements, triangled to military precision. Amongst the senior military staff was General Erasmus, head of the SADF, with whom Karl and Dominic had stayed in Muizenberg during the Cape Tour. Every uniformed chest seemed to be laced with ribbons and medals, the specific meaning of each unknown to Karl, but the overall impression awe-inspiring. Tension on the faces of every man in the church as they stood beside their unsmiling behatted wives. Members of Parliament. The élite of the South African government and army. Newspaper photographers.

The coffin, draped in the orange, white and blue flag, stood elevated on a silver stand before the high wooden pulpit. A magnet to Karl's eyes, solemnly in front of Ma'am and a man who must have been Graham's father. On either side of Mr Sanders and Ma'am's drawn black figure in the front pew between the Generals sat their daughter Jenny and Miss Hope. Ma'am's knee-length black dress was tucked beneath her legs. Her arms, covered in elbow-length sleeves, were clutched to her sides and she held her hands together, clasped taut into an unmoving white ball in her lap. A charcoal lace mantilla woven with a pattern of black orchids covered her hair and cast her face in shadows, making it impossible to discern her expression. Jenny, as tall as her mother and aunt, was the only woman in the church without a hat. She sat sternly, her eyes never venturing from the pulpit. Miss Hope clutched a programme in one hand – the fingers of her other extended on the fabric of the black dress above the knee – gazing into her lap. Other than to stand and sit during the singing, not one of the three women seemed to alter once their initial postures. The father looked around quite a bit, taking in all that was going on. But the two sisters' heads turned only slightly towards the choirs when they sang. The two choirs, men in uniform on one side, boys on the other, had been arranged in a wedge to face each other at the front of Pietermaritzburg's Central Methodist church. In this way the end of the first and second soprano boys linked with the beginning of the male tenor and baritone voices of Infantry School. The men were clad in their green and khaki uniforms and wore no berets. The boys were in grey flannels, black ties and blazers, the blue and white of their concert attire too conspicuous for the occasion. From the centre of the wedge Jacques conducted, his face ashen, none of the usual expressiveness to communicate with the voices before him. Together with the Infantry School men they sang 'Exerce Perfectioni'. And then Dirkie De Villiers's arrangement of Psalm 23. For the Sanctus from Gounod's *Messe solennelle de Ste. Cecile*, Dominic stepped forward and stood to Jacques's left. The conductor in effect allowed the boy to lead while he did little more than guide the combined voices of men and boys from behind. Dominic's voice rose into the church dome, even without microphone ringing above the dominant male timbre. The minister read passages from Exodus and Matthew. He spoke about the greatest gift being the gift of love. Love not only for family, but love of nation and of faith. He said that the biggest and most selfless death was that which occurred in service of love, nation and faith. That Graham's death fulfilled these criteria from whichever angle one tried to understand the loss. 'Mr and Mrs

Sanders. Jenny,' he said, looking down at the two women in the pew below him. 'You have lost a beloved son, a beloved brother. None of us here will ever know or be fully able to share in your grief, your loss. But as incomprehensible as the ways of fate and God might seem to you now, the Word tells us enough for us to understand that your loss has not been in vain. You are the mothers and daughters of this nation. Your sacrifice will be a mark of pride, from here to eternity.' The minister then prayed for strength in the face of adversity, for each man in uniform guarding the borders of South Africa, for courage and strength in the souls of the bereaved. Graham's coffin was again lifted onto the shoulders of his platoon-mates. As they began moving towards the door, the organ and brass played the introduction to 'The Call of South Africa'. During the singing it seemed to Karl that around him every single boy wept as they stood to attention. Jacques too, who stood to one side of the choir, head bowed, lips unmoving. When the congregation sang the final '*At thy will to live or perish, oh South Africa dear land*', it felt to Karl as though for the first time in his life he understood the terrifying meaning of the words. Through his own tears he shuddered as he pictured Bokkie, Bok, Bernice and Lena, standing one day in the place of Ma'am and Jenny.

The choir did not sing at the burial. The boys boarded the buses the moment they left the church. Outside waited the hearse. Flags on the bonnets of the vehicles, preceded by twelve black motorcycles. Behind the hearse followed Ma'am, Jenny and Miss Hope in the back seat of a black Mercedes. Then another eight black vehicles carrying military dignitaries and government VIPs. The streets of Pietermaritzburg were lined with casual onlookers. The entire city seemed to be mourning. Passers-by, white and black, stood quietly and expressionless as the motorcade moved from the church and down the streets.

For the two-and-a-half-hour drive back to school, no one on the packed bus could be heard speaking. No one laughed. Quietly, between Bennie and Dominic somewhere near the middle, sat Karl.

Near Estcourt, as the bus approached the Wagendrift Dam with its sluices open and jets of silver spray pounding the stream below, Dominic put his mouth close to Karl's ear and whispered: 'As bad as Liza Minnelli doing cabaret for the Nazis.' Karl at once shifted his weight from where he had been resting against Dominic's shoulder. He gripped his hands to the silver beam of the seat before him and lay his forehead on his arms, looking down. His black shoes and the turn-ups of his grey flannels vibrated from the engine against the bus floor.

Karl had looked around the foyer and caught himself unconsciously combing the crowd for a face which might resemble the photographs on Jacques's dressing table. They had to be here somewhere, but how to spot them amongst the hundreds of chattering mynahs? The women in their glitz, the men all like penguins. Near the entrance was Mathison, and with him Mr and Mrs Clemence-Gordon and other parents whom Karl knew from sight but couldn't name. Addressing Ma'am, Juffrou Sang behind Karl was saying she'd heard many praise-worthy things about her and that meeting at last was an honour. Lifting her gaze and smile up at the tall woman, Juffrou Sang recalled how she had been the one to motivate Karl to audition for the school. She had spotted his musicality the moment he'd stepped into Kuswag's pre-fab music room. 'Raw out of Zululand,' she laughed. 'But the talent was visible from the moment I laid eyes on him.' Now smiling at Karl, she said that he had come a long way since – 'that first eisteddfod where you sang – what was it again – and you got your first golden diploma?'

'Ek Bemin my Land van Harte.' Karl smiled, shaking his head and shrugging at Lukas and Alette, feigning lapsed memory and diffidence, abashed at being reminded of an amateur eisteddfod career. He deliberately kept his eyes off Lena, all too aware that she was probably in a tizz at the attention being showered on him.

'You also won a gold for recitation, didn't you, Karl?' Bokkie offered, and he felt himself blush. Hoped Bok was still engaged with Uncle Charlie and Mr Walshe.

'So the love of poetry has been there for years?'

'Yes, Ma'am.' He couldn't help but catch Lena's eye. No foam around the mouth.

'Actually, I too remember the first time I saw him,' Ma'am said, winking at Bokkie and Juffrou Sang. 'Rather a poetic moment, if I can call it that.' She cast a playful glance at him. 'Do you mind if I tell them, Karl?'

'I don't know what you mean, Ma'am?' He would have done anything for the bell to ring then.

'Can't you remember the first time I spoke to you? Good heavens, I remember it like yesterday. Lukas, can you? You were all there!'

'Oh yes!' Karl blurted. 'I remember. It was in Miss Holloway's class!'

'Well, thank you!' And she smiled, now also at Bok who had rejoined the group. 'From my classroom I heard a commotion down the veranda.' Bok shook his head, clearly in jest, and said he wasn't sure he wanted to hear this. Ma'am again winked and said there was no need for them to be embarrassed. 'I had seen Mrs Holloway leave, so I suspected the mice were at it. Off I went to inspect the scene of the crime.'

Bokkie shook her head. Ma'am laughed and shot her a smile.

'A little way before I reached the door, I heard a boy's voice,' she paused. 'Very, very expressively.' Her eyes rested on Karl. 'Melodramatically, of course. Reciting Langenhoven's "The Moth and the Flame". There were sporadic bursts of laughter from the class as the boy's voice grew louder and louder and more urgent.' Ma'am looked around the group and then settled her gaze on Karl. 'I was standing on the veranda – out of sight – and I let him continue. And then, there was the crash of something as the voice almost cried out the final lines!' The group laughed. 'I stepped into the doorway to see this young man,' her hand now on Karl's shoulder, 'spread like a corpse over the desk.' Again everyone laughed.

'Where was Miss Holloway?' Bokkie asked, shaking her head, putting on discomfort.

'Running an errand,' Ma'am answered, a look of genuine fondness caressing Karl's face.

'Well, I hope you saw to it he got six of the best,' Bok joked, to which a mix of laughter and mirthful shock erupted. The first bell shrilled into the foyer's din. It was time for members of the audience to take their seats.

'Not at all,' Ma'am answered, and then looking at Juffrou Sang. 'Like you, I knew an exceptional talent when it stared me in the face.' Then, before they left the foyer to come and take their seats, Ma'am asked Karl to make sure he and Lukas said goodbye after the concert.

'We're taking Lukas to the airport, Ma'am, so we won't have much time.'

'Well, I'll meet you right here then. On your way out, okay?'

'Yes, Ma'am.'

'And what about the others, have you already said goodbye? Have you been backstage?'

'No, Ma'am. We'll see how much time there is after the concert. Lukas's plane leaves at ten.'

'Well. They must go and say goodbye to their friends.' She cast Bok a stern look. 'This shouldn't finish later than eight thirty. Surely there's time for that, Mr De Man?' Bok said he'd have to drive like a madman if they were running late. Ma'am smiled. 'Let me find you backstage, then. Directly after the concert, yes?' And they agreed to meet as soon as the performance ended.

The diminuendo brings him back into the hall. Silence reigns and he's amazed that he has missed virtually the entire first movement. He sees Jacques's head turn briefly to Dominic. The boy nods. What's going on, he wonders. Has he missed something? He tells himself to concentrate, to keep himself within the immediacy of the music, not to let his mind wander. Jacques's back, the black of his jacket, is unmoving. Television cameras glide closer to the stage. Someone in the choir coughs. An echo. A hush over the hall.

Jacques lifts his hands. A pause. His arms shoot forward a torrent as choir and orchestra together burst through *Gloria, in excelcis Deo*. A riveting tempo, awesome volume like waves rushing over and back through the audience, colliding with walls, balconies and ceilings. On *et in terra pax hominibus* the male bass voices almost drown the boys' and there's a swift, almost invisible tremble of Jacques's right hand, a single shake of the head at which Karl imagines him scowling at the men; opening his eyes wide and pursing his lips at the boy altos. Remarkable. This is artistry. This is mastery and grandeur unleashed.

There is a largo transition before the *Gratias agimus* that he awaits. There the soloists will come in and he may be able to assess the meaning of Dominic's nod. Is there a problem with his voice? There was last week's slight sniff from which he said he'd recovered completely. Horror if Johan Rademan has to take over halfway. Would spoil everything.

When Dominic's chin rises and his lips open and his notes lift into the *gratias*, joining with Gerhard Conradie's, it is again the voice of an angel. Rich, dark, long, elongated, perfectly pitched and controlled notes. Every tremble of the vibratum just as it has always been. Karl breathes out. His chest swells. His legs tingle in the sound; turn to gooseflesh. Still aware of Alette and Bok on either side of him, he hears Dominic's voice alone, sees nothing but his friend's mouth, the concentration of the body, the slight heaving of the stomach and chest beneath the blue of the waistcoat. Oh Dominic, to have been able to sing like you, he thinks for a moment. For me to have been able to be like you. How I will miss you, Beloved. How I love you. Yes. Love you till eternity comes. Once the bird's beak has made the hollow in Mphafa's boulders, I will begin to stop loving you. That is enough. Yes. To have wanted to be like you would have been avaricious. And I was not. Not when it came to you. What I felt for you and what you were to me is love and to that no impediment can ever be admitted. Star, you were, always, to my every wandering bark. How, ever, could I have resisted? In that June, in your parents' Saxonwold house, in a night when the country must already have been burning, when your mother brought into our room, where you and I lay talking, a can of Condensed Milk. And your father, a moment later, an anthology, *Sonnets For My Scotsman*, from which he said the two of us may want to read. And while I drank from the tin, you read to me:

> *and this, more than any other memory you must have*
> *if time ravages our love and leaves us separate*
> *and these lips no longer give you the joys we've had*
> *should your beauty or my lust go stray, leave me desperate*
> *longing for days, nights we were one as we are now:*
> *when no more than your glance fills me to love's brim*
> *over your voice, skin, teeth, taste, smell of brow*
> *when just thought of you invites mine to never trim*
> *the sky so huge the universe made for us alone*
> *and nothing nor anything is of meaning but you*
> *where no world's treasure's worth a stone*
> *without you lover beloved, no word's more true:*
> > *no altered state we might reach will cut or sham*
> > *that for knowing you: the better, wholer man I am.*

The last Parents' Weekend had offered the two their final chance to be alone with each other, mostly in the Websters' suite at the Champagne Castle Hotel or outside in the car listening to cassettes. At the hotel they had dinner on the Friday evening before the boys had to return to sleep at school, cursing the regulation that no sleep-out was allowed. On Saturday morning Dr Webster collected them again and they were together until Dominic had to return at four p.m. to sleep till six in preparation for the evening concert. Karl had returned to dairy duty with Lukas. And so, while there was the pleasure of being away from the school amongst people he cared for, Karl was all too aware that the break was barely a temporary recess. Each time Dr Webster collected him and Dominic from the parking lot, the fact that they had to return, that there was again a law governing the limits of their liberty, bore down on him and he struggled to enjoy himself. While hotel lunches and suppers with the Websters lifted his spirits, he remained guarded. Being daily in the company of adults now frightened him. That he probably had nothing to fear from the Websters was something he almost accepted as they were kind and generous and Dominic adored them as much as they did him. Still, Karl was cautious. Kept a guard at his lips, not allowing escape to the occasional urges for words he could taste against his pallet.

Unlike what Karl had imagined would be the case, the Websters barely referred to the incident between Dominic and Ma'am. The issue was over and resolved as far as they were concerned. On their part no ill feelings lingered. Instead, talk moved often to Canada, where Dr Webster had bought into a Toronto private practice. It was now definite: Dominic and his family were leaving the country. As Canadian school terms commenced only in September, Dominic would be doing a catching-up course before officially starting school in the second half of 1977. Mrs Webster clinched her teeth at talk of Canada's snow in winter. And while they spoke of a new homeland over lunches and dinners, or lay on the double bed with the two boys between them, Karl thought obsessively about his return to Toti, to Durban, moving into a flat, going to Port Natal. The Websters invited him to visit in Canada. At once he set to a fantasy of running from Bok and Bokkie. Stowing away in a ship like the *Jessye Likes* on which Bok had taken the rhino to America. How he wished he could leave with the Websters. Maybe his parents would be killed in a car crash. That would free him. Instantly he felt sorry for his mother and his sisters. Imagined their despair. He felt nothing for Bok. And he thought he would not mind staying in Durban if only his father would die. Or if his parents could get divorced, then he could take care of his mother in peace and maybe convince her to go to university and train herself so that she could get a job. Make something of herself and be rid of her dependence on Bok. He felt guilty, telling himself over and over that Bokkie had never done anything but her best for him and the girls. She's my mother, he thought. She does love me. Of that I'm sure. But she loves me and the girls too much and her love feels so heavy. Like we could smother. Mother. There's a poem in that. Do I love her or hate her, he wondered even as he glowed with shame. And what with Bernice gone, next year? Who in that house — that flat — will I speak to? Who will be left for me to trust? During the concert for the parents in the Winterton Town Hall he sat in the audience between Dr and Mrs Webster. Throughout found himself again imagining he could leave with them. That he was their son. A prodigal.

As a belated birthday gift Mrs Webster gave him an Abba tape named *Arrival*. Outside the hotel Karl and Dominic sat in the Benz listening to the recording: 'Dancing Queen'; 'Money Money Money' and 'Fernando' — catchy tunes to which both could sing along after a second hearing. For that while alone, in the car only, Karl again allowed Dominic to hold his hand.

They had the whole of Sunday free. They went hiking with the parents to Nandi's Falls and Karl told them the story of Chaka's illegitimate birth, how he had been terrorised by the other Zulu boys, and how, when he later became king, he had taken his revenge on everyone that had been cruel to him and his mother. How when he had grown big and handsome, he bathed naked every day in full view of his underlings so that word could spread throughout Zululand of his physical beauty.

Returning to the hotel from the falls, the boys stuffed themselves at the huge buffet lunch. Karl thought he would burst from too much trifle. When the Websters wanted to take a nap the boys lay between them until they fell asleep and then again went out to the car where they again listened through Abba's *Arrival*. Near sundown, with only hours to go before the parents would have to bid the boys farewell, the Websters drove to the airstrip at El Mirador where Mervyn's father was to take everyone on a flip in his Cessna. The Clemence-Gordons, with Bennie along for the weekend, were there already, waiting. The four boys stood around the cars while first the parents took to the sky. After three years of drop-offs and Parents' Weekends they were all familiar with the Sunday afternoon heaviness. The pending farewell and the return to prison. Dominic said he had just the right thing to cheer them up. He stuck into the player a cassette he said was his mother's favourite. Emmylou Harris blared into the sunshine over the grassy field, and at once all but Karl faked puking sounds, holding their stomachs and wrenching. 'Look, there's Marabou,' Karl shouted and the others spun around, laughed at their own silliness. An even deeper sadness came to cling to the afternoon.

Bennie convinced them that he had to sit beside the pilot as he was the only non-moffie and the only one who wouldn't go hysterical if the plane were to fall. When the craft returned with the Websters exclaiming how breathtaking it had been, the four boys scrambled into the small cabin, Bennie at the front and the three others squashed onto the two seats behind. Karl, his mood lifting with the plane, was filled with awe at seeing the green and brown landscape fold out beneath them, then the mountains jagged, red and shaded to the west, rising like mammoths into the blue. From up there they pointed out the school and the rugby fields – small and insignificant, Karl thought, how pathetic, really, miserably out of place against the landscape, a strange white L or lopsided T possible to erase with one swipe of a rubber – the pool like a tiny blue tile, the game pen where Karl could see zebra and the others said he was lying, and tried to see who could spot the fort, Copper Falls, the Bushmen paintings, to where Sterkspruit wound itself from sight. Soon they had climbed to 3500 metres, approaching the cliffs of Cathedral Peak. Then, on the return flight, with the sun setting and the Drakensberg in a red and pink haze, Dominic started 'Boulder to Birmingham'. The others joined and when they came to the chorus they harmonised, eclipsing with their voices the drone of the engine as they sang: *I would rock my soul, in the bosom of Abraham, I would hold my life, in saving grace.* From behind the control panels Mr Clemence-Gordon hummed along. As they approached the strip to land, he said he wished the choir could sing songs like this instead of all the heavy Latin hocus-pocus. And Mervyn told his father he clearly knew very little about Art with a capital A.

The Clemence-Gordons and the Websters said goodbye to each other and confirmed that Dominic would fly up from the Durban concert with them and Mervyn. The Websters themselves were missing the concert – Mrs Webster said she'd be watching it on TV – as their entire household was being shipped off to Canada around the time of the performance and Dr Webster would already have left.

'So, we'll see you in Jo'burg,' Mrs Webster said to the Clemence-Gordons and then they bade Bennie goodbye. They told him that if he ever came to Canada, he should be sure to look them up. And Bennie smiled and said thank you, but he wasn't sure that was going to happen anytime soon. His one chance of overseas was blown this year.

Mervyn's parents said they'd see Karl again in Durban for a goodbye.

Sunday night the boys had to be in at eight. Karl and Dominic had a small supper with the Websters on the hotel terrace and then they drove down the gravel road from Champagne Castle to the school. Dr Webster again told Karl that he was welcome to visit them in Canada. 'We've grown very fond of you, Karl,' the man said from the front seat. 'And we know that Dominic loves you deeply.' It had felt to Karl as though his heart would bounce from his throat. Instead of feeling gratitude for the Webster generosity, he could only fear that Dominic had told his parents something. In the dark he felt blood rush into his face and he barely managed a thank you from a mouth gone instantly dry. Thank God they were soon leaving the country. Away. Emigrated from his life as if they had never been part of it. 'Then you and I, Karl,' Mrs Webster said over her shoulder, 'can listen to country music as much as we like and leave these two snobs to the classics.' They had laughed. Dominic said Abba wasn't country: it was plain and simple sugar-pop with an extra lick of cream and a cherry on top.

At the school the four of them stood in the night while other families were saying goodbye to their sons. The Websters kissed Dominic goodbye, wishing him good luck for the final performance and again congratulating him on the success of his Grade Eight exam. 'And I'll see you in Toronto, Dom? Make sure this woman dresses warmly, won't you, my boy? She's in for a shock when she walks out into that snow.'

Then, in turns, they embraced Karl. The boy was cold, barely able to lift his arms to return the hugs. 'Don't think that now your voice is breaking you're too big for a nice bear hug,' Dr Webster said and he again pulled Karl to him. This time Karl reciprocated, holding onto the man, clasping his arms tightly around the broad back, feeling a moment of trust. 'You'll come and visit, won't you, Karl?' Mrs Webster asked again. He said he would try his best. That one day he'd perhaps become a Rotary exchange student. Mrs Webster wrapped her arms around him and he took in her scent: Chanel No. 5, Dominic said, all his mother wears to bed. Just like Marilyn.

The Websters left and Karl knew he would never see them again. As fond as he was of them, he told himself he was relieved to see them go. They waved as the rectangular tail-lights diminished and disappeared in the night. They tarried in the dark, just out of reach of the quad lights. Dominic led Karl into the dark, down towards the rock where the school's signpost hung invisibly, highlighted only by the occasional headlights of a car. Here they sat talking – assuaging the drop-off blues – as late arrivals came in to deposit the last of their peers.

'Your voice sounded fine. In the plane, I mean,' Dominic murmured. 'I still think it's ridiculous that Cilliers won't let you sing.'

'It does just what it wants, Dom. You've heard it in class.'

Saying he wanted to see the dairy at night, Dominic steered Karl into the shadows down the embankment above the orchards. When they were a safe distance from the school he pulled Karl closer: 'One kiss, Karl, just one, for old times' sake?'

'Did you tell your mum and dad? About us?' Karl enquired in an urgent whisper.

'What does it matter! You know how easy-going they are. Give me a kiss.' But as he leant forward, Karl held him away and demanded to know what he had told his parents.

'Nothing. I told them nothing. Are you satisfied?'

'I don't believe you.'

'Good! Because I did tell them! In December, the moment we got off that plane from Malawi!' Karl stood as if turned into stone, as though his death sentence had been pronounced. 'This has nothing to do with me or my parents, does it, Karl?' And Dominic had let go of Karl, drawn away, stung by his friend's reluctance. 'For three weeks now you've been sour and sulking and horrible. I'm asking you for the last time to tell me what's going on with you. What's wrong?'

'How could you tell your parents, Dom? How could you do . . .'

'Because they asked whether you were my boyfriend, that's why! What's wrong with you, Karl?' Karl stood in the night, terrified.

'I have the blues, that's all.' And he started up the embankment, wishing the term was over and Dominic gone to Canada and everything, the whole mess, every memory of this place with him.

'Loelovise yokou,' Dominic called from behind.

'Stop it, Dominic.' Karl spun around. 'What happens if someone hears you?'

Dominic ran up the embankment: 'You are being childish and paranoid.'

'No, Dom. You're the childish one, speaking in Gogga when we're fourteen already. That's what's childish.'

'Strange that you could speak to me in Gogga even after you had turned fourteen. Up until three weeks ago, when suddenly I wasn't allowed to come to your bed, when suddenly your voice broke.'

'Please stop, Dominic. If Mathison hears us. Please, please promise you will forget what happened between us. Won't you phone your parents and tell them you were only joking?'

'You are fucking crazy, you know that, Karl De Man? Has anyone ever told you you are actually certifiably living on cloud cuckoo? Not running on all cylinders. Nuts?' And with that, Dominic stalked off. Left Karl standing alone with his fear of the world. His terror of Mathison.

I will not go there, he tells himself, as he tries to hear the music. I will not think of Mathison. Not now, please don't let me remember him. Not ever again. But only when the Gloria ends and there's a silence over the hall do Karl's thoughts return to the choir, having listened to — heard — only the opening sections of the movement. I must listen to this music. I must concentrate. This is the last concert, the last time I'll see them. I must not think of anything other than the music. A bulge is forming in his throat. He swallows; blinks repeatedly. Wants to close his eyes. Forces them to remain on stage.

Arms and body jerk, bring in the instruments, basses, tenor, Credo, Credo, joined by women and sopranos, Credo, Credo, over and over, Deum Patrem. Violins sweeping bows, heads I believe in one God the Father, omnipotentem, almighty, factorem coli et, creator of heaven and terra — terrae — visibilium omnium — genetive plural — et invisibilium, full orchestra, D minor to G and then the wonderful A major. 'See what he does with the change in harmonies as we move to Jesus's time on earth? And remember Beethoven had the gift of synaesthesia, music came to him in colour.' There's the flute solo now. And bassoon, Jissus the bassoon is good, listen, flute is the Holy Spirit, strings, trumpets, timpani, volume, crescendo, Jacques's arms flailing, directing, conducting, controlling instruments and voices, reining in, woman's voices ready to break out of his arms, bordering on chaos ordered perfectly, if Beethoven could hear this, could he ever have imagined it here in Africa, from the heart, may it go to your hearts, yes, yes, may it go to your hearts as he wrote, if Beethoven were backstage to say what he thought, afterwards, only heard twice in his lifetime, already deaf, Vienna, and then he must have not heard it, felt it, maybe, like the vibrations from my chair, can Bokkie feel, beneath my feet, what he wanted from the voice, 'like the Ninth Symphony,' Dom said, similar challenges, odd transitions, so suddenly, new themes. Sensually, sensually, Jacques, said, don't think, this you must feel, every sense here must be at nerve-end, everything that goes on in your body must come to lie beneath the epidermis, that is all that means anything, what touches the body, not the head, don't think, not use head, no head, heart, stomach, each section on its own, no need to understand, feel, feel, feel, this is his monument, after this he dies, sing it at his funeral, a tonal mausoleum, in the Credo is the heart, the centre the nucleus, fugue, explosive. 'He saw music in colours, like a million rainbows appearing in endless patterns. Here I want you to think of bold, brilliant colours. This is an assertion of beliefs: I believe, we believe.' I believe in one Lord Jesus Christ, Christum, filium Dei unigenitum, et ex patre natum ante omnia saecula, not et as it should be, conjunction et thrown out in favour of Credo, each sentence is a statement separately, not simply a part of the greater whole, Deum de Deo, beautiful, beautiful, lumen de lumine, and adagio, here it's only the boys, yes, and was incarnated by the Holy Spirit from the Virgine Maria and was homo factus and was also crucified for us under sub snubbed under Pontio Pilato he suffered and was buried, quartet, Jiss, help Dominic on the Crucifixus forcing sound, why? Dom looks tired, others sound terrific. Okay, again, bases too loud, tenor in on Allegro, whole choir, fantastic, tempo up, timpani, galloping, Rufus, at cliff, then galloping again on the, no et, and, on the third day he rose according to scriptures and ascended into heaven, and, no sedet, sits at the right hand of the Father and shall come again with glory to judge I'll be a judge after I'm a lawyer

one day to judicare, vivos et mortuos, living and dead, his reign shall
have no end, eternity like boulders at Mphafa, I believe in the Holy
Spirit, the Lord, the giver of life 'bright orange', who proceeds from
the father and the son who is worshipped and glorified with the
Father and the Son. Who spoke through the prophets. 'Shimmering
white.' Credo in unu, no unam sanctam catholicam et apostolicam
ecclesiam, I acknowledge one baptism for the remission of sins et
expecto resurrectionem mortuorum. 'You're saying your credo, again
and again, like an incantation, you're going into a trance of belief,
colour your voices. The deepest blue you can imagine.' Listen to
Allegretto, boys, alone, quartet, amen chorus, over over, over, Dom,
perfect, Mike van der Bijlt almost, tonight, like Steven, is he copying
Steven's voice, no, Jacques shudders, stares at Mike, amen, amen,
Dom casts the amen up, settles amen, amen, a long beautiful note over
all.

His eyes are on Jacques's upright back. Now relaxed, almost unmoving, calm as he takes the orchestra into the Sanctus, carefully, gently
with only the lightest gesture of head and hands, brings in the
soloists, one at a time.

'Tell me from the beginning. Everything.' Mathison spoke from
behind his desk.

It had taken the man no more than a moment after the library
lights went on before he said — Come with me — in a sober voice, to
Karl, who cowered across the walkway against the door. Karl would
later recall that there had been no surprise or anger in the voice.
Matter of fact, as he spoke over the humming of the library's fluorescent light. With leaded legs and fear vaulting into his brain, Karl had
followed the man down the stairs, through the hall where tables had
the previous night already been laid for the teachers' breakfast. Along
the corridor to the headmaster's office. Amidst the fear, the casting
around for explanations and mediating circumstances — *any way* to
influence his judge and juror and executioner — he already regretted

everything. His recklessness. His life. How many thoughts could pass through a mind in the time it takes at a quick pace from the library, down the stairs, through the dining hall, to the office? A hundred, a thousand? And how many fragments of thoughts and words suspended halfway into thought?

Karl had crossed the carpet and stood a few paces from the desk behind which the man took his seat. His mouth was dry, tongue like sandpaper. He was vaguely aware of a toe throbbing, blood seeping into his woollen slipper. Facing Mathison, hearing the phrase – tell me from the beginning, everything – Karl's mind was abruptly cleared. He was ready for this. Calm and collected, that's me. I am not going to be afraid. I will not stutter. If only I hadn't smoked that stuff. But that's gone. I'm only tired. I will handle this situation and this man. There will be the caning. That is fine. There will probably be a phone call to Bok and another beating at home. But it is fine. He is prepared. And there is no way they will expel me, never. Surely, never? Jacques will see to that. By hook or by crook. Jacques will – must – find a way to keep him from being expelled. 'Sir,' he had to swallow, licked his parched lips. 'Sir, I picked up this key in the dust on the parking lot. I think it must have fallen from someone's bunch. And then I tried it on all the doors, just for interest sake, Sir. But when I found it was the door to the passage, I just kept it. I know it was wrong, Sir. I'm sorry, Sir.' He waited with bated breath. How many? Surely he would not get more than four? But even six from Mathison would be okay. And Bok could be dealt with later. Take one issue at a time. Remember the lilies of the field . . . Just laps that need to be swum. Turn on the tumble and shoot yourself off.

'And then you used the key to sneak out, tonight?'

'Yes, Sir.'

'And when did you find the key in the parking lot, Karl?'

'About three or four days ago, Sir. It must have been Saturday because I was going down to the stables to see Lukas and it was early afternoon. So, four days ago, Sir.'

'And tonight was the first time you snuck out, right?'

'Yes, Sir. I'm sorry, Sir. I realise I deserve to be punished, Mr Mathison.'

'And what did you do while you were outside, Karl?'

'I just walked around in the veld, Sir. And then down to the river. And, Mr Mathison, I realise it is prohibited but I also went into the orchard to see whether any of the plums are ripe. I'm telling you because you asked for the whole truth, Sir.'

'And, what about the plums?'

'How do you mean, Sir?'

'Were they ripe, Karl? And if so, were they to your liking?' There was a hint of sarcasm in the man's voice and Karl began to suspect a trap. He now saw at once the danger of answering the question.

'I couldn't find the plum trees, Sir.'

'Clever.'

He frowned at the man, indicating he did not understand the comment.

'Yet you spent quite a long time outside, Karl, didn't you? After being unable to locate the plums, I mean.'

'I'm not sure how long, Sir.'

'Look at your watch, Karl, tell me what it says.'

'Three twenty-two, Sir.'

'Half-past three in the morning. What time did you leave F Dorm?'

'I don't know, Sir.'

The man was quiet. When he spoke again his voice carried a tone of resolution, as though, Karl thought, his story had been believed and was now merely there for the summing up: 'So, you found that key in your hand on Saturday on the parking lot and tonight you snuck out for the first time. That key must have fallen from one of the teachers' bunches.' Mathison took the glasses from his face and held them, as if pondering everything he had just heard. 'Ultimately, as I understand it then, just a bit of boyish mischief, right?'

'Yes, Sir. I think the thing with Do – Webster and Ma'am got to me, Mr Mathison. Webster is my friend, Sir, just like Van Rensberg and Oberholzer. And I hate the thought of him leaving and what it will do to the choir to lose his voice. I couldn't sleep, Sir, so I just thought I'd go for a walk. I know that is no excuse, Sir, and I know I deserve to be punished. Severely, Sir.'

Mathison studied Karl for a while. The night was quiet, no sound of crickets or frogs from the orchard. As if everything had stopped. Certain his story had been wholly believed, Karl maintained his outward countenance: frown, pursed lips, while inwardly rejoicing; even imagined being turned into something of a hero when it became known he had been caught and caned for sneaking around outside. The prefects would be green.

Then Mathison dropped his gaze, sat back in his chair and Karl heard the desk drawer slide open. Mathison replaced the glasses, adjusted them over his nose and asked: 'Do you know what I have in here, Karl?'

'No, Sir.' The boy froze. Something was amiss. The man brought his hand from the drawer. Onto the desk he flicked a key. The silver object came to rest near the middle on the bare wooden surface. Unmistakable. *The extra key he had had cut in Amanzimtoti. My locker. Christ. They've been into my locker.* The key in his palm felt like a clot of heated metal. Heated metal in scalding water.

'So, if you found that key in your hand – the one you unlocked the door with tonight – four days ago, Karl, when did you have time to slip into Winterton to have a duplicate made?' There was nothing he could say. For this he was not prepared. 'Or did you walk to Winterton on another night, say, last night and you only lied to me about how many times you've been out. It's actually twice. Twice, isn't it, Karl?'

The boy didn't answer.

'Or, did you send someone to Winterton to cut the key for you? Who could it be that you sent, Karl? One of the servants, or the farm boys? Or was it two keys you found on the parking lot? Not one as you remembered? Or was it perhaps someone else, someone a little closer to your dorm from whom you stole the key? From Uncle Charlie, didn't you? There are only so many people with a key to that door, you know. And I know each one of them. You stole this key, didn't you?' Yet as he said the word 'stole' a light played in his eyes, as if, Karl trembled, he knew the boy had not stolen the object. That in fact it had been given. Oh my God, he knows, he knows, sweet merciful Jesus Christ, he knows. Mathison now leant far forward across the desk. His fist folded over the key. Without warning he barked: 'Now, you are going to start telling the truth! Do you hear me? I have had it with you. You will tell me every word of the truth I want to hear without missing a detail.'

Karl stared at Mathison. Speechless.

'Or must I bring out the book I brought along from your locker for you to swear on?'

A gasp escaped Karl's lips. My diary! Jesus, Christ, the diary, he has the diary! He knows everything, everything. No. No. And his eyes brimmed with tears even as he told himself but it's in Gogga, the worst parts are in Gogga. He can't understand Gogga. But anyone can decipher that, any Grade One freak can decipher that with a little time. Tears now flowed freely down Karl's cheeks. His lips twitched.

'Tell me, you little fool. Tell me everything. I'm going to hear it from your lips. And you may as well stop crying because I will not be taken in by your manipulations. Not in any way.'

The boy couldn't speak. He stood stupefied. Horrified, knowing nothing but that his life was ended. And that he would live it. That he was at last facing the noose of his own making.

'My hand is on this phone, Karl. Do you hear me? I can either pick up this receiver and call your parents. Or you can tell me. Everything.'

Not Bok and Bokkie please. Please. 'I love him,' the words escaped. Suddenly the tears stopped. He wiped his face with one hand and the sleeve of his dressing gown while the other still clung to the key. He looked Mathison in the eye.

'What? I love him, indeed.' Mathison was expressionless. 'Tell me how it started. The whole truth. From the beginning.'

'Which beginning, Sir?'

'The bloody key, Karl, how did you get the key? Tell me where and how you got the key.'

'It was one afternoon, Sir. In March. He told me he would leave it for me in a book in the library where I always go to read. I was reading Shakespeare's *Sonnets*. Ma'am lent them to me so I put the book of *Sonnets* beside A of the encyclopaedia and he left—'

'Who, for goodness' sake, Karl? Stop mincing your words and use his name.'

'Mr Cilliers.' In a whisper.

There is a ghostly silence in the room. Karl hears Mathison swallow, sees his Adam's apple bob repeatedly against his throat. A look of shock, and the boy wonders why the man seems rattled. At first Mathison's expression doesn't change. The eyes are enormous behind the glasses. His lips tense. He stares at Karl and the boy stares at him.

When Mathison speaks again he is calm. An overwhelming tenderness has crept into his voice, the anger seeped from his face. 'Dear Lord, my poor boy. My God. What has he done to you?' Karl frowns. Not able to answer as he imagines he may be expected. 'Where did he molest you? How many times?' Mathison shakes his head. It seems to Karl as if the headmaster is about to weep.

'No, Mr Mathison, he never molested me. I promise. We were just, we . . . were just together.'

'What do you mean, Karl? Just together . . . Why didn't you come and tell me sooner? Dear boy, why, why, why didn't you come to me? You knew you could trust me? You knew I understood these things!'

Karl looks in bewilderment at the man across the table from him. Why the sudden change in attitude? No, he has it all wrong. There was nothing to fear from Jacques. Never.

'He was always good to me, Sir.'

'Karl?'

'When we were together, Mr Mathison.'

'What did he do to you? Where did he touch you?' This was no longer an interrogation. Mathison seemed spellbound in his pity for Karl. Kind, gentle, concerned only for the welfare of the boy in front of him. Relief swept over the boy.

'Everywhere I asked him to, Sir.'

'Karl, Karl, Karl! What has he done to you? You are a child and you have been molested. Don't be afraid of me, Karl. You don't have to fear that he will ever do anything to you again. Speak to me. I'll never allow him to hurt you again. Tell me everything from the beginning.'

'I am never scared of him, Mr Mathison. He would never hurt me.'

'And that's why you're protecting him?'

'I went to him at first, Sir, because I thought it would be an adventure, but then I slowly fell in love with him . . .'

'He forced you to perform disgusting acts with him, didn't he, Karl?'

'No, Mr Mathison. I love him.'

'Karl, he has done the most abominable thing an adult can ever do to a child.' Mathison's eyes now darted around the room, cast around, searched for the right words to say: 'He has indoctrinated you to speak of this aberration as love. Do you know what love is, Karl?'

'Yes, Sir.'

'Tell me.'

'It's a bit long, Sir.'

'Tell me what you think.'

'Love is an ever fixed mark, Sir.'

'Go on, go on . . .'

'That looks on tempests and is never shaken; it's the star to every wandering bark, whose worth's unknown although his height be taken. Love's not time's fool, even though rosy lips and cheeks, within his bending sickle's compass come. Love alters not with his brief hours and weeks, but bears it out even to the edge of doom. Love—'

A frown cut Mathison's forehead. He shook his head.

'That's from Shakespeare, Sir.'

Again Mathison shook his head, pursed tight his eyes. 'No, Karl. No. That's not what love is! Love is what a parent feels for a child. What we as teachers feel for you boys. It is based on trust and caring. It is what a man feels for the woman he marries. Do you understand?' Karl looked at Mathison. Could not find in himself a response. 'Let me tell you what it is, my boy. And mine is from the Word of God, not from Shakespeare.'

Karl watched as Mathison took a Bible from his desk. He placed it in front of him and paged towards the back. The New Testament. 'I want you to listen carefully, Karl. I want you to never forget what I read to you tonight.' He paused and cleared his throat. '*If I had the gift of being able to speak in other languages without learning them, and could speak in every language there is in all of heaven and earth, but didn't love others, I would simply be making a noise. If I had the gift of prophecy and knew all about what is going to happen in the future, knew everything about everything, but didn't love others, what good would it do? Even if I had the gift of faith so that I could speak to a mountain and make it move, I would still be worth nothing at all without love. If I gave everything I had to poor people, and if I were burnt alive for preaching the Gospel, but didn't love others, it would be of no value whatever. Love is very patient and kind, never jealous or envious, never boastful or proud, never haughty or selfish or rude. Love does not demand its own way. It is not irritable or touchy. It does not hold grudges and will hardly even notice when others do wrong. It is never glad about injustice, but rejoices whenever truth wins its way. If you love someone you will be loyal to him no matter what the cost. You will always believe in him, always expect the best of him, and always stand your ground defending him. All the special gifts and powers from God will some day come to an end, but love goes on forever. Some day prophecy, and speaking in unknown languages, and special knowledge — these gifts will disappear. Now we know so little, even with our special gifts, and the inspired preaching of those most gifted is still so poor. But when we have been made perfect and complete, then the need for these inadequate special gifts will come to an end, and they will disappear. It is like this: when I was a child I*

spoke and thought and reasoned as a child does. But when I became a man my
thoughts grew far beyond those of my childhood, and now I have put away the child-
ish things. In the same way, we can see and understand only a little about God now,
as if we were peering in his reflection in a poor mirror; but some day we are going
to see him in his completeness, face to face. Now all that I know is hazy and blurred,
but then I will see everything clearly, just as clearly as God sees into my heart right
now. There are three things that remain — faith, hope, and love — and the greatest
of these is love.'

Even after he had finished the reading, Mathison kept his eyes in
the book. When he spoke, it was in almost a whisper: 'Do you see,
Karl, by these criteria, you could not possibly love this man . . .
Would you still say that you love him?'

But Karl does not hear the question. He is caught in some place
where he searches for a way to please the man in front of him without betraying the man he feels he is poised to. Knows he already has.

'Maybe not, Sir, maybe I don't love him.' Then, finding filtered
from memory a paraphrase of an idea spoken by Jacques, he says:
'Only pleasure is possible, Sir, not love. But he gives me pleasure, Sir.
I never knew how nice it could be to do all those things. So maybe
he's not the one I love, but he is the one who gives me pleasure. The
one I love . . .' It is on the tip of his tongue to say Dominic's name,
when he sees that Mathison's face has turned purple, swollen and
bloated. As if the man's head is about to explode.

'What kind of a perverted child are you, De Man! Have you no
understanding of what you are saying! Last year Mr Buys punished
you in this same office for a similar crime. I told you what it meant.
I warned you, I asked you to come and tell me if you heard about any
of this business! Instead of learning from your — perversion — you go
around engaging in unspeakable filth of the very nature you were
meant to be reporting to me! Worse filth!' Mathison pauses, half
rising from the desk before falling back into his chair. 'You are des-
picable. Do you realise I am about to call your parents and inform
them that you are expelled?'

The boy stands agog. He has no idea what has brought about the renewed anger. He trembles. Silent. But I have tried to tell the truth, he wants to cry. This is what you have asked for. Will I be expelled for telling you what you wanted to hear?

'Speak to me, Karl.'

Tears again run down his cheeks. He now sobs and he snivels: 'I don't know what you want me to say, Sir.'

'Tell me the truth. It is the truth that will set you free.'

'I'm telling you the truth, Sir, I swear, I'm telling you the truth, please, Sir, you . . .'

'Tell me he molested you, tell me everything he did to you, do not stand here telling me about love you don't understand anything of.' Still Karl cannot speak. And then Mathison, again almost in a whisper, sits forward and spits: 'How can you, for one moment, think that you're the only one?' It took Karl a second to comprehend that Mathison was not asking him a question. He was being told something. No, not something. Mathison was letting Karl understand that he knew of others who either had passed through Jacques's chambers or had been asked to pass through there. Still, with the doubt, there was now suddenly another: that Mathison was maybe tricking him. Could it be? But he barely cared. He now just wanted it to be over. Was ready to say anything for now. Later, later he could ask Jacques, warn him that Mathison knew or suspected others. And what does it matter if I wasn't the only one! I don't care. I love him in my own way and I know he loves me in his.

'I don't love him, Sir.'

'Past tense, Karl. Speak in the past tense.'

'I didn't love him, Sir.'

'Say it again, De Man.'

'I didn't love him, Mr Mathison.'

'Say he . . . abused you.'

'He abused me, Sir.'

'Now tell me what he did to you, word for word, moment for

moment. How many times, where, when, where did he touch you?'

And the boy weeps as he stands before the man, and he shakes his head and he says he cannot tell.

'Why not, why can't you speak?'

'Because you're going to chase him away, I know. Like you fired Mr Samuels.'

'What do you know about Mr Samuels?'

'Everybody knows. It was even in the newspapers.'

The headmaster sits, his head resting in his hands. It seems he is waiting for Karl to stop crying. He slowly rises from his chair. Karl raises his head and goes quiet. Mathison again sits down.

'I want you to tell me all the details. Or I will call your parents.'

Exhausted, no longer able to weep, he looks at the man with red, swollen eyes. He no longer fears the man. It is as if he now reads fear from the man's stare. Mathison is the one whom the boy now sees as afraid. What have I said, Karl's mind churns, what over the past hour has suddenly hit home to make this man fearful? And then, with the last of his bravado, mustering something of Dominic's words spoken in a different time in a different place: 'You can phone my parents, Mr Mathison. You can expel me. I don't care anymore, Sir. I'm no longer afraid of anything.'

The headmaster stares at the boy in disbelief. Slowly his stare turns to a look of deep loathing. Karl's hand around the key is sweaty and he drops the object into his gown pocket. Rubs both hands on the towelling fabric. It seems that an hour passes in which the two of them do nothing but stare at each other.

It is Mathison who breaks the silence: 'Karl, let you and me make a pact today. Do you know what a pact is?'

'Yes, Mr Mathison.'

'You are proud of this school, right?'

'Yes, Sir.'

'Given the choice, you would prefer not to be expelled, right?'

'Yes, Mr Mathison.'

'Would you like to see this institution's name dragged through the mud?'

'No, Sir.'

'Then, let us make a pact. That neither you nor I will ever speak about this outside these four walls.' Mathison looks at the boy with a face again become friendly, inviting Karl to trust.

'Yes, Sir.'

'So everything will be just the way it is. Right?' He nods, prodding the boy to agreement. From outside comes the twittering of sparrows and from the distance the gurgling of turkeys. It is almost dawn. 'We will not make a scandal,' Mathison continues. 'So that the newspapers will not destroy what is a sacred and national treasure of our country.' Again he waits for his words to sink in. Karl nods. 'And, so you will go on as if nothing happened, right?'

'You will not do anything to Mr Cilliers, Sir?'

Mathison casts his eyes around the room. 'You just leave that to me, right? That is an issue that has nothing to do with you, right?'

'Yes, Mr Mathison. But if everything is to be the same then Mr Cilliers will be the same. Like he won't be fired and he'll still be the senior conductor. Sir?'

'What is important here is that you don't want to cause damage to this school and neither do I. We will not do anything to do damage to the institution.' An extended pause, before he says: 'I am extremely proud of you, Karl. You must trust me. Do you?'

'Only if you promise not to do anything to Mr Cilliers, Sir.'

Mathison seems agitated. 'I give you my word of honour that I will do nothing to that man that may hurt this institution. Okay?'

'Yes, Sir.'

'And will you now give me your word of honour that you will never repeat to anyone, for as long as you live, what you have told me here tonight?'

'I promise, Mr Mathison. I give you my word of honour.'

Light gleamed on the dew outside Mathison's window. Then, again with extraordinary kindness he asked Karl whether the boy would like him to call the minister: 'How would you feel about talking to the minister about this? Maybe Dominee Steytler. Maybe he can pray with you?'

'No, Sir. Please, Sir, I'd prefer not to.'

'You can trust Dominee Steytler, Karl. He has dealt with everything. He is a man of deep wisdom.'

'No, Sir. I think everything is fine, Mr Mathison.'

'Then, I will pray with you, Karl.' And Mathison came around his desk. Kneeling he asked Karl to do the same. His eyes already closed, Karl suddenly felt sure that he was being looked at. He opened his eyes. He turned to find Mathison's gaze piercing his.

'De Man. Have you been smoking?'

'No, Sir.'

Mathison shook his head. Karl knew that the man knew he was lying. Still, Mathison again closed his eyes. He prayed a long prayer, thanking God for guidance for both himself and Karl, thanking God that he had given them the wisdom to not act rashly and to approach a terrible situation with calm and reason. He asked God's forgiveness for Karl's sins and thanked God for the blessed promise of eternal life given to those who turn from sin. When the prayer was over, he asked Karl for the other key. The boy retrieved it from his pocket, placed it into the waiting hand. As the boy was about to leave, Mathison held out the Bible from which he had read: 'Here,' he said. 'It is yours. You should read it more regularly, Karl. Your salvation lies in those pages. Not in Shakespeare.' Taking the book, Karl felt himself again grow flustered.

'Thank you, Sir.' And it must have been then, as he walked from the office, that it struck him that his diary was hidden in the cut of his mattress. Mathison could not have found it. No one, not even Dominic, knew where it was hidden. He looked down into his trembling hands: *The Living Bible*. On the cover pictures of children with balloons. High-rise buildings. Streets with neon lights. A man smiling.

Trees. Ripe fruit. A young woman with long hair laughing. He opened the covers and looked for the photograph of Alette, found it at Psalm 23. He rushed upstairs. Walked on his toes through C Dorm which was already bathed in light. Into F. Before pulling back the covers, he felt for the hard spot beneath the pillow. The diary was safe. Thank you, thank you, sweet Jesus. You are real after all.

Still thanking God that everything had worked out, he must have fallen asleep. An hour later Uncle Charlie's call of *Wakey, wakey, rise and shine, shorts, vests, takkies* roused him. Groggy and with a headache throbbing against his skull, he dressed for morning PT. He wondered how he was going to be able to run in his exhausted state. He fell in with the others and asked after Dominic. When Mervyn said that Dominic was packed and ready to leave Karl again thought with shock for the first time of the previous day's events. For the first time since using Dominic and Ma'am as a feeble excuse for his sneaking out, his mind now became fixated on anything but himself. He started running with the pack, casting a gaze over his shoulder to see whether Dominic was maybe somewhere at an upstairs window. Should he turn back? Tell the rear prefect he was ill? But the thought of Mathison seeing him, of being found out for gippoing PT a mere few hours after returning from the brink of expulsion, drove him on with the group. With every shock of his running shoes pounding the gravel and while around him boys chattered and laughed until they grew breathless, he thought: please, please, God, Father, Holy Spirit. He prayed: let that woman apologise. Don't let Dominic go. I will become a good Christian. I swear on my mother and father's lives I will never do anything against the Bible again. I will be a good and disciplined boy. I will not do unnatural things with Dominic or Jacques again. With your help, sweet merciful Jesus, these urges will disappear. I will never smoke dagga again and risk becoming a drug addict. I will confess to the world my disgusting sins and be an example of Your Salvation. No more subterfuge in my life, ever.

Please just keep Dominic here for me and I will become a minister of Your Glorious Church. I will become like St Francis of Assisi. I will be selfless, I will be the most humble man on earth. I will become a fisher of souls for Your Church. Or anything You command or expect of me. I will die in Your service. I will listen for Your voice and I will hear You. I will study Your Word and know it by rote as I know the Psalms and the Song of Songs. Just let Dominic stay. That is all I ask of You: let my friend stay with me for he is all I have and all I have ever loved.

By the time they were almost back at school he realised that morning PT had not been the torture he had thought it would be. Either from his intense prayer or from the pounding, the headache had disappeared. He thought of choir, of facing Jacques. He would go to him directly after choir and explain everything about how he had thought that they had found his diary, that Mathison had tricked him. Misled him. Bastard. No, Mathison is a man of God, forgive me, Father. I will tell Jacques that Mathison has been reasonable about the whole thing. If I can get to Dominic before Dr Webster arrives, I can tell Dominic to go and speak to Mathison. Just explain things. How stupid of me, he thought, I should have told Mathison last night that he had to save Dominic. I should have thought of a way. That's what Dominic would have done had he been the one to get caught: he would have tied his silence to my salvation. Instead I was so frightened of what was going to happen to me that I thought only of myself, my own survival. Forgive me, Father. Maybe I can go and speak to Ma'am. Tell her what was wrong with what she said to Dominic. Why it is so hurtful.

Instead of entering F he huffed and puffed and bundled into G with the others. Dominic's bed was stripped. The faded plaid curtain to his locker rolled back. Empty shelves. Could it be that in the half-hour jog Dr Webster had come? That they'd already left? He wanted to run downstairs, to see if his friend was still there. Again the events of the night and the resolutions of the dawn kept him in check.

Instead he rushed to his own locker, dressed and before the bell rang for breakfast found himself downstairs. From classroom to classroom. Peaked into the teachers' dining room. In the foyer he saw Dominic's leather suitcases, his rolled sleeping bag. His music case. Everything packed and stacked against a wall. At least he was still here. He found Dominic in the phone booth beside the dining room. His friend, speaking in soft tones into the handset, looked spent. Had he too not slept the night? The breakfast bell rang, but he waited for Dominic to finish.

'Hold on, Dad. Karl's here.' And smiling at Karl he said, 'Mathison called Dad this morning at six. He had a meeting with Ma'am late into the night and it sounds as if she's going to apologise. Go to breakfast, I'll see you there in a bit.' They smiled at each other and Karl's eyes brimmed with tears as he turned to join the line falling in for breakfast. He prayed a frevent prayer of thanks and praise.

Percy Johnstone was the prefect at breakfast who allowed Karl to reserve a seat even though that was not permitted. Percy, big, fat and jovial, said he hoped Karl was right, that Dominic would indeed be coming to breakfast. And before Buys spotted the bare seat. Grace was said and they fell to eating their porridge. To Karl it seemed that everyone – even at the table behind him – was speaking about Webster this, Webster that. Only Karl himself said nothing and Percy asked why he was so quiet. He answered that he hadn't slept well. Radys, sitting beside Bennie at the bottom end from Karl, quipped that Karl had been crying about his little girlfriend who was being expelled for dungpunching and terrorism. The prefect told Radys to restrain his brutality and to show empathy with those in trouble. While Karl had never much cared for Percy Johnstone, the ungainly older boy momentarily seemed a new best friend.

Breakfast was near over when a hush descended. Dominic was entering the dining hall. He wound through the tables and walked to Buys.

'Permission to join for breakfast, Sir.'

'Go ahead, Webster.' Buys said, deliberate disdain on his face.

The hall remained silent and all eyes followed Dominic as he walked to the counter. Florence and Precious were serving. Florence smiled at Dominic and then, in a voice loud enough for the entire dining hall to hear, Dominic said: 'I won't be leaving after all, Florence. Ma'am will be apologising to me later in the morning, in front of our whole class.' From around him Karl heard an angry murmur ripple through the dining hall. Florence, who barely spoke English, looked at Precious as though she had been made an unwilling accomplice. Dominic said something else that Karl couldn't hear and then walked, head held high, to where he had seen his place reserved.

'Eat your food,' Buys barked and at once the sounds of spoons against porridge plates filled the hall.

'Morning to you all. Lovely day, don't you think?' Dominic said. Only Karl and Percy acknowledged his defiant greeting.

'Pass the sugar, please,' Dominic spoke to Bennie and Radys. Neither moved to pass the container. Karl stretched out his arm only to have Radys pull the bowl just beyond his reach.

'Dietz,' the prefect snapped. 'Pass that sugar bowl to Webster.' Radys, with a smirk, spun the bowl over the linoleum and it settled just beside Dominic's porridge plate.

'You're looking for trouble today, aren't you, Dietz?' the prefect said.

'The trouble's sitting right there next to you, Johnstone,' Radys quipped and went back to eating.

Mathison, at assembly, was freshly shaved and as well groomed as ever. Nothing in his bearing gave away the events of the night. At his announcement that there would be no morning choir, Karl suspected at once that the cancellation had something to do with Jacques. In an instant Dominic, right beside him, was forgotten as he now became obsessed with what was happening to Jacques and whether something could still, after all, go wrong in the agreement he had with Mathison.

No one in class spoke while they awaited Ma'am. A prefect came to tell Dominic that Mathison wanted him in his office. The moment Dominic left class, the hushed speculation began. Would Ma'am be forced to apologise to a snot-nose? It was a disgrace. If she apologised the least Dominic would have to do was apologise to her. What was so terrible about what she had said anyway? *Everyone* hates girlish boys. No secret in that. She said it for his own good. If she apologised she'd be as good as giving him a passport to continue being a fairy. A third of the class participated in the discussion. Two others sat quietly, listening, paging through books, some talking amongst themselves about other things. Karl sat with *The Brothers Karamazov* open in front of him. Reading, but not taking in a word. Eavesdropping on the conversations around him, he tried to turn a page at approximately the time he guessed it would have taken him to read and understand it.

'Here they come!' came a whisper and the room went quiet. Almost at once the class stood as Ma'am and Dominic entered. The class greeted her and she gave them permission to sit.

'I would like you all to know that I have apologised to Dominic for what I said to him in class yesterday. I spoke in a moment of anger, without thinking, I had not intended to hurt him and I regret having spoken the way I did.' She faltered for a moment and then told the class to open their Maths homework.

'Ma'am.'

'Yes, Benjamin?'

'Now that you've apologised to him, don't you think he should apologise to you?' Murmured agreement from the desks in Bennie's corner.

'It's up to Dominic, but as far as I'm concerned the issue is now closed.'

'I will not apologise, Ma'am, with all due respect,' Dominic said quickly from his seat. 'What I said I stand by.' His voice still carried the defiant tone. Karl looked down onto his desk.

'Well, we've got work to get through. Let's look at that Maths homework.' Karl took the Maths book from his desk, certain that he would be in trouble for not having completed a single problem. Yet upon opening his book, it was all there, in his own handwriting, done, obviously during the previous evening's prep. Still, he could not remember ever having seen the sums. Where had he been last night? The entire previous day and most of the events of the night seemed to have vanished from memory. He was suddenly exhausted, barely able to draw the crosses beside the answers.

Shortly before evening choir, Mathison had a prefect call Karl from where he had fallen asleep on his arms at his desk. Still half asleep, he arrived at Mathison's office. The headache had returned. He stood in the same spot from where he had faced Mathison less than twelve hours before. Through a tired smile, Mathison asked Karl whether the idea of helping Lukas and Mr Walshe in the dairy might appeal to him. Karl answered that he had often been a little envious of Lukas, as he too enjoyed the farm.

'We'd like it if from now till the end of the year you helped Lukas in the dairy.'

'What about choir, Sir?'

'I think it best if we agree that Mr Cilliers has called you for a voice test and that your voice is going.'

That was all. All he needed for Karl to know that he would no longer be singing. That he would be telling the others and his family that his voice was breaking.

'You will tell everyone that Mr Cilliers called you for a voice test, right? Because of some odd sounds during choir. And that it was decided you couldn't continue. You understand, right?'

'Yes, Sir.'

'This is a reasonable resolution, right?'

'Yes, Sir.'

'Let your voice jump a few times in class, right? So you'll help out with Lukas in the dairy, right? I'll tell Lukas myself. You're content with that Karl, right?'

'Yes, Sir. And, Sir, my parents?'

'They will never know. As long as you keep our pact. Remember, loose lips sink big ships. Of course you will have to leave the school, though, Karl. In December, of course, once you've finished Standard Six.' He paused, and nodded at Karl. 'Because your voice is breaking, right?'

'Will you not do anything to Mr Cilliers?'

'Your conductor and I have an agreement that is really none of your business. Now leave and forget that this ever happened. Karl, one more thing: you will not speak to Mr Cilliers again. Never. Not on the premises of this school, do you understand? If I as much as see you near him or hear anyone say that you were seen in his company, I will rescind this agreement with immediate effect, right? Both you and he will be out of here at the drop of a hat. Is that clear?'

'Yes, Sir.'

Again Karl rode the seesaw of relief and loss. So that was it. This is okay. I'm safe. He's safe. No one knows. And Dom is staying. Everything is the way it's always been. Bok and Bokkie won't ever know. Leaving Mathison's office, suddenly unable to keep his eyes open and unperturbed at possibly being found by Uncle Charlie, he slouched upstairs to F Dorm. Shoes and all he crept between the covers. He slept, fully clothed, from five in the afternoon till six the next morning, when Uncle Charlie's call woke them for PT.

Again fully engaged in preparations for his Grade Eight exams, Dominic spent most of the next few weeks behind the music room's door in virtual seclusion. Karl no longer went to sit and work at the table behind his friend's back and so the two boys saw little of each other after Ma'am's apology. To Karl's announcement that he was out of choir Dominic, Bennie and Mervyn responded with surprise and incredulity. Dominic expressed regret, for he understood that over the previous months Karl had developed a thorough-going enjoyment of the music, a change that had introduced an element hitherto absent from their relationship. At first Dominic suggested that he would go and speak to Cilliers, convince the man that any cracks in Karl's voice were but temporary and not at all serious. For surely the change had come on all too suddenly to be permanent? In all likelihood the tear had been caused by nothing more than a cold. In a response that seemed to leave Dominic even more perplexed, Karl angrily prohibited him from doing any such thing. He said he was quite happy with the way things had turned out; that the dairy work and additional time for riding with Lukas was more appealing than Beethoven, ad nauseam. Lukas said that having Karl down at the dairy made the job even more pleasant and jokingly he told Dominic to accept that the two of them were now ahead on the road to manhood. 'Quite frankly, Lukas, I don't give a spare shit for where you are in the testosterone race.' Then turning from Lukas and facing Karl: 'And if we were still going overseas,' Dominic asked, scowling at Karl's implied denial of ever having enjoyed the music, 'would you then have taken this so,' he searched for a word, 'so pathetically? Still be staying down here in the barn chewing straw with your new best friend in the whole world?'

'Well, we're not going overseas any longer. So, it's a moot point, isn't it, Dom? Maybe if we were I would have gone begging or something, but not now. Not for one concert and some silly record album. And there's no reason to be sarcastic.'

Being as busy as he was in the next weeks, Dominic's frustration offered little reason to concern Karl. The two saw each other only in class and during meals. As for the rest of his friends and the school, Karl thought he sensed from them and from the teachers a hint of awe, as if his altering voice indeed placed him in a league of maturity alongside Lukas. He drew particular pleasure from the fact that both he and Lukas were still a year younger than the Standard Seven prefects, none of whose voices were showing signs of change. On the phone Bok chuckled, delighted when Karl told him that his voice was going. Bokkie too had a smile in her voice when she said: 'You're turning into a young man now, Karl.'

From his classmates and the schoolboys generally, the initial antagonism towards Dominic soon waned. By the time Parents' Weekend came around, even Bennie was back on speaking terms with the boy he now called the Young Ter. The discomfort and silence between Ma'am and Dominic abated and while Karl sensed that Dominic still kept a guard to his lips, surfaces at least returned, and to all intent and purposes seemed the way they'd always been. Karl himself, now spending choir rehearsal time with Lukas at the dairy or out on the farm, had not been to the fort or to the library since the night with Mathison. The idea of returning to the river frightened him. He prayed at night that Uncle Klaas and his companion had left.

The library was taboo. Jacques passed through there regularly and he didn't want to see him – as much because of Mathison's imperative as from shame at the prospect of having to face the man he now knew he had certainly betrayed. His reading of the encyclopaedias had been abandoned near the middle of D in September, anyway, and now that he was doing farm work there were other obligations and responsibilities that had to be met. He tried not to think about Jacques. To forget that the man had ever been more than his choir master. Once, in class, briefly, he caught himself daydreaming about Uncle Klaas. Why, he wondered, had he not told Mathison that night about the tramp, instead of about Jacques? Or about both? Had he spoken about Uncle Klaas and thought up a better story about the key instead of telling the truth, everything may have been different. Had his betrayal of Jacques after all not been accidental? He pushed these uncomfortable questions from his mind.

In the weeks leading to school's break-up, he would see Jacques only twice and each time from a distance: once as he drove by the dairy in his Mazda, and once when Karl and Lukas were walking across the quad as the choirs spilt from rehearsal. Each time Karl changed direction, finding an excuse to look or head elsewhere. Did he ever see me, Karl wondered. What is he thinking? Does he hate me? When their classmates went to rehearsal – at times for three hours a day – Karl went with Lukas down the hill to the dairy. By keeping to his tasks on the farm and out of the library, he made certain never to cross paths with the conductor. Although Mathison was rarely outside of his office, Karl felt sure he was under surveillance. Eyes were on him, on the corridors, the dairy, the classroom, even when he and Lukas snuck off for a quick ride after milking. He allowed himself only rarely to think of Jacques and then mostly when one of his friends spoke of what was going on in choir. Always there was the fear that even his thoughts would show through on his face and that Mathison himself might read it or that Mathison might hear of it from whomever was Mathison's eyes. Initially, after the first few rehearsals from which he was absent, he had burnt to ask the others how it had been, but he gritted his teeth, relying on information volunteered or overheard in class, in the dorms, on the corridors, in the showers. And when the others asked whether he missed choir, he pulled his nose up and said no, what a silly notion. The thought of sending Jacques a note of explanation and regret had been repressed, again in the face of Mathison's vigilance. Since the fatal night he had not allowed himself to believe that he missed either Jacques or Dominic, the mere thought of intimacy with either causing a heaviness in his legs. He undertook that once Dominic had completed his exam, he would resist from his friend any rekindling of physical closeness that was certain to occur after the other emerged finally from behind the piano. Those were chapters over, closed, written, ripped out and destroyed. They had to be. Yet, they rushed back. How given he now was, more than ever before, to retrospection. How scenes and phrases rushed back to embarrass, haunt, anger and shame like a guilty conscience. I have betrayed twice, he thought. First my friends. Then my lover. Who will

I do in next? Could betrayal, like death and accidents, come in threes? And after that, what would come from that?

He read little outside of the Bible at night during quiet time. His struggle to concentrate was not new. But what struck him as different, what worried him, was the inability to concentrate even when reading fiction. For two or three days after the night with Mathison, he had tried the Dostoyevsky, sometimes at night with his torchlight, but to no avail. He once fell asleep with the book and torch in his hand, waking to find the batteries gone flat and his cheeks wet and hot. He abandoned *The Brothers Karamazov* a bare hundred pages into the text. Instead of trying another novel, he turned for solace to that other book in his locker. It must have been four months since he had read from the Bible and he now plunged in at Genesis, resolving to read it cover to cover, to resist the old ways of singling out favourite passages.

As usual he did his homework only to the extent that he would have something to show to Ma'am in class. Barely aware of the development, he found himself resenting his former mentor. He found it difficult to hold her gaze when she looked at him in class or if they passed each other in the corridors. He was afraid of her, wondering if perhaps she and the other members of staff knew about the thing with Jacques. Caught in a terrible daydream in which the whole school and all the teachers jeered and laughed at him, he found his face aglow, as if he were coming down with fever. He worried about his diary being discovered, vowed to get rid of it, burn it as soon as he could. His passion for writing and drawing had fled. Within days of the events with Mathison he realised he could not complete the statue essay that Ma'am had said held the seeds of promise. Instead of continuing the struggle to complete the essay, he wrote, within an hour of prep, a story about Henry Francis Fynn witnessing 'the vision' of Chaka's great hunt at the confluence of the two Umfolozi Rivers. Already as he placed it on the pile he knew the piece was an embarrassment. Not only was there nothing original to the story, but he had not used Ma'am's Oxford Concise once to correct the abominable spelling. Ma'am's remarks on the returned essay were sparse, the tone curt. He received an abysmal 14/20 and he knew he would receive a B for English. He feared his report. There was no way he was going to get a single A. *Your story seems* — Ma'am wrote — *to be nothing more than another of your excellent ideas into which little or no effort has gone. More like something written at the beginning of the year*, she said, before he had known what metaphor or simile or precise language and idiom were. Certainly before he had gleaned the existence of a thing called a dictionary. Embarrassed, ashamed, angry at himself and her, he undertook to try harder in the final essay. But again he dropped the essay on the pile, feeling ashamed, hating himself for the weakness of his resolve. Art class, too, no longer held him spellbound. He soon experienced both writing and drawing as equally boring to all his other subjects. Art prac he presented in simple black and white. The use of colour and shading seemed to him like too much hard work, a waste of time. Ma'am did not broach the question of what was going on with him until shortly before Parents' Weekend. Keeping him after class she asked whether there was anything he would like to discuss with her, something that may be bothering him.

'Nothing, Ma'am, not at all.'

She asked about his lack of interest in Art and English. He answered that he was preoccupied with leaving at the end of the year and that he would make good for it with the next assignments. She prodded, saying she had heard his parents were not coming up for the weekend. Was that what was bothering him?

'Not at all, Ma'am, I'm going to stay in for the weekend and work on Latin and maybe spend a little time with Lukas's family and maybe a little with the Websters.'

She looked him in the eye and asked: 'Karl, are you trying to punish me? By not working anymore? Are you somehow trying to tell me you're angry about the way I spoke to Dominic?'

'No, Ma'am.' He emphasized the denial, 'No, Ma'am. Why would I be angry about that?'

'You do realise that I said what I said only to help him, don't you, Karl? He must realise what a tough life he faces once he leaves the safe and nurturing environment of this school. The same goes for all you boys. I expressed myself badly, but it was a message I believe the class had to hear. What do you think?'

'I agree, Ma'am. You were right and I think he should have apologised to you. I hope you will not think I'm choosing his side if I spend a little time with him over Parents' Weekend, Ma'am?' And she had said that she held no grudge against Dominic, that she was as fond of him as she had ever been. 'I know, Ma'am. I've never doubted that for a moment.'

'Good. And, Karl, I wanted to ask you something else. While I was away, with . . . the funeral . . . I heard that you and Dominic introduced yourselves to Mr Loveday as Oscar and Johann Sebastian. Is that true?'

'Yes, Ma'am, it was only a joke.'

'Why did you choose the name Oscar? Was it because you read *Dorian Gray*?'

'Yes, Ma'am.'

'Who told you to read Oscar Wilde, anyway?'

'Aag, Ma'am. I just liked the name Oscar, you know, this silly thing of me becoming a writer, and Dominic chose Bach because he's going to compose.'

She smiled and said, Karl, as remarkable a writer as Wilde was, there is no pride attached to the life of that man. He died in disgrace. Because of precisely the sort of thing I warned Dominic about. Why don't you find yourself another role model, William, Isaac, Ernest, any of those. Then she looked at him with grave seriousness: 'Karl, I in no way wish to sound disloyal to this school. This is my bread and butter. But, I want you to count your blessings that your voice is changing. This is an unhealthy environment for boys to be together. Very unhealthy. And someone like you, Karl, could easily go . . . either way in a place like this. Do you understand what I mean, or do I need to spell it out?'

'I understand, Ma'am. And don't worry, Ma'am, I'm too wise to be led astray.'

'You're strong, Karl. And talented. You're the strongest fourteen-year-old I've ever taught. Truly, from all my years of teaching you're one of only two or three I will always remember. Hold on to your strength and you'll make it in the real world out there.'

After the meeting with Ma'am, and in spite of her saying he could have gone either way — a phrase that sucked like a leech at his brain — and knowing he had in some way behaved treacherously by speaking to her about Dominic, he had again felt the urge to write. The term's quota of Afrikaans and English essays had already been completed, but he fell to trying to complete the statue piece. If only as a gesture of thanks to Ma'am. He could give it to her as a thank you for her unqualified support of him as a person. To show how he would never forget what she had taught him. When his statue project went nowhere, he returned to the orange poem, thinking he could just as well give that to her. But the poem still refused to yield more than a list of words which eventually ran to two foolscap pages. He again thought of his diary. Since the night with Mathison, worry had sat astride his thoughts in case the book were somehow discovered and what he'd written exposed. Badly wanting to keep the book, not quite wanting to destroy its contents, he decided to bury it. Along with some of his poems. From Matron Booysen he asked five or six plastic bags — to pack some of my books to take home, Mrs Booysen — into which he then carefully slid the diary and the poems, knotting each plastic Checkers bag before placing the parcel knot-side in the next. When everyone was in choir he took the parcel down to the dairy. From the shed he took a spade and went to dig a hole exactly halfway between the orchard's only two almond trees. Satisfied that no one had followed him and none could see him behind the dense green foliage of a large pomegranate bush, he nervously dug to two feet, then placed the bright yellow package at the bottom before dumping the moist black soil and clay back into the hole. I will come back and fetch you, I promise, he told the parcel as the hole closed in. Just wait for me, I will not forget you. No one will find you here. Only I will know your whereabouts and even of your existence. He covered over the disturbed soil with leaves and twigs, gave the place a last look so that he would remember the location, and saw that it was not at the precise halfway point. It was a little to the left, a little closer to the younger of the two trees. I'll remember. I'll come back. One day. Then he rushed to return the spade and attend the milking before he could be missed by either Mr Walshe or Lukas.

He soon felt himself part of the dynamics of the farm, milking, supervising rides, meeting farm labourers – faces he had known got names – and he and Mr Walshe related well. Without needing to be told, Karl understood that he was there in Lukas's domain and as such there was no rivalry between the boys either in their work or for the affections of the farm foreman. All too aware of Karl's passion for the horses, Lukas seemed deliberately to place the animals in Karl's care while he himself focused instead on the dairy. When a number of the horses had to be shod, Lukas and Mr Walshe spent hours showing Karl how to clip hooves, how to heat the shoes, how to assess the depths of each nail, how to ensure that a horse was not hurt by touching a nerve. Karl kept an open mind, taking in new information like a sponge, executing his tasks with rigour, good humour and discipline. If he could learn this world, he thought, if he could become part of this rhythm for the last month of being there, he could forget almost altogether the other.

Yet, even as he worked at milking the cows, enjoyed the sense of achievement at having cleaned cribs and mixed feedtroughs alongside the workers, he had to acknowledge to himself that he had the blues. Now he thought that the words 'to have the blues' that Bernice and Stephanie had explained to him were inappropriate. It was more like being inside the blues, rather than the blues being inside him. Even as he rode, worked and spoke to the men and Lukas around him, the endless sky and mountain ridges pressed down on him, sometimes so hard that his field of vision seemed narrowed, hulled in a focus of grey mists. A darkness came over the world from inside the sunshine, then, threatening to suffocate him as if he were being systematically encompassed by everything around him in a grip he thought he would never escape. Of this he told no one, and no one could have suspected what was happening. For he continued to talk, to joke, to pretend interest in all that was happening and being said around him on the farm and in class. Only when he was alone did he allow himself to be pressed down, to let go of pretence, to take the full impact of the heaviness. One day he seemed to become hypnotised by the motion of his hands sliding down the teats of an udder: the tss, tss, tss, tss, of the milk squirting against the silver metal bucket between his legs. From then on he looked forward to the task of milking even at the moment he awoke in the morning. At times in the middle of a class discussion or conversation over lunch, he realised he was not hearing a word or a sound from the boys around him, instead he heard the tss, tss, tss, tss of the milk's jetting rhythm against enamel. He now wanted to be in the dairy more than he had ever wanted to be on horseback. The sound of milk hitting the bucket, the thought of himself astride a bench looking at his greased fingers massaging the teats, appealed to him as if the simple task was the only thing of value left in his world.

Then, miraculously, for a few days a week, the world would again look light and beautiful to him. He would awake in the morning and the ominous pressure from the sky had abated as if it had been but a dream and he would know it was gone at the instant — even before — he opened his eyes. On days when with luck or fate on his side his favourite subjects and lessons arrived in those window periods, he felt himself again passionate, excited, playful, even ready to love. He ventured to Dominic's music room, fooled around on horseback, went swimming with Bennie, competing to see who could do more than a length underwater without surfacing for a breath. If this can last, he thought, I will be fine and I will still come to something in the world, I will paint something spectacular, I will write an unforgettable poem. But then, just as suddenly as the sun had risen on a different day, the thick clouds rushed in and he again barely saw the mountains, the colours. Am I sick, he wondered. What is wrong with me? Is there a diagnosis other than the blues and a treatment other than death? He was no longer afraid that Bok and Bokkie would come to hear of Jacques. No, he seemed to fear little, but then little seemed of interest to him anyway. The world did not so much pass him by as oppress him. There seemed little to live for. Yes, this is what's wrong, he thought. Trying to stay alive is all a terrible waste of time. I want to die. At night, in these moments, he lay in bed thinking about the tambotie seeds in his toilet bag, wondered how long it would be before they took effect. Whether it would be a painful death. Knew it would. He dwelled on Bernice in Mkuzi. Vomiting up bile and blood that resembled pieces of raw meat. Saw her again as she was when she came out of hospital: a yellow, shaky praying mantis. But he had to ensure that he could not be found and saved. He would scream in pain, he knew. As she had writhed like a snake wounded by the wheel of a car. He could do it in the bathroom, take his pillow to muffle the cries. Or on a Saturday afternoon, when everyone was at the river, he could sneak to the stables or to the farthest part of the orchard, above Second Rugby Field, and do it there. If only he still had the key he could do it after lights-out anywhere in the veld and they'd take days to find him. How long would it take for the poison to work? This was his only question. These thoughts were unlike the flights of fancy which he had had in sick-bay after the Dr Taylor holiday. In those he had sort of died while still being able to attend his own funeral, there still somehow alive to watch people grieve and to smile a bittersweet smile at them, as in doleful remorse at the memory of how they had treated him they fell upon his grave clawing at the red soil, weeping. Then he had feared hell, for he knew, to kill yourself was the surest one-way ticket to eternal damnation. But now it was different. Rather than think *beyond* death, his thoughts of swallowing the jumping beans stopped at the moment of their effect. Of completion. That was all he could imagine. He had slipped into the world like an overeager bird, Bokkie said, and now he wanted to slip out with the same haste. Beyond that moment of exit was the big oblivion into which the dark clouds would finally descend and take him away. Out of Bok's testicles into the shaft, out of the glans into Bokkie's womb, out of Bokkie's vagina into Arusha, out of Tanzania into the Republic of South Africa, out of South Africa into the where and what of death. But that every out had to have an in no longer mattered. He wanted out of the world, no matter what its concomitant in. With everything over and gone he would not have to worry about anything that had concerned him here, ever again. Least his own funeral.

Dominic seemed to find his friend's altered state excruciating. After the success with his exams the occasion arose that he again wanted to come to Karl's bed. His suggestion was met initially with resistance and finally with a flat refusal. At first Karl told him to wait a few days, but when Dominic insisted, Karl told him that that part of their lives was over. That he had outgrown the pleasure of being in bed with another boy.

'What's going on, Karl?' became a refrain, at least once a day, from Dominic. 'Why don't you ever come to my music room anymore? Why don't you draw anymore? Why can't we be lovers anymore?' All of which Karl deflected, saying in different forms and with different words that things change, that relationships alter, that boys turn into men. And Dominic looked at Karl and said: 'People don't change so suddenly. Circumstances do. What's changed?'

'For one thing, I'm leaving this school and you're staying.'

A few days later Dominic announced that his family would be emigrating to Canada. That he would be attending piano classes with a professor at the University of Toronto. He said his parents had decided three months earlier but had kept it from him from concern that it could influence his concentration. And then when a discussion of the coming Parents' Weekend arose, Dominic asked whether Bok and Bokkie were staying on the farm and Karl had said no, they were not coming because Bernice was writing matric and he was staying at school for the weekend.

'Why don't you come with us? My parents are staying at Champagne.'

'No, I want to stay here and do some Latin. I'm falling behind.'

'You're lying, Karl. You're feeling sorry for yourself about something, aren't you? Cutting off your nose to spite your face. Well, come back to me when you decide to stop your shit. And you're welcome to join us for the weekend. My parents would love it. And I would too.' The discussion was left at that, but Karl silently resented Dominic. Hated the way the Websters could throw around their money, live as though they were in control of the world, able to dish out cash and charity as the whim took them. On a day when Karl again awoke feeling the joy of the world around him, he returned to Dominic's music room. He said he would very much like to join the Websters. Dominic, perhaps taking this as indication that all was again well, put his hand on Karl's shoulder and tried to pull him close. Karl recoiled. He asked Dominic to stop, to promise that he would never do that again.

'No,' Dominic said, 'I will not promise that. I'll wait till you decide you want to come back to me. And you will, I know.' But I didn't, Dom. I didn't come back to you and now I won't. It is all gone and flying off with you in the Clemence-Gordons' plane later tonight or tomorrow morning depending on the weather. And then I now try and picture you after all these years, in the snows of Toronto where you must have fallen in love with the splendid university and the green landscape without fear. Fallen in love, like falling pregnant. Why did we call it fall, Dom, like you're hurting yourself? And did you do what I could not allow myself to imagine then: fall in love

with another boy and when you became men did you live in a
Montreal apartment and speak French? And were you bourgeois and
happy? Bourgeois. How I too wanted to be that word, Dom. More
than almost anything in the world.

For five days Karl and Lukas stayed in the Berg when the Mass choir
went off for the Johannesburg rehearsals. The school was empty and
Lukas moved from G Dorm to F beside Karl to sleep in Fat Du Toit's
bed. With Uncle Charlie also away, the two of them took showers for
as long and as often as they chose. They stayed for hours in the steam
of the Junior showers where they had to go as the hot-water geysers
in the Seniors' bathroom had been turned off. On the long shower
floor they skidded, shooting themselves from wall to wall. Then they
scrubbed again to clear off the clingy fragments of red floor paint
that had come off on their foot soles and white buttocks.

They rode bareback all day in the warm November sun. They
asked Matron Booysen for sandwiches and fruit and Mr Walshe for
his lighter as they wanted to light a fire to make tea — and for the off
chance of finding the hidden cave. Then for hours they explored
paths and trails on which they had never been before, stopping for
lunch in the shade of enormous cabbage trees and yellow-woods,
their bases hidden by brambles and tree ferns hundreds of years
old. Here they made a fire and boiled an empty can of water and
dunked a putrid teabag. Above Copper Falls they followed antelope
paths neatly cut along the mountainside's contours and when they
reached the plateaus they cantered across the veld, green, undulating
like new corn in the breeze. And they had the time to search for and
find the hidden caves. Hisses carried into the back from where dark
shadows returned whispered promises of deeper entrances. From the
moment they entered with Mr Walshe's Bic ablaze, the cave had
become a black cavern filled with flickering ghosts. Without looking
back at the entrance, they moved through a narrow opening into a
second chamber. They heard the twitter of bats and the rapid wings

fluttering; shadows collided as they took to the air and exited the cave.

'Look, they're dancing . . .' said Lukas, and the echo carried: sing, ing, ng

'It's a hunting dance . . . look, this one is pretending to be an ostrich and those are sneaking up on him.'

'It's a woman . . . not a him . . . look . . .'

'Maybe, but it looks like it's the rock, not part of the painting.'

'There,' Lukas said, taking the lighter from Karl and stretching his arm up towards the ceiling, which remained in darkness. 'What's that up there? Can you see?'

'Looks like a bird . . . Maybe a lammergeier. No, it's too far, lift the flame higher.'

He tried to hoist himself up a narrow ledge but couldn't keep his footing.

They took in what seemed to them the tale of a big hunt or a war. In it were ox-wagon and horses, above it what seemed like an odd and meaningless series of circles and stripes.

'Looks like they played noughts and crosses, here,' Lukas said, lifting the flame to the tapestry of criss-crosses.

'Maybe it's their language,' Karl countered. 'Maybe that's how they wrote.'

'The Bushmen couldn't write, Karl, jissis, that much we know.' No, no, o

'No we don't and anyway, these must be signs, saying something.'

'Well, I wish we had found bows and arrows and more Stone Age implements instead of their silly signs. But there's nothing here. This damn thing is getting hot. I better give it a rest.'

He flicked off the lighter and they waited in pitch darkness.

'Karl?' Kaal, kal, al

'Karl?' Kaal, kaal, kal, al, a

'Shhh . . .' Shh, sh, s

'What?' What, wat, at, a

'Listen.' Isten, issn, sn

'What?' Wat, t

'The silence.' Slince, lince, snss

'What about it?' Whatait, whatit, uit, uu

Karl found Lukas's arm. He stood on his toes and brought his lips to Lukas's ear. To cheat the echo, he tried as softly as possible: 'Beautiful.' But he knew the darkness, the earth, the rock was an ear and a mouth and a rib-cage around him. Barely, barely audible, came the clicks of the returning t.

At night Karl's thighs ached. Lukas laughed when he noticed that he could hardly bend his legs. It was as though clutching Rufus's back had demanded the use of muscles he had not known the existence of. But the next day they were out again; bareback again. They let the horses wade in the river while they sat naked above pools where they swam, then lazed in the sun. Lukas spoke about returning to Indwe, being back with Harlequin, about his father importing two new American saddler mares for Swaargenoeg's breeding. Going to school in Queenstown where his brothers had matriculated would probably be a bit of an ordeal at first, with everyone thinking you were a pansy if you came from the Berg. But that would pass once the rugby season started in May. And when Karl spoke he passed over the near future as though the next four years either did not exist or were impossible to imagine. His dreams began at university where he was studying law. Poring over books in an enormous library. There he would be free. Life for him would begin there amongst bright and stimulating lecturers – all of whom were as intelligent and creative as Ma'am.

'And the army?' Lukas asked.

'I'll go after university, once I'm a lawyer.'

'You don't want to be a soldier, do you, Karl?'

He didn't answer. If he spoke he knew he would lie. The warm sun beat down on his face, his arms and chest. The mountains above them rose amber, brown and blue. Birds whose names he didn't know called from every angle around the river. He felt the day and the world light and glorious. He was not going to lie on a day like today. Just for once I'm not going to lie. He looked downstream to where Rufus still stood in the water. King was tugging long strands of kikuyu from the bank.

'Karl?'

'What?'

'You heard me. About not wanting to be a soldier.'

Again he remained quiet. Then he felt Lukas's hand against his shoulder and their eyes met.

'It's okay, Karl. I understand you better than you think.'

'Of course I want to be a soldier, Lukas. Jirre jissis. I just want to get my degree first, that's all.' And he rose to retrieve his shorts and underpants.

Returning to the fort for the first time since Mathison's night, he saw – smelt – at once that Uncle Klaas and the Silent One had left. The fort smelt again of decaying poplar leaves and thatch. Rains had cleared the covering of any smoke scent that may have lingered. As if they had never been here, he thought. Where were they now? Who knows if they're even alive.

Lukas had procured slingshots from the farm workers, and he and Karl shot across the river at a row of empty Coca-Cola cans. For every five cans Lukas toppled, Karl felled one. He thought again of how Bok had taken him down to the Umfolozi to fire the revolver. He saw again Bok walking from the round boulder on the opposite bank, his mpategas crunching into the white sand of the dry riverbed while he waited in the shade of the reeds. Held in both his hands was the tray of copper bullets with their little grey lead heads. And he's sure he sees his fingernails unbitten.

Bok knelt beside him and flicked open the revolver's chamber.

'You see, it's empty,' he said. 'You don't have to fear a revolver. But you must treat it with respect. Here, hold it, Philistine. Both hands.'

And Karl passed the narrow tray of twenty-four bullets to Bok. He placed both hands around the handle, felt the cold metal weight of the open weapon in his fingers, pulling at his shoulders.

'It's heavy, Bok.'

'It won't be, once you grow accustomed to it. Here, let me show you how to put in the rounds.' He took the revolver from Karl's hands.

'Can I shoot now, Bok?'

'Be patient. Watch now, look closely at how I do it because you'll be doing this for the rest of your life.'

One at a time, Bok said, you remove one bullet at a time from the tray and you slip it into its little groove. Like this, you see. They look like a bee's nest, Bok. Ja, but believe me they do more damage than any wasp. These things kill, Karl. Do you understand me? This thing is not something you play with, ever. Okay? Yes, Bok. You don't go near this revolver without my permission, ever. Do you hear me, Philistine? Yes, Bok. And he watched as his father's fingers skilfully filled the honeycomb with bullets before flicking the chamber shut. And now you get yourself into a comfortable position, like this, Bok said, and Karl emulated his father: legs slightly apart, shoulders back. Because you're still small you can take a dead aim on my arm. Bok knelt beside Karl. He held the revolver and told the boy to lean into him so that he could explain the lining up of the sights with the target. This gap here, shut your one eye, Karl, these two little teeth, do you see them? Yes, Bok. Through them you find this little one at the front, do you see it? Yes, Bok, as he squinted, struggled to keep the right eye shut, and tried to line up the little ant between the little teeth. Then you must see the little one at the front of the barrel, and the target – the jerry can – through the two teeth at the back. Okay? Yes, Bok. So, when all three are in place – can you see all three – keep your one eye closed, Philistine, can you see all three? I think so, Bok. Then, if you keep them lined up and you draw the trigger in, like this, you never pull it, okay, because then you lose balance. Gently, you draw it in so that you don't lose the line-up of the revolver with the target. And you keep your eye on the target, always. The target is like a magnet and your eye doesn't waver, not even for a second, okay? Yes, Bok. Okay. Now I'm going to sit here and you stand behind me and you can rest your hands on my arm as a dead rest, okay? Yes, Bok. With his father half in front of him he took dead aim across the hairy arm. Take your time now, Bok spoke softly, almost into his ear. Remember don't pull the trigger, just draw it in gently – after you have the jerry can in your sights. That's good. Beautiful. Can you see it, close your right eye, Karl. Yes, yes, that's nice. Beautiful. Champion. Keep your eye on the target.

Suddenly nervous, Karl said he didn't want to shoot. Bok told him there was nothing to be afraid of. Come on, Karl. Try again. You can do it, you're a big boy. You don't want Lena and Bernice to hear you were too afraid to fire a few little shots, do you? And Karl, fearful but sure that he had the necessary three things lined up, tugged violently at the trigger. A boom and the revolver came alive, jumped from his hands, dropped; sand flew up no more than a pace beyond his father's arm.

'Are you out of your mind! What the hell did I tell you? Keep your eye on the target. Do you want to kill me? Karl? Why don't you listen to me, for God's sake? Look at this revolver, now. Covered in dirt.' When Bok turned from retrieving the revolver where it lay with its barrel in the sand, Karl was weeping. After pacifying the boy, he knelt down behind him. With his hands around Karl's hands, holding the boy's steady at height and around the revolver's handle and placing his finger over the small forefinger already around the trigger, he helped the boy fire the remaining five rounds, each hitting the opposite bank a little closer to the jerry can.

'You're very good for a five-year-old, Philistine. With practice you're going to be as good as your father.'

'I'm almost six, Bok. I'm going to school next year,' he said as they made their way back to where Bokkie waited.

'Well, you're very good for almost six. Now you can tell all the boys at school next year your Dad's already teaching you how to shoot with a revolver. Then no one will mess with you.'

'And Lena and Bernice,' Karl answered and ran ahead to tell his mother.

With Jacques gone he found himself in the library at night. Ignoring the encyclopaedias, he read more about the Bushmen and rock art, contemplated the prints in the large books. As huge, impersonal and empty as the school was, he again felt stirring in himself the prodding of some urge to create. And be happy. In his mind the two seemed in a mysterious way connected. He wanted to draw. Maybe write a poem. He laughed aloud at himself when remembering his silly thoughts of swallowing the tambotie seeds. With solitude he was regaining equilibrium and was certain the blues had fled for ever. He was glad of the fact that he and Lukas spoke less than he and Dominic: in quiet lay peace and tranquillity. This shows that everything happens for the good, he told himself. I needed this time away from everyone to come to terms with everything that has happened. This is God's way of helping me through the dark times, preparing me for next year and the rest of my life. By the fourth and fifth day alone with Lukas he thought he could never again be unhappy. They were free, seeing the teachers only when they went to the teachers' dining hall to collect their food. Then they sat alone in the closed boys' dining hall, eating, only occasionally speaking. They rode, swam, participated in the milking, loading silver milk-cans onto the van that dropped off supplies at the surrounding hotels and smallholdings. They slowly began packing up their lockers.

When he awoke on the morning of the day the rest of the school was due back, so were the blues. Feeling the heaviness on his head, narrowing his view of the ceiling above his bed until it seemed but a tiny strip of white Elastoplast above him, he wanted to weep. He cursed God for doing this to him. Thought at once again of the jumping beans. His spirit lifted, briefly, that afternoon when Dominic arrived at the dairy. But by that night the clouds moved in, pressing him down into the sheets where he could not sleep and he swore never again to believe in God or in the absurd idea of Divine Grace.

As the time to pack and leave the school had drawn near, Lukas asked Karl whether the De Mans could give him a lift to the Louis Botha Airport after the concert. Karl said he would ask Bok but that he was certain there wouldn't be a problem: the airport was right on their way to Amanzimtoti.

'Don't tell my parents I was with Dominic for Parents' Weekend. I told them I was with you.'

'Why?'

'Because my father likes you more than Dominic. You won't tell Dominic, will you?'

And then, from Dominic he asked that he too not tell that he had spent Parents' Weekend with the Websters at Champagne Castle. He said he had promised Bok and Bokkie that he would stay at the school and catch up on homework.

'Do they expect you to sit here while we're all having fun with our parents?'

'No, they didn't tell me to stay. It's just that I want them to know I'm working hard.'

'Why do you lie to your parents? I can lie to the whole world, but never to my parents.'

'Please, Dom. If you see them in Durban, will you not tell?'

'Okay. But I think it's stupid and I don't understand you. This means you can't tell them anything – not about Mum giving you the Abba tape, not about the flight with Mervy's Dad. It's crazy, don't you see?' Karl didn't answer. Stared into the distance. 'How can you hide such small things from the people you love most? If you can't speak to them, you can't speak to anyone. All the small things pile up and you end up hiding a big thing, like robbing a bank or a murder, from them.'

Karl kept looking away, knowing but not caring that what was being said was true. Things hidden. It is not things I hide from the ones I love most. It is everything. Everything of me. And from you, Dominic, from you too I can hide the murderer in me. If only you know how right you are. 'Come on, Dom, it's not such a big deal.'

And again Dominic asked what was wrong, begged to be told what had happened to turn Karl into somebody he felt he scarcely knew. And Karl, now believing himself, said that nothing had happened, that he was just a little sad at leaving the Berg and his friends. And very sad about Dominic and the Websters emigrating. But Dominic said he didn't believe that he was being told the truth. That everything had changed since Ma'am's apology. He asked whether Karl was angry about his refusal to apologise to Ma'am. Karl said no, but none the less asked why Dominic had refused to apologise.

'I believe, really, that she does dislike boys like me,' Dom answered. 'So, I don't believe that she has remorse for what she said. My father also says this apology of hers is a mere formality because of my threat to leave. They shat themselves because my father intervened and they were scared of losing their soloist.'

Karl looked at Dominic, envied him without knowing why.

'Mum also doesn't believe the cow when she says she did not intend to hurt me. On the contrary, Mum and Dad believe she said it so that she could injure me. And not only me, mind you, but at least half the boys in this school. You too. You see, as Dad says, they want to make it impossible for us to love ourselves, because that's the one way to make sure we can never love each other. Mum says that's why most people want to make doubly sure that we hate ourselves. Until Sanders can tell me, explain what she did wrong and show me that she understands, I'll hold a grudge. I'm sure Mum and Dad will agree with me.'

'We must all learn to forgive, Dominic. That's what the Bible says.'

'How many times must I tell you, Karl! That book is a ball of evil. And as for forgiveness, I don't believe in it. It has happened and it cannot be wiped out. Like Dad had an affair when I was smaller and Mum hasn't forgiven him for it and she says she never will because there will always be some hurt and it doesn't change the fact that Dad did it. But Dad explained why he had done it and Mum believed him and that he was sorry and then she accepted that these things happen and that people make mistakes. But people have to learn from their mistakes, Mum says. They have to grow and then we can even accept that a mistake was worthwhile, though it still hurts. But if she didn't believe that Dad had grown through what he did wrong, then she would have left him.'

Karl thought of Beauty. Wondered whether she had forgiven him. Or accepted that he knew what he had done wrong. Really regretted. Would never speak to a Bantu like that again. And Dominic. Was what he had with Jacques the same as Dr Webster had had with his affair, and would Dominic accept that he was sorry if he were to tell him the whole story, express his remorse? But what if he felt no real remorse; remained unable to see what he had done as wrong? Had he indeed tried to prevent Beauty from loving — herself and therefore also others?

The overall of one of the stable boys. While raking and cleaning out the feeding troughs. The front buttons were open to the belly button and the man's taut brown skin set off against the blue fabric. Something to be painted. Karl caught himself staring at the buttons above the tattered crotch. Felt the movement in his own. He dropped the rake against the wall and left the dark hay smell of the stable to stand out in the sun. As he stares into the orchard, Jonas is beside him. Asleep on the mat of fig leaves while he scans the branches for louries. The buttons of his green Parks Board overall are not properly done and Karl peers at the dark skin of his stomach. Up and down as he breathes. Karl stares at the man's sleeping face, still sees the curly black eyelashes closed. Slowly he lifts his arm, brings his hand to the open buttons. Phinias, no, Jonas, who — his hand goes through and down. Rests on the warm soft filafooi. The eyelids bat. The man opens his eyes and looks at Karl staring down at him. Half lifting his chin he looks down at his crotch, at Karl's hand disappearing at the wrist into his overall. He turns his eyes back to the boy. Still holding the gaze he takes hold of the thin white wrist and lifts it out. Places it gently on the child's chest. For a while longer they lie in silence. Then the man gets up and the boy too. Karl wipes twigs and leaves from his back. They walk towards Mbanyana or Charters, where was it — neither speaks. Near Bokkie's row of sisal Jonas takes my hand, rubs my hair.

I'm not going there. I am not evil. I am not an abomination, he told himself. But by the night, when a desperate urge to be with Dominic or Jacques, to hold onto them and be held, snuck up on him, he fumbled through his toilet bag. Finding the seeds in the dark between toothpaste, deodorant, dental floss and a few round pebbles, he lay with them, throbbing in his fist, their stunted movements like the flickers of pulses against his skin. More than anything he wanted to be gone, to end it all. I even desire kaffirs. Bantus. I was going stiff for a stable boy. Always been like that. Even before this school. No, there are no limits, no boundaries to my capacity for perversion. Lust. I am lust incarnate. This, killing himself, would be the only definitive route out. Why don't I do it? Coward. Coward. Coward. He could find no reason other than that there was a glimmer of hope, somewhere amongst the black of the clouds. It was the glimmer rather than the clouds that made him weep. If only the hope would disappear! If only hope could be erased for the slanderous word it is. Then he would be able to chew these beans, with their little worms, and swallow them and fall asleep and rest for ever. It is not love that is the greatest . . . curse. It is hope. And the greatest of these is hope. The greatest lie of all is hope. He fell asleep crying, raging into his pillow, uncaring if Fat Du Toit or anyone else might hear. He dreamt of Dr Taylor standing over him with a Checkers bag filled with spiders. The man was saying: these are the spiders of hope and you will grow healthy and strong if you allow the spiders to bite you. The spiders of hope. Then Dr Taylor untied the bag and Karl awoke panting as the spiders began crawling over his body. He found the tambotie beans jumping against his chest and stomach. And he loathed himself and the world. Wished he could speak to Aunt Lena, wondered if shock treatments could make him better. Maybe he could go and see Dr Taylor again next year. Maybe that was what the dream was telling him. That hope lay with Dr Taylor.

He sat after class at his desk and opened the class Bible. Paul's letter to the Corinthians, he remembered, and flipped the pages to Chapter 13: *Now I will show you the way which surpasses all the others. If I speak with human tongues and angelic as well, but do not have love, I am a noisy gong, a clanging cymbal. If I have the gift of prophecy and, with full knowledge, comprehend all mysteries, if I have faith great enough to move mountains, but have not love, I am nothing. If I give everything I have to feed the poor and hand over my body to be burnt, but have not love, I gain nothing. Love is patient; love is kind. Love is not jealous, it does not put on airs, it is not snobbish. Love is never rude, it is not self-seeking, it is not prone to anger; neither does it brood over injuries. Love does not rejoice in what is wrong but rejoices with the truth. There is no limit to love's forbearance, to its trust, its hope, its power to endure. Love never fails. Prophecies will cease, tongues will be silent, knowledge will pass away. Our knowledge is imperfect and our prophesying is imperfect. When the perfect comes, the imperfect will pass away. When I was a child I used to talk like a child, think like a child, reason like a child. When I became a man I put childish ways aside. Now we see indistinctly, as in a mirror; then we shall see face to face. My knowledge is imperfect now; then shall I know even as I am known. There are in the end three things that last: faith, hope, and love, and the greatest of these is love.*

It was different from what Mathison had read or the way he thought Mathison had read it. And still more different from how it was in the Afrikaans Bible. This, he felt almost sure, was also the passage the Dominee had read at Aunt Lena and Uncle Joe's wedding. But nothing made sense. This version had nothing about loyalty. He was certain he could recall the word loyalty from Mathison's reading. *If you love someone you will be loyal to him no matter what the cost. You will always believe in him, always expect the best of him, and always stand your ground defending him.* That was it, he was sure he had heard Mathison read those words from his own *Living Bible*. But the class Bible didn't have that; nothing like that. What is it, what must I believe? Is there nothing that is true for me to hold on to?

Despondent, he took from Ma'am's desk the Shakespearean *Sonnets* and read a few. Each making him more morbid. Can I not love, he wondered. Like this, like this man loved his beloved? Is all I have in me lust and desire and treason? And what of loyalty? I think I love Dominic, but I go to Jacques's bed. I tell neither one about the other. And of Alette I can scarcely stand to think. Maybe salvation and true love lies with Alette. And does it hurt anyone if I love them all, in my way? And what if I love none? I feel ready to hate, to envy, to reject everyone I think I love in an instant, in the same moment as a wrong word is spoken, a look given or a glance not returned. Will this anger, this passion to hate, disappear when I grow up? Is this a childish thing that will go when I leave fourteen behind and become a young man? What if I am, in my blood and flesh that other word: evil. For what is evil but the inability to love? He closed the *Sonnets*.

With their suitcases packed, and the school emptying, the choirs left Durban for dress rehearsal. The rows of beds in the dormitories had been stripped, covered now only in the striped calico piss-skins. Everything stacked up, turning the place into an enormous abandoned prison cell; an army barracks he recalled from some unnamed movie. All Dominic's luggage he helped carry to the bus. Along with everything of the Standard Sevens who were all leaving. Then he and Lukas helped Mervyn, who had almost double the amount of anyone else: four suitcases, three bags of sheet music — even as most of Mervy and Bennie's clothing remained shelved for their return next year. Mrs Clemence-Gordon had had prints made for all of them of some of their favourite photographs. One of these was of the six of them the previous year on the Copper Falls hike. Almeida and Dom at his sides.

When the buses drove off it was again only Karl and Lukas remaining, due to drive down the following afternoon with Uncle Charlie and Mr Walshe. From waving the buses off they returned upstairs and cleared out their lockers and their shelves. In the late afternoon they had packed everything into suitcases and bags.

From his locker Karl took the tambotie seeds. He flicked them from the window into the quad. He packed everything except his formals and the clothes he was wearing. He and Lukas took their last shower in the Junior bathrooms and Lukas came again to F to sleep on the bed beside him. In the morning they walked to the dairy to say goodbye to the stable boys. To King and Rufus. Cassandra and Dragon's Prince were away in the paddock.

They said goodbye to the cleaning girls. Karl thanked Beauty for everything she had done for him over the three years. They hugged. 'You must learn to eat your Brussels sprouts,' she said with mock severity and Karl, sure he'd been forgiven, wished he had a gift for her.

In the afternoon they dressed in their grey flannels, white cotton shirts, black ties and blazers. They combed their hair and carried their luggage to Uncle Charlie's Audi. They were a good hour early. They strolled down to the fort, picking near-ripe apples as they went, shining them on their flannels like cricket balls. They wondered who would join Mervyn and Bennie in their place at the river next year. They took off their blazers in the afternoon sun and sat above the green pool on the rocks. With the sun above them, Karl stared at himself and the perfect image of his face, his white shirt reflected in the green—

Bravo! Encore! Around him everyone is up. More! more!

For a brief moment he alone is seated. Then he too is on his feet. Shouting with the crowd. Jacques is to the left of the choir and orchestra, lifting his arm. The entire choir of men, women and boys bow, and the shouting increases. They bow again. Jacques points to the orchestra and the volume from the audience is deafening. The chief violinist stands and bows as shouts of praise and encouragement run through the hall. When Jacques holds out his hands to the quartet, there is a rumble of feet, voices, clapping like thunder that may lift the roof. The quartet bows, Dominic's scalp shining in the lights as his head goes down, he comes up, beaming, teeth glimmering. And Jacques shakes the violinist's hand and leaves the stage. The quartet falls back, each taking his place on the stands. Still the clapping continues and the audience stays on its feet and there's a roar when Jacques returns.

He takes his place. The audience sits down. He nods. Dominic takes four paces forward. Once he is again behind the microphone he looks to Jacques and clears his throat. Nods. Jacques lifts his hands. Karl's eyes move between the conductor and Dominic. When the orchestra begins he knows it is Gounod's 'Sanctus'. Standing at the front of the choir, Dominic's voice, enormous and deeper than Karl knows it, leaps up every entry. On the *Sanctus* — before the choir joins — his body seems to twitch, the head is lifted exposing the throat, his shoulders push forward. He is struggling, Karl thinks. He's too tired. Those in the audience who have heard and seen him sing — particularly those who have watched him for three years — must all notice that he is battling. They might hold their breath both times he reaches for the high A, and when, on the first the boy's voice falters — like a rip midway along a thread — and he falls deliberately to an octave lower, they might shudder, knowing that the voice is going. With almost superhuman effort, as though it is the last time he will ever sing the high A, the boy bravely goes up on the final *Pleni* and holds the note a moment too long where it cracks and his chest heaves and even before the music is ended the audience goes berzerk. It is as if to the witnesses the crack in Dominic's voice is a strength, not a weakness. Dominic bows and the audience is screaming for more. The choir bows. Dominic bows, again, his face red and glowing, and beside Karl Bok is grinning and Alette is shouting Bravo and stamping her feet along with what must be a thousand others. But now Jacques shakes his head, even as he smiles at the audience. Once more he motions Dominic forward. Once more, again the roar: men's voices, deep, women, shouting for more. Shoes rattling the floor and walls. And Jacques leaves.

The same man who earlier made the announcement about not clapping between movements, now walks onto stage. Behind him the choir is smiling. After a minute of him, helplessly holding up his hands, quiet at last comes over the hall. Coughing. Laughter.

'Ladies and Gentleman, the Honourable Prime Minister, our television time is up and both choirs are exhausted after a splendid recital. I think we must now allow them to rest.' Applause. 'And a boy can only take so much,' he points to Dominic. Again the audience claps. Once order has returned he clears his throat and says: 'May I now ask you to stand for the singing of the national anthem. For those of you who don't know the text in both official languages, please make use of your programmes, so that you can follow the words. We'll sing half in Afrikaans and half in English.'

Jacques walks to the podium as the audience rises. He raises his arms. The orchestra plays the opening bars. Karl casts a glance at Prime Minister Vorster. As the voices are about to begin Jacques turns and faces the audience. Beside Karl is Bok's strong baritone, and Alette takes the alto score from the choir. Choir and audience, together:

> Uit die blou van onse hemel uit die diepte van ons see
> oor ons ewige gebergtes waar die kranse antwoord gee
> oor ons ver verlate vlaktes met die kreun van ossewa
>
> Calls the spirit of our Country, of the land that gave us birth.
> At thy call we shall not falter, firm and steadfast we shall stand,
> At thy will to live or perish, oh South Africa, dear land.

In the Prime Minster's box, in the cavern of the hall, above every seat, lips open and close. When the song ends, hands move from the sides where they have been at attention. On stage, Dominic's lips are the only ones that have remained shut, whose arms throughout have been locked behind his back, as if standing at ease.

'Five minutes,' Bok tells Karl and Lukas in the foyer. 'You have five minutes and we'll meet you in the Royal parking lot. Lukas, if you want to be on that plane you better run.' With that the boys scurry through the excited crowds to the backstage area.

'Ooops,' a woman's voice behind Karl, 'watch where you're going, you handsome thing.'

'Sorry, Miss,' and they weave their way through the ushers who allow them to pass.

His mind is racing. Already there's a knot in his throat. No time to say goodbye to anyone properly! Dominic, where are you?

'There's Bennie,' Lukas says. 'I'll meet you back here in three minutes, okay?'

'Okay. I'm going to find Dominic. Can you see Ma'am anywhere?'

Then Dominic is beside him, laughing, asking what he thought of the broken note.

'Dom, it was still beautiful. The audience loved it.'

'Cilliers wasn't pissed off, he's in a great mood. Said everything was perfect.'

Karl looks at Dominic. The noise and laughter of boys and adult choir members are blocked from his ears. He sees only Dominic; knows there is nothing left to say. 'I must go, Dom.'

'Are you taking Lukas to the airport?'

Karl nods; not trusting his voice.

'Will you write?'

'You must send me your address in Canada.'

'I will, I promise. Will you write?'

'Yes. I promise. Dom, I must go now, Lukas will miss his plane.'

'I love you, Karl.' Karl's eyes now come alive and he looks around to see whether anyone has heard.

'Loelovise yokou titoo, Didomimineeicoc.'

'No! Say it to me in English. This once, Karl. All the way.' But before the boy can think to respond, Ma'am is at his side.

'So, you made it, Karl.' Smiling. 'Dominic, you were superb.'

'Thank you, Ma'am. Karl and Lukas have to go.' Dominic turns to call Lukas. From where he's talking to Bennie and Radys he signals he needs a minute.

'Well, my boy. This is it, then. You're off into the big world.'

Karl smiles, unsure of what he is expected to say: 'Thank you for everything, Ma'am. You have meant a great deal to me and I won't ever forget it.'

'You must keep writing, Karl. That's your passion and very few people discover their passions as young as you and Dominic.'

'Thank you, Ma'am.'

'Well, off you go. I'm sure I'll hear from my sister how you're doing. You must make use of her, Karl, she's a very special teacher, you know.'

'Thank you, Ma'am.' She stoops to kiss him, her hands briefly on his shoulders. He feels her eyes on him, takes in her scent, even as he looks at Dominic and they glance at each other.

He extends his hand and Dominic his. Palms meet, fingers touch. Against his palm, Karl feels the light tickling of a forefinger and Dominic smiles and looking away from Karl to Ma'am while holding onto the hand, says: 'There will be much more of this when I see you in Canada. I promise.'

'Bye, Dom.' He withdraws his hand.

'Bye, Ma'am.'

He turns to wave at Lukas to make a move on. He is drained and terrified. As he shakes his finger at Lukas to come at once, he hears Ma'am behind him speak to Dominic: 'What a highlight for Mr Cilliers to end his time at the school.'

'Is he leaving, Ma'am? He didn't say anything to us.' Dominic's voice.

'Well yes, it's sort of an open secret amongst the staff. He's going to lecture at—' And Karl doesn't hear the rest as Lukas arrives and shouts a quick goodbye to Ma'am and Dominic. He tugs at Karl's arm. They're moving and Karl tries to resist Lukas's pull.

'Have you said goodbye to Mr Cilliers?' He asks over the throng.

'There isn't time. Come.'

'No, I want to speak to him. I must say goodbye to him.'

'Come on, Karl, I'm going to miss the plane.'

'No, I want to see Mr Cilliers.'

'Karl!' Lukas almost shouts. 'We must go and you know you're not allowed near . . .' Karl swings back, turns his gaze on Lukas. Lukas adds: 'Because I'm going to miss my plane!'

And then they run, through parents and well-wishers, Karl waving at Bennie and Mervyn and other classmates. And all the time Karl is thinking, they fired him, Mathison fired him. They chased him away. Mervyn has now caught up. While they say a few words that Karl will for ever be unable to recall, he sees the back of Jacques's head as it moves into the men's toilet. Without a word to Lukas or Mervyn he slips to the door that has now swung shut. Jacques is standing at the urinal, his back to the door. Karl stands leaning against the door. Wondering where to start.

'Mr Cilliers . . .' Karl waits, but the man at the urinal does not turn; doesn't even acknowledge the boy behind him.

Still Karl continues: 'He . . . Mathison promised they wouldn't do anything to you. I swear I didn't mean . . .' He pauses, suddenly terrified that the man peeing is not the man in the evening suit he is looking for. There are hundreds of black-suited men here. It must be him. 'Where are you going, Jacques? Ma'am said you were . . .' The toilet door swings open and Lukas grabs Karl by the sleeve. They're out of the door, running, bumping into shoulders, heading for the foyer and the door.

*

'There's the statue of John Ross,' Karl says to Lukas as they turn right at the harbour. The Chevrolet leaves the black palms of Durban's esplanade. Bok races up the on ramp that takes them onto the N2 south.

'We're never going to make this flight,' Bokkie says with a nervous edge to her voice. 'But there's no need to drive like you're practising for Kayalami, Bok.' And the boys laugh.

'We'll make it, Bokkie, calm down. Lukas, if you miss the flight you can stay the night and we'll get you on another plane in the morning.'

'My parents would have left the farm already, Uncle Ralph. It's a two-hour drive to East London.'

'We'll make it. Just hold on tight.'

The car flies and the two boys lean forward to see the speedometer reach one hundred and fifty kilometres per hour. While there are frequent silences, each occasionally comments on the concert. About Vorster who looked tired and Bok says it's because it's been a tough year for the old man. There is unrest in all the black locations. From the Transvaal it has spilt out into the entire country. Lukas says it sounded to him as though Dominic's voice was going and Bokkie says she has never heard a voice like that. Bok agrees and they all opine on what will become of Dominic's voice when it changes.

'You never know,' Karl says. 'There may be nothing left after it's broken.'

'Okay. When we get there,' Bok says, 'I'm going to drive to the No Parking area and you two just grab the suitcases and run. If we're lucky the flight might be delayed. Bokkie and I will park and then come and say goodbye, Lukas. Okay?'

'That's fine, Oom Ralph.'

At Louis Botha's domestic departures Bok pulls onto a yellow line fifteen minutes before the plane is due to leave. Lukas grabs his huge suitcase from the boot. With Karl beside him carrying two loose sportsbags, they rush into the almost deserted terminal. They look around for the check-in counter and make a dash to where a stewardess is signalling to them. The counter is about to close. The attendant makes a hasty phone call. While talking into the receiver she motions for a black man to drag the bags onto the conveyor belt. Replacing the receiver she says that Lukas can make it if he runs. The boys have barely turned from the check-in counter when a female voice over the intercom calls: Passenger Van Rensburg holding up flight SAA 349 to East London, Port Elizabeth and Cape Town, please proceed through Gate 4 immediately. They run. At the gate have but a moment to shake hands. As Lukas is about to be hurried through by the waiting air hostess, he turns back to Karl.

'I'm sorry,' he says.

And Karl lifts his shoulders and smiles a frown. 'What for?'

And Lukas, already moving off, says: 'Didn't you know about Cilliers and Almeida?' And he stops.

Either Karl has not heard right or his brain does not want to accept the lingering words that have come from his friend's mouth. 'What do you mean, Lukas?' he asks softly, not sure that any sound actually leaves his throat.

'I wanted to help you,' Lukas says, again starting to move.

'How do you mean?' Karl asks, now registering his own voice speaking, even as he does not want to be asking the question; as he feels his head grow light, like it wants to take flight rather than hear what it has known all along and has been unable to deal with or acknowledge.

'Nothing,' Lukas says, turning to go.

For a fraction of a second Karl thinks of letting it be, but suddenly it is all too much to leave unspoken, at once he feels he must know: 'Tell me!' He almost cries out and takes a few paces after Lukas, who turns, comes to a standstill.

'Almeida told me in Malawi. About Juffrou Roos . . . and about him and Cilliers. I knew he wasn't coming back . . .' He begins to walk away. 'Bye, Karl. Say thanks and goodbye to your folks . . .'

'Lukas!' Karl calls but the boy in the black blazer has disappeared through the gates.

Gone.

Karl turns back into the all but empty terminal. Huge and white like a hospital ward. This is where Bernice will be working next year. For a mere moment he considers pondering what Lukas said. He swallows, blinks. Tells himself to forget it. No, that's not what he meant. No. Not Lukas. Not Steven, he tells himself. I heard wrong. And he promises to not think of it again. At the door he sees the hurried figures of his mother and father enter the departures hall. Bokkie gestures with incredulity when she sees him alone.

'He just made it. He said to say goodbye to you.'

'Well, at least we made it. Let's go.'

And the three of them exit the terminal into the sounds of an approaching helicopter. Sweeping in from the location of Kwamakhuta, the camouflaged craft's blinding lights drop ground-ward, sweeping to and fro. As the family pass onto the parking lot the massive rhythms and sudden blows of great blades beating are above and around them. Bokkie crouches down beneath the battering, her hands clasped over her ears. Bok contorts his face and draws both his wife and son to him. The shudders of churning air take hold of them and Karl can feel the wind like webs in his neck as he and his parents come to a compete standstill. The gusts and lights are a white rush and his heart beats strangely into the rhythm of the terrifying blades, like brute power that simultaneously pushes and pulls. He feels his body want to rise upward, as though the machine is a magnet caressing his tightening skin exactly where it lies against his flesh.

Leaving the airport on the Isipingo flats, the Chevrolet speeds along the South Coast highway and turns up the hill towards Umbogentwini and heads for Toti. The cabin is a world of a thousand unspoken thoughts. Bokkie reminds Bok that the dog Judy has to be spayed before she goes to her new owners. Karl thinks of the

Clemence-Gordons, that he didn't say goodbye to them. Did not thank them for the photos. What did Mervy say backstage? He notes seconds flash by as the headlights touch the staggered white line dividing the road in two. He sees himself tomorrow: I will burn that photograph of us with Almeida; no, first tear it up into shreds and then burn it. No, all of them! No use keeping them: the one Bok took on the day I arrived, with me and Bokkie standing in the parking lot with Cathkin Peak and Champagne Castle behind us in the blue; with Ma'am and the Olvers at Monkey Bay; the one of us in class laughing at Bennie doing a Cassius Clay match on the desk; the three formal choir shots of us in full blue and white concert dress with Mr Selbourne, Mr Roelofse and Jacques — that's the only one I have of him, maybe I could keep just that — no, no, everything or nothing; Dominic and Mervy in front of the SABC building in Auckland Park; Lukas, me and Dominic on the Bree River Bridge; all those with me and Rufus, maybe just one, of the horse, I can keep just one; our fort in spring when the poplar was budding. Yes, tear and burn in the back yard. Before we say goodbye to Judy and pack up and move to the flat in Durban. A thought catches him off guard and he asks, without thinking, whether they have heard anything recently about Uncle Klaas.

'In Klerksdorp, apparently. Arrived there a few weeks ago and is sleeping in Aunt Barbara's servants' quarters. Strong as a horse, unwashed, as disgusting as ever,' Bokkie says.

Again the car is hulled in silence. Bokkie says they're leaving the Dutch Reformed Church. 'For too long we've been slaves to Afrikaner narrowness and hypocrisy! Dressing up and sitting there like dummies. We're going to the Presbyterian Church the moment we set roots in Durban.' She says that he and Lena will have to share a room in the Durban flat. The flat has only two bedrooms and costs three hundred and fifty a month.

And I will go back, he tells himself, to Dr Taylor, yes, yes, Dr Taylor will give me direction. Look up his number in the phone book, won't be in the Toti book, call inquiries 1003, Dr Taylor. A new programme of action. POA. I'll get the money, somehow, ask Aunt Lena. Or Ouma De Man! Yes, she adores me and she's marrying money. Surely she can get money from Mr Shaw? But that might take a bit of time. He'll get Mr Shaw to like him. In the meantime there's Aunt Lena.

'Are the Mackenzies coming for Christmas?'

'Did you know that Uncle Joe's Matilda is in the other time?' Bokkie asks from the front seat.

'What?'

'Four months.' Silence again as Bok takes the off ramp and crosses the highway bridge. Karl's eyes are on the dark stream of the highway below. Soon the bird sanctuary will be on their right.

'Why didn't she go to London to have an abortion?' he asks.

A brief silence before Bokkie answers: 'Why would she? She and that poor white family of hers can milk Joe Mackenzie for maintenance for the rest of their lives.'

'What does Aunt Lena say?'

'Cries a lot. The whole town knows, of course. But she still believes Uncle Joe will change. Begged the Lord to give her guidance about a week ago and that night she had a dream of Saul riding to Damascus on the donkey. Now she believes the Lord has spoken and told her to stay. So she's staying, for God and those children. Phones here every two or three days in tears. Like she has for all these years.'

''n Jakkals is 'n jakkals,' Bok says, flicking his cigarette butt from the window.

'Won't surprise me if she goes mad again. I know her when she's like this. Starts getting visions of angels and Jesus on the cross. I tell you, before Matilda gives birth Lena will be in Tara again having shock treatments. It's the only way to let her forget.'

As they slow down to turn into Bowen Street, Karl's mind speeds. He is driven to make — before they turn in at that gate and park beneath that Natal mahogany — a chain of what he swears are unbreakable resolutions: henceforth I will be an honourable, disciplined and upright young man. No more boisterousness, no more things with other boys, no, it is all over, no thoughts of the mad gene, or any of this stuff. I will begin by no longer thinking of myself as a boy; boyhood will be left behind like a single unbroken dreadful memory. To make forgetting easier, I will no longer flounder around in the memories of the bush either, for letting go means severing all ties, definitively. It is all over and gone. With the photographs. I will be turning fifteen next year, he tells himself. It is a time for new beginnings. Taking the future into my own hands: eyes on nothing but the target. So yes, there may be high-school guys waiting for him at the gates as Lena had said she'd ensure, but he will eat their initial wrath with good cheer and then he'll win them over: initially by doing everything they tell him, by not using his hands, by trying to use as few words as possible with s and t sounds, by not folding his legs at the knee, keeping his handwriting slanted and desisting from twirling the e's. I'll try to stop biting my nails for that only adds to the appearance of nervousness. I will exude confidence without giving lip to anyone. I will learn to laugh scornfully or to feign indifference. Indifference, indifference, indifference: my motto, my salvation. There is, he knows, the problem that everyone knows he can sing – and Ma'am said her sister will be a mentor for his writing. But that I will evade, yes, I will, he thinks, I will not go near Miss Hope, for to become the teacher's pet or to let anyone know I want to be a writer will again undermine the entire programme of action. Just stop it, forget about being a writer, what a stupid idea anyway. Or do it in secret. Yes, writing can be done without anyone knowing. I can do it in secret. Practise with the weights again. I will simply stick to the story that my voice is breaking and after it indeed has, I will say there is no voice left. I will continue swimming, and after swimming season I will for the life of me play rugby. I won't fake injury or illness as so often in the past: I'll become a team player: loyal to the bitter end, not letting down the side. There will be cadets at school! Yes, the military marching will, as surely as my name is Karl De Man, teach me to walk without the swagger that Dominic said his mother called androgynous. And if anyone uses that word in my direction or simply in my presence or any of its synonyms or associative nouns, I'll smile in mock amusement and then let it go, will not remember it beyond the moment of its articulation. And Dominic can write till he's blue in the face; I won't read a word of his evil. I'll practise with my weights. I'll be strong. I'll have occasional fights, even if I can't stand the thought. I will deliberately pick a fight, maybe with someone I suspect a hint weaker than myself. And I will control this tongue: no wisecracks, no slinging of verbal abuse at enemies, I will become friends with the roughest, strongest boys. Go to school movies with Alette. No, I must break up with Alette. To arrive there with an older girlfriend spells trouble. Lena's right. Find another girlfriend, I'm good-looking, smart and charming. I'll find one. I will be loved and admired. I will go to the army to serve this country and get the Pro Patria. Hopefully be injured. Not killed. Please not killed. Wounded and awarded the Honorus Crux for bravery. This country, each and every person who lives here, will be proud of me. I will become exactly what they all want me to be, and more! I will be their man, whatever it costs. But if I die, let me be killed by the enemy, and not in training at the hands of my own people. Then on to university to become a lawyer. With a beautiful wife and two children and I'll buy a house maybe in Cape Town or Muizenberg and I'll go to the beach with my children and my wife and I'll be a success. I will be kind, generous and successful. I will take care of the woman I marry and the bright, beautiful children we beget. I will not end up like Uncle Joe. Or Bok. Uncle Klaas! Never. I will be powerful and wealthy. But in an honest, respectable way. No, I don't want wealth, no, just respectability, to be part of the decent people, the bourgeoisie of this country. Not rich but not poor. And I will try to be quiet, to keep this loud mouth and laughter muted, to not speak, not speak about anything. If I want to keep a secret I'll think it in Gogga — no — too many others can understand that. I'll find a new secret language, create my own new alphabet. No! No secrets, I will have no secrets any more. Transparent as the skin of a gecko. What you see is what there is, that's me. And I will succeed at everything I do. I will be a phenomenal success. I will be silent and no one will know or suspect anything about the other things I was or may have been or might have become. Only I can decide whether it will have occurred. If I don't say a thing, it doesn't exist. If I don't tell the story, it never happened. What is the past other than the story we choose to tell! It's in my hands. Everything.

Starting tomorrow! It will be the first day of the rest of his life. His new life. Life is remarkable, truly, re-mark-able, he mimics the word into syllables, feeling the tongue on his pallet, the lips close, then open into a new shape, lips touching on the b and the tongue's tip coming to rest against the bottom teeth, its front surface rested against the pallet and top teeth, the mouth slightly open. A new Karl De Man! It is going to be fine, everything is going to be just fine. Perfectly, perfectly fine, as they drive through that gate and park beneath the mahogany, he can hear, already feel it! Like applause flowing over him, audience calls of Bravo! More! Massed voices in unison demanding: Encore! Encore! Encore! As he glides back onto stage, beaming, smiling, as if he were back, again poised to perform.

Encore

'From the heart – may it return – to the heart.'

A boy at ten and a bit. The year before I leave my family. I am at the front door dressed in school uniform with my case in one hand after having placed in there my lunchbox and homework book and the jotter with the essay on what I want to do during the holidays. While I gaze from the door, my mother, in the conjugal bedroom, where she is brushing her thick brown hair, is probably frustrated beyond compare at now, again, finding missing what she is looking for in her closet. She possibly tells my dad — who is almost dressed and freshly shaven — that she has had enough, that she cannot take it anymore. When her voice growing angry reaches my ears, and as she slams the door of her closet and calls my name, I know at once what I have done wrong. Many, many years later, I am able to imagine my mother exasperated at a series of associations now activated at finding, again, something missing from her things and knowing for the umpteenth time that it has to have been her son. Yet, at that front door, I clasp the lost object tightly into my free hand. My father, who knows, responding to my mum and to internal echoes of outrage, fear, anger too long dormant in his own memory, glides down the passage towards me. He must be seething with rage, for over the years he must have become increasingly concerned at a series of words and images he suspects his boy of being or becoming. Having heard the commotion from the bedroom and dreading the approach of the father, I am about to unlatch the bottom door to make a hasty escape and catch up with my siblings who are already halfway down the drive. Coming close, my father does not speak, and I simply wait and watch. He stands in front of me motionless. In later years I will recall that I saw or understood or read from my father's cold blue eyes only loathing, hatred, a raging calm ready to explode into hands around my throat, pressing in the place where the Adam's apple would yet appear. My father may say that his anger then was nothing more than an expression of deep concern. Or he may say that no such thing occurred or that if it did he has no such recollection or it happened in a different way, in a different place. But now, still, I picture that father speaking softly, and, when I look down at my brown Bata school shoes, I hear my father telling me to look him in the eye like a man. Perhaps – in some phraseology or another – saying: 'If you ever go into your mother's things again,' holding my gaze, 'I will cut off your filafooi, do you hear me? If you want to be a little girl, I will turn you into a little girl. If you don't want to be a little girl, then I'm warning you: if you ever even think of doing it again, or if I or your mother ever even suspect you of doing it again, or of you imagining yourself doing it again, I will kill you.'

Then, my father turns around and I hear his tread down the passage. Again, later I might imagine Bok and Bokkie glancing at each other as he re-enters the bedroom. In an attempt to save their son from what they suspect, know, the world may make of him and from feeling their own shame at being held responsible, they have decided that a good talking to this time – even more than a beating – can save them and the boy from himself.

Pausing at the front door, I can see the driveway clearly and coldly. I do not have tears in my eyes and I can see that my siblings have long since disappeared. I unlatch the door with my forefinger and may notice that my hand is trembling – particularly the three fingers clasping the loathsome object in my palm. I step out of the house. Then, again, using thumb and forefinger I latch the bottom door behind me and start down the driveway. In that instant I know what I am to do. I will go away. And not just away anywhere. I will take myself, by hook or by crook, to the place I have been told about, the place of the boys in the concert. Through my mind rush the photographs on that programme: trips overseas with the Eiffel Tower and

London Bridge, hikes in the forest, swimming in rivers, and horses, horses in the mountains! Eland and zebra in a game compound. It doesn't matter that Mary-Alice next door says it's mostly singing and music. I suspect – know – that I do not have an extraordinarily good voice and that I can as of yet play only the recorder and that my sight reading is poor. But I have good rhythm, I can carry a tune, I can learn, like one can learn anything. I have resilience and imagination. That is all I've got, I might mutter or growl to myself: a will of iron and imagination. I will go to that place where there are others like me; others with imagination who know how fabulous, how filled with colour, sound, scent and texture the universe really is. A celebration of the senses. Out of this house. Away from them whom I believe despise me and whom I in this instant loathe with the heat of white-hot metal. I have not noticed how the trembling of fear has transfigured surreptitiously to the shaking of hatred. I hate and from hatred I draw strength. I will not, cannot cry. I will leave them, I tell myself, will not love them again, ever. And I feel stronger than I can remember from before.

But this is only a child's rage boiling over in passions of a moment. Who knows how soon all will be forgotten? How soon I will swell with pride at her beauty when she comes to parents' evenings at school and the other fathers fawn over her. How soon I will play cricket on the lawn with him who teaches me to bowl overhand. How soon I will again giggle as one of them bends over the bed to rub Vicks onto my chest and over my back when I have a cold and a blocked nose, how, in delight, I will squirm when tickled. Certainly, from familiar intimacies repeated, I will love them as much as anything, anything that was ever dreamt or ever existed in the staggering memory of the world.

I can imagine myself in so many ways, my entire life lies ahead. Where do I find an erudition that will most succinctly capture what I become or do in the gorgeous future? And, is knowing *those* – the signifiers bouncing within the space and on the contours of the history from within which I today narrate – perhaps of endlessly greater import or interest than the telling only just begun: an agnostic, a braggart, a charmer, a driver, an enemy, a friend, a gardener, a home-owner, an image, a joker, a keeper of hornbills, a lover, a mountaineer, a nobody, an opportunist, a perpetrator, a queer, a radical, a soldier, a traitor, an upstart, a voyeur, a womaniser, a xenophobe, a yuppie, a zealot? This same space from within which I will complete a poem two decades in the writing: Beloved Dearest, contemplate the sphere in your hands: fleshy, sweet, Southern Asia, sour, Spain, fragrance, wax, planet, bright, oranje, red, yellow, tree, citrus, mandarin, navel, pick, ship, auranja, warm, California, fruit, white, mould, river, leaves, colonialism, naranj, nooi, indentations, skins, tangerine, mampoer, Portugal, segments, health, russet, vomit, fish, sugary, lemon, seeds, transparent, juice, narang, veins, succulent, medicinal, round, naranga, blood, Boland, Beauty, hybrid. But when I whisper through passages of a life's infinite inventory each time I take up language's pen, I say none and all of these in a single word: orange. How much is lost, Dearest, in the brutal reduction to concept? Pay heed then as do I, to the elisions of the story and hear me do battle with veracity as it goes to war in the struggle through and against the scars of the tongue. Then, from care-filled recollection and fine weighing of the fruit touching the boniness and skin of your fingers, may you try and grant the writ's inability to say anything but duplicitous and shabby half-truth. Of happiness, shame, envy, pleasure, guilt, hatred, resentment, and of love.

None, some, all of these pulse in my veins awaiting the terrifying page, every breath and each embrace, as I turn that corner and glance back over my shoulder. Case in hand. The street is empty; no one in sight. With a swift motion of my wrist I flick the hairclip into the bushy sidewalk and head for school.

Oslo, 1993 – Cape Town, 1998

Acknowledgements

During the completion and editing of the novel I made use, amongst others of course, of the following texts: Theodor Adorno: 'Alienated Masterpiece – the *Missa Solemnis*', translated by Duncan Smith, in *Telos* 28, 1976, and *Quasi una Fantasia – Essays on Modern Music*, Verso, 1992. R.O. Pearse: *Barrier of Spears*, Howard Timmins, 1973. Elsa Pooley: *A Complete Field Guide to Trees of Natal, Zululand and Transkei*, Natal Flora Publications Trust, 1997, and *A Field Guide to Wild Flowers: KwaZulu-Natal and the Eastern Regions*, Natal Flora Publications Trust, 1998. Ian Player: *Zululand Wilderness, Shadow and Soul*, David Philip, 1997. C.T. Binns: *Dinuzulu – The Death of the House of Chaka*, Longmans, 1968. Donald R. Morris: *The Washing of the Spears – The Rise and Fall of the Zulu Nation*, Jonathan Cape, 1968. Hans Fransen: *Three Centuries of South African Art*, A.D. Donker, 1982. Percy A. Scholes: *The Oxford Companion to Music*, tenth edition, edited by John Owen Ward, Oxford University Press, 1993. E.A. Ritter: *Chaka Zulu*, Penguin, 1986. A.R. Wilcox: *The Rock Art of South Africa*, Thomas Nelson and Sons, 1963. *Roberts' Birds of Southern Africa*, The Trustees of John Voelcker Bird Book Fund/Central News Agency, third edition, 1971, and fifth edition, 1985.

Eugene Marais, C.J. Langenhoven, The Bard, Dickens, Burke and Beethoven are no longer within copyright.

Karl reads the conceptions of calendars from Funk and Wagnall's *New Encyclopedia*, 1972.

I relied on and adapted from the technical analyis of William Drabkin in *Beethoven, Missa Solemnis*, Cambridge University Press, 1991.

Karl's answers during the test on the French Revolution are translated, paraphrased and adapted from J.J. van Jaarsveld, *Geskiedenis vir Standerd Agt*, 1973.

Finally, this novel could not have been written without the teaching, criticism, stories, anger, humour, pain, support, friendship and generosity of people who have in divergent ways at different times and to different degrees touched my life in the years of writing. I thank you, from the heart, for the ever fixed mark.